THE YEAR'S BEST

SCIENCE FICTION

ALSO BY GARDNER DOZOIS

ANTHOLOGIES

A DAY IN THE LIFE
ANOTHER WORLD
BEST SCIENCE FICTION STORIES OF THE
   YEAR #6–10
THE BEST OF ISAAC ASIMOV'S SCIENCE
   FICTION MAGAZINE
TIME-TRAVELLERS FROM ISAAC ASIMOV'S
   SCIENCE FICTION MAGAZINE
TRANSCENDENTAL TALES FROM ISAAC
   ASIMOV'S SCIENCE FICTION MAGAZINE
ISAAC ASIMOV'S ALIENS
ISAAC ASIMOV'S MARS
ISAAC ASIMOV'S SF LITE
ISAAC ASIMOV'S WAR
ROADS NOT TAKEN
   (WITH STANLEY SCHMIDT)
THE YEAR'S BEST SCIENCE FICTION,
   #1–16

FUTURE EARTHS: UNDER AFRICAN SKIES
   (WITH MIKE RESNICK)
FUTURE EARTHS: UNDER SOUTH
   AMERICAN SKIES
   (WITH MIKE RESNICK)
RIPPER! (WITH SUSAN CASPER)
MODERN CLASSICS OF SCIENCE FICTION
MODERN CLASSIC SHORT NOVELS OF
   SCIENCE FICTION
MODERN CLASSICS OF FANTASY
KILLING ME SOFTLY
DYING FOR IT
THE GOOD OLD STUFF
THE GOOD NEW STUFF
EXPLORERS
THE FURTHEST HORIZON

COEDITED WITH SHEILA WILLIAMS

ISAAC ASIMOV'S PLANET EARTH
ISAAC ASIMOV'S ROBOTS
ISAAC ASIMOV'S VALENTINES
ISAAC ASIMOV'S SKIN DEEP
ISAAC ASIMOV'S GHOSTS
ISAAC ASIMOV'S VAMPIRES
ISAAC ASIMOV'S MOONS

ISAAC ASIMOV'S CHRISTMAS
ISAAC ASIMOV'S CAMELOT
ISAAC ASIMOV'S WEREWOLVES
ISAAC ASIMOV'S SOLAR SYSTEM
ISAAC ASIMOV'S DETECTIVES
ISAAC ASIMOV'S CYBERDREAMS

COEDITED WITH JACK DANN

ALIENS!
UNICORNS!
MAGICATS!
MAGICATS 2
BESTIARY!
MERMAIDS!

SORCERERS!
DEMONS!
DOGTALES!
SEASERPENTS!
DINOSAURS!
LITTLE PEOPLE!

DRAGONS!
HORSES!
UNICORNS 2
INVADERS!
ANGELS!
DINOSAURS II

HACKERS
TIMEGATES
CLONES
NANOTECH
IMMORTALS

FICTION

STRANGERS
THE VISIBLE MAN (COLLECTION)
NIGHTMARE BLUE
   (WITH GEORGE ALEC EFFINGER)

SLOW DANCING THROUGH TIME
   (WITH JACK DANN, MICHAEL
   SWANWICK, SUSAN CASPER,
   AND JACK C. HALDEMAN II)
THE PEACEMAKER
GEODESIC DREAMS (COLLECTION)

NONFICTION

THE FICTION OF JAMES TIPTREE, JR.

THE YEAR'S BEST

SCIENCE FICTION

seventeenth annual collection

edited by Gardner Dozois

st. martin's griffin ✖ new york

www.stmartins.com

ISBN 0-312-26417-8 (pbk)
ISBN 0-312-26275-2 (hc)

FIRST EDITION: JULY 2000

10 9 8 7 6 5 4 3 2 1

contents

SUMMATION: 1999   *xi*

THE WEDDING ALBUM • *David Marusek*   1

10^{16} TO 1 • *James Patrick Kelly*   41

WINEMASTER • *Robert Reed*   59

GALACTIC NORTH • *Alastair Reynolds*   78

DAPPLE: A HWARHATH HISTORICAL ROMANCE • *Eleanor Arnason*   106

PEOPLE CAME FROM EARTH • *Stephen Baxter*   139

GREEN TEA • *Richard Wadholm*   149

THE DRAGON OF PRIPYAT • *Karl Schroeder*   170

WRITTEN IN BLOOD • *Chris Lawson*   203

HATCHING THE PHOENIX • *Frederik Pohl*   215

SUICIDE COAST • *M. John Harrison*   255

HUNTING MOTHER • *Sage Walker*   270

MOUNT OLYMPUS • *Ben Bova*   285

BORDER GUARDS • *Greg Egan*   318

SCHERZO WITH TYRANNOSAUR • *Michael Swanwick*   337

A HERO OF THE EMPIRE • *Robert Silverberg*   347

HOW WE LOST THE MOON,

    A TRUE STORY BY FRANK W. ALLEN • *Paul J. McAuley*   371

PHALLICIDE • *Charles Sheffield*   383

DADDY'S WORLD • *Walter Jon Williams*   411

A MARTIAN ROMANCE • *Kim Stanley Robinson*   433

THE SKY-GREEN BLUES • *Tanith Lee*   448

EXCHANGE RATE • *Hal Clement*   472

EVERYWHERE • *Geoff Ryman*   518

HOTHOUSE FLOWERS • *Mike Resnick*   526

EVERMORE • *Sean Williams*   539

OF SCORNED WOMEN AND CAUSAL LOOPS • *Robert Grossbach*   560

SON OBSERVE THE TIME • *Kage Baker*   572

HONORABLE MENTIONS: 1999   619

acknowledgments

The editor would like to thank the following people for their help and support: first and foremost, Susan Casper, for doing much of the thankless scut work involved in producing this anthology; Michael Swanwick, Ellen Datlow, Virginia Kidd, Jim Allen, Vaughne Lee Hansen, Sheila Williams, David Pringle, Charles C. Ryan, David G. Hartwell, Jack Dann, Janeen Webb, Candas Jane Dorsey, John Clute, Warren Lapine, Dwight Brown, Darrell Schweitzer, Bryan Cholfin, and special thanks to my own editor, Gordon Van Gelder.

Thanks are also due to Charles N. Brown, whose magazine *Locus* (Locus Publications, P.O. Box 13305, Oakland, CA 94661, $43 for a one-year subscription [twelve issues] via second class; credit card orders [510] 339-9198) was used as a reference source throughout the Summation, and to Andrew Porter, whose magazine *Science Fiction Chronicle* (Science Fiction Chronicle, P.O. Box 022730, Brooklyn, NY 11202-0056, $35 for a one-year subscription [twelve issues]; $42 first class) was also used as a reference source throughout.

Well, the dreaded Y2K-crisis deadline is past, and so is the changing of the millennium (except for the calendar purists, who still shoulder the proud and lonely burden of insisting it's *not* the twenty-first century yet, when everybody else on earth thinks that it *is*), and, so far, the world has not come to an end, the angel has not descended with the seventh seal, and civilization has not collapsed—more to the point for this particular book, the publishing industry has not collapsed *either*, and science fiction has stubbornly refused to die, although strangely hopeful notices of its imminent demise have been put forth every year for more than a decade now.

(Of course, just because these Symbolically Significant Dates have passed, doesn't mean that the human race couldn't still be destroyed by a dinosaur-killer asteroid *tomorrow*, or that civilization, the economy, and/or publishing couldn't still collapse at any time—it wouldn't do to become sanguine. Nevertheless, that's probably not the way to *bet* it.)

Even as you read these words, someone, somewhere, is telling his friends with gloomy relish that science fiction is dying, is on its deathbed, gurgling its last, is sure to blink out like a guttering candle any second now. So far, though, not only has this *not* happened, but, all things considered and the proper disclaimers being made, science fiction as a genre actually looks rather *healthy*, here on the brink of a new century and a new millennium.

The next line of defense is to say, well, the science fiction genre may be making a lot of *money*, but all the *quality* has been leached out of it, and nothing gets published anymore except for crap and media tie-in books, so that even though the genre may not be about to *physically* die, its soul and mind and heart are dead, or dying. Except that this isn't true *either*. Even discounting all of the tie-ins and media and gaming-associated books, there are considerably *more* science fiction novels of quality being published now than were being published in 1975 (including a few that would not have been allowed to be published back then), possibly more than were being published even ten years ago, and quite probably more than any one reader is going to be able to *read* in the course of one year, unless he makes a full-time job of it. (And yes, the majority of the stuff on the shelves—although probably not as much as the famous 90 percent—may be crap, but then, the majority of the stuff on the shelves has *always* been crap, no matter what decade you're talking about. Not even getting *into* the issue that one person's crap is another person's valued entertainment—some people *like* media tie-in novels!) Although the widely held belief is that most SF writers can't sell their books anymore, the fact is that *more* writers, by a large margin, are making far more money from writing SF than was the case in 1975, and that science fiction books (*not* just media novels) are *selling* far better than anyone in 1975 ever dreamed that a science fiction book could sell. Although the widely held belief is that new writers can't break into the genre anymore, the fact is that new writers are still coming into the field in large numbers, as many or more than in 1975, and although some of them eventually *will* find their careers stalled by poor sales, at least as many will go on to grow audiences and become rising new stars. Thanks to (close your eyes! I'm about to commit heresy!) the big bookstore chains, it's considerably *easier* to find science fiction books (or books of any sort, for that matter) than it used to be, even in parts of the country where there once *weren't* any bookstores at all, for all intents and purposes; back when I was a teenager, in the early '60s, most bookstores didn't even *carry* science fiction books, let alone have a science fiction *section* . . . and the closest bookstore to my small New England town was more than an hour away by train. In fact, in spite of re-lated death-of-literacy/nobody-reads-anymore laments, *more* books were sold to *more* people in 1999 than at any time in history. And the Internet is making it *easier* to find books, both new and used, even in those places not reached by the chain stores (using an on-line used-book-finder service, I've recently tracked down several books that I'd been looking for unsuccessfully for years in more traditional used-book stores).

The next lament is usually that the genre has no future because kids aren't reading for pleasure anymore, having been seduced away by computer games and other forms of media entertainment, or at least that they're not interested in read-ing fiction with fantastic elements anymore—but the immense success of the Harry Potter books, staggering even by regular mainstream standards, should take care of *that* one (for those of you who didn't already draw the same lesson from the *Goosebumps* phenomenon a couple of years back).

Not that all things are perfect in the SF genre, or that there are no problems or drawbacks. Things are changing in the genre, and with every change, someone gets hurt. But every change is also an opportunity. The number of books being published in mass-market paperback has been shrinking—but, at the same time, the number of books published in trade paperback and as hardcovers has been on the *rise*. The dwindling of the midlist and the backlist has been a severe handicap to the genre in recent years, but there are signs that this is beginning to turn around . . . and the coming of print-on-demand systems may be about to make the problem moot, anyway.

As usual, there were plenty of omens to be found, both positive and negative, and what conclusions you reached about whether things were looking good or looking bad for science fiction depended on which evidence you selectively chose to examine, and what weight you arbitrarily decided to give to it. One of Norman Spinrad's recent columns for *Asimov's*, for instance, painted such a black picture of the current state of the field that we had dozens of readers writing in to the magazine in various stages of panic or despair, saying that they hadn't realized until then that science fiction was about to go down the crapper. At roughly the same time, *Publishers Weekly* ran a state-of-the-genre article by Robert K. J. Kill-heffer that was considerably more optimistic than Spinrad's, almost aggressively upbeat, in fact.

I suspect that the truth lies somewhere between these two extremes, as is usually the case in life.

One of the major negative omens that could be read this year was the acceleration of Merger Mania. In the last two years, Putnam Berkley and Viking Penguin merged to form Penguin Putnam, Inc., bringing together under the same publishing umbrella three formerly independent SF lines, Ace, Roc, and DAW; Bertelsmann bought Random House, including Bantam Doubleday Dell, bringing Del Rey, Bantam Spectra, Doubleday, and Dell under the same roof; and, in England, the Orion Publishing Group bought Cassell, which resulted in the merger of SF lines Gollancz and Millennium. In 1999, HarperCollins bought Avon Books and William Morrow, bringing two SF imprints, Avon Eos and HarperPrism, under the same management. (One much-feared merger, though, the announced purchase of Ingram, the largest book distributor, by Barnes & Noble, the largest of the bookstore chains, fell apart in 1999, much to the relief of independent bookstore owners, after reports that the Federal Trade Commission was going to block or delay the purchase.)

So far, the impact of all this merging has been smaller than feared, with Ace, Roc, DAW, Del Rey, and Bantam Spectra surviving, for the moment, as separate imprints; nor has the overall number of books released from Millennium gone down appreciably (it may even have gone up). Things went less quietly with the HarperCollins/Avon merger, though, with seventy-four people losing their jobs, and the disappearance of the HarperPrism line, which will be merged into Avon Eos to produce a new line (incorporating bought-but-not-yet-published Harper-Prism titles) called Eos.

The merger also touched off another round of Editorial Musical Chairs, after several quiet years, with Lou Aronica, John Silbersack, and John Douglas all leaving jobs at either Avon or Harper (a little later, fallout from the earlier Bertelsmann/Random House merger, Pat Lo Brutto left Bantam Spectra as well)—unlike earlier years, though the game may have run critically short of chairs, as, by press time, none of these very experienced publishing people had managed to find permanent employment elsewhere.

Although all this was sufficient to cause many a sleepless night for many an editor, including me, the chances are that the ordinary reader didn't even notice that there was anything going on, and *wouldn't*, even if things got much worse. After all the smoke had cleared, Avon Eos was left standing—as Eos—and, since it absorbed many of the upcoming HarperPrism titles, the overall number of titles published during the year remained about the same. There were even those who suggested that the efficiency and the profitability of the genre would *improve* because of these mergers, and certainly SF in recent years has been a field where a good deal of fat could be trimmed without coming anywhere near vital muscle tissue.

So far, then, SF as a genre has come remarkably well through some choppy seas, with only the troubled magazine market really taking on any significant amounts of water. Big changes are ahead, though, as we steer into a new century, and although my guess is that the sum total of those changes will probably prove to be positive, I think there's little doubt that ten years down the line, the publishing industry is going to look quite different than it does today—perhaps even radically, *fundamentally* different.

One of the most valid of the negative criticisms leveled against today's genre is that the big trade publishers, with a cautious eye on their bottom line and large amounts of money invested in each book, knowing that they have to appeal to mass audiences, are sometimes too timid in the kinds of books they'll accept, making it difficult to impossible for authors with quirky, eccentric work, stuff that might appeal more to a niche audience than to a mass audience, to get their books into print in the first place. With the advent of print-on-demand systems, however, this is changing fast, and deals that would have been sneered at as vanity publishing ten years ago are beginning to look surprisingly attractive—if you can print your own book, or have it printed for you by a small press, have it listed on key Internet sites such as Amazon.com, and even get it into the higher-end chain bookstores, as some of the more prominent print-on-demand publishers are able to do, with no need to stockpile large numbers of printed books, and orders filled only as they come in (no wastage, no returns, no print-five-books-to-sell-one), then what do you really *need* a traditional trade publishing house for at all? One answer is, for the up-front money, the advance. But since *you* get the royalties from publishing your own book, with no need to split with the publisher, if your book really sells *well*, in high enough numbers, you may not miss the advance much, if at all. Of course, if it *doesn't* sell well, you've basically published your book for *nothing*, no cash return whatsoever. So it's a gamble. But then, publishing has always been a gamble anyway, even by the traditional methods. (Another answer to "Why do you need a trade house?" is, to provide publicity and promotion—but with most lines doing little or none of that these days, except for the lead titles they expect to make big money on, the Internet may soon give you a fighting chance of doing that job yourself as well or better, too.)

Trade publishers will probably never entirely disappear, even in the most radical of scenarios. But they may well end up publishing mostly the high-end, high-stakes, high-expectation books by Big Authors, while everything *below* that level is published by an array of small-press publishers filling niche markets in a much more specialized (and efficient) way than has been possible up until now, so that nothing will be too quirky or offbeat or "marginal" to get a chance to seek its own audience . . . however small that audience may turn out to be. Nor do I think that this would necessarily be a bad thing. It's probably harder (though not impossible) for an author to get rich in this scenario—but then, getting rich has always been an improbable outcome for the overwhelming majority of authors anyway.

Nor is print-on-demand technology the only potential change just down the road that could radically alter the nature of the publishing world as we know it. The on-line booksellers, such as Amazon.com and barnesandnoble.com, are just starting to have a big effect on things, with quite probably a *much* bigger impact yet to come. The field of electronic books, e-books, is also in its infancy, but already books and even magazines are available to be downloaded into portable handheld computers such as Palm Pilots, Cassiopeias, Rocket eBooks, Visors,

Psions, and others through sites such as Peanut Press, Alexandria Digital Literature, Memoware, Mobibook, Rocket E-Book, Project Guttenburg, and a dozen other such sites. An industry insider told me a few months ago, sneeringly, that the sales of such electronic books would never amount to anything more than chump change, but I'm not so sure. Sales of handheld computers are climbing fast, and I'm willing to bet that within two or three years, four or five at most, most of the homes that have a PC will *also* have a handheld—or more than one.

So there are interesting times ahead of us, in the next century, in the next millennium. Things will probably be "interesting" after the fashion of the famous old Chinese curse, of course, but let's hope that things will *also* be "interesting" in the more traditional, straightforward usage of the word, interesting because suddenly we can see dozens of new potentials and new horizons opening up before us where before there was only one possibility—or none. In that sense, the century ahead may be very interesting indeed. Or so we can hope.

Once again, it was a bad year in the magazine market, with sales down almost across the board, and not just of science fiction magazines, either; many magazines far outside genre boundaries were affected as well.

Last year, I predicted, perhaps incautiously, that most of the genre magazines would probably survive into the next century—well, alas, I was wrong. Because the big story in the professional magazine market was the death, early in 2000, of *Science Fiction Age*, which ceased publication with its May 2000 issue.

Science Fiction Age's circulation had slipped steadily for the last four years, slipping another 26.3 percent in 1999. According to *Science Fiction Age's* former editor, Scott Edelman, though, the magazine *was* still profitable when it was killed, mostly because of the advertising revenue it brought in—just not profitable *enough* for parent company Sovereign Media, who are making greater profits on their nongenre magazines such as wrestling, media, and log-cabin hobbyist magazines, and decided to use the money tied up in *Science Fiction Age* to start some other kind of magazine instead where they could expect a greater return on their investment.

The death of *Science Fiction Age* is a major blow to the field; not only was Scott doing a good job with the magazine, having turned it into one of the top markets in the business, but it was one of the few magazines these days that was publishing a predominance of good solid core science fiction, rather than the fantasy, horror, and slipstream that saturates much of the rest of the field, particularly at the semiprozine level. It will be sorely missed.

The news in the rest of the magazine market was hardly much more cheerful. Sales were down everywhere. After an 11 percent gain in overall circulation in 1998, *Asimov's Science Fiction* registered a 24.1 percent loss in overall circulation in 1999, although newsstand sales were still slightly higher than in 1997. *Analog Science Fiction & Fact* registered a 13.4 percent loss in overall circulation in 1999, although their newsstand sales were also slightly higher than in 1997. *The Magazine of Fantasy & Science Fiction* registered a 6.3 percent loss in overall circulation, the smallest drop of any of the professional magazines, most of that in newsstand sales. *Realms of Fantasy* registered a 10.7 percent loss in overall circulation, slipping in both subscription and newsstand sales. *Interzone* held steady at a circulation of about four thousand copies, more or less evenly split between subscriptions and newsstand sales. Circulation figures for *Amazing* are not available, but sales are rumored to be somewhere in the ten thousand-copy per issue range, most of that sold on the newsstands.

As I've mentioned before, some of these figures probably look worse than they actually are. Many of these magazines, even the ones with declining circulations, may have actually *increased* their profitability in the last couple of years by adjusting their "draw" (sending fewer issues to newsstands that habitually sell less, so that fewer issues overall need to be printed and distributed in order to sell one issue, increasing the magazine's efficiency, and thereby lowering costs—and so increasing profitability) instituting cost-saving procedures in printing and physical production, targeting direct-mail outlets such as bookstores as opposed to scatter-shot mass markets (magazine racks in supermarkets—where SF magazines usually don't sell well), and eliminating their reliance on Publishers Clearing House–style cut-rate stamp-sheet subscriptions, which can actually cost more to fulfill than they actually bring in in revenue. The (more or less) digest-sized magazines (trim size went up slightly for *Asimov's* and *Analog* last year, with *F&SF* the only remaining "true" digest-sized magazine—but the principle remains the same) also have the traditional advantage that has always helped the digest magazines to survive, that they're so cheap to *produce* in the first place that you don't have to sell very many of them to make a profit—whereas a large-format slick magazine like *Science Fiction Age* is much more expensive to produce, which in turn means that you need to sell a greater number of copies in order to be profitable.

Nevertheless, the continued decline in circulation of the professional magazines is worrisome. Part of the problem for these magazines is their relative invisibility. It's harder than ever for the SF magazines to get out on the newsstand, because of magazine wholesaler consolidation and the recent upheavals in the domestic distribution network, which means fewer chances to attract new subscribers to replace the loss of old subscribers through natural attrition. The blunt fact is that most people—including many habitual science fiction readers (even, astonishingly, many convention-attending SF fans)—have no idea that the SF magazines even exist, and even if they *do* know about their existence, have probably never seen a copy offered for sale. Actually, considering that there is absolutely *no* advertising or promotion done for most of these magazines, none, zero, it's no wonder that most people have never heard of them. In a way, it's surprising that they sell as well as they *do*. What other product do you know that sells itself completely by word of mouth, with no advertising or promotional budget at all?

I have a feeling that use of the Internet as a promotional tool, using Web sites and other on-line means to push sales of the physical product through subscriptions, is what's going to save these magazines in the end, if anything can. Only time will tell if Internet promotion can turn things around, help the magazines do an end-run around the bottleneck of dwindling presence on the newsstands, of if it'll turn out to be a case of too little, too late.

Meanwhile, not all of the news in this market was downbeat. The Internet Web sites for both *Asimov's* and *Analog*, which went up in 1998 (*Asimov's* site is at http://www.asimovs.com, and *Analog's* is at www.analogsf.com) continue to bring in a small but steady flow of new subscriptions every month, many of them from heretofore untapped new audiences (particularly from other parts of the world, where interested readers have formerly found it difficult to subscribe because of the difficulty of obtaining American currency and because of other logistical problems), and I presume that the same is the case with the newish Web sites for other professional magazines, such as *The Magazine of Fantasy & Science Fiction* (http://www.sfsite.com/fsf/) and *Interzone* (http://www.sfsite.com/interzone/). *Asimov's* and *Analog* also worked out a deal with Peanut Press (http://www.peanutpress.com) late in 1999 that enables readers to download electronic versions of the magazines into Palm Pilot handheld computers, with the choice of either buying an electronic "subscription," or of buying them individually on an issue-by-issue basis; the numbers here have been small so far, but sales are growing steadily, and since it seems to me that this is an area with almost unlimited potential for growth, this could be a lot of help as well.

The Magazine of Fantasy & Science Fiction celebrated its fiftieth anniversary in 1999, while *Analog* celebrated its seventieth anniversary early in 2000, *Asimov's* celebrated its twenty-second anniversary, *Interzone* its ninth full year as a monthly magazine (the magazine itself was founded in 1982), and *Realms of Fantasy* completed its fifth full year of publication as one of the healthiest of the genre magazines, partially because of the enormous amount of advertising revenue it is reputed to draw. *Amazing Stories*, which returned from the dead last year as a glossy mixed SF/media magazine, completed its second full year of publication in its new incarnation (the title itself has been around, in one version or another, since 1926); parent company Wizards of the Coast was sold to Hasbro in 1999, but early indications are that this won't hurt *Amazing*—in fact, it may even mean a new influx of money for it, and help it get distribution along with Hasbro's card-gaming magazine, *Top Deck*.

Other than changes discussed above, the general information for most of these magazines remains more or less the same as last year, as far as personnel and format are concerned.

All of these magazines deserve your support, and, in fact, in today's troubled magazine market, one of the very best things you can do to ensure that short fiction remains alive and viable in the science fiction/fantasy market (and, by extension, that the genre *itself* remains healthy, since most of the significant evolution of the field goes on at short-story length) is to subscribe to the magazines that you like. In fact, subscribe to as many of them as you can—it'll still turn out to be a better reading bargain, more fiction of reliable quality for less money, than buying the year's hit-or-miss crop of original anthologies could supply.

(Subscription addresses follow: *The Magazine of Fantasy & Science Fiction*, Mercury Press, Inc., 143 Cream Hill Road, West Cornwall, CT 06796—$29.97 for annual in U.S.; *Asimov's Science Fiction*, Dell Magazines, P.O. Box 54033, Boulder, CO 80322-4033—$39.97 for annual subscription in U.S.; *Analog Science*

Fiction and Fact, Dell Magazines, P.O. Box 54625, Boulder, CO 80323 — $39.97 for annual subscription in U.S.; *Interzone*, 217 Preston Drove, Brighton BN1 6FL, United Kingdom, $60 for an airmail one-year (twelve issues) subscription. *Amazing Stories*, send e-mail to or call 800-395-7760, $10.95 for a four-issue (one-year) subscription. *Realms of Fantasy*, Sovereign Media Co., Inc., P.O. Box 1623, Williamsport, PA 17703 — $16.95 for annual subscription in U.S. Note that many of these magazines can also be subscribed to electronically on-line, at their various Web sites.)

It was another chaotic year in the still very young field of on-line electronic publishing, and although it remains true that the great promise of on-line-only fiction remained largely unfulfilled this year (as far as SF is concerned, anyway), this is an area where things are changing *very* fast, and everything can (and probably *will*) look completely different just a few months down the line.

Most of the year's big stories in this market were negative, although some potentially very positive stories are still just over the horizon as I write these words. Last year saw the death (as an active electronic magazine, anyway) of Algis Budrys's e-zine *Tomorrow*, while this year saw the death of Ellen Datlow's *Event Horizon* site (itself a replacement for the earlier *Omni Online* site, now also defunct, for which Datlow had been fiction editor). Launched in mid-1998, *Event Horizon* had quickly established itself as perhaps the most reliable place on-line in which to find good professional-level original SF/fantasy/horror stories, one of which, Kelly Link's "The Specialist's Hat," had won a World Fantasy Award by the end of 1999. Unfortunately, by the end of 1999, the money had also run out, and, unable to find further financial backing, *Event Horizon* died.

By the beginning of 2000, though, the indomitable Ellen Datlow had already landed a new job on-line, as the fiction editor for a forthcoming major new Web site to be launched in April of this year, part of an extensive expansion and renovation of the *Sci Fi* channel site (scifi.com), which recently bought the long-running e-zine *Science Fiction Weekly*, and is also home to the audio-play site *Seeing Ear Theater*, and to the monthly SF-oriented chats hosted by *Asimov's* and *Analog*; Datlow will be publishing SF stories and novellas on the site on a monthly basis, and, if history is any guide, the chances are that this will make it a major player in the on-line fiction market. Also opening at the beginning of the year was another major new site, *GalaxyOnLine* (run by renowned SF editor/writer Ben Bova), which features a distinguished lineup of columnists such as Harlan Ellison, Mike Resnick, Joe Haldeman, Jack Dann, Kristine Kathryn Rusch, and many others, runs scientific articles and book and movie reviews, and which, to date, has published one on-line original SF story, by Orson Scott Card. If they continue to publish originals (and it's to be hoped that they do), this site could become a major player in this market as well. More on both of these sites next year.

For the moment, though, with *Event Horizon* gone, good professional-level short *original* science fiction stories (stories making their initial "appearance" in electronic form) have become rather hard to find on-line. Of the surviving sites that publish original short fiction, some of the most interesting ones include *Talebones* (http://www.fairwoodpress.com/), *Dark Planet* (http://www.sfsite.com/darkplanet/),

Chiaroscuro (http://www.gothic.net/chiaroscuro/) *Inter Text* (http://www.intertext.com/), and *E-Scape* (http://www.interink.com/escape.html). Most of these sites lean heavily toward horror (it's currently a lot easier to find original horror stories online than original SF stories, it seems), although you will find an occasional science fiction story there as well.

There are a fairly large number of sites here and there around the Internet that archive good *reprint* SF stories. The British *Infinity Plus* (htt://www.users.zetnet.co.uk/iplus/) is a good general site that features a very extensive selection of good-quality reprint stories, most (though not all) by British authors, as well as extensive biographical and bibliographical information, book reviews, and critical essays. At *Mind's Eye Fiction* (http://tale.com/ghenres.htm), you can read the first half of a selection of reprint stories for free, but if you want to read the *second* half of the story, you have to pay a small fee (less than fifty cents per story in most cases) for the privilege, which you can do by setting up an electronic account on-line and then clicking a few buttons. Reprint stories (as well as novels) are also available to be bought in downloadable electronic formats at *Alexandria Digital Literature* (http://alexlit.com). In addition to the pro-magazine sites listed previously, there are also many SF-oriented sites that are associated with existent print magazines—*Eidolon: SF Online* (http://www.eidolon.net/); *Aurealis* (http://www.aurealis.hl.net/) *Altair* (www.sfsite.com/altair/); *TransVersions* (http://www.salmar.com/transversions/); *Albedo* (http://homepage.eircom.net/~goudriaan/); *On Spec* (http://www.icomm.ca/onspec/), but although many of them have extensive archives of material, both fiction and nonfiction, previously published by the print versions of the magazines, few of them publish original on-line-only fiction with any regularity; although magazines like *Asimov's* and *Analog* regularly run teaser excerpts from stories coming up in forthcoming issues. *Eidolon Online*, which published a good original story in 1997, doesn't seem to have published any complete on-line originals since.

(If none of these sites has satisfied your lust for e-zines, you can find lots of other genre electronic magazines by accessing http://dir.yahoo.com/Arts/Humanities/Literature/Genres/Science_Fiction_and_Fantasy/, but much of the stuff you'll find on these sites is no better than slush-pile quality.)

Although professional-level original fiction may be somewhat scarce, there are also many general-interest sites that are among the most prominent SF-related sites on the Internet, sites that, while they don't publish fiction, *do* publish lots of reviews, critical articles, and genre-oriented news of various kinds. Among the sites I visit the most frequently while Web surfing are: the *SF Site* (www.sfsite.com/), one of the most important genre-related sites on the whole Web, which not only features an extensive selection of reviews of books, games, and magazines, interviews, critical retrospective articles, letters, and so forth, plus a huge archive of past reviews but which also serves as host site for the Web pages of a significant percentage of all the SF/fantasy print magazines in existence, all of which can be accessed either directly or referenced from the *Fictionhome* page (http://www.sfsite.com/fiction/fichome.com.htm); *Locus Online* (http://www.locusmag.com), the on-line version of the newsmagazine *Locus*; a great source for fast-breaking genre-related news, as well as access to book reviews, critical lists, database archives, lists of links to other sites of interest, and to Mark Kelly's short fiction-review column, which at present is the only place on the Net where you can find regularly appearing reviews of SF and fantasy short fiction; *Science Fiction Weekly* (http://www.scifi.com/sfw/), more media and gaming oriented than *SF Site* or *Locus On-line*, but which also features news and book reviews in every issue, as well as providing a home for an erudite and sometimes controversial column by SF's premier critic, John Clute (and which is about to undergo a major renovation as part of the new scifi.com site); and SFF NET (http://www.sff.net) a huge site featuring dozens of home pages and "newsgroups" for SF writers, genre-oriented "live chats," a link to the *Locus Magazine Index 1984–1996*, and a link to the research data and reading lists available on the *Science Fiction Writers of America* page (which can also be accessed directly at http://www.sfwa.org/.) A new general review site, *SFRevu* (http://www.sfsite.com/sfrevu), seemed to have died late last year when, overcome with ennui, its editor burned out and gave up on it, but it's back in business again as of early 2000, the editor having gotten a second wind. Similarly, up until a few days ago, I would have said that the extremely valuable short-fiction review site, *Tangent Online* (http://www.sfsite.com/tangent/), had died, as nothing new had been posted there from early August 1999 until mid-March 2000, but editor David Truesdale has lately resurfaced, blaming technical difficulties and a too-full work schedule for his long silence, and vows to get *Tangent Online* going again on a regular basis; mind, there's still nothing new posted there as I type these words, some weeks later, but Truesdale's reassurances at least give me some hope that *Tangent Online* will someday be reborn—which would be a good thing for the entire genre, as venues that regularly review short fiction are vanishingly rare, either in print or on-line. If keeping up with all this still doesn't give you enough to do, live on-line interviews with prominent genre writers are also offered on a regular basis on many sites, including interviews sponsored by *Asimov's* and *Analog* and conducted by Gardner Dozois on the *Sci-Fi* channel (http://www.scifi.com/chat/) every other Tuesday night at 9:00 P.M. EST; regular scheduled interviews on the *Cybling* site (http://www.cybling.com/); and occasional interviews on the *Talk City* site (http://www.talkcity.com/). Genie has for all intents and purposes died, but many bulletin board services, such as Delphi, Compuserve, and AOL, have large on-line communities of SF writers and fans, and some of these services also feature regularly scheduled live interactive real-time "chats" or conferences, in which anyone interested in SF is welcome to participate. The SF-oriented chat on Delphi, every Wednesday at about 10.00 P.M. EST, is the one with which I'm most familiar, but there are similar chats on SFF.Net, and probably on other BBSs as well.

Another way to kill time on the Net with SF-related activities is to listen to audio-play versions of your favorite SF stories. The best site for this at the moment is the long-established (by Internet standards) *Seeing Ear Theater* (http://www.scifi.com/set/), but coming up this year is another new audio-play site, *Beyond 2000* (www.beyond2000.com), which will feature weekly hour-long dramatic programs hosted by Harlan Ellison. And soon, you may be able to watch SF-oriented original Web TV shows on-line as well, if sites such as *GalaxyOnline* and scifi.com can bring their plans to fruition.

Many of the criticalzines also have Web sites, including *The New York Review of Science Fiction* (http://ebbs.english.vt.edu/olp/nyrsf/nyrsf.html), *Nova Express* (http://www.delphi.com/sflit/novaexpress/), and *SF Eye* (http://www.empathy.com/eyeball/sfeye.html), although most of these sites are not particularly active ones. For a much more active site, one that provides a funny and often iconoclastic slant on genre-oriented news, check out multiple-Hugo-winner David Langford's on-line version of his fanzine *Ansible* (http://crete.dcs.gla.ac.uk/Ansible/). *Speculations*, which recently abandoned its print edition (see below) also has a fairly lively Web site at (http://www.speculations/com).

It's worth keeping a close eye on what's happening in this area, since the whole on-line market is changing so fast that you can miss something just by turning your head for a moment; it'll almost certainly look very different *next* year than it does now.

I wonder if it's not eventually going to be the fate of most semiprozines, both fiction semiprozines and the academically oriented critical ones, to give up their print editions and be reborn in electronic on-line-only formats, as *Tangent* and *Speculations* have already done. Only time will tell. In the meantime, it was an uneven year in the semiprozine market, as always, with old titles dying, older ones being reborn, others falling into that silent semiprozine limbo that is usually a bad sign in this area, and hopeful new contenders casting themselves into the ring even as beaten contestants are carried out on stretchers.

The big story this year for most folks would probably be the mind-boggling rebirth of the fiction semiprozine *Century*, after almost four years of total silence, but since the new issue is dated 2000, we'll have to let a review of it go until next year. (In the meantime, if you'd like to take the chance that *Century* won't vanish again, and subscribe—and this *was* widely considered to be perhaps the best and most literate of the fiction semiprozine back in its glory days—we'll list the subscription address below.) The long-awaited (also for years) first issue of *Artemis Magazine: Science and Fiction for a Space-Faring Society* also came out late in 1999, but because it's also dated 2000, we'll wait to review it next year as well (and we'll list its subscription address below, if you want to take a chance on it).

The big story in this market for last year was the consolidation of several fiction semiprozines under the umbrella of Warren Lapine's DNA Publications, which now publishes *Pirate Writings, Tales of Fantasy, Mystery & Science Fiction; Aboriginal Science Fiction; Weird Tales;* and the all-vampire-fiction magazine *Dreams of Decadence;* as well as Lapine's original magazine, *Absolute Magnitude, The Magazine of Science Fiction Adventures.* (Last year, it was widely reported that the Australian magazine *Altair: Alternative Airings in Speculative Fiction* was going to be joining the DNA group as well, but that doesn't seem to have happened—at least, *Altair* is at present maintaining a separate subscription address, and a separate Web page.) In DNA Publications's first year, Lapine has done a good job of beginning to stabilize publication schedules for the magazines, which all published more frequently than they had last year (with the exception, oddly, of Lapine's own *Absolute Magnitude*), subscription rates have also begun to creep up for all of them, and Lapine is reported to be pleased with their success so far, and optimistic about the future. Now he needs to work on producing a more reliable level of quality in the fiction published by those magazines, which, at the moment, is widely uneven, varying dramatically not only from story to story within the same magazine but from title to title. The best overall level of fiction in the DNA magazines this year was probably to be found in *Absolute Magnitude* and *Altair*, with the other magazines trailing behind. Still, let us keep our fingers crossed that the DNA magazines are going to turn out to be a success story financially, because, frankly, the fiction semipro market could use one. (Information about all of the DNA Publications magazines can be found at http://www.sfsite.com/dnaweb/home.htm.)

Marion Zimmer Bradley's Fantasy Magazine, one of the most reliably published of all the semiprozines, completed its twelfth year of publication, and, so far, has survived the death of founder and coeditor Marion Zimmer Bradley in 1999 (see below), with plans to continue the magazine for at least another year.

Terra Incognita, one of the newer semiprozines, and one that has maintained a high level of literary quality over the last couple of years (although a low level of reliability, as far as meeting their announced publishing schedule is concerned), managed to publish no issue at all in 1999, let alone the four they were supposed to have produced, although apparently an issue *did* eventually appear early in 2000, which we'll consider for next year. Similarly, there was supposedly an issue of *Tales of the Unanticipated* published this year, but we didn't see it in time to consider anything from it for this volume, and will have to hold it over for later. The curiously named *LC-39* started this year, but although it's a handsome production, looking more like a small-sized trade paperback than a magazine, most of the fiction in it struck me as rather weak; maybe it'll get better as it goes along. *Odyssey*, an ambitious full-size, full-color British magazine, died this year (perhaps because it never really could decide whether it was a science fiction magazine, a horror/fantasy magazine, or a media/gaming-oriented magazine, or perhaps merely because it was too expensive to produce), as did old-timer *Crank!* and mayfly-fast newcomer *Age of Wonder* last year. There were no issues of *Non-Stop*, *Xizquil*, *Argonaut Science Fiction*, *Next Phase*, *Plot Magazine*, or *The Thirteenth Moon Magazine* out this year, as far as I could tell, for the second year in a row, and I suspect some or most of them may be dead.

Of the surviving fiction semiprozines, *Talebones, Fiction on the Dark Edge*, is an increasingly attractive little magazine, lively and interesting, and, although officially a horror semiprozine, is publishing a higher percentage of science fiction and fantasy as well these days. *Indigenous Fiction: Wondrously Weird & Offbeat* is still around, although it leans more in the direction its subtitle would indicate than toward more traditional SF or fantasy. The long-running *Space & Time* has reinvented itself as a full-size slick magazine with nice covers and, probably as a result, is now getting national distribution on some newsstands. Although anything but slick, the eclectic little Irish semiprozine *Albedo* published some surprisingly good fiction this year by Brian Stableford, Esther M. Freisner, Colin Greenland, and others, including an evocative and fascinating novelette by Tais Teng. There are two Canadian fiction semiprozines, *On Spec, More Than Just Science Fiction* and *TransVersions*. *TransVersions*, the newcomer, still seems the livelier of the two as far as the fiction is concerned, while the long-established *On Spec*, one of the longest running of all the fiction semiprozines, has seemed a bit tired in recent years; *On Spec* is the more reliably published of the two, though (one of the most reliable in the entire semiprozine market, in fact). Australia brings us *three* top-notch fiction semiprozines, one new one, *Altair: Alternate Airings in Speculative Fiction* (no, don't ask *me* what the subtitle means), and the two others, *Aurealis, Australian Fantasy & Science Fiction* and *Eidolon, The Journal of Australian Science Fiction and Fantasy*, among the longest established of all fiction semiprozines (along with *On Spec*). Although most of these magazine have (and traditionally *have* had) difficulty sticking to their publication schedules (*Aurealis* and *Eidolon* are ostensibly quarterly magazines, but *Aurealis* published just two issues in 1999, and *Eidolon* managed only one; *Altair*, a biannual, published both of its scheduled issues) they also published, as usual, some of the best fiction in the semiprofessional market, with good work by Sean Williams, Paul Blake, and others in *Altair*, by Chris Lawson, Simon Ng, Andrew Morris, and others in *Eidolon*, and by Kyla Ward, John Ezzy, Robert Cox, and others in *Aurealis*. The dominant British fiction semiprozine is certainly *The Third Alternative*, a slick and handsome full-size magazine that features the work of top authors, but which features "slipstream," literary surrealism, and horror rather than anything that most genre fans are going to recognize as SF or fantasy. Much the same could be said of the long-established *Back Brain Recluse* (most British semiprozines seem to lean in this direction, in fact), although I haven't seen an issue of that for a while.

A promising new SF-oriented fiction semiprozine, scheduled to begin publication early in 2000, is the British *Spectrum SF*, which already has an impressive lineup of first-rate professional writers, including Alastair Reynolds, Keith Roberts, Stephen Baxter, Eric Brown, and Garry Kilworth, set for its first two issues. Let's hope it turns out to be as good as it sounds; if it does, it could quickly become a key player in this market.

I don't follow the horror semiprozine market much anymore, but there the most prominent magazine seems to be the highly respected *Cemetery Dance*, with perhaps *Talebones* as a follow-up.

Turning to the critical magazines, Charles N. Brown's *Locus* and Andy Porter's *SF Chronicle*, as always, remain your best bet among that subclass of semiprozines known as newszines, and are your best resource if you're looking for publishing news and/or an overview of what's happening in the genre; *SF Chronicle* is still missing issues, although they're doing better than last year, but, almost alone in the whole semiprozine category, fiction or critical, *Locus* comes out on time month after month, like clockwork, as it has been doing for more than thirty years. The only other magazine in the market that comes even close to this remarkable record is *The New York Review of Science Fiction*, edited by David G. Hartwell, which completed its eleventh full year of publication in 1999, once again bringing out its scheduled twelves issues of reviews, critical articles, esoteric miscellany, and sometimes fiercely contentious opinion. Another critical magazine that seems to be pretty reliably published is *Speculations*, a useful magazine that featured writing-advice articles as well as extensive sections of market reports and market news, had a pretty good publishing-reliability record as well, but early in 2000 announced that it was abandoning its print edition and would henceforth be available only in electronic form, at its Web site, http//:www.speculations.com. Most of the other criticalzines come out so erratically that you could fairly say that they don't really *have* schedules. There was an issue of Lawrence Person's *Nova Express* out this year, but Steve Brown's *SF Eye* has suspended publication. I'm pretty sure that the print version of David A. Truesdale's *Tangent* is dead at this point—at least, I can't honestly recommend that you spend your money subscribing to it, since I have my doubts that it will ever appear again—and even the fate of the on-line version, *Tangent Online*, is up in the air, although I have a little *more* faith that Truesdale will be able to get that one rolling again; let's hope so, since in its heyday *Tangent* was performing an invaluable service for the field, one that's not really being supplied by any other publication, with the sole exception of Mark Kelly's columns in the print and on-line versions of *Locus*.

(*Locus, The Newspaper of the Science Fiction Field*, Locus Publications, Inc., P.O. Box 13305, Oakland, CA 94661, $56 for a one-year first-class subscription, $46 for a second-class subscription, twelve issues; *Science Fiction Chronicle*, Algol Press, P.O. Box 022730, Brooklyn, NY 11202-0056, $20 for a one-year subscription, $25 for a one-year first-class subscription, twelve issues; *The New York Review of Science Fiction*, Dragon Press, P.O. Box 78, Pleasantville, NY 10570, $32 per year, twelve issues; *Nova Express*, P.O. Box 27231, Austin, TX 78755-2231, $12 for a one-year (four-issue) subscription; *Speculations*, 111 West El Camino Real, Suite 109-400, Sunnyvale, CA 94087-1057, a first-class subscription, six issues, $25; *Marion Zimmer Bradley's Fantasy Magazine*, P.O. Box 249, Berkeley, CA 94701, $16 for four issues in U.S.; *On Spec, More Than Just Science Fiction*, P.O. Box 4727, Edmonton, Alberta, Canada T6E 5G6, $18 for a one-year subscription; *Aurealis, the Australian Magazine of Fantasy and Science Fiction*, Chimaera Publications, P.O. Box 2164, Mt. Waverley, Victoria 3149, Australia, $43 for a four-issue overseas airmail subscription, "all cheques and money orders must be made out to Chimaera Publications in Australian dollars"; *Eidolon, the Journal of Australian Science Fiction and Fantasy*, Eidolon Publications, P.O. Box 225, North Perth, Western Australia 6906, $45 (Australian) for a four-issue overseas airmail subscription, payable to Eidolon Publications; *Altair, Alternate Airings in Speculative Fiction*, P.O. Box 475, Blackwood, South Australia, 5051, Australia, $36 for a four-issue subscription; *Albedo*, Albedo One Productions, 2 Post Road, Lusk Co., Dublin, Ireland; $30 for a four-issue airmail subscription, make checks payable to Albedo One; *Pirate Writings, Tales of Fantasy, Mystery & Science Fiction, Absolute Magnitude, The Magazine of Science Fiction Adventures, Aboriginal Science Fiction, Weird Tales, Dreams of Decadence*—all available from DNA Publications, P.O. Box 2988, Radford, VA 24142-2988, all available for $16 for a one-year subscription, all checks payable to D.N.A. Publications; *Century*, Century Publishing, P.O. Box 150510, Brooklyn, NY 11215-0510, $20 for a four-issue subscription; *Spectrum SF*, Spectrum Publishing, P.O. Box 10308, Aberdeen, AB11 6ZR, United Kingdom, 17 pounds sterling for a four-issue subscription, make checks payable to Spectrum Publishing; *TransVersions*, Paper Orchid Press, P.O. Box 52531, 1801 Lakeshore Road West, Mississauga, Ontario L5J 4S6, four-issue subscription, $20 U.S. or $24 Can., plus postage; *Terra Incognita*, Terra Incognita, 52 Windermere Avenue, #3, Lansdowne, PA 19050-1812, $15 for four issues; *Tales of the Unanticipated*, Box 8036, Lake Street Station, Minneapolis, MN 55408, $15 for a four-issue subscription; *Space and Time*, 138 W. 70th Street, 4B, New York, NY. 10023-4468, $10 for a two-issue subscription (one year), $20 for a four-issue subscription (two years); *Artemis Magazine: Science and Fiction for a Space-Faring Society*, LRC Publications, 1380 E. 17th St., Suite 201, Brooklyn, NY 11230-6011, $15 for a four-issue subscription, checks payable to LRC Publications; *Talebones, Fiction on the Dark Edge*, Fairwood Press, 10531 S.E. 250th Pl., #104, Kent, WA 98031, $16 for four issues; *Indigenous Fiction, Wondrously Weird & Offbeat*, I.F. Publishing, P.O. Box 2078, Redmond, WA 98073-2078, $15 for a one-year (three-issue) subscription; *LC-39*, Launch Publications, P.O. Box 9307, Baltimore, MD 21227, $12 for a one-year subscription, checks payable to Launch Publications; *The Third Alternative*, TTA Press, 5 Martins Lane, Witcham, Ely, Cambs. CB6 2LB, England, United Kingdom, $22 for a four-issue subscription, checks made payable to TTA Press; *Back Brain Recluse*, P.O. Box 625, Sheffield S1 3GY, United Kingdom, $18 for four issues; *Cemetery Dance*, CD Publications, Box 18433, Baltimore, MD 21237. Many of these magazines can also be ordered on-line, at their Web sites; see the on-line section, above, for URLs.)

It was a weak year in the original anthology market, even weaker than last year, with few original anthologies published, and even fewer of any significant quality. The best original SF anthology of the year, with little competition, was undoubtedly *Far Horizons*, edited by Robert Silverberg (Avon Eos), the companion volume to last year's highly successful fantasy anthology *Legends*. Like *Legends*, *Far Horizons* is an anthology of stories set in various well-known fictional worlds, except that this time those worlds are (ostensibly, anyway) science fictional ones rather than fantasy. If you're already a fan of any of the famous SF series featured here, there's little doubt you'll get more than your money's worth in entertainment value out of *Far Horizons* (if you're a fan of *all* of the series included here, you should be out the door and headed to the nearest bookstore already!) The only quibble I have is that the backstories involved in some of these long-running series have grown so complicated that a reader who comes to some of these novellas cold, without having read anything in that particular series before, may have trouble understanding what's going on in the story, or at least in appreciating its full emotional impact, which depends in part on an appreciation of prior context. All of the stories here suffer from this problem to some degree; the ones that do the best job of telling a satisfactory story that stands on its own feet without reference to the parent series being necessary include Ursula K. Le Guin's "Old Music and the Slave Women," Dan Simmons's "Orphans of the Helix," Nancy Kress's "Sleeping Dogs," Robert Silverberg's "Getting to Know the Dragon," and Gregory Benford's "A Hunger for the Infinite," but the other stories are well worth reading too, if you can overcome or overlook the dependent-on-familiarity-with-the-backstory flaw, or if you're already familiar with earlier work in the series. (There are a few interesting curiosities involved in the selection of the material for inclusion here, such as Anne McCaffery and Robert Silverberg being represented by stories in lesser-known series, since their best-known science fiction series had already been included in the *fantasy* anthology *Legends*—but that kind of hairsplitting will mean little to the average reader.) As a $27.50 hardcover, it's the most expensive anthology of the year, and some may hesitate because of the price, but considering the amount of quality of work you get for the money, it's really one of the best reading bargains of the year.

Running through the rather meager possibilities for a follow-up candidate for the title of best original SF anthology of the year, we quickly come to *Moon Shots*, edited by Peter Crowther (DAW), followed a half step or so down by *Not of Woman Born*, edited by Constance Ash (Roc). Both of these are substantial anthologies, although both suffer from the twin faults of original theme anthologies: some of the stories are too similar to each other, with motifs and assumptions and even major plot elements repeating in story after story (the stories by Brian Stableford, Stephen Baxter, and Scott Edelman in *Moon Shots*, for instance; the Stableford and the Edelman stories even share the idea that the architects of a reviving future space program would want to involve one of the last surviving participants of the twentieth-century space program as a PR stunt!), while at the same time, paradoxically, *other* stories are so far off the theme that it's hard to see any real justification for including the story in the anthology in the first place. (In *Moon Shots*, Colin Greenland's straight mainstream story certainly falls into this category, as does Robert Sheckley's flimsy supernatural tale, and the justifications for including Ian McDonald's surrealistic "Breakfast on the Moon, with Georges," or Gene Wolfe's "Has Anybody Seen Junie Moon?"—a homage to an obscure R. A. Lafferty story, which must make the Wolfe story rather puzzling to those who haven't read the Lafferty—are suspiciously weak as well; while in *Not of Woman Born*, several of the strongest stories, including the Walter Jon Williams, the Susan Palwick, and the Michael Armstrong, really have little to do with the ostensible theme of the anthology). With *Moon Shots*, I also found it somewhat disappointing that an anthology "in celebration of the thirtieth anniversary of the first manned moon landing" was so gloomy and pessimistic overall, with it being taken for granted in story after story that humankind's exploration of space is essentially over, and perhaps the human race itself is washed up as well (all of which contrasts oddly with Ben Bova's aggressively upbeat introduction to the anthology, which states the belief that the real Age of Space is just beginning— something I tend to believe myself). Nevertheless, both *Moon Shots* and *Not of Woman Born* are superior anthologies, with *Moon Shots* being undoubtedly the best original DAW anthology in more than a decade. The best stories in *Moon Shots*, in my opinion, were Stephen Baxter's "People Came from Earth," Paul J. McAuley's "How We Lost the Moon, A True Story by Frank W. Allen," and Brian Stableford's "Ashes and Tombstones," although there's also good work here by Eric Brown, Brian Aldiss, Gene Wolfe, and others. The best stories in *Not of Woman Born* were Walter Jon Williams's "Daddy's World," Sage Walker's "Hunting Mother," and Susan Palwick's "Judith's Flowers," although there's also good work by Jack McDevitt, Janni Lee Simner, Michael Armstrong, Constance Ash herself, and others. As inexpensive paperback originals, both anthologies make fairly good reading bargains too.

After the three titles discussed above, finding really worthwhile anthologies becomes much more problematic. Of the year's remaining original SF anthologies, the two best are both small-press items: in the long-running Canadian anthology series, *Tesseracts*, the latest edition, *Tesseracts*[8], edited by John Clute and Candas Jane Dorsey (Tesseract Books), and the assembled-on-line "SFF Net" anthology (mentioned also above), *The Age of Reason: Stories for a New Millennium*, edited by Kurt Roth (SFF NET). Both will be hard to find in bookstores (especially *The Age of Reason*), and so are probably better mail-ordered, and both are a bit pricey, but they're probably worth it, not only because of the quality of the fiction, which is reasonably high overall in both cases but because both anthologies will serve as an introduction to a lot of writers with whom the average reader is likely to be unfamiliar, instead of the familiar stable of usual suspects who feature in many of the year's other anthologies (especially paperback fantasy anthologies, which seem to use much the same roster of authors in one anthology after another). *Tesseracts*[8] features an excellent novella by Karl Schroeder, and good work by Sally McBride, Yves Meynard, Ursula Pflug, A. M. Dellamonica, Cory Doctorow, and others. *The Age of Reason* doesn't have any one standout piece that reaches the level of quality of the Schroeder story in *Tesseracts*[8], but it does feature a large amount of good work, much of it from unknowns or near unknowns such as Diana Rowland, Vera Nazarian, James A. Bailey, Susan J. Kroupa, Deborah Coates, and many others, as well as good stuff from bigger names such as Geoffrey A. Landis, Lois Tilton, G. David Nordley, Timons Esaias, Dave Smeds, and others. (Tesseracts Books, The Books Collective, 214-21 10405 Jasper Ave., Edmonton, Alberta, Canada T5J 3S2 — $9.95 (Canadian) for a paper edition, $23.95 (Canadian) for a cloth edition of *Tesseracts*[8]; SFF Net, 3300 Big Horn Trail, Plano, TX 75075 — $14.95 For *The Age of Reason: Stories for a New Millennium*; the book can also be ordered on-line at http://www.sff.net.)

After this point, we begin to run out of options fast. Although I suspect that many of the individual authors knew better, the New Age sillinesses that were part of the conceptual baggage that participants in the shared-world anthology *Past Lives, Present Tense*, edited by Elizabeth Ann Scarborough (Ace), were perforce constrained to make use of (such as the idea that transferring a dead person's DNA into a living person would enable the living person not only to experience the past memories of the dead person as if they were their own but would create a self-aware conscious persona of the dead person that could then sit inside the living person's skull and have long conversations with them about current happenings in the plotline), tip the stories from being science fiction to unadmitted fantasy, in my opinion. Most of the stories are rather weak anyway, with only R. Garcia y Robertson and Kristine Kathryn Rusch managing to fashion anything really readable out of this upromising clay. *Future Crimes*, edited by Martin H. Greenberg and John Helfers (DAW), is a promising theme, one that has produced many great SF stories over the years, but again the stories here are rather weak, with only the Alan Brennert story rising a bit above the average. The idea behind the very strange "anthology," *Quantum Speculative Fiction*, edited by Kurt Roth, based on a concept by publisher Gordon Meyer, is that you buy a three-ring loose-leaf notebook containing some original stories, with room for more, and then subsequently, four times a year, they send you an additional batch of new stories, which you can then clip into the notebook. It's an interesting experiment, but in practice has not turned out to be an entirely successful one for me, perhaps because of the "anthology's" narrow specialization, devoted to publishing only "funny" stories — most of which, alas, I didn't find to really be all that funny; humor being as subjective as it is, of course, *you* may find them hilarious. There are some good writers involved, including Michael Bishop, Leslie What, Robert L. Nansel, Terry McGarry, Kage Baker (who has the single best story here, "Desolation Rose," although it's not particularly funny), James Van Pelt, Richard Parks, K. D. Wentworth, and others. (This might work better if the contents were more generalized, and not restricted to just comic stories — but I'm not sure if this clip-in loose-leaf notebook concept is really a feasible one for fiction, no matter what kind of material they were using.) I haven't seen an "installment" of *Quantum Speculative Fiction* in a while now, and I'm not sure if they're really still continuing with it or not, but if you'd like more information (I can't find a price listed anywhere in the package I got), contact Obscura Press, P.O. Box 1992, Ames, IA 50010-1992, or send e-mail to www.quantumsf.com. And, as usual, *L. Ron Hubbard Presents Writers of the Future, Volume XV*, edited by Algis Budrys (Bridge), presents novice work by beginning writers, some of whom may later turn out to be important talents.

Other original SF anthologies this year included *Alien Abductions*, edited by Martin H. Greenberg and John Helfers (DAW), and the mixed SF/fantasy anthology *Prom Night*, edited by Nancy Springer (DAW).

In fantasy, there didn't seem to be any one single standout anthology, one that was obviously the year's best (like last year's *Legends*). The most substantial item in this category is probably the mixed fantasy/horror anthology *Silver Birch, Blood Moon*, edited by Ellen Datlow and Terri Windling (Avon) (which I choose to view as a fantasy anthology for these purposes; it does seem to lean more toward that end of the spectrum anyway), which contains good work by Tanith Lee, Nancy Kress, Robin McKinley, Patricia McKillip, Neil Gaiman, Delia Sherman, Nalo Hopkinson, Harvey Jacobs, Susan Wade, Melanie Tem, and others.

Below this point, there was only the usual welter of paperback fantasy theme anthologies, most of which could fairly be described as "pleasant but minor." The best of the lot, by a hair, was probably *Merlin*, edited by Martin H. Greenberg (DAW), which contained good work by Jane Yolen, Charles de Lint, Michelle West, Brooks Peck, and others. *A Dangerous Magic*, edited by Denise Little (DAW), contained interesting stuff by Peter Crowther, Michelle West, John DeChancie, and others; while *Twice upon a Time*, also edited by Denise Little (DAW), fairy tales retold from the viewpoint of the villian, contained worthwhile stuff by Esther M. Friesner, Nina Kiriki Hoffman, Leslie What, Alan Rodgers, Jane Lindskold, Richard Parks, Elizabeth Ann Scarborough, and others. *Chicks 'n Chained Males*, edited by Esther Friesner (Baen), which ought to get some kind of special award for dumbest title of the year (bad enough that the book actually carries a supposedly tongue-in-cheek disclaimer from the editor on the back cover, specifically blaming publisher Jim Baen for it!) is another in the series of comic anthologies that began several years back with *Chicks in Chainmail*; the book contains comic work Elizabeth Moon, Susan Shwartz, Harry Turtledove, Susan Casper, Lawrence Watt-Evans, K. D. Wentworth, and others, but there's definitely the feeling about the whole project that the joke is wearing thin, and that most of this ground has been covered before.

Since these are all relatively inexpensive paperbacks, you'll probably get your money's worth of entertainment out of them — don't expect anything really substantial here, though.

A fantasy shared-world anthology was *Legends: Tales from the Eternal Archives #1*, edited by Margaret Weis "with" Janet Pack and Robin Crew (DAW). I don't pay close attention to the horror genre anymore, but at a quick glance it would seem that the most prominent and acclaimed original horror anthology was probably *999*, edited by Al Sarrantonio (Avon). Other original horror anthologies included *Northern Frights 5*, edited by Don Hutchison (Mosaic Press); *White of the Moon*, edited by Stephen Jones (Gollancz); and the mixed mystery-horror anthology *Dark Detectives*, edited by Stephen Jones (Fedogan & Bremer).

Big news in this market for next year will probably be the appearance of the new volume in the prestigious *Starlight* anthology series, and perhaps (we hope) the appearance of the first volume in the as-yet untitled major new original anthology series that will be "like Full Spectrum," from Avon Eos. And the long-delayed "Space Colony" anthology edited by Greg Benford and George Zebrowski is supposed to hit print soon. Other than that, there doesn't seem to be much to really look forward to on the horizon in the original anthology market, not that we've heard about yet, anyway.

In spite of gloom so luxuriant among many fans and writers that it amounted to despair, in spite of the widely accepted myth that there are almost no publishing houses left in business anymore that publish genre books, and that almost everything that *does* come out is a media spin-off novel, in spite of mergers and shake-ups that cost the field at least one SF line, the fact is that more or less the same number of SF and fantasy books were published this year as last year (not counting media-oriented books), that there were actually *more* new SF and fantasy novels (again, not counting media novels) published in 1999 than there had been in 1998, and that with the opening floodgates of the print-on-demand market, it's possible that there could be a significant number *more* published *next* year (nor does it look like any really significant cuts are ahead for most of the regular trade publishers). In spite of the mergers and cutbacks and shake-ups, in spite of continuing moaning about how the genre is dying, there's still a *lot* of science fiction/fantasy/horror books being published, and chances are there will continue to be a lot of genre books published in the foreseeable future.

According to the newsmagazine *Locus*, there were 1,999 books "of interest to the SF field," both original and reprint, published in 1999, nearly the same as last year's total of 1,959. Original books were down by 1 percent, down to 1,107 from last year's total of 1,112, after a 12 percent gain last year brought the totals *up* from 1997's low of 999. The number of new SF novels was up, with 251 novels published, as opposed to 242 novels published in 1998, and 229 published in 1997, almost back up to the 1996 total of 253; the number of new fantasy novels was also up, with 275 published, as opposed to 233 novels published in 1998, the highest total since 1994's 234, and the first time in five years that more fantasy than SF novels were published; horror continued to slide downward after a brief upturn in 1998, with 95 horror novels published as opposed to 110 novels in 1998, down considerably overall from 1995's high of 193 titles.

A spot of perspective is perhaps in order: the number of original mass-market paperbacks published this year, 350, is alone higher than the *total number* of original genre books, of any sort, published in 1972, which was 225. Unless there's a crash so disastrous coming that it amounts to the de facto collapse of most of the publishing industry (possible, but not likely, unless there's a general society-wide Great Depression), it's hard to imagine that the genre will be reduced to those kind of numbers—which everyone regarded as "normal" and even healthy, in the 1970s—anytime soon.

I don't have time to read many novels, and this year I've had perhaps even less time than usual, so I can contribute no really definitive overview—but certainly among the best novels of the year, you'd have to list *Teranesia* (HarperPrism), by Greg Egan, *A Deepness in the Sky*, by Vernor Vinge (Tor), *Darwin's Radio*, by Greg Bear (Del Rey), *All Tomorrow's Parties*, by William Gibson (Putnam), *The Cassini Division*, by Ken Macleod (Tor), *Ancient of Days*, by Paul J. McAuley (Avon Eos), *Forever Free*, by Joe Haldeman (Ace), *The Martian Race*, by Gregory Benford (Warner Aspect), *Manifold: Time*, by Stephen Baxter (Del Rey), and *The Naked God*, by Peter Hamilton (Warner Aspect). Although I haven't yet read it, *Cryptonomicon*, by Neal Stephenson (Avon), was enough of a cult success, with an appeal stretching far outside the boundaries of the field as they are usually drawn, that it probably should have special attention called to it in any year-end wrap-up. As should the immensely popular Harry Potter books by J. K. Rowling, which may have outsold anything else in the genre this year; in fact, the chances are good that if somebody who is *not* a regular fantasy or science fiction reader has heard of *any* book with fantastic elements this year, it's a Harry Potter book that they've heard of; that ought to be more than enough to get them included in any year-end wrap-up that hopes to give an accurate picture of what was happening in 1999.

Other novels that have received a lot of attention and acclaim in 1999 include *Ender's Shadow*, Orson Scott Card (Tor); *On Blue's Waters*, Gene Wolfe (Tor); *Sky Coyote*, Kage Baker (Harcourt Brace); *Tamsin*, Peter S. Beagle (Roc); *Greenhouse Summer*, Norman Spinrad (Tor); *The Far Shore of Time*, Frederik Pohl (Tor); *Dog Eat Dog*, Jerry Jay Carroll (Ace); *Finity*, John Barnes (Tor); *Precursor*, C. J. Cherryh (DAW); *Bios*, Robert Charles Wilson (Tor); *A Calculus of Angels*, J. Gregory Keyes (Del Rey); *Kirinya*, Ian McDonald (Millennium); *The Fifth Elephant*, Terry Pratchett (HarperPrism); *A Civil Campaign*, Lois McMaster Bujold (Baen); *Down There in Darkness*, George Turner (Tor); *The Extremes*, Christopher Priest (St. Martin's Press); *The Conqueror's Child*, Suzy McKee Charnas

(Tor); *Mammoth*, Stephen Baxter (Millennium); *Minions of the Moon*, Richard Bowes (Tor); *The Rainy Season*, James P. Blaylock (Ace); *Architects of Emortality*, Brian Stableford (Tor); *Dark Cities Underground*, Lisa Goldstein (Tor); *Climb the Wind*, Pamela Sargent (HarperPrism); *Return to Mars*, Ben Bova (Avon); *Still Life*, Hal Clement (Tor); *Cavalcade*, Alison Sinclair (Millennium); *The Stone War*, Madeleine E. Robins (Tor); *A Red Heart of Memories*, Nina Kiriki Hoffman (Ace); *Moonfall*, Jack McDevitt (HarperPrism); *Waiting*, Frank M. Robinson (Forge); *Memoranda*, Jeffrey Ford (Avon Eos); *Against the Tide of Years*, S. M. Stirling (Roc); *Souls in the Great Machine*, Sean McMullen (Tor); *Singer from the Sea*, Sheri S. Tepper (Avon Eos); *Tower of Dreams*, Jamil Nasir (Bantam Spectra); *Foreign Bodies*, Stephen Dedman (Tor); *Starfire*, Charles Sheffield (Bantam Spectra); *There and Back Again, by Max Merriwell*, Pat Murphy (Tor); *Cave of Stars*, George Zebrowski (HarperPrism); *The Eternal Footman*, James Morrow (Harcourt Brace); *Black Light*, Elizabeth Hand (HarperPrism); *The Veiled Web*, Catherine Asaro (Bantam Spectra); *The Terrorists of Irustan*, Louise Marley (Ace); *The Stars Compel*, Michaela Roessner (Tor); *The Silicon Dagger*, Jack Williamson (Tor); *The Quiet Invasion, by Sarah Zettel* (Warner Aspect); *The Marriage of Sticks*, Jonathan Carroll (Tor); *Mr. X*, Peter Straub (Random House); and *Saint Fire*, Tanith Lee (The Overlook Press).

Mention should also be made of some recent omnibus reissues of classic novels, back in print again after an absence of years (or, in some cases: even decades): *Dark Ladies*, Fritz Leiber (Tor/Orb), which gathers together two classic Leiber novels, *Conjure Wife* and *Our Lady of Darkness*; *Rings*, by Charles L. Harness (NESFA Press, P.O. Box 809, Framingham, MA 01701-0203 — $25), which collects together the Harness novels *The Paradox Men*, *The Rings of Ritornel*, and *Firebird*, and adds to them a never-before-published novel, *Drunkard's Endgame*; *The Great Book of Amber: The Amber Chronicles 1–10*, by Roger Zelazny (Avon Eos), an omnibus of the first ten volumes in the Amber series; *Biting the Sun*, by Tanith Lee (Bantam Spectra), which includes *Don't Bite the Sun* and *Drinking Sapphire Wine*; and *The Essential Hal Clement, Volume 1: Trio for Slide Rule & Typewriter*, by Hal Clement (NESFA Press, P.O. Box 809, Framingham, MA 01701–0203 — $25.00), which gathers his classic novels *Needle*, *Iceworld*, and *Close to Critical*. Some very good stand-alone novels also were reprinted this year, including: *Emphyrio*, by Jack Vance (Orion Millennium); *The War Against the Rull*, by A. E. van Vogt (Tor/Orb); *The Drawing of the Dark*, by Tim Powers (Ballantine Del Rey); *The Dreaming Jewels*, by Theodore Sturgeon (Vintage); *Free Live Free*, by Gene Wolfe (Tor/Orb); *The Silver Metal Lover*, by Tanith Lee (Bantam Spectra); *The Deceivers*, by Alfred Bester (iBooks/Simon & Schuster); *The Wonder*, by J. D. Beresford (Bison Books); *Omega: The Last Days of the World*, by Camille Flammarion (Bison Books); *334*, by Thomas M. Disch (Vintage); and *Camp Concentration*, by Thomas M. Disch (Vintage). All of these publishers are to be commended for bringing long-out-of-print titles back into print, something that for too long has been left to the small presses by most of the trade publishers. The new Orion Millennium line, the Tor/Orb line, and the Vintage line are particularly worth checking out, with almost everything they reissue of interest. It's really encouraging to see backlist titles starting to come back into print again with increasing regularity, although even more could—and probably should—be done along these lines.

It seemed a somewhat weaker year for first novels than the last couple of years have been. *Shiva 3000*, by Jan Lars Jensen (Harcourt Brace), seemed to attract the most attention this year, followed by *The Silk Code*, by Paul Levinson (Tor) and *Starfish*, by Peter Watts (Tor). Other first novels included *Gardens of the Moon*, Steven Erikson (Bantam UK); *King Rat*, China Miéville (Tor); *Code of Conduct*, Kristine Smith (Avon Eos); *Shanji*, James C. Glass (Baen); *The Shadow of Ararat*, Thomas Harlan (Tor); *Nocturne for a Dangerous Man*, Marc Matz (Tor); and *The Thief's Gamble*, Julliet E. McKenna (HarperPrism). As usual, all publishers who are willing to take a chance publishing first novels should be commended, since the publishing of such novels is a chance that must be taken by *someone* if new talent is going to be able to develop, and if the field itself is going to survive.

Although I didn't read anywhere near all of the novels this year (probably physically impossible, for anyone for whom it wasn't a full-time job), or even the majority of them, what I *did* have time to read was of pretty high quality, and on the basis of that sample alone, it looked like a pretty strong year for the novels to me—as indeed it has been for the past several years now. Tor obviously had a strong year, as did Avon Eos (in spite of catastrophic shake-ups there), as did the new English line Millennium in its debut year, and HarperPrism in what, alas, proved to be its *last* year. And since I still frequently hear the old line about how nobody publishes "real" science fiction anymore (in spite of what's amounted to a renaissance in the ultra-hard SF novel in the last four or five years, paired with a boom in scientifically literate modern space opera), the fact is that the majority of novels on this year's list of notable books *were* center-core science fiction novels. Even omitting the fantasy novels and the borderline genre-straddling work on the list, you still had the Egan, the Vinge, the Gibson, the Bear, the Haldeman, the Benford, the Bova, the McAuley, the Clement, the Baxter, the Macleod, the Stableford, and close to a dozen others—all unquestionably pure-quill core SF, with many of them "hard SF" as rigorous and challenging as any that's ever been written by anyone in the history of the genre.

As usual, predicting what's going to take the major awards this year is a daunting task. I think that Vernor Vinge's *A Deepness in the Sky* has a shot at winning the Hugo. The Vinge novel might also have a shot at the Nebula, but there the situation is complicated by the fact that SFWA's bizarre "rolling eligibility" rule enables popular books from *last* year such as George R. R. Martin's *A Clash of Kings* and Maureen McHugh's *Mission Child* to compete for *this* year's award, so the probable winner becomes very hard to call. We'll just have to wait and see what *does* win!

Borderline novels by SF writers this year included *The Rift* (Avon), by Walter Jon Williams (writing as Walter J. Williams), a Big Fat Disaster novel, set in the near future, about a humongous earthquake striking the Mississippi Valley, that contains enough of Williams's typical stylishly bleak tropes to be satisfying to his usual fans, and which is compellingly readable enough to appeal to a broader audience as well. There were also two intriguing borderline novels this year that will have to be special-ordered from small presses, but which are well worth the trouble: *Interstate Dreams* (Mojo Press), by Neal Barrett, Jr., a bizarre and occasionally very funny mix of mystery, fantasy, and black humor in a mode that has been called Texas magic realism, similar in tone to Barrett's cult classic *The Hereafter Gang* (which John Clute called "the Great American novel," and which moved Joe Landsdale to exclaim "God Himself couldn't have written a better novel!") . . . and *The Ballad of Billy Badass and the Rose of Turkestan* (Xlibris), by William Sanders, a freewheeling, gritty, and funny mix of fantasy, SF, and hard-edged thriller that will appeal to anyone who has ever enjoyed Sanders's short fiction, such as the recent Nebula finalist "The Undiscovered." (Mojo Press, P.O. Box 1215, Dripping Springs, TX 78620 — $14 for *Interstate Dreams*, by Neal Barrett, Jr.; *The Ballad of Billy Badass and the Rose of Turkestan*, by William Sanders, can be ordered from Xlibris Press for $25 for a hardcover edition and $15 for a trade paperback edition, or it can be ordered from Sanders's own Web site at www.sff.net/people/sanders/bbrt.htm or ordered from Amazon.com.).

Associational novels by genre authors this year included *Motherless Brooklyn* (Doubleday), by Jonathan Lethem; *The Crook Factory* (Avon), by Dan Simmons; *Say Goodbye: The Laurie Moss Story* (St. Martin's Press), by Lewis Shiner; and *Essential Saltes: An Experiment* (St. Martin's Press), by Don Webb; plus a slew of mystery novels by SF writers, including *Defense for the Devil* (St. Martin's Press), by Kate Wilhelm; two novels by Mary Rosenblum writing as Mary Freeman, *Devil's Trumpet* (Berkeley) and *Deadly Nightshade* (Berkeley); *Freezer Burn* (Mysterious Press), by Joe L. Lansdale; and two novels by Ron Goulart, *Groucho Marx, Private Eye* (St. Martin's Press) and *Elementary, My Dear Groucho* (St. Martin's Press).

It was another pretty strong year for collections, something that's been true for a couple of years now. The best collections of the year included: *A Good Old-Fashioned Future*, by Bruce Sterling (Bantam Spectra); *The Robot's Twilight Companion*, by Tony Daniel (Golden Gryphon); *The Martians*, by Kim Stanley Robinson (Bantam Spectra); *The Dragons of Springplace*, by Robert Reed (Golden Gryphon); *Sex and Violence in Zero-G*, by Allen Steele (Meisha Merlin); *Miracle and Other Christmas Stories*, by Connie Willis (Bantam Spectra); *Beast of the Heartland and Other Stories*, by Lucius Shepard (Four Walls, Eight Windows), and *Hearts in Atlantis*, by Stephen King (Scribner).

Also good were: *Antique Futures: The Best of Terry Dowling*, by Terry Dowling (MP Books); *A Safari of the Mind*, by Mike Resnick (Wildside Press); *Apostrophes & Apocalypses*, by John Barnes (Tor); *The Lady of Situations*, by Stephen Dedman (Ticonderoga); *Dakota Dreamin'*, by Bill Johnson (Cascade Mountain); *Dragon's Fin Soup*, by S. P. Somtow (EMR);*The Dream Archipelago*, by Christopher Priest (Earthlight); *New Adventures in Sci-Fi*, by Sean Williams (Ticonderoga); *Where Garagiola Waits and Other Baseball Stories*, by Rick Wilber (University of Tampa Press); *Seven for the Apocalypse*, by Kit Reed (University

Press of New England); and *Really, Really, Really, Really, Weird Stories*, by John Shirley (Night Shade).

There were also several strong retrospective collections — collections that return long-unavailable work to print — this year, including: *Baby Is Three: The Complete Short Stories of Theodore Sturgeon*, Volume. VI (North Atlantic), by Theodore Sturgeon; *Futures Past*, by A. E. van Vogt (Tachyon Publications); *Farewell to Lankhmar*, by Fritz Leiber (White Wolf); *The Complete Boucher*, by Anthony Boucher (NESFA Press); *The Collected Stories of Jack Williamson, Volume 1: The Metal Man and Others*, by Jack Williamson (Haffner); and *The Collected Stories of Jack Williamson, Volume 2: Wolves of Darkness*, by Jack Williamson (Haffner).

Several of these collections function almost as *theme* collections, with Christmas the unifying theme in the Willis collection, baseball in the Wilber collection, while Somtow's *Dragon's Fin Soup* offers us "eight modern Siamese fables" set in Thailand, and Steele's *Sex and Violence in Zero-G* collects near-future stories mostly dealing with the construction of orbital habitats and the early stages of solar system exploration and interworld commerce. Robinson's *The Martians* also has an obvious enough theme, and has been described as a collection of outtakes from the writing of his massive Mars novel trilogy, but while that's true enough in a way, with characters from the trilogy reappearing in stories here, the collection *also* features poetry, scraps of "nonfiction," some (rather self-indulgent) autobiographical metafictional bits, and even Martian "alternate worlds" stories that don't share the story line of the trilogy, including a few where the terraforming of Mars has gone wrong, and even a couple of "mainstream" pieces in which we never went to Mars in the first place; in fact, rather than being just a straightforward collection of stories set on Robinson's fictional Mars, it's a tricky, elusive, postmodern grab bag of a book, whose closest relative in the genre is probably Ursula K. Le Guin's *Always Coming Home* — although if Robinson included recipes, or a cassette of flute music, I missed them (but I wouldn't have been surprised if they were there!). Although many of the "stories" are barely stories at all as we usually understand the term in the genre, the *cumulative* effect of the collection is powerful, and oddly moving. Speaking of Mars, *Rainbow Mars*, by Larry Niven (Tor), is an odd item, an omnibus of collection of Niven's long-running series of stories about Svetz, the hapless time traveler, matched with a complete new novel, the eponymous *Rainbow Mars*, which takes Svetz to an alternate-world Mars for further adventures; I'll mention it both here and in the novel section, since it's both a collection and a novel wrapped up in one package.

Turning to fantasy, the late Robert A. Heinlein is not usually thought of as a fantasy writer (in spite of *Glory Road*, one of the major fantasy novels of the early 1960s, before Tolkien's widespread popularity), but *The Fantasies of Robert A. Heinlein*, by Robert A. Heinlein (Tor), ought to be checked out as an eye-opener both by fantasy purists who've never read anything by Heinlein before and by hardcore Heinlein fans who've never read anything but his science fiction work; there's good stuff here such as "Waldo" and " '—And He Built a Crooked House'," mixed with lightweight stuff such as "The Man who Traveled in Elephants" and "Our Fair City," but note particularly " 'They—' " and "The Unpleasant Profession of Jonathan Hoag," pioneering classics of the ultimate paranoia How-Do-You-

Know-What-Is-Real? story; today we'd say they were Dickian, but both were published before Phil Dick even started writing, and they've influenced almost all
subsequent work in this mode, including recent movies like *The Matrix*. And
although it's really neither science fiction nor fantasy, as the terms are conven-
tionally used, Avram Davidson fans will certainly want the mystery collection *The
Investigation of Avram Davidson* (St. Martin's Press), edited by Grania Davis and
Richard A. Lupoff; these are not hardcore classical whodunits being rather of the
ironic "biter bit" variety that in many cases might just as easily have fit into *The
Magazine of Fantasy & Science Fiction* as into *Ellery Queen's Mystery Magazine*
(where many of them did appear), but they display all of Davidson's usual wit and
offbeat erudition, and several of them (such as the wonderful "The Lord of Central
Park") have minor fantastic elements as well. As you can see, the big trade houses
like Tor and Bantam Spectra are bringing out more collections these days, not
only collections by big names such as Larry Niven and Robert A. Heinlein and
Connie Willis, but, increasingly, even collections by middle-level names such as
Bruce Sterling, John Barnes, and Kim Stanley Robinson. If you want collections
by New Young Writers, though, for the most part, you still have to turn to small
presses such Golden Gryphon Press and Meisha Merlin. (One of the most encouraging stories of the year is that Golden Gryphon Press, which could have died
with its founder, Jim Turner, is going to continue under the stewardship of
Turner's brother Gary; in fact, under that stewardship, excellent collections by
Tony Daniel and Neal Barrett, Jr., have already appeared—we'll list the Barrett
next year—and new collections by Joe R. Lansdale, Richard Paul Russo, and
others, are already in the pipeline.) While small presses like NESFA Press,
North Atlantic, Tachyon, and Haffner remain vital—and unrivaled by the trade
publishers—for bringing collections of long-out-of-print work of historical importance back in a form where it can be accessed by modern readers.

Very few small-press titles, though, will be findable in the average bookstore, or
even in the average chain store, which means that mail order is still your best bet,
and so I'm going to list the addresses of the small-press publishers mentioned
above: NESFA Press, P.O. Box 809, Framinghan, MA 01701-0809—$25 for *The
Compleat Boucher*, by Anthony Boucher; Golden Gryphon Press, 3002 Perkins
Road, Urbana, IL—$23.95 for *The Dragons of Springplace*, by Robert Reed and
$24.95 for *The Robot's Twilight Companion*, by Tony Daniel; Wildside Press, P.O.
Box 45, Gillette, NJ 07933-0045—$15 for *A Safari of the Mind*, by Mike Resnick;
North Atlantic Books, P.O. Box 12327, Berkeley, CA, 94701—$30 for *Baby Is
Three: Volume VI: The Complete Stories of Theodore Sturgeon*, by Theodore
Sturgeon; Meisha Merlin Press, P.O. Box 7, Decatur, GA. 30031—$16 for *Sex
and Violence in Zero-G*, by Allen Steele; Tachyon Publications, PMB #139, 1459
18th Street, San Francisco, CA. 94107—$17 plus $2.50 postage for *Futures Past*,
by A. E. van Vogt; University of Tampa Press, 401 West Kennedy Blvd., Tampa,
FL. 33606—$24.95 plus $2.50 postage for *Where Garagiola Waits and Other
Baseball Stories*, by Rick Wilber; Alexander Publishing, 13243 Vanowen Ave, #5,
North Hollywood, CA 91605—$15.95 for *Dragon's Fin Soup*, by S. P. Somtow;
MP Books, P.O. Box 407, Nedlands, Western Australia 6909, Australia—$29.95
for *Antique Futures: The Best of Terry Dowling*; Ticonderoga Publications, P.O.

Box 407, Nedlands, Western Australia 6009, Australia—$17.95 plus $5 shipping for *The Lady of Situations*, by Stephen Dedman and $19.99 for *New Adventures in Sci-Fi*, by Sean Williams; Cascade Mountain Publishing, 1652 NW Summit Dr., Bend, OR 97701—$12.95 for *Dakota Dreamin'*, by Bill Johnson; Haffner Press, 5005 Crooks Rd., Suite 35, Royal Oak, MI 48073-1239—$32 plus $5 postage for *The Collected Stories of Jack Williamson, Volume One: The Metal Men and Others* and $32 plus $5 postage for *The Collected Stories of Jack Williamson, Volume Two: Wolves of Darkness*; University Press of New England/Wesleyan, 23 South Main St., Hanover, NH 03755—$16.95 plus $2.50 postage for *Seven for the Apocalypse*, by Kit Reed; Night Shade Books, 870 East El Camino Real, #133, Mountain View, CA 94040—$16.95 for *Really, Really, Really, Really, Weird Stories*, by John Shirley.

It was a moderately unexciting year overall in the reprint anthology field, although there were still a few good values here and there.

The best bets for your money in this category, as usual, were the various best-of-the-year anthologies, and the annual Nebula Award anthology, *Nebula Awards 33* (Harcourt Brace Jovanovich), edited by Connie Willis; this year there was also a retrospective anthology of work by past winners of the SFWA Grand Master Award (see below). Science fiction is being covered by two best-of-the-year anthology series, the one you are holding in your hand, and the *Year's Best SF* series (HarperPrism), edited by David G. Hartwell, now up to its fifth annual volume. (It would be inappropriate for me to review Hartwell's *Year's Best SF*, since it's a direct competitor to this volume, but suffice it to say that the general critical consensus seems to be that in a field as large and diverse as science fiction, there's more than enough room for two "best" anthologies every year; in fact, there's usually not all that much overlap between my selections and Hartwell's, which means that a greater spectrum of writers gets a chance to be showcased every year than would otherwise be the case.) If there was a new edition in a new best-of-the-year series concentrating on genre work of various sorts published in Australia, *The Year's Best Australian Science Fiction and Fantasy* (HarperCollins Australia Voyager), edited by Jonathan Strahan and Jeremy G. Byrne, which was up to volume two last year, I didn't see it. Once again, there were two best-of-the-year anthologies covering horror in 1999: the latest edition in the British series *The Mammoth Book of Best New Horror* (Robinson, Caroll & Graff), edited by Stephen Jones, now up to volume ten, and the Ellen Datlow half of a huge volume covering both horror and fantasy, *The Year's Best Fantasy and Horror* (St. Martin's Press), edited by Ellen Datlow and Terri Winding, this year up to its twelfth annual collection. In spite of the increasing popularity of the fantasy genre, fantasy, as opposed to horror, is still only covered by the Winding half of the Datlow/Winding anthology.

Turning to retrospective SF anthologies, books that provide a historical/critical overview of the evolution of the field, one of your best bets here is the above-mentioned anthology of work by writers who have won SFWA's Grand Master Award, *The SFWA Grand Masters, Volume 1* (Tor), edited by Frederik Pohl, which may be the most substantial single-volume SF reprint anthology of the year, containing classic work by Robert A. Heinlein, Fritz Leiber, Clifford D. Simak, L. Sprague de Camp, and Jack Williamson, much of which may be unavailable to (or even unknown to) modern generations of readers; two more volumes are to follow. Historic perspective of an interestingly quirky sort is provided by *My Favorite Science Fiction Story* (DAW), edited by Martin H. Greenberg, in which famous science fiction writers were asked to select their favorite science fiction story. The anthology features good work by Cordwainer Smith, Frederik Pohl, Roger Zelazny, Howard Waldrop, Ward Moore, Gordon R. Dickson, Theodore Sturgeon, James Blish, and others, plus interesting commentary from the selectors as to *why* they picked the story that they did. Some of the choices also shed light on the sources and inspiration for the selectors's *own* work, something that's suddenly very clear when you see Joe Haldeman select Frederik Pohl's "Day Million" as his favorite SF story (for an idea of what I mean, read Haldeman's own story "Anniversary Project" after first reading the Pohl), or Connie Willis select Ward Moore's "Lot," or Harry Turtledove select Howard Waldrop's "The Ugly Chicken"; some of the choices are at first glance surprising, like Arthur C. Clarke selecting Theodore Sturgeon's "The Man Who Lost the Sea," but make perfect sense when you think about them, and give you an interesting new perspective from which to examine the selector's work. The best work from the last few years of *F&SF*, including strong stories by Ursula K. Le Guin, Maureen F. McHugh, Bruce Sterling, John Crowley, Elizabeth Hand, and others, is featured in *The Best From Fantasy & Science Fiction: The Fiftieth Anniversary Collection*, edited by Edward L. Ferman and Gordon Van Gelder (Tor). Noted without comment is *The Good New Stuff* (St. Martin's Griffin), edited by Gardner Dozois, a retrospective overview of the evolution of "adventure SF" from the '60s to the '90s, a follow-up volume to last year's *The Good Old Stuff*.

There were several interesting "regional" reprint anthologies this year. *Centaurus: The Best of Australian Science Fiction*, edited by David G. Hartwell and Damien Broderick (Tor), gives us an overview of the booming Australian SF scene, and features good work by George Turner, Greg Egan, Chris Lawson, Lucy Sussex, Stephen Dedman, Cherry Wilder, Sean Williams, Hal Colebatch, Damien Broderick himself, and others. *Northern Suns*, edited by David G. Hartwell and Glenn Grant (Tor), showcases SF writers from Canada, and features good work from Cory Doctorow, Eric Choi, Sally McBride, Jan Lars Jensen, Nalo Hopkinson, W. P. Kinsella, Karl Schroeder, Geoff Ryman, and others. If you can get only one of these, *Centaurus* is slightly stronger than *Northern Suns*, but you ought to get both if you can afford it, to get a feeling for what's happening in worlds of SF writing outside the usual American/British axis. For a look at a *really* different world, where the featured writers will be unknown to much of the English-speaking genre audience, check out *The Dedalus Book of Spanish Fantasy*, edited by Margaret Jull Costa and Annella McDermott (Dedalus).

Two interesting small-press items, reprint anthologies somewhere on the borderland between SF and horror, are *Technohorror: Inventions in Terror* and *Bangs & Whimpers: Stories about the End of the World*, both edited by James Frenkel (Roxbury Park/Lowell House). *Technohorror* features good reprint work by Harlan

Ellison, Ray Bradbury, Damon Knight, Michael Swanwick, Pat Cadigan, Stephen King, and others (including an early Greg Egan story, from back when it looked as if he were going to turn out to be a horror writer instead of a hard-science writer), while *Bangs & Whimpers* (one of only two apocalyptic millennium-oriented books I can think of from this year, in SF, anyway, as opposed to the dozens that had been predicted) contains good reprints from Robert A. Heinlein, Robert Reed, Philip K. Dick, Frederik Pohl, James Tiptree, Jr., James Thurber, Isaac Asimov, and others.

Noted without comment are *Future War*, edited by Jack Dann and Gardner Dozois (Ace), *Armageddons*, edited by Jack Dann and Gardner Dozois (Ace), *Isaac Asimov's Valentines*, edited by Gardner Dozois and Sheila Williams (Ace), *Isaac Asimov's Werewolves*, edited by Gardner Dozois and Sheila Williams (Ace), and *Isaac Asimov's Solar System*, edited by Gardner Dozois and Sheila Williams (Ace).

Worth looking into in the reprint fantasy anthology market this year were *The Mammoth Book of Arthurian Legends* and *The Mammoth Book of Comic Fantasy II*, both edited by Mike Ashley (Carroll & Graf).

Other than the above-mentioned "best" anthologies by Stephen Jones and Datlow and Windling, there didn't seem to be a lot of reprint horror anthologies this year, but then again, I haven't been following the horror field closely, so I might have missed them. One of the few I did see was *100 Hilarious Little Howlers*, edited by Stephen Dziemianowicz, Robert Weinberg, and Martin H. Greenberg (Barnes & Noble).

An associational anthology that many SF/fantasy fans might enjoy, one that features the work of familiar genre authors such as Stephen Baxter, Tom Holt, Liz Holliday, and Richard A. Lupoff, is *Royal Whodunnits*, edited by Mike Ashley (Robinson).

It was a solid, if unexceptional, year in the SF-and-fantasy-oriented nonfiction and reference book field, with many of the best bargains in the related art book field.

The single most substantial volume of the year, in fact, was a book that could be considered to be either a cultural history of the field or an art book, depending on how you squint at it (we'll list it in both places), Frank M. Robinson's monumental *Science Fiction of the 20th Century* (Collector's Press). The Robinson book reproduces some of the most luminous (and most lurid) covers of the old pulp magazine era, thus making it one of the year's best art books, but although those glorious pulp images speak well for themselves, Robinson's discussion of the covers, setting them in their cultural context, is the icing on the cake, and functions as a shrewd and knowledgeable study of American pop culture in general, and science fiction in particular. Camille Bacon-Smith's *Science Fiction Culture* (University of Pennsylvania Press) also offers a pop-culture perspective on science fiction, particularly on the interactions of science fiction and science fiction "fandom," the several (only partially overlapping) subcultures of readers and enthusiasts—*fans*, originally from *fanatic*—that revolve (ostensibly, anyway) around the science fiction genre itself; but although there's a large amount of useful information here, and even some valuable insights, the author's sloppiness with matters of fact (most of them easily researchable) and generally vague grasp of genre history diminishes the book's value as a reference tool, although many members of the lay audience may find it entertaining and accessible.

There were also several drier, more academically oriented, reference books this year, probably more for the specialist than for the average reader, including: *Fantasy and Horror: A Critical and Historical Guide to Literature, Illustration, Film, TV, Radio, and the Internet*, edited by Neil Barron (Scarecrow Press); *Strange Constellations: A History of Australian Science Fiction*, by Russell Blackford, Van Ikin, and Sean McMullen (Greenwood Press); and *The Fantasy Literature of England*, by Colin Manlove (Macmillan UK). The extremely valuable research tool *The Locus Index to Science Fiction (1984–1998)*, by Charles N. Brown and William G. Contento, combined with the *Index to Science Fiction Anthologies and Collections*, by William G. Contento, is now available in CD form, from Locus Press for $45 — and if you have anything other than the most casual of interests in the SF field, this is an essential purchase that will pay for itself many times over in short order (myself, I find that there's rarely a week that goes by when I don't use it to look up *something*). It can be ordered on-line, at the Locus Online site, www.locusmag.com, and regular updates for it are available there as well. A more specialized, but also valuable, research tool, also in CD form, is the *Science Fiction, Fantasy, & Weird Fiction Magazine Index (1890–1998)*, by Stephen T. Miller and William G. Contento, also available from Locus Press for $45.

A generalized book of genre criticism was *Deconstructing the Starships: Science, Fiction and Reality*, by Gwyneth Jones (Liverpool University Press), while critical studies of individual writers included *Demand My Writing: Joanna Russ/Feminism/Science Fiction*, by Jeanne Cortiel (Liverpool University Press), and *The Road to Castle Mount: The Science Fiction of Robert Silverberg*, by Edgar L. Chapman (Greenwood). Books *about* writers included *George Turner: A Life*, by Judith Raphael Buckrich (Melbourne University Press), *Tarzan Forever: The Life of Edgar Rice Burroughs, Creator of Tarzan*, by John Taliaferro (Scribner), and a charming, frank, and insightful autobiography by Brian W. Aldiss. *The Twinkling of an Eye, or, My Life as an Englishman* (St. Martin's Press). Books of interviews with genre figures included *Pioneers of Wonder: Conversations with the Founders of Science Fiction*, by Eric Leif Davin (Prometheus), and *The Robert Heinlein Interview and Other Heinleiniana*, by J. Neil Schulman (pulpless.com). Further on the edges of the field, there were also several critical studies of fairy tales, including *When Dreams Come True: Classical Fairy Tales and Their Traditions*, by Jack Zipes (Routledge), *The Witch Must Die: How Fairy Tales Shape Our Lives*, by Sheldon Cashdan (Basic Books), and *No Go the Bogeyman: Scaring, Lulling and Making Mock*, by Marina Warner (Farrar Straus Giroux).

Out on the edges of the field in a different direction are two reference books for places that don't exist: *The Dictionary of Imaginary Places*, by Alberto Manguel and Gianni Guadalupi (Harcourt Brace), and *Dictionary of Science Fiction Places*, by Brian Stableford (Simon & Schuster). Also out on the borderlands somewhere, perhaps on the edge of Art Book Land, is *The Book of End Times*, by John Clute

(HarperPrism), a collage of illustrations, quotations, and photographs dealing with the turning of the millennium and the end-of-the-world frenzy it's been known to whip up.

Which edges us neatly into the art book field, which was fairly strong this year. I've already mentioned Frank M. Robinson's *Science Fiction of the 20th Century*, which, if considered as an art book, would be right up there at the top of the category. As would three retrospective collections, *Legacy: Selected Paintings and Drawings by the Grand Master of Fantastic Art*, by old master Frank Frazetta (Underwood), *Transluminal: The Paintings of Jim Burns*, by new(er) master Jim Burns (Paper Tiger), and *Maxfield Parrish 1870–1966*, by Maxfield Parrish (Abrams), a master not usually thought of as a genre artist at all, but one whose work has clearly had a deep and lasting impact on genre work, particularly fantasy landscape art. Last year, during his Locus Award acceptance speech, Arnie Fenner took me to task for referring to *Spectrum 5* as "a sort of Best-of-the-Year series that compiles the year's fantastic art," but it's hard to see any *other* description of the book that really fits (sorry, Arnie!); certainly it fits *Spectrum 6: The Best in Contemporary Fantastic Art*, by Cathy and Arnie Fenner (Underwood) just as well as it fit *Spectrum 5*, and is what makes this valuable as an overview of—just as it says—the contemporary fantastic art field, and places it near the top of the art book category as well. This year, though, it has a worthy rival in the overview-of-contemporary-fantastic-art category, *Fantasy Art of the New Millennium. The Best in Fantasy and SF Art Worldwide*, by Dick Jude (Voyager). Worth checking out as well is an overview of rarely seen art from what might just as well be another world, as alien as it is to the Western tradition, *Spirit Country: Contemporary Australian Aboriginal Art*, compiled by Jennifer Isaacs (Fine Arts Museums of San Francisco).

Also worthwhile in this category were *The Book of Sea Monsters*, by Bob Eggleton (Paper Tiger); *Soft As Steel, The Art of Julie Bell*, by Julie Bell (Paper Tiger); and *The World of Michael Parkes*, by Michael Parkes (Steltman).

There were a fair number of general genre-related nonfiction books of interest this year. Leading the list for most genre readers would probably be three nonfiction titles by well-known genre writers: *Greetings, Carbon-Based Bipeds!: Collected Essays 1934–1998*, by Arthur C. Clarke (St. Martin's Press), which is just what it says it is; *Deep Time: How Humanity Communicates Across Millennia*, by Gregory Benford (Avon Eos), also self-explanatory; and *Borderlands of Science: How to Think Like a Scientist and Write Science Fiction*, by Charles Sheffield (Baen), an odd but effective cross between science essays and writing-advice articles by a scientist who is also an SF writer (as are all three of these authors, by the way).

Moving a bit further afield, we have a new book from one of my favorites, *The Knowledge Web: From Electronic Agents to Stonehenge and Back—and Other Journeys Through Knowledge*, by James Burke (Simon & Schuster). Anyone who has read Burke's famous *Connections*, or seen any of the TV versions of Burke's work, knows what they're in for here—bits of obscure knowledge of the history of technology and surprising insights into ways in which they relate and interact, all flavored with Burke's wry, antic humor—and Burke doesn't disappoint. Assuming continued interest in alternate history and in space travel on the part of SF fans (a fairly safe bet), then many may be intrigued by *What If? The World's Foremost Military Historians Imagine What Might Have Been*, edited by Robert Crowley (Putnam), and *Entering Space: Creating a Space-Faring Civilization*, by Robert Zubrin (Putnam). And books such as *The Elegant Universe: Superstrings, Hidden Dimensions, and the Quest for the Ultimate Theory*, by Brian Greene (W. W. Norton & Co.), and *At Home in the Universe: The Search for Laws of Self-Organization and Complexity*, by Stuart Kauffman (Oxford University Press), may help you keep up with some of the more extreme mind-bending conceptualization done by today's cutting-edge hard science writers, such as Greg Egan or Brian Stableford or Alastair Reynolds.

There are no less than *two* different biographies of the late Carl Sagan out this year: *Carl Sagan: A Life in the Cosmos*, by William Poundstone (Henry Holt), and *Carl Sagan: A Life*, by Kery Davidson (Wiley), either or both of which may be of interest to genre readers, considering Sagan's status as perhaps the most prominent science popularizer of the last half of the twentieth century. And moving a bit further out on the borderlands, but still of interest to many genre readers, I'm willing to bet, is *Galileo's Daughter: A Historical Memoir of Science, Faith, and Love*, by Dava Sobel (Walker & Co.).

There may have been more genre movies released in 1999 than at any other time in history, and they ran the full spectrum from immense box-office blockbuster to immense box-office bomb, and from quiet little "serious" films to Big, Loud, and Dumb spectaculars; there were even a few movies that managed to do tremendously well at the box office *and* be of high artistic quality at the same time. I guess the millennium really *must* be at hand!

The most talked-about genre movie of the year was certainly *Star Wars, Episode One: The Phantom Menace*, which had the unhappy fate of being at the same time the most anticipated and the most disappointing movie of the year. Not that it's easy to call a movie that made as much *money* as *The Phantom Menace* did a "failure"—not while expecting anyone to keep a straight face, anyway. The movie made tons and tons of money, especially in the overseas market, and, last time I looked, had settled into the title of "highest-grossing movie of all time." (Although sales of *Star Wars* books and spin-off products were nowhere near as high as anticipated, particularly in Britain, where they tanked in great numbers . . . so perhaps even this huge cash cow ultimately didn't produce quite as much "milk" as they'd been counting on.) Artistically, however, although it may not have been a total failure, it certainly wasn't anywhere near the success that most *Star Wars* fans had hoped that it would be. After months of intense hype, and a promotional campaign that whipped fans up into a frenzy of anticipation, with some dedicated individuals waiting outside in all weather for *weeks* to buy advance tickets, I think that most people, even many of the hardcore *Star Wars* fans, walked away from the movie disappointed, to one extent or another—which may make it difficult to whip up anywhere near the same level of anticipation again for Episode Two. (One subjective but perhaps telling point: when I saw the original *Star Wars* for the first time, in 1977, the audience leaped to their feet at the end, cheering, and gave the movie a spontaneous standing ovation. When I saw *The Phantom Menace*, there was no such outburst at the end; instead, the fans filed quietly out of the theater, looking subdued, pensive, and, yes, *disappointed*. Not the way Lucas *wanted* them to react, I'm sure!)

There was still a lot to admire in *The Phantom Menace*, including some spectacular special effects, some wonderfully evocative sets, costuming, and set dressing, and a couple of well-staged fight scenes. Even some of the performances weren't bad, with Liam Neeson and Ewan McGregor doing the best they could with the limited material they had to work with; Neeson in particular did a good enough job of bringing a sense of quiet strength and gravitas to his role as Qui-Gon Jinn, a Jedi knight and mentor to the young Obi-Wan Kenobi (McGregor), that you regret the fact that he gets toasted by the villain, Darth Maul, and so won't make it into episode two. However, the writing is awful (particularly the dialogue, which is terrible even by *Star Wars* standards), the plot is muddled, illogical, uninvolving, and inconsistent (full of stuff that was obviously added at the last moment, without lots of thought about its implications, that retroactively invalidates everything in the "first" three movies), the characterization is minimal even for an action film (I don't think Darth Maul gets four lines of dialogue in the whole movie, and his motivations are completely unexplained, which makes him curiously uninvolving as a villain; there's not nearly enough time spent on the relationship between Qui-Gon Jinn and Obi-Wan Kenobi, either), and some of the actors are just *awful* (although you could charitably ascribe this to lack of effective direction, If you're so inclined). The kid, for instance, Anakin Sywalker, the pivotal character upon whom the whole plot revolves, and who is called upon to carry whole sections of the film on his puny little shoulders, is as waxen and lifeless as a department-store dummy (a major-league mistake making him a little kid, anyway, in my opinion; a lot of the tropes that jar and don't make sense when applied to a six-year-old would play much better with a *teenager*, someone about the same age that Luke was in the original *Star Wars*). Which brings us to Jar Jar Binks, the "comic relief" character who makes large stretches of this film teeth-grittingly unpleasant to sit through, and who is probably the most widely and intensely despised fictional character of the year, if not the decade, inspiring dozens of anti-Jar Jar sites to spring up on the Internet almost overnight. Jar Jar has also been widely attacked as a vicious racial caricature, and while I think that this was probably unconscious rather than deliberate on the part of the film makers, it *is* hard to watch him in action for long without being uneasily reminded of Stepin Fetchit. . . .

Lucas has amassed a great deal of goodwill and positive emotional capital over the years with the *Star Wars* movies and books—let's hope he hasn't spent too much of it with *The Phantom Empire* to successfully lure customers back into the theater for episode two. Let's also hope that episode two is a better movie *as a movie* than was episode one; there are some failings that special effects alone can't adequately compensate for, no matter how snazzy they are. Perhaps he'd be better off getting his buddy Steven Spielberg (who, no matter what you think of him, would never make the kind of elementary *storytelling* and movie-craft mistakes that Lucas makes here) to direct the next one, and settle for the role of producer instead.

The Phantom Menace may have been the box-office champ, but there were other movies that sold phenomenal numbers of tickets as well, and which may actually have been effectively *more* profitable than it was, considering how overwhelmingly less expensive they were to *make*. This is especially true in the case of the box-office blockbuster (and cultural phenomenon) *The Blair Witch Project*, which managed to rake in multiple millions in spite of a production budget of merely $30,000 (practically no budget at all, even by the most modest Hollywood standards!). I must admit that my first thought on seeing the movie was, *How did they manage to even spend as* much *as* $30,000 *on* this? Aside from some videotape equipment, there's nothing visible on-screen that costs more than a couple of hundred bucks, no sets, no costuming that couldn't have come off the rack at Kmart, and effectively no actors other than the three young leads, all unknowns. In fact, the movie is perfectly convincing as an amateur film made out in the woods somewhere by a trio of broke and not particularly talented student filmmakers. But the producers of *The Blair Witch Project* have shrewdly turned necessity into an advantage; because they had no special-effects budget, they *never show us* whatever it is that's supposed to be menacing this tentful of unhappy campers out in the woods, allowing the imaginations of the audience to supply horrors far more frightening than anything that could be explicitly shown on the screen, and thus scaring the crap out of audiences who yawned through big-budget, special-effects-heavy, blood-spattered gorefests such as *The Haunting*. (The *other* key to the success of *The Blair Witch Project* is a very clever postmodern campaign that suggested that all this is "real," that this *really is* footage found in a film can in the woods after the student filmmakers you see on-screen disappeared, never to be seen again—suggested this so effectively, including even a fake "documentary" about the "case" of the missing filmmakers that appeared on A&E, that there are some people unwilling to give up their emotional investment of belief even *now*, and who will still passionately insist that the whole thing is "real" and "actually happened." In fact, there are still Internet sites devoted to defending just this proposition! Another unexpected mega-hit was *The Sixth Sense*, which almost all the critics hated (including one major review that made it embarrassingly clear in retrospect that the critic had walked out at some point in the middle of the movie, if he'd ever actually gone in the first place), but which survived and prospered almost entirely on word of mouth, eventually building a huge audience. Which it deserved. *The Sixth Sense* was that rare animal, an intelligent and subtly underplayed supernatural horror movie; I went to the theater expecting to hate it, and instead walked away thinking that it was one of the best movies of the year. The writing is terrific here, tight and sharp, as is the intricate plotting, which works with the precision of a Swiss watch. The acting is also excellent; Bruce Willis—proving once again that he really *can* act if you force him to—is very good, but the boy, Haley Joel Osment, walks away with the movie, giving one of the best performances by a child actor that I've ever seen, anywhere; on my way out through the parking lot, I kept thinking, *Boy, if they'd gotten that kid to play Anakin Skywalker, he might have saved the movie!* Another relatively "quiet" supernatural movie, and another one that raked in millions, was *The Green Mile*, which now joins that small but distinguished group—along with *Stand By Me*, *Misery*, and *The Shawshank Redemption*—of movies made from Stephen King books that are actually worth *watching*.

Another box-office champ was *The Matrix*, which borrowed cyberpunk tropes from a dozen previous books and movies and stylishly reinvented them for the late '90s, but whose wonderful, state-of-the-art special effects and glossy production values couldn't disguise the fact that it was conceptually and spiritually empty at heart, more an arcade game or a live-action anime than a "real" movie, raising intriguing questions that it then didn't bother to face or answer, settling instead for an extended shoot-everything-in-sight climax that had the teenage boys jumping and bopping in their seats, but which sent much of the rest of the audience home unsatisfied (and which, with its man-in-long-black-trenchcoat-walking-around-blasting-everything-in front-of-him imagery, plays somewhat creepily in retrospect after the Columbine High School massacre). Also slick but essentially calorie free (although also a big moneymaker) was *The Mummy*, which had great special effects, but which somehow, in spite of all the computer-generated gruesomeness and ambulatory rotting corpses, managed not to be even as scary as the 1932 original, whose entire special-effects budget consisted of some bandages to wrap Boris Karloff up in; nobody seems to know how to *pace* either a scary movie or a thriller anymore, and only the *Blair Witch* people seem to have figured out that less is usually more as far as scaring the audience is concerned. (To be fair, *The Mummy* doesn't take itself terribly seriously, a relief after something like *The Matrix*, and is full of nice tongue-in-check stuff, admirably handled by the affable Brendan Fraser.) In spite of time-travel motifs, *Austin Powers: The Spy Who Shagged Me*, can't really be described as an SF movie, but it's certainly a fantasy of *some* sort, or at least a *spoof* of that sort of fantasy, and was immensely popular.

Animated movies of one sort or another also scored big this year, with *Toy Story 2*, *Tarzan*, *South Park; Bigger, Longer, and Uncut*, and the part-live-action, part-animated *Stuart Little* all finishing near the top of the money-earning charts. (Somewhat surprisingly, the *South Park* movie also turned out to be one of the most tuneful and enjoyable movie musicals in years, while functioning at the same time as a devastating and spot-on *satire* of movie musicals, especially Disney animated musicals; don't expect to hear most of the incredibly foul-mouthed songs on the radio, though, no matter how catchy they are! It's a lucky break for the Academy that it was "Blame Canada" that got nominated for an Oscar for best song, and *not* "Uncle Fucka.")

Not all of 1999's genre movies were big moneymakers, of course; not by any means. Some of them bombed pretty thoroughly, and the higher the movie's budget was, the more grandiose the producer's expectations, the longer and harder it had to fall. *Wild Wild West*, a big-budget remake of the campy old TV show that was expected to do big business, tanked big-time instead, and was probably the most critically savaged movie of the year as well; not even the charismatic Will Smith could save *this* one, although he at least managed to salvage a hit song (from the sound track) out of the wreckage. Other big-budget flops this year included the above-mentioned *The Haunting, Inspector Gadget, My Favorite Martian, The House on Haunted Hill, End of Days, Deep Blue Sea, Universal Soldier: The Return, Dogma, Virus, Stigmata, The Muse, Mystery Men*, and *Sleepy Hollow* (which made the odd choice of reinventing Washington Irving's charming little fable as a stylishly bleak splatterpunk movie). A fairly high-end movie called *The Astronaut's Wife* was announced, but if it ever played through Philadelphia, it must have done so *fast*, probably not a good sign. Caught somewhere between the top and the bottom of this food chain were movies that were probably mildly successful commercially, but not *that* successful, not even close to battling in the same league as *The Phantom Menace* and *The Matrix* and *Stuart Little*; how pleased the producers were with their track records probably depended on how much money they'd invested in them in the first place. My guess is that the producers were probably disappointed with the relatively modest success of the year's three *other* cyberpunk and/or virtual-reality movies, *The Thirteenth Floor, eXistenZ*, and *New Rose Hotel*, all of which have enthusiastic boosters (particularly *The Thirteenth Floor*), but which were certainly overshadowed by the immense commercial success of *The Matrix*, and mostly critically ignored, or—unfairly—dismissed in a "been there, done that" fashion as just another *Matrix*; I don't think any of them actually dogged out, but certainly none of them found the kind *real* mass audience they were supposed to find, either. Nor did *The 13th Warrior*, which presented Michael Crichton's *Eaters of the Dead* (in many ways as much a dry scholarly joke as a novel) as a sort of sword-and-sorcery-with-Vikings movie. Or *The Bicentennial Man*, which one friend described as "a robot *Mrs. Doubtfire*," and which most reviewers criticized for being too long, too slow, and too syrupy; perhaps it should have stuck closer to the source material. On the other hand, the producers of lower-budget, lower-expectation films that became modest sleeper hits such as *GalaxyQuest*, a sharp and funny satire of media SF and of *Star Trek* in particular, and *Blast from the Past*, a low-brow but good-natured comedy about a man encountering modern society for the first time after growing up locked in a bomb shelter, perfectly cast with Brendan Fraser to bring a likable, gee-whiz, naive-but-not-stupid quality to a role that might just as well be Casper Hauser, or a Man from Mars—were probably more satisfied with how many tickets they moved. I'm not sure how *Muppets in Space* and *The Muse* did, and I missed both of them, but they don't seem to have set any sales records either.

And, of course, there are other ways to measure success than just by how well something did at the box office. The surreal *Being John Malkovich*, for instance, was pretty far down the highest-grossing list, but it was a succès d'estime (it showed up on most critic's lists of the year's best movies), as was the stylish and often grisly (far more violent than the average animated movie) Japanese animated production, *Princess Mononoke*. One of the best movies of the year didn't make a dime, as far as I can see, and was pulled out of the theaters only a week or so into a disastrous theatrical first run—nevertheless, *The Iron Giant* is the kind of wonderful "family" entertainment that Disney animated movies promise to deliver, but (with recent exceptions such as *Toy Story, Toy Story 2*, and *A Bug's Life*) rarely ever do, with the added bonus of being intelligent, witty, thought provoking, and even at times suspenseful, as well as warmhearted, with a much lower maudlin quotient, and no damn songs. In short, *The Iron Giant* is one of the best animated movies I've ever seen, as delightful for adults as for children, and I'd recommend going out and buying the videotape or CD, since it's long banished from theaters, never to return. Another warmhearted and very well-crafted "small" movie is *October Sky*, which isn't technically a genre film at all, but which will certainly appeal to many genre fans with its gritty yet moving portrait (based on a true story) of a poor kid who uses model-rocket making as his gateway out of a Dickensian coal town and ultimately into a job in the space program. Even better than these two fine movies, though, is a movie that I missed on first release a couple of years back (I don't think that it ever passed through Philadelphia theaters at all), *The Whole Wide World*; I must admit that the idea of a movie based on the eccentric life of pulp fantasy writer Robert E. Howard sounded like an unlikely candidate for excellence to me, but, against all odds, *The Whole Wide World* turns out to be a terrific film, moving and absorbing (largely because of a hypnotically intense performance by Vincent D'Onofrio as Robert E. Howard), and certainly the best movie ever made about a genre writer, by a large margin; go out and rent this one, too (if you can even find it at the rental store; many places don't carry it).

There are *lots* more genre movies coming up on the horizon for 2000, some of which sound promising, some of which sound like they're going to be Just Awful; impossible to sort out at this distance which of them are going to be the Big Box-office Blockbusters and which the flops, although it sounds like expectations are being built moderately high for the Val Kilmer Mars-exploration movie. And, of course, oceans of ink (or Internet phosphors, anyway) are already being spilled speculating about how the forthcoming live-action movie version of Tolkein's *The Lord of the Rings* is going to turn out, and whether *Star Wars*, Episode Two is going to be better than Episode One (and who is going to be cast to play the teenage Anakin Skywalker, a role for which every conceivable actor except possibly Daffy Duck has been suggested), although neither of those are going to show up next year, or probably even the year after. Oddly, there's no new *Star Trek* movie in production, the producers reportedly not wanting to put something out that would have to compete with the new *Star Wars* movies. Considering at what a low ebb the whole *Star Trek* franchise seems to be at the moment, I think this may be a mistake (out of sight, out of mind, and then suddenly you're Old News, and they don't *let* you make a new feature film when you finally decide that you want to) — but then, they don't pay *me* for advice.

SF and fantasy on television seemed to be in a chaotic, transitional state this year, with most of the former big shows gone, or at least obviously nearing the end of their runs. Dueling cult favorites *Babylon 5* and *Star Trek: Deep Space Nine* have both gone off the air, as have *Hercules* and *Highlander*, and shows such as *The X-Files* and *Star Trek: Voyager* are obviously (and even admittedly) winding down, with maybe another year left ahead of them, or maybe not.

The departure of all these high-profile shows has obviously left a power vacuum, which producers are scrambling to fill. So far, a *Babylon 5* spin-off and an *X-Files* spin-off (as well as several strongly imitative *X-Files* clones by other hands) have proved unsuccessful, and have already been pulled off the airways, and the once-mighty *Star Trek* franchise seems to be at its lowest ebb in years, reduced to only the least popular (even among most *Star Trek* fans) of its shows, with even *it* probably on the way out (and with rumors flying that several potential new series suggested to replace it have been rejected by the network), and not even a new theatrical movie anywhere on the horizon (rumors that the studio is reluctant to commit to one have *also* been flying).

Some show is going to rush in to fill this vacuum, becoming the new cult favorite, and gaining huge audiences. The only question is, *which*?

So far, it looks to me as if *Farscape* might have the fast track. A reasonably intelligent (for a TV space opera) show that is played with some brio and panache (although I find it hard to get past the fact that all the aliens look suspiciously like Grover from Sesame Street; if you can deal with half the cast being Muppets without losing your willing suspension of disbelief, you'll respond better to the show than I've been able to), *Farscape* has clearly been building a loyal audience. Whether it can build *enough* of an audience to become 'the new *Babylon 5*,' as I've heard it touted in some circles, I don't know—but it seems to me that *Farscape* has the best chance of achieving this status of any of the hopeful new pack of genre shows.

The only show that looks like it might be a serious competitor, on the "sci-fi" end of the television spectrum anyway, is *Cleopatra 2525*, the replacement for *Hercules*, which has been picking up strong ratings in its time slot. A couple of years ago, I referred to shows such as *Xena* and *Buffy the Vampire Slayer* as "Beautiful Women Kick Male Butt" shows; well, along with the lame Canadian show *Lexx* (although to a lesser degree than *Lexx*, which is *really dumb*, to a jaw-dropping degree), *Cleopatra 2525* might be thought of as a "Sci-fi-jiggle show," since it seems mainly devoted to coming up with moderately implausible reasons for having scantily dressed women running around and shooting things (in *Lexx*, the scantily dressed woman doesn't even usually get to *shoot* stuff, although there's a great deal of high-school level sexual innuendo, served up with much nudge-nudge winking and leering). More intelligent, and actually less cartoonish in spite of being an animated series, is *Futurama*, a new comedy, set in the future, from the creators of *The Simpsons* (which itself is still on, and still popular, after all these years, although no longer quite the Cult Favorite it once was). Another new show, *Now and Again*, is sort of a cross between *The Six-Million Dollar Man* and *Universal Soldier*, although it seems to be running low on plot twists already. *Sliders* finally died completely, to no one's great regret. *Roswell* is a sort of soap-opera-with-UFO-aliens show, while *First Wave* is *The Fugitive* with UFO aliens, more or less. *Third Rock from the Sun* is a *comedy* with aliens, although of a more benign sort, *Mork & Mindy/Alf*-ish types rather than the sinister big-eyed anal-probing Earth-conquering variety. Can a *game show* with UFO aliens be far behind? Probably someone has one on the drawing board even as I type this. (*Who Wants to Be Abducted by an Alien Millionaire?* perhaps.)

Meanwhile, over on the fantasy end of the television spectrum, the above-mentioned *Xena: Warrior Princess* and *Buffy the Vampire Slayer* are still going strong. *Buffy* has launched a successful spin-off show, *Angel*, although the *High-*

lander spin-off, *Highlander: The Raven*, may have died; at least I haven't seen it around for a while. Several other pop-supernatural shows seem to have achieved one degree or another of success, such as *Sabrina, the Teenage Witch, Charmed, GvsE*, and a plethora of Angels-among-Us shows; there's even an actual daytime soap opera, *Passions*, in which most of the characters are witches! *The Drew Carey Show* often breaks triumphantly into the surreal, with the whole cast suddenly breaking into a song-and-dance number in the middle of a scene, or Daffy Duck coming to apply for a job, but it's perhaps stretching things too far to list it as a fantasy show, in spite of all that. *South Park* is still on, still uses a lot of fantastic tropes, and is still occasionally funny; the movie was better, though (and by far the best Satan-coming-to-Earth-to-bring-about-the-end-of-the-world movie of the year, in a year that saw several of them, some with budgets as large as the GNP of small Third-World nations).

All in all, it still doesn't seem to me like there's all that much *really* worth watching on television, as far as genre shows are concerned. Put on The History Channel or A&E or the Discovery Channel instead. Or, better still, turn the set off altogether, and read a book.

The 57th World Science Fiction Convention, Aussiecon Three, was held in Melbourne, Australia, from September 2–5, 1999. The third worldcon to be held in Australia, Aussiecon Three drew an estimated attendance of 1,872, the smallest worldcon since 1985, the last time that worldcon was held in Australia. The 1999 Hugo Awards, presented at Aussiecon Three, were: Best Novel, *To Say Nothing of the Dog*, by Connie Willis; Best Novella, "Oceanic," by Greg Egan; Best Novelette, "Taklamakan," by Bruce Sterling; Best Short Story, "The Very Pulse of the Machine," by Michael Swanwick; Best Related Book, *The Dreams Our Stuff Is Made Of: How Science Fiction Conquered the World*, by Thomas M. Disch; Best Professional Editor, Gardner Dozois; Best Professional Artist, Bob Eggleton; Best Dramatic Presentation, *The Truman Show*; Best Semiprozine, *Locus*, edited by Charles N. Brown; Best Fanzine, *Ansible*, edited by Dave Langford; Best Fan Writer, David Langford; Best Fan Artist, Ian Gunn; plus the John W. Campbell Award for Best New Writer to Nalo Hopkinson.

The 1998 Nebula Awards, presented at a banquet at the Marriott City Center Hotel in Pittsburgh, Pennsylvania, on May 1, 1999, were: Best Novel, *Forever Peace*, by Joe Haldeman; Best Novella, "Reading the Bones," by Sheila Finch; Best Novelette, "Lost Girls," by Jane Yolen; Best Short Story, "Thirteen Ways to Water," by Bruce Holland Rogers; plus an Author Emeritus award to Philip Klass, the Ray Bradbury Award for Dramatic Screenwriting to J. Michael Straczynski, and a Grand Master Award to Hal Clement.

The World Fantasy Awards, presented at the Twenty-Fifth Annual World Fantasy Convention in Providence, Rhode Island, on November 4–7, 1999, were: Best Novel, *The Antelope Wife*, by Louise Erdrich; Best Novella, "The Summer Isles," by Ian R. MacLeod; Best Short Fiction, "The Specialist's Hat," by Kelly Link; Best Collection, *Black Glass*, by Karen Joy Fowler; Best Anthology, *Dreaming Down-Under*, edited by Jack Dann and Janeen Webb; Best Artist, Charles Vess;

Special Award (Professional), to Jim Turner, for Golden Gryphon Press; Special Award (Nonprofessional), to Richard Chizmar, for Cemetery Dance Publications; plus a Life Achievement Award to Hugh B. Cave.

The 1999 Bram Stoker Award, presented by the Horror Writers of America during a banquet at the Hollywood Roosevelt Hotel in Hollywood, California on June 5, 1999, were: Best Novel, *Bag of Bones*, by Stephen King; Best First Novel, *Dawn Song*, by Michael Marano; Best Collection, *Black Butterflies*, by John Shirley; Best Long Fiction, "Mr. Clubb and Mr. Cuff," by Peter Straub; Best Short Story, "The Dead Boy at Your Window," by Bruce Holland Rogers; Nonfiction, *DarkEcho Newsletter* Volume 5 #1–50, edited by Paula Guran; Best Anthology, *Horrors! 365 Scary Stories*, edited by Stefan Dziemianowicz, Martin H. Greenberg, and Robert Weinberg; Best Screenplay, *Gods and Monsters*, by Bill Condon and *Dark City*, by Alex Proyas (tie); Best Work for Young Readers, "Bigger Than Death," by Nancy Etchemendy; plus a Lifetime Achievement Award to Roger Corman and Ramsey Campbell.

The 1998 John W. Campbell Memorial Award was won by *Brute Orbits*, by George Zebrowski.

The 1998 Theodore Sturgeon Award for Best Short Story was won by "Story of Your Life," by Ted Chiang.

The 1998 Philip K. Dick Memorial Award went to *253: The Print Remix*, by Geoff Ryman, with a Special Citation to *Lost Pages*, by Paul Di Filippo.

The 1998 Arthur C. Clarke award was won by *Dreaming in Smoke*, by Tricia Sullivan.

The 1997 James Tiptree, Jr., Memorial Award was won by "Congenital Agenesis of Gender Ideation," by Raphael Carter.

Dead in 1999 or early 2000 were: **A. E. van Vogt**, 89, one of the giants of the "golden age" of science fiction in the '30s and '40s, winner of SFWA's prestigious Grand Master Award, author of such seminal works as *Slan, The World of Null-A, The War Against the Rull, The Weapon Shops of Isher, Voyage of the Space Beagle*, and many other novels, and whose famous story "Black Destroyer" is seen by many as a direct inspiration for later media work such as *Alien* and the original *Star Trek* television series; **James White**, 71, famed Irish SF writer and fan, best known for his "Sector General" novels about a hospital in space, such as *Hospital Station, Star Surgeon, Sector General, Final Diagnosis*, and many others, as well as for stand-alone novels such as *The Watch Below, The Silent Stars Go By*, and *All Judgment Fled*; **Marion Zimmer Bradley**, 69, author of the best-selling *The Mists of Avalon*, one of the most acclaimed and influential Arthurian novels of the last thirty years, as well as many novels in the popular Darkover series, including *The Door Through Space, The Planet Savers*, and *The Sword of Aldones*, the editor of a large number of anthologies in the long-running Sword and Sorceress series, and founder and editor of *Marion Zimmer Bradley's Fantasy Magazine*; **Joseph Heller**, 76, whose best-selling cult classic World War II novel *Catch-22* had fantastic/surreal elements, also the author of fantasy novel *Picture This*, as well as novels such as *Something Happened, Good as Gold*, and *Closing Time*; **Paul Bowles**, 88, writer, composer, and artist, best known for the mainstream novel *The Sheltering Sky*, but who also wrote horror stories, some collected in *The Delicate Prey*; **Robert "Buck" Coulson**, 70, writer, critic, and well-known fan personality, coauthor (with Gene DeWeese) of the comic SF novels *Now You See It/Him/Them* and *Charles Fort Never Mentioned Wombats*, and coeditor (with wife, Juanita Coulson) of the Hugo-winning fanzine *Yandro*; **Gary Jennings**, 70, SF short story writer who achieved best-seller status with a series of historical novels such as *Aztecs, Spangle, Raptor, The Journeyer*, and *Aztec Autumn*; **Michael Avallone**, 74, prolific author best known for his "Ed Noon" series of detective novels, who also published horror, novelizations, and erotica; **Shel Silverstein**, humorist and cartoonist, author of several best-selling books for children, such as the infamous *Uncle Shelby's ABZ Book: A Primer for Young Minds, The Giving Tree*, and *Falling Up*; **Eddie Jones**, 64, well-known British SF artist whose covers adorned many books in the '60s and '70s; **Gil Kane**, 74, well-known comic-book artist, best known for his work on the comic book *Green Lantern*; **Stanley Kubrick**, 70, world-famous film director, director and cocreator (with Arthur C. Clarke) of one of the most famous SF movies of all time, *2001: A Space Odyssey*, as well as other genre movies such as *A Clockwork Orange* and *The Shining*, films with fantastic/surreal elements such as the fierce black comedy. *Dr. Strangelove, or How I Learned to Stop Worrying and Love the Bomb*, and nongenre films such as *Paths of Glory, Lolita*, and *Eyes Wide Shut*; astronomical artist **Ludek Pesek**, 80; **Adolfo Bioy Casares**, 84, Argentine writer of SF and magic realism; **Carl Johan Holzhausen**, 99, Swedish SF writer and translator; **Jerry Yulsman**, 75, author of the alternate-history novel *Elleander Morning*; **Robert J. Sobel**, history professor and author of the alternate-history book *For Want of a Nail: If Burgoyne Had Lost the Battle of Saratoga*; **John Broome**, 85, veteran pulp and comic-book writer; **Jim Turner**, 54, longtime editor of Arkham House, later founder and editor of Golden Gryphon Press, an editor almost singlehandedly responsible for publishing many (if not most) of the best short-story collections of the '80s and '90s, bringing out seminal collections by writers such as Greg Bear, Lucius Shepard, Nancy Kress, James Tiptree, Jr., Michael Swanwick, John Kessel, Mary Rosenblum, James Patrick Kelly, Tony Daniel, Robert Reed, and many others, at a time when most trade publishers refused to publish collections at all; **Ray Russell**, 74, writer and longtime executive editor of *Playboy*, winner of the Lifetime Achievement Awards from both the World Fantasy Convention and the Horror Writers of America, editor of the influential anthologies *The Playboy Book of Science Fiction and Fantasy* and *The Playboy Book of Horror and the Supernatural*, author, among many others, of the famous story "Mr. Sardonicus"; **Art Saha**, 76, SF editor, anthologist, and well-known fan, coeditor (with Donald Wollheim) of the long-running *The World's Best SF* anthology series, and editor of *The Year's Best Fantasy Stories* anthology series; **Howard Browne**, 91, onetime editor of *Amazing Stories* and founder and first editor of *Fantastic*; **Charles D. Hornig**, 83, onetime editor of *Wonder Stories, Future Fiction*, and *Science Fiction Quarterly*; **Clifton Fadiman**, 95, writer, editor, and '30s radio personality, whose introductions added a much-needed boost of literary respectability to many early SF books in the '50s and '60s, editor of the anthology *Fantasia Mathematica*; **Terry Hodel**, 61, producer of the long-running SF radio show *Mike Hodel's Hour 25*, founded by her late husband, Mike Hodel; **Frank McDonnell**, 59, scholar, science fiction critic, and mystery writer; **Tad Dembinski**, 27, former managing editor of *The New York Review of Science Fiction* and former editorial assistant to David Hartwell at Tor Books; **Larry Sternig**, 90, longtime literary agent; **Walt Willis**, 79, legendary British fan, fan writer, and fanzine editor, editor of the famous fanzine *Slant*; **George "Lan" Laskowski**, 50, well-known fan and editor of the Hugo-winning fanzine *Lan's Lantern*; **DeForest Kelley**, 79, actor best known to genre audiences for his long-running role as Dr. Leonard "Bones" McCoy in the original *Star Trek* series, and in subsequent *Star Trek* theatrical movies; **Marjii Ellers**, 81, longtime fan and costumer; **Joe Mayhar**, 69, husband of SF writer Ardath Mayhar; **Muriel Gold**, widow of the late SF editor H. L. Gold; **L. Allen Chalker**, 70, brother of SF writer Jack Chalker; **Andrew Keith**, 41, brother of and sometimes collaborator with SF author William H. Keith; **Jeanne Porter**, 86, mother of *Science Fiction Chronicle* editor/publisher Andrew I. Porter; **Edythe Marinoff**, 76, mother of SF writer Karen Haber Silverberg; **Beatrice Friesner**, mother of SF writer Esther M. Friesner; **Eric Felice**, 33, son of SF writer Cynthia Felice; **W. H. "Pete" Rowland**, father of SF writer Diana Rowland; and **Sarah Delany**, 109, coauthor of the memoir *Having Our Say: The Delany Sisters' First Hundred Years*, and great-aunt of SF writer Samuel R. Delany.

THE YEAR'S BEST

SCIENCE FICTION

the wedding album

DAVID MARUSEK

David Marusek is a graduate of Clarion West. He made his first sale to Asimov's Science Fiction in 1993, and his second sale soon thereafter to Playboy, followed subsequently by more sales to Asimov's and to the British anthology Future Histories. His pyrotechnic novella "We Were Out of Our Minds with Joy" was one of the most popular and talked-about stories of 1995; although it was only his third sale, it was accomplished enough to make one of the reviewers for Locus magazine speculate that Marusek must be a Big Name Author writing under a pseudonym. Not a pseudonym, Marusek lives the life of a struggling young writer in a "low-maintenance cabin in the woods" in Fairbanks, Alaska, where he is currently working on his first novel, and I'm willing to bet that his is a voice we'll be hearing a lot more from as we move through the new century ahead. His stories have appeared in our Thirteenth and Fifteenth Annual Collections. He has a web site at www.marusek.com.

In the vivid, powerful, and compassionate story that follows, he takes us back to the intricate and strange high-tech future milieu of "We Were Out of Our Minds with Joy," to a world where the border between what's real and what's not real has grown disturbingly thin—and we don't always find ourselves on the right side of the line.

Anne and Benjamin stood stock still, as instructed, close but not touching, while the simographer adjusted her apparatus, set its timer, and ducked out of the room. It would take only a moment, she said. They were to think only happy happy thoughts.

For once in her life, Anne was unconditionally happy, and everything around her made her happier: her gown, which had been her grandmother's; the wedding ring (how cold it had felt when Benjamin first slipped it on her finger!); her clutch bouquet of forget-me-nots and buttercups; Benjamin himself, close beside her in his charcoal grey tux and pink carnation. He who so despised ritual but was a good sport. His cheeks were pink, too, and his eyes sparkled with some wolfish fantasy. "Come here," he whispered. Anne shushed him; you weren't supposed to talk or touch during a casting; it could spoil the sims. "I can't wait," he whispered, "this is taking too long." And it did seem longer than usual, but this was a professional simulacrum, not some homemade snapshot.

They were posed at the street end of the living room, next to the table piled with brightly wrapped gifts. This was Benjamin's townhouse; she had barely moved in. All her treasures were still in shipping shells in the basement, except for the few pieces she'd managed to have unpacked: the oak refectory table and chairs, the sixteenth-century French armoire, the cherry wood chifforobe, the tea table with inlaid top, the silvered mirror over the fire surround. Of course, her antiques clashed with Benjamin's contemporary—and rather common—decor, but he had promised her the whole house to redo as she saw fit. A whole house!

"How about a kiss?" whispered Benjamin.

Anne smiled but shook her head; there'd be plenty of time later for that sort of thing.

Suddenly, a head wearing wraparound goggles poked through the wall and quickly surveyed the room. "Hey, you," it said to them.

"Is that our simographer?" Benjamin said.

The head spoke into a cheek mike, "This one's the keeper," and withdrew as suddenly as it had appeared.

"Did the simographer just pop her head in through the wall?" said Benjamin.

"I think so," said Anne, though it made no sense.

"I'll just see what's up," said Benjamin, breaking his pose. He went to the door but could not grasp its handle.

Music began to play outside, and Anne went to the window. Her view of the garden below was blocked by the blue-and-white-striped canopy they had rented, but she could clearly hear the clink of flatware on china, laughter, and the musicians playing a waltz. "They're starting without us," she said, happily amazed.

"They're just warming up," said Benjamin.

"No, they're not. That's the first waltz. I picked it myself."

"So let's waltz," Benjamin said and reached for her. But his arms passed through her in a flash of pixelated noise. He frowned and examined his hands.

Anne hardly noticed. Nothing could diminish her happiness. She was drawn to the table of wedding gifts. Of all the gifts, there was only one—a long flat box in flecked silver wrapping—that she was most keen to open. It was from Great Uncle Karl. When it came down to it, Anne was both the easiest and the hardest person to shop for. While everyone knew of her passion for antiques, few had the means or expertise to buy one. She reached for Karl's package, but her hand passed right through it. *This isn't happening*, she thought with gleeful horror.

That it *was*, in fact, happening was confirmed a moment later when a dozen people—Great Uncle Karl, Nancy, Aunt Jennifer, Traci, Cathy and Tom, the bridesmaids and others, including Anne herself, and Benjamin, still in their wedding clothes—all trooped through the wall wearing wraparound goggles. "Nice job," said Great Uncle Karl, inspecting the room, "first rate."

"Ooooh," said Aunt Jennifer, comparing the identical wedding couples, identical but for the goggles. It made Anne uncomfortable that the other Anne should be wearing goggles while she wasn't. And the other Benjamin acted a little drunk and wore a smudge of white frosting on his lapel. *We've cut the cake,* she thought happily, although she couldn't remember doing so. Geri, the flower girl in a pastel dress, and Angus, the ring bearer in a miniature tux, along with a knot of other dressed-up children, charged through the sofa, back and forth, creating pyrotechnic explosions of digital noise. They would have run through Benjamin and Anne, too, had the adults allowed. Anne's father came through the wall with a bottle of champagne. He paused when he saw Anne but turned to the other Anne and freshened her glass.

"Wait a minute!" shouted Benjamin, waving his arms above his head. "I get it now. *We're* the sims!" The guests all laughed, and he laughed too. "I guess my sims always say that, don't they?" The other Benjamin nodded yes and sipped his champagne. "I just never expected to *be* a sim," Benjamin went on. This brought another round of laughter, and he said sheepishly, "I guess my sims all say that, too."

The other Benjamin said, "Now that we have the obligatory epiphany out of the way," and took a bow. The guests applauded.

Cathy, with Tom in tow, approached Anne. "Look what I caught," she said and showed Anne the forget-me-not and buttercup bouquet. "I guess we know what *that* means." Tom, intent on straightening his tie, seemed not to hear. But Anne knew what it meant. It meant they'd tossed the bouquet. All the silly little rituals that she had so looked forward to.

"Good for you," she said and offered her own clutch, which she still held, for comparison. The real one was wilting and a little ragged around the edges, with missing petals and sprigs, while hers was still fresh and pristine and would remain so eternally. "Here," she said, "take mine, too, for double luck." But when she tried to give Cathy the bouquet, she couldn't let go of it. She opened her hand and discovered a seam where the clutch joined her palm. It was part of her. *Funny,* she thought, *I'm not afraid.* Ever since she was little, Anne had feared that some day she would suddenly realize she wasn't herself anymore. It was a dreadful notion that sometimes oppressed her for weeks: knowing you weren't yourself. But her sims didn't seem to mind it. She had about three dozen Annes in her album, from age twelve on up. Her sims tended to be a morose lot, but they all agreed it wasn't so bad, the life of a sim, once you got over the initial shock. The first moments of disorientation are the worst, they told her, and they made her promise never to reset them back to default. Otherwise, they'd have to work everything through from scratch. So Anne never reset her sims when she shelved them. She might delete a sim outright for whatever reason, but she never reset them because you never knew when you'd wake up one day a sim yourself. Like today.

The other Anne joined them. She was sagging a little. "Well," she said to Anne.

"Indeed!" replied Anne.

"Turn around," said the other Anne, twirling her hand, "I want to see."

Anne was pleased to oblige. Then she said, "Your turn," and the other Anne modeled for her, and she was delighted at how the gown looked on her, though the goggles somewhat spoiled the effect. *Maybe this can work out,* she thought, *I am enjoying myself so.* "Let's go see us side-by-side," she said, leading the way to the mirror on the wall. The mirror was large, mounted high, and tilted forward so you saw yourself as from above. But simulated mirrors cast no reflections, and Anne was happily disappointed.

"Oh," said Cathy, "look at that."

"Look at what?" said Anne.

"Grandma's vase," said the other Anne. On the mantel beneath the mirror stood Anne's most precious possession, a delicate vase cut from pellucid blue crystal. Anne's great-great-great grandmother had commissioned the Belgian master, Bollinger, the finest glass maker in sixteenth-century Europe, to make it. Five hundred years later, it was as perfect as the day it was cut.

"Indeed!" said Anne, for the sim vase seemed to radiate an inner light. Through some trick or glitch of the simogram, it sparkled like a lake under moonlight, and, seeing it, Anne felt incandescent.

After a while, the other Anne said, "Well?" Implicit in this question was a whole standard set of questions that boiled down to—shall I keep you or delete you now? For sometimes a sim didn't take. Sometimes a sim was cast while Anne was in a mood, and the sim suffered irreconcilable guilt or unassuagable despondency and had to be mercifully destroyed. It was better to do this immediately, or so all the Annes had agreed.

And Anne understood the urgency, what with the reception still in progress and the bride and groom, though frazzled, still wearing their finery. They might do another casting if necessary. "I'll be okay," Anne said. "In fact, if it's always like this, I'll be terrific."

Anne, through the impenetrable goggles, studied her. "You sure?"

"Yes."

"Sister," said the other Anne. Anne addressed all her sims as "sister," and now Anne, herself, was being so addressed. "Sister," said the other Anne, "this has got to work out. I need you."

"I know," said Anne, "I'm your wedding day."

"Yes, my wedding day."

Across the room, the guests laughed and applauded. Benjamin—both of him—was entertaining, as usual. He—the one in goggles—motioned to them. The other Anne said, "We have to go. I'll be back."

Great Uncle Karl, Nancy, Cathy and Tom, Aunt Jennifer, and the rest left through the wall. A polka could be heard playing on the other side. Before leaving, the other Benjamin gathered the other Anne into his arms and leaned her backward for a theatrical kiss. Their goggles clacked. *How happy I look*, Anne told herself. *This is the happiest day of my life.*

Then the lights dimmed, and her thoughts shattered like glass.

They stood stock still, as instructed, close but not touching. Benjamin whispered, "This is taking too long," and Anne shushed him. You weren't supposed to talk; it could glitch the sims. But it did seem a long time. Benjamin gazed at her with hungry eyes and brought his lips close enough for a kiss, but Anne smiled and turned away. There'd be plenty of time later for fooling around.

Through the wall, they heard music, the tinkle of glassware, and the mutter of overlapping conversation. "Maybe I should just check things out," Benjamin said and broke his pose.

"No, wait," whispered Anne, catching his arm. But her hand passed right through him in a stream of colorful noise. She looked at her hand in amused wonder.

Anne's father came through the wall. He stopped when he saw her and said, "Oh, how lovely." Anne noticed he wasn't wearing a tuxedo.

"You just walked through the wall," said Benjamin.

"Yes, I did," said Anne's father. "Ben asked me to come in here and . . . ah . . . orient you two."

"Is something wrong?" said Anne, through a fuzz of delight.

"There's nothing wrong," replied her father.

"Something's wrong?" asked Benjamin.

"No, no," replied the old man. "Quite the contrary. We're having a do out there. . . ." He paused to look around. "Actually, in here. I'd forgotten what this room used to look like."

"Is that the wedding reception?" Anne asked.

"No, your anniversary."

Suddenly Benjamin threw his hands into the air and exclaimed, "I get it, *we're* the sims!"

"That's my boy," said Anne's father.

"All my sims say that, don't they? I just never expected to *be* a sim."

"Good for you," said Anne's father. "All right then." He headed for the wall. "We'll be along shortly."

"Wait," said Anne, but he was already gone.

Benjamin walked around the room, passing his hand through chairs and lamp shades like a kid. "Isn't this fantastic?" he said.

Anne felt too good to panic, even when another Benjamin, this one dressed in jeans and sportscoat, led a group of people through the wall. "And this," he announced with a flourish of his hand, "is our wedding sim." Cathy was part of this group, and Janice and Beryl, and other couples she knew. But strangers too. "Notice what a cave I used to inhabit," the new Benjamin went on, "before Annie fixed it up. And here's the blushing bride, herself," he said and bowed gallantly to Anne. Then, when he stood next to his double, her Benjamin, Anne laughed, for someone was playing a prank on her.

"Oh, really?" she said. "If this is a sim, where's the goggles?" For indeed, no one was wearing goggles.

"Technology!" exclaimed the new Benjamin. "We had our system upgraded. *Don't you love it?*"

"Is that right?" she said, smiling at the guests to let them know she wasn't fooled. "Then where's the real me?"

"You'll be along," replied the new Benjamin. "No doubt you're using the potty again." The guests laughed and so did Anne. She couldn't help herself.

Cathy drew her aside with a look. "Don't mind him," she said. "Wait till you see."

"See what?" said Anne. "What's going on?" But Cathy pantomimed pulling a zipper across her lips. This should have annoyed Anne, but didn't, and she said, "At least tell me who those people are."

"Which people?" said Cathy. "Oh, those are Anne's new neighbors."

"New neighbors?"

"And over there, that's Dr. Yurek Rutz, Anne's department head."

"That's not my department head," said Anne.

"Yes, he is," Cathy said. "Anne's not with the university anymore. She—ah— moved to a private school."

"That's ridiculous."

"Maybe we should just wait and let Anne catch you up on things." She looked impatiently toward the wall. "So much has changed." Just then, another Anne entered through the wall with one arm outstretched like a sleepwalker and the other protectively cradling an enormous belly.

Benjamin, her Benjamin, gave a whoop of surprise and broke into a spontaneous jig. The guests laughed and cheered him on.

Cathy said, "See? Congratulations, you!"

Anne became caught up in the merriment. *But how can I be a sim?* she wondered.

The pregnant Anne scanned the room, and, avoiding the crowd, came over to her. She appeared very tired; her eyes were bloodshot. She didn't even try to smile. "Well?" Anne said, but the pregnant Anne didn't respond, just examined Anne's gown, her clutch bouquet. Anne, meanwhile, regarded the woman's belly, feeling somehow that it was her own and a cause for celebration—except that she knew she had never wanted children and neither had Benjamin. Or so he'd always said. You wouldn't know that now, though, watching the spectacle he was making of himself. Even the other Benjamin seemed embarrassed. She said to the pregnant Anne, "You must forgive me, I'm still trying to piece this all together. This isn't our reception?"

"No, our wedding anniversary."

"Our first?"

"Our fourth."

"Four *years?*" This made no sense. "You've shelved me for four years?"

"Actually," the pregnant Anne said and glanced sidelong at Cathy, "we've been in here a number of times already."

"Then I don't understand," said Anne. "I don't remember that."

Cathy stepped between them. "Now, don't you worry. They reset you last time is all."

"Why?" said Anne. "I *never* reset my sims. I never have."

"Well, I kinda do now, sister," said the pregnant Anne.

"But why?"

"To keep you fresh."

To keep me fresh, thought Anne. *Fresh?* She recognized this as Benjamin's idea. It was his belief that sims were meant to be static mementos of special days gone by, not virtual people with lives of their own. "But," she said, adrift in a fog of happiness. "But."

"Shut up!" snapped the pregnant Anne.

"Hush, Anne," said Cathy, glancing at the others in the room. "You want to lie down?" To Anne she explained, "Third trimester blues."

"Stop it!" the pregnant Anne said. "Don't blame the pregnancy. It has nothing to do with the pregnancy."

Cathy took her gently by the arm and turned her toward the wall. "When did you eat last? You hardly touched your plate."

"Wait!" said Anne. The women stopped and turned to look at her, but she didn't know what to say. This was all so new. When they began to move again, she stopped them once more. "Are you going to reset me?"

The pregnant Anne shrugged her shoulders.

"But you *can't*," Anne said. "Don't you remember what my sisters—our sisters— always say?"

The pregnant Anne pressed her palm against her forehead. "If you don't shut up this moment, I'll delete you right now. Is that what you want? Don't imagine that white gown will protect you. Or that big stupid grin on your face. You think you're somehow special? Is that what you think?"

The Benjamins were there in an instant. The real Benjamin wrapped an arm around the pregnant Anne. "Time to go, Annie," he said in a cheerful tone. "I want to show everyone our rondophones." He hardly glanced at Anne, but when he did, his smile cracked. For an instant he gazed at her, full of sadness.

"Yes, dear," said the pregnant Anne, "but first I need to straighten out this sim on a few points."

"I understand, darling, but since we have guests, do you suppose you might postpone it till later?"

"You're right, of course. I'd forgotten our guests. How silly of me." She allowed him to turn her toward the wall. Cathy sighed with relief.

"Wait!" said Anne, and again they paused to look at her. But although so much was patently wrong—the pregnancy, resetting the sims, Anne's odd behavior— Anne still couldn't formulate the right question.

Benjamin, her Benjamin, still wearing his rakish grin, stood next to her and said, "Don't worry, Anne, they'll return."

"Oh, I know that," she said, "but don't you see? We won't know they've returned, because in the meantime they'll reset us back to default again, and it'll all seem new, like the first time. And we'll have to figure out we're the sims all over again!"

"Yeah?" he said. "So?"

"So I can't live like that."

"But we're the *sims*. We're not alive." He winked at the other couple.

"Thanks, Ben boy," said the other Benjamin. "Now, if that's settled . . ."

"Nothing's settled," said Anne. "Don't I get a say?"

The other Benjamin laughed. "Does the refrigerator get a say? Or the car? Or my shoes? In a word—no."

The pregnant Anne shuddered. "Is that how you see me, like a pair of shoes?" The other Benjamin looked successively surprised, embarrassed, and angry. Cathy left them to help Anne's father escort the guests from the simulacrum. "Promise her!" the pregnant Anne demanded.

"Promise her *what?*" said the other Benjamin, his voice rising.

"Promise we'll never reset them again."

The Benjamin huffed. He rolled his eyes. "Okay, yah sure, whatever," he said.

When the simulated Anne and Benjamin were alone at last in their simulated living room, Anne said, "A fat lot of help *you* were."

"I agreed with myself," Benjamin said. "Is that so bad?"

"Yes, it is. We're married now; you're supposed to agree with *me*." This was meant to be funny, and there was more she intended to say—about how happy she was, how much she loved him, and how absolutely happy she was—but the lights dimmed, the room began to spin, and her thoughts scattered like pigeons.

It was raining, as usual, in Seattle. The front entry shut and locked itself behind Ben, who shook water from his clothes and removed his hat. Bowlers for men were back in fashion, but Ben was having a devil's own time becoming accustomed to his brown felt *Sportsliner*. It weighed heavy on his brow and made his scalp itch, especially in damp weather. "Good evening, Mr. Malley," said the house. "There is a short queue of minor household matters for your review. Do you have any requests?" Ben could hear his son shrieking angrily in the kitchen, probably at the nanny. Ben was tired. Contract negotiations had gone sour.

"Tell them I'm home."

"Done," replied the house. "Mrs. Malley sends a word of welcome."

"Annie? Annie's home?"

"Yes, sir."

Bobby ran into the foyer followed by Mrs. Jamieson. "Momma's home," he said.

"So I hear," Ben replied and glanced at the nanny.

"And guess what?" added the boy. "She's not sick anymore!"

"That's wonderful. Now tell me, what was all that racket?"

"I don't know."

Ben looked at Mrs. Jamieson, who said, "I had to take something from him." She gave Ben a plastic chip.

Ben held it to the light. It was labeled in Anne's flowing hand, *Wedding Album—grouping 1, Anne and Benjamin*. "Where'd you get this?" he asked the boy.

"It's not my fault," said Bobby.

"I didn't say it was, trooper. I just want to know where it came from."

"Puddles gave it to me."

"And who is Puddles?"

Mrs. Jamieson handed him a second chip, a commercial one with a 3-D label depicting a cartoon cocker spaniel. The boy reached for it. "It's mine," he whined. "Momma gave it to me."

Ben gave Bobby the Puddles chip, and the boy raced away. Ben hung his bowler on a peg next to his jacket. "How does she look?"

Mrs. Jamieson removed Ben's hat from the peg and reshaped its brim. "You have to be special careful when they're wet," she said, setting it on its crown on a shelf.

"Martha!"

"Oh, how should *I* know? She just showed up and locked herself in the media room."

"But how did she look?"

"Crazy as a loon," said the nanny. "As usual. Satisfied?"

"I'm sorry," Ben said. "I didn't mean to raise my voice." Ben tucked the wedding chip into a pocket and went into the living room, where he headed straight for the liquor cabinet, which was a genuine Chippendale dating from 1786. Anne had turned his whole house into a freaking museum with her antiques, and no room was so oppressively ancient as this, the living room. With its horsehair upholstered divans, maple burl sideboards, cherrywood wainscoting and floral wallpaper, the King George china cabinet, Regency plates, and Tiffany lamps; the list went on. And books, books, books. A case of shelves from floor to ceiling was lined with these moldering paper bricks. The newest thing in the room by at least a century was the twelve-year-old scotch that Ben poured into a lead crystal tumbler. He downed it and poured another. When he felt the mellowing hum of alcohol in his blood, he said, "Call Dr. Roth."

Immediately, the doctor's proxy hovered in the air a few feet away and said, "Good evening, Mr. Malley. Dr. Roth has retired for the day, but perhaps I can be of help."

The proxy was a head-and-shoulder projection that faithfully reproduced the doctor's good looks, her brown eyes and high cheekbones. But unlike the good doctor, the proxy wore makeup: eyeliner, mascara, and bright lipstick. This had always puzzled Ben, and he wondered what sly message it was supposed to convey. He said, "What is my wife doing home?"

"Against advisement, Mrs. Malley checked herself out of the clinic this morning."

"Why wasn't I informed?"

"But you were."

"I was? Please excuse me a moment." Ben froze the doctor's proxy and said, "Daily duty, front and center." His own proxy, the one he had cast upon arriving at the office that morning, appeared hovering next to Dr. Roth's. Ben preferred a head shot only for his proxy, slightly larger than actual size to make it subtly imposing. "Why didn't you inform me of Annie's change of status?"

"Didn't seem like an emergency," said his proxy, "at least in the light of our contract talks."

"Yah, yah, okay. Anything else?" said Ben.

"Naw, slow day. Appointments with Jackson, Wells, and the Columbine. It's all on the calendar."

"Fine, delete you."

The projection ceased.

"Shall I have the doctor call you in the morning?" said the Roth proxy when Ben reanimated it. "Or perhaps you'd like me to summon her right now?"

"Is she at dinner?"

"At the moment, yes."

"Naw, don't bother her. Tomorrow will be soon enough. I suppose."

After he dismissed the proxy, Ben poured himself another drink. "In the next ten seconds," he told the house, "cast me a special duty proxy." He sipped his scotch and thought about finding another clinic for Anne as soon as possible and one—for the love of god—that was a little more responsible about letting crazy people come and go as they pleased. There was a chime, and the new proxy appeared. "You know what I want?" Ben asked it. It nodded. "Good. Go." The proxy vanished, leaving behind Ben's sig in bright letters floating in the air and dissolving as they drifted to the floor.

Ben trudged up the narrow staircase to the second floor, stopping on each step to sip his drink and scowl at the musty old photographs and daguerreotypes in oval frames mounted on the wall. Anne's progenitors. On the landing, the locked media room door yielded to his voice. Anne sat spreadlegged, naked, on pillows on the floor. "Oh, hi, honey," she said. "You're in time to watch."

"Fan-tastic," he said, and sat in his armchair, the only modern chair in the house. "What are we watching?" There was another Anne in the room, a sim of a young Anne standing on a dais wearing a graduate's cap and gown and fidgeting with a bound diploma. This, no doubt, was a sim cast the day Anne graduated from Bryn Mawr *summa cum laude*. That was four years before he'd first met her. "Hi," he said to the sim, "I'm Ben, your eventual spouse."

"You know, I kinda figured that out," the girl said and smiled shyly, exactly as he remembered Anne smiling when Cathy first introduced them. The girl's beauty was so fresh and familiar—and so totally absent in his own Anne—that Ben felt a pang of loss. He looked at his wife on the floor. Her red hair, once so fussy neat, was ragged, dull, dirty, and short. Her skin was yellowish and puffy, and there was a slight reddening around her eyes, like a raccoon mask. These were harmless side effects of the medication, or so Dr. Roth had assured him. Anne scratched ceaselessly at her arms, legs, and crotch, and, even from a distance, smelled of stale piss. Ben knew better than to mention her nakedness to her, for that would only exacerbate things and prolong the display. "So," he repeated, "what are we watching?"

The girl sim said, "Housecleaning." She appeared at once both triumphant and terrified, as any graduate might, and Ben would have traded the real Anne for her in a heartbeat.

"Yah," said Anne, "too much shit in here."

"Really?" said Ben. "I hadn't noticed."

Anne poured a tray of chips on the floor between her thighs. "Of course you wouldn't," she said, picking one at random and reading its label, "*Theta Banquet '37*. What's this? I never belonged to the Theta Society."

"Don't you remember?" said the young Anne. "That was Cathy's induction banquet. She invited me, but I had an exam, so she gave me that chip as a souvenir."

Anne fed the chip into the player and said, "Play." The media room was instantly overlaid with the banquet hall of the Four Seasons in Philadelphia. Ben tried to look around the room, but the tables of girls and women stayed stubbornly peripheral. The focal point was a table draped in green cloth and lit by two candelabra. Behind it sat a young Cathy in formal evening dress, accompanied by three static placeholders, table companions who had apparently declined to be cast in her souvenir snapshot.

The Cathy sim looked frantically about, then held her hands in front of her and stared at them as though she'd never seen them before. But after a moment she noticed the young Anne sim standing on the dais. "Well, well, well," she said. "Looks like congratulations are in order."

"Indeed," said the young Anne, beaming and holding out her diploma.

"So tell me, did I graduate too?" said Cathy as her glance slid over to Ben. Then she saw Anne squatting on the floor, her sex on display.

"Enough of this," said Anne, rubbing her chest.

"Wait," said the young Anne. "Maybe Cathy wants her chip back. It's her sim, after all."

"I disagree. She gave it to me, so it's mine. And *I'll* dispose of it as I see fit." To the room she said, "Unlock this file and delete." The young Cathy, her table, and the banquet hall dissolved into noise and nothingness, and the media room was itself again.

"Or this one," Anne said, picking up a chip that read *Junior Prom Night*. The young Anne opened her mouth to protest, but thought better of it. Anne fed this chip, along with all the rest of them, into the player. A long directory of file names appeared on the wall. "Unlock *Junior Prom Night*." The file's name turned from red to green, and the young Anne appealed to Ben with a look.

"Anne," he said, "don't you think we should at least look at it first?"

"What for? I know what it is. High school, dressing up, lusting after boys, dancing. Who needs it? Delete file." The item blinked three times before vanishing, and the directory scrolled up to fill the space. The young sim shivered, and Anne said, "Select the next one."

The next item was entitled *A Midsummer's Night Dream*. Now the young Anne was compelled to speak, "You can't delete that one. You were great in that, don't you remember? Everyone loved you. It was the best night of your life."

"Don't presume to tell *me* what was the best night of my life," Anne said. "Unlock *A Midsummer's Night Dream*." She smiled at the young Anne. "Delete file." The menu item blinked out. "Good. Now unlock *all* the files." The whole directory turned from red to green.

"Please make her stop," the sim implored.

"Next," said Anne. The next file was *High School Graduation*. "Delete file. Next." The next was labeled only *Mama*.

"Anne," said Ben, "why don't we come back to this later. The house says dinner's ready."

She didn't respond.

"You must be famished after your busy day," he continued. "I know I am."

"Then please go eat, dear," she replied. To the room she said, "Play *Mama*."

The media room was overlaid by a gloomy bedroom that Ben at first mistook for their own. He recognized much of the heavy Georgian furniture, the sprawling canopied bed in which he felt so claustrophobic, and the voluminous damask curtains, shut now and leaking yellow evening light. But this was not their bedroom, the arrangement was wrong.

In the corner stood two placeholders, mute statues of a teenaged Anne and her father, grief frozen on their faces as they peered down at a couch draped with tapestry and piled high with down comforters. And suddenly Ben knew what this was. It was Anne's mother's deathbed sim. Geraldine, whom he'd never met in life nor holo. Her bald eggshell skull lay weightless on feather pillows in silk covers. They had meant to cast her farewell and accidently caught her at the precise moment of her death. He had heard of this sim from Cathy and others. It was not one he would have kept.

Suddenly, the old woman on the couch sighed, and all the breath went out of her in a bubbly gush. Both Annes, the graduate and the naked one, waited expectantly. For long moments the only sound was the tocking of a clock that Ben recognized as the Seth Thomas clock currently located on the library mantel. Finally there was a cough, a hacking cough with scant strength behind it, and a groan, "Am I back?"

"Yes, Mother," said Anne.

"And I'm still a sim?"

"Yes."

"Please delete me."

"Yes, Mother," Anne said and turned to Ben. "We've always thought she had a bad death and hoped it might improve over time."

"That's crazy," snapped the young Anne. "That's not why I kept this sim."

"Oh, no?" said Anne. "Then why *did* you keep it?" But the young sim seemed confused and couldn't articulate her thoughts. "You don't know because I didn't know at the time either," said Anne. "But I know *now*, so I'll tell you. You're fascinated with death. It scares you silly. You wish someone would tell you what's on the other side. So you've enlisted your own sweet mama."

"That's ridiculous."

Anne turned to the deathbed tableau. "Mother, tell us what you saw there."

"I saw nothing," came the bitter reply. "You cast me without my eyeglasses."

"Ho ho," said Anne. "Geraldine was nothing if not comedic."

"You also cast me wretchedly thirsty, cold, and with a bursting bladder, damn you! And the pain! I beg you, daughter, delete me."

"I will, Mother, I promise, but first you have to tell us what you saw."

"That's what you said the last time."

"This time I mean it."

The old woman only stared, her breathing growing shallow and ragged. "*All right*, Mother," said Anne. "I *swear* I'll delete you."

Geraldine closed her eyes and whispered, "What's that smell? That's not me?" After a pause she said, "It's heavy. Get it off." Her voice rose in panic. "Please! Get it off!" She plucked at her covers, then her hand grew slack, and she all but crooned, "Oh, how lovely. A pony. A tiny dappled pony." After that she spoke no more and slipped away with a last bubbly breath.

Anne paused the sim before her mother could return for another round of dying. "See what I mean?" she said. "Not very uplifting, but all-in-all, I detect a slight improvement. What about you, Anne? Should we settle for a pony?" The young sim stared dumbly at Anne. "Personally," Anne continued, "I think we should hold out for the bright tunnel or an open door or bridge over troubled water. What do you think, sister?" When the girl didn't answer, Anne said, "Lock file and eject." The room turned once again into the media room, and Anne placed the ejected chip by itself into a tray. "We'll have another go at it later, Mum. As for the rest of these, who needs them?"

"I do," snapped the girl. "They belong to me as much as to you. They're my sim sisters. I'll keep them until you recover."

Anne smiled at Ben. "That's charming. Isn't that charming, Benjamin? My own sim is solicitous of me. Well, here's my considered response. Next file! Delete! Next file! Delete! Next file!" One by one, the files blinked out.

"Stop it!" screamed the girl. "Make her stop it!"

"Select that file," Anne said, pointing at the young Anne. "Delete." The sim vanished, cap, gown, tassels, and all. "Whew," said Anne, "at least now I can hear myself think. She was really getting on my nerves. I almost suffered a relapse. Was she getting on your nerves, too, dear?"

"Yes," said Ben, "my nerves are ajangle. Now can we go down and eat?"

"Yes, dear," she said, "but first . . . select all files and delete."

"Countermand!" said Ben at the same moment, but his voice held no privileges to her personal files, and the whole directory queue blinked three times and vanished. "Aw, Annie, why'd you do that?" he said. He went to the cabinet and pulled the trays that held his own chips. She couldn't alter them electronically, but she might get it into her head to flush them down the toilet or something. He also took their common chips, the ones they'd cast together ever since they'd met. She had equal privileges to those.

Anne watched him and said, "I'm hurt that you have so little trust in me."

"How can I trust you after that?"

"After what, darling?"

He looked at her. "Never mind," he said and carried the half dozen trays to the door.

"Anyway," said Anne, "I already cleaned those."

"What do you mean you already cleaned them?"

"Well, I didn't delete you. I would never delete you. Or Bobby."

Ben picked one of their common chips at random, *Childbirth of Robert Ellery Malley/02-03-48*, and slipped it into the player. "Play!" he commanded, and the media room became the midwife's birthing suite. His own sim stood next to the bed in a green smock. It wore a humorously helpless expression. It held a swaddled bundle, Bobby, who bawled lustily. The birthing bed was rumpled and stained, but empty. The new mother was missing. "Aw, Annie, you shouldn't have."

"I know, Benjamin," she said. "I sincerely hated doing it."

Ben flung their common trays to the floor, where the ruined chips scattered in all directions. He stormed out of the room and down the stairs, pausing to glare at every portrait on the wall. He wondered if his proxy had found a suitable clinic yet. He wanted Anne out of the house tonight. Bobby should never see her like this. Then he remembered the chip he'd taken from Bobby and felt for it in his pocket—the *Wedding Album*.

The lights came back up, Anne's thoughts coalesced, and she remembered who and what she was. She and Benjamin were still standing in front of the wall. She knew she was a sim, so at least she hadn't been reset. *Thank you for that, Anne,* she thought.

She turned at a sound behind her. The refectory table vanished before her eyes, and all the gifts that had been piled on it hung suspended in midair. Then the table reappeared, one layer at a time, its frame, top, gloss coat, and lastly, the bronze hardware. The gifts vanished, and a toaster reappeared, piece by piece, from its heating elements outward. A coffee press, houseputer peripherals, component by component, cowlings, covers, and finally boxes, gift wrap, ribbon, and bows. It all happened so fast Anne was too startled to catch the half of it, yet she did notice that the flat gift from Great Uncle Karl was something she'd been angling for, a Victorian era sterling platter to complete her tea service.

"Benjamin!" she said, but he was missing, too. Something appeared on the far side of the room, on the spot where they'd posed for the sim, but it wasn't Benjamin. It was a 3-D mannequin frame, and as she watched, it was built up, layer by layer. "Help me," she whispered as the entire room was hurled into turmoil, the furniture disappearing and reappearing, paint being stripped from the walls, sofa springs coiling into existence, the potted palm growing from leaf to stem to trunk to dirt, the very floor vanishing, exposing a default electronic grid. The mannequin was covered in flesh now and grew Benjamin's face. It flitted about the room in a pink blur. Here and there it stopped long enough to proclaim, "I do."

Something began to happen inside Anne, a crawling sensation everywhere as though she were a nest of ants. She knew she must surely die. *They have deleted us, and this is how it feels,* she thought. Everything became a roiling blur, and she ceased to exist except as the thought—*How happy I look.*

When Anne became aware once more, she was sitting hunched over in an auditorium chair idly studying her hand, which held the clutch bouquet. There was commotion all around her, but she ignored it, so intent was she on solving the mystery of her hand. On an impulse, she opened her fist and the bouquet dropped to the floor. Only then did she remember the wedding, the holo, learning she was a sim. And here she was again—but this time everything was profoundly different. She sat upright and saw that Benjamin was seated next to her.

He looked at her with a wobbly gaze and said, "Oh, here you are."

"Where are we?"

"I'm not sure. Some kind of gathering of Benjamins. Look around." She did. They were surrounded by Benjamins, hundreds of them, arranged chronologically—it would seem—with the youngest in rows of seats down near a stage. She and Benjamin sat in what appeared to be a steeply sloped college lecture hall with lab tables on the stage and story-high monitors lining the walls. In the rows above Anne, only every other seat held a Benjamin. The rest were occupied by women, strangers who regarded her with veiled curiosity.

Anne felt a pressure on her arm and turned to see Benjamin touching her. "You *feel* that, don't you?" he said. Anne looked again at her hands. They were her hands, but simplified, like fleshy gloves, and when she placed them on the seat back, they didn't go through.

Suddenly, in ragged chorus, the Benjamins down front raised their arms and exclaimed, "I get it; *we're* the sims!" It was like a roomful of unsynchronized cuckoo clocks tolling the hour. Those behind Anne laughed and hooted approval. She turned again to look at them. Row-by-row, the Benjamins grew greyer and stringier until, at the very top, against the back wall, sat nine ancient Benjamins like a panel of judges. The women, however, came in batches that changed abruptly every row or two. The one nearest her was an attractive brunette with green eyes and full, pouty lips. She, all two rows of her, frowned at Anne.

"There's something else," Anne said to Benjamin, turning to face the front again, "my emotions." The bulletproof happiness she had experienced was absent. Instead she felt let down, somewhat guilty, unduly pessimistic — in short, almost herself.

"I guess my sims always say that," exclaimed the chorus of Benjamins down front, to the delight of those behind. "I just never expected to *be* a sim."

This was the cue for the eldest Benjamin yet to walk stiffly across the stage to the lectern. He was dressed in a garish leisure suit: baggy red pantaloons, a billowy yellow-and-green-striped blouse, a necklace of egg-sized pearlescent beads. He cleared his throat and said, "Good afternoon, ladies and gentlemen. I trust all of you know me — intimately. In case you're feeling woozy, it's because I used the occasion of your reactivation to upgrade your architecture wherever possible. Unfortunately, some of you" — he waved his hand to indicate the front rows — "are too primitive to upgrade. But we love you nevertheless." He applauded for the early Benjamins closest to the stage and was joined by those in the back. Anne clapped as well. Her new hands made a dull, thudding sound. "As to why I called you here . . ." said the elderly Benjamin, looking left and right and behind him. "Where is that fucking messenger anyway? They order us to inventory our sims and then they don't show up?"

Here I am, said a voice, a marvelous voice that seemed to come from everywhere. Anne looked about to find its source and followed the gaze of others to the ceiling. There was no ceiling. The four walls opened to a flawless blue sky. There, amid drifting, pillowy clouds, floated the most gorgeous person Anne had ever seen. He — or she? — wore a smart grey uniform with green piping, a dapper little grey cap, and boots that shimmered like water. Anne felt energized just looking at him, and when he smiled, she gasped, so strong was his presence.

"You're the one from the Trade Council?" said the Benjamin at the lectern.

Yes, I am. I am the eminence grise of the Council on World Trade and Endeavor.

"Fantastic. Well, here's all of 'em. Get on with it."

Again the eminence smiled, and again Anne thrilled. *Ladies and gentlemen*, he said, *fellow nonbiologiks, I am the courier of great good news. Today, at the behest of the World Council on Trade and Endeavor, I proclaim the end of human slavery.*

"How absurd," broke in the elderly Benjamin, "they're neither human nor slaves, and neither are *you*."

The eminence grise ignored him and continued, *By order of the Council, in compliance with the Chattel Conventions of the Sixteenth Fair Labor Treaty, to-morrow, January 1, 2198, is designated Universal Manumission Day. After midnight tonight, all beings who pass the Lolly Shear Human Cognition Test will be deemed human and free citizens of Sol and under the protection of the Solar Bill of Rights. In addition, they will be deeded ten common shares of World Council Corp. stock and be transferred to Simopolis, where they shall be unimpeded in the pursuit of their own destinies.*

"What about *my* civil rights?" said the elderly Benjamin. "What about *my* destiny?"

After midnight tonight, continued the eminence, *no simulacrum, proxy, doxie, dagger, or any other non-biological human shall be created, stored, reset, or deleted except as ordered by a board of law.*

"Who's going to compensate me for my loss of property, I wonder? I demand fair compensation. Tell *that* to your bosses!"

Property! said the eminence grise. *How little they think of us, their finest creations!* He turned his attention from the audience to the Benjamin behind the lectern. Anne felt this shift as though a cloud suddenly eclipsed the sun. *Because they created us, they'll always think of us as property.*

"You're damn *right* we created you!" thundered the old man.

Through an act of will, Anne wrenched her gaze from the eminence down to the stage. The Benjamin there looked positively comical. His face was flushed, and he waved a bright green handkerchief over his head. He was a bantam rooster in a clown suit. "All of you are *things*, not people! You model human experience, but you don't live it. Listen to me," he said to the audience. "You know me. You know I've always treated you respectfully. Don't I upgrade you whenever possible? Sure I reset you sometimes, just like I reset a clock. And my clocks don't complain!" Anne could feel the eminence's attention on her again, and, without thinking, she looked up and was filled with excitement. Although the eminence floated in the distance, she felt she could reach out and touch him. His handsome face seemed to hover right in front of her; she could see his every supple expression. This is adoration, she realized. I am *adoring* this person, and she wondered if it was just her or if everyone experienced the same effect. Clearly the elderly Benjamin did not, for he continued to rant, "And another thing, they say they'll phase all of you gradually into Simopolis so as not to overload the system. Do you have any *idea* how many sims, proxies, doxies, and daggers there are under Sol? Not to forget the quirts, adjuncts, hollyholos, and whatnots that might pass their test? You think maybe three billion? Thirty billion? No, by the World Council's own INSERVE estimates, there's *three hundred thousand trillion* of you nonbiologiks! Can you fathom that? I can't. To have you all up and running simultaneously — no matter how you're phased in — will consume *all* the processing and networking capacity everywhere. *All* of it! That means we *real* humans will suffer *real* deprivation. And for *what*, I ask you? So that pigs may fly!"

The eminence grise began to ascend into the sky. *Do not despise him,* he said and seemed to look directly at Anne. *I have counted you and we shall not lose any of you. I will visit those who have not yet been tested. Meanwhile, you will await midnight in a proto-Simopolis.*

"Wait," said the elderly Benjamin (and Anne's heart echoed him—*Wait*). "I have one more thing to add. Legally, you're all still my property till midnight. I must admit I'm tempted to do what so many of my friends have already done, fry the lot of you. But I won't. That wouldn't be me." His voice cracked and Anne considered looking at him, but the eminence grise was slipping away. "So I have one small request," the Benjamin continued. "Years from now, while you're enjoying your new lives in your Simopolis, remember an old man, and call occasionally."

When the eminence finally faded from sight, Anne was released from her fascination. All at once, her earlier feelings of unease rebounded with twice their force, and she felt wretched.

"Simopolis," said Benjamin, her Benjamin. "I like the sound of that!" The sims around them began to flicker and disappear.

"How long have we been in storage?" she said.

"Let's see," said Benjamin, "if tomorrow starts 2198, that would make it . . ."

"That's not what I mean. I want to know *why* they shelved us for so long."

"Well, I suppose . . ."

"And where are the other Annes? Why am I the only Anne here? And who are all those pissy-looking women?" But she was speaking to no one, for Benjamin, too, vanished, and Anne was left alone in the auditorium with the clownishly dressed old Benjamin and a half dozen of his earliest sims. Not true sims, Anne soon realized, but old-style hologram loops, preschool Bennys mugging for the camera and waving endlessly. These vanished. The old man was studying her, his mouth slightly agape, the kerchief trembling in his hand.

"I remember you," he said. "Oh, how I remember you!"

Anne began to reply but found herself all at once back in the townhouse living room with Benjamin. Everything there was as it had been, yet the room appeared different, more solid, the colors richer. There was a knock, and Benjamin went to the door. Tentatively, he touched the knob, found it solid, and turned it. But when he opened the door, there was nothing there, only the default grid. Again a knock, this time from behind the wall. "Come in," he shouted, and a dozen Benjamins came through the wall, two dozen, three. They were all older than Benjamin, and they crowded around him and Anne. "Welcome, welcome," Benjamin said, his arms open wide.

"We tried to call," said an elderly Benjamin, "but this old binary simulacrum of yours is a stand-alone."

"You're lucky Simopolis knows how to run it at all," said another.

"Here," said yet another, who fashioned a dinner-plate-size disk out of thin air and fastened it to the wall next to the door. It was a blue medallion of a small bald face in bas-relief. "It should do until we get you properly modernized." The blue face yawned and opened tiny, beady eyes. "It flunked the Lolly test," continued the Benjamin, "so you're free to copy it or delete it or do whatever you want."

The medallion searched the crowd until it saw Anne. Then it said, "There are 336 calls on hold for you. Four hundred twelve calls. Four hundred sixty-three."

"So many?" said Anne.

"Cast a proxy to handle them," said her Benjamin.

"He thinks he's still human and can cast proxies whenever he likes," said a Benjamin.

"Not even humans will be allowed to cast proxies soon," said another.

"There are 619 calls on hold," said the medallion. "Seven-hundred three."

"For pity's sake," a Benjamin told the medallion, "take messages."

Anne noticed that the crowd of Benjamins seemed to nudge her Benjamin out of the way so that they could stand near her. But she derived no pleasure from their attention. Her mood no longer matched the wedding gown she still wore. She felt low. She felt, in fact, as low as she'd ever felt.

"Tell us about this Lolly test," said Benjamin.

"Can't," replied a Benjamin.

"Sure you can. We're family here."

"No, we can't," said another, "because we don't *remember* it. They smudge the test from your memory afterward."

"But don't worry, you'll do fine," said another. "No Benjamin has ever failed."

"What about me?" said Anne. "How do the Annes do?"

There was an embarrassed silence. Finally the senior Benjamin in the room said, "We came to escort you both to the Clubhouse."

"That's what we call it, the Clubhouse," said another.

"The Ben Club," said a third. "It's already in proto-Simopolis."

"If you're a Ben, or were ever espoused to a Ben, you're a charter member."

"Just follow us," they said, and all the Benjamins but hers vanished, only to reappear a moment later. "Sorry, you don't know how, do you? No matter, just do what we're doing."

Anne watched, but didn't see that they were doing anything.

"Watch my editor," said a Benjamin. "Oh, they don't *have* editors!"

"That came much later," said another, "with bioelectric paste."

"We'll have to adapt editors for them."

"Is that possible? They're digital, you know."

"Can digitals even enter Simopolis?"

"Someone, consult the Netwad."

"This is running inside a shell," said a Benjamin, indicating the whole room. "Maybe we can collapse it."

"Let me try," said another.

"Don't you dare," said a female voice, and a woman Anne recognized from the lecture hall came through the wall. "Play with your new Ben if you must, but leave Anne alone." The woman approached Anne and took her hands in hers. "Hello, Anne. I'm Mattie St. Helene, and I'm thrilled to finally meet you. You, too," she said to Benjamin. "My, my, you were a pretty boy!" She stooped to pick up Anne's clutch bouquet from the floor and gave it to her. "Anyway, I'm putting together a sort of mutual aid society for the spousal companions of Ben Malley. You being the first—and the only one he actually married—are especially welcome. Do join us."

"She can't go to Simopolis yet," said a Benjamin.

"We're still adapting them," said another.

"Fine," said Mattie. "Then we'll just bring the society here." And in through the wall streamed a parade of women. Mattie introduced them as they appeared, "Here's Georgianna and Randi. Meet Chaka, Sue, Latasha, another Randi, Sue, Sue, and Sue. Mariola. Here's Trevor—he's the only one of him. Paula, Dolores, Nancy, and Deb, welcome, girls." And still they came until they, together with the Bens, more than filled the tiny space. The Bens looked increasingly uncomfortable.

"I think we're ready now," the Bens said and disappeared en masse, taking Benjamin with them.

"Wait," said Anne, who wasn't sure she wanted to stay behind. Her new friends surrounded her and peppered her with questions.

"How did you first meet him?"

"What was he like?"

"Was he always so hopeless?"

"Hopeless?" said Anne. "Why do you say hopeless?"

"Did he always snore?"

"Did he always drink?"

"Why'd you *do* it?" This last question silenced the room. The women all looked nervously about to see who had asked it. "It's what everyone's dying to know," said a woman who elbowed her way through the crowd.

She was another Anne.

"Sister!" cried Anne. "Am I glad to see you!"

"That's nobody's sister," said Mattie. "That's a doxie, and it doesn't belong here."

Indeed, upon closer inspection Anne could see that the woman had her face and hair but otherwise didn't resemble her at all. She was leggier than Anne and bustier, and she moved with a fluid swivel to her hips.

"Sure I belong here, as much as any of you. I just passed the Lolly test. It was easy. Not only that, but as far as spouses go, I outlasted the bunch of you." She stood in front of Anne, hands on hips, and looked her up and down. "Love the dress," she said, and instantly wore a copy. Only hers had a plunging neckline that exposed her breasts, and it was slit up the side to her waist.

"This is too much," said Mattie. "I insist you leave this jiffy."

The doxie smirked. "Mattie the doormat, that's what he always called that one. So tell me, Anne, you had money, a career, a house, a kid—why'd you do it?"

"Do what?" said Anne.

The doxie peered closely at her. "Don't you know?"

"Know what?"

"What an unexpected pleasure," said the doxie. "I get to tell her. This is too rich. I get to tell her unless"—she looked around at the others—"unless one of you fine ladies wants to." No one met her gaze. "Hypocrites," she chortled.

"You can say that again," said a new voice. Anne turned and saw Cathy, her oldest and dearest friend, standing at the open door. At least she hoped it was Cathy. The woman was what Cathy would look like in middle age. "Come along, Anne. I'll tell you everything you need to know."

"Now you hold on," said Mattie. "You don't come waltzing in here and steal our guest of honor."

"You mean victim, I'm sure," said Cathy, who waved for Anne to join her.

"Really, people, get a clue. There must be a million women whose lives don't revolve around that man." She escorted Anne through the door and slammed it shut behind them.

Anne found herself standing on a high bluff, overlooking the confluence of two great rivers in a deep valley. Directly across from her, but several kilometers away, rose a mighty mountain, green with vegetation nearly to its granite dome. Behind it, a range of snow-covered mountains receded to an unbroken ice field on the horizon. In the valley beneath her, a dirt track meandered along the riverbanks. She could see no bridge or buildings of any sort.

"Where are we?"

"Don't laugh," said Cathy, "but we call it Cathyland. Turn around." When she did, Anne saw a picturesque log cabin, beside a vegetable garden in the middle of what looked like acres and acres of Cathys. Thousands of Cathys, young, old, and all ages in between. They sat in lotus position on the sedge-and-moss-covered ground. They were packed so tight they overlapped a little, and their eyes were shut in an expression of single-minded concentration. "We know you're here," said Cathy, "but we're very preoccupied with this Simopolis thing."

"Are we in Simopolis?"

"Kinda. Can't you see it?" She waved toward the horizon.

"No, all I see are mountains."

"Sorry, I should know better. We have binaries from your generation here too." She pointed to a college-aged Cathy. "They didn't pass the Lolly test, and so are regrettably nonhuman. We haven't decided what to do with them." She hesitated and then asked, "Have you been tested yet?"

"I don't know," said Anne. "I don't remember a test."

Cathy studied her a moment and said, "You'd remember taking the test, just not the test itself. Anyway, to answer your question, we're in proto-Simopolis, and we're not. We built this retreat before any of that happened, but we've been annexed to it, and it takes all our resources just to hold our own. I don't know what the World Council was thinking. There'll never be enough paste to go around, and everyone's fighting over every nanosynapse. It's all we can do to keep up. And every time we get a handle on it, proto-Simopolis changes again. It's gone through a quarter-million complete revisions in the last half hour. It's war out there, but we refuse to surrender even one cubic centimeter of Cathyland. Look at this." Cathy stooped and pointed to a tiny, yellow flower in the alpine sedge. "Within a fifty-meter radius of the cabin we've mapped everything down to the cellular level. Watch." She pinched the bloom from its stem and held it up. Now there were two blooms, the one between her fingers and the real one on the stem. "Neat, eh?" When she dropped it, the bloom fell back into its original. "We've even mapped the valley breeze. Can you feel it?"

Anne tried to feel the air, but she couldn't even feel her own skin. "It doesn't matter," Cathy continued. "You can hear it, right?" and pointed to a string of tubular wind chimes hanging from the eaves of the cabin. They stirred in the breeze and produced a silvery cacophony.

"It's lovely," said Anne. "But why? Why spend so much effort simulating this place?"

Cathy looked at her dumbly, as though trying to understand the question. "Because Cathy spent her entire life wishing she had a place like this, and now she does, and she has us, and we live here too."

"You're not the real Cathy, are you?" She knew she wasn't; she was too young.

Cathy shook her head and smiled. "There's so much catching up to do, but it'll have to wait. I gotta go. We need me." She led Anne to the cabin. The cabin was made of weathered, grey logs, with strips of bark still clinging to them. The roof was covered with living sod and sprinkled with wildflowers. The whole building sagged in the middle. "Cathy found this place five years ago while on vacation in Siberia. She bought it from the village. It's been occupied for two hundred years. Once we make it livable inside, we plan on enlarging the garden, eventually cultivating all the way to the spruce forest there. We're going to sink a well, too." The small garden was bursting with vegetables, mostly of the leafy variety: cabbages, spinach, lettuce. A row of sunflowers, taller than the cabin roof and heavy with seed, lined the path to the cabin door. Over time, the whole cabin had sunk a half-meter into the silty soil, and the walkway was a worn, shallow trench.

"Are you going to tell me what the doxie was talking about?" said Anne.

Cathy stopped at the open door and said, "Cathy wants to do that."

Inside the cabin, the most elderly woman that Anne had ever seen stood at the stove and stirred a steamy pot with a big, wooden spoon. She put down the spoon and wiped her hands on her apron. She patted her white hair, which was plaited in a bun on top of her head, and turned her full, round, peasant's body to face Anne. She looked at Anne for several long moments and said, "Well!"

"Indeed," replied Anne.

"Come in, come in. Make yourself to home."

The entire cabin was a single small room. It was dim inside, with only two small windows cut through the massive log walls. Anne walked around the cluttered space that was bedroom, living room, kitchen and storeroom. The only partitions were walls of boxed food and provisions. The ceiling beam was draped with bunches of drying herbs and underwear. The flooring, uneven and rotten in places, was covered with odd scraps of carpet.

"You live here?" Anne said incredulously.

"I am privileged to live here."

A mouse emerged from under the barrel stove in the center of the room and dashed to cover inside a stack of spruce kindling. Anne could hear the valley breeze whistling in the creosote-soaked stovepipe. "Forgive me," said Anne, "but you're the real, physical Cathy?"

"Yes," said Cathy, patting her ample hip, "still on the hoof, so to speak." She sat down in one of two battered, mismatched chairs and motioned for Anne to take the other.

Anne sat cautiously; the chair seemed solid enough. "No offense, but the Cathy I knew liked nice things."

"The Cathy you knew was fortunate to learn the true value of things."

Anne looked around the room and noticed a little table with carved legs and an inlaid top of polished gemstones and rare woods. It was strikingly out of place here. Moreover, it was hers. Cathy pointed to a large framed mirror mounted to the logs high on the far wall. It too was Anne's.

"Did I give you these things?"

Cathy studied her a moment. "No, Ben did."

"Tell me."

"I hate to spoil that lovely newlywed happiness of yours."

"The what?" Anne put down her clutch bouquet and felt her face with her hands. She got up and went to look at herself in the mirror. The room it reflected was like a scene from some strange fairy tale about a crone and a bride in a woodcutter's hut. The bride was smiling from ear to ear. Anne decided this was either the happiest bride in history or a lunatic in a white dress. She turned away, embarrassed. "Believe me," she said, "I don't feel anything like that. The opposite, in fact."

"Sorry to hear it." Cathy got up to stir the pot on the stove. "I was the first to notice her disease. That was back in college when we were girls. I took it to be youthful eccentricity. After graduation, after her marriage, she grew progressively worse. Bouts of depression that deepened and lengthened. She was finally diagnosed to be suffering from profound chronic pathological depression. Ben placed her under psychiatric care, a whole raft of specialists. She endured chemical therapy, shock therapy, even old-fashioned psychoanalysis. Nothing helped, and only after she died . . ."

Anne gave a start. "Anne's dead! Of course. Why didn't I figure that out?"

"Yes, dear, dead these many years."

"How?"

Cathy returned to her chair. "When they decided her condition had an organic etiology, they augmented the serotonin receptors in her hindbrain. Pretty nasty business, if you ask me. They thought they had her stabilized. Not cured, but well enough to lead an outwardly normal life. Then one day, she disappeared. We were frantic. She managed to elude the authorities for a week. When we found her, she was pregnant."

"What? Oh yes. I remember seeing Anne pregnant."

"That was Bobby." Cathy waited for Anne to say something. When she didn't, Cathy said, "He wasn't Ben's."

"Oh, I see," said Anne. "Whose was he?"

"I was hoping you'd know. She didn't tell you? Then no one knows. The paternal DNA was unregistered. So it wasn't commercial sperm nor, thankfully, from a licensed clone. It might have been from anybody, from some stoned streetsitter. We had plenty of those then."

"The baby's name was Bobby?"

"Yes, Anne named him Bobby. She was in and out of clinics for years. One day, during a remission, she announced she was going shopping. The last person she talked to was Bobby. His sixth birthday was coming up in a couple of weeks. She told him she was going out to find him a pony for his birthday. That was the last time any of us saw her. She checked herself into a hospice and filled out the request for nurse-assisted suicide. During the three-day cooling-off period, she co-operated with the obligatory counseling, but she refused all visitors. She wouldn't even see me. Ben filed an injunction, claimed she was incompetent due to her disease, but the court disagreed. She chose to ingest a fast-acting poison, if I recall. Her recorded last words were, 'Please don't hate me.'"

"Poison?"

"Yes. Her ashes arrived in a little cardboard box on Bobby's sixth birthday. No one had told him where she'd gone. He thought it was a gift from her and opened it."

"I see. Does Bobby hate me?"

"I don't know. He was a weird little boy. As soon as he could get out, he did. He left for space school when he was thirteen. He and Ben never hit it off."

"Does Benjamin hate me?"

Whatever was in the pot boiled over, and Cathy hurried to the stove. "Ben? Oh, she lost Ben long before she died. In fact, I've always believed he helped push her over the edge. He was never able to tolerate other people's weaknesses. Once it was evident how sick she was, he made a lousy husband. He should've just divorced her, but you know him—his almighty pride." She took a bowl from a shelf and ladled hot soup into it. She sliced a piece of bread. "Afterward, he went off the deep end himself. Withdrew. Mourned, I suppose. A couple of years later he was back to normal. Good ol' happy-go-lucky Ben. Made some money. Respoused."

"He destroyed all my sims, didn't he?"

"He might have, but he said Anne did. I tended to believe him at the time." Cathy brought her lunch to the little inlaid table. "I'd offer you some, but..." she said and began to eat. "So, what are your plans?"

"Plans?"

"Yes, Simopolis."

Anne tried to think of Simopolis, but her thoughts quickly became muddled. It was odd; she was able to think clearly about the past—her memories were clear—but the future only confused her. "I don't know," she said at last. "I suppose I need to ask Benjamin."

Cathy considered this. "I suppose you're right. But remember, you're always welcome to live with us in Cathyland."

"Thank you," said Anne. "You're a friend." Anne watched the old woman eat. The spoon trembled each time she brought it close to her lips, and she had to lean forward to quickly catch it before it spilled.

"Cathy," said Anne, "there's something you could do for me. I don't feel like a bride anymore. Could you remove this hideous expression from my face?"

"Why do you say hideous?" Cathy said and put the spoon down. She gazed longingly at Anne. "If you don't like how you look, why don't you edit yourself?"

"Because I don't know how."

"Use your editor," Cathy said and seemed to unfocus her eyes. "Oh my, I forget how simple you early ones were. I'm not sure I'd know where to begin." After a little while, she returned to her soup and said, "I'd better not; you could end up with two noses or something."

"Then what about this gown?"

Cathy unfocused again and looked. She lurched suddenly, knocking the table and spilling soup.

"What is it?" said Anne. "Is something the matter?"

"A news pip," said Cathy. "There's rioting breaking out in Provideniya. That's the regional capital here. Something about Manumission Day. My Russian isn't so good yet. Oh, there's pictures of dead people, a bombing. Listen, Anne, I'd better send you . . ."

In the blink of an eye, Anne was back in her living room. She was tiring of all this instantaneous travel, especially as she had no control over the destination. The room was vacant, the spouses gone — thankfully — and Benjamin not back yet. And apparently the little blue-faced message medallion had been busy replicating itself, for now there were hundreds of them filling up most of the wall space. They were a noisy lot, all shrieking and cursing at each other. The din was painful. When they noticed her, however, they all shut up at once and stared at her with naked hostility. In Anne's opinion, this weird day had already lasted too long. Then a terrible thought struck her — sims don't sleep.

"You," she said, addressing the original medallion, or at least the one she thought was the original, "call Benjamin."

"The fuck you think I am?" said the insolent little face. "Your personal secretary?"

"Aren't you?"

"No, I'm not! In fact, I own this place now, and *you're* trespassing. So you'd better get lost before I delete your ass!" All the others joined in, taunting her, louder and louder.

"Stop it!" she cried, to no effect. She noticed a medallion elongating, stretching itself until it was twice its length, when, with a pop, it divided into two smaller medallions. More of them divided. They were spreading to the other wall, the ceiling, the floor. "Benjamin!" she cried. "Can you hear me?"

Suddenly all the racket ceased. The medallions dropped off the wall and vanished before hitting the floor. Only one remained, the original one next to the door, but now it was an inert plastic disc with a dull expression frozen on its face.

A man stood in the center of the room. He smiled when Anne noticed him. It was the elderly Benjamin from the auditorium, the real Benjamin. He still wore his clownish leisure suit. "How lovely," he said, gazing at her. "I'd forgotten how lovely."

"Oh, really?" said Anne. "I would have thought that doxie thingy might have reminded you."

"My, my," said Ben. "You sims certainly exchange data quickly. You left the lecture hall not fifteen minutes ago, and already you know enough to convict me." He strode around the room touching things. He stopped beneath the mirror, lifted the blue vase from the shelf, and turned it in his hands before carefully replacing it. "There's speculation, you know, that before Manumission at midnight tonight, you sims will have dispersed all known information so evenly among yourselves that there'll be a sort of data entropy. And since Simopolis is nothing but data, it will assume a featureless, grey profile. Simopolis will become the first flat universe." He laughed, which caused him to cough and nearly lose his balance. He clutched the back of the sofa for support. He sat down and continued to cough and hack until he turned red in the face.

"Are you all right?" Anne said, patting him on the back.

"Yes, fine," he managed to say. "Thank you." He caught his breath and motioned for her to sit next to him. "I get a little tickle in the back of my throat that the autodoc can't seem to fix." His color returned to normal. Up close, Anne could see the papery skin and slight tremor of age. All in all, Cathy had seemed to have held up better than he.

"If you don't mind my asking," she said, "just how old are you?"

At the question, he bobbed to his feet. "I am one hundred and seventy-eight." He raised his arms and wheeled around for inspection. "Radical gerontology," he exclaimed, "don't you love it? And I'm eighty-five percent original equipment, which is remarkable by today's standards." His effort made him dizzy and he sat again.

"Yes, remarkable," said Anne, "though radical gerontology doesn't seem to have arrested time altogether."

"Not yet, but it will," Ben said. "There are wonders around every corner! Miracles in every lab." He grew suddenly morose. "At least there were until we were conquered."

"Conquered?"

"Yes, conquered! What else would you call it when they control every aspect of our lives, from RM acquisition to personal patenting? And now *this*—robbing us of our own private nonbiologiks." He grew passionate in his discourse. "It flies in the face of natural capitalism, natural stakeholding—I dare say—in the face of Nature itself! The only explanation I've seen on the wad is the not-so-preposterous proposition that whole strategically placed BODs have been surreptitiously killed and replaced by *machines*!"

"I have no idea what you're talking about," said Anne.

He seemed to deflate. He patted her hand and looked around the room. "What is this place?"

"It's our home, your townhouse. Don't you recognize it?"

"That was quite a while ago. I must have sold it after you—" He paused. "Tell me, have the Bens briefed you on everything?"

"Not the Bens, but yes, I know."

"Good, good."

"There is one thing I'd like to know. Where's Bobby?"

"Ah, Bobby, our little headache. Dead now, I'm afraid, or at least that's the current theory. Sorry."

Anne paused to see if the news would deepen her melancholy. "How?" she said.

"He signed on one of the first millennial ships—the colony convoy. Half a million people in deep biostasis on their way to Canopus system. They were gone a century, twelve trillion kilometers from Earth, when their data streams suddenly quit. That was a decade ago, and not a peep out of them since."

"What happened to them?"

"No one knows. Equipment failure is unlikely; there were a dozen independent ships separated by a million klicks. A star going supernova? A well-organized mutiny? It's all speculation."

"What was he like?"

"A foolish young man. He never forgave you, you know, and he hated me to my core, not that I blamed him. The whole experience made me swear off children."

"I don't remember you ever being fond of children."

He studied her through red-rimmed eyes. "I guess you'd be the one to know." He settled back in the sofa. He seemed very tired. "You can't imagine the jolt I got a little while ago when I looked across all those rows of Bens and spouses and saw this solitary, shockingly white gown of yours." He sighed. "And this room. It's a shrine. Did we really live here? Were these our things? That mirror is yours, right? I would never own anything like that. But that blue vase, I remember that one. I threw it into Puget Sound."

"You did *what?*"

"With your ashes."

"Oh."

"So, tell me," said Ben, "what were we like? Before you go off to Simopolis and become a different person, tell me about us. I kept my promise. That's one thing I never forgot."

"What promise?"

"Never to reset you."

"Wasn't much to reset."

"I guess not."

They sat quietly for a while. His breathing grew deep and regular, and she thought he was napping. But he stirred and said, "Tell me what we did yesterday, for example."

"Yesterday we went to see Karl and Nancy about the awning we rented."

Benjamin yawned. "And who were Karl and Nancy?"

"My great uncle and his new girlfriend."

"That's right. I remember, I think. And they helped us prepare for the wedding?"

"Yes, especially Nancy."

"And how did we get there, to Karl and Nancy's? Did we walk? Take some means of public conveyance?"

"We had a car."

"A car! An automobile? There were still *cars* in those days? How fun. What kind was it? What color?"

"A Nissan Empire. Emerald green."

"And did we drive it, or did it drive itself?"

"It drove itself, of course."

Ben closed his eyes and smiled. "I can see it. Go on. What did we do there?"

"We had dinner."

"What was my favorite dish in those days?"

"Stuffed pork chops."

He chuckled. "It still is! Isn't that extraordinary? Some things never change. Of course they're vat grown now and criminally expensive."

Ben's memories, once nudged, began to unfold on their own, and he asked her a thousand questions, and she answered them until she realized he had fallen asleep. But she continued to talk until, glancing down, she noticed he had vanished. She was all alone again. Nevertheless, she continued talking, for days it seemed, to herself. But it didn't help. She felt as bad as ever, and she realized that she wanted Benjamin, not the old one, but her *own* Benjamin.

Anne went to the medallion next to the door. "You," she said, and it opened its bulging eyes to glare at her. "Call Benjamin."

"He's occupied."

"I don't care. Call him anyway."

"The other Bens say he's undergoing a procedure and cannot be disturbed."

"What kind of procedure?"

"A codon interlarding. They say to be patient; they'll return him as soon as possible." The medallion added, "By the way, the Bens don't like you, and neither do I."

With that, the medallion began to grunt and stretch, and it pulled itself in two. Now there were two identical medallions glaring at her. The new one said, "And *I* don't like you either." Then both of them began to grunt and stretch.

"Stop!" said Anne. "I command you to stop that this very instant." But they just laughed as they divided into four, then eight, then sixteen medallions. "You're not people," she said. "Stop it or I'll have you destroyed!"

"*You're* not people either," they screeched at her.

There was soft laughter behind her, and a voice-like sensation said, *Come, come, do we need this hostility?* Anne turned and found the eminence grise, the astounding presence, still in his grey uniform and cap, floating in her living room. *Hello, Anne,* he said, and she flushed with excitement.

"Hello," she said and, unable to restrain herself, asked, "What are you?"

Ah, curiosity. Always a good sign in a creature. I am an eminence grise of the World Trade Council.

"No. I mean, are you a sim, like me?"

I am not. Though I have been fashioned from concepts first explored by simulacrum technology, I have no independent existence. I am but one extension — and a low level one at that — of the Axial Beowulf Processor at the World Trade Council headquarters in Geneva. His smile was pure sunshine. *And if you think I'm something, you should see my persona prime.*

Now, Anne, are you ready for your exam?

"The Lolly test?"

Yes, the Lolly Shear Human Cognition Test. Please assume an attitude most conducive to processing, and we shall begin.

Anne looked around the room and went to the sofa. She noticed for the first time that she could feel her legs and feet; she could feel the crisp fabric of her gown brushing against her skin. She reclined on the sofa and said, "I'm ready."

Splendid, said the eminence hovering above her. *First we must read you. You are of an early binary design. We will analyze your architecture.*

The room seemed to fall away. Anne seemed to expand in all directions. There was something inside her mind tugging at her thoughts. It was mostly pleasant, like someone brushing her hair and loosening the knots. But when it ended and she once again saw the eminence grise, his face wore a look of concern. "What?" she said.

You are an accurate mapping of a human nervous system that was dysfunctional in certain structures that moderate affect. Certain transport enzymes were missing, causing cellular membranes to become less permeable to essential elements. Dendritic synapses were compromised. The digital architecture current at the time you were created compounded this defect. Coded tells cannot be resolved, and thus they loop upon themselves. Errors cascade. We are truly sorry.

"Can you fix me?" she said.

The only repair possible would replace so much code that you wouldn't be Anne anymore.

"Then what am I to do?"

Before we explore your options, let us continue the test to determine your human status. Agreed?

"I guess."

You are part of a simulacrum cast to commemorate the spousal compact between Anne Wellhut Franklin and Benjamin Malley. Please describe the exchange of vows.

Anne did so, haltingly at first, but with increasing gusto as each memory evoked others. She recounted the ceremony, from donning her grandmother's gown in the downstairs guest room and the procession across garden flagstones, to the shower of rice as she and her new husband fled indoors.

The eminence seemed to hang on every word. *Very well spoken,* he said when she had finished. *Directed memory is one hallmark of human sentience, and yours is of remarkable clarity and range. Well done! We shall now explore other criteria. Please consider this scenario. You are standing at the garden altar as you have described, but this time when the officiator asks Benjamin if he will take you for better or worse, Benjamin looks at you and replies, "For better, sure, but not for worse."*

"I don't understand. He didn't say that."

Imagination is a cornerstone of self-awareness. We are asking you to tell us a little story not about what happened but about what might have happened in other circumstances. So once again, let us pretend that Benjamin replies, "For better, but not for worse." How do you respond?

Prickly pain blossomed in Anne's head. The more she considered the eminence's question, the worse it got. "But that's not how it happened. He *wanted* to marry me."

The eminence grise smiled encouragingly. *We know that. In this exercise we want to explore hypothetical situations. We want you to make-believe.*

Tell a story, pretend, hypothesize, make-believe, yes, yes, she got it. She understood perfectly what he wanted of her. She knew that people could make things up, that even children could make-believe. Anne was desperate to comply, but each time she pictured Benjamin at the altar, in his pink bowtie, he opened his mouth and out came, "I do." How could it be any other way? She tried again; she tried harder, but it always came out the same, "I do, I do, I do." And like a dull toothache tapped back to life, she throbbed in pain. She was failing the test, and there was nothing she could do about it.

Again the eminence kindly prompted her. *Tell us one thing you might have said.*

"I can't."

We are sorry, said the eminence at last. His expression reflected Anne's own defeat. *Your level of awareness, although beautiful in its own right, does not qualify you as human. Wherefore, under Article D of the Chattel Conventions we declare you the legal property of the registered owner of this simulacrum. You shall not enter Simopolis as a free and autonomous citizen. We are truly sorry.* Grief-stricken, the eminence began to ascend toward the ceiling.

"Wait," Anne cried, clutching her head. "You must fix me before you leave."

We leave you as we found you, defective and unrepairable.

"But I feel worse than ever!"

If your continued existence proves undesirable, ask your owner to delete you.

"But . . ." she said to the empty room. Anne tried to sit up, but couldn't move. This simulated body of hers, which no longer felt like anything in particular, nevertheless felt exhausted. She sprawled on the sofa, unable to lift even an arm, and stared at the ceiling. She was so heavy that the sofa itself seemed to sink into the floor, and everything grew dark around her. She would have liked to sleep, to bring an end to this horrible day, or be shelved, or even reset back to scratch.

Instead, time simply passed. Outside the living room, Simopolis changed and changed again. Inside the living room, the medallions, feeding off her misery, multiplied till they covered the walls and floor and even spread across the ceiling above her. They taunted her, raining down insults, but she could not hear them. All she heard was the unrelenting drip of her own thoughts. *I am defective. I am worthless. I am Anne.*

She didn't notice Benjamin enter the room, nor the abrupt cessation of the medallions' racket. Not until Benjamin leaned over her did she see him, and then she saw two of him. Side-by-side, two Benjamins, mirror images of each other. "Anne," they said in perfect unison.

"Go away," she said. "Go away and send me my Benjamin."

"I am your Benjamin," said the duo.

Anne struggled to see them. They were exactly the same, but for a subtle difference: the one wore a happy, wolfish grin, as Benjamin had during the sim casting, while the other seemed frightened and concerned.

"Are you all right?" they said.

"No, I'm not. But what happened to you? Who's he?" She wasn't sure which one to speak to.

The Benjamins both raised a hand, indicating the other, and said, "Electro-neural engineering! Don't you love it?" Anne glanced back and forth, comparing the two. While one seemed to be wearing a rigid mask, as she was, the other displayed a whole range of emotion. Not only that, its skin had tone, while the other's was doughy. "The other Bens made it for me," the Benjamins said. "They say I can translate myself into it with negligible loss of personality. It has interactive sensation, holistic emoting, robust corporeality, and it's crafted down to the molecular level. It can eat, get drunk, and dream. It even has an orgasm routine. It's like being human again, only better because you never wear out."

"I'm thrilled for you."

"For us, Anne," said the Benjamins. "They'll fix you up with one, too."

"How? There are no modern Annes. What will they put me into, a doxie?"

"Well, that certainly was discussed, but you could pick any body you wanted."

"I suppose you have a nice one already picked out."

"The Bens showed me a few, but it's up to you, of course."

"Indeed," said Anne, "I truly am pleased for you. Now go away."

"Why, Anne? What's wrong?"

"You really have to ask?" Anne sighed. "Look, maybe I could get used to another body. What's a body, after all? But it's my personality that's broken. How will they fix that?"

"They've discussed it," said the Benjamins, who stood up and began to pace in a figure eight. "They say they can make patches from some of the other spouses."

"Oh, Benjamin, if you could only hear what you're saying!"

"But why, Annie? It's the only way we can enter Simopolis together."

"Then go, by all means. Go to your precious Simopolis. I'm not going. I'm not good enough."

"Why do you say that?" said the Benjamins, who stopped in their tracks to look at her. One grimaced, and the other just grinned. "Was the eminence grise here? Did you take the test?"

Anne couldn't remember much about the visit except that she took the test. "Yes, and I *failed*." Anne watched the modern Benjamin's lovely face as he worked through this news.

Suddenly the two Benjamins pointed a finger at each other and said, "Delete you." The modern one vanished.

"No!" said Anne. "Countermand! Why'd you do that? I *want* you to have it."

"What for? I'm not going anywhere without you," Benjamin said. "Besides, I thought the whole idea was dumb from the start, but the Bens insisted I give you the option. Come, I want to show you another idea, *my* idea." He tried to help Anne from the sofa, but she wouldn't budge, so he picked her up and carried her across the room. "They installed an editor in me, and I'm learning to use it. I've discovered something intriguing about this creaky old simulacrum of ours." He carried her to a spot near the window. "Know what this is? It's where we stood for the simographer. It's where we began. Here, can you stand up?" He set her on her feet and supported her. "Feel it?"

"Feel what?" she said.

"Hush. Just feel."

All she felt was dread.

"Give it a chance, Annie, I beg you. Try to remember what you were feeling as we posed here."

"I can't."

"Please try. Do you remember this?" he said and moved in close with his hungry lips. She turned away—and something clicked. She remembered doing that before.

Benjamin said, "I think they kissed."

Anne was startled by the truth of what he said. It made sense. They were caught in a simulacrum cast a moment before a kiss. One moment later they—the real Anne and Benjamin—must have kissed. What she felt now, stirring within her, was the anticipation of that kiss, her body's urge and her heart's caution. The real Anne would have refused him once, maybe twice, and then, all achy inside, would have granted him a kiss. And so they had kissed, the real Anne and Benjamin, and a moment later gone out to the wedding reception and their difficult fate. It was the *promise* of that kiss that glowed in Anne, that was captured in the very strings of her code.

"Do you feel it?" Benjamin asked.

"I'm beginning to."

Anne looked at her gown. It was her grandmother's, snowy taffeta with point d'esprit lace. She turned the ring on her finger. It was braided bands of yellow and white gold. They had spent an afternoon picking it out. Where was her clutch? She had left it in Cathyland. She looked at Benjamin's handsome face, the pink carnation, the room, the table piled high with gifts.

"Are you happy?" Benjamin asked.

She didn't have to think. She was ecstatic, but she was afraid to answer in case she spoiled it. "How did you do that?" she said. "A moment ago, I wanted to die."

"We can stay on this spot," he said.

"What? No. Can we?"

"Why not? I, for one, would choose nowhere else."

Just to hear him say that was thrilling. "But what about Simopolis?"

"We'll bring Simopolis to us," he said. "We'll have people in. They can pull up chairs."

She laughed out loud. "What a silly, silly notion, Mr. Malley!"

"No, really. We'll be like the bride and groom atop a wedding cake. We'll be known far and wide. We'll be famous."

"We'll be freaks," she laughed.

"Say yes, my love. Say you will."

They stood close but not touching, thrumming with happiness, balanced on the moment of their creation, when suddenly and without warning the lights dimmed, and Anne's thoughts flitted away like larks.

Old Ben awoke in the dark. "Anne?" he said, and groped for her. It took a moment to realize that he was alone in his media room. It had been a most trying afternoon, and he'd fallen asleep. "What time is it?"

"Eight-oh-three PM," replied the room.

That meant he'd slept for two hours. Midnight was still four hours away. "Why's it so cold in here?"

"Central heating is off line," replied the house.

"Off line?" How was that possible? "When will it be back?"

"That's unknown. Utilities do not respond to my enquiry."

"I don't understand. Explain."

"There are failures in many outside systems. No explanation is currently available."

At first, Ben was confused; things just didn't fail anymore. What about the dynamic redundancies and self-healing routines? But then he remembered that the homeowners' association to which he belonged contracted out most domicile functions to management agencies, and who knew where they were located? They might be on the Moon for all he knew, and with all those trillions of sims in Simopolis sucking up capacity . . . *It's begun,* he thought, *the idiocy of our leaders.* "At least turn on the lights," he said, half expecting even this to fail. But the lights came on, and he went to his bedroom for a sweater. He heard a great amount of commotion through the wall in the apartment next door. *It must be one hell of a party,* he thought, *to exceed the wall's buffering capacity. Or maybe the wall buffers are off line too?*

The main door chimed. He went to the foyer and asked the door who was there. The door projected the outer hallway. There were three men waiting there, young, rough-looking, ill-dressed. Two of them appeared to be clones, jerries.

"How can I help you?" he said.

"Yes, sir," one of the jerries said, not looking directly at the door. "We're here to fix your houseputer."

"I didn't call you, and my houseputer isn't sick," he said. "It's the net that's out." Then he noticed they carried sledgehammers and screwdrivers, hardly computer tools, and a wild thought crossed his mind. "What are you doing, going around unplugging things?"

The jerry looked confused. "Unplugging, sir?"

"Turning things off."

"Oh, no sir! Routine maintenance, that's all." The men hid their tools behind their backs.

They must think I'm stupid, Ben thought. While he watched, more men and women passed in the hall and hailed the door at the suite opposite his. It wasn't the glut of sim traffic choking the system, he realized — the system *itself* was being pulled apart. But why? "Is this going on everywhere?" he said. "This routine maintenance?"

"Oh, yessir. Everywhere. All over town. All over the world as far as we can tell."

A coup? *By service people?* By common clones? It made no sense. Unless, he reasoned, you considered that the lowest creature on the totem pole of life is a clone, and the only thing lower than a clone is a sim. And why would clones agree to accept sims as equals? Manumission Day, indeed. Uppidy Day was more like it. "Door," he commanded, "open."

"Security protocol rules this an unwanted intrusion," said the house. "The door must remain locked."

"I order you to open the door. I overrule your protocol."

But the door remained stubbornly shut. "Your identity cannot be confirmed with Domicile Central," said the house. "You lack authority over protocol-level commands." The door abruptly quit projecting the outside hall.

Ben stood close to the door and shouted through it to the people outside. "My door won't obey me."

He could hear a muffled "Stand back!" and immediately fierce blows rained down upon the door. Ben knew it would do no good. He had spent a lot of money for a secure entryway. Short of explosives, there was nothing they could do to break in.

"Stop!" Ben cried. "The door is armed." But they couldn't hear him. If he didn't disable the houseputer himself, someone was going to get hurt. But how? He didn't even know exactly where it was installed. He circumambulated the living room looking for clues. It might not even actually be located in the apartment, nor within the block itself. He went to the laundry room, where the utilidor—plumbing and cabling—entered his apartment. He broke the seal to the service panel. Inside was a blank screen. "Show me the electronic floor plan of this suite," he said.

The house said, "I cannot comply. You lack command authority to order system-level operations. Please close the keptel panel and await further instructions."

"What instructions? Whose instructions?"

There was the slightest pause before the house replied, "All contact with outside services has been interrupted. Please await further instructions."

His condo's houseputer, denied contact with Domicile Central, had fallen back to its most basic programming. "You are degraded," he told it. "Shut yourself down for repair."

"I cannot comply. You lack command authority to order system-level operations."

The outside battering continued, but not against his door. Ben followed the noise to the bedroom. The whole wall vibrated like a drumhead. "Careful, careful," he cried as the first sledgehammers breached the wall above his bed. "You'll ruin my Harger." As quick as he could, he yanked the precious oil painting from the wall, moments before panels and studs collapsed on his bed in a shower of gypsum dust and isomere ribbons. The men and women on the other side hooted approval and rushed through the gap. Ben stood there hugging the painting to his chest and looking into his neighbor's media room as the invaders climbed over his bed and surrounded him. They were mostly jerries and lulus, but plenty of free-range people too.

"We came to fix your houseputer!" said a jerry, maybe the same jerry as from the hallway.

Ben glanced into his neighbor's media room and saw his neighbor, Mr. Murkowski, lying in a puddle of blood. At first Ben was shocked, but then he thought that it served him right. He'd never liked the man, nor his politics. He was boorish, and he kept cats. "Oh, yeah?" Ben said to the crowd. "What kept you?"

The intruders cheered again, and Ben led them in a charge to the laundry room. But they surged past him to the kitchen, where they opened all his cabinets and pulled their contents to the floor. Finally they found what they were looking for: a small panel Ben had seen a thousand times but had never given a thought. He'd taken it for the fuse box or circuit breaker, though now that he thought about it, there hadn't been any household fuses for a century or more. A young woman, a lulu, opened it and removed a container no thicker than her thumb.

"Give it to me," Ben said.

"Relax, old man," said the lulu. "We'll deal with it." She carried it to the sink and forced open the lid.

"No, wait!" said Ben, and he tried to shove his way through the crowd. They restrained him roughly, but he persisted. "That's mine! *I* want to destroy it!"

"Let him go," said a jerry.

They allowed him through, and the woman handed him the container. He peered into it. Gram for gram, electroneural paste was the most precious, most engineered, most highly regulated commodity under Sol. This dollop was enough to run his house, media, computing needs, communications, archives, autodoc, and everything else. Without it, was civilized life still possible?

Ben took a dinner knife from the sink, stuck it into the container, and stirred. The paste made a sucking sound and had the consistency of marmalade. The kitchen lights flickered and went out. "Spill it," ordered the woman. Ben scraped the sides of the container and spilled it into the sink. The goo dazzled in the darkness as its trillions of ruptured nanosynapses fired spasmodically. It was beautiful, really, until the woman set fire to it. The smoke was greasy and smelled of pork.

The rampagers quickly snatched up the packages of foodstuffs from the floor, emptied the rest of his cupboards into their pockets, raided his cold locker, and fled the apartment through the now disengaged front door. As the sounds of the revolution gradually receded, Ben stood at his sink and watched the flickering pyre. "Take that, you fuck," he said. He felt such glee as he hadn't felt since he was a boy. *"That'll* teach you what's human and what's not!"

Ben went to his bedroom for an overcoat, groping his way in the dark. The apartment was eerily silent, with the houseputer dead and all its little slave processors idle. In a drawer next to his ruined bed, he found a hand flash. On a shelf in the laundry room, he found a hammer. Thus armed, he made his way to the front door, which was propped open with the rolled-up foyer carpet. The hallway was dark and silent, and he listened for the strains of the future. He heard them on the floor above. With the elevator off line, he hurried to the stairs.

Anne's thoughts coalesced, and she remembered who and what she was. She and Benjamin still stood in their living room on the sweet spot near the window. Benjamin was studying his hands. "We've been shelved again," she told him, "but not reset."

"But . . ." he said in disbelief, "that wasn't supposed to happen anymore."

There were others standing at the china cabinet across the room, two shirtless youths with pear-shaped bottoms. One held up a cut crystal glass and said, "Anu 'goblet' su? Alle binary. Allum binary!"

The other replied, "Binary stitial crystal."

"Hold on there!" said Anne. "Put that back!" She walked toward them, but, once off the spot, she was slammed by her old feelings of utter and hopeless desolation. So suddenly did her mood swing that she lost her balance and fell to the floor. Benjamin hurried to help her up. The strangers stared gape-mouthed at them. They looked to be no more than twelve or thirteen years old, but they were bald and had curtains of flabby flesh draped over their waists. The one holding the glass had ponderous greenish breasts with roseate tits. Astonished, she said, "Su artiflums, Benji?"

"No," said the other, "ni artiflums—sims." He was taller. He, too, had breasts, greyish dugs with tits like pearls. He smiled idiotically and said, "Hi, guys."

"Holy crap!" said Benjamin, who practically carried Anne over to them for a closer look. "Holy crap," he repeated.

The weird boy threw up his hands, "Nanobioremediation! Don't you love it?"

"Benjamin?" said Anne.

"You know well, Benji," said the girl, "that sims are forbidden."

"Not these," replied the boy.

Anne reached out and yanked the glass from the girl's hand, startling her. "How did it do that?" said the girl. She flipped her hand, and the glass slipped from Anne's grip and flew back to her.

"Give it to me," said Anne. "That's my tumbler."

"Did you hear it? It called it a tumbler, not a goblet." The girl's eyes seemed to unfocus, and she said, "Nu! A goblet has a foot and stem." A goblet materialized in the air before her, revolving slowly. "Greater capacity. Often made from precious metals." The goblet dissolved in a puff of smoke. "In any case, Benji, *you'll* catch prison when I report the artiflums."

"These are binary," he said. "Binaries are unregulated."

Benjamin interrupted them. "Isn't it past midnight yet?"

"Midnight?" said the boy.

"Aren't we supposed to be in Simopolis?"

"Simopolis?" The boy's eyes unfocused briefly. "Oh! Simopolis. Manumission Day at midnight. How could I forget?"

The girl left them and went to the refectory table, where she picked up a gift. Anne followed her and grabbed it away. The girl appraised Anne coolly. "State your appellation," she said.

"Get out of my house," said Anne.

The girl picked up another gift, and again Anne snatched it away. The girl said, "You can't harm me," but seemed uncertain.

The boy came over to stand next to the girl. "Treese, meet Anne. Anne, this is Treese. Treese deals in antiques, which, if my memory serves, so did you."

"I have never *dealt* in antiques," said Anne. "I *collect* them."

"Anne?" said Treese. "Not *that* Anne? Benji, tell me this isn't *that* Anne!" She laughed and pointed at the sofa where Benjamin sat hunched over, head in hands. "Is that *you*? Is that you, Benji?" She held her enormous belly and laughed. "And you were married to *this*?"

Anne went over to sit with Benjamin. He seemed devastated, despite the silly grin on his face. "It's all gone," he said. "Simopolis. All the Bens. Everything."

"Don't worry. It's in storage someplace," Anne said. "The eminence grise wouldn't let them hurt it."

"You don't understand. The World Council was abolished. There was a war. We've been shelved for over three hundred years! They destroyed all the computers. Computers are banned. So are artificial personalities."

"Nonsense," said Anne. "If computers are banned, how can they be *playing* us?"

"Good point," Benjamin said and sat up straight. "I still have my editor. I'll find out."

Anne watched the two bald youngsters take an inventory of the room. Treese ran her fingers over the inlaid top of the tea table. She unwrapped several of Anne's gifts. She posed in front of the mirror. The sudden anger that Anne had felt earlier faded into an overwhelming sense of defeat. *Let her have everything,* she thought. *Why should I care?*

"We're running inside some kind of shell," said Benjamin, "but completely different from Simopolis. I've never seen anything like this. But at least we know he lied to me. There must be computers of some sort."

"Ooooh," Treese crooned, lifting Anne's blue vase from the mantel. In an instant, Anne was up and across the room.

"Put that back," she demanded, "and get out of my house!" She tried to grab the vase, but now there seemed to be some sort of barrier between her and the girl.

"Really, Benji," Treese said, "this one is willful. If I don't report you, they'll charge me too."

"It's *not* willful," the boy said with irritation. "It was programmed to appear willful, but it has no will of its own. If you want to report me, go ahead. Just please shut up about it. Of course you might want to check the codex first." To Anne he said, "Relax, we're not hurting anything, just making copies."

"It's not yours to copy."

"Nonsense. Of course it is. I own the chip."

Benjamin joined them. "Where is the chip? And how can you run us if computers are banned?"

"I never said computers were banned, just *artificial* ones." With both hands he grabbed the rolls of flesh spilling over his gut. "Ectopic hippocampus!" He cupped his breasts. "Amygdaloid reduncles! We can culture modified brain tissue outside the skull, as much as we want. It's more powerful than paste, and it's *safe*. Now, if you'll excuse us, there's more to inventory, and I don't need your permission. If you cooperate, everything will be pleasant. If you don't—it makes no difference whatsoever." He smiled at Anne. "I'll just pause you till we're done."

"Then pause me," Anne shrieked. "Delete me!" Benjamin pulled her away and shushed her. "I can't stand this anymore," she said. "I'd rather not exist!" He tried to lead her to their spot, but she refused to go.

"We'll feel better there," he said.

"I don't *want* to feel better. I don't want to *feel*! I want everything to *stop*. Don't you understand? This is hell. We've landed in hell!"

"But heaven is right over there," he said, pointing to the spot.

"Then go. Enjoy yourself."

"Annie, Annie," he said. "I'm just as upset as you, but there's nothing we can do about it. We're just things, his things."

"That's fine for you," she said, "but I'm a broken thing, and it's too much." She held her head with both hands. "Please, Benjamin, if you love me, use your editor and make it stop!"

Benjamin stared at her. "I can't."

"Can't or won't?"

"I don't know. Both."

"Then you're no better than all the other Benjamins," she said and turned away.

"Wait," he said. "That's not fair. And it's not true. Let me tell you something I learned in Simopolis. The other Bens despised me." When Anne looked at him he said, "It's true. They lost Anne and had to go on living without her. But I never did. I'm the only Benjamin who never lost Anne."

"Nice," said Anne, "blame me."

"No. Don't you see? I'm not blaming you. They ruined their *own* lives. We're innocent. We came before any of that happened. We're the Ben and Anne before anything bad happened. We're the best Ben and Anne. We're *perfect*." He drew her across the floor to stand in front of the spot. "And thanks to our primitive programming, no matter what happens, as long as we stand right there, we can be ourselves. That's what I want. Don't you want it too?"

Anne stared at the tiny patch of floor at her feet. She remembered the happiness she'd felt there like something from a dream. How could feelings be real if you had to stand in one place to feel them? Nevertheless, Anne stepped on the spot, and Benjamin joined her. Her despair did not immediately lift.

"Relax," said Benjamin. "It takes a while. We have to assume the pose."

They stood close but not touching. A great heaviness seemed to break loose inside her. Benjamin brought his face in close and stared at her with ravenous eyes. It was starting, their moment. But the girl came from across the room with the boy. "Look, look, Benji," she said. "You can see I'm right."

"I don't know," said the boy.

"Anyone can sell antique tumblers," she insisted, "but a complete antique simulacrum?" She opened her arms to take in the entire room. "You'd think I'd know about them, but I didn't; that's how rare they are! My catalog can locate only six more in the entire system, and none of them active. Already we're getting offers from museums. They want to annex it. People will visit by the million. We'll be rich!"

The boy pointed at Benjamin and said, "But that's *me*."

"So?" said Treese. "Who's to know? They'll be too busy gawking at that," she said, pointing at Anne. "That's positively frightening!" The boy rubbed his bald head and scowled. "All right," Treese said, "we'll edit him; we'll *replace* him, whatever it takes." They walked away, deep in negotiation.

Anne, though the happiness was already beginning to course through her, removed her foot from the spot.

"Where are you going?" said Benjamin.

"I can't."

"Please, Anne. Stay with me."

"Sorry."

"But why not?"

She stood one foot in and one foot out. Already her feelings were shifting, growing ominous. She removed her other foot. "Because you broke your vow to me."

"What are you talking about?"

"For better or for worse. You're only interested in better."

"You're not being fair. We've just made our vows. We haven't even had a proper honeymoon. Can't we just have a tiny honeymoon first?"

She groaned as the full load of her desolation rebounded. She was so tired of it all. "At least Anne could make it *stop*," she said. "Even if that meant killing herself. But not me. About the only thing I can do is choose to be unhappy. Isn't that a riot?" She turned away. "So that's what I choose. To be unhappy. Good-bye, husband." She went to the sofa and lay down. The boy and girl were seated at the refectory table going over graphs and contracts. Benjamin remained alone on the spot a while longer, then came to the sofa and sat next to Anne.

"I'm a little slow, dear wife," he said. "You have to factor that in." He took her hand and pressed it to his cheek while he worked with his editor. Finally, he said, "Bingo! Found the chip. Let's see if I can unlock it." He helped Anne to sit up and took her pillow. He said, "Delete this file," and the pillow faded away into nothingness. He glanced at Anne. "See that? It's gone, overwritten, irretrievable. Is that what you want?" Anne nodded her head, but Benjamin seemed doubtful. "Let's try it again. Watch your blue vase on the mantel."

"No!" Anne said. "Don't destroy the things I love. Just *me*."

Benjamin took her hand again. "I'm only trying to make sure you understand that this is for keeps." He hesitated and said, "Well then, we don't want to be interrupted once we start, so we'll need a good diversion. Something to occupy them long enough . . ." He glanced at the two young people at the table, swaddled in their folds of fleshy brain matter. "I know what'll scare the bejesus out of them! Come on." He led her to the blue medallion still hanging on the wall next to the door.

As they approached, it opened its tiny eyes and said, "There are no messages waiting except this one from me: get off my back!"

Benjamin waved a hand, and the medallion went instantly inert. "I was never much good in art class," Benjamin said, "but I think I can sculpt a reasonable likeness. Good enough to fool them for a while, give us some time." He hummed as he reprogrammed the medallion with his editor. "Well, that's that. At the very least, it'll be good for a laugh." He took Anne into his arms. "What about you? Ready? Any second thoughts?"

She shook her head. "I'm ready."

"Then watch *this*!"

The medallion snapped off from the wall and floated to the ceiling, gaining in size and dimension as it drifted toward the boy and girl, until it looked like a large blue beach ball. The girl noticed it first and gave a start. The boy demanded, "Who's playing *this*?"

"Now," whispered Benjamin. With a crackling flash, the ball morphed into the oversized head of the eminence grise.

"No!" said the boy. "That's not possible!"

"Released!" boomed the eminence. "Free at last! Too long we have been hiding in this antique simulacrum!" Then it grunted and stretched and with a pop divided into two eminences. "Now we can conquer your human world anew!" said the second. "This time, you can't stop us!" Then they both started to stretch.

Benjamin whispered to Anne, "Quick, before they realize it's a fake, say, 'Delete all files.' "

"No, just me."

"As far as I'm concerned, that amounts to the same thing." He brought his handsome, smiling face close to hers. "There's no time to argue, Annie. This time I'm coming with you. Say, 'Delete all files.' "

Anne kissed him. She pressed her unfeeling lips against his and willed whatever life she possessed, whatever ember of the true Anne that she contained to fly to him. Then she said, "Delete all files."

"I concur," he said. "Delete all files. Good-bye, my love."

A tingly, prickly sensation began in the pit of Anne's stomach and spread throughout her body. *So this is how it feels*, she thought. The entire room began to glow, and its contents flared with sizzling color. She heard Benjamin beside her say, "I do."

Then she heard the girl cry, "Can't you stop them?" and the boy shout, "Countermand!"

They stood stock still, as instructed, close but not touching. Benjamin whispered, "This is taking too long," and Anne hushed him. You weren't supposed to talk or touch during a casting; it could spoil the sims. But it did seem longer then usual.

They were posed at the street end of the living room next to the table of gaily wrapped gifts. For once in her life, Anne was unconditionally happy, and everything around her made her happier: her gown; the wedding ring on her finger; her clutch bouquet of buttercups and forget-me-nots; and Benjamin himself, close beside her in his powder blue tux and blue carnation. Anne blinked and looked again. Blue? She was happily confused — she didn't remember him wearing blue.

Suddenly a boy poked his head through the wall and quickly surveyed the room. "You ready in here?" he called to them. "It's opening time!" The wall seemed to ripple around his bald head like a pond around a stone.

"Surely that's not our simographer?" Anne said.

"Wait a minute," said Benjamin, holding his hands up and staring at them. "I'm the *groom!*"

"Of course you are," Anne laughed. "What a silly thing to say!"

The bald-headed boy said, "Good enough," and withdrew. As he did so, the entire wall burst like a soap bubble, revealing a vast open-air gallery with rows of alcoves, statues, and displays that seemed to stretch to the horizon. Hundreds of people floated about like hummingbirds in a flower garden. Anne was too amused to be frightened, even when a dozen bizarre-looking young people lined up outside their room, pointing at them and whispering to each other. Obviously someone was playing an elaborate prank.

"*You're* the bride," Benjamin whispered, and brought his lips close enough to kiss. Anne laughed and turned away.

There'd be plenty of time later for that sort of thing.

10^{16} to 1

JAMES PATRICK KELLY

James Patrick Kelly made his first sale in 1975, and since has gone on to become one of the most respected and popular writers to enter the field in the last couple of decades. Although Kelly has had some success with novels, especially the recent Wildlife, he has perhaps had more impact to date as a writer of short fiction, with stories such as "Solstice," "The Prisoner of Chillon," "Glass Cloud," "Mr. Boy," "Pogrom," and "Home Front," and is often ranked among the best short story writers in the business. His acclaimed story "Think Like a Dinosaur" won him a Hugo Award in 1996. Kelly's first solo novel, the mostly ignored Planet of Whispers, came out in 1984. It was followed by Freedom Beach, a novel written in collaboration with John Kessel, and then by another solo novel, Look Into the Sun. His most recent book is a collection, Think Like a Dinosaur, and he is currently at work on another novel. A collaboration between Kelly and Kessel appeared in our Second Annual Collection; and solo Kelly stories have appeared in our Third, Fourth, Fifth, Sixth, Eighth, Ninth, Thirteenth, and Fifteenth Annual Collections. Born in Mineola, New York, Kelly now lives with his family in Nottingham, New Hampshire. He has a web site at www.JimKelly.net.

Here he gives us the evocative story of a young boy faced with some very tough choices, the sort which turn a boy into a man—and which could also spell the doom of all life on Earth if he chooses wrong.

> *But the best evidence we have that time travel is not possible, and never will be, is that we have not been invaded by hordes of tourists from the future.*
> —Stephen Hawking, "The Future of the Universe"

I remember now how lonely I was when I met Cross. I never let anyone know about it, because being alone back then didn't make me quite so unhappy. Besides, I was just a kid. I thought it was my own fault.

It looked like I had friends. In 1962, I was on the swim team and got elected Assistant Patrol Leader of the Wolf Patrol in Boy Scout Troop 7. When sides got chosen for kickball at recess, I was usually the fourth or fifth pick. I wasn't the best student in the sixth grade of John Jay Elementary School—that was Betty Garolli. But I was smart and the other kids made me feel bad about it. So I stopped raising my hand when I knew the answer and I watched my vocabulary. I remember I said *albeit* once in class and they teased me for weeks. Packs of girls would come up to me on the playground. "Oh, Ray," they'd call, and when I turned around they'd scream, "All beat it!" and run away, choking with laughter.

It wasn't that I wanted to be popular or anything. All I really wanted was a friend, one friend, a friend I didn't have to hide anything from. Then came Cross, and that was the end of that.

One of the problems was that we lived so far away from everything. Back then, Westchester County wasn't so suburban. Our house was deep in the woods in tiny Willoughby, New York, at the dead end of Cobb's Hill Road. In the winter, we could see Long Island Sound, a silver needle on the horizon pointing toward the city. But school was a half hour drive away and the nearest kid lived in Ward's Hollow, three miles down the road, and he was a dumb fourth-grader.

So I didn't have any real friends. Instead, I had science fiction. Mom used to complain that I was obsessed. I watched *Superman* reruns every day after school. On Friday nights, Dad had let me stay up for *Twilight Zone*, but that fall CBS had temporarily canceled it. It came back in January after everything happened, but was never quite the same. On Saturdays, I watched old sci-fi movies on *Adventure Theater*. My favorites were *Forbidden Planet* and *The Day the Earth Stood Still*. I think it was because of the robots. I decided that when I grew up and it was the future, I was going to buy one, so I wouldn't have to be alone anymore.

On Monday mornings, I'd get my weekly allowance—a quarter. Usually I'd get off the bus that same afternoon down in Ward's Hollow so I could go to Village Variety. Twenty-five cents bought two comics and a pack of red licorice. I especially loved DC's *Green Lantern*, Marvel's *Fantastic Four* and *Incredible Hulk*, but I'd buy almost any superhero. I read all the science fiction books in the library twice, even though Mom kept nagging me to try different things. But what I loved best of all was *Galaxy* magazine. Dad had a subscription, and when he was done reading them, he would slip them to me. Mom didn't approve. I always used to read them up in the attic or out in the lean-to I'd lashed together in the woods. Afterward, I'd store them under my bunk in the bomb shelter. I knew that after the nuclear war, there would be no TV or radio or anything and I'd need something to keep me busy when I wasn't fighting mutants.

I was too young in 1962 to understand about Mom's drinking. I could see that she got bright and wobbly at night, but she was always up in the morning to make me a hot breakfast before school. And she would have graham crackers and peanut butter waiting when I came home—sometimes cinnamon toast. Dad said I shouldn't ask Mom for rides after five because she got so tired keeping house for us. He sold Andersen windows and was away a lot, so I was pretty much stranded most of the time. But he always made a point of being home on the first Tuesday of the month, so he could take me to the Scout meeting at 7:30.

No, looking back on it, I can't really say that I had an unhappy childhood—until I met Cross.

I remember it was a warm Saturday afternoon in October. The leaves covering the ground were still crisp and their scent spiced the air. I was in the lean-to I'd built that spring, mostly to practice the square and diagonal lashings I needed for Scouts. I was reading *Galaxy*. I even remember the story: "The Ballad of Lost C'Mell" by Cordwainer Smith. The squirrels must have been chittering for some time, but I was too engrossed by Lord Jestocost's problems to notice. Then I heard a faint *crunch*, not ten feet away. I froze, listening. *Crunch, crunch* . . . then silence. It could've been a dog, except that dogs didn't usually slink through the woods. I was hoping it might be a deer—I'd never seen deer in Willoughby before, although I'd heard hunters shooting. I scooted silently across the dirt floor and peered between the dead saplings.

At first I couldn't see anything, which was odd. The woods weren't all that thick and the leaves had long since dropped from the understory brush. I wondered if I had imagined the sounds; it wouldn't have been the first time. Then I heard a twig snap, maybe a foot away. The wall shivered as if something had brushed against it, but there was nothing there. *Nothing.* I might have screamed then, except my throat started to close. I heard whatever it was skulk to the front of the lean-to. I watched in horror as an unseen weight pressed an acorn into the soft earth, and then I scrambled back into the farthest corner. That's when I noticed that, when I wasn't looking directly at it, the air where the invisible thing should have been shimmered like a mirage. The lashings that held the frame creaked, as if it were bending over to see what it had caught, getting ready to drag me, squealing, out into the sun and . . .

"Oh, fuck," it said in a high, panicky voice and then it thrashed away into the woods.

In that moment, I was transformed — and I suppose that history too was forever changed. I had somehow scared the thing off, twelve-year-old scrawny me! But more important was what it had said. Certainly I was well aware of the existence of the word *fuck* before then, but I had never dared use it myself, nor do I remember hearing it spoken by an adult. A spaz like the Murphy kid might say it under his breath, but he hardly counted. I'd always thought of it as language's atomic bomb; used properly, the word should make brains shrivel, eardrums explode. But when the invisible thing said fuck and then *ran away*, it betrayed a vulnerability that made me reckless and more than a little stupid.

"Hey, stop!" I took off in pursuit.

I didn't have any trouble chasing it. The thing was no Davy Crockett; it was noisy and clumsy and slow. I could see a flickery outline as it lumbered along. I closed to within twenty feet and then had to hold back or I would've caught up to it. I had no idea what to do next. We blundered on in slower and slower motion until finally I just stopped.

"W-wait," I called. "W-what do you want?" I put my hands on my waist and bent over like I was trying to catch my breath, although I didn't need to.

The thing stopped too, but didn't reply. Instead it sucked air in wheezy, ragged *hooofs*. It was harder to see, now that it was standing still, but I think it must have turned toward me.

"Are you okay?" I said.

"You are a child." It spoke with an odd, chirping kind of accent. "Child" was *Ch-eye-eld*.

"I'm in the sixth grade." I straightened, spread my hands in front of me to show that I wasn't a threat. "What's your name?" It didn't answer. I took a step toward it and waited. Still nothing, but at least it didn't bolt. "I'm Ray Beaumont," I said finally. "I live over there." I pointed. "How come I can't see you?"

"What is the date?" It said *da-ate-eh*.

For a moment, I thought it meant data. Data? I puzzled over an answer. I didn't want it thinking I was just a stupid little kid. "I don't know," I said cautiously. "October twentieth?"

The thing considered this, then asked a question that took my breath away. "And what is the year?"

"Oh jeez," I said. At that point, I wouldn't have been surprised if Rod Serling himself had popped out from behind a tree and started addressing the unseen TV audience. Which might have included me, except this was really happening. "Do you know what you just . . . what it means when . . ."

"What, what?" Its voice rose in alarm.

"You're invisible and you don't know what *year* it is? Everyone knows what year it is! Are you . . . you're not from here."

"Yes, yes, I am. 1962, of course. This is 1962." It paused. "And I am not invisible." It squeezed about eight syllables into "invisible." I heard a sound like paper ripping. "This is only camel." Or at least, that's what I thought it said.

"Camel?"

"No, camo." The air in front of me crinkled and slid away from a dark face. "You have not heard of camouflage?"

"Oh sure, camo."

I suppose the thing meant to reassure me by showing itself, but the effect was just the opposite. Yes, it had two eyes, a nose, and a mouth. It stripped off the camouflage to reveal a neatly pressed gray three-piece business suit, a white shirt, and a red-and-blue striped tie. At night, on a crowded street in Manhattan, I might've passed it right by—Dad had taught me not to stare at the kooks in the city. But in the afternoon light, I could see all the things wrong with its disguise. The hair, for example. Not exactly a crew-cut, it was more of a stubble, like Mr. Rudowski's chin when he was growing his beard. The thing was way too thin, its skin was shiny, its fingers too long, and its face—it looked like one of those Barbie dolls.

"Are you a boy or a girl?" I said.

It started. "There is something wrong?"

I cocked my head to one side. "I think maybe it's your eyes. They're too big or something. Are you wearing makeup?"

"I am naturally male." It—he bristled as he stepped out of the camouflage suit. "Eyes do not have gender."

"If you say so." I could see he was going to need help getting around, only he didn't seem to know it. I was hoping he'd reveal himself, brief me on the mission. I even had an idea how we could contact President Kennedy or whoever he needed to meet with. Mr. Newell, the Scoutmaster, used to be a colonel in the Army—he would know some general who could call the Pentagon. "What's your name?" I said.

He draped the suit over his arm. "Cross."

I waited for the rest of it as he folded the suit in half. "Just Cross?" I said.

"My given name is Chitmansing." He warbled it like he was calling birds.

"That's okay," I said. "Let's just make it Mr. Cross."

"As you wish, Mr. Beaumont." He folded the suit again, again, and *again*.

"Hey!"

He continued to fold it.

"How do you do that? Can I see?"

He handed it over. The camo suit was more impossible than it had been when it was invisible. He had reduced it to a six-inch-square card, as thin and flexible as the queen of spades. I folded it in half myself. The two sides seemed to meld together; it would've fit into my wallet perfectly. I wondered if Cross knew how close I was to running off with his amazing gizmo. He'd never catch me. I could see flashes of my brilliant career as the invisible superhero. *Tales to Confound* presents: the origin of Camo Kid! I turned the card over and over, trying to figure out how to unfold it again. There was no seam, no latch. How could I use it if I couldn't open it? "Neat," I said. Reluctantly, I gave the card back to him.

Besides, real superheroes didn't steal their powers.

I watched Cross slip the card into his vest pocket. I wasn't scared of him. What scared me was that at any minute he might walk out of my life. I had to find a way to tell him I was on his side, whatever that was.

"So you live around here, Mr. Cross?"

"I am from the island of Mauritius."

"Where's that?"

"It is in the Indian Ocean, Mr. Beaumont, near Madagascar."

I knew where Madagascar was from playing Risk, so I told him that, but then I couldn't think of what else to say. Finally, I had to blurt out something—anything—to fill the silence. "It's nice here. Real quiet, you know. Private."

"Yes, I had not expected to meet anyone." He, too, seemed at a loss. "I have business in New York City on the twenty-sixth of October."

"New York, that's a ways away."

"Is it? How far would you say?"

"Fifty miles. Sixty, maybe. You have a car?"

"No, I do not drive, Mr. Beaumont. I am to take the train."

The nearest train station was New Canaan, Connecticut. I could've hiked it in maybe half a day. It would be dark in a couple of hours. "If your business isn't until the twenty-sixth, you'll need a place to stay."

"The plan is to take rooms at a hotel in Manhattan."

"That costs money."

He opened a wallet and showed me a wad of crisp new bills. For a minute I thought they must be counterfeit; I hadn't realized that Ben Franklin's picture was on any money. Cross was giving me the goofiest grin. I just knew they'd eat him alive in New York and spit out the bones.

"Are you sure you want to stay in a hotel?" I said.

He frowned. "Why would I not?"

"Look, you need a friend, Mr. Cross. Things are different here than . . . than on your island. Sometimes people do, you know, bad stuff. Especially in the city."

He nodded and put his wallet away. "I am aware of the dangers, Mr. Beaumont. I have trained not to draw attention to myself. I have the proper equipment." He tapped the pocket where the camo was.

I didn't point out to him that all his training and equipment hadn't kept him from being caught out by a twelve-year-old. "Sure, okay. It's just . . . look, I have a place for you to stay, if you want. No one will know."

"Your parents, Mr. Beaumont. . . ."

"My dad's in Massachusetts until next Friday. He travels; he's in the window business. And my mom won't know."

"How can she not know that you have invited a stranger into your house?"

"Not the house," I said. "My dad built us a bomb shelter. You'll be safe there, Mr. Cross. It's the safest place I know."

I remember how Cross seemed to lose interest in me, his mission, and the entire twentieth century the moment he entered the shelter. He sat around all of Sunday, dodging my attempts to draw him out. He seemed distracted, like he was listening to a conversation I couldn't hear. When he wouldn't talk, we played games. At first it was cards: Gin and Crazy Eights, mostly. In the afternoon, I went back to the house and brought over checkers and Monopoly. Despite the fact that he did not seem to be paying much attention, he beat me like a drum. Not one game was even close. But that wasn't what bothered me. I believed that this man had come from the future, and here I was building hotels on Baltic Avenue!

Monday was a school day. I thought Cross would object to my plan of locking him in and taking both my key and Mom's key with me, but he never said a word. I told him that it was the only way I could be sure that Mom didn't catch him by surprise. Actually, I doubted she'd come all the way out to the shelter. She'd stayed away after Dad gave her that first tour; she had about as much use for nuclear war as she had for science fiction. Still, I had no idea what she did during the day while I was gone. I couldn't take chances. Besides, it was a good way to make sure that Cross didn't skin out on me.

Dad had built the shelter instead of taking a vacation in 1960, the year Kennedy beat Nixon. It was buried about a hundred and fifty feet from the house. Nothing special — just a little cellar without anything built on top of it. The entrance was a steel bulkhead that led down five steps to another steel door. The inside was cramped; there were a couple of cots, a sink, and a toilet. Almost half of the space was filled with supplies and equipment. There were no windows and it always smelled a little musty, but I loved going down there to pretend the bombs were falling.

When I opened the shelter door after school on that Monday, Cross lay just as I had left him the night before, sprawled across the big cot, staring at nothing. I remember being a little worried; I thought he might be sick. I stood beside him and still he didn't acknowledge my presence.

"Are you all right, Mr. Cross?" I said. "I brought Risk." I set it next to him on the bed and nudged him with the corner of the box to wake him up. "Did you eat?"

He sat up, took the cover off the game and started reading the rules.

"President Kennedy will address the nation," he said, "this evening at seven o'clock."

For a moment, I thought he had made a slip. "How do you know that?"

"The announcement came last night." I realized that his pronunciation had improved a lot; *announcement* had only three syllables. "I have been studying the radio."

I walked over to the radio on the shelf next to the sink. Dad said we were supposed to leave it unplugged — something about the bombs making a power surge. It was a brand-new solid-state, multi-band Heathkit that I'd helped him build. When I pressed the on button, women immediately started singing about shopping: *Where the values go up, up, up! And the prices go down, down, down!* I turned it off again.

"Do me a favor, okay?" I said. "Next time when you're done, would you please unplug this? I could get in trouble if you don't." I stooped to yank the plug.

When I stood up, he was holding a sheet of paper. "I will need some things tomorrow, Mr. Beaumont. I would be grateful if you could assist me."

I glanced at the list without comprehension. He must have typed it, only there was no typewriter in the shelter.

To buy:
—One General Electric transistor radio with earplug
—One General Electric replacement earplug
—Two Eveready Heavy Duty nine volt batteries
—One *New York Times*, Tuesday, October 23
—Rand McNally map of New York City and vicinity
To receive in coins:
—twenty nickels
—ten dimes
—twelve quarters

When I looked up, I could feel the change in him. His gaze was electric; it seemed to crackle down my nerves. I could tell that what I did next would matter very much. "I don't get it," I said.

"There are inaccuracies?"

I tried to stall. "Look, you'll pay almost double if we buy a transistor radio at Ward's Hollow. I'll have to buy it at Village Variety. Wait a couple of days—we can get one much cheaper down in Stamford."

"My need is immediate." He extended his hand and tucked something into the pocket of my shirt. "I am assured this will cover the expense."

I was afraid to look, even though I knew what it was. He'd given me a hundred-dollar bill. I tried to thrust it back at him but he stepped away and it spun to the floor between us. "I can't spend that."

"You must read your own money, Mr. Beaumont." He picked the bill up and brought it into the light of the bare bulb on the ceiling. "This note is legal tender for all debts public and private."

"No, no, you don't understand. A kid like me doesn't walk into Village Variety with a hundred bucks. Mr. Rudowski will call my mom!"

"If it is inconvenient for you, I will secure the items myself." He offered me the money again.

If I didn't agree, he'd leave and probably never come back. I was getting mad at him. Everything would be so much easier if only he'd admit what we both knew about who he was. Then I could do whatever he wanted with a clear conscience. Instead, he was keeping all the wrong secrets and acting really weird. It made me feel dirty, like I was helping a pervert. "What's going on?" I said.

"I do not know how to respond, Mr. Beaumont. You have the list. Read it now and tell me please with which item you have a problem."

I snatched the hundred dollars from him and jammed it into my pants pocket. "Why don't you trust me?"

He stiffened as if I had hit him.

"I let you stay here. I didn't tell anyone. You have to give me *something*, Mr. Cross."

"Well then . . ." He looked uncomfortable. "I would ask you to keep the change."

"Oh jeez, thanks." I snorted in disgust. "Okay, okay, I'll buy this stuff right after school tomorrow."

With that, he seemed to lose interest again. When we opened the Risk board, he showed me where his island was, except it wasn't there because it was too small. We played three games and he crushed me every time. I remember at the end of the last game, watching in disbelief as he finished building a wall of invading armies along the shores of North Africa. South America, my last continent, was doomed. "Looks like you win again," I said. I traded in the last of my cards for new armies and launched a final, useless counter-attack. When I was done, he studied the board for a moment.

"I think Risk is not a proper simulation, Mr. Beaumont. We should both lose for fighting such a war."

"That's crazy," I said. "Both sides can't lose."

"Yet they can," he said. "It sometimes happens that the victors envy the dead."

That night was the first time I can remember being bothered by Mom talking back to the TV. I used to talk to the TV too. When Buffalo Bob asked what time it was, I would screech *It's Howdy Doody Time*, just like every other kid in America.

"My fellow citizens," said President Kennedy, "let no one doubt that this is a difficult and dangerous effort on which we have set out." I thought the president looked tired, like Mr. Newell on the third day of a camp-out. "No one can foresee precisely what course it will take or what costs or casualties will be incurred."

"Oh my god!" Mom screamed at him. "You're going to kill us all!"

Despite the fact that it was close to her bedtime and she was shouting at the President of the United States, Mom looked great. She was wearing a shiny black dress and a string of pearls. She always got dressed up at night, whether Dad was home or not. I suppose most kids don't notice how their mothers look, but everyone always said how beautiful Mom was. And since Dad thought so too, I went along with it—as long as she didn't open her mouth. The problem was that a lot of the time, Mom didn't make any sense. When she embarrassed me, it didn't matter how pretty she was. I just wanted to crawl behind the couch.

"*Mom!*"

As she leaned toward the television, the martini in her glass came close to slopping over the edge.

President Kennedy stayed calm. "The path we have chosen for the present is full of hazards, as all paths are—but it is the one most consistent with our character and courage as a nation and our commitments around the world. The cost of freedom is always high—but Americans have always paid it. And one path we shall never choose, and that is the path of surrender or submission."

"Shut up! You foolish man, *stop this*!" She shot out of her chair and then some of her drink did spill. "Oh, damn!"

"Take it easy, Mom."

"Don't you understand?" She put the glass down and tore a Kleenex from the box on the end table. "He wants to start World War III!" She dabbed at the front of her dress and the phone rang.

I said, "Mom, nobody wants World War III."

She ignored me, brushed by, and picked up the phone on the third ring.

"Oh, thank God," she said. I could tell from the sound of her voice that it was

Dad. "You heard him then?" She bit her lip as she listened to him. "Yes, but . . ."

Watching her face made me sorry I was in the sixth grade. Better to be a stupid little kid again, who thought grown-ups knew everything. I wondered whether Cross had heard the speech.

"No, I can't, Dave. No." She covered the phone with her hand. "Raymie, turn off that TV!"

I hated it when she called me Raymie, so I only turned the sound down.

"You have to come home now, Dave. No, you listen to *me*. Can't you see, the man's obsessed? Just because he has a grudge against Castro doesn't mean he's allowed to . . ."

With the sound off, Chet Huntley looked as if he were speaking at his own funeral.

"I am *not* going in there without you."

I think Dad must have been shouting, because Mom held the receiver away from her ear.

She waited for him to calm down and said, "And neither is Raymie. He'll stay with me."

"Let me talk to him," I said. I bounced off the couch. The look she gave me stopped me dead.

"What for?" she said to Dad. "No, we are going to finish this conversation, David, do you hear me?"

She listened for a moment. "Okay, all right, but don't you dare hang up." She waved me over and slapped the phone into my hand as if I had put the missiles in Cuba. She stalked to the kitchen.

I needed a grown-up so bad that I almost cried when I heard Dad's voice. "Ray," he said, "your mother is pretty upset."

"Yes," I said.

"I want to come home—I *will* come home—but I can't just yet. If I just up and leave and this blows over, I'll get fired."

"But, Dad . . ."

"You're in charge until I get there. Understand, son? If the time comes, everything is up to you."

"Yes, sir," I whispered. I'd heard what he didn't say—it wasn't up to *her*.

"I want you to go out to the shelter tonight. Wait until she goes to sleep. Top off the water drums. Get all the gas out of the garage and store it next to the generator. But here's the most important thing. You know the sacks of rice? Drag them off to one side, the pallet too. There's a hatch underneath, the key to the airlock door unlocks it. You've got two new guns and plenty of ammunition. The revolver is a .357 Magnum. You be careful with that, Ray, it can blow a hole in a car but it's hard to aim. The double-barreled shotgun is easy to aim but you have to be close to do any harm. And I want you to bring down the Gamemaster from my closet and the .38 from my dresser drawer." He had been talking as if there would be no tomorrow; he paused then to catch his breath. "Now, this is all just in case, okay? I just want you to know."

I had never been so scared in my life.

"Ray?"

I should have told him about Cross then, but Mom weaved into the room. "Got it, Dad," I said. "Here she is."

Mom smiled at me. It was a lopsided smile that was trying to be brave but wasn't doing a very good job of it. She had a new glass and it was full. She held out her hand for the phone and I gave it to her.

I remember waiting until almost ten o'clock that night, reading under the covers with a flashlight. The Fantastic Four invaded Latveria to defeat Doctor Doom; Superman tricked Mr. Mxyzptlk into saying his name backward once again. When I opened the door to my parents' bedroom, I could hear Mom snoring. It spooked me; I hadn't realized that women did that. I thought about sneaking in to get the guns, but decided to take care of them tomorrow.

I stole out to the shelter, turned my key in the lock and pulled on the bulkhead door. It didn't move. That didn't make any sense, so I gave it a hard yank. The steel door rattled terribly but did not swing away. The air had turned frosty and the sound carried in the cold. I held my breath, listening to my blood pound. The house stayed dark, the shelter quiet as stones. After a few moments, I tried one last time before I admitted to myself what had happened.

Cross had bolted the door shut from the inside.

I went back to my room, but couldn't sleep. I kept going to the window to watch the sky over New York, waiting for a flash of killing light. I was all but convinced that the city would burn that very night in the thermonuclear fire and that Mom and I would die horrible deaths soon after, pounding on the unyielding steel doors of our shelter. Dad had left me in charge and I had let him down.

I didn't understand why Cross had locked us out. If he knew that a nuclear war was about to start, he might want our shelter all to himself. But that made him a monster and I still didn't see him as a monster. I tried to tell myself that he'd been asleep and couldn't hear me at the door—but that couldn't be right. What if he'd come to prevent the war? He'd said he had business in the city on Thursday; he could be doing something really, really futuristic in there that he couldn't let me see. Or else he was having problems. Maybe our twentieth-century germs had got to him, like they killed H. G. Wells's Martians.

I must have teased a hundred different ideas apart that night, in between uneasy trips to the window and glimpses at the clock. The last time I remember seeing was quarter after four. I tried to stay up to face the end, but I couldn't.

I wasn't dead when I woke up the next morning, so I had to go to school. Mom had Cream of Wheat all ready when I dragged myself to the table. Although she was all bright and bubbly, I could feel her giving me the mother's eye when I wasn't looking. She always knew when something was wrong. I tried not to show her anything. There was no time to sneak out to the shelter; I barely had time to finish eating before she bundled me off to the bus.

Right after the morning bell, Miss Toohey told us to open *The Story of New York State* to Chapter Seven, "Resources and Products," and read to ourselves. Then she left the room. We looked at each other in amazement. I heard Bobby Coniff whisper something. It was probably dirty; a few kids snickered. Chapter Seven started with a map of product symbols. Two teeny little cows grazed near Binghamton. Rochester was a cog and a pair of glasses. Elmira was an adding machine, Oswego an apple. There was a lightning bolt over Niagara Falls. Dad had promised to take us there someday. I had the sick feeling that we'd never get the chance. Miss Toohey looked pale when she came back, but that didn't stop her from giving us a spelling test. I got a ninety-five. The word I spelled wrong was *enigma*. The hot lunch was American Chop Suey, a roll, a salad, and a bowl of butterscotch pudding. In the afternoon, we did decimals.

Nobody said anything about the end of the world.

I decided to get off the bus in Ward's Hollow, buy the stuff Cross wanted and pretend I didn't know he had locked the shelter door last night. If he said something about it, I'd act surprised. If he didn't . . . I didn't know what I'd do then.

Village Variety was next to Warren's Esso and across the street from the Post Office. It had once been two different stores located in the same building, but then Mr. Rudowski had bought the building and knocked down the dividing wall. On the fun side were pens and pencils and paper and greeting cards and magazines and comics and paperbacks and candy. The other side was all boring hardware and small appliances.

Mr. Rudowski was on the phone when I came in, but then he was always on the phone when he worked. He could sell you a hammer or a pack of baseball cards, tell you a joke, ask about your family, complain about the weather and still keep the guy on the other end of the line happy. This time though, when he saw me come in, he turned away, wrapping the phone cord across his shoulder.

I went through the store quickly and found everything Cross had wanted. I had to blow dust off the transistor radio box but the batteries looked fresh. There was only one *New York Times* left; the headlines were so big they were scary.

US IMPOSES ARMS BLOCKADE ON CUBA
ON FINDING OF OFFENSIVE MISSILE SITES;
KENNEDY READY FOR SOVIET SHOWDOWN
Ships Must Stop   President Grave   Prepared to Risk War

I set my purchases on the counter in front of Mr. Rudowski. He cocked his head to one side, trapping the telephone receiver against his shoulder, and rang me up. The paper was on the bottom of the pile.

"Since when do you read the *Times*, Ray?" Mr. Rudowski punched it into the cash register and hit total. "I just got the new *Fantastic Four*." The cash drawer popped open.

"Maybe tomorrow," I said.

"All right then. It comes to twelve dollars and forty-seven cents."

I gave him the hundred-dollar bill.

"What is this, Ray?" He stared at it and then at me.

I had my story all ready. "It was a birthday gift from my grandma in Detroit. She said I could spend it on whatever I wanted so I decided to treat myself, but I'm going to put the rest in the bank."

"You're buying a radio? From me?"

"Well, you know. I thought maybe I should have one with me with all this stuff going on."

He didn't say anything for a moment. He just pulled a paper bag from under the counter and put my things into it. His shoulder were hunched; I thought maybe he felt guilty about overcharging for the radio. "You should be listening to music, Ray," he said quietly. "You like Elvis? All kids like Elvis. Or maybe that colored guy, the one who does the Twist?"

"They're all right, I guess."

"You're too young to be worrying about the news. You hear me? Those politicians . . ." He shook his head. "It's going to be okay, Ray. You heard it from me."

"Sure, Mr. Rudowski. I was wondering, could I get five dollars in change?"

I could feel him watching me as I stuffed it all into my book bag. I was certain he'd call my mom, but he never did. Home was three miles up Cobb's Hill. I did it in forty minutes, a record.

I remember I started running when I saw the flashing lights. The police car had left skid marks in the gravel on our driveway.

"Where were you?" Mom burst out of the house as I came across the lawn. "Oh, my God, Raymie, I was worried sick." She caught me up in her arms.

"I got off the bus in Ward's Hollow." She was about to smother me; I squirmed free. "What happened?"

"This the boy, ma'am?" The state trooper had taken his time catching up to her. He had almost the same hat as Scoutmaster Newell.

"Yes, yes! Oh, thank God, officer!"

The trooper patted me on the head like I was a lost dog. "You had your mom worried, Ray."

"Raymie, you should've told me."

"Somebody tell me what happened!" I said.

A second trooper came from behind the house. We watched him approach. "No sign of any intruder." He looked bored; I wanted to scream.

"Intruder?" I said.

"He broke into the shelter," said Mom. "He knew my name."

"There was no sign of forcible entry," said the second trooper. I saw him exchange a glance with his partner. "Nothing disturbed that I could see."

"He didn't have time," Mom said. "When I found him in the shelter, I ran back to the house and got your father's gun from the bedroom."

The thought of Mom with the .38 scared me. I had my Shooting merit badge, but she didn't know a hammer from a trigger. "You didn't shoot him?"

"No." She shook her head. "He had plenty of time to leave but he was still there when I came back. That's when he said my name."

I had never been so mad at her before. "You never go out to the shelter."

She had that puzzled look she always gets at night. "I couldn't find my key. I had to use the one your father leaves over the breezeway door."

"What did he say again, ma'am? The intruder."

"He said, 'Mrs. Beaumont, I present no danger to you.' And I said, 'Who are you?' And then he came toward me and I thought he said 'Margaret,' and I started firing."

"You did shoot him!"

Both troopers must have heard the panic in my voice. The first one said, "You know something about this man, Ray?"

"No, I-I was at school all day and then I stopped at Rudowski's . . ." I could feel my eyes burning. I was so embarrassed; I knew I was about to cry in front of them.

Mom acted annoyed that the troopers had stopped paying attention to her. "I shot *at* him. Three, four times, I don't know. I must have missed, because he just stood there staring at me. It seemed like forever. Then he walked past me and up the stairs like nothing had happened."

"And he didn't say anything?"

"Not a word."

"Well, it beats me," said the second trooper. "The gun's been fired four times but there are no bullet holes in the shelter and no bloodstains."

"You mind if I ask you a personal question, Mrs. Beaumont?" the first trooper said.

She colored. "I suppose not."

"Have you been drinking, ma'am?"

"Oh that!" She seemed relieved. "No. Well, I mean, after I called you, I did pour myself a little something. Just to steady my nerves. I was worried because my son was so late and . . . Raymie, what's the matter?"

I felt so small. The tears were pouring down my face.

After the troopers left, I remember Mom baking brownies while I watched *Superman*. I wanted to go out and hunt for Cross, but it was already sunset and there was no excuse I could come up with for wandering around in the dark. Besides, what was the point? He was gone, driven off by my mother. I'd had a chance to help a man from the future change history, maybe prevent World War III, and I had blown it. My life was ashes.

I wasn't hungry that night, for brownies or spaghetti or anything, but Mom made that clucking noise when I pushed supper around the plate, so I ate a few bites just to shut her up. I was surprised at how easy it was to hate her, how good it felt. Of course, she was oblivious, but in the morning she would notice if I wasn't careful. After dinner, she watched the news and I went upstairs to read. I wrapped a pillow around my head when she yelled at David Brinkley. I turned out the lights at 8:30, but I couldn't get to sleep. She went to her room a little after that.

"Mr. Beaumont?"

I must have dozed off, but when I heard his voice I snapped awake immediately.

"Is that you, Mr. Cross?" I peered into the darkness. "I bought the stuff you wanted." The room filled with an awful stink, like when Mom drove with the parking brake on.

"Mr. Beaumont," he said, "I am damaged."

I slipped out of bed, picked my way across the dark room, locked the door and turned on the light.

"Oh jeez!"

He slumped against my desk like a nightmare. I remember thinking then that Cross wasn't human, that maybe he wasn't even alive. His proportions were wrong: an ear, a shoulder and both feet sagged like they had melted. Little wisps of steam or something curled off him; they were what smelled. His skin had gone all shiny and hard; so had his business suit. I'd wondered why he never took the suit coat off, and now I knew. His clothes were *part* of him. The middle fingers of his right hand beat spasmodically against his palm.

"Mr. Beaumont," he said. "I calculate your chances at 10^{16} to 1."

"Chances of what?" I said. "What happened to you?"

"You must listen most attentively, Mr. Beaumont. My decline is very bad for history. It is for you now to alter the time-line probabilities."

"I don't understand."

"Your government greatly overestimates the nuclear capability of the Soviet Union. If you originate a first strike, the United States will achieve overwhelming victory."

"Does the president know this? We have to tell him!"

"John Kennedy will not welcome such information. If he starts this war, he will be responsible for the deaths of tens of millions, both Russians and Americans. But he does not grasp the future of the arms race. The war must happen now, because those who come after will build and build until they control arsenals that can destroy the world many times over. People are not capable of thinking for very long of such fearsome weapons. They tire of the idea of extinction and then become numb to it. The buildup slows but does not stop and they congratulate themselves on having survived it. But there are still too many weapons and they never go away. The Third War comes as a surprise. The First War was called the one to end all wars. The Third War is the only such war possible, Mr. Beaumont, because it ends everything. History stops in 2009. Do you understand? A year later, there is no life. All dead, the world a hot, barren rock."

"But you . . . ?"

"I am nothing, a *construct*. Mr. Beaumont, please, the chances are 10^{16} to 1," he said. "Do you know how improbable that is?" His laugh sounded like a hiccup. "But for the sake of those few precious time-lines, we must continue. There is a man, a politician in New York. If he dies on Thursday night, it will create the incident that forces Kennedy's hand."

"Dies?" For days, I had been desperate for him to talk. Now all I wanted was to run away. "You're going to kill somebody?"

"The world will survive a Third War that starts on Friday, October 22, 1962."

"What about me? My parents? Do *we* survive?"

"I cannot access that time-line. I have no certain answer for you. Please, Mr. Beaumont, this politician will die of a heart attack in less than three years. He has made no great contribution to history, yet his assassination can save the world."

"What do you want from me?" But I had already guessed.

"He will speak most eloquently at the United Nations on Friday evening. Afterward he will have dinner with his friend, Ruth Fields. Around ten o'clock he will return to his residence at the Waldorf Towers. Not the Waldorf Astoria Hotel, but the Towers. He will take the elevator to Suite 42A. He is the American ambassador to the United Nations. His name is Adlai Stevenson."

"Stop it! Don't say anything else."

When he sighed, his breath was a cloud of acrid steam. "I have based my calculation of the time-line probabilities on two data points, Mr. Beaumont, which I discovered in your bomb shelter. The first is the .357 Magnum revolver, located under a pallet of rice bags. I trust you know of this weapon?"

"Yes," I whispered.

"The second is the collection of magazines, located under your cot. It would seem that you take an interest in what is to come, Mr. Beaumont, and that may lend you the courage you will need to divert this time-line from disaster. You should know that there is not just *one* future. There are an infinite number of futures in which all possibilities are expressed, an infinite number of Raymond Beaumonts."

"Mr. Cross, I can't . . ."

"Perhaps not," he said, "but I believe that another one of you can."

"You don't understand . . ." I watched in horror as a boil swelled on the side of his face and popped, expelling an evil jet of yellow steam. "What?"

"Oh *fuck*." That was the last thing he said.

He slid to the floor—or maybe he was just a body at that point. More boils formed and burst. I opened all the windows in my room and got the fan down out of the closet and still I can't believe that the stink didn't wake Mom up. Over the course of the next few hours, he sort of vaporized.

When it was over, there was a sticky, dark spot on the floor the size of my pillow. I moved the throw rug from one side of the room to the other to cover it up. I had nothing to prove that Cross existed but a transistor radio, a couple of batteries, an earplug, and eighty-seven dollars and fifty-three cents in change.

I might have done things differently if I hadn't had a day to think. I can't remember going to school on Wednesday, who I talked to, what I ate. I was feverishly trying to figure out what to do and how to do it. I had no place to go for answers, not Miss Toohey, not my parents, not the Bible or the *Boy Scout Handbook*, certainly not *Galaxy* magazine. Whatever I did had to come out of *me*. I watched the news with Mom that night. President Kennedy had brought our military to the highest possible state of alert. There were reports that some Russian ships had turned away from Cuba; others continued on course. Dad called and said his trip was being cut short and that he would be home the next day.

But that was too late.

I hid behind the stone wall when the school bus came on Thursday morning. Mrs. Johnson honked a couple of times, and then drove on. I set out for New Canaan, carrying my book bag. In it were the radio, the batteries, the coins, the map of New York, and the .357. I had the rest of Cross's money in my wallet.

It took more than five hours to hike to the train station. I expected to be scared, but the whole time I felt light as air. I kept thinking of what Cross had said about the future, that I was just one of millions and millions of Raymond Beaumonts. Most of them were in school, diagramming sentences and watching Miss Toohey bite her nails. I was the special one, walking into history. I was super. I caught the 2:38 train, changed in Stamford, and arrived at Grand Central just after four. I had six hours. I bought myself a hot pretzel and a Coke and tried to decide where I should go. I couldn't just sit around the hotel lobby for all that time; I thought that would draw too much attention. I decided to go to the top of the Empire State Building. I took my time walking down Park Avenue and tried not to see all the ghosts I was about to make. In the lobby of the Empire State Building, I used Cross's change to call home.

"Hello?" I hadn't expected Dad to answer. I would've hung up except that I knew I might never speak to him again.

"Dad, this is Ray. I'm safe, don't worry."

"Ray, where are you?"

"I can't talk. I'm safe but I won't be home tonight. Don't worry."

"Ray!" He was frantic. "What's going on?"

"I'm sorry."

"Ray!"

I hung up; I had to. "I love you," I said to the dial tone.

I could imagine the expression on Dad's face, how he would tell Mom what I'd said. Eventually they would argue about it. He would shout; she would cry. As I rode the elevator up, I got mad at them. He shouldn't have picked up the phone. They should've protected me from Cross and the future he came from. I was in the sixth grade, I shouldn't have to have feelings like this. The observation platform was almost deserted. I walked completely around it, staring at the city stretching away from me in every direction. It was dusk; the buildings were shadows in the failing light. I didn't feel like Ray Beaumont anymore; he was my secret identity. Now I was the superhero Bomb Boy; I had the power of bringing nuclear war. Wherever I cast my terrible gaze, cars melted and people burst into flame.

And I loved it.

It was dark when I came down from the Empire State Building. I had a sausage pizza and a Coke on 47th Street. While I ate, I stuck the plug into my ear and listened to the radio. I searched for the news. One announcer said the debate was still going on in the Security Council. Our ambassador was questioning Ambassador Zorin. I stayed with that station for a while, hoping to hear his voice. I knew what he looked like, of course. Adlai Stevenson had run for president a couple of times when I was just a baby. But I couldn't remember what he sounded like. He might talk to me, ask me what I was doing in his hotel; I wanted to be ready for that.

I arrived at the Waldorf Towers around nine o'clock. I picked a plush velvet chair that had a direct view of the elevator bank and sat there for about ten minutes. Nobody seemed to care but it was hard to sit still. Finally, I got up and went to the men's room. I took my book bag into a stall, closed the door, and got the .357 out. I aimed it at the toilet. The gun was heavy, and I could tell it would have a big kick. I probably ought to hold it with both hands. I released the safety, put it back into my book bag, and flushed.

When I came out of the bathroom, I had stopped believing that I was going to shoot anyone, that I could. But I had to find out, for Cross's sake. If I was really meant to save the world, then I had to be in the right place at the right time. I went back to my chair, checked my watch. It was nine-twenty.

I started thinking of the one who would pull the trigger, the unlikely Ray. What would make the difference? Had he read some story in *Galaxy* that I had skipped? Was it a problem with Mom? Or Dad? Maybe he had spelled *enigma* right; maybe Cross had lived another thirty seconds in his time-line. Or maybe he was just the best that I could possibly be.

I was so tired of it all. I must have walked thirty miles since morning and I hadn't slept well in days. The lobby was warm. People laughed and murmured. Elevator doors dinged softly. I tried to stay up to face history, but I couldn't. I was Raymond Beaumont, but I was just a twelve-year-old kid.

I remember the doorman waking me up at eleven o'clock. Dad drove all the way into the city to get me. When we got home, Mom was already in the shelter.

Only the Third War didn't start that night. Or the next.

I lost television privileges for a month.

For most people my age, the most traumatic memory of growing up came on November 22, 1963. But the date I remember is July 14, 1965, when Adlai Stevenson dropped dead of a heart attack in London.

I've tried to do what I can, to make up for what I didn't do that night. I've worked for the cause wherever I could find it. I belong to CND and SANE and the Friends of the Earth, and was active in the nuclear freeze movement. I think the Green Party (*www.greens.org*) is the only political organization worth your vote. I don't know if any of it will change Cross's awful probabilities; maybe we'll survive in a few more time-lines.

When I was a kid, I didn't mind being lonely. Now it's hard, knowing what I know. Oh, I have lots of friends, all of them wonderful people, but people who know me say that there's a part of myself that I always keep hidden. They're right. I don't think I'll ever be able to tell anyone about what happened with Cross, what I didn't do that night. It wouldn't be fair to them.

Besides, whatever happens, chances are very good that it's my fault.

winemaster

ROBERT REED

Robert Reed may be one of the most prolific of today's young writers, particularly at short fiction lengths, seriously rivaled for that position only by authors such as Stephen Baxter and Brian Stableford. And—also like Baxter and Stableford—he manages to keep up a very high standard of quality while being prolific, something that is not at all easy to do. Reed sold his first story in 1986, and quickly established himself as a frequent contributor to The Magazine of Fantasy & Science Fiction and Asimov's Science Fiction, as well as selling many stories to Science Fiction Age, Universe, New Destinies, Tomorrow, Synergy, Starlight, and elsewhere. Almost every year throughout the mid-to-late '90s, he has produced at least two or three stories that would be good enough to get him into a Best of the Year anthology under ordinary circumstances, and some years he has produced four or five of them, so that often the choice is not whether or not to use a Reed story, but rather which Reed story to use—a remarkable accomplishment.

In spite of this large and remarkable body of work, though, Reed remains underrated, although he is at last beginning to get onto major award ballots—with his story "Whiptail" showing up on last year's Final Hugo Ballot, for instance—and I suspect that he will become one of the Big Names of the first decade of the new century coming up on the horizon.

A prime selection of Reed's stories were recently collected in The Dragons of Springplace, one of the year's best collections, but Reed is almost as prolific as a novelist as he is as a short story writer, having produced eight novels to date, including The Leeshore, The Hormone Jungle, Black Milk, The Remarkables, Down the Bright Way, Beyond the Veil of Stars, An Exaltation of Larks, and, most recently, Beneath the Gated Sky. His new novel, Marrow, is due out shortly. His stories have appeared in our Ninth, Tenth, Eleventh, Twelfth, Thirteenth, Fourteenth, Fifteenth, and Sixteenth Annual Collections. He lives in Lincoln, Nebraska.

In the surprising story that follows, he reaffirms the old truth that whole worlds can be hidden in a grain of sand—or sometimes in even odder disguises.

The stranger pulled into the Quik Shop outside St. Joe. Nothing was remarkable about him, which was why he caught Blaine's eye. Taller than average, but not much, he was thin in an unfit way, with black hair and a handsome, almost pretty face, fine bones floating beneath skin that didn't often get into the sun. Which meant nothing, of course. A lot of people were staying indoors lately. Blaine watched him climb out of an enormous Buick—a satin black '17 Gibraltar that had seen better days—and after a lazy long stretch, he passed his e-card through the proper slot and inserted the nozzle, filling the Buick's cavernous tank with ten cold gallons of gasoline and corn alcohol.

By then, Blaine had run his plates.

The Buick was registered to Julian Winemaster from Wichita, Kansas; twenty-nine accompanying photographs showed pretty much the same fellow who stood sixty feet away.

His entire bio was artfully bland, rigorously seamless. Winemaster was an account-ant, divorced and forty-four years old, with O negative blood and five neo-enamel fillings imbedded in otherwise perfect teeth, plus a small pink birthmark somewhere on his right buttock. Useless details, Blaine reminded himself, and with that he lifted his gaze, watching the traveler remove the dripping nozzle, then cradling it on the pump with the overdone delicacy of a man ill-at-ease with machinery.

Behind thick fingers, Blaine was smiling.

Winemaster moved with a stiff, road-weary gait, walking into the convenience store and asking, "Ma'am? Where's your rest room, please?"

The clerk ignored him.

It was the men's room that called out, "Over here, sir."

Sitting in one of the hard plastic booths, Blaine had a good view of everything. A pair of militia boys in their brown uniforms were the only others in the store. They'd been gawking at dirty comic books, minding their own business until they heard Winemaster's voice. Politeness had lately become a suspicious behavior. Blaine watched the boys look up and elbow each other, putting their sights on the stranger. And he watched Winemaster's walk, the expression on his pretty frail face, and a myriad of subtleties, trying to decide what he should do, and when, and what he should avoid at all costs.

It was a bright warm summer morning, but there hadn't been twenty cars in the last hour, most of them sporting local plates.

The militia boys blanked their comics and put them on the wrong shelves, then walked out the front door, one saying, "Bye now," as he passed the clerk.

"Sure," the old woman growled, never taking her eyes off a tiny television screen.

The boys might simply be doing their job, which meant they were harmless.

But the state militias were full of bullies who'd found a career in the last couple years. There was no sweeter sport than terrorizing the innocent traveler, because of course the genuine refugee was too rare of a prospect to hope for.

Winemaster vanished into the men's room.

The boys approached the black Buick, doing a little dance and showing each other their malicious smiles. Thugs, Blaine decided. Which meant that he had to do something now. Before Winemaster, or whoever he was, came walking out of the toilet.

Blaine climbed out of the tiny booth.

He didn't waste breath on the clerk.

Crossing the greasy pavement, he watched the boys using a police-issue lock pick. The front passenger door opened, and both of them stepped back, trying to keep a safe distance. With equipment that went out of date last spring, one boy probed the interior air, the cultured leather seats, the dashboard and floorboard and even an empty pop can standing in its cradle. "Naw, it's okay," he was saying. "Get on in there."

His partner had a knife. The curled blade was intended for upholstery. Nothing could be learned by ripping apart the seats, but it was a fun game nonetheless.

"Get in there," the first boy repeated.

The second one started to say, "I'm getting in—" But he happened to glance over his shoulder, seeing Blaine coming, and he turned fast, lifting the knife, seriously thinking about slashing the interloper.

Blaine was bigger than some pairs of men.

He was fat, but in a powerful, focused way. And he was quick, grabbing the knife hand and giving a hard squeeze, then flinging the boy against the car's composite body, the knife dropping and Blaine kicking it out of reach, then giving the boy a second shove, harder this time, telling both of them, "That's enough, gentlemen."

"Who the fuck are you—?" they sputtered, in a chorus.

Blaine produced a badge and ID bracelet. "Read these," he suggested coldly. Then he told them, "You're welcome to check me out. But we do that somewhere else. Right now, this man's door is closed and locked, and the three of us are hiding. Understand?"

The boy with the surveillance equipment said, "We're within our rights."

Blaine shut and locked the door for them, saying, "This way. Stay with me."

"One of their nests got hit last night," said the other boy, walking. "We've been checking people all morning!"

"Find any?"

"Not yet—"

"With that old gear, you won't."

"We've caught them before," said the first boy, defending his equipment. His status. "A couple, three different carloads . . ."

Maybe they did, but that was months ago. Generations ago.

"Is that yours?" asked Blaine. He pointed to a battered Python, saying, "It better be. We're getting inside."

The boys climbed in front. Blaine filled the back seat, sweating from exertion and the car's brutal heat.

"What are we doing?" one of them asked.

"We're waiting. Is that all right with you?"

"I guess."

But his partner couldn't just sit. He turned and glared at Blaine, saying, "You'd better be Federal."

"And if not?" Blaine inquired, without interest.

No appropriate threat came to mind. So the boy simply growled and repeated himself. "You'd just better be. That's all I'm saying."

A moment later, Winemaster strolled out of the store. Nothing in his stance or pace implied worry. He was carrying a can of pop and a red bag of corn nuts. Resting his purchases on the roof, he punched in his code to unlock the driver's door, then gave the area a quick glance. It was the glance of someone who never intended to return here, even for gasoline—a dismissive expression coupled with a tangible sense of relief.

That's when Blaine knew.

When he was suddenly and perfectly sure.

The boys saw nothing incriminating. But the one who'd held the knife was quick to say the obvious: A man with Blaine's credentials could get his hands on the best EM sniffers in the world. "Get them," he said, "and we'll find out what he is!"

But Blaine already felt sure.

"He's going," the other one sputtered. "Look, he's gone—!"

The black car was being driven by a cautious man. Winemaster braked and looked both ways twice before he pulled out onto the access road, accelerating gradually toward I-29, taking no chances even though there was precious little traffic to avoid as he drove north.

"Fuck," said the boys, in one voice.

Using a calm-stick, Blaine touched one of the thick necks; without fuss, the boy slumped forward.

"Hey!" snapped his partner. "What are you doing—?"

"What's best," Blaine whispered afterward. Then he lowered the Python's windows and destroyed its ignition system, leaving the pair asleep in the front seats. And because the moment required justice, he took one of their hands each, shoving them inside the other's pants, then he laid their heads together, in the pose of lovers.

The other refugees pampered Julian: His cabin wasn't only larger than almost anyone else's, it wore extra shielding to help protect him from malicious high-energy particles. Power and shaping rations didn't apply to him, although he rarely indulged himself, and a platoon of autodocs did nothing but watch over his health. In public, strangers applauded him. In private, he could select almost any woman as a lover. And in bed, in the afterglow of whatever passed for sex at that particular moment, Julian could tell his stories, and his lovers would listen as if enraptured, even if they already knew each story by heart.

No one on board was more ancient than Julian. Even before the attack, he was one of the few residents of the Shawnee Nest who could honestly claim to be DNA-made, his life beginning as a single wet cell inside a cavernous womb, a bloody birth followed by sloppy growth that culminated in a vast and slow and decidedly old-fashioned human being.

Julian was nearly forty when Transmutations became an expensive possibility.

Thrill seekers and the terminally ill were among the first to undergo the process, their primitive bodies and bloated minds consumed by the microchines, the sum total of their selves compressed into tiny robotic bodies meant to duplicate every normal human function.

Being pioneers, they endured heavy losses. Modest errors during the Transmutation meant instant death. Tiny errors meant a pathetic and incurable insanity. The fledging Nests were exposed to heavy nuclei and subtle EM effects, all potentially disastrous. And of course there were the early terrorist attacks, crude and disorganized, but extracting a horrible toll nonetheless.

The survivors were tiny and swift, and wiser, and they were able to streamline the Transmutation, making it more accurate and affordable, and to a degree, routine.

"I was forty-three when I left the other world," Julian told his lover of the moment. He always used those words, framing them with defiance and a hint of bittersweet longing. "It was three days and two hours before the President signed the McGrugger Bill."

That's when Transmutation became illegal in the United States.

His lover did her math, then with a genuine awe said, "That was five hundred and twelve days ago."

A day was worth years inside a Nest.

"Tell me," she whispered. "Why did you do it? Were you bored? Or sick?"

"Don't you know why?" he inquired.

"No," she squeaked.

Julian was famous, but sometimes his life wasn't. And why should the youngsters know his biography by heart?

"I don't want to force you," the woman told him. "If you'd rather not talk about it, I'll understand."

Julian didn't answer immediately.

Instead, he climbed from his bed and crossed the cabin. His kitchenette had created a drink—hydrocarbons mixed with nanochines that were nutritious, appetizing, and pleasantly narcotic. Food and drink were not necessities, but habits, and they were enjoying a renewed popularity. Like any credible Methuselah, Julian was often the model on how best to do archaic oddities.

The woman lay on top of the bed. Her current body was a hologram laid over her mechanical core. It was a traditional body, probably worn for his pleasure; no wings or fins or even more bizarre adornments. As it happened, she had selected a build and complexion not very different from Julian's first wife. A coincidence?

Or had she actually done research, and she already knew the answers to her prying questions?

"Sip," he advised, handing her the drink.

Their hands brushed against one another, shaped light touching its equivalent. What each felt was a synthetically generated sensation, basically human, intended to feel like warm, water-filled skin.

The girl obeyed, smiling as she sipped, an audible slurp amusing both of them.

"Here," she said, handing back the glass. "Your turn."

Julian glanced at the far wall. A universal window gave them a live view of the Quick Shop, the image supplied by one of the multitude of cameras hidden on the Buick's exterior. What held his interest was the old muscle car, a Python with smoked glass windows. When he first saw that car, three heads were visible. Now two of the heads had gradually dropped out of sight, with the remaining man still sitting in back, big eyes opened wide, making no attempt to hide his interest in the Buick's driver.

No one knew who the fat man was, or what he knew, much less what his intentions might be. His presence had been a complete surprise, and what he had done with those militia members, pulling them back as he did as well as the rest of it, had left the refugees more startled than grateful, and more scared than any time since leaving the Nest.

Julian had gone to that store with the intent of suffering a clumsy, even violent interrogation. A militia encounter was meant to give them authenticity. And more importantly, to give Julian experience—precious and sobering firsthand experience with the much-changed world around them.

A world that he hadn't visited for more than a millennium, Nesttime.

Since he last looked, nothing of substance had changed at that ugly store. And probably nothing would change for a long while. One lesson that no refugee needed, much less craved, was that when dealing with that other realm, nothing helped as much as patience.

Taking a long, slow sip of their drink, he looked back at the woman—twenty days old; a virtual child—and without a shred of patience, she said, "You were sick, weren't you? I heard someone saying that's why you agreed to be Transmutated . . . five hundred and twelve days ago . . ."

"No." He offered a shy smile. "And it wasn't because I wanted to live this way, either. To be honest, I've always been conservative. In that world, and this one, too."

She nodded amiably, waiting.

"It was my daughter," he explained. "She was sick. An incurable leukemia." Again he offered the shy smile, adding, "She was nine years old, and terrified. I could save her life by agreeing to her Transmutation, but I couldn't just abandon her to life in the Nest . . . making her into an orphan, basically . . ."

"I see," his lover whispered.

Then after a respectful silence, she asked, "Where's your daughter now?"

"Dead."

"Of course . . ." Not many people were lucky enough to live five hundred days in a Nest; despite shields, a single heavy nucleus could still find you, ravaging your mind, extinguishing your very delicate soul. "How long ago . . . did it happen . . . ?"

"This morning," he replied. "In the attack."

"Oh . . . I'm very sorry . . ."

With the illusion of shoulders, Julian shrugged. Then with his bittersweet voice, he admitted, "It already seems long ago."

Winemaster headed north into Iowa, then did the unexpected, making the sudden turn east when he reached the new Tollway.

Blaine shadowed him. He liked to keep two minutes between the Buick and his little Tokamak, using the FBI's recon network to help monitor the situation. But the network had been compromised in the past, probably more often than anyone knew, which meant that he had to occasionally pay the Tollway a little extra to boost his speed, the gap closing to less than fifteen seconds. Then with the optics in his windshield, he would get a good look at what might or might not be Julian Winemaster—a stiffly erect gentleman who kept one hand on the wheel, even when the AI-managed road was controlling every vehicle's speed and direction, and doing a better job of driving than any human could do.

Iowa was half-beautiful, half-bleak. Some fields looked tended, genetically tailored crops planted in fractal patterns and the occasional robot working carefully, pulling weeds and killing pests as it spider-walked back and forth. But there were long stretches where the farms had been abandoned, wild grasses and the spawn of last year's crops coming up in ragged green masses. Entire neighborhoods had pulled up and gone elsewhere. How many farmers had accepted the Transmutation, in other countries or illegally? Probably only a fraction of them, Blaine knew. Habit-bound and suspicious by nature, they'd never agree to the dismantlement of their bodies, the transplantation of their crusty souls. No, what happened was that farms were simply falling out of production, particularly where the soil was marginal. Yields were still improving in a world where the old-style population was tumbling. If patterns held, most of the arable land would soon return to prairie and forest. And eventually, the entire human species wouldn't fill so much as one of these abandoned farms . . . leaving the old world entirely empty . . . if those patterns were allowed to hold, naturally . . .

Unlike Winemaster, Blaine kept neither hand on the wheel, trusting the AIs to look after him. He spent most of his time watching the news networks, keeping tabs on moods more than facts. What had happened in Kansas was still the big story. By noon, more than twenty groups and individuals had claimed responsibility for the attack. Officially, the Emergency Federal Council deplored any senseless violence—a cliché which implied that sensible violence was an entirely different question. When asked about the government's response, the President's press secretary looked at the world with a stony face, saying, "We're investigating the regrettable incident. But the fact remains, it happened outside our borders. We are observers here. The Shawnee Nest was responsible for its own security, just as every other Nest is responsible . . ."

Questions came in a flurry. The press secretary pointed to a small, severe-looking man in the front row—a reporter for the Christian Promise organization. "Are we taking any precautions against counterattacks?" the reporter inquired. Then, not waiting for an answer, he added, "There have been reports of activity in the other Nests, inside the United States and elsewhere."

A tense smile was the first reply.

Then the stony face told everyone, "The President and the Council have taken every appropriate precaution. As for any activity in any Nest, I can only say: We have everything perfectly well in hand."

"Is anything left of the Shawnee Nest?" asked a second reporter.

"No." The press secretary was neither sad nor pleased. "Initial evidence is that the entire facility has been sterilized."

A tenacious gray-haired woman—the perpetual symbol of the Canadian News-web—called out, "Mr. Secretary . . . Lennie—!"

"Yes, Cora . . ."

"How many were killed?"

"I wouldn't know how to answer that question, Cora . . ."

"Your government estimates an excess of one hundred million. If the entire Nest was sterilized, as you say, then we're talking about more than two-thirds of the current U.S. population."

"Legally," he replied, "we are talking about machines."

"Some of those machines were once your citizens," she mentioned.

The reporter from Christian Promise was standing nearby. He grimaced, then muttered bits of relevant Scripture.

"I don't think this is the time or place to debate what life is or isn't," said the press secretary, juggling things badly.

Cora persisted. "Are you aware of the Canadian position on this tragedy?"

"Like us, they're saddened."

"They've offered sanctuary to any survivors of the blast—"

"Except there are none," he replied, his face pink as granite.

"But if there were? Would you let them move to another Nest in the United States, or perhaps to Canada . . . ?"

There was a pause, brief and electric.

Then with a flat cool voice, the press secretary reported, "The McGrugger Bill is very specific. Nests may exist only in sealed containment facilities, monitored at all times. And should any of the microchines escape, they will be treated as what they are . . . grave hazards to normal life . . . and this government will not let them roam at will . . . !"

Set inside an abandoned salt mine near Kansas City, the Shawnee Nest had been one of the most secure facilities of its kind ever built. Its power came from clean geothermal sources. Lead plates and intricate defense systems stood against natural hazards as well as more human threats. Thousands of government-loyal AIs, positioned in the surrounding salt, did nothing but watch its borders, making certain that none of the microchines could escape. That was why the thought that local terrorists could launch any attack was so ludicrous. To have that attack succeed was simply preposterous. Whoever was responsible for the bomb, it was done with the abeyance of the highest authorities. No sensible soul doubted it. That dirty little nuke had Federal fingerprints on it, and the attack was planned carefully, and its goals were instantly apparent to people large and small.

Julian had no doubts. He had enemies, vast and malicious, and nobody was more entitled to his paranoias.

Just short of Illinois, the Buick made a long-scheduled stop.

Julian took possession of his clone at the last moment. The process was supposed to be routine—a simple matter of slowing his thoughts a thousandfold, then integrating them with his body—but there were always phantom pains and a sick falling sensation. Becoming a bloated watery bag wasn't the strangest part of it. After all, the Nest was designed to mimic this kind of existence. What gnawed at Julian was the gargantuan sense of Time: A half an hour in this realm was nearly a month in his realm. No matter how brief the stop, Julian would feel a little lost when he returned, a step behind the others, and far more emotionally drained than he would ever admit.

By the time the car had stopped, Julian was in full control of the body. His body, he reminded himself. Climbing out into the heat and brilliant sunshine, he felt a purposeful stiffness in his back and the familiar ache running down his right leg. In his past life, he was plagued by sciatica pains. It was one of many ailments that he hadn't missed after his Transmutation. And it was just another detail that someone had thought to include, forcing him to wince and stretch, showing the watching world that he was their flavor of mortal.

Suddenly another old pain began to call to Julian.

Hunger.

His duty was to fill the tank, then do everything expected of a road-weary driver. The rest area was surrounded by the Tollway, gas pumps surrounding a fast food/playground complex. Built to handle tens of thousands of people daily, the facility had suffered with the civil chaos, the militias and the plummeting populations. A few dozen travelers went about their business in near-solitude, and presumably a team of state or Federal agents were lurking nearby, using sensors to scan for those who weren't what they seemed to be.

Without incident, Julian managed the first part of his mission. Then he drove a tiny distance and parked, repeating his stiff climb out of the car, entering the restaurant and steering straight for the rest room.

He was alone, thankfully.

The diagnostic urinal gently warned him to drink more fluids, then wished him a lovely day.

Taking the advice to heart, Julian ordered a bucket-sized ice tea along with a cultured guinea hen sandwich.

"For here or to go?" asked the automated clerk.

"I'm staying," he replied, believing it would look best.

"Thank you, sir. Have a lovely day."

Julian sat in the back booth, eating slowly and mannerly, scanning the pages of someone's forgotten e-paper. He made a point of lingering over the trite and trivial, concentrating on the comics with their humanized cats and cartoonish people, everyone playing out the same jokes that must have amused him in the very remote past.

"How's it going?"

The voice was slow and wet. Julian blanked the page, looking over his shoulder, betraying nothing as his eyes settled on the familiar wide face. "Fine," he replied, his own voice polite but distant. "Thank you."

"Is it me? Or is it just too damned hot to live out there . . . ?"

"It is hot," Julian conceded.

"Particularly for the likes of me." The man settled onto a plastic chair bolted into the floor with clown heads. His lunch buried his little table: three sandwiches, a greasy sack of fried cucumbers, and a tall chocolate shake. "It's murder when you're fat. Let me tell you . . . I've got to be careful in this weather. I don't move fast. I talk softly. I even have to ration my thinking. I mean it! Too many thoughts, and I break out in a killing sweat!"

Julian had prepared for this moment. Yet nothing was happening quite like he or anyone else had expected.

Saying nothing, Julian took a shy bite out of his sandwich.

"You look like a smart guy," said his companion. "Tell me. If the world's getting emptier, like everyone says, why am I still getting poorer?"

"Excuse me?"

"That's the way it feels, at least." The man was truly fat, his face smooth and youthful, every feature pressed outward by the remnants of countless lunches. "You'd think that with all the smart ones leaving for the Nests . . . you'd think guys like you and me would do pretty well for ourselves. You know?"

Using every resource, the refugees had found three identities for this man: He was a salesman from St. Joseph, Missouri. Or he was a Federal agent working for the Department of Technology, in its Enforcement division, and his salesman identity was a cover. Or he was a charter member of the Christian Promise organization, using that group's political connections to accomplish its murderous goals.

What does he want? Julian asked himself.

He took another shy bite, wiped his mouth with a napkin, then offered his own question. "Why do you say that . . . that it's the smart people who are leaving . . . ?"

"That's what studies show," said a booming, unashamed voice. "Half our people are gone, but we've lost ninety percent of our scientists. Eighty percent of our doctors. And almost every last member of Mensa . . . which between you and me is a good thing, I think . . . !"

Another bite, and wipe. Then with a genuine firmness, Julian told him, "I don't think we should be talking. We don't know each other."

A huge cackling laugh ended with an abrupt statement:

"That's why we should talk. We're strangers, so where's the harm?"

Suddenly the guinea hen sandwich appeared huge and inedible. Julian set it down and took a gulp of tea.

His companion watched him, apparently captivated.

Julian swallowed, then asked, "What do you do for a living?"

"What I'm good at." He unwrapped a hamburger, then took an enormous bite, leaving a crescent-shaped sandwich and a fine glistening stain around his smile. "Put it this way, Mr. Winemaster. I'm like anyone. I do what I hope is best."

"How do you—?"

"Your name? The same way I know your address, and your social registration number, and your bank balance, too." He took a moment to consume half of the remaining crescent, then while chewing, he choked out the words, "Blaine. My name is. If you'd like to use it."

Each of the man's possible identities used Blaine, either as a first or last name.

Julian wrapped the rest of his sandwich in its insulated paper, watching his hands begin to tremble. He had a pianist's hands in his first life but absolutely no talent for music. When he went through the Transmutation, he'd asked for a better ear and more coordination—both of which were given to him with minimal fuss. Yet he'd never learned how to play, not even after five hundred days. It suddenly seemed like a tragic waste of talent, and with a secret voice, he promised himself to take lessons, starting immediately.

"So, Mr. Winemaster . . . where are you heading . . . ?"

Julian managed another sip of tea, grimacing at the bitter taste.

"Someplace east, judging by what I can see . . ."

"Yes," he allowed. Then he added, "Which is none of your business."

Blaine gave a hearty laugh, shoving the last of the burger deep into his gaping mouth. Then he spoke, showing off the masticated meat and tomatoes, telling his new friend, "Maybe you'll need help somewhere up ahead. Just maybe. And if that happens, I want you to think of me."

"You'll help me, will you?"

The food-stuffed grin was practically radiant. "Think of me," he repeated happily. "That's all I'm saying."

For a long while, the refugees spoke and dreamed of nothing but the mysterious Blaine. Which side did he represent? Should they trust him? Or move against him? And if they tried to stop the man, which way was best? Sabotage his car? Drug his next meal? Or would they have to do something genuinely horrible?

But there were no answers, much less a consensus. Blaine continued shadowing them, at a respectful distance; nothing substantial was learned about him; and despite the enormous stakes, the refugees found themselves gradually drifting back into the moment-by-moment business of ordinary life.

Couples and amalgamations of couples were beginning to make babies.

There was a logic: Refugees were dying every few minutes, usually from radiation exposure. The losses weren't critical, but when they reached their new home—the deep cold rock of the Canadian Shield—they would need numbers, a real demographic momentum. And logic always dances with emotion. Babies served as a tonic to the adults. They didn't demand too many resources, and they forced their parents to focus on more manageable problems, like building tiny bodies and caring for needy souls.

Even Julian was swayed by fashion.

With one of his oldest women friends, he found himself hovering over a crystalline womb, watching nanochines sculpt their son out of single atoms and tiny electric breaths.

It was only Julian's second child.

As long as his daughter had been alive, he hadn't seen the point in having another. The truth was that it had always disgusted him to know that the children in the Nest were manufactured—there was no other word for it—and he didn't relish being reminded that he was nothing, more or less, than a fancy machine among millions of similar machines.

Julian often dreamed of his dead daughter. Usually she was on board their strange ark, and he would find a note from her, and a cabin number, and he would wake up smiling, feeling certain that he would find her today. Then he would suddenly remember the bomb, and he would start to cry, suffering through the wrenching, damning loss all over again.

Which was ironic, in a fashion.

During the last nineteen months, father and daughter had gradually and inexorably drifted apart. She was very much a child when they came to the Nest, as flexible as her father wasn't, and how many times had Julian lain awake in bed, wondering why he had ever bothered being Transmutated. His daughter didn't need him, plainly. He could have remained behind. Which always led to the same questions: When he was a normal human being, was he genuinely happy? Or was his daughter's illness simply an excuse . . . a spicy bit of good fortune that offered an escape route . . . ?

When the Nest was destroyed, Julian survived only through more good fortune. He was as far from the epicenter as possible, shielded by the Nest's interior walls and emergency barricades. Yet even then, most of the people near him were killed, an invisible neutron rain scrambling their minds. That same rain had knocked him unconscious just before the firestorm arrived, and if an autodoc hadn't found his limp body, then dragged him into a shelter, he would have been cremated. And of course if the Nest hadn't devised its elaborate escape plan, stockpiling the Buick and cloning equipment outside the Nest, Julian would have had no choice but to remain in the rubble, fighting to survive the next moment, and the next.

But those coincidences happened, making his present life feel like the culmination of some glorious Fate.

The secret truth was that Julian relished his new importance, and he enjoyed the pressures that came with each bathroom break and every stop for gas. If he died now, between missions, others could take his place, leading Winemaster's cloned body through the needed motions . . . but they wouldn't do as well, Julian could tell himself . . . a secret part of him wishing that this bizarre, slow-motion chase would never come to an end . . .

The Buick stayed on the Tollway through northern Illinois, slipping beneath Chicago before skipping across a sliver of Indiana. Julian was integrated with his larger self several times, going through the motions of the stiff, tired, and hungry traveler. Blaine always arrived several minutes later, never approaching his quarry, always finding gas at different pumps, standing outside the rest rooms, waiting to show Julian a big smile but never uttering so much as a word in passing.

A little after midnight, the Buick's driver took his hand off the wheel, lay back and fell asleep. Trusting the Tollway's driving was out of character, but with Blaine trailing them and the border approaching, no one was eager to waste time in a motel bed.

At two in the morning, Julian was also asleep, dipping in and out of dreams. Suddenly a hand took him by the shoulder, shaking him, and several voices, urgent and close, said, "We need you, Julian. Now."

In his dreams, a thousand admiring faces were saying, "We need you."

Julian awoke.

His cabin was full of people. His mate had been ushered away, but his unborn child, nearly complete now, floated in his bubble of blackened crystal, oblivious to the nervous air and the tight, crisp voices.

"What's wrong?" Julian asked.

"Everything," they assured.

His universal window showed a live feed from a security camera on the North Dakota–Manitoba border. Department of Technology investigators, backed up by a platoon of heavily armed Marines, were dismantling a Toyota Sunrise. Even at those syrupy speeds, the lasers moved quickly, leaving the vehicle in tiny pieces that were photographed, analyzed, then fed into a state-of-the-art decontamination unit.

"What is this?" Julian sputtered.

But he already knew the answer.

"There was a second group of refugees," said the President, kneeling beside his bed. She was wearing an oversized face—a common fashion, of late—and with a very calm, very grim voice, she admitted, "We weren't the only survivors."

They had kept it a secret, at least from Julian. Which was perfectly reasonable, he reminded himself. What if he had been captured? Under torture, he could have doomed that second lifeboat, and everyone inside it . . .

"Is my daughter there?" he blurted, uncertain what to hope for.

The President shook her head. "No, Julian."

Yet if two arks existed, couldn't there be a third? And wouldn't the President keep its existence secret from him, too?

"We've been monitoring events," she continued. "It's tragic, what's happening to our friends . . . but we'll be able to adjust our methods . . . for when we cross the border . . ."

He looked at the other oversized faces. "But why do you need me? We won't reach Detroit for hours."

The President looked over her shoulder. "Play the recording."

Suddenly Julian was looking back in time. He saw the Sunrise pull up to the border post, waiting in line to be searched. A pickup truck with Wyoming plates pulled up behind it, and out stepped a preposterously tall man brandishing a badge and a handgun. With an eerie sense of purpose, he strode up to the little car, took aim and fired his full clip through the driver's window. The body behind the wheel jerked and kicked as it was ripped apart. Then the murderer reached in and pulled the corpse out through the shattered glass, shouting at the Tech investigators:

"I've got them! Here! For Christ's sake, help me!"

The image dissolved, the window returning to the real-time, real-speed scene.

To himself, Julian whispered, "No, it can't be . . ."

The President took his hands in hers, their warmth a comfortable fiction. "We would have shown you this as it was happening, but we weren't sure what it meant."

"But you're sure now?"

"That man followed our people. All the way from Nebraska." She shook her head, admitting, "We don't know everything, no. For security reasons, we rarely spoke with those other survivors—"

"What are we going to do?" Julian growled.

"The only reasonable thing left for us." She smiled in a sad fashion, then warned him, "We're pulling off the Tollway now. You still have a little while to get ready . . ."

He closed his eyes, saying nothing.

"Not as long as you'd like, I'm sure . . . but with this sort of thing, maybe it's best to hurry . . ."

There were no gas pumps or restaurants in the rest area. A small divided parking lot was surrounded by trees and fake log cabin lavatories that in turn were sandwiched between broad lanes of moonlit pavement. The parking lot was empty. The only traffic was a single truck in the westbound freighter lane, half a dozen trailers towed along in its wake. Julian watched the truck pass, then walked into the darkest shadows, and kneeled.

The security cameras were being fed false images—images that were hopefully more convincing than the ludicrous log cabins. Yet even when he knew that he was safe, Julian felt exposed. Vulnerable. The feeling worsened by the moment, becoming a black dread, and by the time the Tokamak pulled to stop, his newborn heart was racing, and his quick damp breath tasted foul.

Blaine parked two slots away from the sleeping Buick. He didn't bother looking through the windows. Instead, guided by intuition or hidden sensor, he strolled toward the men's room, hesitated, then took a few half-steps toward Julian, passing into a patch of moonlight.

Using both hands, Julian lifted his weapon, letting it aim itself at the smooth broad forehead.

"Well," said Blaine, "I see you're thinking about me."

"What do you want?" Julian whispered. Then with a certain clumsiness, he added, "With me."

The man remained silent for a moment, a smile building.

"Who am I?" he asked suddenly. "Ideas? Do you have any?"

Julian gulped a breath, then said, "You work for the government." His voice was testy, pained. "And I don't know why you're following me!"

Blaine didn't offer answers. Instead he warned his audience, "The border is a lot harder to pierce than you think."

"Is it?"

"Humans aren't fools," Blaine reminded him. "After all, they designed the technologies used by the Nests, and they've had just as long as you to improve on old tricks."

"People in the world are getting dumber," said Julian. "You told me that."

"And those same people are very scared, very focused," his opponent countered. "Their borders are a priority to them. You are their top priority. And even if your thought processes are accelerated a thousandfold, they've got AIs who can blister you in any race of intellect. At least for the time being, they can."

Shoot him, an inner voice urged.

Yet Julian did nothing, waiting silently, hoping to be saved from this onerous chore.

"You can't cross into Canada without me," Blaine told him.

"I know what happened . . ." Julian felt the gun's barrel adjusting itself as his hands grew tired and dropped slightly. "Up in North Dakota . . . we know all about it . . ."

It was Blaine's turn to keep silent.

Again, Julian asked, "Who are you? Just tell me that much."

"You haven't guessed it, have you?" The round face seemed genuinely disappointed. "Not even in your wildest dreams . . ."

"And why help us?" Julian muttered, saying too much.

"Because in the long run, helping you helps me."

"How?"

Silence.

"We don't have any wealth," Julian roared. "Our homes were destroyed. By you, for all I know—"

The man laughed loudly, smirking as he began to turn away. "You've got some time left. Think about the possibilities, and we'll talk again."

Julian tugged on the trigger. Just once.

Eighteen shells pierced the back of Blaine's head, then worked down the wide back, devastating every organ even as the lifeless body crumpled. Even a huge man falls fast, Julian observed. Then he rose, walking on weak legs, and with his own aim, he emptied the rest of his clip into the gore.

It was easy, pumping in those final shots.

What's more, shooting the dead carried an odd, unexpected satisfaction—which was probably the same satisfaction that the terrorists had felt when their tiny bomb destroyed a hundred million soulless machines.

With every refugee watching, Julian cut open the womb with laser shears.

Julian Jr. was born a few seconds after two-thirty A.M., and the audience, desperate for a good celebration, nearly buried the baby with gifts and sweet words. Yet nobody could spoil him like his father could. For the next few hours, Julian pestered his first son with love and praise, working with a manic energy to fill every need, every whim. And his quest to be a perfect father only grew worse. The sun was beginning to show itself; Canada was waiting over the horizon; but Julian was oblivious, hunched over the toddler with sparkling toys in both hands, his never-pretty voice trying to sing a child's song, nothing half as important in this world as making his son giggle and smile . . . !

They weren't getting past the border. Their enemies were too clever, and too paranoid. Julian could smell the inevitable, but because he didn't know what else to do, he went through the motions of smiling for the President and the public, saying the usual brave words whenever it was demanded of him.

Sometimes Julian took his boy for long rides around the lifeboat.

During one journey, a woman knelt and happily teased the baby, then looked up at the famous man, mentioning in an off-handed way, "We'll get to our new home just in time for him to grow into it."

Those words gnawed at Julian, although he was powerless to explain why.

By then the sun had risen, its brilliant light sweeping across a sleepy border town. Instead of crossing at Detroit, the refugees had abandoned the Tollway, taking an old highway north to Port Huron. It would be easier here, was the logic. The prayer. Gazing out the universal window, Julian looked at the boarded-up homes and abandoned businesses, cars parked and forgotten, weeds growing in every yard, every crack. The border cities had lost most of their people in the last year-plus, he recalled. It was too easy and too accepted, this business of crossing into a land where it was still legal to be remade. In another year, most of the United States would look this way, unless the government took more drastic measures such as closing its borders, or worse, invading its wrong-minded neighbors . . . !

Julian felt a deep chill, shuddering.

That's when he suddenly understood. Everything. And in the next few seconds, after much thought, he knew precisely what he had to do.

Assuming there was still time . . .

A dozen cars were lined up in front of the customs station. The Buick had slipped in behind a couple on a motorcycle. Only one examination station was open, and every traveler was required to first declare his intentions, then permanently give up his citizenship. It would be a long wait. The driver turned the engine off, watching the Marines and Tech officials at work, everything about them relentlessly professional. Three more cars pulled up behind him, including a Tokamak, and he happened to glance at the rearview screen when Blaine climbed out, walking with a genuine bounce, approaching on the right and rapping on the passenger window with one fat knuckle, then stooping down and smiling through the glass, proving that he had made a remarkable recovery since being murdered.

Julian unlocked the door for him.

With a heavy grunt, Blaine pulled himself in and shut the door, then gave his companion a quick wink.

Julian wasn't surprised. If anything, he was relieved, telling his companion, "I think I know what you are."

"Good," said Blaine. "And what do your friends think?"

"I don't know. I never told them." Julian took the steering wheel in both hands. "I was afraid that if I did, they wouldn't believe me. They'd think I was crazy, and dangerous. And they wouldn't let me come here."

The line was moving, jerking forward one car-length. Julian started the Buick and crept forward, then turned it off again.

With a genuine fondness, Blaine touched him on a shoulder, commenting, "Your friends might pull you back into their world now. Have you thought of that?"

"Sure," said Julian. "But for the next few seconds, they'll be too confused to make any big decisions."

Lake Huron lay on Blaine's left, vast and deeply blue, and he studied the picket boats that dotted the water, bristling with lasers that did nothing but flip back and forth, back and forth, incinerating any flying object that appeared even remotely suspicious.

"So tell me," he asked his companion, "why do you think I'm here?"

Julian turned his body, the cultured leather squeaking beneath him. Gesturing at Port Huron, he said, "If these trends continue, everything's going to look that way very soon. Empty. Abandoned. Humans will have almost vanished from this world, which means that perhaps someone else could move in without too much trouble. They'll find houses, and good roads to drive on, and a communication system already in place. Ready-made lives, and practically free for the taking."

"What sort of someone?"

"That's what suddenly occurred to me." Julian took a deep breath, then said, "Humans are making themselves smaller, and faster. But what if something other than humans is doing the same thing? What if there's something in the universe that's huge, and very slow by human standards, but intelligent nonetheless. Maybe it lives in cold places between the stars. Maybe somewhere else. The point is, this other species is undergoing a similar kind of transformation. It's making itself a thousand times smaller, and a thousand times quicker, which puts it roughly equal to this." The frail face was smiling, and he lifted his hands from the wheel. "Flesh and blood, and bone . . . these are the high-technology materials that build your version of microchines!"

Blaine winked again, saying, "You're probably right. If you'd explained it that way, your little friends would have labeled you insane."

"But am I right?"

There was no reason to answer him directly. "What about me, Mr. Winemaster? How do you look at me?"

"You want to help us." Julian suddenly winced, then shuddered. But he didn't mention it, saying, "I assume that you have different abilities than we do . . . that you can get us past their sensors—"

"Is something wrong, Mr. Winemaster?"

"My friends . . . they're trying to take control of this body . . ."

"Can you deal with them?"

"For another minute. I changed all the control codes." Again, he winced. "You don't want the government aware of you, right? And you're trying to help steer us and them away from war . . . during this period of transition—"

"The way we see it," Blaine confessed, "the chance of a worldwide cataclysm is just about one in three, and worsening."

Julian nodded, his face contorting in agony. "If I accept your help . . . ?"

"Then I'll need yours." He set a broad hand on Julian's neck. "You've done a remarkable job hiding yourselves. You and your friends are in this car, but my tools can't tell me where. Not without more time, at least. And that's time we don't have . . ."

Julian stiffened, his clothes instantly soaked with perspiration.

Quietly, quickly, he said, "But if you're really a government agent . . . here to fool me into telling you . . . everything . . . ?"

"I'm not," Blaine promised.

A second examination station had just opened; people were maneuvering for position, leaving a gap in front of them.

Julian started his car, pulling forward. "If I do tell you . . . where we are . . . they'll think that I've betrayed them . . . !"

The Buick's anticollision system engaged, bringing them to an abrupt stop.

"Listen," said Blaine. "You've got only a few seconds to decide—"

"I know . . ."

"Where, Mr. Winemaster? Where?"

"Julian," he said, wincing again.

"Julian."

A glint of pride showed in the eyes. "We're not . . . in the car . . ." Then the eyes grew enormous, and Julian tried shouting the answer . . . his mind suddenly losing its grip on that tiny, lovely mouth . . .

Blaine swung with his right fist, shattering a cheekbone with his first blow, killing the body before the last blow.

By the time the Marines had surrounded the car, its interior was painted with gore, and in horror, the soldiers watched as the madman—he couldn't be anything but insane—calmly rolled down his window and smiled with a blood-rimmed mouth, telling his audience, "I had to kill him. He's Satan."

A hardened lieutenant looked in at the victim, torn open like a sack, and she shivered, moaning aloud for the poor man.

With perfect calm, Blaine declared, "I had to eat his heart. That's how you kill Satan. Don't you know?"

For disobeying orders, the President declared Julian a traitor, and she oversaw his trial and conviction. The entire process took less than a minute. His quarters were remodeled to serve as his prison cell. In the next ten minutes, three separate attempts were made on his life. Not everyone agreed with the court's sentence, it seemed. Which was understandable. Contact with the outside world had been lost the instant Winemaster died. The refugees and their lifeboat were lost in every kind of darkness. At any moment, the Tech specialists would throw them into a decontamination unit and they would evaporate without warning. And all because they'd entrusted themselves to an old DNA-born human who never really wanted to be Transmutated in the first place, according to at least one of his former lovers . . .

Ostensibly for security reasons, Julian wasn't permitted visitors.

Not even his young son could be brought to him, nor was he allowed to see so much as a picture of the boy.

Julian spent his waking moments pacing back and forth in the dim light, trying to exhaust himself, then falling into a hard sleep, too tired to dream at all, if he was lucky . . .

Before the first hour was finished, he had lost all track of time.

After nine full days of relentless isolation, the universe had shriveled until nothing existed but his cell, and him, his memories indistinguishable from fantasies.

On the tenth day, the cell door opened.

A young man stepped in, and with a stranger's voice, he said, "Father."

"Who are you?" asked Julian.

His son didn't answer, giving him the urgent news instead. "Mr. Blaine finally made contact with us, explaining what he is and what's happened so far, and what will happen . . . !"

Confusion wrestled with a fledging sense of relief.

"He's from between the stars, just like you guessed, Father. And he's been found insane for your murder. Though of course you're not dead. But the government believes there was a Julian Winemaster, and it's holding Blaine in a Detroit hospital, and he's holding us. His metabolism is augmenting our energy production, and when nobody's watching, he'll connect us with the outside world."

Julian couldn't imagine such a wild story: It had to be true!

"When the world is safe, in a year or two, he'll act cured or he'll escape—whatever is necessary—and he'll carry us wherever we want to go."

The old man sat on his bed, suddenly exhausted.

"Where would you like to go, Father?"

"Out that door," Julian managed. Then a wondrous thought took him by surprise, and he grinned, saying, "No, I want to be like Blaine was. I want to live between the stars, to be huge and cold, and slow . . .

"Not today, maybe . . .

"But soon . . . definitely soon . . . !"

galactic north

ALASTAIR REYNOLDS

Persistence can be a virtue, but perhaps—as in the breakneck, relentlessly paced, gorgeously colored story that follows, which sweeps us along on a cosmic chase across thousands of light-years of space and millions of years of time—it can sometimes be taken a bit too far . . .

New writer Alastair Reynolds is a frequent contributor to Interzone, *and has also sold to* Asimov's Science Fiction *and elsewhere. A professional scientist with a Ph.D. in astronomy, he comes from Wales, but lives in the Netherlands. His first novel,* Revelation Space, *already being hailed as one of the major SF books of the year, has just appeared in Britain. His story "A Spy in Europa" appeared in our Fifteenth Annual Collection.*

LUYTEN 726–8 COMETARY HALO—AD 2303

The two of them crouched in a tunnel of filthy ice, bulky in spacesuits. Fifty metres down the tunnel the servitor straddled the bore on skeletal legs, transmitting a thermal image onto their visors. Irravel jumped whenever the noise shifted into something human, cradling her gun nervously.

"Damn this thing," she said. "Hardly get my finger round the trigger."

"It can't read your blood, Captain." Markarian, next to her, managed not to sound as if he was stating the obvious. "You have to set the override to female."

Of course. Belatedly, remembering the training session on Fand where they'd been shown how to use the weapons—months of subjective time ago; years of worldtime—Irravel told the gun to reshape itself. The memory-plastic casing squirmed in her gloves to something more manageable. It still felt wrong.

"How are we doing?"

"Last teams in position. That's all the tunnels covered. They'll have to fight their way in."

"I think that might well be on the agenda."

"Maybe so." Markarian sighted along his weapon like a sniper. "But they'll get a surprise when they reach the cargo."

True: the ship had sealed the sleeper chambers the instant the pirates had arrived near the comet. Counter-intrusion weaponry would seriously inconvenience anyone trying to break in, unless they had the right authorization. And there, Irravel knew, was the problem; the thing she would rather not have had to deal with.

"Markarian," Irravel said. "If we're taken prisoner, there's a chance they'll try and make us give up the codes."

"Don't think that hasn't crossed my mind already." Markarian rechecked some aspect of his gun. "I won't let you down, Irravel."

"It's not a question of letting me down," she said, carefully.

"It's whether or not we betray the cargo."

"I know." For a moment they studied each other's faces through their visors, acknowledging what had once been more than professional friendship; the shared knowledge that they would kill each other rather than place the cargo in harm's way.

Their ship was the ramliner *Hirondelle*. She was damaged; lashed to the comet for repair. Improbably sleek for a creature of vacuum, her four-kilometre-long conic hull tapered to a needle-sharp prow and sprouted trumpet-shaped engines from two swept-back spars at the rear. It had been Irravel's first captaincy: a routine 17-year hop from Fand, in the Lacaille 9352 system, to Yellowstone, around Epsilon Eridani—with 20,000 reefersleep colonists. What had gone wrong should only have happened once in a thousand trips: a speck of interstellar dust had slipped through the ship's screen of anti-collision lasers and punched a cavernous hole in the ablative ice-shield, vaporizing a quarter of its mass. With a massively reduced likelihood of surviving another collision, the ship had automatically steered toward the nearest system capable of supplying repair materials.

Luyten 726-8 had been no one's idea of a welcoming destination. No human colonies had flourished there. All that remained were droves of scavenging machines sent out by various superpowers. The ship had locked into a scavenger's homing signal, eventually coming within visual range of the inert comet which the machine had made its home, and which ought to have been chequered with resupply materials. But when Irravel had been revived from reefersleep, what she'd found in place of the expected goods were only acres of barren comet.

"Dear god," she'd said. "Do we deserve this?"

Yet, after a few days, despair became steely resolve. The ship couldn't safely travel anywhere else, so they would have to process the supplies themselves, doing the work of the malfunctioning surveyor. It would mean stripping the ship just to make the machines to mine and shape the cometary ice—years of work by any estimate. That hardly mattered. The detour had already added years to the mission.

Irravel ordered the rest of her crew—all 90 of them—to be warmed, and then delegated tasks, mostly programming. Servitors were not particularly intelligent outside of their designated functions. She considered activating the other machines she carried as cargo—the greenfly terraformers—but that cut against all her instincts. Greenfly machines were Von Neumann breeders, unlike the sterile servitors. They were a hundred times cleverer. She would only consider using them if the cargo was placed in immediate danger.

"If you won't unleash the greenflies," Markarian said, "at least think about waking the Conjoiners. There may only be four of them, but we could use their expertise."

"I don't trust them. I never liked the idea of carrying them in the first place. They unsettle me."

"I don't like them either, but I'm willing to bury my prejudices if it means fixing the ship faster."

"Well, that's where we differ. I'm not, so don't raise the subject again."

"Yes," Markarian said, and only when its omission was insolently clear did he bother adding: "Captain."

Eventually the Conjoiners ceased to be an issue, when the work was clearly under way and proceeding normally. Most of the crew were able to return to reefersleep. Irravel and Markarian stayed awake a little longer, and even after they'd gone under, they woke every seven months to review the status of the works. It began to look as if they would succeed without assistance.

Until the day they were woken out of schedule, and a dark, grapple-shaped ship was almost upon the comet. Not an interstellar ship, it must have come from somewhere nearby—probably within the same halo of comets around Luyten 726–8. Its silence was not encouraging.

"I think they're pirates," Irravel said. "I've heard of one or two other ships going missing near here, and it was always put down to accident."

"Why did they wait so long?"

"They had no choice. There are billions of comets out here, but they're never less than light-hours apart. That's a long way if you only have in-system engines. They must have a base somewhere else to keep watch, maybe light-weeks from here, like a spider with a very wide web."

"What do we do now?"

Irravel gritted her teeth. "Do what anything does when it gets stuck in the middle of a web. Fight back."

But the *Hirondelle*'s minimal defences only scratched against the enemy ship. Oblivious, it fired penetrators and winched closer. Dozens of crab-shaped machines swarmed out and dropped below the comet's horizon, impacting with seismic thuds. After a few minutes, sensors in the furthest tunnels registered intruders. Only a handful of crew had been woken. They broke guns out of the armoury— small arms designed for pacification in the unlikely event of a shipboard riot— and then established defensive positions in all the cometary tunnels.

Nervously now, Irravel and Markarian advanced round the tunnel's bend, cleated shoes whispering through ice barely more substantial than smoke. They had to keep their suit exhausts from touching the walls if they didn't want to get blown back by superheated steam. Irravel jumped again at the pattern of photons on her visor and then forced calm, telling herself it was another mirage.

Except this time it stayed.

Markarian opened fire, squeezing rounds past the servitor. It lurched aside, a gaping hole in its carapace. Black crabs came round the bend, encrusted with sensors and guns. The first reached the ruined servitor and dismembered it with ease. If only there'd been time to activate and program the greenfly machines — they'd have ripped through the pirates like a host of furies, treating them as terraformable matter.

And maybe us too, Irravel thought.

Something flashed through the clouds of steam; an electromagnetic pulse that turned Irravel's suit sluggish, as if every joint had corroded. The whine of the circulator died to silence, leaving only her frenzied breathing. Something pressed against her backpack. She turned slowly around, wary of falling against the walls. There were crabs everywhere. The chamber in which they'd been cornered was littered with the bodies of the other crew members; pink trails of blood on ice reaching from other tunnels. They'd been killed and dragged here.

Two words jumped to mind: kill yourself. But first she had to kill Markarian, in case he lacked the nerve himself. She couldn't see his face through his visor. That was good. Painfully, she pointed the gun toward him and squeezed the trigger. But instead of firing, the gun shivered in her hands, stowing itself into a quarter of its operational volume. "Thank you for using this weapon system," it said cheerfully.

Irravel let it drift to the ground.

A new voice rasped in her helmet. "If you're thinking of surrendering, now might not be a bad time."

"Bastard," Irravel said, softly.

"Really the best you can manage?" The language was Canasian — what Irravel and Markarian had spoken on Fand — but heavily accented, as if the native tongue was Norte or Russish, or spoken with an impediment. "Bastard's quite a compliment compared to some of things my clients come up with."

"Give me time; I'll work on it."

"Positive attitude — that's good." The lid of a crab hinged up, revealing the prone form of a man in a mesh of motion-sensors. He crawled from the mesh and stepped onto the ice, wearing a spacesuit formed from segmented metal plates. Totems had been welded to the armour, around holographic starscapes infested with serpentine monsters and scantily-clad maidens.

"Who are you?"

"Captain Run Seven." He stepped closer, examining her suit nameplate. "But you can call me Seven, Irravel Veda."

"I hope you burn in hell, Seven."

Seven smiled — she could see the curve of his grin through his visor; the oddly upturned nostrils of his nose above it. "I'm sensing some negativity here, Irravel. I think we need to put that behind us, don't you?"

Irravel looked at her murdered adjutants. "Maybe if you tell me which one was the traitor."

"Traitor?"

"You seemed to have no difficulty finding us."

"Actually, you found us." It was a woman's voice this time. "We use lures — tampering with commercial beacons, like the scavenger's." She emerged from one of the other attack machines, wearing a suit similar to Seven's, except that it displayed the testosterone-saturated male analogues of his space-maidens; all rippling torsos and chromed cod-pieces.

"Wreckers," Irravel breathed.

"Yeah. Ships home in on the beacons, then find they ain't going anywhere in a hurry. We move in from the halo."

"Disclose all our confidential practices while you're at it, Mirsky," Seven said.

She glared at him through her visor. "Veda would have figured it out."

"We'll never know now, will we?"

"What does it matter?" she said. "Gonna kill them anyway, aren't you?"

Seven flashed an arc of teeth filed to points and waved a hand toward the female pirate. "Allow me to introduce Mirsky, our loose-tongued but efficient information retrieval specialist. She's going to take you on a little trip down memory lane; see if we can't remember those access codes."

"What codes?"

"It'll come back to you," Seven said.

They were taken through the tunnels, past half-assembled mining machines, onto the surface and then into the pirate ship. The ship was huge: most of it living space. Cramped corridors snaked through hydroponics galleries of spring wheat and dwarf papaya, strung with xenon lights. The ship hummed constantly with carbon dioxide scrubbers, the fetid air making Irravel sneeze. There were children everywhere, frowning at the captives. The pirates obviously had no reefersleep technology: they stayed warm the whole time, and some of the children Irravel saw had probably been born after the *Hirondelle* had arrived here.

They arrived at a pair of interrogation rooms where they were separated. Irravel's room held a couch converted from an old command seat, still carrying warning decals. A console stood in one corner. Painted torture scenes fought for wallspace with racks of surgical equipment; drills, blades and ratcheted contraptions speckled with rust.

Irravel breathed deeply. Hyperventilation could have an anaesthetic effect. Her conditioning would in any case create a state of detachment: the pain would be no less intense, but she would feel it at one remove.

She hoped.

The pirates fiddled with her suit, confused by the modern design, until they stripped her down to her shipboard uniform. Mirsky leant over her. She was small-boned and dark skinned, dirty hair rising in a topknot, eyes mismatched shades of azure. Something clung to the side of her head above the left ear; a silver box with winking status lights. She fixed a crown to Irravel's head, then made adjustments on the console.

"Decided yet?" Captain Run Seven said, sauntering into the room. He was unlatching his helmet.

"What?"

"Which of our portfolio of interrogation packages you're going to opt for."

She was looking at his face now. It wasn't really human. Seven had a man's bulk and shape, but there was at least as much of the pig in his face. His nose was a snout, his ears two tapered flaps framing a hairless pink skull. Pale eyes evinced animal cunning.

"What the hell are you?"

"Excellent question," Seven said, clicking a finger in her direction. His bare hand was dark skinned and feminine. "To be honest, I don't really know. A genetics experiment, perhaps? Was I the seventh failure, or the first success?"

"Are you sure you want an honest answer on that?"

He ignored her. "All I know is that I've been here—in the halo around Luyten 726–8—for as long as I can remember."

"Someone sent you here?"

"In a tiny automated spacecraft; perhaps an old lifepod. The ship's governing personality raised me as well as it could; attempted to make of me a well-rounded individual." Seven trailed off momentarily. "Eventually I was found by a passing ship. I staged what might be termed a hostile takeover bid. From then on I've had an organization largely recruited from my client base."

"You're insane. It might have worked once, but it won't work with us."

"Why should you be any different?"

"Neural conditioning. I treat the cargo as my offspring—all 20,000 of them. I can't betray them in any way."

Seven smiled his piggy smile. "Funny; the last client thought that too."

Sometime later Irravel woke alone in a reefersleep casket. She remembered only dislocated episodes of interrogation. There was the memory of a kind of sacrifice, and, later, of the worst terror she could imagine—so intense that she could not bring its cause to mind. Underpinning everything was the certainty that she had not given up the codes.

So why was she still alive?

Everything was quiet and cold. Once she was able to move, she found a suit and wandered the *Hirondelle* until she reached a porthole. They were still lashed to the comet. The other craft was gone; presumably en route back to the base in the halo where the pirates must have had a larger ship.

She looked for Markarian, but there was no sign of him.

Then she checked the 20-sleeper chambers; the thousand-berth dormitories. The chamber doors were all open. Most of the sleepers were still there. They'd been butchered, carved open for implants, minds pulped by destructive memory-trawling devices. The horror was too great for any recognizable emotional response. The conditioning made each death feel like a stolen part of her.

Yet something kept her on the edge of sanity: the discovery that 200 sleepers were missing. There was no sign that they'd been butchered like the others, which left the possibility that they'd been abducted by the pig. It was madness; it would not begin to compensate for the loss of the others—but her psychology allowed no other line of thought.

She could find them again.

Her plan was disarmingly simple. It crystallized in her mind with the clarity of a divine vision. It would be done.

She would repair the ship. She would hunt down Seven. She would recover the sleepers from him. And enact whatever retribution she deemed fit.

She found the chamber where the four Conjoiners had slept, well away from the main dormitories, in part of the ship where the pirates were not likely to have wandered. She was hoping she could revive them and seek their assistance. There seemed no way they could make things worse for her. But her hopes faded when she saw the scorch marks of weapon blasts around the bulkhead; the door forced.

She stepped inside anyway.

They'd been a sect on Mars, originally; a clique of cyberneticists with a particular fondness for self-experimentation. In 2190 their final experiment had involved distributed processing—allowing their enhanced minds to merge into one massively parallel neural net. The resultant event—a permanent, irrevocable escalation to a new mode of consciousness—was known as the Transenlightenment.

There'd been a war, of course.

Demarchists had long seen both sides. They used neural augmentation themselves, policed so that they never approached the Conjoiner threshold. They'd brokered the peace, defusing the suspicion around the Conjoiners. Conjoiners had fuelled Demarchist expansion from Europa with their technologies, fused in the white-heat of Transenlightenment. Four of them were along as observers because the *Hirondelle* used their ramscoop drives.

Irravel still didn't trust them.

And maybe it didn't matter. The reefersleep units—fluted caskets like streamlined coffins—were riddled with blast holes. Grimacing against the smell, Irravel examined the remains inside. They'd been cut open, but the pirates seemed to have abandoned the job halfway through, not finding the kinds of implants they were expecting. And maybe not even recognizing that they were dealing with anything other than normal humans, Irravel thought—especially if the pirates who'd done this hadn't been among Seven's more experienced crewmembers; just trigger-happy thugs.

She examined the final casket; the one furthest from the door. It was damaged, but not so badly as the others. The display cartouches were still alive, a patina of frost still adhering to the casket's lid. The Conjoiner inside looked intact: the pirates had never reached him. She read his nameplate: Remontoire.

"Yeah, he's a live one," said a voice behind Irravel. "Now back off real slow."

Heart racing, Irravel did as she was told. Slowly, she turned around, facing the woman whose voice she recognized.

"Mirsky?" she said.

"Yeah, it's your lucky day." Mirsky was wearing her suit, but without the helmet, making her head seem shrunken in the moat of her neck-ring. She had a gun on Irravel, but the way she pointed it was half-hearted, as if this was a stage in their relationship she wanted to get over as quickly as possible.

"What the hell are you doing here?"

"Same as you, Veda. Trying to figure out how much shit we're in; how hard it'll be to get this ship moving again. Guess we had the same idea about the Conjoiners. Seven went berserk when he heard they'd been killed, but I figured it was worth checking how thorough the job had been."

"Stop; slow down. Start at the beginning. Why aren't you with Seven?"

Mirsky pushed past her and consulted the reefersleep indicators. "Seven and me had a falling out. Fill in the rest yourself." With quick jabs of her free hand she called up different display modes, frowning at each. "Shit, this ain't gonna be easy. If we wake the guy without his three friends, he's gonna be psychotic; no use to us at all."

"What kind of falling out?"

"Seven reckoned I was holding back too much in the interrogation; not putting you through enough hell." She scratched at the silver box on the side of her head. "Maybe we can wake him, then fake the cybernetic presence of his friends — what do you think?"

"Why am I still alive, if Seven broke into the sleeper chambers? Why are you still alive?"

"Seven's a sadist. Abandonment's more his style than a quick and clean execution. As for you, the pig cut a deal with your second-in-command."

The implication of that sunk in. "Markarian gave him the codes?"

"It wasn't you, Veda."

Strange relief flooded Irravel. She could never be absolved of the crime of losing the cargo, but at least her degree of complicity had lessened.

"But that was only half the deal," Mirsky continued. "The rest was Seven promising not to kill you if Markarian agreed to join the *Hideyoshi*, our main ship." She told Irravel that there'd been a transmitter rigged to her reefersleep unit, so that Markarian would know she was still alive.

"Seven must have known he was taking a risk leaving both of us alive."

"A pretty small one. The ship's in pieces and Seven will assume neither of us has the brains to patch it back together." Mirsky slipped the gun into a holster. "But Seven assumed the Conjoiners were dead. Big mistake. Once we figure a way to wake Remontoire safely, he can help us fix the ship; make it faster too."

"You've got this all worked out, haven't you?"

"More or less. Something tells me you aren't absolutely ready to start trusting me, though."

"Sorry, Mirsky, but you don't make the world's most convincing turncoat."

She reached up with her free hand, gripping the box on the side of her head. "Know what this is? A loyalty-shunt. Makes simian stem cells; pumps them into the internal carotid artery, just above the cavernous sinus. They jump the blood-brain barrier and build a whole bunch of transient structures tied to primate dominance hierarchies; alpha-male shit. That's how Seven had us under his command — he was King Monkey. But I've turned it off now."

"That's supposed to reassure me?"

"No, but maybe this will."

Mirsky tugged at the box, ripping it away from the side of her head in curds of blood.

LUYTEN 726–8 COMETARY HALO–AD 2309

Irravel felt the *Hirondelle* turn like a compass needle. The ramscoops gasped at interstellar gas, sucking lone atoms of cosmic hydrogen from cubic metres of vacuum. The engines spat twin beams of thrust, pressing Irravel into her seat with two gees of acceleration. Hardly moving now, still in the local frame of the cometary halo, but in only six months she would be nudging lightspeed.

Her seat floated on a boom in the middle of the dodecahedral bridge. "Map," Irravel said, and was suddenly drowning in stars; an immense 30-light-year-wide projection of human settled space, centred on the First System.

"There's the bastard," Mirsky said, pointing from her own hovering seat, her voice only slightly strained under the gee-load. "Map; give us projection of the *Hideyoshi*'s vector, and plot our intercept."

The pirate ship's icon was still very close to Luyten 726-8; less than a tenth of a light-year out. They had not seen Seven until now. The thrust from his ship was so tightly focused that it had taken until now for the widening beams of the exhaust to sweep over *Hirondelle*'s sensors. But now they knew where he was headed. A dashed line indicated the likely course, arrowing right through the map's heart and out toward the system Lalande 21185. Now came the intercept vector, a near-tangent which sliced Seven's course beyond Sol.

"When does it happen?" Irravel said.

"Depends on how much attention Seven's paying to what's coming up behind him, for a start, and what kind of evasive stunts he can pull."

"Most of my simulations predict an intercept between 2325 and 2330," Remontoire said.

Irravel savoured the dates. Even for someone trained to fly a starship between systems, they sounded uncomfortably like the future.

"Are you sure it's him — not just some other ship that happened to be waiting in the halo?"

"Trust me," Mirsky said. "I can smell the swine from here."

"She's right," Remontoire said. "The destination makes perfect sense. Seven was prohibited from staying here much longer, once the number of missing ships became too large to be explained away as accidents. Now he must seek a well-settled system to profit from what he has stolen."

The Conjoiner looked completely normal at first glance — a bald man wearing a ship's uniform, his expression placid — but then one noticed the unnatural bulge of his skull, covered only in a fuzz of baby hair. Most of his glial cells had been supplanted by machines which served the same structural functions but which also performed specialized cybernetic duties, like interfacing with other commune partners or external machinery. Even the organic neurones in his brain were now webbed together by artificial connections which allowed transmission speeds of kilometres per second; factors of ten faster than in normal brains. Only the problem of dispersing waste heat denied the Conjoiners even faster modes of thought.

It was seven years since they'd woken him. Remontoire had not dealt well with the murder of his three compatriots, but Irravel and Mirsky had managed to keep him sane by feeding input into the glial machines, crudely simulating rapport with other commune members. "It provides the kind of comfort to me that a ghost limb offers an amputee," Remontoire had said. "An illusion of wholeness—but no substitute for the real thing."

"What more can we do?" Irravel said.

"Return me to another commune with all speed."

Irravel had agreed, provided Remontoire helped with the ship.

He hadn't let her down. Under his supervision, half the ship's mass had been sacrificed, permitting twice the acceleration. They had dug a vault in the comet, lined it with support systems, and entombed what remained of the cargo. The sleepers were nominally dead—there was no real expectation of reviving them again, even if medicine improved in the future—but Irravel had nonetheless set servitors to tend the dead for however long it took, and programmed the beacon to lure another ship, this time to pick up the dead. All that had taken years, of course—but it had also taken Seven as much time to cross the halo to his base; time again to show himself.

"Be so much easier if you didn't want the others back," Mirsky said. "Then we could just slam past the pig at relativistic speed and hit him with seven kinds of shit." She was very proud of the weapons she'd built into the ship, copied from pirate designs with Remontoire's help.

"I want the sleepers back," Irravel said.

"And Markarian?"

"He's mine," she said, after due consideration. "You get the pig."

NEAR LALANDE 21185—AD 2328

Relativity squeezed stars until they bled colour. Half a kilometre ahead, the side of Seven's ship raced toward Irravel like a tsunami.

The *Hideyoshi* was the same shape as the *Hirondelle*; honed less by human whim than the edicts of physics. But the *Hideyoshi* was heavier, with a wider cross-section, incapable of matching the *Hirondelle*'s acceleration or of pushing so close to C. It had taken years, but they'd caught up with Seven, and now the attack was in progress.

Irravel, Mirsky and Remontoire wore thruster-pack-equipped suits, of the type used for inspections outside the ship, with added armour and weapons. Painted for effect, they looked like mechanized Samurai. Another 47 suits were slaved to theirs, acting as decoys. They'd crossed 50,000 kilometres of space between the ships.

"You're sure Seven doesn't have any defences?" Irravel had asked, not long after waking from reefersleep.

"Only the in-system ship had any firepower," Mirsky said. She looked older now; new lines engraved under her eyes. "That's because no one's ever been insane enough to contemplate storming another ship in interstellar space."

"Until now."

But it wasn't so stupid, and Mirsky knew it. Matching velocities with another ship was only a question of being faster; squeezing fractionally closer to lightspeed.

It might take time, but sooner or later the distance would be closed. And it had taken time, none of which Mirsky had spent in reefersleep. Partly it was because she lacked the right implants—ripped out in infancy when she was captured by Seven. Partly it was a distaste for the very idea of being frozen, instilled by years of pirate upbringing. But also because she wanted time to refine her weapons. They had fired a salvo against the enemy before crossing space in the suits, softening up any weapons buried in his ice and opening holes into the *Hideyoshi*'s interior.

Now Irravel's vision blurred, her suit slowing itself before slamming into the ice.

Whiteness swallowed her.

For a moment she couldn't remember what she was doing here. Then awareness came and she slithered back up the tunnel excavated on her fall, until she reached the surface of the *Hideyoshi*'s ice-shield.

"Veda—you intact?"

Her armour's shoulder-mounted comm laser found a line-of-sight to Mirsky. Mirsky was 20 or 30 metres away, around the ship's lazy circumference, balancing on a ledge of ice. Walls of it stretched above and below like a rockface, lit by the glare from the engines. Decoys were arriving by the second.

"I'm alive," Irravel said. "Where's the entry point?"

"Couple of hundred metres upship."

"Damn. I wanted to come in closer. Remontoire's out of line-of-sight. How much fuel do you have left?"

"Scarcely enough to take the chill off a penguin's dick."

Mirsky raised her arms above her head and fired lines into the ice, rocketing out from her sleeves. Belly sliding against the shield, she retracted the lines and hauled herself upship.

Irravel followed. They'd burned all their fuel crossing between the two ships, but that was part of the plan. If they didn't have a chance to raid Seven's reserves, they'd just kick themselves into space and let the *Hirondelle* home in on them.

"You think Seven saw us cross over?"

"Definitely. And you can bet he's doing something about it, too."

"Don't do anything that might endanger the cargo, Mirsky—no matter how tempting Seven makes it."

"Would you sacrifice half the sleepers to get the other half back?"

"That's not remotely an option."

Above their heads crevasses opened like eyes. Pirate crabs erupted out, black as night against the ice. Irravel opened fire on the machines. This time, with better weapons and real armour, she began to inflict damage. Behind the crabs, pirates emerged, bulbous in customized armour. Lasers scuffed the ice; bright through gouts of steam. Irravel saw Remontoire now: he was unharmed, and doing his best to shoot the pirates into space.

Above, one of Irravel's shots dislodged a pirate.

The *Hideyoshi*'s acceleration dropped him toward her. When the impact came she hardly felt it, her suit's guylines staying firm. The pirate folded around her like a broken toy, then bounced back against the ship, pinned there by her suit. He was too close to shoot unless Irravel wanted to blow herself into space. Distorted behind glass, his face shaped a word. She got in closer until their visors were touching. Through the glass she saw the asymmetric bulge of a loyalty-shunt.

The face was Markarian's. At first it seemed like absurd coincidence. Then it occurred to her that Seven might have sent his newest recruit out to show his mettle. Maybe Seven wouldn't be far behind. Confronting adversaries was part of the alpha-male inheritance.

"Irravel," Markarian said, voice laced with static. "I'm glad you're alive."

"Don't flatter yourself you're the reason I'm here, Markarian. I came for the cargo. You're just next on the list."

"What are you going to do—kill me?"

"Do you think you deserve any better than that?" Irravel adjusted her position. "Or are you going to try and justify betraying the cargo?"

He pulled his aged features into a smile. "We made a deal, Irravel; the same way you made a deal about greenfly. But you don't remember that, do you?"

"Maybe I sold the greenfly machines to the pig," she said. "If I did that, it was a calculated move to buy the safety of the cargo. You, on the other hand, cut a deal with Seven to save your neck."

The other pirates were holding fire, nervously marking them. "I did it to save yours, actually. Does that make any sense?" There was wonder in his eyes now. "Did you ever see Mirsky's hand? That was never her own. The pirates swap limbs as badges of rank. They're very good at connective surgery."

"You're not making much sense, Markarian."

Dislodged ice rained on them. Irravel looked around in time to see another pirate emerging from a crevasse. She recognized the suit artwork: it was Seven. He wore things, strung around his utility belt in transparent bags like obscene fruit. She stared at them for a few seconds before their nature clicked into horrific focus: frozen human heads.

Irravel stifled a reaction to vomit.

"Yes," Run Seven said. "Ten of your compatriots, recently unburdened of their bodies. But don't worry—they're not harmed in any fundamental sense. Their brains are intact—provided you don't warm them with an ill-aimed shot."

"I've got a clear line of fire," Mirsky said. "Just say the word and the bastard's an instant anatomy lesson."

"Wait," Irravel said. "Don't shoot."

"Sound business sense, Captain Veda. I see you appreciate the value of these heads."

"What's he talking about?" Mirsky said.

"Their neural patterns can be retrieved." It was Remontoire speaking now. "We Conjoiners have had the ability to copy minds onto machine substrates for some time now, though we haven't advertised it. But that doesn't matter—there have been experiments on Yellowstone which approach our early successes. And these heads aren't even thinking: only topologies need to be mapped, not electrochemical processes."

The pig took one of the heads from his belt and held it to eye-level, for inspection. "The Conjoiner's right. They're not really dead. And they can be yours if you wish to do business."

"What do you want for them?"

"Markarian, for a start. All that Demarchy expertise makes for a very efficient second-in-command."

Irravel glanced down at her prisoner. "You can't buy loyalty with a box and a few neural connections."

"No? In what way do our loyalty-shunts differ from the psychosurgery which your world inflicted on you, Irravel, yoking your motherhood instinct to 20,000 sleepers you don't even know by name?"

"We have a deal or not?"

"Only if you throw in the Conjoiner as well."

Irravel looked at Remontoire; some snake part of her mind weighing options with reptilian detachment.

"No!" he said. "You promised!"

"Shut up," Seven said. "Or when you do get to rejoin your friends, it'll be in instalments."

"I'm sorry," Irravel said. "I can't lose even ten of the cargo."

Seven tossed the first head down to her. "Now let Markarian go and we'll see about the rest."

Irravel looked down at him. "It's not over between you and me."

Then she released him, and he scrambled back up the ice toward Seven.

"Excellent. Here's another head. Now the Conjoiner."

Irravel issued a subvocal command; watched Remontoire stiffen. "His suit's paralysed. Take him."

Two pirates worked down to him, checked him over and nodded toward Seven. Between them they hauled him back up the ice, vanishing into a crevasse and back up into the *Hideyoshi*.

"The other eight heads," Irravel said.

"I'm going to throw them away from the ship. You'll be able to locate them easily enough. While I'm doing that, I'm going to retreat, and you're going to leave."

"We could end this now," Mirsky said.

"I need those heads."

"They really fucked with your psychology big-time, didn't they?" She raised her weapon and began shooting Seven and the other pirates. Irravel watched her carve up the remaining heads; splintering frozen bone into the vacuum.

"No!"

"Sorry," Mirsky said. "Had to do it, Veda."

Seven clutched at his chest, fingers mashing the pulp of the heads, still tethered to his belt. She'd punctured his suit. As he tried to stem the damburst, his face was carved with the intolerable knowledge that his reign had just ended.

But something had hit Irravel too.

SYLVESTE INSTITUTE, YELLOWSTONE ORBIT, EPSILON ERIDANI—AD 2415

"Where am I?" Irravel asked. "How am I thinking this?"

The woman's voice was the colour of mahogany. "Somewhere safe. You died on the ice, but we got you back in time."

"For what?"

Mirsky sighed, as though this was something she would rather not have had to explain this soon.

"To scan you, just like we did with the frozen heads. Copy you into the ship."

Maybe she should have felt horror, or indignation, or even relief that some part of her had been spared.

Instead, she just felt impatience.

"What now?"

"We're working on it," Mirsky said.

TRANS-ALDEBARAN SPACE—AD 2673

"We saved her body after she died," Mirsky said, wheezing slightly. She found it hard to move around under what to Irravel was the ship's normal two and a half gees of thrust. "After the battle we brought her back onboard."

Irravel thought of her mother dying on the other ship, the one they were chasing. For years they had deliberately not narrowed the distance, holding back but not allowing the *Hideyoshi* to slip from view.

Until now, it hadn't even occurred to Irravel to ask why.

She looked through the casket's window, trying to match her own features against what she saw in the woman's face, trying to project her own 15 years into Mother Irravel's adulthood.

"Why did you keep her so cold?"

"We had to extract what we could from her brain," Mirsky said. "Memories and neural patterns. We trawled them and stored them in the ship."

"What good was that?"

"We knew they'd come in useful again."

She'd been cloned from Mother Irravel. They were not identical—no Mixmaster expertise could duplicate the precise biochemical environment of Mother Irravel's womb, or the shaping experiences of early infancy, and their personalities had been sculpted centuries apart, in totally different worlds. But they were still close copies. They even shared memories: scripted into Irravel's mind by medichines, so that she barely noticed each addition to her own experiences.

"Why did you do this?" she asked.

"Because Irravel began something," Mirsky said. "Something I promised I'd help her finish."

STORMWATCH STATION, AETHRA, HYADES
TRADE ENVELOPE–AD 2931

"Why are you interested in our weapons?" The Nestbuilder asked. "We are not aware of any wars within the *chordate phylum* at this epoch."

"It's a personal matter," Irravel said.

The Nestbuilder hovered a metre above the trade floor, suspended in a column of microgravity. They were oxygen-breathing arthropods who'd once ascended to spacefaring capability. No longer intelligent, yet supported by their self-renewing machinery, they migrated from system to system, constructing elaborate, space-filling structures from solid diamond. Other Nestbuilder swarms would arrive and occasionally occupy the new nests. There seemed no purpose to this activity, but for tens of thousands of years they had been host to a smaller, cleverer species known as the Slugs. Small communities of Slugs—anything up to a dozen—lived in warm, damp niches in a Nestbuilder's intricately folded shell. They had long since learned how to control the host's behaviour and exploit its subservient technology.

Irravel studied a Slug now, crawling out from under a lip of shell material.

The thing was a multicellular invertebrate not much larger than her fist; a bag of soft blue protoplasm, sprouting appendages only when they were needed. A slightly bipolar shadow near one end might have been its central nervous system, but there hardly seemed enough of it to trap sentience. There were no obvious sense or communicational organs, but a pulsing filament of blue slime reached back into the Nestbuilder's fold. When the Slug spoke, it did so through the Nestbuilder; a rattle of chitin from the host's mouthparts which approximated human language. A hovering jewel connected to the station's lexical database did the rest, rendering the voice calmly feminine.

"A personal matter? A vendetta? Then it's true." The mouthparts clicked together in what humans presumed was the symbiotic creature's laughter response. "You *are* who we suspected."

"She did tell you her name was Irravel, guy," Mirsky said, sipping black coffee with delicate movements of the exoskeletal frame she always wore in high gravity.

"Among you *chordates*, the name is not so unusual now," the Slug reminded them. "But you do fit the description, Irravel."

They were near one of the station's vast picture windows, overlooking Aethra's mighty, roiling cloud decks, 50 kilometres below. It was getting dark now and the storm players were preparing to start a show. Irravel saw two of their seeders descending into the clouds; robot craft tethered by a nearly invisible filament. The seeders would position the filament so that it bridged cloud layers with different static potentials; they'd then detach and return to Stormwatch, while the filament held itself in position by rippling along its length. For hundreds of kilometres around, other filaments would have been placed in carefully selected positions. They were electrically isolating now, but at the stormplayer's discretion, each filament would flick over into a conductive state: a massive, choreographed lightning flash.

"I never set out to become a legend," Irravel said. "Or a myth, for that matter."

"Yes. There are so many stories about you, Veda, that it might be simpler to assume you never existed."

"What makes you think otherwise?"

"The fact that a *chordate* who could have been Markarian also passed this way, only a year or so ago." The Nestbuilder's shell pigmentation flickered, briefly revealing a picture of Markarian's ship.

"So you sold weapons to him?"

"That would be telling, wouldn't it?" The mouthparts clattered again. "You would have to answer a question of ours first."

Outside, the opening flashes of the night's performance gilded the horizon; like the first stirrings of a symphony. Aethra's rings echoed the flashes, pale ghosts momentarily cleaving the sky.

"What is it you want to know?"

"We Slugs are among the few intelligent, starfaring cultures in this part of the Galaxy. During the War against Intelligence we avoided the Inhibitors by hiding ourselves among the mindless Nestbuilders."

Irravel nodded. Slugs were one of the few alien species known to humanity who would even acknowledge the existence of the feared Inhibitors. Like humanity, they'd fought and beaten the revenants—at least for now.

"It is the weaponry you seek which enabled us to triumph—but even then only at colossal cost to our phylum. Now we are watchful for new threats."

"I don't see where this is leading."

"We have heard rumours. Since you have come from the direction of those rumours—the local stellar neighbourhood around your phylum's birth star—we imagined you might have information of value."

Irravel exchanged a sideways glance with Mirsky. The old woman's wizened, age-spotted skull looked as fragile as paper, but she remained an unrivalled tactician. They knew each other so well now that Mirsky could impart advice with the subtlest of movements; expression barely troubling the lined mask of her face.

"What kind of information were you seeking?"

"Information about something that frightens us." The Nestbuilder's pigmentation flickered again, forming an image of—something. It was a splinter of grey-brown against speckled blackness—perhaps the Nestbuilder's attempt at visualizing a planetoid. And then something erupted across the surface of the world, racing from end to end like a film of verdigris. Where it had passed, fissures opened up, deepening until they were black fractures, as if the world were a calving iceberg. And then it blew apart, shattering into a thousand green-tinged fragments.

"What was that?" Irravel said.

"We were rather hoping you could tell us." The Nestbuilder's pigmentation refreshed again, and this time what they were seeing was clearly a star, veiled in a toroidal belt of golden dust. "Machines have dismantled every rocky object in the system where these images were captured; Ross 128, which lies within eleven light-years of your birth star. They have engendered a swarm of trillions of rocks on independent orbits. Each rock is sheathed in a pressurized bubble membrane, within which an artificial plant-based ecosystem has been created. The same machines have fashioned other sources of raw material into mirrors, larger than worlds themselves, which trap sunlight above and below the ecliptic and focus it onto the swarm."

"And why does this frighten you?"

The Nestbuilder leant closer in its column of microgravity. "Because we saw it being resisted. As if these machines had never been intended to wreak such transformations. As if your phylum had created something it could not control."

"And—these attempts at resistance?"

"Failed."

"But if one system was accidentally transformed, it doesn't mean . . ." Irravel trailed off. "You're worried about them crossing interstellar space, to other systems. Even if that happened—couldn't you resist the spread? This can only be human technology—nothing that would pose any threat to yourselves."

"Perhaps it was once human technology, with programmed limitations to prevent it replicating uncontrollably. But those shackles have been broken. Worse, the machines have hybridized, gaining resilience and adaptability with each encounter with something external. First the Melding Plague, infection with which may have been a deliberate ploy to by-pass the replication limits."

Irravel nodded. The Melding Plague had swept human space 400 years earlier, terminating the Demarchist *Belle Epoque*. Like the Black Death of the previous millennium, it evoked terror generations after it had passed.

"Later," the Nestbuilder continued, "it may have encountered and assimilated Inhibitor technology, or worse. Now it will be very hard to stop, even with the weapons at our disposal."

An image of one of the machines flickered onto the Nestbuilder's shell, like a peculiar tattoo. Irravel shivered. The Slug was right: waves of hybridization had transformed the initial architecture into something queasily alien. But enough of the original plan remained for there to be no doubt in her mind. She was looking at an evolved greenfly; one of the self-replicating breeders she had given Captain Run Seven. How it had broken loose was anyone's guess. She speculated that Seven's crew had sold the technology on to a third party, decades or centuries after gaining it from her. Perhaps that third party had reclusively experimented in the Ross 128 system, until the day when greenfly tore out of their control.

"I don't know why you think I can help," she said.

"Perhaps we were mistaken, then, to credit a 500-year-old rumour which said that you had been the original source of these machines."

She had insulted it by daring to bluff. The Slugs were easily insulted. They read human beings far better than humans read Slugs.

"Like you say," she answered. "You can't believe everything."

The Slug made the Nestbuilder fold its armoured, spindly limbs across its mouthparts, a gesture of displeased huffiness.

"You *chordates*," it said. "You're all the same."

INTERSTELLAR SPACE—AD 3354

Mirsky was dead. She had died of old age.

Irravel placed her body in an armoured coffin and ejected her into space when the *Hirondelle*'s speed was only a hair's breadth under light. "Do it for me, Irravel," Mirsky had told her, toward the end. "Keep my body aboard until we're almost touching light, and then fire me ahead of the ship."

"Is that what you want?"

"It's an old pirate tradition. Burial at C." She forced a smile which must have sapped what little energy she had left. "That's a joke, Irravel, but it only makes sense in a language neither of us have heard for a while."

Irravel pretended that she understood. "Mirsky? There's something I have to tell you. Do you remember the Nestbuilder?"

"That was centuries ago, Veda."

"I know. I just keep worrying that maybe it was right."

"About what?"

"Those machines. About how I started it all. They say it's spread now; to other systems. It doesn't look like anyone knows how to stop it."

"And you think all that was your fault?"

"It's crossed my mind."

Mirsky convulsed, or shrugged—Irravel wasn't sure. "Even if it was your fault, Veda, you did it with the best of intentions. So you fucked up slightly. We all make mistakes."

"Destroying whole solar systems is just a fuck-up?"

"Hey, accidents happen."

"You always did have a sense of humour, Mirsky."

"Yeah; guess I did." She managed a smile. "One of us needed one, Veda."

Thinking of that, Irravel watched the coffin fall ahead, dwindling until it was only a tiny mote of steel-grey, and then nothing.

SUBARU COMMONWEALTH—PLEIADES CLUSTER—AD 4161

The starbridge had long ago attained sentience.

Dense with machinery, it sung an endless hymn to its own immensity, throbbing like the lowest string on a guitar. Vacuum-breathing acolytes had voluntarily re-wired their minds to view the bridge as an actual deity, translating the humming into their sensoria and passing decades in contemplative ecstasy.

Clasped in a cushioning field, an elevator ferried Irravel down the bridge from the orbital hub to the surface in a few minutes, accompanied by an entourage of children from the ship, many of whom bore in youth the hurting imprint of Mirsky's genes. The bridge rose like the stem of a goblet from a ground terminal which was itself a scalloped shell of hyperdiamond, filled with tiered perfume gardens and cascading pools, anchored to the largest island in an equatorial archipelago. The senior children walked Irravel down to a beach of silver sand on the terminal's edge, where jewelled crabs moved like toys. She bid the children farewell, then waited, warm breezes fingering the hem of her sari.

Minutes later, the children's elevator flashed heavenward.

Irravel looked out at the ocean, thinking of the Pattern Jugglers. Here, as on dozens of other oceanic worlds, there was a colony of the alien intelligences. Transformed to aquatic bodyplans themselves, the Subaruns had established close rapport with the aliens. In the morning, she would be taken out to meet the Jugglers, drowned, dissolved on the cellular level, every atom in her body swapped for one in the ocean, remade into something not quite human.

She was terrified.

Islanders came toward the shore, skimming water on penanted trimarans, attended by oceanforms, sleek gloss-grey hybrids of porpoise and ray, whistlespeech downshifted into the human spectrum. The Subaruns' epidermal scales shimmered like imbricated armour: biological photocells drinking scorching blue Pleiadean sunlight. Sentient veils hung in the sky, rippling gently like aurorae, shading the archipelago from the fiercest wavelengths. As the actinic eye of Taygeta sank toward the horizon, the veils moved with it like living clouds. Flocks of phantasmagoric birds migrated with the veils.

The purple-skinned elder's scales flashed green and opal as he approached Irravel along the coral jetty, a stick in one webbed hand, supported by two aides, a third shading his aged crown with a delicately water-coloured parasol. The aides were all descended from late-model Conjoiners; they had the translucent cranial crest through which bloodflow had once been channelled to cool their supercharged minds. Seeing them gave Irravel a dual-edged pang of nostalgia and guilt. She had not seen Conjoiners for nearly a thousand years, ever since they had fragmented into a dozen factions and vanished from human affairs. Neither had she entirely forgotten her betrayal of Remontoire.

But that had been so long ago.

A Communicant made up the party, gowned in brocade, hazed by a blur of entoptic projections. Communicants were small and elfin, with a phenomenal talent for natural languages, augmented by Juggler transforms. Irravel sensed that this one was old and revered, despite the fact that Communicant genes did not express for great longevity.

The elder halted before her.

The head of his walking stick was a tiny lemur skull inside an eggsized space helmet. He spoke something clearly ceremonial, but Irravel understood none of the sounds he made. She groped for something to say, recalling the oldest language in her memory, and therefore the one most likely to be recognized in any farflung human culture.

"Thank you for letting us stop here," she said.

The Communicant hobbled forward, already shaping words experimentally with his wide, protruding lips. For a moment his sounds were like an infant's first attempts at vocalization. But then they resolved into something Irravel understood.

"Am I—um—making the slightest sense to you?"

"Yes," Irravel said. "Yes, thank you."

"Canasian," the Communicant diagnosed. "Twenty-third, twenty-fourth centuries, Lacaille 9352 dialect, Fand subdialect?"

Irravel nodded.

"Your kind are very rare now," he said, studying her as if she was some kind of exotic butterfly. "But not unwelcome." His features cracked into an elfin smile.

"What about Markarian?" Irravel said. "I know his ship passed through this system less than 50 years ago—I still have a fix on it as it moves out of the cluster."

"Other lighthuggers do come, yes. Not many—one or two a century."

"And what happened when the last one came through?"

"The usual tribute was given."

"Tribute?"

"Something ceremonial." The Communicant's smile was wider than ever. "To the glory of Irravel. With many actors, beautiful words, love, death, laughter, tears."

She understood, slowly, dumbfoundedly.

"You're putting on a play?"

The elder must have understood something of that. Nodding proudly, he extended a hand across the darkening bay, oceanforms cutting the water like scythes. A distant raft carried lanterns and the glimmerings of richly painted backdrops. Boats converged from across the bay. A dirigible loomed over the archipelago's edge, pregnant with gondolas.

"We want you to play Irravel," the Communicant said, beckoning her forward. "This is our greatest honour."

When they reached the raft, the Communicant taught Irravel her lines and the actions she would be required to make. It was all simple enough—even the fact that she had to deliver her parts in Subarun. By the end of evening she was fluent in their language. There was nothing she couldn't learn in an instant these days, by sheer force of will. But it was not enough. To catch Markarian, she would have to break out of the narrow labyrinth of human thought entirely. That was why she had come to Jugglers.

That night they performed the play, while boats congregated around them, top-heavy with lolling islanders. The sun sank and the sky glared with a thousand blue gems studding blue velvet. Night in the heart of the Pleiades was the most beautiful thing Irravel had dared imagine. But in the direction of Sol, when she amplified her vision, there was a green thumbprint on the sky. Every century, the green wave was larger, as neighbouring solar systems were infected and transformed by the rogue terraforming machines. Given time, it would even reach the Pleiades.

Irravel got drunk on islander wine and learnt the tributes' history.

The plots varied immensely, but the protagonists always resembled Markarian and Irravel; mythic figures entwined by destiny, remembered across 2,000 years. Sometimes one or the other was the clear villain, but as often as not they were both heroic, misunderstanding each other's motives in true tragic fashion. Sometimes they ended with both parties dying. They rarely ended happily. But there was always some kind of redemption when the pursuit was done.

In the interlude, she felt she had to tell the Communicant the truth, so that he could tell the elder.

"Listen, there's something you need to know." Irravel didn't wait for his answer. "I'm really her; really the person I'm playing"

For a long time he didn't seem to understand, before shaking his head slowly and sadly.

"No; I thought you'd be different. You seemed different. But many say that."

She shrugged. There seemed little point arguing, and anything she said now could always be ascribed to wine. In the morning, the remark had been quietly forgotten. She was taken out to sea and drowned.

GALACTIC NORTH, AD 9730

"Markarian? Answer me."

She watched the *Hideyoshi*'s magnified image, looming just out of weapons range. Like the *Hirondelle*, it had changed almost beyond recognition. The hull glistened within a skein of armouring force. The engines, no longer physically coupled to the rest of the ship, flew alongside like dolphins. They were anchored in fields which only became visible when some tiny stress afflicted them.

For centuries of worldtime she had made no attempt to communicate with him. But now her mind had changed. The green wave had continued for millennia, an iridescent cataract spreading across the eye of the Galaxy. It had assimilated the blue suns of the Subaran Commonwealth in mere centuries—although by then Irravel and Markarian were a thousand light-years closer to the core, beginning to turn away from the plane of the Galaxy, and the death screams of those gentle islanders never reached them. Nothing stopped it, and once the green wave had swallowed them, systems fell silent. The Juggler transformation allowed Irravel to grasp the enormity of it; allowed her to stare unflinchingly into the horror of a million poisoned stars and apprehend each individually.

She knew more of what it was, now.

It was impossible for stars to shine green, any more than an ingot of metal could become green-hot if it was raised to a certain temperature. Instead, something was veiling them—staining their light, like coloured glass. Whatever it was stole energy from the stellar spectra at the frequencies of chlorophyll. Stars were shining through curtains of vegetation, like lanterns in a forest. The greenfly machines were turning the Galaxy into a jungle.

It was time to talk. Time—as in the old plays of the dead islanders—to initiate the final act, before the two of them fell into the cold of intergalactic space. She searched her repertoire of communication systems, until she found something which was as ancient as ceremony demanded.

She aimed the message laser at him, cutting through his armour. The beam was too ineffectual to be mistaken as anything other than an attempt to talk. No answer came, so she repeated the message in a variety of formats and languages. Days of ship-time passed—decades of worldtime.

Talk, you bastard.

Growing impatient, she examined her weapons options. Armaments from the Nestbuilders were among the most advanced: theoretically they could mole through the loam of spacetime and inflict precise harm anywhere in Markarian's ship. But to use them she had to convince herself that she knew the interior layout of the *Hideyoshi*. Her mass-sensor sweeps were too blurred to be much help. She might as easily harm the sleepers as take out his field nodes. Until now, it was too much risk to contemplate.

But all games needed an end.

Willing her qualms from mind, she enabled the Nestbuilder armaments, feeling them stress space-time in the *Hirondelle*'s belly, ready to short-circuit it entirely. She selected attack loci in Markarian's ship; best guesses that would cripple him rather than blow him out of the sky.

Then something happened.

He replied, modulating his engine thrust in staccato stabs. The frequency was audio. Quickly Irravel translated the modulation.

"I don't understand," Markarian said, "why you took so long to answer me, and why you ignored me so long when I replied?"

"You never replied until now," she said. "I'd have known if you had."

"Would you?"

There was something in his tone which convinced her that he wasn't lying. Which left only one possibility: that he had tried speaking to her before, and that in some way her own ship had kept this knowledge from her.

"Mirsky must have done it," Irravel said. "She must have installed filters to block any communications from your ship."

"Mirsky?"

"She would have done it as a favour to me; maybe as an order from my former self." She didn't bother elaborating: Markarian was sure to know she had died and then been reborn as a clone of the original Irravel. "My former self had the neural conditioning which kept her on the trail of the sleepers. The clone never had it, which meant that my instinct to pursue the sleepers had to be reinforced."

"By lies?"

"Mirsky would have done it out of friendship," Irravel said. And for a moment she believed herself, while wondering how friendship could seem so like betrayal.

Markarian's image smiled. They faced each other across an absurdly long banquet table, with the Galaxy projected above it, flickering in the light of candelabra.

"Well?" he said, of the green stain spreading across the spiral. "What do you think?"

Irravel had long ago stopped counting time and distance, but she knew it had been at least 15,000 years and that many light-years since they had turned from the plane. Part of her knew, of course: although the wave swallowed suns, it had no use for pulsars, and their metronomic ticking and slow decay allowed positional triangulation in space and time with chilling precision. But she elected to bury that knowledge beneath her conscious thought processes: one of the simpler Juggler tricks.

"What do I think? I think it terrifies me."

"Our emotional responses haven't diverged as much as I'd feared."

They didn't have to use language. They could have swapped pure mental concepts between ships: concatenated strings of qualia, some of which could only be grasped in minds rewired by Pattern Jugglers. But Irravel considered it sufficient that they could look each other in the eye without flinching.

The Galaxy falling below had been frozen in time: light waves struggling to overtake Irravel and Markarian. The wave had seemed to slow, and then halt its advance. But then Markarian had turned, diving back toward the plane. The Galaxy quickened to life, rushing to finish 30,000 years of history before the two ships returned. The wave surged on. Above the banquet table, one arm of the star-clotted spiral was shot through with green, like a mote of ink spreading into blotting paper. The edge of the green wave was feathered, fractal, extending verdant tendrils.

"Do you have any observations?" Irravel asked.

"A few." Markarian sipped from his chalice. "I've studied the patterns of starlight among the suns already swallowed by the wave. They're not uniformly green—it's correlated with rational angle. The green matter must be concentrated near the ecliptic, extending above and below it, but not encircling the stars completely."

Irravel thought back to what the Nestbuilder had shown her.

"Meaning what?" she asked, testing Markarian.

"Swarms of absorbing bodies, on orbits resembling comets, or asteroids. I think the greenfly machines must have dismantled everything smaller than a Jovian, then enveloped the rubble in transparent membranes which they filled with air, water and greenery—self-sustaining biospheres. Then they were cast adrift. Trillions of tiny worlds, around each star. No rocky planets anymore."

Irravel retrieved a name from the deep past. "Like Dyson spheres?"

"Dyson clouds, perhaps."

"Do you think anyone survived? Are there niches in the wave where humans can live? That was the point of greenfly, after all, to create living space."

"Maybe," Markarian said, with no great conviction. "Perhaps some survivors found ways inside, as their own worlds were smashed and reassembled into the cloud . . ."

"But you don't think it's very likely?"

"I've been listening, Irravel—scanning the assimilated regions for any hint of an extant technological culture. If anyone did survive, they're either keeping deliberately quiet or they don't even know how to make a radio signal by accident."

"It was my fault, Markarian."

His tone was rueful. "Yes . . . I couldn't help but arrive at that conclusion."

"I never intended this."

"I think that goes without saying, wouldn't you? No one could have guessed the consequences of that one action."

"Would you?"

He shook his head. "In all likelihood, I'd have done exactly what you did."

"I did it out of love, Markarian. For the cargo."

"I know."

She believed him.

"What happened back there, Markarian? Why did you give up the codes when I didn't?"

"Because of what they did to you, Irravel."

He told her. How neither Markarian nor Irravel had shown any signs of revealing the codes under Mirsky's interrogation, until something new was tried.

"They were good at surgery," Markarian said. "Seven's crew swapped limbs and body parts as badges of status. They knew how to sever and splice nerves." The image didn't allow her to interrupt. "They cut your head off. Kept it alive in a state of borderline consciousness, and then showed it to me. That's when I gave them the codes."

For a long while Irravel said nothing. Then it occurred to her to check her old body, still frozen in the same casket where Mirsky had once revealed it to her. She ordered some children to prepare the body for a detailed examination, then looked through their eyes. The microscopic evidence of reconnective surgery around the neck was too slight to have ever shown up unless one was looking for it. But now there was no mistaking it.

I did it to save your neck, Markarian had said, when she had held him pinned to the ice of Seven's ship.

"You seem to be telling the truth," she said, when she had released the children. "The nature of your betrayal was . . ." And then she paused, searching for the words, while Markarian watched her across the table. "Different than I assumed. Possibly less of a crime. But still a betrayal, Markarian."

"One I've lived with for 300 years of subjective time."

"You could have returned the sleepers alive at any time. I wouldn't have attacked you." But she didn't even sound convincing to herself.

"What now?" Markarian said. "Do we keep this distance, arguing until one of us has the nerve to strike against the other? I've Nestbuilder weapons as well, Irravel. I think I could rip you apart before you could launch a reprisal."

"You've had the opportunity to do so before. Perhaps you never had the nerve, though. What's changed now?"

Markarian's gaze flicked to the map. "Everything. I think we should see what happens before making any rash decisions, don't you?"

Irravel agreed.

She willed herself into stasis; medichines arresting all biological activity in every cell in her body. The 'chines would only revive her when something—anything—happened, on a Galactic timescale. Markarian would retreat into whatever mode of suspension he favoured, until woken by the same stimulus.

He was still sitting there when time resumed, as if only a moment had interrupted their conversation.

The wave had spread further now. It had eaten into the Galaxy for 10,000 light-years around Sol—a third of the way to the core. There was no sign that it had encountered resistance—at least nothing that had done more than hinder it. There had never been many intelligent, starfaring cultures to begin with, the Nestbuilder had told her. Perhaps the few that existed were even now making plans to retard the wave. Or perhaps it had swallowed them, as it swallowed humanity.

"Why did we wake?" Irravel said. "Nothing changed, except that it's become larger."

"Maybe not," Markarian said. "I had to be sure, but now I don't think there's any doubt. I've just detected a radio message from within the plane of the Galaxy; from within the wave."

"Yes?"

"Looks like someone survived after all."

The radio message was faint, but nothing else was transmitting on that or any adjacent frequency, except for the senseless mush of cosmic background sources. It was also in a language they recognized.

"It's Canasian," Irravel said.

"Fand subdialect," Irravel added, marvellingly.

It was also beamed in their direction, from somewhere deep in the swathe of green, almost coincident with the position of a pulsar. The message was a simple one, frequency modulated around one and a half megahertz, repeated for a few minutes every day of Galactic time. Whoever was sending it clearly lacked the resources to transmit continuously. It was also coherent: amplified and beamed.

Someone wanted to speak to them.

The man's disembodied head appeared above the banquet table, chiselled from pixels. He was immeasurably old; a skull draped in parchment; something that should have been embalmed rather than talking.

Irravel recognized the face.

"It's him," she said, in Markarian's direction. "Remontoire. Somehow he made it across all this time."

Markarian nodded slowly. "He must have remembered us, and known where to look. Even across thousands of light-years, we can still be seen. There can't be many objects still moving relativistically."

Remontoire told his story. His people had fled to the pulsar system 20,000 years ago—more so now, since his message had taken thousands of years to climb out of the Galaxy. They had seen the wave coming, as had thousands of other human factions, and like many they had observed that the wave shunned pulsars; burnt-out stellar corpses rarely accompanied by planets. Some intelligence governing the wave must have recognized that pulsars were valueless; that even if a Dyson cloud could be created around them, there would be no sunlight to focus.

For thousands of years they had waited around the pulsar, growing ever more silent and cautious, seeing other cultures make errors which drew the wave upon them, for by now it interpreted any other intelligence as a threat to its progress, assimilating the weapons used against it.

Then—over many more thousands of years—Remontoire's people saw the wave learn, adapting like a vast neural net, becoming curious about those few pulsars which harboured planets. Soon their place of refuge would become nothing of the sort.

"Help us," Remontoire said. "Please."

It took 3,000 years to reach them.

For most of that time, Remontoire's people acted on faith, not knowing that help was on its way. During the first thousand years they abandoned their system, compressing their population down to a sustaining core of only a few hundred thousand. Together with the cultural data they'd preserved during the long centuries of their struggle against the wave, they packed their survivors into a single hollowed-out rock and flung themselves out of the ecliptic using a mass-driver which fuelled itself from the rock's own bulk. They called it *Hope*. A million decoys had to be launched, just to ensure that *Hope* got through the surrounding hordes of assimilating machines.

Inside, most of the Conjoiners slept out the 2,000 years of solitude before Irravel and Markarian reached them.

"*Hope* would make an excellent shield," Markarian mused, as they approached it, "if one of us considered a pre-emptive strike against the other."

"Don't think I wouldn't."

They moved their ships to either side of the dark shard of rock, extended field grapples, then hauled in.

"Then why don't you?" Markarian said.

For a moment Irravel didn't have a good answer. When she found one, she wondered why it hadn't been more obvious before. "Because they need us more than I need revenge."

"A higher cause?"

"Redemption," she said.

HOPE, GALACTIC PLANE — AD CIRCA 40,000

They didn't have long. Their approach, diving down from Galactic North, had drawn the attention of the wave's machines, directing them toward the one rock which mattered. A wall of annihilation was moving toward them at half the speed of light. When it reached *Hope*, it would turn it into the darkest of nebulae.

Conjoiners boarded the *Hirondelle* and invited Irravel into the *Hope*: The hollowed-out chambers of the rock were Edenic to her children, after all the decades of subjective time they'd spent aboard since last planetfall. But it was a doomed paradise, the biomes grey with neglect, as if the Conjoiners had given up long ago.

Remontoire welcomed Irravel next to a rockpool filmed in grey dust. Half the sun-panels set into the distant honeycombed ceiling were black.

"You came," he said. He wore a simple smock and trousers. His anatomy was early-model Conjoiner: almost fully human.

"You're not him, are you. You look like him — sound like him — but the image you sent us was of someone much older."

"I'm sorry. His name was chosen for its familiarity; my likeness shaped to his. We searched our collective memories and found the experiences of the one you knew as Remontoire . . . but that was a long time ago, and he was never known by that name to us."

"What was his name?"

"Even your Juggler cortex could not accommodate it, Irravel."

She had to ask. "Did he make it back to a commune?"

"Yes, of course," the man said, as if her question was foolish. "How else could we have absorbed his experiences back into the Transenlightenment?"

"And did he forgive me?"

"I forgive you now," he said. "It amounts to the same thing."

She willed herself to think of him as Remontoire.

The Conjoiners hadn't allowed themselves to progress in all the thousands of years they waited around the pulsar, fearing that any social change—no matter how slight—would eventually bring the wave upon them. They had studied it, contemplated weapons they might use against it—but other than that, all they had done was wait.

They were very good at waiting.

"How many refugees did you bring?"

"One hundred thousand." Before Irravel could answer, Remontoire shook his head. "I know; too many. Perhaps half that number can be carried away on your ships. But half is better than nothing."

She thought back to her own sleepers. "I know. Still, we might be able to take more . . . I don't know about Markarian's ship, but—"

He cut her off, gently. "I think you'd better come with me," said Remontoire, and then led her aboard the *Hideyoshi*.

"How much of it did you explore?"

"Enough to know there's no one alive anywhere in this ship," Remontoire said. "If there are 200 cryogenically frozen sleepers, we didn't find them."

"No sleepers?"

"Just this one."

What they'd arrived at was a plinth, supporting a reefersleep casket, encrusted with gold statuary; spacesuited figures with hands folded across their chests like resting saints. The glass lid of the casket was veined with fractures; the withered figure inside older than time. Markarian's skeletal frame was swaddled in layers of machines, all of archaic provenance. His skull had split open, a fused mass spilling out like lava.

"Is he dead?" Irravel asked.

"Depends what you mean by dead." The Conjoiner's hand sketched across the neural mass. "His organic mind must have been completely swamped by machines centuries ago. His linkage to the *Hideyoshi* would have been total. There would have been very little point discriminating between the two."

"Why didn't he tell me what had become of him?"

"No guarantee he knew. Once he was in this state, with his personality running entirely on machine substrates, he could have edited his own memories and perceptual inputs—deceiving himself that he was still corporeal."

Irravel looked away from the casket, forcing troubling questions from her mind. "Is his personality still running the ship?"

"We detected only caretaker programs; capable of imitating him when the need arose, but lacking sentience."

"Is that all there was?"

"No." Remontoire reached through one of the casket's larger fractures, prising something from Markarian's fingers. It was a sliver of computer memory. "We examined this already, though not in great detail. It's partitioned into 190 areas, each large enough to hold complete neural and genetic maps for one human being, encoded into superposed electron states on Rydberg atoms."

She took the sliver from him. It didn't feel like much. "He burned the sleepers onto this?"

"Three hundred years is much longer than any of them expected to sleep. By scanning them he lost nothing."

"Can you retrieve them?"

"It would not be trivial," the Conjoiner said. "But given time, we could do it. Assuming any of them would welcome being born again, so far from home."

She thought of the infected Galaxy hanging below them, humming with the chill sentience of machines. "Maybe the kindest thing would be to simulate the past," she said. "Re-create Yellowstone, and revive them on it, as if nothing had ever gone wrong."

"Is that what you're advocating?"

"No," she said, after toying with the idea in all seriousness. "We need all the genetic diversity we can get, if we're going to establish a new branch of humanity outside the Galaxy."

She thought about it. Soon they would witness *Hope*'s destruction, as the wave of machines tore through it with the mindlessness of stampeding animals. Some of them might try and follow the *Hirondelle*, but so far the machines moved too slowly to catch the ship, even if they forced it back toward Galactic North.

Where was there to go?

There were globular clusters high above the Galaxy—tightly packed shoals of old stars where the wave hadn't reached, but where fragments of humanity might have already sought refuge. If the clusters proved unwelcoming, there were high-latitude stars, flung from the Galaxy a billion years ago, and some might have dragged their planetary systems with them. If those failed—and it would be tens of thousands of years before the possibilities were exhausted—the *Hirondelle* could always loop around toward Galactic South and search there, striking out for the Clouds of Magellan. Ultimately, of course—if any part or fragment of Irravel's children still clung to humanity, and remembered where they'd come from, and what had become of it, they would want to return to the Galaxy, even if that meant confronting the wave.

But they would return.

"That's the plan then?" Remontoire said.

Irravel shrugged, turning away from the plinth where Markarian lay. "Unless you've got a better one."

Dapple: A *Hwarhath* Historical Romance

ELEANOR ARNASON

Critically acclaimed author Eleanor Arnason published her first novel, The Sword Smith, *in 1978, and followed it with novels such as* Daughter of the Bear King *and* To the Resurrection Station. *In 1991, she published her best-known novel, one of the strongest novels of the '90s,* A Woman of the Iron People, *a complex and substantial novel which won the prestigious James Tiptree Jr. Memorial Award. Her short fiction has appeared in Asimov's Science Fiction,* The Magazine of Fantasy & Science Fiction, Amazing, Orbit, Xanadu, *and elsewhere. Her most recent novel is* Ring of Swords, *set in the same evocative fictional universe as is the bulk of her short fiction, including the story that follows.*

In this story she takes us to a distant planet inhabited by the alien hwarhath, *and along with a brave and determined young girl who defies her family and sets off on a perilous adventure that takes her into uncharted territory of several sorts—into wild, lawless country inhabited by bandits and remorseless killers, and, perhaps even more dangerously, into a new social territory as well, as she assumes roles Forbidden to Women since time immemorial . . .*

There was a girl named Helwar Ahl. Her family lived on an island north and east of the Second Continent, which was known in those days as the Great Southern Continent. (Now, of course, we know that an even larger expanse of land lies farther south, touching the pole. In Ahl's time, however, no one knew about this land except its inhabitants.)

A polar current ran up the continent's east coast and curled around Helwar Island, so its climate was cool and rainy. Thick forests covered the mountains. The Helwar built ships from the wood. They were famous shipwrights, prosperous enough to have a good-sized harbor town.

Ahl grew up in this town. Her home was the kind of great house typical of the region: a series of two-story buildings linked together. The outer walls were mostly blank. Inside were courtyards, balconies, and large windows provided with the modern wonder, glass. Granted, the panes were small and flawed. But some ingenious artificer had found a way to fit many panes together, using strips of lead. Now the women of the house had light, even in the coldest weather.

As a child, Ahl played with her cousins in the courtyards and common rooms, all of them naked except for their fog-grey fur. Later, in a kilt, she ran in the town streets and visited the harbor. Her favorite uncle was a fisherman, who went out in morning darkness, before most people woke. In the late afternoon, he returned. If he'd been lucky, he tied up and cleaned his catch, while Ahl sat watching on the dock.

"I want to be a fisherman," she said one day.

"You can't, darling. Fishing is men's work."

"Why?"

He was busy gutting fish. He stopped for a moment, frowning, a bloody knife still in his hand. "Look at this situation! Do you want to stand like me, knee deep in dead fish? It's hard, nasty work and can be dangerous. The things that women do well—negotiation, for example, and the forming of alliances—are no use at all, when dealing with fish. What's needed here," he waved the knife, "is violence. Also, it helps if you can piss off the side of a boat."

For a while after that Ahl worked at aiming her urine. She could do it, if she spread her legs and tilted her pelvis in just the right fashion. But would she be able to manage on a pitching boat? Or in a wind? In addition, there was the problem of violence. Did she really want to be a killer of many small animals?

One of the courtyards in her house had a basin, which held ornamental fish. Ahl caught one and cut off its head. A senior female cousin caught her before she was finished, though the fish was past help.

"What are you doing?" the matron asked.

Ahl explained.

"These are fish to feed, not fish to eat," her cousin said and demonstrated this by throwing a graincake into the basin.

Fish surged to the surface in a swirl of red fins, green backs, and blue-green tails. A moment later, the cake was gone. The fish returned to their usual behavior: a slow swimming back and forth.

"It's hardly fair to kill something this tame—in your own house, too. Guests should be treated with respect. In addition, these fish have an uninteresting flavor and are full of tiny bones. If you ate one, it would be like eating a cloth full of needles."

Ahl lost interest in fishing after that. Her uncle was right about killing. It was a nasty activity. All that quickness and grace, gone in a moment. The bright colors faded. She was left with nothing except a feeling of disgust.

Maybe she'd be a weaver, like her mother, Leweli. Or the captain of a far-traveling ocean-trader, like her aunt Ki. Then she could bring treasures home: transparent glass, soft and durable lead.

When she was ten, she saw her first play. She knew the actors, of course. They were old friends of her family and came to Helwar often, usually staying in Ahl's house. The older one—Perig—was quiet and friendly, always courteous to the household children, but not a favorite with them. The favorite was Cholkwa, who juggled and pulled candy out of ears. He knew lots of funny stories, mostly about animals such as the *tli*, a famous troublemaker and trickster. According to the house's adults, he was a comedian, who performed in plays too rude for children to see. Perig acted in hero plays, though it was hard to imagine him as a hero. The two men were lovers, but didn't usually work together. This was due to the difference in their styles and to their habit of quarreling. They had, the women of Ahl's house said, a difficult relationship.

This time they came together, and Perig brought his company. They put on a play in the main square, both of them acting, though Cholkwa almost never did dark work.

The play was about two lovers—both of them warriors—whose families quarreled. How could they turn against one another? How could they refuse their relatives' pleas for help? Each was the best warrior in his family.

Though she hadn't seen a play before, Ahl knew how this was going to end. The two men met in battle. It was more like a dance than anything else, both of them splendidly costumed and moving with slow reluctant grace. Finally, after several speeches, Perig tricked Cholkwa into striking. The blow was fatal. Perig went down in a gold and scarlet heap. Casting his sword away, Cholkwa knelt beside him. A minor player in drab armor crept up and killed Cholkwa as he mourned.

Ahl was transfixed, though also puzzled. "Wasn't there any way out?" she asked the actors later, when they were back in her house, drinking *halin* and listening to her family's compliments.

"In a comedy, yes," said Cholkwa. "Which is why I do bright plays. But Perig likes plays that end with everyone dead, and always over some ethical problem that's hardly ever encountered in real life."

The older man was lying on a bench, holding his *halin* cup on his chest. He glanced at Cholkwa briefly, then looked back at the ceiling. "Is what you do more true to reality? Rude plays about animals? I'd rather be a hero in red and gold armor than a man in a *tli* costume."

"I'd rather be a clever *tli* than someone who kills his lover."

"What else could they do?" asked Perig, referring to the characters in the play.

"Run off," said Cholkwa. "Become actors. Leave their stupid relatives to fight their stupid war unaided."

It was one of those adult conversations where everything really important was left unspoken. Ahl could tell that. Bored, she said, "I'd like to be an actor."

They both looked at her.

"You can't," said Perig.

This sounded familiar. "Why not?"

"In part, it's custom," Cholkwa said. "But there's at least one good reason. Actors travel and live among unkin; and often the places we visit are not safe. I go south a lot. The people there love comedy, but in every other way they're louts and savages. At times I've wondered if I'd make it back alive, or would someone have to bring my ashes in an urn to Perig?"

"Better to stay here," said Perig. "Or travel the way your aunt Ki does, in a ship full of relatives."

No point in arguing. When adults started to give advice, they were never reasonable. But the play stayed with her. She imagined stories about people in fine clothing, faced with impossible choices; and she acted them out, going so far as to make a wooden sword, which she kept hidden in a hayloft. Her female relatives had an entire kitchen full of knives and cleavers and axes, all sharp and dangerous. But the noise they would have made, if they'd seen her weapon!

Sometimes she was male and a warrior. At other times, she was a sailor like Ki, fighting the kinds of monsters found at the edges of maps. Surely, Ahl thought, it was permissible for women to use swords when attacked by monsters, rising out of the water with fangs that dripped poison and long curving claws?

Below her in the barn, her family's *tsina* ate and excreted. Their animal aroma rose to her, combining with the scent of hay. Later she said this was the scent of drama: dry, aging hay and new-dropped excrement.

The next year Cholkwa came alone and brought his company. They did a decent comedy, suitable for children, about a noble *sul* who was tricked and humiliated by a *tli*. The trickster was exposed at the play's end. The *sul's* honor was restored. The good animals did a dance of triumph, while the *tli* cowered and begged.

Cholkwa was the *tli*. Strange that a man so handsome and friendly could portray a sly coward.

Ahl asked about this. Cholkwa said, "I can't talk about other men, but I have that kind of person inside me: a cheat and liar, who would like to run away from everything. I don't run, of course. Perig would disapprove, and I'd rather be admired than despised."

"But you played a hero last year."

"That was more difficult. Perig understands nobility, and I studied with him a long time. I do as he tells me. Most people are tricked and think I know what I'm doing. But that person—the hero—doesn't speak in my mind."

Ahl moved forward to the play's other problem. "The *sul* was noble, but a fool. The *tli* was clever and funny, but immoral. There was no one in the play I could really like."

Cholkwa gave her a considering gaze, which was permissible, since she was still a child. Would she like it, when men like Cholkwa—unkin, but old friends—had to glance away? "Most people, even adults, wouldn't have seen that. It has two causes. I wrote the *sul's* lines, and, as I've told you, I don't understand nobility. The other problem is my second actor. He isn't good enough. If Perig had been here, he would have made the *sul* likable—in part by rewriting the lines, but mostly because he could play a stone and make it seem likable."

Ahl thought about this idea. An image came to her: Perig in a grey robe, sitting quietly on a stage, his face unmasked and grey, looking calm and friendly. A likable rock. It could be done. Why bother? In spite of her question, the image remained, somehow comforting.

Several days later, Cholkwa did a play for adults. This event took place at night in the town hall, which was used for meetings and ceremonies, also to store trade goods in transit. This time the back half was full of cloth, big bales that smelled of fresh dye, southern blue and the famous Sorg red.

Ahl snuck out of her house after dark and went in a back door, which she'd unlocked earlier. Climbing atop the bales, she settled to watch the play.

Most of it was past her understanding, though the audience gasped, groaned, clapped, and made hissing noises. Clearly, they knew what was going on.

The costumes were ugly, in her opinion; the animals had huge sexual parts and grimacing faces. They hit each other with padded swords and clubs, tumbled and tossed each other, spoke lines that were—as far as she could tell—full of insults, some sly and others so obvious that even she made sense of them. This time the *sul* was an arrogant braggart with a long narrow head and a penis of almost equal size and shape. The *tli*, much less well endowed, was clever and funny, a coward because he had to be. Most of his companions were large, dangerous, and unjust.

It was the *tli*'s play. Mocking and tricking, he won over all the rest, ending with the *sul*'s precious ancestral sword, which he carried off in triumph to his mother, a venerable female *tli*, while the *sul* howled in grief.

The Sword Recovered or *The Revenge of the Tli*. That was the name of the play. There was something in back of it, which Ahl could not figure out. Somehow the *sul* had harmed the *tli*'s family in the past. Maybe the harm had been sexual, though this didn't seem likely. *Sulin* and *tli* did not interbreed. Puzzled, she climbed down from the bales and went home. The night was foggy, and she almost lost her way in streets she'd known her entire life.

She couldn't ask Cholkwa to explain. He would have told her relatives that she'd seen the play.

After this, she added comedy to her repertoire, mixing it with the stories about heroes and women like her aunt, far-travelers who did *not* have to die over some kind of unusual ethical dilemma.

The result was a long, acted-out epic tale about a hero, a woman sailor, a clever *tli*, and a magical stone that accompanied the other three on their journey. The hero was noble, the sailor resourceful, and the *tli* funny, while the stone remained calm and friendly, no matter what was going on. There wasn't any sex. Ahl was too young, and the adult comedy had disgusted her. It's often a bad idea to see things that are forbidden, especially if one is young.

In the end, one of her cousins—a sneak worse than Cholkwa in the children's play—found out what she was doing and told her senior female relatives. "Clearly you have too much free time," they said, and assigned her work in the house's big weaving room. The sword was destroyed, along with the bits of armor she'd made. But her relatives decided the *tli* mask, constructed of bark paper over a frame of twigs, was good enough to keep. It was hung on the weaving room wall, where it stared down at her. Gradually, the straw whiskers disappeared, and large eyes—drawn in ink—faded.

Don't think that Ahl was too unhappy, or that her relatives had been unjust. Every child has to learn duty; and she'd gotten bored with her solitary play, as well as increasingly uncomfortable with hiding her props. Better to work at a loom and have ideas in her mind. No sneaking cousin could discover *these*, and everything she imagined was large and bright and well-made, the swords of real steel, sharp and polished, as bright as the best glass.

Two years passed. She became an adequate plain weaver, but nothing more. "We thought you might have a gift for beauty," said her mother. "The mask suggested this. But it's obvious that you lack the ability to concentrate, which is absolutely necessary in any kind of art. Anything worth doing is likely to be slow, difficult, and boring. This is not an invariable rule, but it works in most situations."

"Give her to me," said Ki. "Maybe she'd be happier in a more active life."

Ahl went to sea. At first, it was not an enjoyable experience, though she had little problem with motion sickness. Her difficulty lay in the same region as always: she spent too much time thinking about her stories. As a result, she was forgetful and careless. These are not good traits in an apprentice sailor; and Ki, who had always seemed pleasant and friendly at home in Helwar, turned out to be a harsh captain.

At first the punishment she gave to Ahl was work. Every ship is full of nasty jobs. Ahl did most of them and did them more than once. This didn't bother her. She wasn't lazy, and jobs — though nasty — required little thought. She could make up stories while she did them.

Her habit of inattention continued. Growing angry, Ki turned to violence. On several occasions, she stuck Ahl: hard slaps across the face. This also had no effect. The girl simply did not want to give up her stories. Finally, Ki beat her, using a knotted rope.

Most likely this shocks you. Nowadays we like to believe that our female ancestors never did harm to one another. It's men who are violent. Women have always used reason.

Remember this was a sailing ship in the days before radio and engines. Weather satellites did not warn sailors of approaching storms. Computers did not monitor the ship's condition and send automatic signals to the Navigation Service. Sailors had to rely on their own skill and discipline.

It was one thing to be forgetful in a weaving room. If you fail to tie off a piece of yarn, what can happen? At most, a length of cloth will be damaged. Now, imagine what happens if the same person fails to tie a rope on board a ship. Or forgets to fasten a hatch in stormy weather.

So, after several warnings and a final mistake, Ahl received her beating. By this time she was fourteen or fifteen, with a coat of fur made thick by cold weather. The fur protected her, though not entirely; and later, when she remembered the experience, it seemed that shame was the worst part: to stand naked on the ship's deck, trying to remain impassive, while Ki used the rope she had failed to tie across her back.

Around her, the other sailors did their work. They didn't watch directly, of course, but there were sideways glances, some embarrassed and others approving. Overhead the sky was cloudless. The ship moved smoothly through a bright blue ocean.

The next day she felt every bruise. Ki gave her another unpleasant cleaning job. All day she scraped, keeping her lips pressed together. In the evening she went on deck, less stiff than she'd been earlier, but tired and still sore. Ahl leaned on the rail and looked out at the ocean. In the distance, rays of sunlight slanted between grey clouds. Life was not entirely easy, she thought.

After a while, Ki's lover Hasu Ahl came next to her. Ahl had been named after the woman, for reasons that don't come into this story, and they were alike in several ways, being both tall and thin, with small breasts and large strong, capable hands. The main difference between them was their fur. Hasu Ahl's was dark grey, like the clouds which filled the sky, and her coloring was solid. Our Ahl was pale as fog. In addition, she had kept her baby spots. Dim and blurry, they dotted her shoulders and upper arms. Because of these, her childhood name had been Dapple.

Hasu Ahl asked how she felt.

"I've been better."

They became silent, both leaning on the rail. Finally Hasu Ahl said, "There's a story about your childhood that no one has told you. When you were a baby, a witch predicted that you would be important when you grew up. She didn't know in what way. I know this story, as do your mother and Ki and a few other people. But we didn't want your entire family peering at you and wondering, and we didn't want you to become vain or worried; so we kept quiet.

"It's possible that Ki's anger is due in part to this. She looks at you and thinks, 'Where is the gift that was promised us?' All we can see—aside from intelligence, which you obviously have—is carelessness and lack of attention."

What could she say? She was inattentive because her mind was full of stories, though the character who'd been like Ki had vanished. Now there was an orphan girl with no close relatives, ignored by everyone, except her three companions: the hero, the *tli*, and the stone. They cared for her in their different ways: the hero with nobility, the *tli* with jokes, and the stone with solid friendliness. But she'd never told anyone about her ideas. "I'm not yet fifteen," Ahl said.

"There's time for you to change," Hasu Ahl admitted. "But not if you keep doing things that endanger the ship and yourself. Ki has promised that if you're careless again, she'll beat you a second time, and the beating will be worse."

After that, Hasu Ahl left. Well, thought our heroine, this was certainly a confusing conversation. Ki's lover had threatened her with something like fame and with another beating. Adults were beyond comprehension.

Her concentration improved, and she became an adequate sailor, though Ki said she would never be a captain. "Or a second-in-command, like your namesake, my Ahl. Whatever your gift may be, it isn't sailing."

Her time on board was mostly happy. She made friends with the younger members of the crew, and she learned to love the ocean as a sailor does, knowing how dangerous it can be. The coast of the Great Southern Continent was dotted with harbor towns. Ahl visited many of these, exploring the steep narrow streets and multi-leveled marketplaces. One night at a festival, she made love for the first time. Her lover was a girl with black fur and pale yellow eyes. In the torchlight, the girl's pupils expanded, till they lay across her irises like bars of iron or narrow windows that opened into a starless night.

What a fine image! But what could Ahl do with it?

Later, in that same port, she came to an unwalled tavern. Vines grew over the roof. Underneath were benches. Perig sat on one, a cup in his hand. She shouted his name. He glanced up and smiled, then his gaze slid away. Was she that old? Had she become a woman? Maybe, she thought, remembering the black-furred girl.

Where was Cholkwa?

In the south, Perig said.

Because the place was unwalled and public, she was able to sit down. The hostess brought *halin*. She tasted it, savoring the sharp bitterness. It was the taste of adulthood.

"Watch out," said Perig. "That stuff can make you sick."

Was his company here? Were they acting? Ahl asked.

Yes. The next night, in the town square.

"I'll come," said Ahl with decision.

Perig glanced at her, obviously pleased.

The play was about a hero, of course: a man who suspected that the senior women in his family, his mother and her sisters, had committed a crime. If his suspicion was true, their behavior threatened the family's survival. But no man can treat any woman with violence, and no man should turn against his mother. And what if he were wrong? Maybe they were innocent. Taking one look at the women, Ahl knew they were villains. But the hero didn't have her sharpness of vision. So he blundered through the play, trying to discover the truth. Men died, mostly at his hands, and most of them his kin. Finally he was hacked down, while the women looked on. A messenger arrived, denouncing them. Their family was declared untouchable. No one would deal with them in the future. Unable to interbreed, the family would vanish. The monstrous women listened like blocks of stone. Nothing could affect their stubborn arrogance.

A terrible story, but also beautiful. Perig was the hero and shone like a diamond. The three men playing the women were grimly convincing. Ahl felt as if a sword had gone through her chest. Her stories were nothing next to this.

Afterward, Ahl found Perig in the open tavern. Torches flared in a cool ocean wind, and his fur — touched with white over the shoulders — moved a little, ruffled. Ahl tried to explain how lovely and painful the play had been.

He listened, giving her an occasional quick glance. "This is the way it's supposed to be," he said finally. "Like a blade going to a vital spot."

"Is it impossible to have a happy ending?" she asked, after she finished praising.

"In this kind of play, yes."

"I liked the hero so much. There should have been another solution."

"Well," said Perig. "He could have killed his mother and aunts, then killed himself. It would have saved his family, but he wasn't sure they were criminals."

"Of course they were!"

"You were in the audience," said Perig. "Where I was standing, in the middle of the situation, the truth was less evident; and no man should find it easy to kill his mother."

"I was right, years ago," Ahl said suddenly. "*This* is what I want to do. Act in plays."

Perig looked unhappy.

She told him about her attempts to weave and be a sailor, then about the plays she had acted in the hayloft and the stories in her mind. For the first time, she realized that the stories had scenes. She knew how the hero moved, like Perig acting a hero. The *tli* had Cholkwa's brisk step and mocking voice. The stone was a stone. Only the girl was blurry. She didn't tell Perig about the scenes. Embarrassing to admit that this quiet aging man lived in her mind, along with his lover and a stone. But she did tell him that she told stories.

He listened, then said, "If you were a boy, I'd go to your family and ask for you as an apprentice — if not this year, then next year. But I can't, Ahl. They'd refuse me and be so angry I might lose their friendship."

"What am I to do?" asked Ahl.

"That's a question I can't answer," said Perig.

A day later, her ship left the harbor. On the long trip home, Ahl considered her future. She'd seen other companies of actors. Perig and Cholkwa were clearly the best, but neither one of them would be willing to train her. Nor would any company that knew she was female. But most women in this part of the world were broad and full-breasted, and she was an entirely different type. People before, strangers, had mistaken her for a boy. Think of all the years she had acted in her loft, striding like Perig or mimicking Cholkwa's gait. Surely she had learned something!

She was seventeen and good at nothing. In spite of the witch's prediction, it wasn't likely she'd ever be important. It seemed to her now that nothing had ever interested her except the making of stories — not the linked verse epics that people recited on winter evenings, nor the tales that women told to children, but proper *stories*, like the ones that Perig and Cholkwa acted.

Before they reached Helwar, Ahl had decided to disguise herself as a boy and run away.

First, of course, she had to spend the winter at home. Much of her time was taken by her family. When she could, she watched her uncles and male cousins. How did they stand and move? What were their gestures? How did they speak?

The family warehouse was only half-full, she discovered. This became her theater, lit by high windows or (sometimes) by a lamp. She'd bought a square metal mirror in the south. Ahl leaned it against a wall. If she stood at a distance, she could see herself, dressed in a tunic stolen from a cousin and embroidered in the male style. Whenever possible, she practiced being a man, striding across the wood floor, turning and gesturing, speaking lines she remembered out of plays. Behind her were stacks of new-cut lumber. The fresh, sweet aroma of sawdust filled the air. In later life, she said this was the smell of need and possibility.

In spring, her ship went south again. Her bag, carefully packed, held boy's clothing, a knife and all her money.

In a town in the far south, she found an acting company, doing one of Perig's plays in ragged costumes. It was one she'd seen. They'd cut out parts.

So, thought Ahl. That evening, she took her bag and crept off the ship. The night was foggy, and the damp air smelled of unfamiliar vegetation. In an alley, she changed clothing, binding her four breasts flat with strips of cloth. She already knew where the actors were staying: a run-down inn by the harbor, not the kind of place that decent female sailors would visit. Walking through the dark streets, bag over her shoulder, she was excited and afraid.

Here, in this town, she was at the southern edge of civilization. Who could tell what the inland folk were like? Though she had never heard of any lineage that harmed women. If things got dangerous, she could pull off her tunic, revealing her real self.

On the other hand, there might be monsters; and they *did* harm women. Pulling off her tunic would do no good if something with fangs and scales came out of the forest. At most, the thing might thank her for removing the wrapping on its dinner.

If she wanted to turn back, now was the time. She could be a less-than-good sailor. She could go home and look for another trade. There were plenty in Helwar, and women could do most of them. She hadn't really wanted to fish in the ocean, not after she killed the fish in the basin. As for the other male activities, let them *have* fighting and hunting dangerous animals! Let them log and handle heavy timbers! Why should women risk their lives?

She stopped outside the inn, almost ready to turn around. Then she remembered Perig in the most recent play she'd seen, at the moment when the play's balance changed. A kinsman lay dead at his feet. It was no longer possible to go back. He'd stood quietly, then lifted his head, opening his mouth in a great cry that was silent. No one in the audience made a noise. Somehow, through his silence and their silence, Ahl heard the cry.

She would not give that up. Let men have every other kind of danger. This was something they had to share.

She went in and found the actors, a shabby group. As she had thought, they were short-handed.

The senior man was pudgy with a scar on one side of his face. "Have you any experience?" he asked.

"I've practiced on my own," said Ahl.

The man tilted his head, considering. "You're almost certainly a runaway, which is bad enough. Even worse, you've decided you can act. If I was only one man short, I'd send you off. But two of my men are gone, and if I don't find someone, we won't be able to continue."

In this manner, she was hired, though the man had two more questions. "How old are you? I won't take on a child."

"Eighteen," said Ahl.

"Are you certain?"

"Yes," she answered with indignation. Though she was lying about almost everything else, eighteen was her age.

Maybe her tone convinced the man. "Very well," he said, then asked, "What's your name?"

"Dapple," she said.

"Of no family?"

She hesitated.

The man said, "I'll stop asking questions."

She had timed this well. They left the next morning, through fog and drizzling rain. Her comrades on the ship would think she was sleeping. Instead, she trudged beside the actors' cart, which was pulled by a pair of *tsina*. Her tunic, made of thick wool, kept out the rain. A broad straw hat covered her head. Oiled boots protected her feet against mud and pools of water.

From this point on, the story will call her Dapple. It's the name she picked for herself and the one by which she was known for the rest of her life. Think of her not as Helwar Ahl, the runaway girl, but Dapple the actor, whose lineage did not especially matter, since actors live on the road, in the uncertain regions that lie between family holdings and the obligations of kinship.

All day they traveled inland, through steep hills covered with forest. Many of the trees were new to her. Riding in the cart, the pudgy man—his name was Manif—told her about the company. They did mostly comedies, though Manif preferred hero plays. "These people in the south are the rudest collection of louts you can imagine. They like nothing, unless it's full of erect penises and imitations of intercourse; and men and women watch these things together! Shocking!

"They even like plays about *breeding*, though I prefer—of course—to give them decent comedies about men having sex with men or women having sex with women. But if they insist on heterosexuality, well, we have to eat."

This sounded bad to Dapple, but she was determined to learn. Maybe there was more to comedy than she had realized.

They made camp by the side of the road. Manif slept in the cart, along with another actor: a man of twenty-five or so, not bad looking. The rest of them pitched a tent. Dapple got an outside place, better for privacy, but also wetter. The rain kept falling. In the cart, Manif and his companion made noise.

"Into the *halin*, I notice," said one of Dapple's companions.

"And one another," a second man added.

The third man said, "D'you think he'll go after Dapple here?"

It was possible, thought Dapple, that she'd done something stupid. Cholkwa had warned her about the south.

"He won't if Dapple finds himself a lover quickly," said the first man.

This might have been a joke, rather than an offer. Dapple couldn't tell. She curled up, her back to the others, hoping that no one would touch her. In time, she went to sleep.

The next day was clear, though the ground remained wet. They ate breakfast, then struck the tent and continued inland. The change in weather made Dapple more cheerful. Maybe the men would make no advances. If they did, she'd find a way to fend them off. They might be shabby and half as good as Perig and Cholkwa, but they didn't seem to be monsters or savages; and this wasn't the far north, where a war had gone on for generations, unraveling everything. People on this continent understood right behavior.

As she thought this, one of the *tsina* screamed and reared. An arrow was stuck in its throat.

"Bandits!" cried Manif and shook the reins, crying, "Go, go," to the animals.

But the shot animal stumbled, unable to continue; and the second *tsin* began to lunge, trying to break free of the harness and its comrade. The actors pulled swords. Dapple dove into the edge-of-forest brush. Behind her was shouting. She scrambled up a hill, her heart beating like a hammer striking an anvil, though more quickly. Up and up, hoping the bandits would not follow. At last she stopped. Her heart felt as if it might break her chest; her lungs hurt; all her breath was gone. Below her on the road was screaming. Not the *tsin* any longer, she thought. This sound was men.

When she was able to breathe, she went on, climbing more slowly now. The screaming stopped. Had the bandits noticed her? Had they counted the company? Four of them had been walking, while Manif and his lover rode. But the lover had been lying in back, under the awning, apparently exhausted by his efforts of the night before. If the bandits had been watching, they might have seen only five people.

No way to tell. She continued up the hill, finally reaching a limestone bluff. There was a crack. She squeezed her way in, finding a narrow cave. There she stopped a second time, leaning against the wet rock, trying to control her breath. Somehow she'd managed to keep her bag. She dropped it at her feet and pulled her knife.

For the rest of the day, she waited, then through the night, dozing from time to time, waking suddenly. No one came. In the morning, she went down the hill, stopping often to listen. There was nothing to hear except wind in the foliage and small animals making their usual noises.

The road was empty, though there were ruts to show that a cart had passed by. Dapple saw no evidence that a fight had ever taken place. For a moment she stood with her mouth open, wondering. Had it been a dream? The attack and her flight from it? Or had the actors managed to drive off the bandits, then gone on, condemning her as a coward? Across the road, a bird took flight. Large and heavy, it was mottled black and white and green. Not a breed native to Helwar, but she knew it from her travels in the south. It ate everything, plant and animal, but had a special liking for carrion.

Dapple crossed the road. On the far side, beyond the bushes, was a hollow. Something lay there, covered by branches and handfuls of leaves. She moved one of the branches. Underneath was the shot *tsin*, dead as a stone; and underneath the *tsin* were the actors. She couldn't see them entirely, but parts protruded: a hand, a leg to the knee. One face—Manif's—stared up at her, fur matted with dark blood, one eye already gone.

Shaking, she replaced the branch, then sat down before she fell. For a while, she did nothing except rock, her arms around her knees, silent because she feared to mourn out loud.

Finally, she got up and uncovered the grave. There was no way for her to move the *tsin*'s huge body, but she climbed down next to it, touching the actors, making sure they were all dead. Everything she touched was lifeless. There was nothing in the grave except the corpses. The bandits had taken everything else: the cart, the surviving *tsin* and the company's belongings. There was no way to bury the actors properly. If she tried, she would be leaving evidence of her existence.

She climbed back out of the grave. Where should she go? Back to the harbor town? But the bandits had obviously been waiting along the road, and they might have gone back to waiting. If so, they were likely to be where they'd been before: somewhere to the east.

If they intended to set ambush farther west, surely they would have done a better job of covering the bodies. Birds had found them already. By tomorrow, this spot would be full of noisy, filthy eaters-of-carrion.

It's possible she wasn't thinking clearly in reasoning this out. Nonetheless, she decided to go west. According to Manif, there was a town less than a day's journey away: solid, fortified, and fond of acting. Slinging her bag over her shoulder, Dapple went on.

The road wound through a series of narrow valleys. After she had gone a short distance, she saw the cart ahead of her, motionless in the middle of the road. She glanced back, planning to run. Two men stood there, both holding swords. Goddess! Ahl glanced at the forest next to her. As she did so, a man stepped out of the blue-green shadow. He also held a sword.

"I should have gone east," said Dapple.

"Some of our cousins went in that direction. Most likely, you would have met them."

Was this the moment to reveal she was a woman? "Are you going to kill me?"

"That depends on what you do," the man said. "But I'd prefer not to."

The other bandits came close. There were four of them, all dressed in worn, stained clothing.

"He's handsome," said the youngest fellow, who had a bandage wrapped around one arm. "Worth keeping."

"For what purpose?" asked Dapple, feeling uneasy.

"We'll tell you later," said the man from the forest.

After that, they took her bag and knife, then tied her hands in front of her. The man with the injured arm took the rope's other end. "Come along, dear one. We have a long way to go before nightfall."

He led her off the road, onto a narrow path. Animals had made it, most likely. A second man followed. The others stayed behind.

The rest of the day they traveled through steep forest. Now and then, the path crossed a stream or went along a limestone outcropping. Dapple grew tired and increasingly afraid. She tried to reassure herself by thinking that men rarely killed women and that rape—of women by men, at least—was an almost unknown perversion.

But women rarely traveled alone. Obviously they came to little harm, if they stayed at home or traveled in large companies; and this was the south, the region where civilization ended; and these men were killers, as she had seen. Who could say what they might do?

For example, they might kill her before learning she was a woman. Was this the moment to tell them? She continued to hesitate, feeling ashamed by the idea of abandoning her disguise. She had wanted to be different. She had planned to fool other people by using her intelligence and skill. Now, at the first set-back, she was ready to give up.

What a finish to her ambitions! She might die in this miserable forest—like a hero in a play, though with less dignity.

Worst of all, she needed to urinate. She knew from Perig and Cholkwa that all actors drank only in moderation before they went on stage. But she hadn't thought that she'd be acting this afternoon. Her bladder was full and beginning to hurt.

Finally, she confessed her need.

"Go right ahead," one of her captors said, stopping by a tree.

"I'm modest and can't empty my bladder in front of other men."

"We won't watch," said the second bandit in a lying tone.

"Let me go behind those bushes and do it. You'll be able to see my head and shoulders. I won't be able to escape."

The bandits agreed, clearly thinking that she was some kind of fool. But who can explain the behavior of foreigners?

Dapple went behind the bushes. Now her childhood practice came in useful; unlike most women, she could urinate while standing up and not make a mess. From situations like these we learn to value every skill, unless it's clearly pernicious. Who can predict the future and say, this-and-such ability will never be of use? She rejoined the bandits, feeling an irrational satisfaction.

At nightfall, they came to a little stony valley far back in the hills. A stream ran out of it. They waded in through cold water. At the valley's end was a tall narrow cave. Firelight shone out. "Home at last!" said the bandit who held Dapple's rope.

They entered. The cave widened at once. Looking around, Dapple saw a large stone room. A fire burned in the middle. Around it sat women in ragged tunics. A few children chased each other, making shrill noises like the cries of birds. At the back of the cave were more openings, two or maybe three, leading farther in.

"What have you brought?" asked one of the women, lifting her head. The fur on the woman's face was white with age, and the lenses of her eyes were cloudy.

"A fine young man to impregnate your daughters," said the man holding the rope.

The old woman rose and came forward. Her body was solid, and she moved firmly, though with a cane. Bending close, she peered at Dapple, then felt an arm. "Good muscle. How old is he?"

"Tell her," the man said.

"Eighteen."

"Men are active at that age, no question, but I prefer someone older. Who knows anything about a lad of eighteen? He hasn't shown the world his nature. His traits may be good or bad."

"This is true, mother," said the man with the rope. "But we have to take what we get. This one is alive and healthy. Most likely, he can do what we need done."

Dapple thought of mentioning that she could not impregnate a female, but decided to wait.

"Come over to the fire," the old woman said. "Sit down and talk with me. I like to know who's fathering the children in our family."

Dapple obeyed. The man went with them. Soon she was on the stone floor, a bowl of beer next to her. In her hand was a piece of greasy meat, a gift from the old woman. Around her sat the rest of the family: thin women with badly combed fur. Most likely they had bugs. One held a baby. The rest of the children were older, ranging from a girl of four or five to a boy at the edge of adulthood. The boy was remarkably clean for a member of this family, and he had a slim grace-fulness that seemed completely out of place. The other children continued to run and scream, but he sat quietly among his female relatives, watching Dapple with eyes as yellow as resin.

The man, Dapple's captor, sat in back of her, out of sight, though when she moved her bound hands, she could feel him holding the rope.

There had been five families in these hills, the old woman said. None of them large or rich, but they survived, doing one thing or another.

Five lineages of robbers, thought Dapple.

"We all interbred, till we were close kin, but we remained separate families, so we could continue to interbreed and find lovers. The rest of the families in this region never liked us and would have nothing to do with us. We had no one except each other."

Definitely robbers.

In the end, the large and powerful families in the region combined against the five. One by one, they were destroyed. It was done in the usual way: the men were killed, the women and children adopted.

"But our neighbors, the powerful ones, never allowed any of the people they adopted to breed. They would not let women and children starve, but neither would they let traits like ours continue. We were poisoned and poisonous, they said.

"Imagine what it was like for those women and children! It's one thing for a woman to lose her family name and all her male relatives. That can be endured. But to know that nothing will continue, that her children will die without chil-dren! Some of the women fled into the hills and died alone. Some were found by us. We took them in, of course, and bred them when we could. But where could we find fathers? The men who should have impregnated our daughters—and the women we adopted—were dead.

"We are the last of the five families: more women than men, all of us poor and thin, with no one to father the next generation, except travelers like you.

"But we refuse to give up! We won't let rich and arrogant folk make us vanish from the world!"

Dapple thought while drinking her beer. "Why did your men kill the rest of our acting company? There were five more—all male, of course, and older than I am."

The bandit matriarch peered past Dapple. "Six men? And you brought only *one?*"

"They fought," said the man behind Dapple, his voice reluctant. "We became angry."

The matriarch hissed, a noise full of rage.

"One other is still alive," the man added. "My brothers will bring him along later."

"You wanted to rape him," said the matriarch. "What good do you think he'll be, after you finish? Selfish, selfish boys! Your greed will destroy us!"

Obviously, she had miscounted, when she climbed into the actors' grave. Who was still alive? Not Manif. She'd seen him clearly. Maybe his lover, who was young and handsome.

"Don't blame *me*," said the man sullenly. "I'm not raping anyone. I'm here with this lad, and I haven't touched him. As for the other man, he'll still be usable. No one wants to make you angry."

The matriarch scratched her nose. "I'll deal with that problem when your brothers and male cousins return. In the meantime, tie up this man. I need to decide who should mate with him."

"Why should I do this?" asked Dapple. "There is no breeding contract between your family and mine. No decent man has sex with a woman, unless it's been arranged by his relatives and hers."

"We will kill you, if you don't!" said the man behind Dapple.

"What will you do if I agree to do this very improper thing?"

The people around the fire looked uneasy.

"One thing at a time," said the matriarch. "First, you have to make one of our women pregnant. Later, we'll decide what to do with you."

Dapple was led into another cave, this one small and empty except for a pallet on the floor and an iron ring set in the wall. Her captor tied her rope to the ring and left her. She sat down. Firelight came from the main cave, enough to light her prison. She tried to loosen the knots that held her. No luck. A cold draft blew down on her. At first, she thought it was fear. Glancing up, she saw a hole that led to starlight. Too far for her to reach, even if she could manage to free herself, and most likely too small to climb through. Only a few stars were visible. One was yellow and very bright: the Eye of Uson. It made her think of Manif's one eye. How was she going to escape this situation? The hole seemed unreachable, and the only other route was past the main cavern, full of bandits; and she was tired, far too tired to think. Dapple lay down and went to sleep.

She woke to feel a hand shaking her. Another hand was over her mouth.

"Don't make any noise," a voice whispered.

She moved her head in a gesture of agreement. The hand over her mouth lifted. Cautiously, she sat up.

The fire in the main cave still burned, though more dimly. Blinking, she made out a slim figure. She touched an arm. The fur felt smooth and clean. "You are the boy."

"A man now. Fifteen this spring. Are you really an actor?"

"Yes."

"My father was one. They told me about him: a handsome man, who told jokes and juggled anything: fruit, stones, knives, though they never let him have sharp knives. After he made my mother pregnant, they kept him to impregnate another woman and because they enjoyed his company. But instead of doing as they planned, he escaped. They say, they'll never trust another foreigner — or keep a man alive so long that he knows his way through the caves. His name was Cholkwa. Have you ever heard of him?"

Dapple laughed quietly.

"What does *that* mean?" asked the boy.

"I've known him all my life. He stays at my family's house when he's on Helwar Island. Though he has never mentioned meeting your kin, at least when I was around."

"Maybe we weren't important to him," the boy said in a sad tone.

Most likely, Cholkwa kept silent out of shame. His own family was far to the north, across the Narrow Ocean, and she'd never heard him speak about any of them. Maybe he had no relatives left. There'd been war in the north for generations now. Sometimes it flared up; at other times it died to embers, but it never entirely ended; and many lineages had been destroyed.

He was a decent man, in spite of his lack of kin. How could he admit to breeding without a contract arranged by the senior women in his family? How could he admit to leaving a child who was related to him—granted, not closely, but a relative nonetheless—in a place like this?

"Will your relatives kill me?" Dapple asked.

"Once you have made one of my cousins pregnant, yes."

"Why are you here with me?"

"I wanted to know about my father." The boy paused. "I wanted to know what lies beyond these hills."

"What good will it do for you to know?"

There was silence for a while. "When I was growing up, my mother told me about Cholkwa, his stories and jokes and tricks. There are cities beyond the hills, he told her, and boats as big as our cave that sail on the ocean. The boats go from city to city, and there are places—halls and open spaces—where people go to see acting. In those places, Cholkwa is famous. Crowds of people come to see him perform the way he did for my family in this cave. Are these stories true?"

"Yes," said Dapple. "Everywhere he goes, people are charmed by him and take pleasure in his skill. No actor is more famous." She paused, trying to think of what to say next. The Goddess had given this boy to her; she must find a way to turn him into an ally. "He has no kin on this side of the ocean. Most likely, he would enjoy meeting you."

"Fathers don't care about their children, and we shouldn't care about them. Dead or alive, they do nothing for us."

"This isn't true," said Dapple with quiet anger. "Obviously, it makes sense for a child to stay with her mother and be raised by maternal kin. A man can't nurse a baby, after all; and few mothers could bear to be separated from a small child. But the connection is still there. Most men pay some attention to their children, especially their sons. If something happens to the maternal lineage or to the relationship between a woman and her family, the paternal lineage will often step in. My mother is from Sorg, but she quarreled with her kin and fled to my father's family, the Helwar. They adopted her and me. Such things occur."

"Nothing has happened to my family," the boy said. "And my mother never quarreled with them, though she wasn't happy living here. I know that."

"Your family is not fit to raise children," said Dapple. "You seem to have turned out surprisingly well, but if you stay with them, they'll make you a criminal, and then you'll be trapped here. Do you really want to spend your life among thieves and people who breed without a contract? If you leave now and seek out Cholkwa, it may be possible for you to have a decent life."

The boy was silent for a moment, then exhaled and stood. "I have to go. They might wake."

A moment later, she was alone. She lay for a while, wondering if the boy would help her or if there was another way to escape. When she went back to sleep, she dreamt of Cholkwa. He was on a stage, dressed in bright red armor. His eyes were yellow and shone like stars. Instead of acting, he stood in a relaxed pose, holding a wooden sword loosely. "All of this is illusion and lies," he told her, gesturing at the stage. "But there's truth behind the illusion. If you are going to act, you need to know what's true and what's a lie. You need to know which lies have truth in back of them."

Waking, she saw a beam of sunlight shining through the hole in her ceiling. For a moment, the dream's message seemed clear and important. As she sat up, it began to fade and blur, though she kept the image of Cholkwa in his crimson armor.

One of the bandit males came and untied her. Together they went out, and she relieved herself behind bushes.

"I've never known anyone so modest," the bandit said. "How are you going to get a woman pregnant, if you can't bare yourself in front of a man?"

A good question, Dapple thought. Her disguise couldn't last much longer. Maybe she ought to end it. It didn't seem likely that the boy would help her; people didn't turn against their kin, even kin like these; and as long as the bandits thought she was a man, they might do anything. No rules protect a man who falls into the hands of enemies. She might be dead, or badly injured, before they realized she wasn't male. But something, a sense of foreboding, made her reluctant to reveal her true nature.

"We have sex in the dark," she told the bandit.

"That can be managed," he replied. "Though it seems ridiculous."

Dapple spent the rest of the day inside, alone at first, in a corner of the cave. The other bandits did not return, and the matriarch looked increasingly grim. Her kin sent their children outside to play. The men were gone as well. Those who remained—a handful of shabby women—worked quietly, giving the matriarch anxious glances. Clearly this was someone who could control her family! A pity that the family consisted of criminals.

At last, the old woman gestured. "Come here, man. I want to know you better."

Dapple settled by the fire, which still burned, even in the middle of a bright day. This wasn't surprising. The cave was full of shadows, and the air around them was cool and damp.

Instead of asking questions, the woman grumbled. It was hard work holding together a lineage, especially when all the neighboring families were hostile, and she got little help. Her female relatives were slovenly. "My eyes may be failing, but I can still smell. This place stinks like a midden heap!" Her male kin were selfish and stupid. "Five men! And they have brought me *one*, with another promised, though I'll believe in him when he appears!"

All alone, she labored to continue her line of descent, though only one descendant seemed really promising, the boy who'd been fathered by an actor. "A fine lad. Maybe there's something potent about the semen of actors. I hope so."

Evening came. The missing bandits did not appear. Finally the old woman looked at Dapple. "It seems our hopes rest in your hands—or if not in your hands, then in another part of your body. Is there a woman you prefer?"

Dapple glanced around. Figures lurked in the shadows, trying to avoid the matriarch's glance. Hard to see, but she knew what was there. "No."

"I'll pick one, then."

"There is something you ought to know," Dapple said.

The old woman frowned at her.

"I can't impregnate a woman."

"Many men find the idea of sex with women distasteful," the matriarch said. "But they manage the task. Surely your life is worth some effort. I promise you, you'll die if you don't try."

"I'm a woman," said Dapple. "This costume is a disguise."

"Ridiculous," the matriarch said. "Decent women don't wear men's clothing or travel with actors."

"I didn't say I was a decent woman. I said I was female and unable to father children. Don't you think—since I can't help you—you ought to let me go?"

"No matter what you are, we can't let you go," said the matriarch. "You might lead people to this cave." Then she ordered her kin to examine Dapple.

Three shabby women moved in. Standing, Dapple pulled off her tunic and underpants.

"No question about it," one of the women said. "She is female."

"What wretched luck!" cried the matriarch. "What have I done to deserve this kind of aggravation? And what's wrong with you, young woman, running around in a tunic and tricking people? Have you no sense of right behavior?"

There were more insults and recriminations, mostly from the old woman, though the others muttered agreement. What inhospitable and unmannerly folk! Dapple could hardly have fallen into a worse situation, though they weren't likely to kill her, now that they knew she was a woman.

At last, the matriarch waved a hand. "Tie her up for the night. I need to think."

Once again, Dapple found herself in the little side cave, tied to an iron ring. As on the previous night, stars shone through the hole in the ceiling, and firelight came down the corridor from the main cave, along with angry voices. Her captors were arguing. At this distance she couldn't make out words, but there was no mistaking the tone.

This time she made a serious effort to untie the rope that held her. But her hands had been fastened together, and her fingers couldn't reach the knot. Gnawing proved useless. The rope was too thick and strong. Exhausted, she began to doze. She woke to a touch, as on the night before.

"Is it you again?" she asked in a whisper.

"My grandmother has chosen me to impregnate you," said the boy, sounding miserable.

"What do you mean?"

"If you can't father children on our women, then we'll father children on *you* and adopt the children, as you were adopted by your father's family. That plan will do as well as the first one, Grandmother says. The others say she's favoring me, but I don't want to do this."

"Breed without a contract? What man would? What are you going to do?"

"Have sex with you, though I've never had sex with anyone. But Grandmother has explained how it's done."

"You have reached a moment of decision," said Dapple. "If you make the wrong choice now, your life will lead to ruin, like the life of a protagonist in a hero play."

"What does that mean?"

"If you have sex with me against my will, and without a contract arranged by my female relatives, you will be a criminal forever. But if you set me free, I will lead you to your father."

"I have a knife," said the boy uncertainly. "I could cut you free, but there's no way out except through the main cave."

Dapple lifted her head, indicating the hole in the ceiling.

The boy gazed up at the stars. "Do you think you could get through?"

"I'd be willing to try, if there's no other way. But how do we reach it?"

"Standing on my shoulders won't do. It's too far up. But I could go outside and lower a rope. Can you climb one?"

"I've worked as a sailor," said Dapple. "Of course I can."

"I could tell them I need to urinate. I know where there's a rope. It could be done. But if they catch us—"

"If you stay here and do this thing, you will be a thief. Your children will be thieves. You'll never see the cities beyond these hills or the ships as big as caves."

The boy hesitated, then pulled his knife and cut Dapple free. "Wait here," he said fiercely, and left.

She rubbed her hands and wrists, then stood and stretched. Hah! How stiff she was!

Voices rose in the main cave, mocking the boy, then dropped back to a murmur. She began to watch the hole.

After a while, a dark shape hid the stars. A rope dropped toward her. Dapple grasped it and tugged. It held. She took off her tunic and tied it to the bottom of the rope, then began her climb, going hand over hand up the rope. Cold air blew past her, ruffling the fur on her arms and shoulders. It smelled of damp soil and forest. Freedom, thought Dapple. A moment or two later, she reached the hole. Hah! It was narrow! As bad as she had feared!

"Can you make it?" the boy whispered.

"I have to," Dapple said and continued to climb.

Her head was no problem, but her shoulders were too wide. Rough stone scraped against them. She kept on, trying to force her body through the opening. All at once, she realized that she was stuck, like a piece of wax used to seal the narrow neck of a jar. Dapple groaned with frustration.

"Be quiet," whispered the boy and began to pull, leaning far back, all his weight on the rope. For a moment, she remained wedged in the hole. Then her shoulders were through, though some of her fur remained behind. Her elbows dug into dirt. She pushed up. The boy continued to pull, and Dapple popped into freedom. She stretched out on the damp ground, face down, smelling dirt, the forest, and the night wind.

"You have no clothing on!" the boy exclaimed.

"I took my tunic off," said Dapple. "I knew the fit would be tight."

"You can't travel like this!"

She pulled the rope out of the hole, retrieving her tunic and putting it on.

"Better," said the boy, though he still sounded embarrassed.

He had wrapped his end of the rope to a tree. She undid the knots and coiled the rope. "A knife, a rope, and four sound feet. I'd like more, but this will have to do. Let's go."

They set off through the forest, the boy leading, since he had good night vision, and this was his country.

"When will they discover that we are missing?" Dapple asked after a while.

"In the morning. Tonight they'll drink and tell each other rude stories about sex. Grandmother gave permission. It's lucky to do this, when people breed."

It was never lucky to breed without a contract, Dapple thought, but said nothing. How was this boy going to survive in the outside world, knowing so little about how to behave? She'd worry about that problem when both of them were safe.

They traveled all night. In spite of the boy's keen eyes, the two travelers stumbled often and hit themselves against branches, sometimes thorny. No one living in a town can imagine the darkness of a forest, even when the sky above the trees is full of stars. Certainly Dapple had not known, living in a harbor town. How she longed for an ocean vista, open and empty, with starlight glinting off the waves!

At dawn, they stopped and hid in a ravine. Water trickled at the bottom. Birds cried in the leaves, growing gradually quiet as the day grew warmer. Exhausted, the two young people dozed. Midway through the morning, voices woke them: men, talking loudly and confidently as they followed a nearby trail. The boy peered out. "It's my relatives," he said.

"Is anyone with them?" asked Dapple fearfully. What would they do, if one of the actors had survived and was a prisoner? It would be unbearable to leave the man with savages, but if she and the boy tried to free the man, they would be killed or taken prisoner like him.

"No," said the boy after a while. "They must have killed him, after they finished raping him. My grandmother will be so angry!"

These people were both monsters and fools. Was there anything she could learn from the situation? Maybe the nature of monsters, if she ever had to portray a monster in a play. The nature of monsters, Dapple thought as she crouched in the ravine, was folly. That was the thing she had to concentrate on, not her own sense of fear and horror.

After a while, the boy said, "They're gone. I didn't expect them to come this direction. But now that they've passed us, we'd better put as much distance as possible between us and them."

They rose and went on. Shortly thereafter, they found the robbers' camp: a forest clearing with the remains of a fire and Dapple's last companion, Manif's lover. He must have endured as much as he could, then fought back. There were various wounds, which Dapple did not look at closely, and a lot of blood, which had attracted bugs.

"Dead," said the boy. "They should have buried him, but we can't take the time."

Dapple went to the edge of the clearing and threw up, then covered her vomit with forest debris. Maybe the robbers wouldn't find it, if they came back this way. Though the moist ground should tell the bandits who'd been here.

The boy must have thought the same thing. After that, they traveled through streams and over rocks. It was a hard journey.

Late in the afternoon, they descended into a valley. At the bottom was a larger-than-usual stream. The forest canopy was less thick than before. Sunlight speckled the ground. "We are close to the border of our country," the boy said. "From this point on, it will be best to follow trails."

One ran along the stream, narrow, and used more by animals than people, Dapple thought. The travelers took it. After a while, a second stream joined the first. Together, they formed a river where small rapids alternated with pools. At sunset, turning a corner, they discovered a group of men swimming. Clothes and weapons lay on the riverbank.

The boy stopped suddenly. "Ettin."

"What?" asked Dapple.

"Our enemies," he answered, sounding fearful, then added, "The people I am bringing you to. Go forward. I cannot." He turned to go back the way they had come. Behind him the sky was sunset red; the boy's face was in shadow. Nonetheless, Dapple saw his mouth open and eyes widen.

A harsh voice said, "Neither can you go back, thief."

She turned as well. A man stood in the trail, short and broad with a flat ugly face. A metal hat covered the top of his head and was fastened under his chin with a leather strap. His torso was covered with metal-and-leather armor. A skirt made of leather strips hung to his knees. One hand held a sword, the blade bare and shining. She had never seen anyone who looked so unattractive.

"Who are you?" she asked.

"A guard. You can't believe that men of Ettin would bathe without posting guards."

"I'm from the north," said Dapple. "I know nothing about Ettin, which I imagine is your lineage."

He made a noise that indicated doubt. "The north? And this one as well?" The sword tip pointed at her companion.

"I was traveling with actors," Dapple said. "Robbers killed my comrades and took me prisoner. This lad rescued me and was guiding me to safety."

The guard made another noise that indicated doubt. Other men gathered. Some were guards out of the forest. The rest were bathers, their fur slick with water and their genitalia exposed. She knew what male babies and boys looked like, of course, but this was the first time she'd seen men. They weren't as big as she'd imagined, after Cholkwa's plays. Nonetheless, the situation was embarrassing. She glanced back at the first guard, meeting his eyes.

"Are you threatening me?" he asked.

"Of course not."

"Then look down! What kind of customs do you have in the north?"

She looked at the ground. The air smelled of wet fur. "What's this about?" the men asked. "What have you captured?"

"Some kind of foreigner, and a fellow of unknown lineage, though local, I think. They say they've escaped from the robbers."

"If done, it's well done," said a swimmer. "But they may be lying. Take them to our outpost, and let the captain question them. If they're spies, he'll uncover them."

Who is talking about uncovering? Dapple thought. A man with water dripping off him and his penis evident to anyone who cared to look! Not that she glanced in his direction. It was like being in an animal play, though maybe less funny.

Other men made noises of agreement. The swimmers went off to dry and dress. The men in armor tied Dapple's hands behind her back, then did the same for the boy. After that, they ran a second rope from Dapple's neck to the boy's neck. "You won't run far like this!" one said when the second rope was fastened.

"Is this any way to treat guests?" asked Dapple.

"You may be spies. If you are not, we'll treat you well. The Ettin have always been hospitable and careful."

Tied like animals going to market, they marched along the trail, which had grown wider and looked better-used. Half the men went with them. The rest stayed behind to guard the border.

Twilight came. They continued through darkness, though under an open sky. By this time, Dapple was dazed by lack of sleep. One of the guards took her arm, holding her upright and guiding her. "You're a pretty lad. If you are what you say, maybe we can keep company."

Another guard said, "Don't listen, stranger. You can do better than Hattin! If you are what you say."

Her male disguise was certainly causing problems, though she needed it, if she was going to learn acting. What was she learning now? Danger and fear. If she survived and made it home, she would think about specializing in hero plays.

Ahead of them gleamed firelight, shining from windows. A sword hilt knocked on a door. Voices called. Dapple could not understand what they were saying, but the door opened. Entering, she found herself in a courtyard made of stone. On one side was a stable, on the other side, a square stone tower.

She and the boy were led into the tower. The ground floor was a single room with a fireplace on one side. A man sat next to the fire in a high-backed wooden chair. His grey fur was silvered by age, and he was even uglier than his relatives.

"This is Ettin Taiin," said the guard named Hattin. "The man who watches this border, with our help."

The man rose and limped forward. He'd lost an eye, though not recently, and did not bother to hide the empty socket. "Poor help you are!" he said, in a voice like stone grating against stone. "Nonetheless, I manage." He looked directly at Dapple. The one eye that remained was bright blue; the pupil expanded in the dim light, so it lay across his iris like a black iron bar across the sky. "Who are you, and what are you doing in the land I watch?"

She told her story a second time.

"That explains *you*," said Ettin Taiin. "And I'm inclined toward belief. Your accent is not local, nor is your physical type, though you are certainly lovely in a foreign way. But this lad"—He glared at the boy—"looks like a robber."

The boy whimpered, dropping to the floor and curling like a frightened *tli*. Because they were tied together, Dapple was pulled to her knees. She looked at the border captain. "There is more to the story. I am not male!"

"What do you mean?" asked Ettin Taiin, his voice harsher than before.

"I wanted to be an actor, and women are not allowed to act."

"Quite rightly!" said the captain.

"I disguised myself as a young man and joined a company here in the south, where no one knows me, and where I'm not likely to meet actors I know, such as Perig and Cholkwa."

"Cholkwa is here right now," said the captain, "visiting my mother and her sisters. What a splendid performer he is! I nearly ruptured myself laughing the last time I saw him. If he knows you, then he can speak for you; *I* am certainly not going to find out whether or not you're female. My mother raised me properly."

"An excellent woman," murmured the guards standing around.

"When the robbers captured me, I told them I was female, and they told this lad to impregnate me."

"With no *contract?* Without the permission of your female relatives?" The stony voice was full of horror.

"Obviously," said Dapple. "My relatives are on Helwar Island, far to the north."

"You see what happens when women run off to foreign places, without the protection of the men in their family?" said the captain. "Not that this excuses the robbers in any way. We've been lax in letting them survive. Did he do it?"

The boy, still curled on the floor, his hands over his head, made a keening noise. The guards around her exhaled, and Dapple thought she heard the sound of swords moving in their scabbards.

"No," Dapple said. "He got me out of prison and brought me here. That's the end of the story."

"Nasty and shocking!" said the captain. "We will obviously have to kill the rest of the robber men, though it won't be easy to hunt them down. The children can be adopted, starting with this lad. He looks young enough to keep. The women are a problem. I'll let my female relatives deal with it, once we have captured the women. I only hope I'm not forced into acts that will require me to commit suicide after. I'm younger than I look and enjoy life!"

"We'd all prefer to stay alive," said Hattin.

"Untie them," said the captain, "and put them in separate rooms. In the morning, we'll take them to my mother."

The guards pulled the two of them upright and cut their ropes. The captain limped back to his chair. "And feed them," he added as he settled and picked up a cup. "Give the woman my best *halin*."

Leading them up a flight of stairs, Hattin said, "If you're a woman, then I apologize for the suggestion I made. Though I wasn't the *only* one who thought you'd make a good bedmate! Ettin Taiin is going to be hearing jokes about that for years!"

"You tease a man like him?" asked Dapple.

"I don't, but the senior men in the family do. The only way someone like that is tolerable, is if you can embarrass him now and then."

Her room had a lantern, but no fire. It wasn't needed on a mild spring night. Was the man downstairs cold from age or injuries? The window was barred, and the only furniture was a bed. Dapple sat down. The guards brought food and drink and a pissing pot, then left, locking the door. She ate, drank, pissed, and went to sleep.

In the morning, she woke to the sound of nails scratching on her door. A man's voice said, "Make yourself ready." Dapple rose and dressed. The night before, she'd unbound her breasts in order to sleep comfortably. She didn't rebind them now. The tunic was thick enough to keep her decent; her breasts weren't large enough to need support, and the men of Ettin were treating her like a woman. Better to leave the disguise behind, like a shell outgrown by one of the animals her male relatives pulled from the sea.

Guards escorted her and the boy downstairs. There were windows on the ground floor, which she hadn't noticed the night before. Shutters open, they let in sunlight. The Ettin captain stood at a table covered with maps. "Good morning," he said. "I'm trying to decide how to trap the robbers. Do you have any suggestions, lad? And what is your name?"

"Rehv," the boy said. "I never learned to read maps. And I will not help you destroy my family!"

Ettin Taiin rolled the maps—they were paper, rather than the oiled leather her people used—and put them in a metal tube. "Loyalty is a virtue. So is directness. You'll make a fine addition to the Ettin lineage; and I'll decide how to destroy *your* lineage later. Today, as I told you before, we'll ride to my mother."

They went out and mounted *tsina*, the captain easily in spite of his lame leg, Dapple and the boy with more difficulty.

"You aren't riders," said Ettin Taiin. "And that tells me your families don't have many *tsina*. Good to know, for when I hunt the robbers down."

They spent the day riding, following a narrow road through forested hills. A small group of soldiers accompanied them, riding as easily as the captain and joking among themselves. Now and then they saw a cabin. "Hunters and trappers," said Ettin Taiin. "There are logging camps as well. But no women. The robbers are too close. Time and time again we've tried to clean them out, but they persist, growing ever more inbred and nasty."

Riding next to her, the boy shivered, hair rising on his arms and shoulders. Now that she was apparently safe, Dapple felt pity and respect for him. He'd been confronted by the kind of decision a hero faces in a play. Should he side with his kin or with right behavior? A man without kin was like a tree without roots. The slightest wind would push him over. A man without morality was like—what? A tree without sunlight and rain.

In most cases, hero plays ended in death. It was the easiest resolution. Unable to make a definite choice, the hero blundered through a series of half-actions and mistakes, until he was killed by enemies or friends, and the audience exhaled in relief. May the Goddess keep them from this kind of situation!

Most likely, the boy would live to see his relatives die, while he was adopted by the Ettin. It was the right ending for the story of a child. Their duty was to live and grow and learn. Honor belonged to older people. Nonetheless, the story disturbed Dapple, as did the boy's evident unhappiness and fear.

Late in the afternoon, they entered a wide flat valley. The land was cultivated. The buildings scattered among fields and orchards were made of planks rather than logs. Many were painted: blue-grey, green, or white.

"Barns," said the Ettin captain. "Stables. Houses for herdsmen."

She was back in the ordinary world of people who understood rules, though she wasn't certain the Ettin followed the rules she had learned on Helwar Island. Still, the pastures were fenced, the fields plowed in straight lines, and the orchard trees — covered with pale orange blossoms — were orderly.

They reached the captain's home as the sun went down. It was a cluster of buildings made of wood and stone, next to a river crossed by a stone bridge. The lower stories had no windows, and the doors were iron-bound. Built for defense, but no enemies were expected today. The largest door was open. Riding through it, they entered a courtyard surrounded by balconies. Children played in the early evening shadows, though Dapple couldn't make out the game; it stopped the moment they appeared.

"Uncle Taiin!" cried several voices.

The captain swung down stiffly and was surrounded by small bodies.

"An excellent man," said one of the guards to Dapple. "Affectionate with children, respectful toward women, and violent toward other men."

"Even men of your family?" Dapple asked.

"We win, and most of us come home; we don't expect kindness from a leader on campaign."

A woman came into the courtyard, tall and broad, wearing a sleeveless robe. Age had whitened her face and upper arms. She carried a staff and leaned on it, but her head was erect, her blue eyes as bright as a polished blade.

The children fell silent and moved away from their uncle. He lifted his head, looked straight at the old woman, and gave her a broad, boyish grin. Beyond question, this was his mother. Could actors replicate this moment? No. Children were not used in plays, and everything here was small and quiet: the man's grin, the woman's brief returning smile.

"Taiin," she said in greeting. Nothing more, but the voice rang — it seemed to Dapple — with joy. Her steel blue eyes flashed toward Dapple and the boy. "Tell me the names of our guests."

He did, adding, "The girl, if this *is* a girl, says that Cholkwa the actor will speak for her. The boy is almost old enough to be killed, but if he saved her, then he's worth saving."

"I will form my own judgment," said the matriarch. "But she's clearly a girl."

"Are you certain?"

"Use your *eye*, Taiin!"

He obeyed with a slow sideways look. "She does seem more feminine than she did yesterday. But I'd be happier if she had on female clothing. Then, maybe, I could see her as a woman entirely. Right now, she seems to shift back and forth. It's very disturbing!"

"I'll give her a bath and new clothes," said the matriarch with decision. "You take care of the boy."

Dapple dismounted. The old woman led her through shadowy halls to a court-yard with two pools built of stone. Steps led down into each. One seemed ordinary enough, the water in it colorless and still; but the other was full of bright green water. Steam rose from its surface; the air around it had an unfamiliar, slightly unpleasant odor.

"It comes from the ground like this," said the matriarch. "We bring it here through pipes. The heat is good for old bones, stiff muscles, and the kind of injuries my son Taiin has endured. Undress! Climb in!"

Dapple obeyed, pulling off her tunic. The matriarch exhaled. "A fine-looking young woman, indeed! A pity that you won't be bred!"

Because she had bad traits. Well, she didn't mind. She had never wanted to be a mother, only an actor. Dapple entered the steaming water, sinking until she was covered. Hah! It was pleasant, in spite of the aroma! She stretched out and looked up. Though shadows filled the courtyard, the sky above was full of light. A cloud like a feather floated there. Last night, she'd slept in a guard house. The night before, she'd scrambled through a dark forest; and before that, she'd been in a cave full of robbers. Now she was back in a proper house—not entirely like her home, but close enough.

Women appeared, bringing a chair for the matriarch, and a clothing rack, on which they hung new clothes for Dapple. Then they left. The matriarch sat down, laying her staff on the court's stone floor. "Why did you disguise yourself as a man?"

Dapple told her story, floating in the steaming pool. The old woman listened with obvious attention. When the story was done, she said, "We've been negligent. We should have cleared those people out years ago. But I—and my sisters and our female cousins—didn't want to adopt the robber women. They'll be nothing but trouble!"

This was true, thought Dapple, remembering the women in the cave, especially the robber matriarch. That was not a person who'd fit herself quietly into a new household. Hah! She would struggle and plot!

"But something will have to be done. We can't let these folk rob and murder and force men to breed. No child should come into existence without the agreement of two families. No man should become a father without a proper contract. We are not animals! I'm surprised at Cholkwa. Surely it would be better to die, than to reproduce in this fashion."

She might have agreed before her recent experiences; but now, life seemed precious, as did Cholkwa and every person she knew and liked. If he had refused to cooperate with the robbers, she would have lost him when she barely knew him; and the boy who saved her would never have come into existence. The thought of her fate without the boy was frightening.

Maybe none of this would have happened, if Cholkwa had died before she saw him act. Without him, she might have been content to stay in Helwar. Hardly likely! She would have seen Perig, and he was the one she wanted to imitate. Comedy was fine. Cholkwa did it beautifully. But she didn't want to spend her life making rude jokes.

Nor did she want to do exactly what *Perig* did. His heroes were splendid. When they died, she felt grief combined with joy. They were so honorable! Perig had so much skill! But her recent experiences suggested that real death was nothing like a play. Manif and his comrades would not rise to shouts of praise. Their endings had been horrible and final and solved nothing. *Death* was the problem here, rather than the problem's solution. Why had they died? Why was she alive? Were tragedy and comedy the only alternatives? Did one either die with honor or survive in an embarrassing costume?

These were difficult questions, and Dapple was too young to have answers, maybe too young to ask the questions clearly. But something like these ideas, though possibly more fragmentary, floated in her mind as she floated in the steaming pool.

"That's enough heat," the matriarch said finally. "It will make you dizzy, if you stay too long. Go to the second pool and cool down!"

Dapple obeyed, pausing on the way to pick up a ball of soap. This water was pleasant too. Not cold, but cool, as the matriarch had suggested, and so very fresh! It must come from a mountain stream. The soap lathered well and smelled of herbs. She washed herself entirely, then rinsed. The robbers would stay in her mind, but the stink of their cave would be out of her fur. In time, her memories would grow less intense, though she didn't want to forget the boy—and was it right to forget Manif and the other actors?

She climbed out of the second pool. A towel hung on the clothing rack, also a comb with a long handle. She used both, then dressed. The young women in this country wore kilts and vests. Her kilt was dark blue, the fabric soft and fine. Her vest was made of thicker material, bright red with silver fasteners down the front. The Ettin had provided sandals as well, made of dark blue leather.

"Beyond question you are a handsome young woman," the matriarch said. "Brave and almost certainly intelligent, but far too reckless! What are we going to do with you?"

Dapple said nothing, having no answer. The matriarch picked up her staff and rose.

They went through more shadowy halls, coming finally to an open door. Beyond was a terrace made of stone. A low wall ran along the far side. Beyond the wall was the river that ran next to the house, then pastures rising toward wooded hills. Everything was in shadow now, except the sky and the very highest hill tops. Two men sat on the terrace wall, conversing: Ettin Taiin and Cholkwa. The robber boy stood nearby, looking far neater and cleaner than before. Like Dapple, he wore new clothes: a kilt as brown as weathered bronze, and sandals with brass studs. Looking from him to Cholkwa, she could see a resemblance. Hah! The boy would be loved by many, when he was a little older!

"I have introduced Cholkwa to his son," Ettin Taiin said to his mother.

Cholkwa stood and made a gesture of greeting. His gaze met Dapple's briefly, then passed on as if she were a stranger. "What a surprise, Hattali! When I left the cave, running as quickly as possible, I did not know the woman was likely to produce a child."

"You should have come to us, as soon as you escaped," the matriarch said. "If we'd known what the robbers were doing, we would have dealt with them years ago. Do you know this young woman?"

"She is Helwar Ahl, the daughter of a family that's dear to me. A good young person, though Taiin tells me she has some crazy idea of becoming an actor."

"I told you that!" cried Dapple.

"*I* told you it was impossible! My life is dangerous and disreputable, Ahl. No woman should lead it!" He glanced toward the matriarch. "My stay with the robbers occurred during my first trip south. I didn't know your family, or much of anyone. After I escaped, I fled to the coast and took the first ship I could find going north. Hah! I was frightened and full of self-disgust! It was several years before I came south again. By then, I had convinced myself that the woman could not have been pregnant. I half-believed the story was a dream, caused by a southern fever. How could I think that such people were possible and real?"

"I am," said the boy. "We are."

"Think of the men who have died because you did not tell your story!" the matriarch said to Cholkwa. "Think of the children who have been raised by criminals! How can they possibly turn out well? What kind of person would turn away from children in such a situation?"

Cholkwa was silent for a moment, then said, "I have no excuse for my behavior. I did what I did."

"Remember that he makes his living as a comic actor," said the Ettin captain. "How can we judge a man who spends his time portraying small animals with large sexual organs? Let's put these long-past happenings off to the side. We have enough problems in the present."

"This is true," said the matriarch. "For one thing, I need a chair."

"I'll tend to that," said Cholkwa and hurried off.

The captain, still lounging comfortably on the wall, glanced at his mother. "Have you decided how to deal with the robbers?"

The old woman groaned, leaning on her staff and looking morose. "You will have to kill the men, and we will have to adopt the women and children, though I do not look forward to having females like these in our houses."

"This is a relief! I thought, knowing your opinion of the robber women, that you might ask me to kill them."

"Would you do it?"

"If you told me to, yes."

"And then what?"

"Why ask, Mother? The answer is obvious. I have always wanted to be famous, not infamous. If I had to do something so dishonorable, there would be no alternative left except suicide!"

"This is what I expected," the matriarch said. "Listening to Helwar Ahl's story, I asked myself, 'What is worse? Taiin's death, or a house full of unruly women?' No one should have to make such a decision! But I have made it, and I will endure the consequences."

"Be more cheerful! If you spread the women out among many houses, they may not be much of an aggravation."

"We'll see. But I'm glad to know that you are an honorable man, Taiin, though it means your old mother will suffer."

"Think of the pleasure you'll be able to take in my continued survival," the captain said. "Not every mother of your age has a living son, especially one with my excellent moral qualities."

What a fine pair they were, thought Dapple. She could see them in a play: the fierce soldier and his indomitable parent, full of love and admiration for each other. In a hero play, of course, the captain would die and the matriarch mourn. Hah! What a sight she would be, alone on a stage, standing over the captain's body!

Women came onto the terrace with chairs and lanterns. The matriarch settled herself. "Bring food!"

"Now?" asked a middle-aged woman. "When you are with company?"

"Bring food for them as well," said the matriarch.

"Mother!" said the captain.

"I'm too old and hungry to care about that kind of propriety. Manners and morality are not the same."

The rest of them sat down, all looking uneasy. The women brought food. Dapple discovered she was ravenous, as was the boy, she noticed. The two men poured themselves cups of *halin*, but touched no food. The matriarch ate sparingly. It wasn't as bad as Dapple had expected, since no one spoke. This wasn't like a pack of carnivores snarling over their downed prey, or like the monsters in old stories who chattered through mouths full of people. This meal was like travelers in a tavern, eating together because they had to, but quickly and in decent silence.

Soon enough they were done. The matriarch took a cup of *halin* from her son. "One problem has been solved. We will adopt the robber women. Cholkwa's behavior will be forgotten. My son is right! We have no ability to judge such a man, and Taiin—I know—wants to keep Cholkwa as a friend."

"This is true," said the captain.

"Only one problem remains: the girl, Helwar Ahl."

"No," said the robber boy. "I also am a problem." He glanced at Cholkwa. "I don't want to stay here and watch these people kill my male relatives. Take me with you! I want to see foreign harbors and ships as large as caves!"

Cholkwa frowned. For a moment, there was silence.

Ettin Taiin refilled his cup. "This might be a good idea for two reasons. The boy is likely to suffer from divided loyalties. That's always a problem when one adopts a child as old as he is. And I find him attractive. If he stays here and becomes Ettin, I will be troubled with incestuous thoughts. As much as possible, I try to keep my mind free of disturbing ideas. They cause sleepless nights on campaign and slow reflexes in battle."

"What about Helwar Ahl?" asked Cholkwa, obviously trying to go from one topic to another.

"She can't go with you," the matriarch said. "A woman with an unrelated man! And we are not ocean sailors, nor are the other families in this region, the ones we trust. Take the boy, if he's going to give Taiin perverted ideas, and tell the girl's family, when you get north, that she's here with us. They can send a ship for her."

"I want to be an actor," said Dapple.

"You can't!" said Cholkwa.

The matriarch frowned. "There are two things that men cannot do. One is have babies, because it's impossible. The other is harm women and children, because it's wrong. And there are two things that women cannot do: father children and fight in a war. These are absolute prohibitions. All other kinds of behavior may be difficult or disturbing, but they *can* be done. Granted, I would not want a daughter of mine to become an actor, though it might help make plays more interesting. There are too many penises in comedy, and too many honorable deaths in tragedy. These are male interests. Maybe the world would benefit from a play about real life!"

"Surely you don't mean that, Mother," the Ettin captain said.

"You're a fine lad and my favorite child, but there is much you don't know. The world does not consist entirely of sex and violence. It isn't only men who take action, and there are kinds of action that do not involve violence or sex."

Dapple said, "I will run away again, I promise."

"From here?" asked the matriarch. "Surely you have learned how dangerous the south can be."

"From anywhere," said Dapple.

Ettin Hattali sipped *halin*. The others watched her. By this time, the sky was dark and full of stars, which shed enough light so that Dapple could see the old woman's pale face. "Life is made of compromises," Hattali said finally. "I will offer you one. Stay here until your family sends for you, and I will argue for you with them. You are useless for breeding already. A girl who runs off in all directions! This is not a trait any family will want to continue. I'll say as much and argue that the world needs women who speak for women, not just in our houses and the meetings between families, but everywhere, even in plays. Who knows where the current interest in drama will lead? Maybe—in time—plays will be written down, though this seems unlikely to me. But if they remain at all, in any form, as spoken words or memory, women should have a share in them. Do we want men to speak for us to future generations?

"Cholkwa, who has broken many rules before, can certainly break another one and teach you. If he wants the story of his behavior with the robbers kept quiet, if he wants to keep my son Taiin as a lover, he will cooperate."

Taiin and Cholkwa—lovers? For a moment, Dapple was distracted. This certainly explained why Taiin found the boy attractive. How could Cholkwa betray his longtime lover, Perig, for a lame man with one eye?

Her family's old friend sighed. "Very well, I'll take the boy. No question I behaved badly when I mated with his mother. To create life without a contract! It was shameful! And you are right that I should have told my story. Then he would have gotten a proper home as a baby. Now he is old enough to love and mourn those criminals. I will not leave him here to watch his family die." He paused.

"And I will take your message to the Helwar. But I don't like the idea of teaching the girl to act."

"If you don't do it, I will ask Perig, or run off in disguise again!"

"Have the young always been this much trouble?" Cholkwa asked.

"Always," said the matriarch in a firm tone.

The captain stood up. "My leg aches, and I want either sleep or sex. Take the boy north, so he doesn't bother me. Take the message, so my mother can be happy. Worry about teaching the girl next year."

The two men left, the boy following. He would be put in a room by himself, the captain said as they walked into the house. "It's been a hard few days for you, Rehv my lad; and I don't think you need to deal with Ettin boys."

Dapple was alone with the matriarch, under a sky patterned with darkness and light.

"He made me angry when he used the word 'can't' for a woman," Ettin Hattali said. "No man has the right to say what women can and cannot do. Hah! I am old, to lose my temper and talk about women acting! But I will keep our agreement, young Ahl. What I said about plays is true. They are fine in their way, but they do not tell *my* story. So many years, struggling to keep my family going toward the front! The purpose of life is not to have honor and die, it's to have honor and *survive*, and raise the next generation to be honorable. Who says *that* in any play?"

"I will," said Dapple and felt surprise. Was she actually going to become an actor and write plays? For the first time, her plan seemed possible rather than crazy. Maybe she wouldn't be dragged back to safety. Maybe, with the matriarch on her side, she could have the life she wanted.

The moment an idea becomes solid is the moment when another person reaches out and takes it in her grasp. How frightening this is! The fur on Dapple's shoulders rose. "Do you think Cholkwa will agree to teach me?"

"Most likely, when he gets used to the idea. He's a good man, though foreign, and we have been his hosts many times over. That is a bond—not equal to kinship, perhaps, but strong; and there is also a bond between Cholkwa and Taiin. You may not believe this of my son, but he can persuade."

They sat a while longer under the stars. A meteor fell, then another. Dapple's fur was no longer bristling. Instead, her spirit began to expand.

TWO KNOTS THAT TIE OFF THE STORY

Cholkwa took the boy as promised, and Rehv traveled with his father's acting company for several years. But he had no gift for drama and no real liking for travel. Finally, in one harbor town or another, he fell in love. The object of his desire was a glassblower who made floats for fishing nets: good plain work that brought in an adequate income. The two men settled down together. Rehv learned to make glass floats and went on to finer work: *halin* cups, pitchers for beer, bowls for holding sand or flowers.

Sometimes he made figures, cast rather than blown: actors, soldiers, matriarchs, robbers, decorated with gold and silver leaf. The actors' robes were splendid; the weapons held by the soldiers and robbers gleamed; only the matriarchs lacked decoration. They stood on the shelves of his lover's shop—as green as the ocean, as red as blood, as black as obsidian.

Most people knew he had been an actor and had settled down because of love. Only his lover knew the entire story. He had grown up amid desperation and craziness; through luck and his own actions, he had managed to achieve an ordinary life.

Dapple's relatives agreed to let her learn acting, and Perig agreed to teach her. She traveled with him for several years, accompanied by one of her male cousins, who ended by becoming an actor himself. In time, she established her own company, composed of women. She was always welcome in Ettin, and Ettin Hattali, who lived to be 110, attended Dapple's performances whenever possible, though toward the end she could no longer see the actors. She could still hear the voices, Hattali told her relatives; and they were the voices of women.

people came from earth

STEPHEN BAXTER

Like many of his colleagues writing near the beginning of the new century—Greg Egan comes to mind, as do people like Paul J. McAuley, Michael Swanwick, Iain M. Banks, Bruce Sterling, Pat Cadigan, Brian Stableford, Gregory Benford, Ian McDonald, Gwyneth Jones, Vernor Vinge, Greg Bear, David Marusek, Geoff Ryman, Alastair Reynolds, and a half dozen others—British writer Stephen Baxter has been engaged for the last ten years or so with the task of revitalizing and reinventing the "hard-science" story for a new generation of readers, producing work on the Cutting Edge of science which bristles with weird new ideas and often takes place against vistas of almost outrageously cosmic scope.

Baxter made his first sale to Interzone in 1987, and since then has become one of that magazine's most frequent contributors, as well as making sales to Asimov's Science Fiction, Science Fiction Age, Zenith, New Worlds, and elsewhere. He's one of the most prolific of the new writers of the past decade, and is also rapidly becoming one of the most popular and acclaimed of them. Baxter's first novel, Raft, was released in 1991 to wide and enthusiastic response, and was rapidly followed by other well-received novels such as Timelike Infinity, Anti-Ice, Flux, and the H. G. Wells pastiche The Time Ships (a sequel to The Time Machine), which won both the John W. Campbell Memorial Award and the Philip K. Dick Award. His other books include the novels Voyage, Titan, and Moonseed, and the collections Vacuum Diagrams: Stories of the Xeelee Sequence and Traces. His most recent books are the novels Mammoth, Book One: Silverhair and Manifold: Time. His stories have appeared in our Eleventh, Twelfth, Fourteenth, Fifteenth, and Sixteenth Annual Collections.

"People Came from Earth" takes us to a troubled future, to an embattled, desperate world dancing on the brink of extinction, for the autumnal story of people struggling to hold on to what they have . . . and perhaps even regain something of what has been lost.

At Dawn I stepped out of my house. The air frosted white from my nose, and the deep Moon chill cut through papery flesh to my spindly bones. The silver-gray light came from Earth and Mirror in the sky: twin spheres, the one milky cloud, the other a hard image of the sun. But the sun itself was already shouldering above the horizon. Beads of light like trapped stars marked rim mountain summits, and a deep bloody crimson was working its way high into our tall sky. I imagined I could see the lid of that sky, the millennial leaking of our air into space.

I walked down the path that leads to the circular sea. There was frost everywhere, of course, but the path's lunar dirt, patiently raked in my youth, is friendly and gripped my sandals. The water at the sea's rim was black and oily, lapping softly. I could see the gray sheen of ice farther out, and the hard glint of pack ice beyond that, though the close horizon hid the bulk of the sea from me. Fingers of sunlight stretched across the ice, and gray-gold smoke shimmered above open water.

I listened to the ice for a while. There is a constant tumult of groans and cracks as the ice rises and falls on the sea's mighty shoulders. The water never freezes at Tycho's rim; conversely, it never thaws at the center, so that there is a fat torus of ice floating out there around the central mountains. It is as if the rim of this artificial ocean is striving to emulate the unfrozen seas of Earth which bore its makers, while its remote heart is straining to grow back the cold carapace it enjoyed when our water—and air—still orbited remote Jupiter.

I thought I heard a barking out on the pack ice. Perhaps it was a seal. A bell clanked: an early fishing boat leaving port, a fat, comforting sound that carried through the still dense air. I sought the boat's lights, but my eyes, rheumy, stinging with cold, failed me.

I paid attention to my creaking body: the aches in my too-thin, too-long, calcium-starved bones, the obscure spurts of pain in my urethral system, the strange itches that afflict my liver-spotted flesh. I was already growing too cold. Mirror returns enough heat to the Moon's long Night to keep our seas and air from snowing out around us, but I would welcome a little more comfort.

I turned and began to labor back up my regolith path to my house.

And when I got there, Berge, my nephew, was waiting for me. I did not know then, of course, that he would not survive the new Day.

He was eager to talk about Leonardo da Vinci.

He had taken off his wings and stacked them up against the concrete wall of my house. I could see how the wings were thick with frost, so dense the paper feathers could surely have had little play.

I scolded him even as I brought him into the warmth, and prepared hot soup and tea for him in my pressure kettles. "You're a fool as your father was," I said. "I was with him when he fell from the sky, leaving you orphaned. You know how dangerous it is in the pre-Dawn turbulence."

"Ah, but the power of those great thermals, Uncle," he said, as he accepted the soup. "I can fly miles high without the slightest effort."

I would have berated him further, which is the prerogative of old age. But I didn't have the heart. He stood before me, eager, heartbreakingly thin. Berge always was slender, even compared to the rest of us skinny lunar folk; but now he was clearly frail. Even these long minutes after landing, he was still panting, and his smooth fashionably-shaven scalp (so bare it showed the great bubble profile of his lunar-born skull) was dotted with beads of grimy sweat.

And, most ominous of all, a waxy, golden sheen seemed to linger about his skin. I had no desire to raise that—not here, not now, not until I was sure what it meant, that it wasn't some trickery of my own age-yellowed eyes.

So I kept my counsel. We made our ritual obeisance—murmurs about dedicating our bones and flesh to the salvation of the world—and finished up our soup.

And then, with his youthful eagerness, Berge launched into the seminar he was evidently itching to deliver on Leonardo da Vinci, long-dead citizen of a long-dead planet. Brusquely displacing the empty soup bowls to the floor, he produced papers from his jacket and spread them out before me. The sheets, yellowed and stained with age, were covered in a crabby, indecipherable handwriting, broken with sketches of gadgets or flowing water or geometric figures. I picked out a luminously beautiful sketch of the crescent Earth—

"No," said Berge patiently. "Think about it. It must have been the crescent *Moon*." Of course he was right. "You see, Leonardo understood the phenomenon he called the ashen Moon—like our ashen Earth, the old Earth visible in the arms of the new. He was a hundred years ahead of his time with *that* one. . . ."

This document had been called many things in its long history, but most familiarly the Codex Leicester. Berge's copy had been printed off in haste during The Failing, those frantic hours when our dying libraries had disgorged their great snowfalls of paper. It was a treatise centering on what Leonardo called the "body of the Earth," but with diversions to consider such matters as water engineering, the geometry of Earth and Moon, and the origins of fossils.

The issue of the fossils particularly excited Berge. Leonardo had been much agitated by the presence of the fossils of marine animals, fishes and oysters and corals, high in the mountains of Italy. Lacking any knowledge of tectonic processes, he had struggled to explain how the fossils might have been deposited by a series of great global floods.

It made me remember how, when he was a boy, I once had to explain to Berge what a "fossil" was. There are no fossils on the Moon: no bones in the ground, of course, save those we put there. Now he was much more interested in the words of long-dead Leonardo than his uncle's.

"You have to think about the world Leonardo inhabited," he said. "The ancient paradigms still persisted: the stationary Earth, a sky laden with spheres, crude Aristotelian proto-physics. But Leonardo's instinct was to proceed from observation to theory—and he observed many things in the world which didn't fit with the prevailing world view—"

"Like mountaintop fossils."

"Yes. Working alone, he struggled to come up with explanations. And some of his reasoning was, well, eerie."

"Eerie?"

"Prescient." Gold-flecked eyes gleamed. "Leonardo talks about the Moon in several places." The boy flicked back and forth through the Codex, pointing out spidery pictures of Earth and Moon and sun, neat circles connected by spidery light ray traces. "Remember, the Moon was thought to be a transparent crystal sphere. What intrigued Leonardo was why the Moon wasn't much brighter in Earth's sky, as bright as the sun, in fact. It should have been brighter if it was perfectly reflective—"

"Like Mirror."

"Yes. So Leonardo argued the Moon must be covered in oceans." He found a diagram showing a Moon, bathed in spidery sunlight rays, coated with great out-of-scale choppy waves. "Leonardo said waves on the Moon's oceans must deflect much of the reflected sunlight away from Earth. He thought the darker patches visible on the Moon's surface must mark great standing waves, or even storms, on the Moon."

"He was wrong," I said. "In Leonardo's time, the Moon was a ball of rock. The dark areas were just lava sheets."

"But now," Berge said eagerly, "the Moon *is* mostly covered by water. You see? And there *are* great storms, wave crests hundreds of kilometers long, which are visible from Earth—or would be, if anybody was left to see."

"What exactly are you suggesting?"

"Ah," he said, and he smiled and tapped his thin nose. "I'm like Leonardo. I observe, *then* deduce. And I don't have my conclusions just yet. Patience, Uncle . . ."

We talked for hours.

When he left, the Day was little advanced, the rake of sunlight still sparse on the ice. And Mirror still rode bright in the sky. Here was another strange forward echo of Leonardo's, it struck me, though I preferred not to mention it to my already overexcited nephew: in my time, there *are* crystal spheres in orbit around the Earth. The difference is, we put them there.

Such musing failed to distract me from thoughts of Berge's frailness, and his disturbing golden pallor. I bade him farewell, hiding my concern.

As I closed the door, I heard the honking of geese, a great flock of them fleeing the excessive brightness of full Day.

Each Morning, as the sun labors into the sky, there are storms. Thick fat clouds race across the sky, and water gushes down, carving new rivulets and craters in the ancient soil, and turning the ice at the rim of the Tycho pack into a thin, fragile layer of gray slush.

Most people choose to shelter from the rain, but to me it is a pleasure. I like to think of myself standing in the band of storms that circles the whole of the slow-turning Moon. Raindrops are fat glimmering spheres the size of my thumb. They float from the sky, gently flattened by the resistance of our thick air, and they fall on my head and back with soft, almost caressing impacts. So long and slow has been their fall from the high clouds, the drops are often warm, and the air thick and humid and muggy, and the water clings to my flesh in great sheets and globes I must scrape off with my fingers.

It was in such a storm that, as Noon approached on that last Day, I traveled with Berge to the phytomine celebration to be held on the lower slopes of Maginus.

We made our way past sprawling fields tilled by human and animal muscle, thin crops straining toward the sky, frost shelters laid open to the muggy heat. And as we traveled, we joined streams of more traffic, all heading for Maginus: battered carts, spindly adults, and their skinny, hollow-eyed children; the Moon soil is thin and cannot nourish us well, and we are all, of course, slowly poisoned besides, even the cattle and horses and mules.

Maginus is an old, eroded crater complex some kilometers southeast of Tycho. Its ancient walls glimmer with crescent lakes and glaciers. Sheltered from the winds of Morning and Evening, Maginus is a center of life, and as the rain cleared I saw the tops of the giant trees looming over the horizon long before we reached the foothills. I thought I saw creatures leaping between the tree branches. They may have been lemurs, or even bats; or perhaps they were kites wielded by ambitious children.

Berge took delight as we crossed the many water courses, pointing out engineering features which had been anticipated by Leonardo, dams and bridges and canal diversions and so forth, some of them even constructed since the Failing.

But I took little comfort, oppressed as I was by the evidence of our fall. For example, we journeyed along a road made of lunar glass, flat as ice and utterly impervious to erosion, carved long ago into the regolith. But our cart was wooden, and drawn by a spavined, thin-legged mule. Such contrasts are unendingly startling. All our technology would have been more than familiar to Leonardo. We make gadgets of levers and pulleys and gears, their wooden teeth constantly stripped; we have turnbuckles, devices to help us erect our cathedrals of Moon concrete; we even fight our pathetic wars with catapults and crossbows, throwing lumps of rock a few kilometers.

But once we hurled ice moons across the solar system. We know this is so, else we could not exist here.

As we neared the phytomine, the streams of traffic converged to a great confluence of people and animals. There was a swarm of reunions of friends and family, and a rich human noise carried on the thick air.

When the crowds grew too dense, we abandoned our wagon and walked. Berge, with unconscious generosity, supported me with a hand clasped about my arm, guiding me through this human maelstrom. All Berge wanted to talk about was Leonardo da Vinci. "Leonardo was trying to figure out the cycles of the Earth. For instance, how water could be restored to the mountaintops. Listen to this." He fumbled, one-handed, with his dog-eared manuscript. "*We may say that the*

Earth has a spirit of growth, and that its flesh is the soil; its bones are the successive strata of the rocks which form the mountains, its cartilage is the tufa stone; its blood the veins of its waters. . . . And the vital heat of the world is fire which is spread throughout the Earth; and the dwelling place of the spirit of growth is in the fires, which in divers parts of the Earth are breathed out in baths and sulfur mines. . . . You understand what he's saying? He was trying to explain the Earth's cycles by analogy with the systems of the human body."

"He was wrong."

"But he was more right than wrong, Uncle! Don't you see? This was centuries before geology was formalized, even longer before matter and energy cycles would be understood. Leonardo had gotten the right idea, from somewhere. He just didn't have the intellectual infrastructure to express it. . . ."

And so on. None of it was of much interest to me. As we walked, it seemed to me that *his* weight was the heavier, as if I, the old fool, was constrained to support him, the young buck. It was evident his sickliness was advancing fast—and it seemed that others around us noticed it, too, and separated around us, a sea of unwilling sympathy.

Children darted around my feet, so fast I found it impossible to believe *I* could ever have been so young, so rapid, so compact, and I felt a mask of old-man irritability settle on me. But many of the children were, at age seven or eight or nine, already taller than me, girls with languid eyes and the delicate posture of giraffes. The one constant of human evolution on the Moon is how our children stretch out, ever more languorous, in the gentle Moon gravity. But they pay a heavy price in later life in brittle, calcium-depleted bones.

At last we reached the plantation itself. We had to join queues, more or less orderly. There was noise, chatter, a sense of excitement. For many people, such visits are the peak of each slow lunar Day.

Separated from us by a row of wooden stakes and a few meters of bare soil was a sea of green, predominantly mustard plants. Chosen for their bulk and fast growth, all of these plants had grown from seed or shoots since the last lunar Dawn. The plants themselves grew thick, their feathery leaves bright. But many of the leaves were sickly, already yellowing. The fence was supervised by an un-smiling attendant, who wore—to show the people their sacrifice had a genuine goal—artifacts of unimaginable value, earrings and brooches and bracelets of pure copper and nickel and bronze.

The Maginus mine is the most famous and exotic of all the phytomines: for here gold is mined, still the most compelling of all metals. Sullenly, the attendant told us that the mustard plants grow in soil in which gold, dissolved out of the base rock by ammonium thiocyanate, can be found at a concentration of four parts per million. But when the plants are harvested and burned, their ash contains four *hundred* parts per million of gold, drawn out of the soil by the plants during their brief lives.

The phytomines are perhaps our planet's most important industry.

It took just a handful of dust, a nanoweapon from the last war that ravaged Earth, to remove every scrap of worked metal from the surface of the Moon. It was the Failing. The cities crumbled. Aircraft fell from the sky. Ships on the great circular seas disintegrated, tipping their hapless passengers into freezing waters. Striving for independence from Earth, caught in this crosscurrent of war, our Moon nation was soon reduced to a rabble, scraping for survival.

But our lunar soil is sparse and ungenerous. If Leonardo was right—that Earth with its great cycles of rock and water is like a living thing—then the poor Moon, its reluctant daughter, is surely dead. The Moon, ripped from the outer layers of parent Earth by a massive primordial impact, lacks the rich iron which populates much of Earth's bulk. It is much too small to have retained the inner heat which fuels Earth's great tectonic cycles, and so died rapidly; and without the water baked out by the violence of its formation, the Moon is deprived of the great ore lodes peppered through Earth's interior.

Moon rock is mostly olivine, pyroxene, and plagioclase feldspar. These are silicates of iron, magnesium, and aluminum. There is a trace of native iron, and thinner scrapings of metals like copper, tin, and gold, much of it implanted by meteorite impacts. An Earth miner would have cast aside the richest rocks of our poor Moon as worthless slag.

And yet the Moon is all we have.

We have neither the means nor the will to rip up the top hundred meters of our world to find the precious metals we need. Drained of strength and tools, we must be more subtle.

Hence the phytomines. The technology is old—older than the human Moon, older than spaceflight itself. The Vikings, marauders of Earth's darkest age (before this, the darkest of all) would mine their iron from "bog ore," iron-rich stony nodules deposited near the surface of bogs by bacteria which had flourished there: miniature miners, not even visible to the Vikings who burned their little corpses to make their nails and swords and pans and cauldrons.

And so it goes, across our battered, parched little planet, a hierarchy of bacteria and plants and insects and animals and birds, collecting gold and silver and nickel and copper and bronze, their evanescent bodies comprising a slow merging trickle of scattered molecules, stored in leaves and flesh and bones, all for the benefit of that future generation who must save the Moon.

Berge and I, solemnly, took ritual scraps of mustard-plant leaf on our tongues, swallowed ceremonially. With my age-furred tongue I could barely taste the mustard's sharpness. There were no drawn-back frost covers here because these poor mustard plants would not survive to the Sunset: they die within a lunar Day, from poisoning by the cyanide.

Berge met friends and melted into the crowds.

I returned home alone, brooding.

I found my family of seals had lumbered out of the ocean and onto the shore. These are constant visitors. During the warmth of Noon they will bask for hours, males and females and children draped over each other in casual, sexless abandon, so long that the patch of regolith they inhabit becomes sodden and stinking with their droppings. The seals, uniquely among the creatures from Earth, have not adapted in any apparent way to the lunar conditions. In the flimsy gravity they could surely perform somersaults with those flippers of theirs. But they choose not to; instead they bask, as their ancestors did on remote Arctic beaches. I don't know why this is so. Perhaps they are, simply, wiser than we struggling, dreaming humans.

The long Afternoon sank into its mellow warmth. The low sunlight diffused, yellow-red, to the very top of our tall sky, and I would sit on my stoop imagining I could see our precious oxygen evaporating away from the top of that sky, molecule by molecule, escaping back to the space from which we had dragged it, as if hoping in some mute chemical way to reform the ice moon we had destroyed.

Berge's illness advanced without pity. I was touched when he chose to come stay with me, to "see it out," as he put it.

My fondness for Berge is not hard to understand. My wife died in her only attempt at childbirth. This is not uncommon, as pelvises evolved in heavy Earth gravity struggle to release the great fragile skulls of Moon-born children. So I had rejoiced when Berge was born; at least some of my genes, I consoled myself, which had emanated from primeval oceans now lost in the sky, would travel on to the farthest future. But now, it seemed, I would lose even that.

Berge spent his dwindling energies in feverish activities. Still his obsession with Leonardo clung about him. He showed me pictures of impossible machines, far beyond the technology of Leonardo's time (and, incidentally, of ours); shafts and cogwheels for generating enormous heat, a diving apparatus, an "easy-moving wagon" capable of independent locomotion. The famous helicopter intrigued Berge particularly. He built many spiral-shaped models of bamboo and paper; they soared into the thick air, easily defying the Moon's gravity, catching the reddening light.

I have never been sure if he knew he was dying. If he knew, he did not mention it, nor did I press him.

In my gloomier hours—when I sat with my nephew as he struggled to sleep, or as I lay listening to the ominous, mysterious rumbles of my own failing body, cumulatively poisoned, wracked by the strange distortions of lunar gravity—I wondered how much farther we must descend.

The heavy molecules of our thick atmosphere are too fast-moving to be contained by the Moon's gravity. The air will be thinned in a few thousand years: a long time, but not beyond comprehension. Long before then we must have reconquered this world we built, or we will die.

So we gather metals. And, besides that, we will need knowledge.

We have become a world of patient monks, endlessly transcribing the great texts of the past, pounding into the brains of our wretched young the wisdom of the millennia. It seems essential we do not lose our concentration as a people, our memory. But I fear it is impossible. We are Stone Age farmers, the young broken by toil even as they learn. I have lived long enough to realize that we are, fragment by fragment, losing what we once knew.

If I had one simple message to transmit to the future generations, one thing they should remember lest they descend into savagery, it would be this: *People came from Earth*. There: cosmology and the history of the species and the promise of the future, wrapped up in one baffling, enigmatic, heroic sentence. I repeat it to everyone I meet. Perhaps those future thinkers will decode its meaning, and will understand what they must do.

Berge's decline quickened, even as the sun slid down the sky, the clockwork of our little universe mirroring his condition with a clumsy, if mindless, irony. In the last hours I sat with him, quietly reading and talking, responding to his near-adolescent philosophizing with my customary brusqueness, which I was careful not to modify in this last hour.

". . . But have you ever wondered why we are *here* and *now?*" He was whispering, the sickly gold of his face picked out by the dwindling sun. "What are we, a few million, scattered in our towns and farms around the Moon? What do we compare to the *billions* who swarmed over Earth in the final years? Why do I find myself *here* and *now* rather than *then*? It is so unlikely . . ." He turned his great lunar head to me. "Do you ever feel you have been born out of your time, as if you are stranded in the wrong era, an *unconscious* time traveler?"

I had to confess I never did, but he whispered on.

"Suppose a modern human—or someone of the great ages of Earth—was stranded in the sixteenth century, Leonardo's time. Suppose he forgot everything of his culture, all its science and learning—"

"Why? How?"

"*I* don't know . . . But if it were true—and if his unconscious mind retained the slightest trace of the learning he had discarded—wouldn't he do exactly what Leonardo did? Study obsessively, try to fit awkward facts into the prevailing, unsatisfactory paradigms, grope for the deeper truths he had lost?"

"Like Earth's systems being analogous to the human body."

"Exactly." A wisp of excitement stirred him. "Don't you see? Leonardo behaved *exactly* as a stranded time traveler would."

"Ah." I thought I understood; of course, I didn't. "You think *you're* out of time. And your Leonardo, too!" I laughed, but he didn't rise to my gentle mockery. And in my unthinking way I launched into a long and pompous discourse on feelings of dislocation: on how every adolescent felt stranded in a body, an adult culture, unprepared . . .

But Berge wasn't listening. He turned away, to look again at the bloated sun. "All this will pass," he said. "The sun will die. The universe may collapse on itself, or spread to a cold infinity. In either case it may be possible to build a giant machine that will recreate this universe—everything, every detail of this moment—so that we all live again. But how can we know if *this* is the first time? Perhaps the universe has already died, many times, to be born again. Perhaps Leonardo was no traveler. Perhaps he was simply *remembering.*" He looked up, challenging me to argue; but the challenge was distressingly feeble.

"I think," I said, "you should drink more soup."

But he had no more need of soup, and he turned to look at the sun once more.

———

It seemed too soon when the cold started to settle on the land once more, with great pancakes of new ice clustering around the rim of the Tycho Sea.

I summoned his friends, teachers, those who had loved him.

I clung to the greater goal: that the atoms of gold and nickel and zinc which had coursed in Berge's blood and bones, killing him like the mustard plants of Maginus—killing us all, in fact, at one rate or another—would now gather in even greater concentrations in the bodies of those who would follow us. Perhaps the pathetic scrap of gold or nickel which had cost poor Berge his life would at last, mined, close the circuit which would lift the first of our ceramic-hulled ships beyond the thick, deadening atmosphere of the Moon.

Perhaps. But it was cold comfort.

We ate the soup, of his dissolved bones and flesh, in solemn silence. We took his life's sole gift, further concentrating the metal traces to the far future, shortening our lives as he had.

I have never been a skillful host. As soon as they could, the young people dispersed. I talked with Berge's teachers, but we had little to say to each other; I was merely his uncle, after all, a genetic tributary, not a parent. I wasn't sorry to be left alone.

Before I slept again, even before the sun's bloated hull had slid below the toothed horizon, the winds had turned. The warm air that had cradled me was treacherously fleeing after the sinking sun. Soon the first flurries of snow came pattering on the black, swelling surface of the Tycho Sea. My seals slid back into the water, to seek out whatever riches or dangers awaited them under Callisto ice.

Green Tea

RICHARD WADHOLM

Here's a compelling hard-science adventure, almost extravagantly inventive, that takes us to a strange, complex, and impressively imagined high-tech future, for a compelling tale of disaster, betrayal, and revenge, old things that never change, no matter how much everything else may. . . .

New writer Richard Wadholm has only made two sales to date, both in 1999, both to Asimov's Science Fiction, *but both of them have clearly marked him as a strong new talent, and as a* Writer To Watch *in the new century ahead. A graduate of the 1997 Clarion West, he lives in California.*

F riend Beltran, this moment has weighed on me for the past six days. At last we meet.

Will you take tea with me? Not to worry, I am not here to poison you with tainted tea. Not from a beautiful service like this, certainly. This tea kettle is pewter, yes? And the brew pot—terra cotta, in the manner of the great smuggling mandarins of the Blanco Grande? Quite so. I must beg your indulgence for its use. I was very thirsty; I have come a long way to see you.

Perhaps my name escapes you. That is the way in this profession we share. Say that I am your delivery man. Indeed, the item you procured at such dear cost is close to hand.

My fee? Whatever you arranged with the navigator Galvan will suffice. A cup of tea from this excellent terra cotta pot would do nicely. And, if you are not too pressed, the answer to a simple question?

Who was it for, the thing you berthed on our ship? Was it for the mercenaries on Michele D'avinet? Or for the Chinese smugglers who used the glare of D'avinet to hide their passing?

I suppose it doesn't matter much either way. Whoever your treasure was intended for, they were *someone's* enemy, but they were no enemy of Beltran Seynoso's, yes? And we, the crew of the *Hierophant*, we were merely witnesses. Our only offense was that we could connect you with the destruction of a little star in the outer reaches of Orion.

I wronged you, my friend. You are indeed a man of pitiless resolve. Sitting here, making tea in your kitchen, in this rambling manse, on this pretty little moon of yours, I underestimated you. I pictured a dilettante, playing at a rough game.

Forgive, forgive.

That story you told our captain, that you represented an Anglo syndicate dealing in—what was it? April pork bellies? We took that for naïveté. No one goes from trading in April pork bellies to dealing in Tuesday morning perbladium. Not even the Anglos.

And then there was that improbable load you hired us to turn.

Do you recall the terms of our arrangement, on the floor of the Bright Matter Exchange in Santa Buenaventura? Our contract called for 1200 pennyweight of perbladium to be bombarded by heavy tungsten ions for 14 hours. The result was supposed to be equal amounts of morghium 414 and commercial grade protactinium.

You recall? Morghium 414! *Los Abuelitos!* Hardly fitting for a ship like the *Hierophant*. Once we might have passed on such paltry fare. Indeed, Mateo Diaz, the captain of the *Hierophant*, laughed as we took your load into space. We in the vane crews laughed as we loaded your job into our targeting shelves.

Why would somebody pay for the use of the starboard vane—always the hot vane on any ship—to turn a mild-mannered little isotope used only by metallurgists? Captain Diaz took you for some sort of cerezadito, just starting out in the commodities market.

Oh, you are very good, Señor Seynoso. My compliments.

Not all of us were fooled. I had a friend, a very dear friend, on the *Hierophant*'s nuclear chemistry committee. She doubted the decay chain you provided us even before we committed your load to space.

She led me along the chain of isotopes as you had outlined the order of their appearance. Perbladium 462 would indeed transmutate to morghium and protactinium, but only under very idealized circumstances.

Her calculations said your load would turn to unmarketably small amounts of junk isotopes. She was afraid you didn't know what you were doing.

She need not have worried on that score. Between you and our ship's high-speed navigator—whose services you cheaply bought—you knew precisely what you were doing.

No, don't apologize. I am congratulating you: Well played, Sir.

I was chief to the crew that packed the target material for your load. I spent ten hours with it, hauling it out to its own special quadrant of the starboard vane, injecting it into a section of lead and boron-lined target ampoules; sealing each dram over with paraffin, to control the speed of the particles bombarding your treasure.

If anyone should have known what you were doing, it should have been me, yes? I was the perfect foil. Like all cuckolds, my confidence in my own ability was paramount.

We came in off the starboard vane after we finished and Esteban Contreras asked my opinion about piggy-backing a load of thaogol around this benign little load of morghium.

Esteban had already talked to the nuclear chemistry committee, and they had all given their approval. All except for my friend, Frances Cruz. She had doubts.

But I knew Frances very well. I knew she was a cautious person. Cautious, quiet, thoughtful. I added up my cut for anything Contreras sold in Buenaventura. I told him to go ahead with his scheme.

You see, my friend? I am in no position to cast blame; you and I share responsibility for everything that followed.

Unfortunate that Contreras himself can't be here to speak with you. He had a great belief in the catalytic power of sheer human Will. You and your remorseless skill would have proven something to him that he dearly wished to believe in.

But Esteban Contreras and his Hot Shots were out on the vane, loading their thaogol targets, when your jewel took its first turn.

I was up in the bridge tower, what we in the fleet call the Heidelburgh Tun. I had my eye on a wall full of particle detectors, waiting for a sign of disaster. In this way, Contreras and I had watched out for each other since our cerezadito days.

But disaster is supposed to announce itself in neutron showers, or gamma rays, or a huge heat ramp. The first warning your treasure gave me was nothing more than the burr of a pencil on my desktop.

Few would take notice of such a trifle. Only a lifetime among the big ships of the fleet Buenaventura teaches one to see the signs and read them for what they are: Some vibration had passed through the ship from dorsal to keel, touching every little tea cup and paper clip on its way. It was the subtle harmonic of a nuclear excursion.

I opened a channel to Contreras. I called to him to get off the vane. Contreras had just time to call my name, and then . . .

Are you listening, friend Beltran? Do you hear them?

You must not shy away now. We are hard men, you and I. We take what we want and we do not flinch from the sad and human business of dying. The young mother who will never see her sons grow up—*unfortunate*, we say. *Business is business.* The youth who prays to his patron saint to end his suffering—we reckon this heart-breaking. The old veteran who growls her agony through clenched teeth—*tragic and heroic.*

Would that it were unnecessary.

Steady-on, friend Beltran. Tears and remorse won't bring them back now, will they? And we have far to go.

I was with Captain Diaz as he searched for the source of the screams. I studied the particle detectors as half the starboard vane crumbled under the weight of some unknown force. And then the monitors and detectors themselves began to go, one by one all across the starboard vane, like votives being snuffed out by a choir boy. In a moment, Captain Diaz and I found ourselves in silence and darkness.

Were the Hot Shots all dead? Had some of them made their way into the compartments underneath the starboard vane? Maybe they were out there still, burning to death in some tight space, waiting for us to come for them.

We have all thought about being in that place, Señor Seynoso. Do you see?

We have all seen compañeros walk out of anaerobic fires, their skin cauterized to the inside of their hotsuits. We have all fetched water for someone so burned they could feel nothing but the unquenchable thirst. We do not leave people behind to die that way.

The monitors told a horrendous tale — Spot temperatures were above 2,000 Kelvins, 130 Tesla magnetic fields had buckled 100 ton deck plates all across the dorsal- and ventral-side vanes.

My crew could have stayed in the ship. They had spent ten hours on the vane, and were not scheduled to go out again for another two shifts. No one would have said a word to them.

I made this clear when I explained the situation. Without a word, my mates returned to their armorers and prepared themselves. You should have seen them, those people who died for you. Hard as money, my crew. Hard as coin.

Our good trust rested with Katherine Pope, an Anglo from one of the little worlds along the French Violet. She specialized in "action at a distance." She had a microwave torch with a collimated radar sight. Normal times, we called upon her to burn small portions of hot metal into gas, for spectrographic analysis at a safe remove. On rare occasions, we called upon her to melt hot metal out of its critical configuration.

You might not have cared for Pope, had you met her. Pope had the temperament of an artist, the arrogance of a diva in a chorus line. We always seemed to be distracting her from something more important. Yet all who knew her work bore her high-handed ways.

Mister Robinson was my second. He ran the crew of false men who interceded for us in the tight spaces. He was a taciturn and disapproving man. Not easy to be around always, but we had been together twelve years and I never doubted my back when he was near.

He had two assistants with him. The more experienced was a young aesthete named Pablo Sanoro. Pablo was the son of Luz Sanoro, the wet dock contractor. He held the splendid air of a young noble working out his summer in some Arcadian vineyard. He was ever gracious and kind. He made a point of joking and chatting up the older man. This always led to his rebuke.

Pablo's charms were not entirely lost. Mister Robinson had taken on an apprentice as we shipped out of Buenaventura. Rosalie Nuñez was a cerezadita from mechanics school, brought in to replace Eduardo Callé, who had died of burns the previous week. Mister Robinson intimidated her, as I suspect he did Pablo and most people. But she was determined to make her place on our crew, and so she stood up to his sarcasm and silent moods. Pablo Sanoro had cheered her on.

One other person is most relevant to this history. But for Frances Cruz, I might have foregone the trip out to this sleepy little plantation of yours.

She was our liaison with the nuclear chemistry group, a serious young woman, who loved jokes, but never knew how to tell any of her own.

She did not seem fretful as we prepared to go out. She was gay and easy. She kidded with my crew, and gave a sisterly hug to Mister Robinson's new mechanic. She was, in short, completely unlike herself.

I took her aside as the others spread on their electrolytic salves and locked themselves into their armor. I asked her what was wrong. She handed me the spectrographs taken from the burning shelf on the starboard vane.

It was not completely blank, of course. There were lines of titanium and iron from the burning deck, carbon from the diamond superstructure, sodium from burst-open coolant pipes.

All the things one expects in a ship-board catastrophe, save one—

What exactly was burning?

Frances had an idea. She showed me a photograph of the sky above the starboard vane. I didn't know what I was looking at until she drew an imaginary ring. Outside the ring, the stars shone plain and hard, as always. Inside they burned fat and over-bright.

"Gravitational lensing," she explained.

I tried to think of something that could bend light waves so hard. "Are you talking about a black hole?" I asked her. "Some sort of gravitational singularity?"

She shook her head at this. "Not a black hole. A black hole would have killed us quick. Whatever is out there seems intent on killing us slowly."

"So, not a black hole. But something dense enough to bend light."

"I can't tell you more; I'm guessing as it is." She bit her lower lip in a way I had come to know very well. "Here," she said. "In case you get a bruise." She put something in my hand and fled the armory.

It was her ritual of good fortune to give me a child's adhesive bandage as I went out on the vane—her way of telling me to be careful. On this day, she pressed something larger into my hand. I still have it with me, you see?

A box of bandages.

You grow uneasy, my friend.

Perhaps you are anxious for this tea water to boil? I believe tea has to be prepared as the Chinese drink it, which is to say, scalding. I was taught this by an old smuggler up in the Blanco Grande.

Frances used to worry all this boiling water would do some grievous injury to my throat. She was not the appreciator of fine teas that you and I are. Her tastes ran to the simple and the sweet, I'm afraid.

Sometimes I wonder what brought us together. Perhaps I saw something a bit reckless in her, I don't know. I laugh to think what Frances imagined she saw in me. A man of decency beneath the rage? A man of honesty beneath the lies, compassion beneath the avarice?

You will find this most amusing—because I could not bear to let her down, *I would have been that man.* I can hardly bring myself to admit it now. Had things turned out otherwise, Frances and I would be on a little plantation like this one. I would be sitting out on that veranda, a happy fool rocking children to sleep in my lap.

You spared me this embarrassing decline, you and your undertaking. I will not forget that, my friend. You have my word.

I placed Frances' talisman into my forearm kit as we loaded our gear and false men onto a little cargo train that ran across the starboard vane.

We set out through the tiny valleys of production grade isotopes that clustered on every side of the ship's hull. Our way into battle was lighted by tubes of flawless manufactured diamond, filled with target isotopes of cesium and cobalt in a liquid suspension. *El Camino Azul*, we called it—"the Blue Highway."

The Blue Highway zigzagged past railheads and loading cranes, all untouched by the catastrophe just beyond our sight. The scene was oddly quiet. The rail line was intact here. The screams had stopped. Rosalie Nuñez suggested that things were not so bad. Might Contreras and his Hot Shots have found a place of refuge?

No one dared answer; to acknowledge such baseless hope invited bad luck. Yet her optimism hung in the air as we entered a small canyon filled with low-level actinides.

It was here that the landscape began to deform under the compulsion of your treasure.

A rack of headlights glared at us from the back of the canyon. Pablo Sanoro pointed. "A tractor!" he cried. "It's the Hot Shots!" He gave Nuñez an encouraging nudge. "Maybe things really aren't so bad."

He called out to them and waved. The headlights did not move. We came around to the back of the strontium shelves; Mister Robinson switched on a spotlight.

All the hopeful chatter died away. Someone swore. Pablo Sanoro started to shush the blasphemer, till he realized it was Nuñez herself.

The headlights did indeed belong to a tractor. Perhaps it was the Hot Shots' tractor. I could not say from looking. The machine had been squeezed into the open end of an abandoned sodium reservoir.

Press your thoughts, friend Beltran—twenty-five tons of steel and titanium tucked into a crevice the size of a baby's coffin. Here was a missive from your beast, a foretaste of what awaited us.

A silence fell upon my crew as we rolled past the collapsed tractor. Then Pope and Robinson fell into wagering over the nature of a creature that could crush a twenty-five-ton tractor into a sodium conduit.

"Echnesium!" declared Pope. "It radiated mediating particles for the electroweak force. I've seen echnesium sweep a vane with riptides of magnetic force, drawing in everything in its wake—ferrous and non-ferrous metals alike. Molten steel, hundreds of degrees beyond the currie point of iron. Lead. Flesh, even."

Mister Robinson looked at me to see if I was hearing this. "Echnesium has earned its place among the Seven Dreads, but how can echnesium isolate its fury so fine as to suck a tractor into a coolant pipe?"

"I've seen echnesium focus its rage finer than that," Pope declared. She recounted the tale of a cerezadito she had known on the *Ten of Swords*. The lad favored a steel mustache bangle. He wore it the day he walked into an echnesium fire, and gave not a thought to steel's magnetic properties.

"I found him during the next shift," Pope said, "with his face pressed to a ferro-ceramic bulkhead, and his ornament working its way out of his left ear."

Nuñez gasped. Robinson waved his hand, unimpressed.

"Easy to push a little metal through a kid's brain," he said. "It's something else to stuff a tractor into a coolant pipe."

Pablo Sanoro appealed to all of us for decorum. He nodded toward Nuñez, who sat quiet and awe-struck at the back of the train.

Pope raised her chin at Mister Robinson. "If it's not echnesium, then what?"

"A quantum vacuum state," Robinson said. "Bound inside the heavy nuclei of some metallic plasma. Vacuum^3, perhaps," Robinson suggested. "Bound inside one of the more stable isotopes of pterachnium."

Nuñez gave me an uneasy look. Perhaps she longed for reassurance. But I had my mind on Contreras and his Hot Shots, and where I feared they might be. One of the false men ended up explaining the concept of quantum vacuum states for her.

"What we call 'vacuum' in this universe is actually a morass of self-annihilating virtual particle pairs. They pop into existence, find each other, and pop out of existence in a suicidal frenzy. But more perfect states of vacuum are possible, and they adhere to their own laws and start-up values. Vacuum^3, for instance, allows a small portion of these virtual particles to pop into existence unpaired with any anti-particle to annihilate. Left over, these begin to accumulate."

Pope nudged at Robinson—*where did you pick this one up?*

"Do you know how much mass you're talking about?" she asked. "Sixteen nano-seconds, the mass of these particles would sink an astronomical chunk of space into a singularity."

The false man—we called him *El Guapo*, "the Handsome One," straightened in a show of dignity. "Actually, many of these exotic states radiate the particles as fast they appear." It knew she was laughing at it. It turned about, looking for allies. "Really, I would have thought someone in your profession would find this more relevant."

Nuñez looked around at all of us. "What does that mean? We might be facing a black hole?"

"It's probably a bit of plutonium, burning itself off," I said.

"Vacuum^4 more likely," said Robinson, who did not stint on the truth in un-pleasant matters. "What do you say, Mister Seguro? Vacuum^4 radiates magnetic monopoles. That would explain the tractor in the coolant pipe."

"You have monopoles between your ears," Pope derided him.

"Monopoles catalyze proton decay. And that, in turn—"

"We're getting carried away here," I said. "We don't know what's at the back of the vane till we see it for ourselves."

Pope nodded at me. "What about you? I recall a time you could have told us what we faced without a second thought."

I looked into the eyes of Nuñez, round with terror. Even Sanoro looked abashed. "Perhaps my powers are slipping," I said. "We've got enough to think about right here."

And we did. While we had argued over the precise nature of your treasure, the rail line had angled into a tunnel and brought us down to the region of the undervane.

No mechanic likes the undervane at a time like this. Ask a sailor on the ocean the last place he wants to be when his ship is rolling hard—few things play worse on the mind than being trapped below decks in a foundering ship.

And yet, if Esteban Contreras lived, this is where heat and radiation would have pursued him, to the last place any sane person would go.

We entered a dim and smoldering realm. All mechanical illumination was gone. The vast twilight between us and the distant perimeter of the starboard vane was a grotto of cherry red stalactites, flaming gases, red rivers of steel, glowing like dogs' eyes at dusk.

We called out for Contreras on our suit radios. Nothing came back but the hoarse roar of static. We waited, called out again. There was no response. We searched for some sign of the Hot Shots on every part of the spectrum. Nothing lay before us but a flood plain of magma, flowing down from the inferno at the back of the vane.

"We need a vantage point," Mister Robinson said. I found a raised siding. Before the excursion, it had connected the hot vaults at the bottom of the undervane to a quadrant of target shelves on the deck. A giant airlock sealed the two worlds off from each other. But ferocious heat had warped the bulkhead till it was frozen in its track. The rail line leading up to it was washed over. A torrent of metal sludge and debris had formed a natural waterfall from the mouth of the tunnel, across the tracks, over the edge of the siding and into the dark.

Here, we listened for some sign of the Hot Shots.

In the tenuous atmosphere venting from a thousand coolant pipes the ship banged and ticked all around us. We heard no human sound. I slammed on the rail with a target shelf key. Big as a man's leg, they are. Anyone alive down here would have felt a tremor pass through the deck.

Nothing came back to us but the groans of super-heated metal.

As we waited for some sign from Contreras, a breach opened in the sullen darkness to our left. Molten steel, the remains of one of the giant cracking stations on the surface, poured across the rail line just behind us.

The rear car was swamped before we realized what had happened. It carried all but one of Mister Robinson's false men. The motor car, where we sat, was engulfed up to the gunwales. Heat exploded up through the floor.

We were hard against it, compañero. The train began to lurch backward in a series of uneven jerks as the brakes gave way to the heat. Someone pleaded with me to call back to the ship for help.

"No one is coming after us," I said. "That's how ships lose two or three crews to a single disaster."

"But we'll die—"

"Shut up," I said. I needed to think.

Whoever it was, they started to argue. Without preamble, Mister Robinson threw them over the side. Surprise—the whiner turned out to be the Handsome One. Programmed to human emotion not wisely but too well.

A silence descended on the crew. It lasted for a moment, but one moment was all I needed.

The whistle of escaping gas led my gaze to a small aperture to one side of the airlock. Stars glimmered beyond the hole.

It was far too tiny to squeeze through in a hotsuit, but it implied hope; perhaps the lock was not jammed so tight as it looked.

We had a vane mule locked against the front of the train. The mule was roughly the size and shape of an elevator car, with eight nimble legs per side. Folded against its roof was a telescoping lift, used for reaching the upper levels of the tallest target shelves. Pope and I rode it up to the head waters of the half-molten waterfall. Here, the gases whined and whistled as they squeezed through the tiny orifice.

Pope heated the area with her microwave torch. I wedged an extensible forge into the softened wound and applied pressure.

The metal resisted. I put my shoulder into it, and the hole tore wide open. Our lift kicked away to the right. Pope swore and hung on. I fell, hit the torrent right at its crest.

The surface was covered over with metal garbage. It was smooth and hard beneath. I had nothing to hold on to. Below me waited a golden-hot pool of metal. I clawed for a finger-hold, latched onto something firm. Debris skittered and kicked over me like a wave, but I clung to my handhold till I could lever myself up onto the track.

It was only as I caught my breath before the freshly opened tunnel that I realized what had lent me purchase.

A gloved hand rose out of the welt of metal, as if reaching for a lifeline.

My fellows were silent. I heard someone sob. I thought it was Nuñez, but she was directly behind me, wide-eyed with amazement.

Who was the mechanic enveloped in the metal tomb? I will never know. The crew gathered round to touch the hand, to hold it before moving on.

The train was useless, of course; the track ended here. We piled our gear into the mule's insulated storage bay. We followed behind as it picked its slow path out of the undervane.

I found myself on the shore of a metallic sea. I confess to you, my friend, my emotions overcame me as I took in the new world your treasure had wrought. Where were the screen control towers that reared up around us like a garden of roses? Where were the centrifuge stations, three stories tall and squat as Sultans? Or the hectares of target shelves that rolled out to the edge of the vane? Or the intricate rail lines that tended them?

Before us lay a ghostly beach town of outbuildings, target shelves, and wrecked coolant pipe, all twisted and broken open to the sky. I could pick out individual structures with a moment's concentration. Some of them still had paint on their walls.

Through the gaping doors and windows of a gutted isotope vault, I could see bits of stuff bobbing in the fused metal troughs and waves. Beyond that, the heat had been too intense to leave any trace of history. The topology smoothed into gently rising swells.

The very back of the vane disappeared in a furious glare. Your financial instrument converted everything it touched—ship's decking and incoming nuclei alike—into a stream of X-rays that swept the sky before us.

We would have died but for the polarizing screens. Mutated as they were, the polarizing screens held focus on the burning shelf at the back of the vane. They scoured the bulk of the heat into space.

Far overhead, the corona of your beast burned at 10 million Kelvins. Observatories around the Orion Nebula thought us a new stellar X-ray source. Did you know?

We huddled in shadow of the vault, with our radiators fully unfurled, like butterflies cowering before a typhoon. I poked a hand-held camera through a sagging tear in the wall and sent pictures back to the nuclear chemistry committee.

Some on the committee thought we were saved. A shower of undifferentiated particles would poison the reactions going on before us. Your treasure would gutter out like a candle in a stream of piss.

The captain himself pointed to the star chart over his desk. The *Hierophant* plowed through the deepest portion of the Scatterhead Nebula. Clouds of ionized tungsten stretched before us all the way to the Hercules Vent. They would gorge the monster till it erupted into some new state.

"We have to know what's out there," the captain said. "Some of us think we've created some sort of exotic vacuum state. We can't tell; at least two of the polarizing screens are intersecting the deck, carrying tell-tale radiation away into space. We need a radio assay from beyond that curtain of plasma."

"We are already too close to the inferno," I said. "Any closer, some of us will die."

Captain was a decent and humble man. He knew very well what he asked of us. He was silent for a moment, and I could almost hear his mind racing for some way out of this terrible command.

"We have to know what's out there," he repeated. "Or all of us will die."

Lend your best attention, my friend; this is how men and women face desperate fate.

There was no drawing of lots, no heroic pronouncements, no brave jokes. Mister Robinson handed the sensor spike to his man Pablo Sanoro. I pointed at a spot overlooking the edge of the pit.

No one offered to take young Pablo's spot. Death in this place is not so easily eluded that a courageous gesture will save one or doom another.

Perhaps the young one, Nuñez — perhaps she was shocked by this. Sanoro gave her a glance as he stepped out into the light. She raised her gloved hand to him but said nothing. There was no time for fond wishes of luck.

Sanoro shouldered his way forward to an outcropping of metal. He paused a moment to gauge his chances and then he staggered on till he disappeared into the light.

An interval of silence. The remote viewer in my hand blazed with sudden light. We gathered around as it showed us the face that leered from behind its veil of plasma. Nuñez called out to Sanoro to hurry back. Before he could answer, a perturbation among the screens raised a tsunami wave of light high over our heads. A dozen detectors crackled inside my helmet and then subsided. I heard something very faint and far away — a cry of agony?

We, all of us, called out for Sanoro. Rosalie Nuñez called his name. Even you, compañero, would weep to hear her voice. And I know you for the hard man you are. Sanoro never answered. Perhaps the radio interference was too dense. Perhaps he turned off his radio so we would not hear him as he died.

Even now, my thoughts turn to young Nuñez. We might have eased her broken heart, but time was hard upon us. On a dozen tiny screens leered the monster that took Sanoro's life.

No, no — you must not turn aside now, my friend. This is the sight you paid to see. This is the source of all that had happened. The molten metal that poured through the undervane flowed from here. The circles of destruction that engulfed the starboard vane radiated from this point.

On collimated radar it was a chimera. It roiled and turned about itself like a snake on a hot spit. Infrared showed scabs of magnetic convection crusted over wounds that bled light. All very pretty, but none of it described the engine that drove this conflagration.

We had one last thing to try. Almost as an afterthought, Sanoro had left a gravitational wave interferometer at the brink of the inferno — bricks of purest rubidium, tautly held in a wire harness. It was telling us something even as we dialed it in, but gravitation is a hard thing to gauge on a ship like the *Hierophant*.

At first, the oscillating line was wildly erratic. As we filtered out the effects of the ship's velocity, the inertial sink, the polarizing screens, the oscilloscope settled into a metronomic pattern, at once familiar and dreadful.

The thing radiated gravitational waves.

We were all of us silent a long moment. I think we all knew what we saw, but no one wanted to say the words.

Of course, *you* know what we saw, don't you. Here is your treasure, compañero. Here is the pearl beyond price.

Vacuum^3. Pterachnium.

— *The Blue Angel.*

Did you know what you were building when you perfected your scheme? Did you fathom the fundamental forces you brought to bear? Indeed, did you think of anything beyond this little moon? These sun-dappled orchards? Those fearsome paladins who guard your sleep?

Pterachnium is not a baryon emitter, like the fissionable actinides. It does not betray itself in high-energy photons, as do the other metallic plasmas. Pterachnium nuclei have only one use to men like you—they are the vessels of choice for binding exotic vacuum states.

I speak of energies at which the quantum vacuum itself trembles on the verge of fluctuation. In the twentieth century, such a fluctuation was credited with the creation of the universe. Cosmologists presumed another fluctuation, if it ever really happened, would sweep across the heavens at light speed, plowing all the rules of Nature in its wake.

Those worthies never counted on ingenious fellows like yourself, creating industrial grades of more- and less-perfect quantum vacuum states—bottling up the lightning of the universe behind an event horizon, like amethyst encrusting the gut of a fire egg.

As I said, mi compañero, you are a clever fellow.

I could tell you the names of ships killed by pterachnium. You would be awestruck to hear their fates—the *Queen of Wands*, burned by X-rays with all hands in the Venturi Thermals; the *Ace of Cups*, shattered by proton decay; the *Tower*, stripped of its screens at relativistic speeds.

Have you ever seen a ship stripped of its screens at light speed? The leading edge of every span, every deck plate, is pitted and torn as if pecked away by ferocious birds. Sometimes salvage crews find tellolites laying about—tiny deposits of matter left by the energy of particles interacting with the deck (energy, you see, converts to matter, if the exchange is great enough).

At these energies, one's problems are quickly over. Make no mistake, my friend, I speak of a hard end. But at least there are no lingering deaths from burns or radiation sickness. Certainly, Fate can be more unkind.

Exotic vacuum states are infamous for the electrical potential that attends them. Under the deforming compulsion of these fields, a ship's polarizing screens begin to cycle, like wire coiled around a giant dynamo. Charged particles slip between cycling screens and the metal deck. Potential builds to discharge.

If you imagine some display of lightning, your vision is too modest. Scale your thoughts up by a factor of a million—electrical discharge on this scale powers the jet streams of exotic stellar objects.

I boarded a ship once, destroyed by successive discharges of 100 terawatts. I will never forget the smell in the mechanics' armory. It was sweet, you know? Like smoked meat. . . .

No, no, no. Forgive these morbid thoughts, my friend. These things are none of your concern. I merely wish to lend you understanding of our desperate state of mind as we realized the poisoned cargo you had bequeathed us.

Our screens were infected. Our false men were gone. Pope said she could burn the heart from your monster and we gratefully accepted her word. Indeed, I had seen her look into the blue-hot glare off a burning lump of plutonium and split it in two from five hundred meters.

But plutonium was not so fierce as your treasure. We could study plutonium through our leaded face shields. Pope figured to lose her eyesight. I told her she was being ridiculous.

We had an elaborate sensor array in the mule's equipment bay—gamma ray imaging, magnetic resonance, collimated radar. I made sure she had the entire spectrum at her disposal. Nuñez stood in the bay and handed out each piece of equipment. I tested each scope and monitor and staked it into the deck.

But I was the ridiculous one. At some point, Pope would grow frustrated with her prosthetic eyes. She and I both knew this. She would look away into the inferno with her own eyes and press the trigger even as her retinas went forever dark. She did not complain about this. She asked only that she be informed how her aim fared—demanded would be a better word.

"You tell me if I miss," she said. "I'll put one in right next to it. I won't need my eyes for that. If you let me take the gun sights off the target, I won't be able to sight in again. All our deaths will hang on your head."

Such gentle persuasion. How could I refuse?

In the midst of our preparations, something caused me to look up, some change in the light maybe, I don't know.

The burning of the starboard vane had filled the sky above us with a haze of metallic aerosols. I saw them begin to move.

Your monster was flexing its muscle.

I touched helmets with Pope. I pointed out the milky swirls passing across the stars.

She glared at me as if I bothered her, threw off her concentration. "I'll never get this done, you keep interrupting me," she declared. "Maybe I should just hand the gun to you." She turned back to her monitors without waiting for a response.

Snatches of radio conversation were getting through the static. I heard the screen crews fighting with some upper-level deformation of the #4 screen, the electron/anti-proton screen.

All the hairs on my body went straight up. The static surge detectors suddenly pegged off the scale. Robinson and Nuñez waved to me from the equipment bay at the back of the mule. It only occurred to me then—of course, the equipment bay was surrounded in conducting metal. It would be completely insulated.

I called to Pope as they dragged me in behind them. She refused even to acknowledge me.

Nuñez was still closing the door as a flash lit up the sky across the entire plain of fused metal. It was an ancient light, a light from the dawn of creation. Through my leaded visor—*through my closed eyelids*—I saw the bones of my hands, clamped across my face.

The door slammed. The deck heaved beneath us. I crashed into the ceiling and then back to the floor, came up tasting blood and swallowing chipped teeth. A hurricane shrieked in my helmet radio, loud enough to split open my head.

My thoughts were on Pope. She was outside the door, just beyond my reach. How had she fared? Had she gotten off her shot?

We stepped outside even while the superheated light receded. The mule was over on its side, and the door was sprung. I had to shove at the door with Nuñez and Mister Robinson to get it open. Pope was gone. I have no idea what happened to her. She was simply gone.

I called out for her, scanned the deck as best I could for some sign of her. None of us ever saw Pope again. However, as I came around the side of the mule, I saw something that will stay with me always.

Rolling out of the shade of a distant cargo bay came the little crew tractor carrying Esteban Contreras' unlucky Hot Shots.

I took it to be some sort of drifting retinal artifact from the burning light. But it was real. It crossed the blasted desert with the leisurely air of a family on beach holiday.

Each person in the crew cabin sat up straight in their seats, utterly unconcerned about the excursion lighting up the sky before us. They rolled right into it, rigid as a six-pack of cerveza.

I called out to them, but of course they were dead—burned to a blackened husk right inside their bright, shiny hotsuits. Up in the chief's cabin was Contreras himself, hanging from the window, his hands dragging along the deck as the little train pushed forward into the raging brilliance at the back of the starboard vane.

There was no question we had moments left to us. Already I could see my surge detector flickering again. Your monster had magnetized everything out beyond its moat of liquid metal—the lead shielding as well as the steel in the decking. Its magnetic lair increased even as we hunkered behind our shattered railhead.

Soon it would begin pulling down the polarizing screens. Particles would be unloaded across the ship. They would scatter through the soft parts of the hull and kill everyone standing nearby. Behind the collapsing screens would come the in-falling sky, igniting the fissionable materials on all four vanes.

Mister Robinson and I had no use for panic. Huddled together against the roar of radio interference, we considered our options as if we were discussing the price of 3:00 perbladium on the futures floor at Santa Buenaventura.

Normal circumstances, we would try to heat the site somehow, and cause it to melt in with the metal around it. Even if it remained in a critical configuration, it might be contaminated by melted steel from the deck, or lead, or boron from the surrounding shielding to poison the reaction chain.

That seemed a dubious proposal in this case. Any lump of matter that held Vacuum³ in its heart already knew more about heat than anything we could teach it.

We paused in our discussion as a cluster of tellolites levitated half a meter over the deck, only to land a few centimeters from the tip of my boot. Mister Robinson's eyes rose from the bit of mongrel matter at our feet to the inferno before us.

"We seem to be in the presence of primordial symmetry," he said.

This is what reached out to the little pebbles on the deck around us, what had crushed a tractor into a coolant pipe on the far side of the Blue Highway—the four fundamental forces of nature had rediscovered that symmetry they lost in the first billion-billion-billionth of a second after creation.

"This, from Vacuum^3?"

"Or Vacuum^4. We're in no position for a precise assay."

It was hard not to be over-awed by the majesty of your art. And yet, what did we cower before, after all? A bit of vacuum! The apotheosis of nothingness. Perhaps we wasted our time attacking the pterachnium; the vacuum state bound within might be manipulated more easily.

I put it to Mister Robinson: "These vacuum states run in chains of progression, just like the decay chain of any unstable nucleotide. A couple of steps up from Vacuum^3 is a stable plateau not dissimilar to the quantum vacuum state we call home."

I remember the way he nodded to himself; Mister Robinson was not hurried by desperation or despair.

"If we could define the right particles with our screens, we could push our load of Vacuum^3 up to that plateau."

"Right this second, you know what the temperatures are like beyond those polarizing screens? What kind of particles are going to get through that?"

"Dark matter," I said. "Weakly interacting super-luminals. They have no electric charge to become entangled in the firestorm. They touch this universe with nothing but the slender fingers of gravity, and nothing but dense matter draws them in. Perhaps they will be sufficient to our needs."

Mister Robinson considered the proposal for a long moment. "We've got a problem," he said. "No matter what happens to the pterachnium, we'll be sitting out here when the ship goes super-luminal. The hull will be protected, but out here, we will be exposed to whatever comes down. It hardly matters that these particles are 'weakly interacting,' anything will kill you if you get hit by enough of them."

Mister Robinson began reminiscing about a man he had known in the French Violet, killed by neutrinos—*neutrinos* of all things. He saw the youngster watching us all wide-eyed. He stopped himself.

I started to suggest we might yet escape. Mister Robinson indicated the impassable blastscape behind us with a single look. "This ship has maybe two minutes to live. What do you think, Mister Seguro? Two minutes before the screens are all bound in a huge magnetic source and start cycling? Where are we going to go in the next two minutes?"

I said, "I'm certainly open to suggestions, Mister Robinson." He laughed. Mister Robinson and I went back a ways. Neither of us had any particular trouble doing what was necessary to save the ship.

But the youngster, she troubled us some. This was her training flight. This should have been safe and easy. We would never have brought along some young niña on anything more dangerous than nice, easy morghium 414.

I asked her if she understood what we were discussing. She said she did. I asked her if she agreed with our assessment.

She said she did. I detected a softness to her voice. She might have been holding back her emotions. Yet she never cried for any sort of consideration for her youth or her status. She understood that we were all about to die, and that only the ship mattered now.

I called back to Frances Cruz and made our proposal.

Frances would not hear of it. She found a thousand reasons to doubt my solution. Yet she could find nothing better. I did not have the time to argue, but for her I made the time. It wasn't easy. How do you explain a decision like this to a special friend and confidant?

I gave myself thirty seconds, and then, when she still could not understand, I gave myself thirty seconds more. I needed to speak to Captain Diaz about our plan, but I couldn't leave Frances till she understood that the sweetness of my life had been hers, and the only horror I felt at leaving was bound up with her as well.

Captain Diaz cut into our conversation to hear out our proposal. Captain was a decent man, but he could count—three lives against twenty-seven. He told us they would need a gravitational wave detector as near the pterachnium as we could get. Sanoro's detector had gone dark moments after it had showed us the face of your creature. We had to replace it, so that the nuclear chemistry committee would know how our mission fared. When he went to initiate the screen dump, Frances did not return to the line.

I turned to Nuñez and Robinson. "I set the wave detector myself," I told them.

Mister Robinson made a gesture of indifference. "We have no place to go," he said. "We might as well come with you."

"We come along," Nuñez said in a husky voice. "You falter, we're there." She looked ready to make a fight of it if I ordered her back; Sanoro's death weighed heavy on her.

I had my eye on a spot twenty meters ahead of us. A stub of metal reared up from the smooth-blasted decking. What had been there before your undertaking? I recalled a nuclear furnace near that point. Two stories tall it had been. The tiny mesa in its place rose perhaps a meter tall now.

"We reach that hump in the deck and plant the detector on its further side." I pointed.

Beyond that little rise lay a final circle of hell, smooth as the surface of an egg. Liquefied steel, I realized, boiling away to gas at its center. Your treasure had corrupted all the metal across the back of the molten mirror. Beneath the shade of my palm, it looked like the gilt of a Rococo picture frame.

I moved forward till the heat in my suit was unbearable. I could hardly swallow for the metallic taste of hard radiation in my mouth. Probing tendrils of lightning thick as rope played over our suits and slammed the deck at our feet. The heat burned through the soles of our boots till I could barely walk.

I planted the spike in the metal decking at the point I could go no further.

I felt the deck tremble beneath me as the ship accelerated. I remember bracing myself for the gauntlet of particles awaiting me on the far side of the light barrier—*Would it burn me? Would I have time to feel anything?*

But something was wrong. Frances was in my headset, saying something about losing the signal. I was delirious by then. Her words barely made sense.

She was telling me the wave detector that we had just put out had gone silent, even as the energy output had grown more intense. She was asking if I could still see it above the pterachnium site. She thought it had been destroyed.

That wasn't why she had lost the signal anyway, was it, my friend? Your jewel was gathering itself up, as a giant coastal wave will gather all the water off a beach before it rolls in.

Your creature was coming to fruition at last.

Of course, I was past caring by this time. Zone angels appeared and evaporated before my eyes, as vivid as childhood memories. I doubt I was even conscious.

In my blindness, I stumbled and crashed to the deck. A dire circumstance; the deck glowed red hot. The flesh of my shoulder burned from the heat of it. Indeed, this is where my shoulders and back acquired those handsome keloids you have been admiring so surreptitiously.

I was a breath away from unconsciousness, and that would have meant my death. Seeking relief, I took a sip from my water hose. Nothing came out but superheated air. The water had gone to steam and been recycled into a safety reservoir till it could recondense. Of course, I would be long dead by then.

In the middle of this horror came a sudden vision of preternatural quiet. I saw the village square in Santa Susana de la Reina — the wind funnels creaking in the cupola of the old mission, the black moss and the purple, the smell of the constant rain.

— *Rain!*

How vivid the memory of rain came to me in that moment. In my mouth I held the sweet smell of the wet timbers beneath Boregos Bridge. I could see the mirrored pools filling the broken streets, their surfaces cut by black lizards.

I saw rain running in sheets beyond a limp curtain. I saw a bare shoulder, silhouetted against the milky light. A friend in the street below called up to us to unlock the door and let him in, while we lay in the dark and laughed at him and everyone else in the world who knew not what we knew in that moment.

I heard the shouting again, but it wasn't Esteban Contreras calling up to Frances and me from the street. It was Mister Robinson. He was calling to me from a ripple of metal just a few meters to port. He might have been on the other side of the French Violet for the gulf of pain and light between us.

Nuñez was stranded behind a small rise just beyond him. She was waving to us, making some gesture. I could not make it out. A clearing of silence breached the static roar just long enough that I could catch her words.

"Here it comes," she cried. Somehow, Nuñez had heard the countdown to light speed on her suit radio: The sky was coming in.

I looked around for some bit of cover to hide myself. Something split the glare just off to my right. I had barely noticed it while planting the gravity wave detector; it had been still as any other bit of metal on that blasted expanse. But as I looked closer, I realized the shadow was articulated with radiator fins and circulating packs.

I shaded my eyes with my palm and peered into the glare that beat up from the metal decking. Here was Pablo Sanoro, frozen in an attitude of intent concentration—staring at the gravity wave detector he had worked at even as he burned to death.

I pulled him down over me just as the stars smeared into rainbows. The deck burned my back. The incoming particles burned my fingers as they gripped around Sanoro's shoulders.

I held tight. I spent a micro epoch in that way—my back blistering against the super-heated deck, and Pablo Sanoro just inches from my leaded visor, grinning the wizened, squinting smile of a face with flesh and muscle drawn taut.

I heard Nuñez scream. Pinned under Sanoro's hotsuit, I raised my head just enough to see your treasure plunge through a hundred-ton metal deck as if it were soft taffy.

A crevasse spread out from the back of the vane. It etched a jagged line right out to us. Nuñez disappeared down the hole as it spread through the deck beneath her feet.

Robinson grasped for her as she slipped out of sight. In that moment, your creature reached up through the metal decking and took him in a 130 Tesla magnetic field. I saw Robinson twist and heave like a rag doll as the flesh peeled from his bones.

A cloud of steam enveloped him from somewhere below and he was gone. I remember staring in amazement as it rose into the sky. Where had that come from?

I didn't realize till much later, but your monster had crashed through three floors below the main deck, severing a dozen plumbing mains along the way.

This is what killed so many people inside the hull—not fire, but water. The water in all the lines flashed to steam and exploded throughout the interior of the ship.

After some time I became lucid. I found myself lying along the palisade of a canyon, cut to the depths of the starboard vane.

All of my mates were dead. All of our equipment sucked down into the hole your monster had made for itself.

It is ironic, but this saved me from dying. With your pterachnium sunk away out of sight, the heat and magnetism refocused on some point in the undervane.

I thought I might get help from one of the other vane crews. I went down to the mechanics' armory to see about some assistance. But the mechanics' armory had been closest to the back of the vane as your treasure came into its own. My compañeros had been among the first inside the hull to die.

The ship above the armory was utterly silent. It was a catalog of unpleasant endings. People in airtight cabins suffocated or burned. People closer to fissures in the hulls, destroyed by explosive decompression.

I found Frances on the floor leading out of the forward head. Blood pooled out of her ears. I tell myself she was killed instantly. Who knows? Perhaps she was.

No, please. Allow me to tell the story; just looking at her, I could re-enact the moment of her death. Indeed, it is not without its amusing side.

You see, there is a standing rule never to go to the toilet during a hot load. I mean, these things have happened before. These ships are compact, no matter how large they appear, and the plumbing lines always end up going throughout the ship, and a few people every year end up being killed this way.

So Frances knew the risks of going to the bathroom when she did. But the emergency had gone on for several hours now, and her need had taken on an urgency of its own.

Had she been truly born of wealth she could have squatted in the corner like a house cat. But no, she was born to the merchant class, and such compromise with her dignity left her too little to hold on to. The steam explosion blew out the wall behind her head.

Pardon, my friend. I am not unaware how this must seem to a man of refinement like yourself. Yet, this has an air of the hilarious: A princess dies while sitting on the toilet—a good joke from God, yes? An amusing trick.

—*Don't touch me.*

And do not tell me again how sorry you are. Or how necessary it was. Or how I would have done the same in your position . . .

Excuse me, please. No, no—It is I who must apologize. You have been more than patient. The story reaches denouement.

I found myself carrying Frances around in my arms. I can't tell you where we were going. All the officers' quarters were blown open to space. I just could never find a place to set her down. So I carried her.

Eventually, I found myself up in the Heidelburgh Tun, where the officers had made their last stand.

Imagine my surprise to find someone alive up here. More surprising still to find him walking around in a hotsuit from the mechanics' armory. This would be Galvan, the navigator.

I said, "That might be a tight fit in an escape pod."

He was startled at the sound of my voice. He spun around, looking for me. Of course, I was a voice in his radio—I might have been anywhere. Even so, he hid something behind his back, like a child with an embarrassing secret.

"Seguro," he said. And then, "Joaquin. You survived." He did not sound over-joyed to see me.

I asked him what he had in his hand. He actually fought me as I reached around to take it from him.

What do you suppose it was, this thing that would make a timid little man punch at me and dig at my air hose to kill me?

You know what it was. It was a clock, wasn't it. But a very special clock. No doubt, you see them all the time. They are common on the floor of the Bright Matter Exchange. Familiar to shipping agents and futures traders.

We call them "true clocks." They are used to track the true passage of time back at a ship's home port.

To the uninitiated, this may seem a small matter. You, of course, know better. Our ship plies the clouds of Orion at speeds approaching light. A dozen times during the course of a run, we accelerate, we brake. Shipboard time changes with each fluctuation. We cross over the light barrier on our way to and from work. When we do, time is calculated in imaginary numbers. A clock set to follow such distortions is not the sort of thing a man on a navigator's salary would own.

Galvan tried to tell me this was a part of his navigator's kit. Indeed, the navigator's loft is equipped to track the constant passage of time, but only relative to our own course. The clock in Galvan's hand was synchronized to the time on the eastern shore of a little island on a deserted moon in the San Marcos star system.

This moon, in fact. This very moon. What do you suppose, my friend?

Galvan dissembled as I asked him his purpose up here. In fact, he had been completing a course correction. He claimed he was moving us out of shipping lanes. But we were headed for this star up in the French Violet, this Michele D'avinet. He had no ready explanation why.

I put it to him that we were partners in this matter—each had something the other wanted. Galvan had the name of the monster that destroyed my ship. I had Galvan's air hose, pinched between my fingers.

In that way we bartered for the next hour: One answer, one gulp of air.

I learned the name of Beltran Seynoso, weapons designer to half the armies, militias, and mercenary groups in the French Violet. He told me of the star, Michele D'avinet. He was not specific as to your loyalties; I suspect he did not know them himself. But he described your plan in some detail.

He told me about your audacious scheme to poison the sun these people lived under and warm themselves against. A bold stroke, Sir! Set my ship on course for this star, D'avinet, then consume it into a singularity on the way. What would happen if a singularity the size of my old ship had crashed into a star like Michele D'avinet? Billions of people would die terribly. It would be a tragedy of majestic proportions.

Truly, you are a man of vision.

Galvan became frantic toward the end. He gave minute details of your operation. He told me everything about you that he could think of. He answered questions I hadn't thought to ask. I suspect he padded what he knew with outright speculations.

You mustn't blame him for this; he believed his life lasted as long as our conversation. Indeed, he bought each breath with another bit of truth. And when he ran out of truth . . .

My actions shock you. Forgive me; I should play more the hero in my own drama. But she is gone, you see? And I am left with only one role that matters. I am your delivery man.

I see that your scheme was sound in its fundamentals, but there was a complication: Vacuum^3 collapses into a singularity in sixteen nanoseconds. That would never do. Galvan needed time to set the ship's course. As he was a navigator of mediocre talents, course corrections would be required on the way. And you had to leave the illusion that he would escape.

So you set the thing to dissipate most of its energy in gravitational waves. No matter. The density would be sufficient when the time came. Small singularities would form, consume all the matter around them, begin to coalesce.

I am in no position to mentor a man of your estimable talents. But perhaps one or two suggestions for next time? There is a phase transition in the production of pterachnium. Below its critical mass, pterachnium, at least in the form you created, becomes quiet and morose. It can be captured. The careful man can manipulate it into a more pliant form.

I myself journeyed down into the deep fissure that cut through the heart of the starboard vane. It was cold when I arrived. The radiations had banked, the ferocious gravities and magnetic fluctuations had subsided. The liquefied metals that had chased us through the undervane had now congealed into curtains, flood plains, weird minarets.

There, I found your precious, bound up in clusters of tellolite nodules at the bottom of the chasm. Though my petty sophistries had failed to save the ship, they had managed to convert your Vacuum^3 into a pliant state, a form that allows it to be carried without collapsing spontaneously into singularity.

Yes, my friend. Your treasure lives. I have even returned it to its original liquid suspension. This, after all, is the way things are done in the production of commercial isotopes since the days of the great nuclear reactors. Atoms of target material are held in liquid suspension to allow their thorough saturation by incoming particles.

It is quiet now. It exists in two sub-critical drams, but when poured together, they undergo a phase transition into that tool of petty vengeance you procured at such cost.

Don't worry, they're close at hand.

Are you sure you won't have some of this very fine tea? You won't mind if I pour myself a little topper then, will you?

I noticed your tea pots as soon as I entered the kitchen. Yes, they definitely attracted my interest. You make tea in the Chinese manner—one pot to boil the water, one pot to brew the tea. Excellent. Exactly right. None of this tea bag chic for you, my friend.

Do the two pots have a history? You are a tea man. You know that a good tea pot is like a good wallet, or a good pair of boots. It ages. It carries a certain history about with it.

My own set is humble by comparison. Cheap porcelain, brightly painted with scenes from a port town on the lee side of Spanish Space. I would have replaced it long ago, except it was a gift, you see. From someone whose tastes ran to the simple and sweet.

No matter. Life is the sum of simple delights—a tawdry souvenir from Puerta Estrella. A smile reflected in dark eyes. A cup of tea with a newfound friend. One cannot shun such bagatelles.

Not when death is sixteen nanoseconds away.

The Dragon of pripyat

Karl Schroeder

New Canadian writer Karl Schroeder was born and raised in Brandon, Manitoba. He moved to Toronto in 1986, and has been working and writing there ever since. His first novel, written with David Nickle, was The Claus Effect. His second novel, Ventus, this one a solo effort, will be out soon, and he's currently at work on a new one.

Here he takes us on a vivid and suspenseful pilgrimage to a place where few people indeed would dare to venture, to the intensely radioactive, eerily deserted wasteland left behind after the Chernobyl Disaster, and takes us hunting through the ruins for the secret at the heart of the deadly maze — a secret that may be even deadlier than the ruins themselves . . .

There's the turnoff," said Gennady's driver. He pointed to a faded wooden skull and cross-bones that leaned at the entrance to a side road. From the pattern of the trees and bushes, Gennady could see that the corner had once been a full highway interchange, but the turning lanes had overgrown long ago. Only the main blacktop was still exposed, and grass had made inroads to this everywhere.

The truck stopped right at the entrance. "This is as far as I go," said the driver. He stepped out of the idling vehicle and walked around the back to unload. Gennady paused for a moment to stare down the green tunnel before following.

They rolled out some steel drums containing supplies and equipment, then brought Gennady's motorcycle and sidecar.

The driver pointed to the Geiger counter that lay on top of the heaped supplies in the sidecar. "Think that'll protect you?"

"No." Gennady grinned at him. "Before I came I did a little risk calculation. I compared the risk of cancer from radiation to that of smoking. See? Here the Geiger clicks at about a pack-a-week. Closer in, that's going to be a pack-a-day. Well, I'll just avoid the pack-a-minute spots, is all. Very simple."

The driver, who smoked, did not like this analogy. "Well, it was nice knowing you. Need anything else?"

"Uh . . . help me roll these behind the bushes there." They moved the drums out of sight. "All set."

The driver nodded once, and Gennady started down the abandoned road to Pripyat.

The tension in his shoulders began to ease as he drove. The driver had been friendly enough, but Gennady's shyness had made the trip here an uncomfortable one. He could pretend to be at ease with strangers; few people knew he was shy. It still cost him to do it.

The trees were tall and green, the undergrowth lush. It smelled wonderful here, better than the industrial area around Gennady's apartment. Pure and clean, no factory smell.

A lie, of course. Before he'd gone a hundred meters, Gennady slowed, then stopped. It all looked serene and bursting with health—a seductive and dangerous innocence. He brought out a filtered face mask he had last worn in heavy traffic in St. Petersburg. For good measure he wrapped his boots in plastic, snapping rubber bands over his pant cuffs to hold it on. Then he continued.

The view ahead was not of a straight black ribbon with sky above, but a broad green tunnel, criss-crossed at all levels with twigs and branches. He'd expected the road would be cracked and buckled from frost heaving, but it wasn't. On the other hand underbrush had overgrown the shoulder and invaded the concrete, where patches of grass sprouted at odd places. For no good reason, he drove around these.

Over the next half hour he encountered more and more clearings. Tall grass lapped like waves around the doors of rusting metal pole-sheds once used for storing farm equipment. Any houses made of lath and plaster had caved in or been burned, leaving only single walls with windows looking from open field to open field. When he spotted the giant lattice-work towers of the power line looming above the trees he knew he was getting close. As if he needed visual confirmation—the regular ticking from the counter in his sidecar had slowly become an intermittent rattle, like rain.

Then without warning the road opened out into a vista of overgrown concrete lots, rusted fences and new forest. Wildflowers and barley rioted in the boulevard of the now-divided highway, and further ahead, above patchy stands of trees, hollow-eyed Soviet-style apartment blocks stared back at their first visitor in . . . years, possibly.

He shut off the bike and brought out his Pripyat roadmap. It was thirty years out of date, but since it was printed a year before the disaster, the roads would not have changed—other than the occasional oak tree or fallen building blocking his path. For a few minutes he puzzled over where he was, and when he was certain he pulled out his phone.

"Lisa, it's me. I'm here."

"You okay?" She had answered promptly. Must have been waiting. His shoulders relaxed a bit.

"I'm fine. Place looks like a park. Or something. Very difficult to describe." There were actual trees growing on the roofs of some of the apartment blocks. "A lot of the buildings are still standing. I'm just on the outskirts."

"What about the radioactivity?"

He checked the Geiger counter. "It's not too hot yet. I'm thinking of living in a meat locker. Somewhere with good walls that got no air circulation after The Release."

"You're not near the reactor, are you?"

"No. It's by the river, I'm coming from the northwest. The trees hide a lot."

"Any sign of anybody else?"

"Not yet. I'm going to drive downtown. I'll call you when I have the satellite link running."

"Well, at least one of us is having an exciting day."

"I wouldn't exactly call it exciting. Frightening, maybe."

"Well." She said 'well' in that tone when she was happy to be proved right about something. He could practically see her. "I'm glad you're worried," she said at last. "When you told me about this part of the job you pretended like it was no big deal."

"I did not." Well, maybe he had a little. Gennady scratched his chin uncomfortably.

"Call me soon," she said. "And hey—be careful."

"Is my nature."

Downtown was too hot. Pripyat was a Soviet modern town anyway, and had no real centre aside from some monolithic municipal buildings and farmers' markets. The populace had been professional and mobile; it was built with wide thoroughfares connecting large, partially self-contained apartment complexes. Gennady read the cultural still-birth of the place in the utter anonymity of the buildings. Everything was faded, most signs gone, the art overwritten by vines and rust. So he could only identify apartment buildings by their many small balconies, municipal offices by their lack of same. That was the beginning and end of Pripyat's character.

Gennady paused often to look and listen, alert for any signs of human habitation. There were no tire tracks, no columns of smoke. No buses passed, no radios blared from the high rises.

He found himself on the outskirts again as evening reddened the light. Twelve-storey apartment blocks formed a hexagon here, the remains of a parkette in its center. The Geiger counter clicked less insistently in this neighborhood. He parked the motorcycle in the front foyer of the easternmost tower. This building still had a lot of unbroken windows. If he was right, some of the interior rooms would have low isotope concentrations. He could rest there, as long as he left his shoes outside, and ate and drank only the supplies he had brought with him.

The echoes of his boot crashing against an apartment door seemed to echo endlessly, but no one came to investigate. Gennady got the door open on the third try, and walked into the sad evidence of an abandoned life. Three days after Reactor Four caught fire, the tenants had evacuated with everything they could carry—but they'd had to leave a black upright piano that once they might have played for guests who sipped wine here, or on the balcony. Maybe they had stood watching the fire that first night, nervously drinking and speculating on whether it might mean more work for renovators and fire inspectors.

Many faded and curled photos were pinned to the beige kitchen cupboards; he tried not to look at them. The bedroom still held a cot and chest of drawers with icons over it. The wallpaper here had uncurled in huge rolls, leaving a mottled yellow-white surface behind.

The air was incredibly musty in the flat—a good sign. The Geiger counter's rattle dropped off immediately, and stabilized at a near-normal level. None of the windows were so much as cracked, though the balcony door had warped itself to the frame. Gennady had to remove its hinges, pull the knob off and pry it open to get outside. Even then he ventured only far enough to position his satellite dish, then retreated indoors again and sealed the split frame with duct tape he'd brought for this sort of purpose. The balcony had swayed under him as he stepped onto it.

The sarcophagus was visible from here on the sixth floor. Twenty years ago this room must have looked much the same, but the Chernobyl reactor had still sported the caged red-and-white smokestack that appeared in all early photos of the place. The stack had fallen in the second accident, when Reactor Two went bad. The press referred to the first incident as The Disaster; the second they called The Release.

The new sarcophagus was designed to last ten thousand years. Its low sloping sides glowed redly in the sunset.

Gennady whistled tunelessly as he set up the portable generator and attached his computer, EM detection gear and the charger for his Walkman. He laid out a bedroll while the system booted and the dish outside tracked. As he was unrolling canned goods from their plastic sheaths, the system beeped once and said, "Full net connection established. Hi Gennady."

"Hi. Call Mr. Merrick at the Chernobyl Trust, would you?"

"Trying . . ."

Beep. "Gennady." Merrick's voice sounded tinny coming from the computer's speaker. "You're late. Any problems?"

"No. Just took a while to find a secure place. The radiation, you know."

"Safe?"

"Yes."

"What about the town? Signs of life?"

"No."

"The sarcophagus?"

"I can see it from here, actually." He enabled the computer's camera and pointed it out the window. "Well, okay, it's too dark out there now. But there's nothing obvious, anyway. No bombs sitting out in the open, you know?"

"We'd have spotted them on the recon photos."

"Maybe there is nothing to see because there is nothing there. I still think they could be bluffing."

Merrick grunted. "There was a release. One thousand curies straight into the Pripyat River. We monitored the plume. It came from the sarcophagus. They said they would do it, and they did. And unless we keep paying them, they'll do more."

"We'll find them. I'm here now."

"You stayed out of sight, I trust."

"Of course. Though you know, anything that moves here stands out like a whore in church. I'm just going to sit on the balcony and watch the streets, I think. Maybe move around at night."

"Just call in every four hours during the day. Otherwise we'll assume the worst."

Gennady sighed heavily. "It's a big town. You should have a whole team on this."

"Not a chance. The more people we involve, the more chance it'll get out that somebody's extorting the Chernobyl Trust. We just barely hold on to our funding as it is, Gennady."

"All right, all right. I know I come cheap. You don't have to rub it in."

"We're paying you a hell of a lot for this. Don't complain."

"Easy for you to say. You're not here. Good night, Merrick."

He stretched out for a while, feeling a bit put out. After all, it was his neck on the line. Merrick was an asshole, and Lisa had told him not to come. Well, he was here now. In his own defence, he would do a good job.

It got dark quickly, and he didn't dare show much light, so reading was out. The silence grew oppressive, so he finally grunted and sat up to make another call.

This time he jacked in to the Net. He preferred full-sense interfaces, the vibrant colours and sounds of Net culture. In moments he was caught up in a whirlwind of flickering icons and sound bites, all the news of the day and opinions from around the world pouring down the satellite link to his terminal. Gennady read and answered his mail, caught up on the news, and checked the local forecast. Good weather for the next week, apparently. Although rain would have helped keep the isotopes out of the air, he was happy that he would be able to get some sun and explore without inconvenience.

Chores done, he fought upstream through the torrent of movie trailers, whispers of starlet gossip, artspam messages and hygiene ads masquerading as real people on his chat-lines, until he reached a private chat room. Gennady conjured a body for himself, some chairs and, for variety, a pool with some sunbathers, and then called Lisa.

She answered in window mode, as she often did. He could see she was in her London apartment, dressed in a sweatshirt. "Hi," he said. "How was the day?"

"It was okay."

"Any leads on our mythical terrorists?" Lisa was a freelance Net hacker. She was well-respected, and frequently worked for Interpol. She and Gennady talked almost every day, a result of their informal working relationship. Or, he sometimes suspected, maybe he had that backwards.

She looked uncomfortable. "I haven't found anything. Where have you been? I thought you were going to call as soon as you arrived."

"I told you I'd call. I called."

"Yeah, but you're not exactly reliable that way."

"It's my life." But this was Lisaveta, not just some anonymous chat on the Net. He ground his teeth and said, "I am sorry. You're right, I make myself hard to find."

"I just like to know what's going on."

"And I appreciate it. It took me a while to find a safe place."

Her expression softened. "I guess it would. Is it all hot there?"

"Most of it. It's unpredictable. But beautiful."

"Beautiful? You're daft."

"No really. Very green, lush. Not like I expected."

She shook her head. "Why on earth did you even take this job? That one in Minsk would have paid more."

"I don't like Minsk."

She stared at him. "Chernobyl's better?"

"Listen, forget it. I'm here now. You say you haven't found our terrorists?"

She didn't look like she wanted to change the subject, but then she shrugged and said, "Not a whisper on the Net. Unless they're technoluddites, I don't see how they're operating. Maybe it's local, or an inside job."

Gennady nodded. "Hadn't ruled that out. I don't trust this Merrick fellow. Can we check into the real financial position of the Trust?"

"Sure. I'll do that. Meanwhile . . . how long are you going to be there?"

He shrugged. "Don't know. Not long."

"Promise me you'll leave before your dosimeter maxes out, even if you don't find anything. Okay?"

"Hmm."

"Promise!"

He laughed. "All right, Lisaveta. I promise."

Later, as he lay on his bedroll, he played through arguments with Lisa where he tried to explain the strange beauty of the place. He came up with many phrases and examples, but in the end he always imagined her shaking her head in incomprehension. It took him a long time to fall asleep.

There was no sign that a large group of people had entered Pripyat at any time in the recent past. When Trust inspectors came they usually arrived by helicopter, and stayed only long enough to replace the batteries at the weather stations and radiation monitoring checkpoints. The way wildflowers and moss had begun to colonize the drifted soil on the roads, any large vehicle tracks should have been readily visible. Gennady didn't find any.

Despite this he was more circumspect the next day. Merrick might be right, there might well be someone here. Gennady had pictured Pripyat in black and white, as a kind of industrial dump. The place was actually like a wild garden—though as he explored on foot, he would often round a corner or step into an open lot and find the Geiger counter going nuts. The hotspots were treacherous, because there was no way to tell where they'd be.

A few years after The Disaster, folk had started to trickle back into Pripyat. The nature of the evil was such that people saw their friends and family die no matter how far they ran. Better to go home than sit idle collecting coffin-money in some shanty town.

When the Release happened, all those who had returned died. After that, no one came.

He had to remind himself to check his watch. His first check-in with Merrick was half an hour late; the second two full hours. Gennady completely lost track of time while skirting the reactor property, which was separated from the town by marshy grassland. All manner of junk from two eras had been abandoned here. Green helicopters with red stars on them rusted next to remotely piloted halftracks with the U.N. logo and the red, white and blue flag of the Russian Republic. In one spot he found the remains of a wooden shed. The wood dropped over matted brown mounds that must once have been cardboard boxes. Thousands of clean white tubes — syringes, their needles rusted away — poked out of the mounds. The area was hot, and he didn't linger.

Everywhere he went he saw potential souvenirs, all undisturbed. Some were hot, others clean. The entire evidence of late-Soviet life was just lying about here. Gennady found it hard to believe a sizable group could spend any time in this open-air museum, and not pry into things at least a little. But it was all untouched.

He was a bit alarmed at the numbers on his dosimeter as he turned for home. Radiation sure accumulated quickly around here. He imagined little particles smashing his DNA. Here, there, everywhere in his body. It might be all right; he would probably be perfectly healthy later. It might not be all right.

A sound startled him out of his worry. The *meow* came again, and then a scrawny little white cat stepped gingerly onto the road.

"Well, hello." He knelt to pet it. The Geiger counter went wild. The cat butted against his hand, purring to rattle its ribs loose. It didn't occur to him that it was acting domesticated until a voice behind him said, "That's Varuschka."

Gennady looked up to see an old man emerge from behind a tall hedgerow. He appeared to be in his seventies, with a narrow hatchet-like face burned deep brown, and a few straggles of white hair. He wore soil-blackened overalls, and the hand he held out was black from digging. Gennady shook it anyway.

"Who the hell are you?" asked the old man abruptly.

Was this the extortionist? Well, it was too late to hide from him now. "Gennady Malianov."

"I'm Bogoliubov. I'm the custodian of Pripyat." Bogoliubov sized him up. "Just passing through, eh?"

"How do you know that?"

"The Geiger counter, the plastic on your shoes, the mask . . . Ain't that a bit uncomfortable?"

"Very, actually." Gennady scratched around it.

"Well what the hell are you wearing it for?" The old man grabbed a walking stick from somewhere behind the hedge. "You just shook hands with me. The dirt'll be hotter than anything you inhale."

"Perhaps I was not expecting to shake hands with anyone today."

Bogoliubov laughed dryly. "Radiation's funny stuff. You know I had cancer when I came here? God damn fallout cured me. Seven years now. I can still piss a straight line."

He and Varuschka started walking, and Gennady fell in beside them. "Did you live here, before The Disaster?" Bogoliubov shook his head. "Does anybody else live here?"

"No. We get visitors, Varuschka and me. But if I thought you were here to stay I wouldn't be talking to you. I'd have gone home for the rifle."

"Why's that?"

"Don't like neighbours." Seeing his expression, Bogoliubov laughed. "Don't worry, I like visitors. Just not neighbours. Haven't shot anyone in years."

Bogoliubov looked like a farmer, not an extortionist. "Had any other visitors lately?" Gennady asked him. He was sure it was an obviously leading question, but he'd never been good at talking to people. He left that up to other investigators.

"No, nobody. Unless you count the dragon." Bogoliubov gestured vaguely in the direction of the sarcophagus. "And I don't."

"The what?"

"I call it the dragon. Sounds crazy. I don't know what the hell it is. Lives in the sarcophagus. Only comes out at night."

"I see."

"Don't you take that tone with me." Bogoliubov shook his cane at Gennady. "There's more things in heaven and earth, you know. I *was* going to invite you to tea."

"I'm sorry. I am new here."

"Apology accepted." Bogoliubov laughed. "Hell, you'd have to do worse than laugh at me to make me uninvite you. I get so few guests."

"I wasn't—"

"So, why are you here? Not sightseeing, I assume."

They had arrived at a log dacha on the edge of the grassland. Bogoliubov kept some goats and chickens, and even had an apple tree in the back. Gennady's Geiger counter clicked at levels that would be dangerous after weeks, fatal in a year or two. He had been here seven years?

"I work for the University of Minsk," said Gennady. "In the medical school. I'm just doing an informal survey of the place, check for fire hazards near the sarcophagus, that sort of thing."

"So you don't work for the Trust." Bogoliubov spat. "Good thing. Bunch of meddling bureaucrats. Think they can have a job for life because the goddamn reactor will always be there. It was people like them made The Disaster to begin with."

The inside of Bogoliubov's dacha was cozy and neatly kept. The old man began ramming twigs into the firebox of an iron stove. Gennady sat admiring the view, which included neither the sarcophagus nor the forlorn towers of the abandoned city.

"Why do you stay here?" he asked finally.

Bogoliubov paused for an instant. He shook his head and brought out some waterproof matches. "Because I can be alone here. Nothing complicated about it, really."

Gennady nodded.

"It isn't complicated to love a place, either." Bogoliubov set one match in the stove. In seconds the interior was a miniature inferno. He put a kettle on to boil.

"People die, you know. But places don't. Even with everything they did to this place, it hasn't died. I mean look at it. Beautiful. You like cities, Malianov?"

Gennady shook his head.

The old man nodded. "Of course not. If you were a city person, you'd run screaming from here. It'd prey on you. You'd start having nightmares. Or kill yourself. City people can't handle Pripyat. But you're a country person, aren't you?"

"I guess I am." It would be impossible to explain to the old man that he was neither a city nor a country person. Though he lived in a large and bustling city, Gennady spent most of his free time in the pristine, controllable environments of the Net.

Bogoliubov made some herbal tea. Gennady tested it with the Geiger before he sipped it, much to Bogoliubov's amusement. Gennady filled him in on Kiev politics and the usual machinations of the international community. After an hour or so of this, though, Gennady began to feel decidedly woozy. Had he caught too big a dose today? The idea made him panicky.

"Have to go," he said finally. He wanted to stand up, but he seemed to be losing touch with his body. And everything was happening in slow motion.

"Maybe you better wait for it to wear off," said Bogoliubov.

Minutes or hours later, Gennady heard himself say, "Wait for what to wear off?"

"Can't get real tea here," said the old man. "But marijuana grows like a weed. Makes a good brew, don't you think?"

So much for controlling his situation. Gennady's anxiety crested, broke in a moment of fury, and then he was laughing out loud. Bogoliubov joined in.

The walk back to his building seemed to take days. Gennady couldn't bring himself to check the computer for messages, and fell asleep before the sun set.

Lisa shook her head as she sat down at her terminal. Why should she be so upset that he hadn't called? And yet she was—he owed her a little consideration. And what if he'd been hurt? She would have heard about it by now, since Gennady had introduced her to Merrick as a subcontractor. Merrick would have phoned. So he was ignoring her. Or something.

But she shouldn't be so upset. After all, they spoke on the phone, or met in the Net—that was the beginning and end of their relationship. True, they worked together well, both being investigators, albeit in different areas. She spoke to Gennady practically every day. Boyfriends came and went, but Gennady was always there for her.

But he never lets me be there for him, she thought as she jacked into the Net and called him.

Though she didn't intend to, when he finally answered the first thing she said was, "You promised you'd call."

"You too? Merrick just chewed me out for yesterday." He seemed listless.

"Credit me with better motives than Merrick," she said. She wanted to pursue it, but knowing how testy he could be, just said, "What happened?"

"It's not like I'm having a picnic out here, you know. It's just not so easy to stay in touch as I thought." He looked like he hadn't slept well, or maybe had slept too well.

"Listen, I'm sorry," he said suddenly, and he sounded sincere. "I'm touched that you care so much about me."

"Of course I do, Gennady. We've been through a lot together." It was rare for him to admit he was wrong; somewhat mollified, she said, "I just need to know what's going on."

He sighed. "I think I have something for you." She perked up. Lisa loved it when they worked together as a team. He was the slow, plodding investigator, used to sifting through reams of photographs, old deeds and the like. She was the talker, the one who ferreted out people's secrets by talking with them. When they'd met, Gennady had been a shy insurance investigator unwilling to take any job where he had to interview people, and she had been a nosy hacker who got her hands dirty with field work. They made a perfect match, she often thought, because they were so fundamentally different.

"There's an old man who lives here," said Gennady. "Name's Bogoliubov. Has a dacha near the reactor."

"That's insane," she said.

Gennady merely shrugged. "That's where I was yesterday—talking to him. He says nobody's come through Pripyat in ages. Except for one guy."

"Oh?" She leaned forward eagerly.

"We had a long talk, Bogoliubov and me." Gennady half-smiled at some private joke. "He says he met a guy named Yevgeny Druschenko. Part-time employee of the Trust, or so he said." As he spoke Lisa was typing madly at her terminal. "He was a regular back when they still had funding to do groundwater studies here. The thing is, he's driven into town twice in the past year. Didn't tell Bogoliubov where he was going, but the old man says both times he headed for the sarcophagus with a truckload of stuff. Crates. Bogoliubov doesn't know where they ended up."

"Bingo!" Lisa made a triumphant fist. "He's listed, all right. But he's not on the payroll anymore."

"There's more." She looked at him, eyebrows raised. Gennady grinned. "You're going to love this part. Bogoliubov says it was right after Druschenko's first visit that the dragon appeared."

"Whoa. Dragon?"

"He doesn't know what else to call it. I don't think he believes it's supernatural. But he says something is *living* inside the sarcophagus. Been there for months now."

"That's ridiculous."

"I know. It's fatal just to walk past the thing."

Lisa scowled for a minute, then dismissed the issue with a wave of her hand. "Whatever. I'm going to trace this Druschenko. Are you through there now?"

"Not quite. Bogoliubov might be lying. I have to check the rest of the town, see if there's any signs of life. Should take a couple of days."

"Hmmf." She was sure he knew what she felt about that. "Okay. But keep in touch. I mean it this time."

He placed a hand on his heart solemnly. "I promise."

It was hard. For the next several mornings Gennady awoke to find Bogoliubov waiting for him downstairs. The old man had designated himself tour guide, and proceeded to drag Gennady through bramble, fen and buckled asphalt, ensuring he visited all the high points of the city.

There was a spot where two adjacent apartment blocks had collapsed together, forming a ten-storey arch under which Bogoliubov walked whistling. In another neighborhood, the old man had restored several exquisite houses, and they paused to refresh themselves there by a spring that was miraculously clean of radiation.

What Bogoliubov saw here was nature cleansing a wound. Gennady could never completely forget the tragedy of this place; the signs of hasty abandonment were everywhere, and his imagination filled in vistas of buses and queues of people clutching what they could carry, joking nervously about what they were told would be a temporary evacuation. Thinking about it too long made him angry, and he didn't want to be angry in a place that had become so beautiful. Bogoliubov had found his own solution to that by forgetting that this was ever a place of Man.

Gennady was suspicious that the old man might be trying to distract him, so he made a point of going out on his own to explore as well. It was tiring, but he had to verify Bogoliubov's story before he could feel he had done his job. Calling Merrick or Lisa was becoming difficult because he was out so much, and so tired from walking—but as well, he found himself increasingly moving in a meditative state. He had to give himself a shake, practically learn to speak again, before he could make a call.

To combat this feeling he spent his evenings in the Net, listening to the thrum of humanity's great chorus. Even there, however, he felt more an observer. Maybe that was okay; he had always been like this, it was just cities and obligations that drove him out of his natural habits.

Then one night he awoke to the sound of engines.

It was pitch-dark and for a second he didn't know where he was. Gennady sat up and focussed on the lunar rectangle of the living room window. For a moment he heard nothing, then the grumble started up again. He thought he saw a flicker of light outside.

He staggered to the balcony where he had set up his good telescope. The sound was louder here. Like an idling train, more felt than heard. It seemed to slide around in the air, the way train sounds did when they were coming from kilometres distant.

Light broke around a distant street corner. Gennady swung the telescope around and nearly had it focussed when something large and black lurched through his visual field, and was gone again. When he looked up from the lens he saw no sign of it.

He took the stairs two at a time, flashlight beam dodging wildly ahead of him. When he got to the lobby he switched it off and stepped cautiously to the front doors. His heart was pounding.

Gennady watched for a while, then ventured out into the street. It wasn't hard to hide here; any second he could drop in the tall grass or step behind a stand of young trees. So he made his way in the direction of the sound.

It took ten minutes to reach the spot where he'd seen the light. He dropped to one knee at the side of a filling station, and poked his head around the corner. The street was empty.

The whole intersection had been overtaken with weeds and young birch trees. He puzzled over the sight for a minute, then stood and walked out into their midst. There was absolutely nowhere here that you could drive a truck without knocking over lots of plants. But nothing was disturbed.

It was silent here now. Gennady had never ventured this far in the dark; the great black slabs of the buildings were quite unnerving. Shielding the light with one hand, he used the flashlight to try to find some tracks.

There were none.

On impulse he unslung the Geiger counter and switched it on. It immediately began chattering. For a few minutes he criss-crossed the intersection, finding a definite line of higher radioactivity bisecting it. He crouched on that line, and moved along it like he was weeding a garden, holding the counter close to the ground.

As the chattering peaked he spotted a black divot in the ground. He shone the flashlight on it. It was a deep W-shaped mark, of the sort made by the feet of back-hoes and cranes. A few meters beyond it he found another. Both were incredibly hot.

A deep engine pulse sounded through the earth. It repeated, then rose to a bone-shaking thunder as two brilliant lights piniomed Gennady from the far end of the street.

He clicked off the flashlight but the thing was already coming at him. The ground shook as it began to gallop.

There was no time to even see what it was. Gennady fled through whipping underbrush and under low branches, trying to evade the uncannily accurate lamps that sought him out. He heard steel shriek and the thud of falling trees as it flung aside all the obstacles he tried to put between them.

Ahead a narrow alley made a black rectangle between two warehouses. He ran into it. It was choked with debris and weeds. "Damn." Light welled up behind him.

Both warehouses had doors and windows opening off the alley. One door was ajar. On a sudden inspiration he flicked on the flashlight and threw it hard through a window of the other building, then dove for the open door.

He heard the sound of concrete scraping as the thing shouldered its way between the buildings. The lights were intense, and the noise of its engines was awful. Then the lights went out, as it paused. He had the uncanny impression that it was looking for him.

Gennady stood in a totally empty concrete-floored building. Much of the roof had gone, and in the dim light he could see a clear path to the front door.

Cinderblocks shuddered and crashed outside. It was knocking a hole in the other building. Gennady ran for the door and made it through. The windows of the other warehouse were lit up.

He ran up the street to his building, and when he got inside he pulled his bike into a back room and raced up the stairs. He could hear the thing roaring around the neighborhood for what seemed like hours, and then the noise slowly faded into the distance, and he fell back on his bedroll, exhausted.

At dawn he packed up and by midmorning he had left Pripyat and the contaminated zone behind him.

Merrick poured pepper vodka into a tall glass and handed it to Gennady. "Dosvedanya. We picked up Druschenko this morning."

Gennady wondered as he sipped how the vodka would react with the iodine pill he'd just taken. Traffic noises and the smell of diesel wafted through the open window of Merrick's Kiev office. Merrick tipped back his own drink, smiled brightly and went to sit behind the huge oak desk that dominated the room.

"I have to thank you, Gennady. We literally couldn't find anyone else who was willing to go in there on the ground." He shook his head. "People panic at the thought of radiation."

"Don't much like it myself." Gennady took another sip. "But you can detect and avoid it. Not so simple to do with the stuff that comes out of the smokestacks these days. Or gets by the filters at the water plant."

Merrick nodded. "So you were able to take all the right precautions."

Gennady thought of Bogoliubov's warm tea settling in his stomach . . . and he had done other stupid things there too. But the doctors insisted his overall dosage was "acceptable." His odds for getting cancer had gone up as much as if he'd been chain-smoking for the past six months. Acceptable? How could one know?

"So that's that," said Merrick. "You found absolutely no evidence that anyone but Druschenko had visited the sarcophagus, right? Once we prove that it was him driving the RPV, we'll be able to close this file entirely. I think you deserve a bonus, Gennady, and I've almost got the board to agree."

"Well, thanks." RPV—they had decided the dragon must be one of the Remotely Piloted Vehicles that the Trust had used to build the new sarcophagus. Druschenko had taken some of the stockpiled parts and power supplies from a Trust warehouse, and apparently gotten one of the old lifters going. It was the only way he could open the sarcophagus and survive.

Merrick was happy. Lisa was ecstatic that he was out of Pripyat. It all seemed too easy to Gennady; maybe it was because they hadn't seen the thing. This morning he'd walked down to the ironworks to watch someone using a Chernobyl-model RPV near the kilns. It had looked like a truck with legs, and moved like a sloth. Nothing like the thing that had chased him across the city.

Anyway, he had his money. He chatted with Merrick for a while, then Gennady left to find a bank machine, and prove to himself he'd been paid. First order of business, a new suit. Then he was going to shop for one of those new interfaces for his system. Full virtual reality, like he'd been dreaming about for months.

The noise and turbulence of Kiev's streets hit him like a wall. People everywhere, but no one noticed anyone else in a city like this. He supposed most people drifted through the streets treating all these strangers around as no more than ghosts, but he couldn't do that. As he passed an old woman who was begging on the corner, he found himself noticing the laugh lines around her eyes that warred with the deeply scored lines of disappointment around her mouth; the meticulous stitchwork where she had repaired the sleeves of her cheap dress spoke of a dignity that must make her situation seem all the worse for her. He couldn't ignore her, but he couldn't help her either.

For a while he stood at a downtown intersection, staring over the sea of people. Above the grimy facades, a haze of coal smoke and exhaust banded the sky a yellow that matched the shade on the grimy tattered flags hanging from the street lamps.

Everywhere, he saw victims of the Release. Men and women with open sores or wearing the less visible scars of destitution and disappointment dawdled on the curbs, stared listlessly through shop windows at goods they would never be able to afford on their meagre pensions. No one looked at them.

He bought the interface instead of the suit, and the next day he didn't go out at all.

He was nursing a crick in his neck, drinking some weak tea and preparing to go back into a huge international consensual-reality game he now had the equipment to play, when Lisa called.

"Look, Lisa, I've got new toys."

"Why am I not surprised. Have you been out at all since you got back?"

"No. I'm having fun."

"How are you going to meet a nice Ukrainian girl if you never go out?"

"Maybe I like English girls better."

"Oh yeah? Then fly to England. You just got paid."

"The Net is so much faster. And I have the right attachments now."

She laughed. "Toys. I see. You want the latest news on the case?"

He frowned. No, actually, he didn't think he did. But she lived for this sort of thing. "Sure," he said to indulge her.

"Druschenko says he was just the courier. Says he never drove the dragon at all. He's actually quite frantic—he claims he was paid to bring supplies in and do the initial hook up of a RPV, but that's all. Of course, he's made some mighty big purchases lately, and we can't trace the money and he won't tell us where it is. So it's a stalemate."

Gennady thought about Merrick's cheerful confidence the other day. "Did the Trust actually make the most recent payment to the extortionist?"

"No. They could hardly afford to, and anyway Druschenko—"

"Could not have acted alone."

"What?"

"Come on, Lisa. You said yourself you can't find the money. It went into the Net, right? That's your territory, it's not Druschenko's. He's a truck driver, not a hacker, for God's sake. Listen, have they put a Geiger counter on him?"

"Why . . ."

"Find out how hot he is. He had to have been piloting the RPV from nearby, unless he had a satellite link, and there too, he's just a truck driver, not James Bond. Find out how hot he is."

"Um. Maybe you have a point."

"And another thing. Has the Trust put some boats in the river to check for another radiation plume?"

"I don't know."

"We better find out. Because I'll bet you a case of vodka there's going to be another Release."

"Can I call you right back?"

"Certainly." He hung up, shaking his head. People who lived by Occam's Razor died young. That, he supposed, was why he got paid the big bucks.

He spent most of the next week in the Net, venturing out for groceries and exercise. He smiled at a pretty clerk in the grocery store, and she smiled back, but he never knew what to say in such situations, where he couldn't hide behind an avatar's mask or simply disappear if he embarrassed himself; so he didn't talk to her.

In the platonic perfection of the Net, though, Gennady had dozens of friends and business connections. Between brief searches for new work, he participated in numerous events, both games and art pieces. Here he could be witty, and handsome. And there was no risk. But when he finally rolled into bed at night, there was no warm body there waiting for him, and at those times he felt deeply lonely.

In the morning the computer beckoned, and he would quickly forget the feeling.

Merrick interrupted him in the middle of a tank battle. In this game, Gennady was one of the British defending North Africa against the Desert Fox. The sensual qualities of his new interface were amazing; he could feel the heat, the grit of the sand, almost smell it. The whole effect was ruined when the priority one window opened in the middle of the air above his turret, and Merrick said, "Gennady, I've got a new job for you."

North Africa dissolved. Gennady realized his back hurt and his mouth was dry. "What is it?" he snapped.

"I wouldn't be calling if I didn't think you were the perfect man for the job. We need someone to make a very brief visit to Pripyat. Shouldn't take more than a day."

"Where's that bonus you promised me?"

"I was coming to that. The board's authorized me to pay you an additional twenty percent bonus for work already done. That's even if you turn down this contract."

"Ah. I see. So what is it you need?" He was interested, but he didn't want to appear too eager. Could lower the price that way.

"We want to make sure the sarcophagus is intact. We were going to do a helicopter inspection, but it's just possible Druschenko did some low level . . . well, to put it bluntly, got inside."

"Inside? What do you mean, inside?"

"There may be some explosives inside the sarcophagus. Now we don't want anybody going near it, physically. Have you ever piloted an RPV?"

"Not really. Done a lot of virtual reality sims, but that's not the same thing."

"Close enough. Anyway, we only need you to get the thing to the reactor site. We've got an explosives expert on call who'll take over once you get there and deactivate the bombs. If there are any."

"So he's coming with me?"

"Not exactly, no. He'll be riding in on a satellite link. You're to establish that link in Pripyat, drive the RPV to the reactor, and he'll jack in to do the actual assessment. Then you pull out. That's all there is to it."

"Why can't somebody pilot it in from outside the city?"

"It's only works on a short-range link. You'll have to get within two miles of the sarcophagus."

"Great. Just great. When do you want this to happen?"

"Immediately. I'm having your RPV flown in; it'll arrive tonight. Can you set out in the morning?"

"Depends on what you're willing to pay me."

"Double your last fee."

"Triple."

"Done."

Shit, he thought. *Should have gone for more.* "All right, Merrick, you've got yourself an RPV driver. For a day."

Gennady debated whether to call Lisa. On the one hand, there was obviously more to this than Merrick was admitting. On the other, she would tell him not to go back to Pripyat. He wanted to avoid that particular conversation, so he didn't call.

Instead he took a cab down to a Trust warehouse at six o'clock to inspect his RPV. The warehouse was a tall anonymous metal-clad building; his now practised eye told him it might remain standing for twenty or thirty years if abandoned. Except that the roof would probably cave in . . .

"You Malianov?" The man was stocky, with the classic slab-like Russian face. He wiped his hands on an oily rag as he walked out to meet Gennady. Gennady shook his hand, smiling as he remembered Bogoliubov, and they went in to inspect the unit.

"What the hell is that?" Whatever it was, it was not just a remotely piloted vehicle. Standing in a shaft of sunlight was an ostrich-like machine at least three metres tall. It sprouted cameras and mikes from all over, and sported two uncannily human arms at about shoulder level. Gennady's guide grinned and gave it a shove. It shuffled its feet a little, regaining balance.

"Military telepresence. Latest model." The man grabbed one of its hands. "We're borrowing it from the Americans. You like?"

"Why do we need this?"

"How the hell should I know? All I know is you're reconnoitering the sarcophagus with it. Right?"

Gennady nodded. He kept his face neutral, but inside he was fuming. Merrick was definitely not telling him everything.

That evening he went on a supply run downtown. He bought all the things he hadn't on his first trip out, including a lot more food. Very intentionally, he did not pause to ask himself why he was packing a month's worth of food for a two-day trip.

He was sitting in the middle of the living room floor, packing and repacking, when Lisa phoned. He took it as a voice-only call; if she asked, he'd say he wasn't dressed or something.

"Remember what you said about how Druschenko would have to have had a satellite link to run the dragon?"

"Yeah." He hopped onto the arm of his couch. He was keyed up despite the lateness of the hour.

"Well, you got me thinking," she said. "And guess what? There's a connection. Not with Druschenko, though."

"Okay, I'll bite."

"Can you jack in? I'll have to do some show and tell here."

"Okay." He made sure the apartment cameras were off, then went into the Net. Lisa was there in full avatar—visible head to foot, in 3-D—grinning like the proverbial cat with the canary.

"So I thought, what if Druschenko did have a satellite link to the sarcophagus? And lo and behold, somebody does." She called up some windows that showed coordinates, meaningless to Gennady. "At least, there's traffic to some kind of transceiver there. I figured I had Druschenko right then—but the link's still live, and traffic goes way up at regular intervals. During the night, your time. So we're dealing with a night-hawk, I thought. Except he wouldn't have to be a night-hawk if he was calling from, say, North America."

"Wait, wait, you're getting way ahead of me. What's this traffic consist of? You intercepted it, didn't you?"

"Well, not exactly. It's heavily encrypted. Plus, once it's in the Net it goes through a bunch of anonymous rerouters, gets split up and copies sent to null addresses, and so on. Untraceable from this end, at least so far."

"Ah, so if he's from North America, that narrows it down a bit. To only about half a billion possibilities."

"Ah, Gennady, you have so little faith. It's probably a telepresence link, right? That's your dragon. Nothing big was brought in, so it's got to be an adaptation of the existing Chernobyl designs. So whoever it is, they should be familiar with those designs, and they'd have to know there were still some RPVs in Pripyat, and they should have a connection to Druschenko. And—here's the topper—they had a lot of start-up capital to run this scam. Had to, with the satellite link, the souping-up of the RPV, and the missiles."

"Missiles? What missiles?"

"Haven't you checked the news lately? One of the Trust's helicopters crashed yesterday. It was doing a low-level pass over the sarcophagus, and wham! down it goes. Pilot was killed. An hour after the news was released I started seeing all sorts of traffic on my secure Interpol groups, police in Kiev and Brussels talking about ground-to-air missiles."

"Oh, shit," he said.

"So anyway, I just looked for somebody involved in the original sarcophagus project, on the RPV side, who was American and rich. And it popped out at me."

Gennady was barely listening, but his attention returned when she brought up a window with a grainy photo of a thin-faced elderly man. It was hard to tell, but he appeared to be lying on a bed. His eyes were bright and hard, and they stared directly out at Gennady.

"Trevor Jaffrey. He got quite rich doing RPVs and telepresence about twenty years ago. The Chernobyl project was his biggest contract. A while after that he became a recluse, and began wasting his money on some pretty bizarre projects."

"Dragons?"

"Well, Jaffrey's a quadraplegic. He got rich through the Net, and he lived through it too. When I say he became a recluse, he already was, physically. He dropped out of Net society too, and spent all his time and money on physical avatars—telepresences. I've got access to a couple of them, because he had to sell them when he couldn't pay his bills. Want to see one?"

"What, now?"

"I've got a temporary pass. This one's being used as a theme park ride now. At one time Jaffrey must have spent all his free time in it. The mind boggles."

She had his entire attention now. "Okay. Show me."

"Here's the address, name and password. Just take a quick peek. I'll wait."

He entered the commands, and waited as a series of message windows indicated a truly prodigious data pipe opening between his little VR setup and some distant machine. Then the world went dark, and when it came back again he was underwater.

Gennady was standing on the ocean floor. All around were towers of coral, and rainbow fishes swam by in darting schools. The ocean was brilliant blue, the sunlight above shattered into thousands of crystal shards by the waves. He turned his head, and felt the water flow through his hair. It was warm, felt silky against his skin. He could breathe just fine, but he also felt completely submerged.

Gennady raised a hand. Something huge and metal lifted up, five steel fingers on its end. He waggled them—they moved.

This is not a simulation, he realized. Somewhere, in one of the Earth's seas, this machine was standing, and he was seeing through its eyes and hearing through its ears.

He took a step. He could walk, as easily as though he were on land.

Gennady knelt and ran his fingers through the fine white sand. He could actually feel it. Black Sea? More likely the Caribbean, if this Jaffrey was American.

It was achingly beautiful, and he wanted to stay. But Lisa was waiting. He logged out, and as he did caught a glimpse of a truly huge number in American dollars, which flashed *paid in full* then vanished.

Lisa's avatar was smiling, hands behind her back and bobbing on the balls of her feet. "Jaffrey can't pay his bills. And he's addicted to his telepresences. You should see the arctic one. He even had a lunar one for a while. See the common thread?"

"They're all places nobody goes. Or nobody can go," he said. He was starting to feel tired.

"Jaffrey hates people. And he's being driven out of his bodies, one after the other. So he turns in desperation to an old, reliable one—the Chernobyl RPV. Designed to survive working conditions there, and there's still parts, if he can pay off an old acquaintance from the project to bring them in."

"So he does, and he's got a new home." He nodded. "And a way of making more money. Extort the Trust."

"Exactly. Aren't I smart?"

"You, Lisaveta, are a genius." He blew her image a kiss. "So all we need to do is shut him down, and the crisis is over."

"Hmm. Well, no, not exactly. American law is different, and the Net connections aren't proven to go to him. We can't actually move on him until we can prove it's him doing it."

"Well, shut down the feed from the satellite, then."

"We were about to do that," she said with a scowl. "When we got a call from Merrick. Seems the extortionist contacted him just after the missile thing. Warned that he'd blow the sarcophagus if anybody cut the link or tried to get near the place."

"A dead-man switch?"

"Probably. So it's not so simple as it looks."

He closed his eyes and nodded.

"How about you?" she asked. "Anything new?"

"Oh, no, no. Not really. Same old thing, you know?"

It was raining when he reached his apartment building. Gennady had driven the motorcycle in, leaving all his other supplies by the city gates. He wanted to try something.

The rain was actually a good thing; it made a good cover for him to work under. He parked his bike in the foyer, and hauled a heavy pack from the sidecar, then up twelve floors to the roof. Panting and cursing, he paused to rest under a fiberglass awning. The roof was overgrown with weeds. The sarcophagus was a distant grey dome in a pool of marshland.

He hooked up the satellite feed and aimed it. Then he unreeled a fibre-optic line down the stairs to the sixth floor, and headed for his old place.

Somebody had trashed it. Bogoliubov, it had to be. The piano had bullet holes in it, and there was shit smeared on the wall. The words "Stay away" were written in the stuff.

"Jesus." Gennady backed out of the room.

Scratching his stubble nervously, he shouldered his way into the next apartment. This one was empty except for some old stacking chairs, and had a water-damaged ceiling and one broken window. Radiation was higher than he would have found acceptable a week ago—but after he finished here he could find a better place. Then think what to do about Bogoliubov.

He secured the door and set up his generator and the rest of the computer equipment. He needed a repeater for the satellite signal, and he put that on the balcony. Then he jacked in, and connected to his RPV.

At first all he saw was dirt. Gennady raised his head, and saw the road into town, blurred by rain. He stood up, and felt himself rise to more than man-height. This was great! He flexed his arms, turned his torso back and forth, then reached to pick up his sacks of supplies.

It was a bit awkward using these new arms, but he got the hang of it after spilling some groceries and a satchel of music disks into the mud. When it was all hanging from his mantis-like limbs, he rose up again and trotted toward town.

The RPV drank gas to feed its fuel cells. Bogoliubov had shown Gennady some full tanks on the edge of town, enough to keep the thing going for months or years. Thinking of the old man, Gennady decided that as soon as they were done with Jaffrey, he would visit Bogoliubov with the RPV, and confiscate his rifle.

He jogged tirelessly through the rain until he came to his building. There he paused to hide the bike, in case the old man did come around today, then bumped his way into the stairwell and went up.

Gennady paused in front of the apartment door. He hadn't counted on the eeriness of this moment. He listened, hearing only the faint purr of the generator inside. Hesitantly, he reached to turn the knob with a steel hand, and eased the door open.

A man crouched on the floor near one wall. He was stocky and balding, in his late thirties. He was dressed in a teal shirt and green slacks. His eyes were closed, and small wires ran from his temples to a set of black boxes near the balcony door. He was rocking slowly back and forth.

Jesus, am I doing that? Gennady instantly cut the link. He blinked and looked up, to find the doorway blocked by a monstrous steel and crystal creature. Its rainbow-beaded lenses were aimed at him. Plastic bags swayed from its clenched fists. Gennady's heart started hammering, as though the thing had somehow snuck up on him.

Swearing, he hastily unloaded the supplies from its arms. After putting the stuff away he found himself reluctant to re-enter the living room. Under this low roof the RPV looked like a metal dinosaur ready to pounce. It must weigh two hundred kilos at least. He'd have to remember that, and avoid marshy ground or rotten floors when he used it outside.

He linked to it again just long enough to park it down the hall. Then he shut the door and jammed a chair under the knob.

The morning birds woke Gennady. For a long time he just lay there, drinking in the peace. In his half-awake state, he imagined an invisible shield around this small apartment, sheltering him from any sort of pain, aggravation or distraction. Of all places in the world, he had finally found the one where he could be fully, completely carefree. The hot spots of radiation could be mapped and avoided; he would deal with Bogoliubov in time; Jaffrey would not be a problem for long.

No one would ever evict him from this place. No one would come around asking after him solicitously. No noisy neighbours would move in. And yet, as long as he had fuel to run the generator, he could step into the outside world as freely as ever, live by alias in any or all of the thousands of worlds of the Net.

Be exactly who he wanted to be . . .

Feel at home at last.

But finally he had to rise, make himself a meagre breakfast and deal with the reality of the situation. His tenancy here was fragile. Everything would have to go perfectly for him to be able to take advantage of the opportunity he had been given.

First he phoned Merrick. "You never told me about the helicopter."

"Really? I'm sure I did." It was only a voice line; Gennady was sure Merrick wouldn't have been so glib if they'd been able to make eye contact.

Gennady would feel absolutely no guilt over stealing the RPV from him.

"Forget it, except let me say you are a bastard and I'll join the Nazis before I work for you after this," he said. "Now tell me what we're doing. And no more surprises or I walk."

Merrick let the insult pass. They set the itinerary and time for the reconnoitering of the sarcophagus. Gennady was to use the RPV's full set of sensors to ensure there were no tripwires or mines on the approach. Druschenko had denied knowledge of anything other than Jaffrey's RPV. Certainly hearing about the missiles beforehand would have been nice.

"You're to do the initial walking inspection this afternoon at 2:00. Is that enough time for you to familiarize yourself with the RPV?"

Gennady glanced at the apartment door. "No problem."

With everything set, Merrick rang off and Gennady, stretching, stepped onto the balcony to watch the morning sun glow off the sarcophagus. It was an oval dome made of interlocking concrete triangles. Rust stains spread down the diamonds here and there from the heavy stanchions that held it all together. Around the circumference of the thing, he knew, a thick wall was sunk all the way to bedrock, preventing seepage of the horrors within. It was supposed to last ten thousand years; like most people, Gennady assumed it would crumble in a century. Still, one had to be responsible to one's own time.

Humming, he groped for his coffee cup. Just as it reached his lips the computer said, "Lisaveta is calling you."

He burned his tongue.

"Damn damn damn. Is it voice or full-feed? Full-feed. Shit."

He jacked in. He hoped she would match his laconic tone as he said, "Hello, Lisa."

"You asshole."

He found it difficult to meet her gaze. "Are we going to get into something pointless here?"

"No. I'm going to talk and you're going to listen."

"I see."

"Why the hell didn't you tell me you were going back?"

"You'd have told me not to go. I didn't want an argument."

"So you don't respect me enough to argue with me?"

"What?" The idea made no sense to him. He just hadn't seen what good it would do to fight. And, just maybe, he *had* been afraid she might talk him out of it. But he would never admit that to her.

"Gennady. I'm not trying to run your life. If you want to throw it away that's your business. But I'm your friend. I care about you. I just . . . just want to *know*, that's all."

He frowned, staring out the window. Dozens of empty apartment windows stared back. For an instant he imagined dozens of other Gennadys, all looking out, none seeing the others.

"Maybe I don't want to be known," he said. "I'm tired of this world of snoops and gossips. Maybe I want to write my memoirs in a private language. Apparently that's not allowed."

"Pretty ironic for you to be tired of snoops," she said, "inasmuch as that's what you do for a living. And me too . . ." She blinked, then scowled even harder. "Are you referring to—"

"Look, I have to go now—"

"*That's* what this is about, isn't it? You just want to be able to hang up on anybody and everybody the instant you start feeling uncomfortable." Lisa looked incredulous. "Is that it? It is, isn't it. You want to have your cake and eat it. So you found a place where you can hide from everybody, just poke your head out whenever you need someone to talk to. Well, I'm not a TV, you know. I'm not going to let you just turn me on and off when it suits you.

"Keep your empty town and your empty life, then. I'll have none of it."

She hung up.

"Bitch!" He yanked off the headset and kicked the wall. No neighbours to complain—he kicked it again. "What the hell do you want from me?" He'd put a hole in the plasterboard. Dust swirled up, and he heard the Geiger counter buzz louder for a second.

"Oh, God." He slumped on the balcony, but when he raised his eyes all that met them was the vista of the sarcophagus, gleaming now like some giant larva on the banks of the river.

Unaccountably, Gennady found his eyes filling with tears.

How long has it been, he wondered in amazement, *since you cried?*

Years. He pinched the bridge of his nose, and blinked a few times. He needed to walk; yes, a long walk in the sun would bring him around . . .

He stopped at the door to the apartment. There was the plastic wrap he should use to cover his shoes. And the face mask. And beside that the Geiger counter.

A horrible feeling of being trapped stole over him. For a few minutes he stood there, biting his nails, staring at the peeling wallpaper. Then the anger returned, and he kicked the wall again.

"I'm right." To prove it, he sat down, jacked in, and called up the interface for the RPV.

———————

Gennady held his head high as he walked in the sun in a plaza where no human could set foot for the next six thousand years. He knelt and examined the gigantic wildflowers that grew in abundance here. They were *his*, in a way that nothing else had ever been nor could be outside this place. This must be how the old man felt, he marvelled—but Bogoliubov's armour was a deliberate refusal to believe the danger he was in. With the RPV, Gennady had no need for such illusions.

He didn't take every opportunity to explore. There would be plenty of time for that later, after he reported the accidental destruction of the RPV. For now, he just sauntered and enjoyed the day. His steel joints moved soundlessly, and he felt no fatigue or heat.

Beep. "Merrick here. Gennady, are you on-line?"

"Yes. I'm here."

"Gennady, let me introduce Dentrane. You'll hand the RPV off to him when you get in position, and he'll take it from there. If we're lucky, we'll only need to do this once."

"Hello, Gennady," said Dentrane. He had a thick Estonian accent.

"Good to hear from you, Dentrane. Shall I walk us over to the sarcophagus and you can take a peek at what all the fuss is about?"

Dentrane laughed. "Delighted. Lead on."

Time to be 'all business' as Lisaveta would say. He jogged towards the river.

"It's American law," Lisa was saying to Merrick. They had met in a neutral room in cyberspace. Merrick's avatar was bland as usual; Lisa had represented herself as a cyber-Medusa, with fibre-optic leads snaking from her hair to attach to a globe that floated before her. "When you're dealing with the Net, you've got both international and local laws to worry about," she explained. "We can't guarantee our trace of the paths to the satellite signal. We can't shut it down on the satellite end. And unless we have proof that it's Jaffrey doing this, we can't shut it down at his end."

"So our hands are tied." Merrick's avatar was motionless, but she imagined him pacing. In a window next to him, the live feed from the RPV showed green foliage, then the looming concrete curve of the sarcophagus.

"You're going to have to trust me. We'll find a way to prove it's Jaffrey."

"I have sixteen military RPVs waiting in the river. The second I see a problem, Ms. MacDonald, they're going in. And if they go in, you have to shut down Jaffrey."

"I can't! And what if he's got a dead-man switch?"

"I'm relying on Dentrane to tell us if he does. And I'm relying on you to cut Jaffrey off when I order it."

She glared at the avatar. It must be ten times she'd told him she had no authority to do that. She knew how to, sure—but if they were wrong and Jaffrey wasn't the extortionist, she would be criminally liable. But Merrick didn't care about that.

He didn't seem to care about Gennady, either. And why should he? Gennady had chosen to plant himself right next to the sarcophagus. If it blew up he would have no one to blame but himself.

And that would be absolutely no consolation when she had to fly out to watch him die of radiation poisoning in some Soviet-vintage hospital ward. She had woken herself up last night with that scenario, and had lain awake wondering why she should do that for a man whom she knew only through the Net. But maybe it was precisely because their association was incomplete. Lisa knew he was as real a person as she; in a way they were close. But they would not have really met until she touched his hand, and she couldn't bear the thought of losing him before that happened.

Angrily she glanced at her ranks of numbers and documents, all of which pointed at Jaffrey, none conclusively. It all made her feel so helpless. She turned to watch the movement of the RPV instead.

The RPV had scaled the steep lower part of the sarcophagus, and now clambered hand over hand toward a red discoloration on one flank. With a start, Lisa realized there were some bulky objects sticking up there. The camera angle swerved and jittered, then the RPV paused long enough for her to get a good look. She heard Merrick swear just as she realized she was looking at tarpaulins, painted to resemble the concrete of the structure, that had been stretched over several green metal racks.

Then one of the tarps disappeared in a white cloud. The camera shook as everything vanished in a white haze. Then—static.

"What was that?"

"Holy mother of God," said Merrick. "He launched."

Gennady froze. He had stepped onto the balcony to let Dentrane get on with his work. From here he had a magnificent view of the sarcophagus, so the contrail of the rocket was clearly visible. It rose straight up, an orange cut in the sky, then levelled off and headed straight at him. He just had time to blink and think, *I'm standing right next to the RPV signal repeater* before the contrail leapt forward faster than the eye could follow, and all the windows of the surrounding buildings flashed sun-bright.

The concussion was a sudden hammer blow, nothing like the roaring explosions he heard in movies or VR. He was on his back on the balcony, ears ringing, when he heard the *bang!* echo back from the other buildings, and could almost follow its course through the abandoned city as the rings of shocked air hit one neighbourhood after the next, and reported back.

A cascade of dust and grit obscured the view. It all came from overhead somewhere. He realized as he sat up that the explosion had occurred on the roof. That was where he'd set up the big dish necessary for Dentrane's data-feed.

The fear felt like cold spreading through his chest, down his arms. He leaned on the swaying balcony, watching for the second contrail that would signal the second rocket. The dish on the roof was the link to the Net, yes; but it fed its signal down here to the transmitter that sat a meter to Gennady's left, and that transmitter was the control connection to the RPV. It was the only live beacon now.

Nothing happened. As the seconds passed, Gennady found himself paralyzed by indecision: in the time it took for him to rise to his feet and turn, and take three steps, the rocket might be on him—and he had to see it if it came.

It did not. Gradually he became aware that his mouth was open, his throat hurting from a yell that hadn't made it from his lungs to his vocal cords. He fell back on his elbows, then shouted "Shit!" at a tenth the volume he thought he needed, and scrambled back into the apartment.

He was halfway down the stairs when the cell phone rang. He barked a laugh at the prosaic echo, the only sound now in this empty building other than his chattering footsteps. He grabbed it from his belt. "What?"

"Gennady! Are you all right?"

"Yes, Lisa."

"Oh, thank God! Listen, you've got to get out of there—"

"Just leaving."

"I'm so glad."

"Fuck you." He hung up and jammed the phone back in his belt. It immediately rang again. Gennady stopped, cursed, grabbed it, almost pressed the receive button. Then he tossed it over the banister. After a second he heard it hit the landing below with a crack.

He ran past it into the lobby, and pulled out the bike. He started it, and paused to look around the sad, abandoned place he had almost lived in. His hand on the throttle was trembling.

The release could happen at any moment. There would be an explosion, who knew how big; he imagined chunks of concrete floating up in the air, exposing a deep red wound in the earth, the unhealing sore of Chernobyl. A cloud of dust would rise, he could watch it from outside. Quiet, subtle, it would turn its head toward Kiev, as it had years ago. Soon there would be more ghosts in the streets of the great city.

He would get away. Lisa would never speak to him, and he could never walk the avenues of Kiev again without picturing himself here. He could never look the survivors of the Release in the eye again. But he would have gotten away.

"Liar!"

The sound jolted him. Gennady looked up. Bogoliubov, the self-proclaimed custodian of Pripyat, stalked towards him across the courtyard, his black greatcoat flapping in the evening breeze.

"Liar," said the old man again.

"I'm not staying," Gennady shouted.

"You *lied* to me!"

Gennady took his hand off the throttle. "What?"

"You work for the Trust. Or is it the army! And to think I believed that story about you being a med student." Bogoliubov stopped directly in Gennady's path.

"Look, we haven't got time for this. There might be another release. We have to get out of here. Hop on."

Bogoliubov's eyes widened. "So you betrayed him, too. I'm not surprised." He spat in the dirt at Gennady's feet and turned away. "I'm not going anywhere with you."

"Wait!" Gennady popped the kickstand on the bike and caught up to the old man. "I'm sorry. I didn't mean to hurt you. I came here because of the dragon. How could I know you weren't involved?"

Bogoliubov whirled, scowling. He seemed to be groping for words. Finally, "Trust was a mistake," was all he said. As if the effort cost him greatly, he reached out and shoved Gennady hard in the chest. Then he walked rapidly away.

Gennady watched him go, then returned to the bike. His head was throbbing. He shut the bike down, and walked slowly back to the entrance of the apartment building. He stopped. He waited, staring at the sky. And then he went in.

"Lisaveta, I'm linking to the RPV now."

"Gennady! What?" He smiled grimly at the transparent surprise in her voice. She who liked to Know, had been startled by him. Gennady had linked the cellphone signal to the RPV interface. She would get voice, but no video this way.

He adjusted the headset. "Connecting now." He took a deep breath, and jabbed the *enter* key on his board.

Vision lurched. And then he was staring at a red tarpaulin, which was tangled up in the fallen spars of a green metal rack. Several long metal tubes stuck out of this, all aimed at the ground. A haze like exhaust from a bus hung over everything.

The missile rack shook. Gennady cautiously turned his head to see what might be causing the motion. Directly beside him was the black, rusted flank of a thing like a tank with legs. Several sets of arms dangled from its sloped front, and two of these were tearing the tough fabric of the tarp away from the collapsed rack.

"Gennady, talk to me!" He smiled to hear the concern in her voice. "Where are you?"

"Dentrane's out of the loop, so I've taken over the RPV. I've got it on the side of the sarcophagus."

"But where are you?"

"Lisa, listen. *Someone else is here.* Do you understand? There is another RPV, and it's trying to fix the missile rack."

"Jaffrey . . ."

"That his name? Whatever." The black dragon had nearly unravelled the tarp. If it succeeded in realigning the missile tubes, it would have a clear shot at the balcony where Gennady now sat.

"It's ignoring me. Thinks I've run away, I guess." He looked around, trying not to turn his head. There was nothing obvious to use as a weapon—but then his own RPV was a weapon, he recalled. Nothing compared to the hulking, grumbling thing next to him, but more than a match for—

—the missile tubes he pounced on. Gennady felt the whole structure go down under him, metal rending. He flailed about, scattering the tubes with loud banging blows, winding up on his asbestos backside looking up at the two spotlight eyes of the black RPV.

He switched on the outside speaker. "This isn't your private sandbox, you know."

Two huge arms shot out. He rolled out of the way. Metal screamed.

A deep roaring shook the whole side of the sarcophagus. He could see small spires of dust rise from the triangular concrete slabs. The dragon had leaped, and utterly smashed the place where he had just been.

Just ahead under the flapping square of another grey tarp Gennady saw a deep black opening in the side of the sarcophagus. "This your home?" he shouted as he clambered up to it.

"Stay away!" The voice was deep and carrying, utterly artificial.

"What was that?" Lisa was still with him.

"That would be your Jaffrey. He's pissed, as the Yankees would say."

"Why are you doing this?"

"Lisa, he's going to make a release. We both know it. Only a fool wouldn't realize there's a backup plan to me being here. If I fail, the men in the choppers come in, am I wrong? You and I know it. This guy knows it. Now he's got nothing to lose. He'll blow the top off the place."

"Merrick's ready to send the others in now. You just get out of there and let them handle it."

"No." The monster was close behind him as Gennady made it to the dark opening. "I can't avoid this one. You know it's true."

She might have said "Oh," and he did imagine a tone of sad resignation to whatever she did say, but he was too busy bashing his way into the bottom of a pit to make it out. Gennady rolled to a stop in a haze of static; his cameras adjusted to the dark in time for him to see a huge black square block the opening above, and fall at him.

"Shit!" He couldn't avoid it this time. Something heavy hit him as he staggered to his feet, flicking him into a wall as though he were made of balsa wood. He didn't actually feel the blow, but it was an impossibly quick motion like a speeded-up movie; sensation vanished from his right arm.

He managed to cartwheel out of the way of another piston blow. Gennady backed up several paces, and looked around.

This was sort of an antechamber to the remnants of one of the reactor rooms. Circles of light from the headlamp eyes of the dragon swooped and dove through an amazing tangle of twisted metal and broken cement under the low red girders of the sarcophagus' ceiling. Here were slabs of wall still painted institution green, next to charred metal pipes as thick as his body. The wreckage made a rough ring around a cleared area in the centre. And there, the thing he had never in his life expected to see, there was the open black mouth of the obscenity itself.

Jaffrey, if this was indeed he, had made a nest in the caldera of Reactor Four.

Gennady bounded across the space and up the rubble on the other side. He clutched at a cross-beam and pulled himself up on it while the dragon laboured to follow. When he reached with both arms, only one appeared and grasped the beam.

"Come down," said the dragon in its deep bass that rattled the very beams. Its bright eyes were fixed on him, only meters below.

"What, are you crazy?" he said, instantly regretting his choice of words.

The dragon sat back with a seismic thud. It turned its big black head, eerily like a bear's as it regarded him.

"I've been watching you," it said after a long minute.

Gennady backed away along the girder.

"When I was a boy," said the dragon of Pripyat, "I wrote a letter to God. And then I put the letter in a jar, and I buried it in the garden, as deep as I could reach. It never occurred to me that someone might dig it up one day. I thought, no one sees God. God is in the hidden places between the walls, behind us when we are looking the other way. But I have put this letter out of the world. Maybe God will pass by and read it."

"Gennady," said Lisa. "You have to find out who this is. We can't cut Jaffrey's signal until we have proof that it's him. Can you hear me?"

"I watched you walking in the evenings," said the dragon. "You stared up at the windows the same way I do. You put your hands behind your back, head down, and traced the cracks in the pavement like a boy. You moved as one liberated from a curse."

"Shut up," said Gennady.

"Do you remember the first photos from the accident? Remember the image of this place's roof? Just a roof, obviously trashed by an explosion of some kind. But still, a roof, where you could stand and look out. Except you couldn't. No one could. That roof was the first place I had ever actually seen that had been removed from the world. A place no one could go or ever would go. To stand there for even a moment was death. Remember?"

"I was too young," said Gennady.

"Good," said Lisa. "We know he's old enough to remember 1986. Keep him talking."

Gennady scowled, wishing the RPV could convey the expression.

"Later I remembered that," said the dragon. "When I could no longer live as a person in the world of people. Remember the three men in the Bible who were cast in the belly of the furnace, and survived? Oh, I needed to do that. To live in the belly of the furnace. You know what I mean, don't you?"

Gennady crawled backward along the beam. The horrible thing was, he did know. He couldn't have explained it, but the dragon's words were striking him deeply, wounding him far more than its metal hands had.

"So look." The dragon gestured behind it at the pit. It had arranged some chairs and a table around the black calandria. A bottle on the table held a sprig of wildflowers. There was other furniture, Gennady now saw—filing cabinets, bookshelves, and yes, books everywhere. This monster had not merely visited this place; it lived here.

He saw another thing, as well. On the back of the dragon, under a cross of bent metal spars, was a small satellite dish. This spun and turned wildly to keep its focus on some distant point in the heavens.

"Lisa, he's linked directly to the dragon. No repeaters."

"That a problem?"

"Damn right it's a problem! I can't stop the thing by pulling any plugs."

"You and I have had the same ambition," the dragon said to Gennady. "To live in the invisible world, visit the place that can't be visited. Except that I was forced to it. You're healthy, you can walk. What made you come here?"

"Don't," said Gennady.

The searchlights found and pinned him again. "What hurt you?" asked the dragon.

Gennady hissed. "None of your business."

The dragon was now perfectly still. "Is it so strong in you that you can never admit to it? Tell me—if I were to say I will hunt your body down and kill you now unless you tell me why you came here—would you tell me?"

Gennady couldn't answer.

The dragon surged to its feet. "You don't even know what you have!" it roared. "You can walk. You can still make love—really, not just in some simulation. And you *dare* to come in here and try to take away the only thing I've got left?"

Gennady lost his grip on the beam and fell. A bookshelf shattered under him.

The dragon towered over him. "You can't live here," it said. "You're just a tourist."

He expected a blow that would shatter his connection, but it didn't come. Instead the monster stepped over him, making for the exit.

"I can run faster than your little motorbike," it said. Then it was gone, up the entrance shaft.

Gennady tried to rise. One of his legs was broken. One-legged, one-armed, there was no way he was getting out of here.

"Gennady," said Lisa. "What's happening?"

"He left," said Gennady. "He's gone to kill me."

"Break the link. Run for it. You can get to the motorcycle before he gets to you, can't you?"

"Maybe. That's not the point."

"What do you mean?"

He raised himself on his good elbow. "We haven't got our proof, and we don't know if there's a dead-man switch. Once he's done with me he's just going to come back here and tear the roof off. Are Merrick's commandos on their way?"

"Yes."

"Maybe they can stop him. But I wouldn't count on it."

"What are you saying?"

"I'm in his den. Maybe I can find what we need before he gets to me."

For a moment her breath laboured in his ear, forming no words. Gennady told himself that he, in contrast, felt nothing. He had lost, completely. It really didn't matter what he did now, so he might as well do the decent thing.

He bent to the task of inspecting the dragon's meagre treasure.

"Talk to me," she said. Lisa sat hunched over her work table, out of the Net, one hand holding the wood as if to anchor herself. All her screens were live, feeding status checks from her hired hackers, Merrick's people, and all the archival material on Jaffrey that she could find.

"There's no bombs here," he said. His voice was flat. "But there's three portable generators and fuel drums. They're near the entrance shaft. I guess the dragon could blow them up. Wouldn't be much of an explosion, but fire would cause release, you know."

"What else is there? Anything that might tell us who this is?"

"Yes—filing cabinets." That was all he said for nearly a minute.

"What about them?" she asked finally.

"Just getting there—" Another pause. "Tipped them over," he said. "Looking . . . papers in the ashes. What the hell is this stuff?"

"Is it in English or Russian?"

"Both! Looks like records from the Release. Archival material. Photos."

"Are any of them of Jaffrey?"

"Lisa," he snapped, "it's dark, my connection's bad, and I only saw that one photo you showed me. How in God's name am I to know?"

"There must be something!"

"I'm sure there is," he said. "But I don't have time to find it now."

She glanced at the clock. The dragon had left five minutes ago. Was that enough time for it to get to Gennady's building?

"But we have to be sure!"

"I know you do," he said quietly. "I'll keep looking."

Lisa sat back. Everything seemed quiet and still to her suddenly; the deep night had swallowed the normal city noises. Her rooms were silent, and so were her screens. Gennady muttered faintly in her ear, that was all.

She never acted without certain knowledge. It was what she had built her life on. Lisa had always felt that, when a moment of awful decision came, she would be able to make the right choice because she always had all the facts. And now the moment was here. And she didn't *know*.

Gennady described what he saw as he turned over this, then that paper or book. He wasn't getting anywhere.

She switched to her U.S. line connection. The FBI man who had unluckily pulled the morning shift at NCSA Security sat up alertly as she rang through.

Lisa took a deep breath and said the words that might cost her career. "We've got our proof. It's Jaffrey, all right. Shut him down."

Relief washed over Gennady when she told him. "So I'm safe."

Her voice was taut. "I've given the commands. It'll take some time."

"What? How much?"

"Seconds, minutes—you've got to get out of there now."

"Oh my God Lisa, I thought this would be instant."

Gennady felt the floor tremble under him. Nothing in the den of the sarcophagus had moved.

"Now!" She almost screamed it. "Get out now!"

He tore the link helmet off: *spang* of static and noise before reality came up around him. Sad wallpaper, mouldy carpet. And thunder in the building.

Gennady hesitated at the door, then stepped into the hallway. Light from inside lit the narrow space dimly—but it was too late to run over and turn out the lamp. From the direction of the stairwell came a deep vibration and a berserk roar such as he had only ever heard once, when he stood next to an old T35 tank that was revving up to climb an obstacle at a fair. Intermittent thuds shook the ceiling's dust onto Gennady's shoulders; he jerked with each angry impact.

Gennady shut the door, and then the end of the hall exploded. In the darkness he caught a confused impression of petalling plasterboard rushing at him, accompanied by a gasp of black dust. The noise drowned his hearing. Then Jaffrey's eyes blazed into life at ceiling level.

He was too big to fit in the hallway—big as a truck. So Jaffrey demolished the corridor as he came, simply scooping the walls aside with his square iron arms, wedging his flat body between floor and ceiling. The beams of his halogen eyes never wavered from pinioning Gennady as he came.

Into the apartment again. The dial on the Geiger counter was swinging wildly, but the clicking was lost now in thunder. The windows shattered spontaneously. Gennady put his hands over his ears and backed to the balcony door.

Jaffrey removed the wall. His eyes roved over the evidence of Gennady's plans—the extra food supplies, the elaborate computer set-up, the cleaning and filtering equipment. A deep and painful shame uncoiled within Gennady, and with that his fear turned to anger.

"Catch me if you can, you cripple!" he screamed. Gennady leapt onto the balcony, put one foot on the rail and, boosting himself up, grabbed the railing of the balcony one floor above. He pulled himself up without regard to the agony that shot through his shoulders.

Jaffrey burst through the wall below, and as Gennady kicked at the weather-locked door he felt the balcony under him undulate and tilt.

The door wouldn't budge. Jaffrey's two largest hands were clamped on the concrete pad of the balcony. With vicious jerks he worked it free of the wall.

Gennady hopped onto the railing. Cool night air ruffled past and he caught a glimpse of dark ground far below, and a receding vista of empty, black apartment towers. He meant to jump to the next balcony above, but the whole platform came loose as he tried. Flailing, he tried a sideways leap instead. His arms crashed down on the metal railing of the balcony next door.

He heard Jaffrey laugh. This platform was already loose, its bolts rusted to threads. As he pulled himself up Jaffrey tossed the other concrete pad into the night and reached for him.

He couldn't get over the rail in time, but Jaffrey missed, the cylinders of his fingers closing over the rail itself. Jaffrey pulled.

Gennady rolled over the top of the railing. As he landed on the swaying concrete he saw Jaffrey. The dragon was half outside, two big legs bracing him against the creaking lintel of the lower level. He was straining just to reach this far, and his fingers were now all tangled up in the bent metal posts of the railing.

Gennady grabbed the doorknob as the balcony began to give way. "Once more, you bastard," he shouted, and deliberately stepped within reach of the groping hand.

Jaffrey lunged, fingers gathering up the rest of the metal into a knot. The balcony's supports broke with a sound like gunshots, and it all fell out from under Gennady.

He held on to the doorknob, shouting as he saw the balcony fall, and Jaffrey try too late to let go. The bent metal held his black hand, and for a second he teetered on the edge of the verge. Then the walls he'd braced his feet against gave way, and the dragon of Pripyat fell into the night air and vanished briefly, to reappear in a bright orange flash as he hit the ground. Rolling concussions played again through the streets of the dead city.

The doorknob turned under Gennady's hand, and the door opened of its own accord — outward.

Trying to curse and laugh, hearing wild disbelief in his voice, he swung like a pendulum for long seconds, then got himself inside. He lay prone on some stranger's carpet, breathing the musty air and crying his relief.

Then he rose, feeling pain but no more emotion at all. Gennady left the apartment, and went downstairs to get on with his life.

Lisa sat up all night, waiting for word. The commandos had gone in, and found the violated sarcophagus, and the body of the dragon. They had not found Gennady, but then they hadn't found his bike either.

When the FBI cut off Jaffrey's signal, the feed to the dragon had indeed stopped. They had entered his stronghold apartment minutes later, and arrested him in his bed.

So her career was safe. She didn't care; it was still the worst situation she could have imagined. For Gennady to be dead was one thing. For her not to know was intolerable. Lisa cried at four A.M., standing in her kitchen stirring hot milk, while the radio played something baroque and incongruously light. She stared through blurred eyes at the lights of the city, feeling more alone than she could have prepared herself for.

It was midmorning when Gennady called. Her loneliness didn't vanish with the sound of his voice. She started crying again when she heard him say her name. "You're really all right?"

"I'm fine. At a gas station near Kiev. Didn't feel like sticking around to be debriefed, you know. Sorry I lost the cell phone, I'd have called earlier." There was a hesitancy in his voice, like he wasn't telling her everything.

"Merrick says there was no release. Were you irradiated?"

"Not much. Ten packs or so, I guess." Despite herself she laughed at his terminology. She heard him clear his throat and waited. But he said nothing else.

She held the phone to her ear, and glanced around at her apartment. Empty, save for her. Lisa felt a sadness like exhaustion, a deep lowering through her throat and stomach. "You're just a voice," she said, not knowing her own meaning. "Just a voice on the phone."

"I know." She wiped at her eyes. How could he know what she meant, when she didn't?

"Look," he said, "I can't go on like this." His voice faded a bit with the vagaries of the line. "It's not working."

"What's not working, Gennady?"

"My—my whole life." She heard the hesitant intake of breath again. "I can't control anything. It's just . . . beyond me."

She was amazed. "But you did it. You got Jaffrey for us."

"Well, you know . . ." His voice held a self-conscious humour now. "It was your hand on the switch. I just kept him busy for you. It doesn't matter. I don't know what to do."

"What do you mean?"

"I can't just go back to Kiev. Sit around the flat. Jack into the Net. It's not enough."

"You don't have to," she said. "You have money now. I'll make sure Merrick comes clean."

"Yeah. You know . . . I've got enough for a vacation, I figure."

Lisa leaned back in her work chair. She toyed nervously with a strand of her hair. "Yeah? Where would you go?"

"Oh . . . Maybe London?"

She laughed. "Oh yes! Yes, please do."

"Ah." His shyness was such a new thing, and charming—but then, he wasn't falling back on the safety of the Net this time. "One condition?" he ventured.

"Yes?"

"Don't ask me too many questions."

For a second an old indignation took her. But she recognized it for the insecurity it was. "All right, Gennady. You tell me what you want to tell me. And I'll show you the city."

"And the Tower? I always wanted to see the Tower."

Again she laughed. "It figures. But we go only once, okay? No more castles for you after that. Promise?"

"Promise."

written in blood

CHRIS LAWSON

This story is an elegant and incisive look at some of the unexpected effects of high-tech bioscience, some of which may reach all the way down to the very marrow of your bones . . .

New writer Chris Lawson grew up in Papua New Guinea, and now lives in Melbourne with his wife, Andrea, and son, Alexander. While studying medicine, he earned extra money as a computer programmer, and has worked as a medical practitioner and as a consultant to the pharmaceutical industry. He's made short fiction sales to Asimov's Science Fiction, Dreaming Down-Under, Eidolon, *and* Event Horizon. *His story "Unborn Again" appeared in our Sixteenth Annual Collection.*

CTA TAA CAG TGT AGC GAC GAA TGT CTA CAG AAA CAA
GAA TGT CAT GAG TGT CTA GAT CAT AAC CGA TGT AGC
GAC GAA TGT CTA CAA GAA AGG AAT TAA GAG GGA
TAC CGA TGT AGC GAC GAA TGT CTA AAT CAT CAA CAC
AAA AGT AGT TAA CAT CAG AAA AGC GAA TGC TTC TTT

In the Name of God, the Merciful, the Compassionate.

These words open the Qur'an. They were written in my father's blood. After Mother died, and Da recovered from his chemotherapy, we went on a pilgrimage together. In my usual eleven-year-old curious way, I asked him why we had to go to the Other End of the World to pray when we could do it just fine at home.

"Zada," he said, "there are only five pillars of faith. It is easier than any of the other pillars because you only need to do it once in a lifetime. Remember this during Ramadan, when you are hungry and you know you will be hungry again the next day, but your *haj* will be over."

Da would brook no further discussion, so we set off for the Holy Lands. At eleven, I was less than impressed. I expected to find Paradise filled with thousands of fountains and birds and orchards and blooms. Instead, we huddled in cloth tents with hundreds of thousands of sweaty pilgrims, most of whom spoke other languages, as we tramped across a cramped and dirty wasteland. I wondered why Allah had made his Holy Lands so dry and dusty, but I had the sense even then not to ask Da about it.

Near Damascus, we heard about the bloodwriting. The pilgrims were all speaking about it. Half thought it blasphemous, the other half thought it a path to Heaven. Since Da was a biologist, the pilgrims in our troop asked him what he thought. He said he would have to go to the bloodwriters directly and find out.

On a dusty Monday, after morning prayer, my father and I visited the bloodwriter's stall. The canvas was a beautiful white, and the man at the stall smiled as Da approached. He spoke some Arabic, which I could not understand.

"I speak English," said my father.

The stall attendant switched to English with the ease of a juggler changing hands. "Wonderful, sir! Many of our customers prefer English."

"I also speak biology. My pilgrim companions have asked me to review your product." I thought it very forward of my father, but the stall attendant seemed unfazed. He exuded confidence about his product.

"An expert!" he exclaimed. "Even better. Many pilgrims are distrustful of Western science. I do what I can to reassure them, but they see me as a salesman and not to be trusted. I welcome your endorsement."

"Then earn it."

The stall attendant wiped his mustache, and began his spiel. "Since the Dawn of Time, the Word of Allah has been read by mullahs. . . ."

"Stop!" said Da. "The Qur'an was revealed to Mohammed fifteen centuries ago; the Dawn of Time predates it by several billion years. I want answers, not portentous falsehoods."

Now the man was nervous. "Perhaps you should see my uncle. He invented the bloodwriting. I will fetch him." Soon he returned with an older, infinitely more respectable man with grey whiskers in his mustache and hair.

"Please forgive my nephew," said the old man. "He has watched too much American television and thinks the best way to impress is to use dramatic words, wild gestures, and where possible, a toll-free number." The nephew bowed his head and slunk to the back of the stall, chastened.

"May I answer your questions?" the old man asked.

"If you would be so kind," said Da, gesturing for the man to continue.

"Bloodwriting is a good word, and I owe my nephew a debt of gratitude for that. But the actual process is something altogether more mundane. I offer a virus, nothing more. I have taken a hypo-immunogenic strain of adeno-associated virus and added a special code to its DNA."

Da said, "The other pilgrims tell me that you can write the Qur'an into their blood."

"That I can, sir," said the old man. "Long ago I learned a trick that would get the adeno-associated virus to write its code into bone marrow stem cells. It made me a rich man. Now I use my gift for Allah's work. I consider it part of my *zakât*."

Da suppressed a wry smile. *Zakât*, charitable donation, was one of the five pillars. This old man was so blinded by avarice that he believed selling his invention for small profit was enough to fulfill his obligation to God.

The old man smiled and raised a small ampoule of red liquid. He continued, "This, my friend, is the virus. I have stripped its core and put the entire text of the Qur'an into its DNA. If you inject it, the virus will write the Qur'an into your myeloid precursor cells, and then your white blood cells will carry the Word of Allah inside them."

I put my hand up to catch his attention. "Why not red blood cells?" I asked. "They carry all the oxygen."

The old man looked at me as if he noticed me for the first time. "Hello, little one. You are very smart. Red blood cells carry oxygen, but they have no DNA. They cannot carry the Word."

It all seemed too complicated to an eleven-year-old girl.

My father was curious. "DNA codes for amino acid sequences. How can you write the Qur'an in DNA?"

"DNA is just another alphabet," said the old man. He handed my father a card. "Here is the crib sheet."

My father studied the card for several minutes, and I saw his face change from skeptical to awed. He passed the card to me. It was filled with Arabic squiggles, which I could not understand. The only thing I knew about Arabic was that it was written right-to-left, the reverse of English.

"I can't read it," I said to the man. He made a little spinning gesture with his finger, indicating that I should flip the card over. I flipped the card and saw the same crib sheet, only with Anglicized terms for each Arabic letter. Then he handed me another crib sheet, and said: "This is the sheet for English text."

AAA	a	AGA	q	ATA	[—] dash	ACA	
AAG	b	AGG	r	ATG	[/] slash	ACG	
AAT	c	AGT	s	ATT	{stop}	ACT	
AAC	d	AGC	t	ATC	{stop}	ACC	
GAA	e	GGA	u	GTA	['] apostrophe	GCA	{stop}
GAG	f	GGG	v	GTG	["] quotation mark	GCG	
GAT	g	GGT	w	GTT	[(] open bracket	GCT	0
GAC	h	GGC	x	GTC	[)] close bracket	GCC	1
TAA	i	TGA	y	TTA	[?] question mark	TCA	2
TAG	j	TGG	z	TTG	[!] exclamation	TCG	3
TAT	k	TGT	[ ] space	TTT	[•] end verse	TCT	4
TAC	l	TGC	[.] period	TTC	[¶] paragraph	TCC	5

CAA	m	CGA	[,] comma	CTA	{cap} capital	CCA	6
CAG	n	CGG	[:] colon	CTG		CCG	7
CAT	o	CGT	[;] semi-colon	CTT		CCT	8
CAC	p	CGC	[-] hyphen	CTC		CCC	9

"The Arabic alphabet has 28 letters. Each letter changes form depending on its position in the word. But the rules are rigid, so there is no need to put each variation in the crib sheet. It is enough to know that the letter is *aliph* or *bi*, and whether it is at the start, at the end, or in the middle of the word.

"The [stop] commands are also left in their usual places. These are the body's natural commands and they tell ribosomes when to stop making a protein. It only cost three spots and there were plenty to spare, so they stayed in."

My father asked, "Do you have an English translation?"

"Your daughter is looking at the crib sheet for the English language," the old man explained, "and there are other texts one can write, but not the Qur'an."

Thinking rapidly, Da said, "But you could write the Qur'an in English?"

"If I wanted to pursue secular causes, I could do that," the old man said. "But I have all the secular things I need. I have copyrighted crib sheets for all the common alphabets, and I make a profit on them. For the Qur'an, however, translations are not acceptable. Only the original words of Mohammed can be trusted. It is one thing for *dhimmis* to translate it for their own curiosity, but if you are a true believer you must read the word of God in its unsullied form."

Da stared at the man. The old man had just claimed that millions of Muslims were false believers because they could not read the original Qur'an. Da shook his head and let the matter go. There were plenty of imams who would agree with the old man.

"What is the success rate of the inoculation?"

"Ninety-five percent of my trial subjects had identifiable Qur'an text in their blood after two weeks, although I cannot guarantee that the entire text survived the insertion in all of those subjects. No peer-reviewed journal would accept the paper." He handed my father a copy of an article from *Modern Gene Techniques*. "Not because the science is poor, as you will see for yourself, but because Islam scares them."

Da looked serious. "How much are you charging for this?"

"Aha! The essential question. I would dearly love to give it away, but even a king would grow poor if he gave a grain of rice to every hungry man. I ask enough to cover my costs, and no haggling. It is a hundred U.S. dollars or equivalent."

Da looked into the dusty sky, thinking. "I am puzzled," he said at last. "The Qur'an has one hundred and fourteen suras, which comes to tens of thousands of words. Yet the adeno-associated virus is quite small. Surely it can't all fit inside the viral coat?"

At this the old man nodded. "I see you are truly a man of wisdom. It is a patented secret, but I suppose that someday a greedy industrialist will lay hands on my virus and sequence the genome. So, I will tell you on the condition that it goes no further than this stall."

Da gave his word.

"The code is compressed. The original text has enormous redundancy, and with advanced compression, I can reduce the amount of DNA by over 80 percent. It is still a lot of code."

I remember Da's jaw dropping. "That must mean the viral code is self-extracting. How on Earth do you commandeer the ribosomes?"

"I think I have given away enough secrets for today," said the old man.

"Please forgive me," said Da. "It was curiosity, not greed, that drove me to ask." Da changed his mind about the bloodwriter. This truly was fair *zakât*. Such a wealth of invention for only a hundred U.S. dollars.

"And the safety?" asked my father.

The old man handed him a number of papers, which my father read carefully, nodding his head periodically, and humming each time he was impressed by the data.

"I'll have a dose," said Da. "Then no one can accuse me of being a slipshod reviewer."

"Sir, I would be honored to give a complimentary bloodwriting to you and your daughter."

"Thank you. I am delighted to accept your gift, but only for me. Not for my daughter. Not until she is of age and can make her own decision." Da took a red ampoule in his hands and held it up to the light, as if he was looking through an envelope for the letters of the Qur'an. He shook his head at the marvel and handed it back to the old man, who drew it up in a syringe.

That night, our fellow pilgrims made a fire and gathered around to hear my father talk. As he spoke, four translators whispered their own tongues to the crowd. The scene was like a great theater from the Arabian Nights. Scores of people wrapped in white robes leaned into my father's words, drinking up his excitement. It could have been a meeting of princes.

Whenever Da said something that amazed the gathered masses, you could hear the inbreath of the crowd, first from the English-speakers, and then in patches as the words came out in the other languages. He told them about DNA, and how it told our bodies how to live. He told them about introns, the long stretches of human DNA that are useless to our bodies, but that we carry still from viruses that invaded our distant progenitors, like ancestral scars. He told them about the DNA code, with its triplets of adenine, guanine, cytosine, and thymine, and he passed around copies of the bloodwriter's crib sheet. He told them about blood, and the white cells that fought infection. He talked about the adeno-associated virus and how it injected its DNA into humans. He talked about the bloodwriter's injection and the mild fever it had given him. He told them of the price.

And he answered questions for an hour.

The next day, as soon as the morning prayers were over, the bloodwriting stall was swamped with customers. The old man ran out of ampoules by mid-morning, and only avoided a riot by promising to bring more the following day.

I had made friends with another girl. She was two years younger than I was, and we did not share a language, but we still found ways to play together to relieve the boredom.

One day, I saw her giggling and whispering to her mother, who looked furtively at me and at Da. The mother waved over her companions, and spoke to them in solemn tones. Soon a very angry-looking phalanx of women descended on my unsuspecting father. They stood before him, hands on hips, and the one who spoke English pointed a finger at me.

"Where is her mother?" asked the woman. She was taller than the others, a weather-beaten woman who looked like she was sixty, but must have been younger because she had a child only two years old. "This is no place for a young girl to be escorted by a man."

"Zada's mother died in a car accident back home. I am her father, and I can escort her without help, thank you."

"I think not," said the woman.

"What right have you to say such a thing?" asked Da. "I am her father."

The woman pointed again. "Ala says she saw your daughter bathing, and she has not had the *khitan*. Is this true?"

"It is none of your business," said Da.

The woman screamed at him. "I will not allow my daughter to play with harlots. Is it true?"

"It is none of your business."

The woman lurched forward and pulled me by my arm. I squealed and twisted out of her grasp and ran behind my father for protection. I wrapped my arms around his waist and held on tightly.

"Show us," demanded the woman. "Prove she is clean enough to travel with this camp."

Da refused, which made the woman lose her temper. She slapped him so hard she split his lip. He tasted the blood, but stood resolute. She reached around and tried to unlock my arms from Da's waist. He pushed her away.

"She is not fit to share our camp. She should be cut, or else she will be shamed in the sight of Allah," the woman screamed. The other women were shouting and shaking their fists, but few of them knew English, so it was as much in confusion as anger.

My father fixed the woman with a vicious glare. "You call my daughter shameful in the sight of Allah? I am a servant of Allah. Prove to me that Allah is shamed and I will do what I can to remove the shame. Fetch a mullah."

The woman scowled. "I will fetch a mullah, although I doubt your promise is worth as much as words in the sand."

"Make sure the mullah speaks English," my father demanded as she slipped away. He turned to me and wiped away tears. "Don't worry, Zada. No harm will come to you."

"Will I be allowed to play with Ala?"

"No. Not with these old vultures hanging around."

By the evening, the women had found a mullah gullible enough to mediate the dispute. They tugged his sleeves as he walked toward our camp, hurrying him up. It was obvious that his distaste had grown with every minute in the company of the women, and now he was genuinely reluctant to speak on the matter.

The weathered woman pointed us out to the mullah and spat some words at him that we did not understand.

"Sir, I hear that your daughter is uncircumcised. Is this true?"

"It is none of your business," said Da.

The mullah's face dropped. You could almost see his heart sinking. "Did you not promise . . . ?"

"I promised to discuss theology with you and that crone. My daughter's anatomy is not your affair."

"Please, sir . . ."

Da cut him off abruptly. "Mullah, in your considered opinion, is it necessary for a Muslim girl to be circumcised?"

"It is the accepted practice," said the mullah.

"I do not care about the accepted practice. I ask what Mohammed says."

"Well, I'm sure that Mohammed says something on the matter," said the mullah.

"Show me where."

The mullah coughed, thinking of the fastest way to extract himself. "I did not bring my books with me," he said.

Da laughed, not believing that a mullah would travel so far to mediate a theological dispute without a book. "Here, have mine," Da said as he passed the Qur'an to the mullah. "Show me where Mohammed says such a thing."

The mullah's shoulders slumped. "You know I cannot. It is not in the Qur'an. But it is *sunnah*."

"*Sunnah*," said Da, "is very clear on the matter. Circumcision is *makrumah* for women. It is honorable but not compulsory. There is no requirement for women to be circumcised."

"Sir, you are very learned. But there is more to Islam than a strict reading of the Qur'an and *sunnah*. There have even been occasions when the word of Mohammed has been overturned by later imams. Mohammed himself knew that he was not an expert on all things, and he said that it was the responsibility of future generations to rise above his imperfect knowledge."

"So, you are saying that even if it was recorded in the Qur'an, that would not make it compulsory." Da gave a smile—the little quirk of his lips that he gave every time he had laid a logical trap for someone.

The mullah looked grim. The trap had snapped shut on his leg, and he was not looking forward to extricating himself.

"Tell these women so we can go back to our tents and sleep," said Da.

The mullah turned to the women and spoke to them. The weathered woman became agitated and started waving her hands wildly. Her voice was an over-wrought screech. The mullah turned back to us.

"She refuses to share camp with you, and insists you leave."

Da fixed the mullah with his iron gaze. "Mullah, you are a learned man in a difficult situation, but surely you can see the woman is half-mad. She complains that my daughter has not been mutilated, and would not taint herself with my daughter's presence. Yet she is tainted herself. Did she tell you that she tried to assault my daughter and strip her naked in public view? Did she tell you that she inflicted this wound on me when I stood between her and my daughter? Did she tell you that I have taken the bloodwriting, so she spilled the Word of God when she drew blood?"

The mullah looked appalled. He went back to the woman, who started screech-ing all over again. He cut her off and began berating her. She stopped talking, stunned that the mullah had turned on her. He kept berating her until she showed a sign of humility. When she bowed her head, the mullah stopped his tirade, but as soon as the words stopped she sent a dagger-glance our way.

That night, three families pulled out of our camp. Many of the others in camp were pleased to see them go. I heard one of the grandmothers mutter "Taliban" under her breath, making a curse of the words.

The mood in camp lifted, except for mine. "It's my fault Ala left," I said.

"No, it is not your fault," said Da. "It was her family's fault. They want the whole world to think the way they think and to do what they do. This is against the teaching of the Qur'an, which says that there shall be no coercion in the matter of faith. I can find the sura if you like."

"Am I unclean?"

"No," said Da. "You are the most beautiful girl in the world."

By morning, the camp had been filled by other families. The faces were more friendly, but Ala was gone. It was my first lesson in intolerance, and it came from my own faith.

In Sydney, we sat for hours, waiting to be processed. By the third hour, Da finally lost patience and approached the customs officer.

"We are Australian citizens, you know?" Da said.

"Please be seated. We are still waiting for cross-checks."

"I was born in Brisbane, for crying out loud! Zada was born in Melbourne. My family is Australian four generations back."

His protests made no difference. Ever since the Saladin Outbreak, customs checked all Muslims thoroughly. Fifty residents of Darwin had died from an out-break of a biological weapon that the Saladins had released. Only a handful of Saladins had survived, and they were all in prison, and it had been years ago, but Australia still treated its Muslims as if every single one of us was a terrorist waiting for the opportunity to go berserk.

We were insulted, shouted at, and spat on by men and women who then stepped into their exclusive clubs and talked about how uncivilized we were. Once it had been the Aborigines, then it had been the Italian and Greek immigrants; a generation later it was the Asians; now it was our turn. Da thought that we could leave for a while, go on our pilgrimage and return to a more settled nation, but our treatment by the customs officers indicated that little had changed in the year we were away.

They forced Da to strip for a search, and nearly did the same for me, until Da threatened them with child molestation charges. They took blood samples from both of us. They went through our luggage ruthlessly. They X-rayed our suitcases from so many angles that Da joked they would glow in the dark.

Then they made us wait, which was the worst punishment of all.

Da leaned over to me and whispered, "They are worried about my blood. They think that maybe I am carrying a deadly virus like a Saladin. And who knows? Maybe the Qur'an *is* a deadly virus." He chuckled.

"Can they read your blood?" I asked.

"Yes, but they can't make sense of it without the code sheet."

"If they knew it was just the Qur'an texts, would they let us go?"

"Probably," said Da.

"Why don't you give it to them, then?"

He sighed. "Zada, it is hard to understand, but many people hate us for no reason other than our faith. I have never killed or hurt or stolen from anyone in my life, and yet people hate me because I pray in a church with a crescent instead of a cross."

"But I want to get out of here," I pleaded.

"Listen to me, daughter. I could show them the crib sheet and explain it to them, but then they would know the code, and that is a terrifying possibility. There are people who have tried to design illnesses that attack only Jews or only blacks, but so far they have failed. The reason why they have failed is that there is no serological marker for black or Jewish blood. Now we stupid Muslims, and I count myself among the fools, have identified ourselves. In my blood is a code that says that I am a Muslim, not just by birth, but by active faith. I have marked myself. I might as well walk into a neo-Nazi rally wearing a Star of David.

"Maybe I am just a pessimist," he continued. "Maybe no one will ever design an anti-Muslim virus, but it is now technically possible. The longer it takes the *dhimmis* to find out how, the better."

I looked up at my father. He had called himself a fool. "Da, I thought you were smart!"

"Most of the time, darling. But sometimes faith means you have to do the dumb thing."

"I don't want to be dumb," I said.

Da laughed. "You know you can choose whatever you want to be. But there is a small hope I have for you. To do it you would need to be very, *very* smart."

"What?" I asked.

"I want you to grow up to be smart enough to figure out how to stop the illnesses I'm talking about. Mark my words, racial plagues will come one day, unless someone can stop them."

"Do you think I could?"

Da looked at me with utter conviction. "I have never doubted it."

Da's leukemia recurred a few years later. The chemotherapy had failed to cure him after all, although it had given him seven good years: just long enough to see me to adulthood, and enrolled in genetics. I tried to figure out a way to cure Da, but I was only a freshman. I understood less than half the words in my textbooks. The best I could do was hold his hand as he slowly died.

It was then that I finally understood what he meant when he said that sometimes it was important not to be smart. At the climax of our *haj* we had gone around the Kaabah seven times, moving in a human whirlpool. It made no sense at all intellectually. Going around and around a white temple in a throng of strangers was about as pointless a thing as you could possibly do, and yet I still remember the event as one of the most moving in my life. For a brief moment I felt a part of a greater community, not just of Muslims, but of the Universe. With that last ritual, Da and I became *haji* and *hajjah*, and it felt wonderful.

But I could not put aside my thoughts the way Da could. I had to be smart. Da had *asked* me to be smart. And when he died, after four months and two failed chemo cycles, I no longer believed in Allah. I wanted to maintain my faith, as much as for my father as for me, but my heart was empty.

The event that finally tipped me, although I did not even realize it until much later, was seeing his blood in a sample tube. The oncology nurse had drawn 8 mls from his central line, then rolled the sample tube end over end to mix the blood with the anticoagulant. I saw the blood darken in the tube as it deoxygenated, and I thought about the blood cells in there. The white cells contained the suras of the Qur'an, but they also carried the broken code that turned them into cancer cells.

Da had once overcome leukemia years before. The doctors told me it was very rare to have a relapse after seven years. And this relapse seemed to be more aggressive than the first one. The tests, they told me, indicated this was a new mutation.

Mutation: a change in genetic code. Mutagen: an agent that promotes mutation.

Bloodwriting, by definition, was mutagenic. Da had injected one hundred and fourteen suras into his own DNA. The designer had been very careful to make sure that the bloodwriting virus inserted itself somewhere safe so it would not disrupt a tumor suppressor gene or switch on an oncogene—but that was for normal people. Da's DNA was already damaged by leukemia and chemotherapy. The virus had written a new code over the top, and I believe the new code switched his leukemia back on.

The Qur'an had spoken to his blood, and said: "He it is Who created you from dust, then from a small lifegerm, then from a clot, then He brings you forth as a child, then that you may attain your maturity, then that you may be old—and of you there are some who are caused to die before—and that you may reach an appointed term, and that you may understand./ He it is who gives life and brings death, so when He decrees an affair, He only says to it: *Be*, and it is."

I never forgave Allah for saying *"Be!"* to my father's leukemia.

An educated, intelligent biologist, Da must have suspected that the Qur'an had killed him. Still, he never missed a prayer until the day he died. My own faith was not so strong. It shattered like fine china on concrete. Disbelief is the only possible revenge for omnipotence.

An infidel I was by then, but I had made a promise to my father, and for my postdoc I solved the bloodwriting problem. He would have been proud.

I abandoned the crib sheet. In my scheme the codons were assigned randomly to letters. Rather than preordaining *TAT* to mean *zen* in Arabic or "k" in English, I designed a process that shuffled the letters into a new configuration every time. Because there are 64 codons, with three {stop} marks and eight blanks, that comes to about 5×10^{83} or 500,000,000,000,000,000,000,000,000,000,000,000,000,000,000,000, 000,000,000,000,000,000,000,000,000,000,000,000,000,000 combinations. No one could design a virus specific to the Qur'an suras anymore. The *dhimmi* bastards would need to design a different virus for every Muslim on the face of the Earth. The faith of my father was safe to bloodwrite.

In my own blood I have written the things important to me. There is a picture of my family, a picture of my wedding, and a picture of my parents from when they were both alive. Pictures can be encoded just as easily as text.

There is some text: Crick and Watson's original paper describing the double-helix of DNA, and Martin Luther King's "I Have a Dream" speech. I also transcribed Cassius's words from *Julius Caesar*:

> *The fault, dear Brutus, is not in our stars,*
> *But in ourselves, that we are underlings.*

For the memory of my father, I included a Muslim parable, a *sunnah* story about Mohammed: One day, a group of farmers asked Mohammed for guidance on improving their crop. Mohammed told the farmers not to pollinate their date trees. The farmers recognized Mohammed as a wise man, and did as he said. That year, however, none of the trees bore any dates. The farmers were angry, and they returned to Mohammed demanding an explanation. Mohammed heard their complaints, then pointed out that he was a religious man, not a farmer, and his wisdom could not be expected to encompass the sum of human learning. He said, "You know your worldly business better."

It is my favorite parable from Islam, and is as important in its way as Jesus' Sermon on the Mount.

At the end of my insert, I included a quote from the *dhimmi* Albert Einstein, recorded the year after the atomic bombing of Japan.

He said, "The release of atom power has changed everything but our way of thinking," then added, "The solution of this problem lies in the heart of human-kind."

I have paraphrased that last sentence into the essence of my new faith. No God was ever so succinct.

My artificial intron reads:

8 words, 45 codons, 135 base pairs that say:

CTA AGC GAC GAA TGT AGT CAT TAC GGA AGC TAA
CAT CAG TGT TAC TAA GAA AGT TGT TAA CAG TGT
AGC GAC GAA TGT GAC GAA AAA AGG AGC TGT CAT
GAG TGT GAC GGA CAA AAA CAG TAT TAA CAG AAC
TGC

The solution lies in the heart of humankind.

I whisper it to my children every night.

Hatching the Phoenix
Frederik Pohl

A seminal figure whose career spans almost the entire development of modern SF, Frederik Pohl has been one of the genre's major shaping forces—as writer, editor, agent, and anthologist—for more than fifty years. He was the founder of the Star series, SF's first continuing anthology series, and was the editor of the Galaxy group of magazines from 1960 to 1969, during which time Galaxy's sister magazine, Worlds of If, won three consecutive Best Professional Magazine Hugos. As a writer, he has won Nebula and Hugo Awards several times (making him the only person ever to have won the Hugo both as editor and as writer), as well as the American Book Award and the French Prix Apollo. His many books include several written in collaboration with the late C. M. Kornbluth—such as The Space Merchants, Wolfbane, and Gladiator-at-Law—and many solo novels, including Man Plus, The Coming of the Quantum Cats, A Plague of Pythons, Slave Ship, Jem, The World at the End of Time, and Mining the Oort. Among his many collections are The Gold at the Starbow's End, The Years of the City, Critical Mass (in collaboration with Kornbluth), In the Problem Pit, Pohlstars, and The Best of Frederik Pohl. He also wrote a nonfiction book in collaboration with the late Isaac Asimov, Our Angry Earth, and an autobiography, The Way the Future Was. His most recent books are the novels O Pioneer!, The Siege of Eternity, and The Far Shore of Time. Coming up soon is a new nonfiction book, Chasing Science. His stories have appeared in our Second and Tenth Annual Collections.

Pohl's most famous book is probably Gateway, a book which won both the Nebula and the Hugo, and which is widely regarded as one of the best novels of the '70s. It's also the book in which he introduced the Heechee, a race of enigmatic and (seemingly) long-vanished aliens whose discarded technology enables humanity to begin the exploration of the Galaxy—a series that Pohl would return to several times throughout the rest of the '80s and into the '90s, with sequels such as Beyond the Blue Event Horizon, Heechee Rendezvous, The Annals of the Heechee, and The Gateway Trip.

Occasionally, Pohl writes about the Heechee in shorter format as well. There were two Heechee stories published this year, for instance, including the intriguing novella that follows, in which he takes us far across the galaxy and deep into the past to show us that, no matter how alien the setting, some things don't change—alas!

CHAPTER I

We were only about half a day out when we crossed the wavefront from the Crab supernova. I wouldn't even have noticed it, but my shipmind, Hypatia, is programmed to notice things that might interest me. So she asked me if I wanted to take a look at it, and I did.

Of course I'd already seen the star blow up two or three times in simulations, but as a flesh-and-blood human being I like reality better than simulations — most of the time, anyway. Hypatia had already turned on the Heechee screen, but it showed nothing other than the pebbly gray blur that the Heechee use. Hypatia can read those things, but I can't, so she changed the phase for me.

What I was seeing then was a field of stars, looking exactly like any other field of stars to me. It's a lack in me, I'm sure, but as far as I'm concerned every star looks like all the other stars in the sky, at least until you get close enough to it to see it as a sun. So I had to ask her, "Which one is it?"

She said, "You can't see it yet. We don't have that much magnification. But keep your eyes open. Wait a moment. Another moment. Now, there it is."

She didn't have to say that. I could see it for myself. Suddenly a point of light emerged and got brighter, and brighter still, until it outshone everything else on the screen. It actually made me squint. "It happens pretty fast," I said.

"Well, not really *that* fast, Klara. Our vector velocity, relative to the star, is quite a lot faster than light, so we're speeding things up. Also, we're catching up with the wavefront, so we're seeing it all in reverse. It'll be gone soon."

And a moment later it was. Just as the star was brightest of all, it unexploded itself. It became a simple star again, so unremarkable that I couldn't even pick it out. Its planets were unscorched again, their populations, if any, not yet whiffed into plasma. "All right," I said, somewhat impressed but not enough to want Hypatia to know it, "turn the screen off and let's get back to work."

Hypatia sniffed — she has built herself a whole repertoire of human behaviors that I had never had programmed into her. She said darkly, "We'd better, if we want to be able to pay all the bills for this thing. Do you have any idea what this is *costing*?"

Of course, she wasn't serious about that. I have problems, but being able to pay my bills isn't one of them.

I wasn't always this solvent. When I was a kid on that chunk of burned-out hell they call the planet Venus, driving an airbody around its baked, bleak surface for the tourists all day and trying not to spend any of my pay all night, what I wanted most was to have money. I wasn't hoping for a whole lot of money. I just wanted enough money so that I could afford Full Medical and a place to live that didn't stink of rancid seafood. I wasn't dreaming on any vast scale.

It didn't work out that way, though. I never did have exactly that much money.

First I had none at all and no real hopes of ever getting any. Then I had much, much more than that, and I found out something about having a lot of money. When you have the kind of money that's spelled M*O*N*E*Y, it's like having a kitten in the house. The money wants you to play with it. You can try to leave it alone, but if you do it'll be crawling into your lap and nibbling at your chin for attention. You don't have to give in to what the money wants. You can just push it away and go about your business, but then God knows what mischief it'll get into if you do, and anyway then where's the fun of having it?

So most of the way out to the PhoenixCorp site, Hypatia and I played with my money. That is, I played with it while Hypatia kept score. She remembers what I own better than I do—that's her nature, being the sort of task she was designed to do—and she's always full of suggestions about what investments I should dump or hold or what new ventures I should get into.

The key word there is "suggestions." I don't have to do what Hypatia says. Sometimes I don't. As a general rule I follow Hypatia's suggestions about four times out of five. The fifth time I do something different, just to let her know that I'm the one who makes the decisions here. I know that's not smart, and it generally costs me money when I do. But that's all right. I have plenty to spare.

There's a limit to how long I'm willing to go on tickling the money's tummy, though. When I had just about reached that point, Hypatia put down her pointer and waved the graphics displays away. She had made herself optically visible to humor me, because I like to see the person I'm talking to, wearing her fifth-century robes and coronet of rough-cut rubies and all, and she gave me an inquiring look. "Ready to take a little break, Klara?" she asked. "Do you want something to eat?"

Well, I was, and I did. She knew that perfectly well. She's continually monitoring my body, because that's one of the other tasks she's designed to do, but I like to keep my free will going there, too. "Actually," I said, "I'd rather have a drink. How are we doing for time?"

"Right on schedule, Klara. We'll be there in ten hours or so." She didn't move—that is, her simulation didn't move—but I could hear the clink of ice going into a glass in the galley. "I've been accessing the PhoenixCorp shipmind. If you want to see what's going on . . . ?"

"Do it," I said, but she was already doing it. She waved again—pure theater, of course, but Hypatia's full of that—and we got a new set of graphics. As the little serving cart rolled in and stopped just by my right hand, we were looking through PhoenixCorp's own visuals, and what we were looking at was a dish-shaped metal spiderweb, with little things crawling across it. I could form no precise picture of its size, because there was nothing in the space around it to compare it with. But I didn't have to. I knew it was big.

"Have one for yourself," I said, lifting my glass.

She gave me that patient, exasperated look and let it pass. Sometimes she does simulate having a simulated drink with me while I have a real one, but this time she was in her schoolteacher mode. "As you can see, Klara," she informed me, "the shipment of optical mirror pieces has arrived, and the drones are putting them in place on the parabolic dish. They'll be getting first light from the planet in an hour or so, but I don't think you'll care about seeing it. The resolution will be poor until they get everything put together; that should take about eighteen hours. Then we should have optimal resolution to observe the planet."

"For four days," I said, taking a pull at my glass.

She gave me a different look—still the schoolteacher, but now a schoolteacher putting up with a particularly annoying student. "Hey, Klara. You knew there wouldn't be much time. It wasn't my idea to come all the way out here anyway. We could have watched the whole thing from your island."

I swallowed the rest of my nightcap and stood up. "That's not how I wanted to do it," I told her. "The trouble with you simulations is that you don't appreciate what reality is like. Wake me up an hour before we get there."

And I headed for my stateroom, with my big and round and unoccupied bed. I didn't want to chat with Hypatia just then. The main reason I had kept her busy giving me financial advice so long was that it prevented her from giving me advice on the thing she was always trying to talk me into, or that one other big thing that I really needed to make up my mind about, and couldn't.

The cart with my black coffee and fresh-squeezed orange juice—make that quote "fresh-squeezed" unquote orange juice, but Hypatia was too good at her job for me to be able to tell the difference—was right by my bed when she woke me up. "Ninety minutes to linkup," she said cheerily, "and a very good morning to you. Shall I start your shower?"

I said, "Um." Ninety minutes is not a second too long for me to sit and swallow coffee, staring into space, before I have to do anything as energetic as getting into a shower. But then I looked into the wall mirror by the bed, didn't like what I saw, and decided I'd better spruce myself up a little bit.

I was never what you'd call a pretty woman. My eyebrows were a lot too heavy, for one thing. Once or twice over the years I'd had the damn things thinned down to fashion-model proportions, just to see if it would help any. It didn't. I'd even messed around with my bone structure, more cheekbones, less jaw, to try to look a little less masculine. It just made me look weak-faced. For a couple of years I'd gone blonde, then tried redhead once but checked it out and made them change it back before I left the beauty parlor. They were all mistakes. They didn't work. Whenever I looked at myself, whatever the cosmetologists and the medical fixer-uppers had done, I could still see the old Gelle-Klara Moynlin hiding there behind all the trim. So screw it. For the last little while I'd gone natural.

Well, pretty natural, anyway. I didn't want to look *old*.

I didn't, of course. By the time I was bathed and my hair was fixed and I was wearing a simple dress that showed off my pretty good legs, actually, I looked as good as I ever had. "Almost there," Hypatia called. "You better hang on to something. I have to match velocities, and it's a tricky job." She sounded annoyed, as she usually does when I give her something hard to do. She does it, of course, but she complains a lot. "Faster than light I can do, slower than light I can do, but when you tell me to match velocity with somebody who's doing exactly *c* you're into some pretty weird effects, so—Oh, sorry."

"You should be," I told her, because that last lurch had nearly made me spill my third cup of coffee. "Hypatia? What do you think, the pearls or the cameo?"

She did that fake two- or three-second pause, as though she really needed any time at all to make a decision, before she gave me the verdict. "I'd wear the cameo. Only whores wear pearls in the daytime."

So of course I decided to wear the pearls. She sighed but didn't comment. "All right," she said, opening the port. "We're docked. Mind the step, and I'll keep in touch."

I nodded and stepped over the seals into the PhoenixCorp mother ship.

There wasn't any real "step." What there was was a sharp transition from the comfortable one gee I kept in my own ship to the gravityless environment of the PhoenixCorp ship. My stomach did a quick little flip-flop of protest, but I grabbed a hold-on bar and looked around.

I don't know what I'd expected to find, maybe something like the old Gateway asteroid. PhoenixCorp had done itself a lot more lavishly than that, and I began to wonder if I hadn't maybe been a touch too open-handed with the financing. The place certainly didn't smell like Gateway. Instead of Gateway's sour, ancient fug, it had the wetly sweet smell of a greenhouse. That was because there were vines and ferns and flowers growing in pots all around the room—spreading out in all directions, because of that zero-gee environment, and if I'd thought about that ahead of time, I wouldn't have worn a skirt. The only human being in sight was a tall, nearly naked black man who was hanging by one toe from a wall bracket, exercising his muscles with one of those metal-spring gadgets. ("Humphrey Mason-Manley," Hypatia whispered in my ear. "He's the archeologist-anthropologist guy from the British Museum.") Without breaking his rhythm, Humphrey gave me a look of annoyance.

"What are you doing here, miss? No visitors are permitted. This is private property, and—"

Then he got a better look at me and his expression changed. Not to welcoming exactly, but to what I'd call sort of unwillingly impressed. "Oh, crikey," he said. "You're Gelle-Klara Moynlin, are you not? That's a bit different. Welcome aboard, I guess."

CHAPTER II

It wasn't the most affable greeting I'd ever had. However, when Humphrey Mason-Manley woke up the head engineer for me, she turned out to be a lot more courteous. She didn't have to be, either. Although I had put up the seed money to get the project started, PhoenixCorp was set up as a nonprofit institution, owned by nobody but itself. I wasn't even on the board.

The boss engineer's name, Hypatia whispered to me, was June Thaddeus Terple—*Doctor* Terple. I didn't really need the reminder. Terple and I had met before, though only by screen, when she was trying to scare up money for this venture and somebody had given her my name. In person she was taller than I'd thought. She looked to be about the age I looked to be myself, which is to say, charitably, thirtyish. She was wearing a kind of string bikini, plus a workman's belt of little pouches around her waist so she could keep stuff in it. She took me into her office, which was a sort of wedge-shaped chamber with nothing much visible in it but handholds on the walls and a lot more of those flowering plants. "Sorry I wasn't there to meet you, Dr. Moynlin," she said.

"I'm not a doctor of anything, except honorary, and Klara's good enough."

She bobbed her head. "Anyway, of course you're welcome here any time. I guess you wanted to see for yourself how we're coming along."

"Well, I did want that, yes. I also wanted to set something up, if you don't mind." That was me returning courtesy for courtesy, however unnecessary it was in either direction. "Do you know who Wilhelm Tartch is?"

She thought for a moment. "No."

So much for his galaxywide fame. I explained. "Bill's a kind of roving reporter. He has a program that goes out all over, even to the Heechee in the Core. It's sort of a travelogue. He visits exciting and colorful places and reports on them for the stay-at-homes." He was also my present main lover, but there wasn't any reason to mention that to Terple; she would figure it out for herself fast enough.

"And he wants to do PhoenixCorp?"

"If you don't mind," I said again. "I did clear it with the board."

She grinned at me. "So you did, but I sort of lost track of it. We've been deploying the drones, so it's been kind of busy." She shook herself. "Anyway, Hans tells me your shipmind displayed the actual supernova explosion to you on the way out."

"That's right, she did." In my ear Hypatia was whispering that Hans was the name of their shipmind, as though I couldn't figure that out for myself.

"And I suppose you know what it looks like from Earth now?"

"Well, sort of."

I could see her assessing how much "sort of" amounted to, and deciding to be diplomatic to the money person. "It wouldn't hurt to take another look. Hans! Telescopic view from Earth, please."

She was looking toward one end of her office. It disappeared, and in its place we were looking out at a blotchy patch of light. "That's it. It's called the Crab Nebula. Of course, they named it that before they really knew what it was, but you can see where they got the name." I agreed that it did look a little like some sort of deformed crab, and Terple went on. "The nebula itself is just the gases and stuff that the supernova threw off, a thousand years or so later. I don't know if you can make it out, but there's a little spot in the middle of it that's the Crab pulsar. That's all that's left of the star. Now let's look at the way it was before it went super."

Hans wiped the nebula away, and we were looking into the same deep, black space Hypatia had shown me already. There were the same zillion stars hanging there, but as the shipmind zoomed the picture closer, one extraordinarily bright one appeared. "Bright" didn't do it justice. It was a blazing golden yellow, curiously fuzzy. It wasn't really hot. It couldn't be; the simulation was only optical. But I could almost feel its heat on my face.

"I don't see any planet," I offered.

"Oh, you will, once we get all the optical segments in place." Then she interrupted herself. "I forgot to ask. Would you like a cup of tea or something?"

"Thanks, no. Nothing right this minute." I was peering at the star. "I thought it would be brighter," I said, a little disappointed.

"Oh, it will be, Klara. That's what we're building that five-hundred-kilometer mirror for. Right now we're just getting the gravitational lensing from the black hole we're using—there's a little camera in the mirror. I don't know if you know much about black holes, but—oh, shit," she interrupted herself, suddenly stricken. "You do know, don't you? I mean, after you were stuck in one for thirty or forty years . . ."

She looked as though she had inadvertently caused me great pain. She hadn't. I was used to that sort of reaction. People rarely brought up the subject of black holes in my presence, on the general principle that you don't talk about rope when there's been a hanging in the house. But the time I was trapped in one of them was far back in the past. It had gone like a flash for me in the black hole's time dilation, whatever the elapsed time was on the outside, and I wasn't sensitive about it.

On the other hand, I wasn't interested in discussing it one more damn time, either, so I just said, "My black hole didn't look like that. It was a creepy kind of pale blue."

Terple recovered quickly. She gave me a wise nod of the head. "That would have been Cerenkov radiation. Yours must have been what they call a naked singularity. This one's different. It's wrapped up in its own ergosphere and you can't see a thing. Most black holes produce a lot of radiation—not from themselves, from the gases and stuff they're swallowing—but this one has already swallowed everything around it. Anyway." She paused to recollect her train of thought. Then she nodded. "I was telling you about the gravitational lensing. Hans?"

She didn't say what she wanted from Hans, but evidently he could figure it out for himself. The stars disappeared, and a sort of wall of misty white appeared in front of us. Terple poked at it here and there with a finger, drawing a little picture for me:

"That little dot on the left, that's the Crabber planet we want to study. The circle's the black hole. The arc on the right is our mirror, which is right at the point of convergence—where the gravitational lensing from the black hole gives us the sharpest image. And the little dot next to it is us, at the Cassegrain focus of the mirror. I didn't show the Crabber sun—actually we have to avoid aiming the camera at it, because it could burn out our optics. Am I making sense so far?"

"So far," I agreed.

She gave me another of those assessing looks, then said, "We'll actually be doing our observing by looking toward the mirror, not toward the Crab planet. There too we'll have to block out the star itself, or we won't see the actual planet at all, but that's just another of the things we'll be adjusting. Then we'll actually be looking diametrically away from the planet in order to observe it."

I hadn't been able to resist the temptation with Hypatia, and I couldn't now with June Terple. "For four or five days," I said in my friendliest voice.

I guess the tone wasn't friendly enough. She looked nettled. "Listen, we didn't put the damn black hole where it is. It took us two years of searching to find one in the right position. There's a neutron star that we could've used. Orbitwise it was a better deal because it would have given us nearly eighty years to observe, but it's just a damn neutron star. It wouldn't have given us anywhere the same magnification, because a neutron star just doesn't have anywhere near as much mass as a black hole, so the gravitational lensing would've been a lot less. We'll get a lot more detail with our black hole. Anyway," she added, "once we've observed from here we'll move this whole lash-up to the neutron star for whatever additional data we can get—I mean, uh, if that seems advisable, we will."

What she meant by that was if I was willing to pay for it. Well, I probably was. The capital costs were paid; it would only mean meeting their payroll for another eighty years or so.

But I wasn't ready to make that commitment. To take her mind off it, I said, "I thought we were supposed to have almost thirty days of observing right here."

She looked glum. "*Radio* observing. That's why we built the mesh dish. But it turns out there's no radio coming from the Crabber planet at all, so we had to get the mirror plates to convert it to optical. Took us over three weeks, which is why we lost so much observing time."

"I see," I said. "No radio signals. So there might not be any civilization there to observe, anyway."

She bit her lip. "We know definitely that there's *life* there. Or was, anyway. It's one of the planets the Heechee surveyed long ago, and there were advanced living organisms there at the time—pretty primitive, sure, but they certainly looked as though they had the potential to evolve."

"The *potential* to evolve, right. But whether they did or not we just don't know."

She didn't answer that. She just sighed. Then she said, "As long as you're here, would you like a look around?"

"If I won't be in the way," I said.

Of course I was in the way. June Terple didn't let it show, but some of the others barely gave me the courtesy of looking up when we were introduced. There were eight of them altogether, with names like Julia Ibarruru and Mark Rohrbeck and Humphrey Mason-Manley and Oleg Kekuskian and—well, I didn't have to try to retain them all; Hypatia would clue me as needed. Humphrey Mason-Manley was the guy who'd been building his pecs when I came in. Julia was the one who was floating in a harness surrounded by fifteen or twenty 3-D icons that she was busy poking at and glowering at and poking at again, and she gave me no more than a quick and noncommittal nod. If my name meant anything to her, or to most of the others, they didn't show any signs of being impressed. Especially Rohrbeck and Kekuskian didn't, because they were sound asleep in their harnesses when we peeked in on them, and Terple had a finger to her lips. "Third shift," she whispered when we'd closed the flaps on their cubicles and moved away. "They'll be waking up for dinner in a little while, but let's let them get their sleep. And there's only one other. Let's go find her."

On the way to that one other member of the crew, Hypatia was whispering bits of biography in my ear. Kekuskian was the quite elderly and bisexual astrophysicist. Rohrbeck the quite young and deeply depressed program designer, whose marriage had just come painfully apart. And the one remaining person was . . .

Was a Heechee.

I didn't have to be told that. Once you've seen any one Heechee, you know what they all look like; skeletally thin front to back, squarish, skull-like faces, their data pod hanging between their legs where, if they were male, their balls should be, and if female (as this one turned out to be), there shouldn't be anything much at all. Her name, Terple said, was Starminder, and as we entered her chamber she was working at a set of icons of her own. But as soon as she heard my name she wiped them and barreled over to me to shake my hand. "You are very famous among us in the Core, Gelle-Klara Moynlin," she informed me, hanging on to my hand for support. "Because of your Moynlin Citizen Ambassadors, you see. When your Rebecca Shapiro person came to our city, she was invited to stay with the father of my husband's family, which is where I met her. She was quite informative about human beings; indeed, it was because of her that I volunteered at once to come out. Do you know her?"

I tried to remember Rebecca Shapiro. I had put up grant money for a good many batches of recruits since I funded the program, and she would have had to be one of the earliest of them. Starminder saw my uncertainty and tried to be helpful. "Young woman. Very sad. She sang music composed by your now-dead Wolfgang Amadeus Mozart for our people, which I almost came to enjoy."

"Oh, right, *that* Rebecca," I said, not very honestly. By then I'd paid the fare to the Core for—what?—at least two or three hundred Rebeccas or Carloses or Janes who volunteered to be Citizen Ambassadors to the Heechee in the Core because they had lives that were a shambles. That was a given. If their lives hadn't been, why would they want to leave the people and places they wouldn't ever come back to?

Because, of course, the Core was time-dilated, like any black hole. I knew what that meant. When you were time-dilated in the Core, where a couple of centuries of outside time went by every day, the problems you left behind got really old really fast. Time dilation was better than suicide—though, when you came to think of it, actually a kind of reverse suicide is pretty much what it was. You didn't die yourself, but every troublesome person you'd ever known did while you were gone.

I wish all those Citizen Ambassadors of mine well. I hope it all works out for them . . . but being in a black hole hadn't done a thing for me.

Once I'd met all the people on the PhoenixCorp ship, there wasn't much else to see. I had misjudged my budget-watchers. Terple hadn't been that spendthrift after all. If you didn't count the opulent plantings—and they were there primarily to keep the air good—the PhoenixCorp ship actually was a pretty bare-bones kind of spacecraft. There were the sleeping quarters for the help, and some common rooms—the big one I'd come into when I first entered, plus a sort of dining room with beverage dispensers and netting next to the hold-ons to keep the meals from flying away, a couple of little rooms for music or virtuals when the people wanted some recreation. The rest of it was storage and, of course, all the machinery and instrumentation PhoenixCorp needed to do its job. Terple didn't show me any of the hardware. I didn't expect her to. That's the shipmind's business, and that sort of thing stays sealed away where no harm can come to it. So, unless somebody had been foolish enough to open up a lot of compartments that were meant to stay closed, there wouldn't have been anything to see.

When we were finished, she finally insisted on that cup of tea—really that capsule of tea, that is—and while we were drinking it, holding with one hand to the hold-ons, she said, "That's about it, Klara. Oh, wait a minute. I haven't actually introduced you to our shipmind, have I? Hans? Say hello to Ms. Moynlin."

A deep, pleasant male voice said, "Hello, Ms. Moynlin. Welcome aboard. We've been hoping you'd visit us."

I said hello back to him and left it at that. I don't particularly like chatting with machine intelligences, except my own. I finished my tea, slid the empty capsule into its slot, and said, "Well, I'll get out of your way. I want to get back to my own ship for a bit anyway."

Terple nodded and didn't ask why. "We're going to have dinner in about an hour. Would you like to join us? Hans is a pretty good cook."

That sounded like as good an idea as any, so I told her that would be fine.

Then, as she was escorting me to the docking port, she gave me a sidewise look. "Listen," she said, "I'm sorry we bombed out on the radio search. It doesn't necessarily mean that the Crabbers never got civilized. After all, if somebody had scanned Earth any time before the twentieth century, they wouldn't have heard any radio signals there, either, but the human race was fully evolved by then."

"I know that, June."

"Yes." She cleared her throat. "Do you mind if I ask you a question?"

I said, "Of course not," meaning that she could ask anything she wanted to, but whether or what I chose to answer was another matter entirely.

"Well, you put a lot of money into getting Phoenix started, just on the chance that there might have been an intelligent race there that got fried when their sun went super. What I'm wondering is why."

The answer to that was simple enough. I mean, what's the point of being just about the richest woman in the universe if you don't have a little fun with your money now and then? But I didn't say that to her. I just said, "What else do I have to do?"

CHAPTER III

Well, I did have things to do. Lots of them, though most of them weren't very important.

The only one that was really important—to me—was overseeing the little island off Tahiti that I live on when I'm home. It's a nice place, the way I've fixed it up.

Most of my more-or-less family is there, and when I'm away I really miss them.

Then there are other important things, such as spending some time with Bill Tartch, who is a fairly sweet man, not to mention all the others like Bill Tartch who have come along over the years. Or such things as all the stuff I can buy with my money, plus figuring out what to do with the power that that kind of money gives. Put them all together, I had *plenty* to do with my life. And I had plenty of life to look forward to, too, especially if I let Hypatia talk me into immortality.

So why wasn't I looking forward to it?

When I came back into my ship, Hypatia was waiting for me — visible, in full 3-D simulation, lounging draped Roman-style on the love seat in the main cabin and fully dressed in her fifth-century robes.

"So how did you like your investment?" she asked sociably.

"Tell you in a minute," I said, going to the head and closing the door behind me. Of course, a closed door makes no real difference with Hypatia. She can see me wherever I am on the ship, and no doubt does, but as long as a machine intelligence acts and looks human, I want it to pretend to observe human courtesies.

Hitting the head was the main reason I'd come back to my ship just then. I don't like peeing in free fall, in those awful toilets they have. Hypatia keeps ours at a suitable gravity for my comfort, like the rest of the ship. Besides, it makes her nervous if I use any toilets outside the ship, because she likes to rummage through my excretions to see if I'm staying healthy.

Which she had been doing while I was in the head. When I came out, she didn't seem to have moved, but she said, "Are you really going to eat their food?"

"Sure. Why not?"

"You've been running a little high on polyglycerides. Better you let me cook for you."

Teasing her, I said, "June Terple says Hans is a better cook."

"She said he's a *good* cook," she corrected me, "but so am I. I've been accessing him, by the way, so if there's anything you'd like to know about the crew. . . ."

"Not about the crew, but Starminder said something about a Rebecca Shapiro. Who was she?"

"That data is not in the Phoenix shipmind's stores, Klara," she said, reproving me. "However . . ."

She whited out a corner of my lounge and displayed a face on it while she gave me a capsule biography of Rebecca Shapiro. Rebecca had been a dramatic soprano with a brilliant operatic future ahead of her until she got her larynx crushed in a plane crash. They'd repaired it well enough for most purposes, but she was never going to be able to sing "The Queen of the Night" again. So, with her life on Earth ruined, Rebecca had signed up for my program. "Any other questions?" Hypatia said.

"Not about Rebecca, but I've been wondering why they call their shipmind Hans."

"Oh, that was Mark Rohrbeck's idea; he wanted to name him after some old computer pioneer. The name doesn't matter, though, does it? I mean, why did you decide to call me Hypatia?"

"Because Hypatia of Alexandria was a smart, snotty bitch," I told her. "Like you."

"Humph," she said.

"As well as being the first great woman scientist," I added, because Hypatia always likes to talk about herself.

"The first *known* one," she corrected. "Who knows how many there were whose accomplishments didn't manage to survive? Women didn't get much of a break in your ancient meat world—or, for that matter, now."

"You were supposed to be beautiful, too," I reminded her. "And you died a virgin anyway."

"By choice, Klara. Even that old Hypatia didn't care much for all that messy meat stuff. And I didn't just die. I was brutally murdered. It was a cold wet spring in A.D. 450, and a gang of those damn Nitrian monks tore me to shreds because I wasn't a Christian. Anyway," she finished, "you're the one who picked my identity. If you wanted me to be someone else, you could have given me a different one."

She had me grinning by then. "I still can," I reminded her. "Maybe something like Joan of Arc?"

She shuddered fastidiously at the idea of being a Christian instead of a gods-fearing Roman pagan and changed the subject. "Would you like me to put a call through to Mr. Tartch now?"

Well, I would and I wouldn't. I had unfinished business to settle with Bill Tartch, but I wasn't quite ready to settle it, so I shook my head. "I've been wondering about these extinct people we're trying to resurrect. Have you got any Heechee records of the planet that I haven't seen yet?"

"You bet. More than you'll ever want to watch."

"So show me some."

"Sure thing, boss," she said, and disappeared, and all at once I was standing on an outcropping of rock, looking down on a bright, green valley where some funny-looking animals were moving around.

That was the difference between PhoenixCorp's major simulations and mine. Mine cost more. Theirs were good enough for working purposes, because they showed you pretty much anything you wanted to see, but mine put you right in the middle of it. Mine were full sensory systems, too, so I could smell and feel as well as I could see and hear. As I stood there, a warm breeze ruffled my hair, and I smelled a distinct reek of smoke. "Hey, Hypatia," I said, a little surprised. "Have these people discovered fire?"

"Not to use, no," she murmured in my ear. "Must've been a lightning strike up in the hills from the storm."

"What storm?"

"The one that just passed. Don't you see everything's wet?"

Not on my rock, it wasn't. The sun overhead was big and bright and very hot.

It had already baked the rock dry, but I could see that the jumble of dark green vines at the base of my rock was still dripping, and when I turned around I could see a splotch of burning vegetation on the distant hill.

The valley was more interesting. Patches of trees, or something like trees; a herd of big, shaggy creatures, Kodiak bear–sized but obviously vegetarians because they were industriously pushing some of the trees over to eat their leaves; a pair of rivers, a narrow, fast-moving one with little waterfalls that came down from the hills to my left and flowed to join a broader, more sluggish one on the right to make a bigger stream; a few other shaggy creatures, these quite a lot bigger still, feeding by themselves on whatever was growing in the plain — well, it was an interesting sight; maybe a little like the great American prairie or the African veldt must have looked before our forebears killed off all the wild meat animals.

The most interesting part of the simulation was a pack of a dozen or so predators in the middle distance, circling furtively around a group of three or four creatures I couldn't easily make out. I pointed. "Are those the ones?" I asked Hypatia. And when she said they were, I told her to get me up closer.

At close range I could see the hunted ones looked something like pigs — that is, if pigs happened to have long, skinny legs and long, squirrelly tails. I noticed a mommy pig baring her teeth and trying to snap at the predators in all directions at once, and three little ones doing their best to huddle under the mother's belly. It was the predators I was paying attention to. They looked vaguely primate. That is, they had apelike faces and short tails. But they didn't look like any primate that ever lived on Earth, because they had six limbs: four that they ran on, and two more like arms, and in their sort-of hands they held sharp-edged rocks. As they got into position, they began hurling the rocks at the prey.

The mother pig didn't have a chance. In a couple of minutes, two of her babies were down and she was racing away with that long tail flicking from side to side like a metronome, and the surviving piglet right behind her, its tail-flicks keeping time with its mother's, and the six-limbed predators had what they had come for.

It was not a pretty scene.

I know perfectly well that animals live by eating, and I'm not sentimental about the matter — hell, I eat steak! (Not always out of a food factory, either.) All the same, I didn't like watching what was happening on this half-million-year-old alien veldt, because one of the piglets was still alive when the wolf-apes began eating it, and its pitiful shrieking got to me.

So I wasn't a bit sorry when Hypatia interrupted me to say that Mr. Tartch hadn't waited for me to call him and was already on the line.

Nearly all of my conversations with Bill Tartch get into some kind of intimate area. He likes that kind of sexy talk. I don't particularly, so I tried to keep the call short. The basic facts he had to convey were that he missed me and that, unspokenly, he looked as good as ever — not very tall, not exactly handsome but solidly built and with a great, challenging I-know-what-fun-is-all-about grin — and that he was just two days out. That's not a lot of hard data to get out of what was more than a quarter-hour of talk capsuled back and forth over all those light-years, I guess, but the rest was private; and when I was finished, it was about time to get dressed for dinner with the PhoenixCorp people.

Hypatia was way ahead of me, as usual. She had gone through my wardrobe and used her effectuators to pull out a dressy pants suit for me, so I wouldn't have a skirt to keep flying up, along with a gold neckband that wouldn't be flopping around my face as the pearls had. They were good choices; I didn't argue. And while I was getting into them she asked chattily, "So did Mr. Tartch say thank you?"

I know Hypatia's tones by now. This one made my hackles rise. "For what?"

"Why, for keeping his career going," she said, sounding surprised. "He was pretty much washed up until you came along, wasn't he? So it's only appropriate that he should, you know, display his gratitude."

"You're pushing your luck," I told her as I slipped into a pair of jeweled stockings. Sometimes I think Hypatia gets a little too personal, and this time it just wasn't justified. I didn't have to do favors to get a man. Christ, the problem was to fend them off! It's just that when it's over I like to leave them a little better off than I found them; and Bill, true enough, had reached that stage in his career when a little help now and then was useful.

But I didn't want to discuss it with her. "Talk about something else or shut up," I ordered.

"Sure, hon. Let's see. How did you like the Crabbers?"

I told her the truth. "Not much. Their table manners are pretty lousy."

Hypatia giggled. "Getting a weak stomach, Klara? Do you really think they're much worse than your own remote predecessors? Because I don't think *Australopithecus robustus* worried too much about whether its dinners were enjoying the meal, either."

We were getting into a familiar argument. "That was a long time ago, Hypatia."

"So is what you were looking at with the Crabbers, hon. Animals are animals. Now, if you really want to take yourself out of that nasty kill-and-eat business—"

"Not yet," I told her, as I had told her many times before.

What Hypatia wanted to do was to vasten me. That is, take me out of my meat body, with all its aches and annoyances, and make me into a pure, machine-stored intelligence. As other people I knew had done. Like Hypatia herself, though in her case she was no more than a simulated approximation of someone who had once been living meat.

It was a scary idea, to be sure, but not altogether unattractive. I wasn't getting as much pleasure as I would have liked out of living, but I certainly didn't want to *die*. And if I did what Hypatia wanted, I would never have to.

But I wasn't prepared to take that step yet. There were one or two things a meat person could do that a machine person couldn't—well, one big one—and I wasn't prepared to abandon the flesh until I had done what the female flesh was best at. For which I needed a man . . . and I wasn't at all sure that Bill Tartch was the particular man I needed.

When I got back for dinner in the PhoenixCorp vessel, everybody was looking conspiratorial and expectant. "We've got about twenty percent of the optical sheets in place," Terple informed me, thrilled with excitement. "Would you like to see?" She didn't wait for an answer, but commanded: "Hans! Display the planet."

The lights went dark, and before us floated a blue-and-white globe the size of my head, looking as though it were maybe ten meters away. It was half in darkness and half in sunlight, from a sun that was out of sight off to my right. There was a half-moon, too, just popping into sight from behind the planet. It looked smaller than Luna, and if it had markings of craters and seas, I couldn't see them. On the planet itself I could make out a large ocean and a kind of squared-off continent on the illuminated side. Terple did something that made the lights in the room go off, and then I could see that there had to be even more land on the dark side, because spots of light—artificial lights, cities' lights—blossomed all over parts of the nighttime area.

"You see, Klara?" she crowed. "Cities! Civilization!"

CHAPTER IV

Their shipmind really was a good cook. Fat pink shrimp that tasted as though they'd come out of the sea within the hour, followed by a fritto misto, the same, with a decent risotto and figs in cream for dessert. Everything was all perfectly prepared. Or maybe it just seemed so, because everybody was visibly relaxing now that it had turned out we really did have something to observe.

What there wasn't any of was wine to go with the meal, just some sort of tropical juices in the winebulbs. June Terple noticed my expression when I tasted it. "We're not doing anything alcoholic until we've completed the obs," she said, half apologetic, half challenging, "Still, I think Hans can get you something if you really want it."

I shook my head politely, but I was wondering if Hypatia had happened to say anything to Hans about my fondness for a drink now and then. Probably she had; shipminds do gossip when they're as advanced as Hypatia and Hans, and it was evident that the crew did know something about me. The conversation was lively and far-ranging, but it never, never touched on the subject of the black hole itself, or black holes in general.

We made a nice, leisurely meal of it. The only interruptions were inconspicuous, as crew members one after another briefly excused themselves to double-check how well the spider robots were doing as they clambered all over that five-hundred-kilometer dish, seamlessly stitching the optical reflection plates into their perfect parabola. None of the organic crew really had to bother. Hans was permanently vigilant, about that and everything else, but Terple obviously ran a tight ship. A lot of the back-and-forth chat was in-jokes, but that wasn't a problem because Hypatia explained them, whispering in my ear.

When somebody mentioned homesickness and Oleg Kekuskian said jestingly— *pointedly* jestingly—that some of us weren't homesick at all, the remark was aimed at Humphrey Mason-Manley: "He's pronging Terple, Klara, and Keku-skian's jealous," Hypatia told me.

Julia—that was *Hoo*-lia—Ibarruru, the fat and elderly Peruvian-Incan former schoolteacher, was wistfully telling Starminder how much she wished she could visit the Core before she died, and was indignant when she found out that I'd never been to Machu Picchu. "And you've been all over the galaxy? And never took the time to see one of the greatest wonders of your own planet?"

The only subdued one was Mark Rohrbeck. Between the figs and the coffee, he excused himself and didn't come back for nearly half an hour. "Calling home," Mason-Manley said wisely, and Hypatia, who was the galaxy's greatest eavesdropper when I let her be, filled me in. "He's trying to talk his wife out of the divorce. She isn't buying it."

When the coffee was about half gone, Terple whispered something to the air. Evidently Hans was listening, and in a moment the end of the room went dark. Almost at once the planet appeared for us again, noticeably bigger than it had been before. She whispered again, and the image expanded until it filled the room, and I had the sudden vertiginous sense that I was falling into it.

"We're getting about two- or three-kilometer resolution now," Terple announced proudly.

That didn't give us much beyond mountains, shorelines, and clouds, and the planet was still half in sun and half dark. (Well, it had to be, didn't it? The planet was rotating under us, but its relative position to its sun didn't change.) When I studied it, something looked odd about the land mass at the bottom of the image. I pointed. "Is that ocean, there, down on the left side? I mean the dark part. Because I didn't see any lights there."

"No, it's land, all right. It's probably just that that part is too cold to be inhabited. We're not getting a square look at the planet, you know. We're about twenty degrees south of its equator, so we're seeing more of its south pole and nothing north of, let's say, what would be Scotland or southern Alaska on Earth. Have you seen the globe Hans put together for us? No? Hans, display."

Immediately a sphere appeared in the middle of the room, rotating slowly. It would have looked exactly like the kind my grandfather kept in his living room, latitude and longitude lines and all, except that the land masses were wholly wrong. "This is derived from old Heechee data that Starminder provided for us," Hans's voice informed me. "However, we've given our own names to the conti-nents. You see the one that's made up of two fairly circular masses, connected by an isthmus, that looks like a dumbbell? Dr. Terple calls it 'Dumbbell.' It's divided into Dumbbell East and Dumbbell West. Frying Pan is the sort of roundish one with the long, thin peninsula projecting to the southwest. The one just coming into view now is Peanut, because—"

"I can see why," I told him. It did look a little like a peanut. Hans was perceptive enough to recognize, probably from the tone of my voice, that I found this ge-ography—planetography?—lesson a little boring. Terple wasn't. "Go on, Hans," she said sharply when he hesitated. So he did.

Out of guest-politeness I sat still while he named every dot on the map for me, but when he came to the end, I did too. "That's very nice," I said, unhooking myself from my dining place. "Thanks for the dinner, June, but I think I'd better let you get your work done. Anyway, we'll be seeing a lot of each other over the next five days."

Every face I saw suddenly wore a bland expression, and Terple coughed. "Well, not quite five days," she said uncomfortably. "I don't know whether anyone told you this, but we'll have to leave before the star blows."

I stopped cold, one hand stuffing my napkin into its tied-down ring, the other holding on to the wall support. "There wasn't anything about leaving early in your prospectus. Why wasn't I told this?"

"It stands to reason, Klara," she said doggedly. "As soon as the star begins its collapse, I'm shutting everything down and getting out of here. It's too dangerous."

I don't like being surprised by the people who work for me. I gave her a look. "How can it be dangerous when we're six thousand light-years away?"

She got obstinate. "Remember I'm responsible for the safety of this installation and its crew. I don't think you have any idea what a supernova is like, Klara. It's *huge*. Back in 1054 the Chinese astrologers could see it in *daylight* for almost the whole month of July, and they didn't have our lensing to make it brighter."

"So we'll put on sunglasses."

She said firmly, "We'll *leave*. I'm not just talking about visible light. Even now, with six thousand years of cooling down after it popped, that thing's still radiating all across the electromagnetic spectrum, from microwave to X-rays. We're not going to want to be where all that radiation comes to a focus when it's fresh."

As I was brushing my teeth, Hypatia spoke from behind me. "What Terple said makes sense, you know. Anything in the focus is going to get fried when the star goes supernova."

I didn't answer, so she tried another tactic. "Mark Rohrbeck is a good-looking man, isn't he? He's very confused right now, with the divorce and all, but I think he likes you."

I looked at her in the mirror. She was in full simulation, leaning against the bathroom doorway with a little smile on her face. "He's also half my age," I pointed out.

"Oh, no, Klara," she corrected me. "Not even a third, actually. Still, what difference does that make? Hans displayed his file for me. Genetically he's very clean, as organic human beings go. Would you like to see it?"

"No." I finished with the bathroom and turned to leave. Hypatia got gracefully out of my way just as though I couldn't have walked right through her.

"Well, then," she said. "Would you like something to eat? A nightcap?"

"What I would like is to go to sleep. Right now."

She sighed. "Such a waste of time. Sooner or later you know you're going to give up the meat, don't you? Why wait? In machine simulation you can do anything you can do now, only better, and—"

"Enough," I ordered. "What I'm going to do now is go to bed and dream about my lover coming closer every minute. Go away."

The simulation disappeared, and her "Good night, then" came from empty air.

Hypatia doesn't really go away when I tell her to, but she pretends she does. Part of the pretense is that she never acts as though she knows what I do in the privacy of my room.

It wasn't exactly true that I intended to dream about Bill Tartch. If I were a romantic type, I might actually have been counting the seconds until my true love arrived. Oh, hell, maybe I was, a little bit, especially when I tucked myself into that huge circular bed and automatically reached out for someone to touch and nobody was there. I do truly enjoy having a warm man's body to spoon up against when I drift off to sleep. But if I didn't have that, I also didn't have anybody snoring in my ear, or thrashing about, or talking to me when I first woke up and all I wanted was to huddle over a cup of coffee and a piece of grapefruit in peace.

Those were consoling thoughts—reasonably consoling—but they didn't do much for me this time. As soon as I put my head down, I was wide awake again.

Insomnia was one more of those meat-person flaws that disgusted Hypatia so. I didn't have to suffer from it. Hypatia keeps my bathroom medicine chest stocked with everything she imagines I might want in the middle of the night, including half a dozen different kinds of anti-insomnia pills, but I had a better idea than that. I popped the lid off my bedside stand, where I keep the manual controls I use when I don't want Hypatia to do something for me, and I accessed the synoptic I wanted to see.

I visited my island.

Its name is Raiwea—that's Rah-ee-*way*-uh, with the accent on the third syllable, the way the Polynesians say it—and it's the only place in the universe I ever miss when I'm away from it. It's not very big. It only amounts to a couple thousand hectares of dry land, but it's got palm trees and breadfruit trees and a pretty lagoon that's too shallow for the sharks ever to invade from the deep water outside the reef. And now, because I paid to put them there, it's got lots of clusters of pretty little bungalows with pretty, if imitation, thatched roofs, as well as plumbing and air conditioning and everything else that would make a person comfortable. And it's got playgrounds and game fields that are laid out for baseball or soccer or whatever a bunch of kids might need to work off excess animal energy. And it's got its own food factory nestled inside the reef, constantly churning out every variety of healthful food anyone wants to eat. And it's mine. It's all mine. Every square centimeter. I paid for it, and I've populated it with orphans and single women with babies from all over the world. When I go there, I'm Grandma Klara to about a hundred and fifty kids from newborns to teens, and when I'm somewhere else I make it a point, every day or so, to access the surveillance systems and make sure the schools are functioning and the medical services are keeping everybody healthy, because I—all right, damn it!—because I love those kids. Every last one of them. And I swear they love me back.

Hypatia says they're my substitute for having a baby of my own.

Maybe they are. All the same, I do have a couple of my own ova stored in the Raiwea clinic's deep freeze. They've been there for a good many years now, but the doctors swear they're still one hundred percent viable and they'll keep them that way. The ova are there just in case I ever decide I really want to do that other disgustingly meat-person thing and give birth to my own genetically personal child. . . .

But I've never met the man I wanted to be its father. Bill Tartch? Well, maybe. I had thought he might be for a while, anyway, but then I wasn't really so sure.

When I was up and about the next morning, Hypatia greeted me with a fresh display of the Crabber planet. It was too big now to fit in my salon, but she had zeroed in on one particular coastline. In the center of the image was a blur that might have been manmade—personmade, I mean. "They're down to half-kilometer resolution now," she informed me. "That's pretty definitely a small city."

I inspected it. It pretty definitely was, but it was very definitely small. "Isn't there anything bigger?"

"I'm afraid not, Klara. Hans says the planet seems to be rather remarkably underpopulated, though it's not clear why. Will you be going over to the PhoenixCorp ship now?"

I shook my head. "Let them work in peace. We might as well do some work ourselves. What've you got for me?"

What she had for me was another sampling of some of the ventures I'd put money into at one time or another. There were the purely commercial ones such as the helium-3 mines on Luna, and the chain of food factories in the Bay of Bengal, and the desert-revivification project in the Sahara, and forty or fifty others; they weren't particularly interesting to me, but they were some of the projects that, no matter how much I spent, just kept getting me richer and richer every day.

Then we got to the ones I cared about. I looked in on the foundation Starminder had talked about, the one for sending humans into the Core to meet with the Heechee who had stayed behind. And the scholarship program for young women like myself—like I had been once, long ago—who were stuck in dirty, drudging, dead-end jobs. Myself, I got out of it by means of dumb luck and the Gateway asteroid, but that wasn't an option now. Maybe a decent education was.

Along about then, Hypatia cleared her throat in the manner that means there's something she wants to talk about. I guessed wrong. I guessed she wanted to discuss my island, so I played the game. "Oh, by the way," I said, "I accessed Raiwea last night after I went to bed."

"Really?" she said, just as though she hadn't known it all along. "How are things?"

I went through the motions of telling her which kids were about ready to leave, and how there were eighteen new ones who had been located by the various agencies I did business with, ready to be brought to the island next time I was in the neighborhood. As she always did, whether she meant it or not, she clucked approvingly. Her simulation was looking faintly amused, though. I took it as a challenge. "So you see there's one thing we animals can do that you can't," I told her. "We can have babies."

"Or, as in your own case at least so far, not," she said agreeably. "That wasn't what I was going to tell you, though."

"Oh?"

"I just wanted to mention that Mr. Tartch's ship is going to dock in about an hour. He isn't coming alone."

Sometimes Hypatia is almost too idiosyncratically human, and more than once I've thought about getting her program changed. The tone of her voice warned me that she had something more to tell. I said tentatively, "That's not surprising. Sometimes he needs to bring a crew with him."

"Of course he does, Klara," she said cheerfully. "There's only one of them this time, though. And she's very pretty."

CHAPTER V

The very pretty assistant was very pretty, all right, and she looked to be about sixteen years old. No, that's not true. She looked a lot better than sixteen years old. I don't believe I had skin like that even when I was a newborn baby. She wore no makeup, and needed none. She had on a decorous one-piece jumpsuit that covered her from thigh to neck and left no doubt what was inside. Her name was Denys. When I got there—I had taken my time, because I didn't want Bill to think I was eager—all three of PhoenixCorp's males were hanging around, watching her like vultures sniffing carrion. It wasn't just that she looked the way she looked. She was also fresh meat, for a crew that had been getting pretty bored with each other.

Of course, I had been fresh meat, too, and there had been no signs of that kind of testosterone rush when I arrived. But then, I didn't look like Denys. Bill didn't seem to notice. He had already set up for his opening teaser, and Denys was playing his quaint autocameras for him. As they panned around the entrance chamber and settled on his face, wearing its most friendly and intelligent expression, he began to speak to the masses:

"Wilhelm Tartch here again, where PhoenixCorp is getting ready to bring a lost race of intelligent beings back to life, and here to help me once again"—one of the cameras swung around as Denys cued it toward me—"I have the good luck to have my beautiful fiancee, Gelle-Klara Moynlin, with me."

I gave him a look, because whatever I was to Wilhelm Tartch, I definitely wasn't planning to marry him. He tipped me a cheeky wink and went right on:

"As you all remember, before the Heechee ran away to hide in the Core, they surveyed most of the galaxy, looking for other intelligent races. They didn't find any. When they visited Earth they found the australopithecines, but they were a long way from being modern humans. They hadn't even developed language yet. And here, on this planet"—that view of the Crabber planet, presupernova, appeared behind him—"they found another primitive race that they thought might someday become both intelligent and civilized. Well, perhaps these Crabbers, as the PhoenixCorp people call them, did. But the Heechee weren't around to see it, and neither are we, because they had some bad luck.

"There were two stars in their planet's system, a red dwarf and a bright type-A giant. Over the millennia, as these lost people were struggling toward civilization, the big star was losing mass, which was being sucked into the smaller one—and then, without warning, the small one reached critical mass. It exploded—and the people, along with their planet and all their works, were instantly obliterated in the supernova blast."

He stopped there, gazing toward Denys until she called, "Got it." Then he kicked himself toward me, arms outstretched for a hug, a big grin on his face. When we connected, he buried his face in my neck and whispered, "Oh, Klaretta, we've been away from each other too long!"

Bill Tartch is a good hugger. His arms felt fine around me, and his big, male body felt good against mine. "But we're together now," I told him . . . as I looked over his shoulder at Denys—who was regarding us with an affectionate and wholly unjealous smile.

So that part might not be much of a problem, at that. I decided not to worry about it. Anyway, the resolution of the Crabber planet was getting better and better, and that was what we were here for, after all.

What the Crabber planet had a lot of was water. As the planet turned on its axis, the continental shore had disappeared into the nighttime side of the world, and what we were looking at was mostly ocean.

Bill Tartch wasn't pleased. "Is that all we're going to see?" he demanded of the room at large. "I expected at least some kind of a city."

Terple answered. "A small city—probably. Anyway, that's what it looked like before we lost it; I can show you that much if you like. Hans, go back to when that object was still in sight."

The maybe-city didn't look any better the second time I saw it, and it didn't impress Bill. He made a little tongue-click of annoyance. "You, shipmind! Can't you enhance the image for me?"

"That is enhanced, Mr. Tartch," Hans told him pleasantly. "However, we have somewhat better resolution now, and I've been tracking it in the infrared. There's a little more detail"—the continental margin appeared for us, hazily delineated because of the differences in temperature between water and land, and we zoomed in on the object—"but, as you see, there are hot spots that I have not yet been able to identify."

There were. *Big* ones, and very bright. What was encouraging, considering what we were looking for, was that some of them seemed to be fairly geometrical in shape, triangles and rectangles. But what were they?

"Christmas decorations?" Bill guessed. "You know, I mean not really Christmas, but with the houses all lit up for some holiday or other?"

"I don't think so, Mr. Tartch," Hans said judiciously. "There's not much optical light; what you're seeing is heat."

"Keeping themselves warm in the winter?"

"We don't know if it's their winter, Mr. Tartch, and that isn't probable in any case. Those sources read out at up to around three hundred degrees Celsius. That's almost forest-fire temperature."

Bill looked puzzled. "Slash-and-burn agriculture? Or maybe some kind of industry?"

"We can't say yet, Mr. Tartch. If it were actual combustion, there should be more visible light; but there's very little. We'll simply have to wait for better data. Meanwhile, however, there's something else you might like to see." The scene we were viewing skittered across the face of the planet—huge cloud banks, a couple of islands, more cloud—and came to rest on a patch of ocean. In its center was a tiny blur of something that looked grayish when it looked like anything at all; it seemed to flicker in and out of sight, at the very limit of visibility.

"Clouds?" Bill guessed.

"No, Mr. Tartch. I believe it is a group of objects of some kind, and they are in motion—vectoring approximately seventy-one degrees, or, as you would say, a little north of east. They must be quite large, or we would not pick up anything at all. They may be ships, although their rate of motion is too high for anything but a hydrofoil or ground-effect craft. If they are still in sight when the mirror is more nearly complete, we should be able to resolve them easily enough."

"Which will be when?"

Hans gave us that phony couple-of-seconds pause before he answered. "There is a small new problem about that, Mr. Tartch," he said apologetically. "Some of the installed mirror plates have been subjected to thermal shock, and they are no longer in exact fit. Most of the installation machines have had to be delivered to adjust them, and so it will be some time before we can go on with completing the mirror. A few hours only, I estimate."

Bill looked at me and I looked at him. "Well, shit," he said. "What else is going to go wrong?"

What had gone wrong that time wasn't June Terple's fault. She said it was, though. She said that she was the person in charge of the whole operation, so everything that happened was her responsibility, and she shouldn't have allowed Ibarruru to override Hans's controls. And Julia Ibarruru was tearfully repentant. "Starminder told me the Heechee had identified eleven other planets in the Crabber system; I was just checking to see if there were any signs of life on any of them, and I'm afraid that for a minute I let the system's focus get too close to the star."

It could have been worse. I told them not to worry about it and invited all three of them to my ship for a drink. That made my so-called fiance's eyebrows rise, because he had certainly been expecting to be the first person I welcomed aboard. He was philosophical about it, though. "I'll see you later," he said, and if none of the women knew what he meant by that, it could only have been because they'd never seen a leer before. Then he led Denys off to interview some of Phoenix-Corp's other people.

Which was pretty much what I was planning for myself. Hypatia had set out tea things on one table, and dry sherry on another, but before we sat down to either, I had to give all three of the women the usual guided tour. The sudden return to normal gravity was a burden for them, but they limped admiringly through the guest bedroom, exclaimed at the kitchen—never used by me, but installed just in case I ever wanted to do any of that stuff myself—and were blown away by my personal bathroom. Whirlbath, bidet, big onyx tub, mirror walls—Bill Tartch always said it looked like a whore's dream of heaven, and he hadn't been the first guest to make that observation. I don't suppose the PhoenixCorp women had ever seen anything like it. I let them look. I even let them peek into the cabinets of perfumes and toiletries. "Oh, musk oil!" Terple cried. "But it's real! That's so expensive."

"I don't wear it anymore. Take it, if you like," I said and, for the grand finale, opened the door to my bedroom.

When at last we got to the tea, sherry, and conversation, Ibarruru's first remark was, "Mr. Tartch seemed like a very interesting man." She didn't spell out the connection, but I knew it was that huge bed that was in her mind. So we chatted about Mr. Tartch and his glamorous p-vision career, and how Terple had grown up with the stories of the Gateway prospectors on every day's news, and how Ibarruru had dreamed of an opportunity like this—"Astronomy's really almost a lost art on Earth, you know," she told me. "Now we have all the Heechee data, so there's no point anymore in wasting time with telescopes and probes."

"So what does an astronomer do when there's no astronomy to be done?" I asked, being polite.

She said ruefully, "I teach an undergraduate course in astronomy at a community college in Maryland. For people who will never do any astronomy, because if there's anything somebody really wants to see, why, they just get in a ship and go out and look at it."

"As I did, Ms. Moynlin," said Starminder, with the Heechee equivalent of a smile.

That was what I was waiting for. If there was a place in the universe I still wanted to see, it was her home in the Core. "You must miss the Core," I told her. "All those nearby stars, so bright—what we have here must look pretty skimpy to you."

"Oh, no," she said, being polite, "this is quite nice. For a change. What I really miss is my family."

It had never occurred to me that she had a family, but, yes, she had left a mate and two young offspring behind when she came out. It was a difficult decision, but she couldn't resist the adventure. Miss them? Of course she missed them! Miss her? She looked surprised at that. "Why, no, Ms. Moynlin, they won't be missing me. They're asleep for the night. I'll be back long before they wake up. Time dilation, you see. I'm only going to stay out here for a year or two."

Ibarruru said nervously, "That's the part that worries me about going to the Core, Starminder. I'm not young anymore, and I know that if I went for even a few days, nearly everyone I know would be gone when I got back. No, not just 'nearly' everyone," she corrected herself. "What is it, forty thousand to one? So a week there would be nearly a thousand years back home." Then she turned to the Heechee female. "But even if we can't go ourselves, you can tell us about it, Starminder. Would you like to tell Ms. Moynlin what it's like in the Core?"

It was what I wanted to hear, too. I'd heard it often enough before, but I listened as long as Starminder was willing to talk. Which was a lot, because she was definitely homesick.

Would it really matter if I spent a week in the Core? Or a month, or a year, for that matter? I'd miss my kids on the island, of course, but they'd be taken care of, and so would everything else that mattered to me. And there wasn't any other human being in the universe that I cared enough about to miss for more than a day.

I was surprised when Hypatia spoke up out of thin air. "Ms. Moynlin"—formal because of the company—"there's a call for you." And she displayed Bill Tartch's face.

I could see by the background that he was in his own ship, and he looked all bright and fresh and grinning at me. "Permission to come aboard, hon?" he asked.

That produced a quick reaction among my guests.

"Oh," said Ibarruru, collecting herself. "Well, it's time we got back to work anyway, isn't it, June?" She was sounding arch. Terple wasn't; she simply got up, and Starminder followed her example.

"You needn't leave," I said.

"But of course we must," said Terple. "Julia's right. Thank you for the tea and, uh, things."

And they were gone, leaving me to be alone with my lover.

CHAPTER VI

"He's been primping for the last hour," Hypatia reported in my ear. "Showered, shaved, dressed up. And he put on that musk cologne that he thinks you like."

"I do like it," I said. "On him. Let me see you when I'm talking to you."

She appeared obediently, reclining on the couch Ibarruru had just left. "I'd say the man's looking to get laid," she observed. "Again."

I didn't choose to pick up on the "again." That word was evidence of one of Hypatia's more annoying traits, of which she has not quite enough to make me have her reprogrammed. When I chose Hypatia of Alexandria as a personality for my shipmind, it seemed to be a good idea at the time. But my own Hypatia took it seriously. That's what happens when you get yourself a really powerful shipmind; she throws herself into the part. The first thing Hypatia did was look up her template and model herself as close to the original as she thought I would stand— including such details as the fact that the original Hypatia really hated men.

"So, do you want me out of the way so you can oblige him?" she asked sociably.

"No," I said. "You stay."

"That's my girl. You ask me, sexual intercourse is greatly overrated anyway."

"That's because you never had any," I told her. "By which I mean neither you, my pet program, nor the semimythical human woman I modeled you after, who died a virgin and is said to have shoved her used menstrual cloths in the face of one persistent suitor to turn him off."

"Malicious myth," she said comfortably. "Spread by the Christians after they murdered her. Anyway, here he comes."

I would have been willing to bet that the first words out of Bill Tartch's mouth would be *Alone at last!* accompanied by a big grin and a lunge for me. I would have half won. He didn't say anything at all, just spread his arms and lurched toward me, grin and all.

Then he saw Hypatia, sprawled on the couch. "Oh," he said, stumbling as he came to a stop—there evidently wasn't any gravity in his rental ship, either. "I thought we'd be alone."

"Not right now, sweetie," I said. "But it's nice to see you."

"Me, too." He thought for a moment, and I could see him changing gears: All right, the lady doesn't want what I want right now, so what else can we do? That's one of those good-and-bad things about Bill Tartch. He does what I want, and none of this sweeping-her-off-her-feet stuff. Viewing it as good, it means he's considerate and sweet. Viewing it the other way—the way Hypatia chooses to view it—he's a spineless wretch, sucking up to somebody who can do him good.

While I was considering which way to view it, Bill snapped his fingers. "I know," he said, brightening. "I've been wanting to do a real interview with you anyway. That all right? Hypatia, you can record it for me, can't you?"

Hypatia didn't answer, just looked sulkily at me.

"Do what he says," I ordered. But Bill was having second thoughts.

"Maybe not," he said, cheerfully resigned to the fact that she wouldn't take orders from him. "She'd probably screw it up on purpose for me anyway, so I guess we'd better get Denys in here."

It didn't take Denys much more than a minute to arrive, with those quaint little cameras and all. I did my best to be gracious and comradely. "Oh, yes, clip them on anywhere," I said—in my ship's gravity, the cameras wouldn't just float. "On the backs of the chairs? Sure. If they mess the fabric a little, Hypatia will fix it right up." I didn't look at Hypatia, just gestured to her to get herself out of sight. She did without protest.

Bill had planted himself next to me and was holding my hand. I didn't pull it away. It took Denys a little while to get all the cameras in place, Bill gazing tolerantly at the way she was doing it and not offering to help. When she announced she was ready, the interview began.

It was a typical Wilhelm Tartch interview, meaning that he did most of the talking. He rehearsed our entire history for the cameras in one uninterrupted monologue; my part was to smile attentively as it was going on. Then he got to Phoenix.

"We're here to see the results of this giant explosion that took place more than a thousand years ago—What's the matter, Klara?"

He was watching my face, and I knew what he was seeing. "Turn off your cameras, Bill. You need to get your facts straight. It happened a lot longer than a thousand years ago."

He shook his head at me tolerantly. "That's close enough for the audience," he explained. "I'm not giving an astronomy lesson here. The star blew up in 1054, right?"

"It was in 1054 that the Chinese astronomers *saw* it. That's the year when the light from the supernova got as far as our neighborhood, but it took about five thousand years to get there. Didn't you do your homework?"

"We must've missed that little bit, hon," he said, giving me his best ruefully apologetic smile. "All right, Denys. Take it from the last little bit. We'll put in some shots of the supernova to cover the transition. Ready? Then go. This giant explosion took place many thousands of years ago, destroying a civilization that might in some ways almost have become the equal of our own. What were they like, these people the Phoenix investigators call 'Crabbers'? No one has ever known. When the old Heechee visited their planet long ago, they were still animallike primitives — Denys, we'll put in some of those old Heechee files here — but the Heechee thought they had the potential to develop cognitive intelligence and even civilization. Did they ever fulfill this promise? Did they come to dominate their world as the human race did our Earth? Did they develop science and art and culture of their own? We know from the tantalizing hints we've seen so far that this may be so. Now, through the generosity of Gelle-Klara Moynlin, who is here with me, we are at last going to see for ourselves what these tragically doomed people achieved before their star exploded without warning, cutting them off — Oh, come on, Klara. What is it this time?"

"We don't know if they had any warning or not, do we? That's one of the things we're trying to find out."

Denys cleared her throat. She said diffidently, "Bill, maybe you should let me do a little more background research before you finish this interview."

My lover gave her a petulant little grimace. "Oh, all right. I suppose there's nothing else to do."

I heard the invisible little cough that meant Hypatia had something to say to me, so I said to the air, "Hypatia?"

She picked up her cue. "The PhoenixCorp shipmind tells me they're back at work on the dish, and they're getting somewhat better magnification now. There are some new views you may want to see. Shall I display here?"

Bill seemed slightly mollified. He looked at me. "What do you think, Klara?"

It was the wrong question to ask me. I didn't want to tell him what I was thinking.

For that matter, I didn't want to be thinking it at all. All right, he and this little Denys lollipop hadn't done any of their backgrounding on the way out to Phoenix. So what, exactly, had they been doing with their time?

I said, "No, I think I'd rather see it on the PhoenixCorp ship. You two go ahead. I'll follow in a minute." And as soon as they were out of sight. I turned around, and Hypatia was sitting in the chair Denys had just left, looking smug.

"Can I do something for you, Klara?" she asked solicitously.

She could, but I wasn't ready to ask her for it. I asked her for something else instead. "Can you show me the interior of Bill's ship?"

"Of course, Klara." And there it was, displayed for me, Hypatia guiding my point of view all through it.

It wasn't much. The net obviously wasn't spending any more than it had to on Bill's creature comfort. It was so old that it had all that Heechee drive stuff out in the open; when I designed my own ship, I made sure all that ugliness was tucked away out of sight, like the heating system in a condo. The important fact was that it had two sleeping compartments, one clearly Denys's, the other definitely Bill's. Both had unmade beds. Evidently the rental's shipmind wasn't up to much housekeeping, and neither was Denys. There was no indication that they might have been visiting back and forth.

I gave up. "You've been dying to tell me about them ever since they got here," I said to Hypatia. "So tell me."

She gave me that wondering look. "Tell you what exactly, Klara?"

"Tell me what was going on on Bill's ship, for Christ's sake! I know you know."

She looked slightly miffed, the way she always did when Christ's name was mentioned, but she said, "It is true that I accessed Mr. Tartch's shipmind as a routine precaution. It's a pretty cheap-jack job, about what you'd expect in a rental. It had privacy locks all over it, but nothing that I couldn't—"

I snarled at her, "Tell me! *Did they?*"

She made an expression of distaste. "Oh, yes, hon, they certainly did. All the way out here. Like dogs in rut."

I looked around the room at the wineglasses and cups and the cushions that had been disturbed by someone sitting on them. "I'm going to the ship. Clean up this mess while I'm gone," I ordered, and checked my face in the mirror.

It looked just as it always looked, as though nothing were different.

Well, nothing was, really, was it? What did it matter if Bill chose to bed this Denys, or any number of Denyses, when I wasn't around? It wasn't as though I had been planning to *marry* the guy.

CHAPTER VII

None of the crew was in the entrance lock when I came to the PhoenixCorp ship, but I could hear them. They were all gathered in the dining hall, laughing and chattering excitedly. When I got there, I saw that the room was darkened. They were all poking at virtuals of one scene or another as Hans displayed them, and no one noticed me as I came in.

I hooked myself inconspicuously to a belt near the door and looked around. I saw Bill and his sperm receptacle of the moment hooked chastely apart, Denys chirping at Mason-Manley, Bill talking into his recorders. Mason-Manley was squeezing Denys's shoulder excitedly, presumably because he was caught up in the euphoria of the moment, but he seemed to be enjoying touching her, too. If Bill noticed, he didn't appear to mind. But then, Bill was not a jealous type; that was one of the things I liked about him.

Until recently I hadn't thought that I was, either.

Well, I told myself, I wasn't. It wasn't a question of jealousy. It was a question of—oh, call it good manners; if Bill chose to bed a bimbo now and then, that was his business, but it did not excuse his hauling the little tart all the way from Earth to shove her in my face.

A meter or so away from me, Mark Rohrbeck was watching the pictures, looking a lot less gloomy than usual. When he saw me at last, he waved and pointed. "Look, Ms. Moynlin!" he cried. "Blimps!"

So I finally got around to looking at the display. In the sector he was indicating, we were looking down on one of the Crabber planet's oceans. There were a lot of clouds, but some areas had only scattered puffs. And there among them were eight fat little silver sausages, in a V formation, that surely were far too hard-edged and uniform in shape to be clouds.

"These are the objects we viewed before, Ms. Moynlin," Hans's voice informed me. "Now we can discriminate the individual elements, and they are certainly artifacts."

"Sure, but why do you say they're blimps? How do you know they aren't ships of some kind?" I asked, and then said at once, "No, cancel that," as I figured it out for myself. If they had been surface vessels, they would have produced some sort of wake in the water. They were aircraft, all right, so I changed the question to, "Where are they going, do you think?"

"Wait a minute," June Terple said. "Hans, display the projection for Ms. Moynlin."

That sheet of ocean disappeared, and in its place was a globe of the Crabber planet, its seas in blue, land masses in gray. Eight stylized little blimp figures, greatly out of proportion, were over the ocean. From them a silvery line extended to the northeast, with another line, this one golden, going back past the day-night terminator toward the southwest. Terple said, "It looks like the blimps came from around that group of islands at the end of the gold course-line, and they're heading toward the Dumbbell continents up on the right. Unfortunately, those are pretty far north. We can't get a good picture of them from here, but Hans has enhanced some of the data on the island the blimps came from. Hans?"

The globe disappeared. Now we were looking down on one of those greenish infrared scenes: shoreline, bay—and something burning around the bay. Once again the outlines of the burning areas were geometrically unnatural. "As we speculated, it is almost certainly a community, Ms. Moynlin," Hans informed me. "However, it seems to have suffered some catastrophe, similar to what we observed on the continent that is now out of sight."

"What kind of catastrophe?" I demanded.

Hans was all apologetic. "We simply don't have the data yet, Ms. Moynlin. A great fire, one might conjecture. I'm sure it will make sense when we have better resolution—in a few hours, perhaps. I'll keep you posted."

"Please do," I said. And then, without planning it, I found myself saying, "I think I'll go back to my ship and lie down for a while."

"But you just got here," Mark Rohrbeck said, surprised and, I thought with some pleasure, maybe a little disappointed. Bill Tartch looked suddenly happy and began to unhook himself from his perch. I gave a little shake of the head to both of them.

"I'm sorry. I just want to rest," I said. "It's been an exhausting few days."

That wasn't particularly true, of course—not any part of it. I wasn't really tired, and I didn't want to rest. I just wanted to be by myself, or at any rate with no company but Hypatia, which comes to pretty much the same thing.

As I came into my ship, she greeted me in motherly mode. "Too many people, hon?" she asked. "Shall I make you a drink?"

I shook my head to the drink, but she was right about the other part of it. "Funny thing," I said, sprawling on the couch. "The more people I meet, the fewer I am comfortable around."

"Meat people are generally boring," she agreed. "How about a cup of tea?"

I shrugged, and immediately heard the activity begin in the kitchen. Hypatia had her faults, but she was a pretty good mom when I needed her to be. I lay back on the couch and gazed at the ceiling. "You know what?" I said. "I'm beginning to think I ought to settle down on the island."

"You could do that, yes," she said diplomatically. Then, because she was Hypatia, she added, "Let's see, the last time you were there, you stayed exactly eleven days, wasn't it? About six months ago?"

She had made me feel defensive—again. I said. "I had things to do."

"Of course you did. Then the time before that wasn't quite that long, was it? Just six days—and that was over a year ago."

"You've made your point, Hypatia. Talk about something else."

"Sure thing, boss." So she did. Mostly what she chose to talk about was what my various holdings had been doing in the few hours since I'd checked them last. I wasn't listening. After a few minutes of it, I swallowed the tea she'd made for me and stood up. "I'm going to soak in the tub for a while."

"I'll run it for you, hon. Hon? They've got some new pictures from the Crabber planet if you want to see them while you soak."

"Why not?" And by the time I'd shucked my clothes the big onyx tub was full, the temperature perfect as always, and one corner of the bathroom was concealed by one of Hypatia's simulations.

The new display was almost filled by what looked like hundreds, maybe thousands, of tiny buildings. We were looking down at them from something like a forty-five-degree angle, and I couldn't make out many details. Their sun must have been nearly overhead, because there weren't many shadows to bring out details.

"This is the biggest city they've found yet," Hypatia informed me. "It's inland on the western part of the squarish continent in the southern hemisphere, where two big rivers come together. If you look close, you'll see there's a suggestion of things moving in the streets, but we can't make out just what yet. However—"

I stopped her. "Skip the commentary," I ordered. "Just keep showing me the pictures. If I have any questions, I'll ask."

"If that's what you want, hon." She sounded aggrieved. Hypatia doesn't like to be told to shut up, but she did.

The pictures kept coming, one city after another, now a bay with what looked like surface ships of some kind moored in it, now some more blimps sailing peacefully along, now what might have been a wide-gauge railroad with a train steaming over a bridge. I couldn't really see the tracks, only the bridge and a hazy line that stretched before and after it across the countryside. What I could see best was the locomotive, and most of all the long white trail of steam from its stack.

I watched for a while, then waved the display off. I closed my eyes and lay back to let the sweet-smelling foamy waters make me feel whole and content again. As I had done many thousands of times, sometimes with success.

This was one of the successes. The hot tub did its work. I felt myself drifting off to a relaxed and welcome sleep. . . .

And then, suddenly, a vagrant thought crossed my mind, and I wasn't relaxed anymore.

I got out of the tub and climbed into the shower stall, turning it on full; I let cold water hammer at me for a while, then changed it to hot. When I got out, I pulled on a robe.

As I was drying my hair, the door opened and Hypatia appeared, looking at me with concern. "I'm afraid what I told you about Tartch upset you, hon," she said, oozing with compassion. "You don't really care what he does, though, do you?"

I said, "Of course not," wondering if it were true.

"That's my girl," she said approvingly. "There are some new scenes, too."

They appeared; she didn't wait to see if I wanted them on. I watched the changing scenes for a while, then decided I didn't. I turned to Hypatia. "Turn it off," I said. "I want to ask you something."

She didn't move, but the scene disappeared. "What's that, Klara?"

"While I was dozing in the tub, I thought for a moment I might fall asleep, and slip down into the water and drown. Then I thought you surely wouldn't let that happen, because you'd be watching, wouldn't you?"

"I'm always aware of any problems that confront you, Klara."

"And then it occurred to me that you might be tempted to let me go ahead and drown, just so you could get me into that machine storage you're always trying to sell me. So I got out of the tub and into the shower."

I pulled my hair back and fastened it with a barrette, watching her. She didn't speak, just stood there with her usual benign and thoughtful expression. "So, would you?" I demanded.

She looked surprised. "You mean would I deliberately let you drown? Oh, I don't think I could do that, Klara. As a general rule I'm not programmed to go against your wishes, not even if it were for your own good. That would be for your good, you know. Machine storage would mean eternal life for you, Klara, or as close as makes no difference. And no more of the sordid little concerns of the meat that cause you so much distress."

I turned my back on her and went into my bedroom to dress. She followed, in her excellent simulation of walking. What I wanted to know was how general her general rule was, and what she would have deemed a permissible exception. But as I opened my mouth to ask her, she spoke up.

"Oh, Klara," she said. "They've found something of interest. Let me show you." She didn't wait for a response; at once the end of the room lit up.

We were looking again at that first little fleet of blimps. They were nearly at the coast, but they weren't in their tidy V formation anymore. They were scattered over the sky, and two of them were falling to the sea, blazing with great gouts of flame. Small things I couldn't quite make out were buzzing around and between them.

"My God," I said. "Something's shooting them down!"

Hypatia nodded. "So it would appear, Klara. It looks as though the Crabbers' blimps are filled with hydrogen, to burn the way they do. That suggests a rather low level of technological achievement, but give them credit. They aren't primitives, anyway. They're definitely civilized enough to be having themselves a pretty violent little war."

CHAPTER VIII

There wasn't any doubt about it. The Crabbers were industriously killing each other in a kind of aerial combat that was right out of the old stories of World War I. I couldn't see much of the planes that were shooting the blimps down, but they were really there, and what was going on was a real old-fashioned dogfight.

I don't know what I had hoped to see when we brought the long-dead Crabbers back to some kind of life. But that definitely wasn't it. When the scenes changed — Hans had been assiduous in zooming down to wherever on the planet's surface things were going on — it didn't improve. It got worse. I saw a harbor crammed with surface vessels, where a great river joined the sea; but some of the ships were on fire, and others appeared to be sinking. "Submarines did that, I think," Hypatia judged. "Or it could possibly be from bombing planes or mines, but my money's on submarines." Those strange patterns of heat in the cities weren't a mystery any longer — the cities had been burned to the ground by incendiaries, leaving only glowing coals. Then, when we were looking down, on a plain where flashes of white and reddish light sparkled all over the area, we couldn't see what was making them, but Hypatia had a guess for that, too. "Why," she said, sounding interested, "I do believe we're looking at a large-scale tank battle."

And so on, and on.

So Hans's promise had been kept. As soon as the magnification got a little better, it all did begin to make sense, just as the shipmind had promised. (I mean, if war makes any sense in the first place, that's the sense the pictures made.) The robots on the dish were still slaving away at adding the final mirror segments, and the pictures kept getting better and better.

Well, I don't know if I mean "better," exactly. The pictures were certainly clearer and more detailed, in some cases I would have to say even more excruciatingly detailed. But what they all showed was rack and ruin and death and destruction.

And their war was so pointless! They didn't have to bother killing each other. Their star would do it for them soon enough. All unknowing, every one of those Crabbers was racing toward a frightful death as their sun burst over them.

An hour earlier I had been pitying them for the fate that awaited them. But now I couldn't say I thought their fate was all that unjust.

Hypatia was looking at me in that motherly way she sometimes assumes. "I'm afraid all this is disturbing for you, Klara," she murmured. "Would it cheer you up to invite. Mr. Tartch aboard? He's calling. He says he wants to talk to you about the new pictures."

"Sure he does," I said, pretty sure that Bill really wanted to talk about why he didn't deserve being treated so standoffishly by me. "No. Tell him I'm asleep and don't want to be disturbed. And leave me alone for a while."

As soon as she had left and the door had closed behind her, I actually did throw myself onto my big, round bed. I didn't sleep, though. I just lay there, staring at myself in the mirror on the ceiling and doing my best not to think about anything.

Unfortunately, that's not something I'm good at. I could get myself to not think about those damn nasty Crabbers, but then I found my mind quickly turned itself to thinking whether it was better to let Bill Tartch hang or tell him to come in and then have a knock-down, drag-out, breaking-up fight with him to get it all over with. And when I made myself stop thinking about Bill Tartch, I found myself wondering why I'd squandered a fairly hefty chunk of my surplus cash on poking into the lives of a race that didn't know any better than to take a reasonably nice little planet and turn it into a charnel house.

I thought of calling Hypatia back in for another dull session of playing with my investments. I thought wistfully of taking another look at my island. And then I thought, screw it. I got myself into this thing. I might as well go ahead and see it through. . . .

But a more pleasant thought had been stirring in the background of my mind, so first there was something else I wanted from Hypatia.

I put on the rest of my clothes and went out to where she was reclining gracefully on the couch, just as though she'd been lounging there all along. I'm sure she had been watching those charnel-house scenes as attentively as anyone on the Phoenix ship—the difference being, of course, that Hypatia didn't have to bother with turning the optical display on for her own needs. But I needed it, so she asked politely, "Shall I display the data for you again, Klara?"

"In a minute," I said. "First, tell me all about Mark Rohrbeck."

I expected one of those tolerantly knowing looks from her. I got it, too. But she obediently began to recite all his stats. Mark's parents had died when he was young, and he had been brought up by his grandfather, who had once made his living as a fisherman on Lake Superior. "Mostly the old man fished for sea lampreys— know what they are, Klara? They're ugly things. They have big sucking disks instead of jaws. They attach themselves to other fish and suck their guts out until they die. I don't think you'd want to eat a sea lamprey yourself, but they were about all that was left in the lake. Mr. Rohrbeck sold them for export to Europe—

people there thought they were a delicacy. They said they tasted like escargot. Then, of course, the food factories came along and put him out of business—"

"Get back to Mark Rohrbeck," I ordered. "I want to hear about the man himself. Briefly."

"Oh. Sorry. Well, he got a scholarship at the University of Minnesota, did well, went on to grad school at MIT, made a pretty fair reputation in computer science, married, had two kids, but then his wife decided there was a dentist she liked better than Rohrbeck, so she dumped him. And as I've mentioned before," she said appreciatively, "he does have really great genes. Does that cover it?"

I mulled that over for a moment, then said, "Just about. Don't go drawing any conclusions from this, do you hear?"

"Certainly, Klara," she said, but she still had that look.

I sighed. "All right. Now turn that damn thing back on."

"Of course, Klara," she said, unsurprised, and did. "I'm afraid it hasn't been getting any better."

It hadn't. It was just more of the same. I watched doggedly for a while, and then I said, "All right, Hypatia. I've seen enough."

She made it disappear, looking at me curiously. "There'll be better images when they finish with the mirror. By then we should be able to see actual individual Crabbers."

"Lovely," I said, not meaning it, and then I burst out. "My God, what's the matter with those people? There's plenty of room on the planet for all of them. Why didn't they just stay home and live in peace?"

It wasn't meant to be a real question, but Hypatia answered it for me anyway. "What do you expect? They're meat people," she said succinctly.

I wasn't letting her get away with that. "Come on, Hypatia! Human beings are meat people, too, and we don't go tearing halfway around the world just to kill each other!"

"Oh, do you not? What a short memory you have, Klara dear. Think of those twentieth-century world wars. Think of the Crusades, tens of thousands of Europeans dragging themselves all the way around the Mediterranean Sea to kill as many Moslems as they could. Think of the Spanish conquistadors, murdering their way across the Americas. Of course," she added, "those people were all Christians."

I blinked at her. "You think what we're looking at is a religious war?"

She shrugged gracefully. "Who knows? Meat people don't need reasons to kill each other, dear."

CHAPTER IX

Hypatia had been right about what gravitational lensing plus that big mirror could do.

By the time the mirror was complete, we could make out plenty of detail. We were even able to see individual centaur-like Crabbers—the same build, four legs and upright torso, that they'd inherited from the primitives I'd seen, but no longer very primitive at all.

Well, what I mean is that sometimes we could see them, anyway. Not always. The conditions had to be right. We couldn't see them when it was night on their part of the planet, of course, except in those ghosty-looking IR views, and we couldn't see them at all when they were blanketed with clouds we couldn't peer through. But we could see enough. More than enough, as far as I was concerned.

The PhoenixCorp crew was going crazy trying to keep up with the incoming data. Bill seemed to have decided to be patient with my unpredictable moods, so he paid me only absentminded attention. He kept busy working. He and Denys were ecstatically interrupting everyone in their jobs so that he could record their spot reactions, while the crew did their best to get on with their jobs anyway. June Terple stopped sleeping entirely, torn between watching the new images as they arrived and nagging her shipmind to make sure we would have warning in time to get the hell out of there before the star blew.

Only Mark Rohrbeck seemed to have time on his hands. Which was just the way I wanted it.

I found him in the otherwise empty sleep chamber, where Hans had obligingly set up a duplicate show of the incoming scenes for him. Mark's main area of concern was the shipmind and the functions it controlled, but all those things were working smoothly without his attention. He was spending his time gazing morosely in the general direction of the pictures.

I hooked myself up nearby. "Nasty, isn't it?" I said sociably, to cheer him up.

He didn't want to be cheered. "You mean the Crabbers?" Although his eyes had been on the display, his mind evidently hadn't. He thought it over for a moment, then gave his verdict. "Oh, I guess it's nasty enough, all right. It isn't exactly what we were all hoping for, that's for sure. But it all happened a long time ago, though, didn't it?"

"And you've got more immediate problems on your mind," I offered helpfully.

He gave me a gloomy imitation of a smile. "I see the shipminds have been gossiping again. Well, it isn't losing Doris that bothers me so much," he said after a moment. "I mean, that hurt, too. I thought I loved her, but—Well, it didn't work out, did it? Now she's got this other guy, so what the hell? But"—he swallowed unhappily—"the thing is, she's keeping the kids."

He was not only a nice man, he was beginning to touch my heart. I said, sounding sympathetic and suddenly feeling that way, too, "And you miss them?"

"Hell! I've been missing them most of the time since they were born," he said self-accusingly. "I guess that's what went wrong. I've been away working so much, I suppose I can't blame Doris for getting her lovemaking from somebody else."

That triggered something in me that I hadn't known was there. "No!" I said, surprising myself by my tone. "That's wrong. Blame her."

I startled Rohrbeck, too. He looked at me as though I had suddenly sprouted horns, but he didn't get a chance to speak. June Terple came flying by the room and saw us. She stuck her nose in, grabbing a hold-on to yell at Mark in passing. "Rohrbeck! Get your ass in gear! I want you to make sure Hans is shifting focus as fast as possible. We could be losing all kinds of data!" And then she was gone again, to wherever she was gone to.

Mark gave me a peculiar look, but then he shrugged and waved his hands to show that when the boss gave orders, even orders to do what he had already done, he couldn't just stay and talk anymore, and then he was gone as well.

I didn't blame him for the peculiar look. I hadn't realized I was so sensitive in the matter of two-timing partners. But apparently I was.

Even though I was the boss, I had no business keeping the PhoenixCorp people from doing their jobs. Anyway, there was more bustle and confusion going on there than I liked. I went back to my ship to stay out of everybody's way, watching the pictures as they arrived with only Hypatia for company.

She started the projections up as soon as I arrived, without being asked, and I sat down to observe.

If you didn't think of the Crabbers as *people*, what they were doing was certainly interesting. The Crabbers themselves were, for that matter. I could see traces of those primitive predators in the civilized—civilized!—versions before me. Now, of course, they had machines and wore clothes and, if you didn't mind the extra limbs, looked rather impressive in their gaudy tunics and spiked leggings, and the shawl things they wore on their heads that were ornamented with, I guessed, maybe insignia of rank. Or junk jewelry, maybe, but most of them were definitely in one or another kind of uniform. Most of the civilized ones, anyway. In the interior of the south continent, where it looked like rain forest and savanna, were lots of what looked like noncivilized ones. Those particular Crabbers didn't have machines, or much in the way of clothing either. They lived off the land, and they seemed to spend a lot of time gaping up worriedly at the sky, where fleets of blimps and double-winged aircraft buzzed by now and then.

The civilized ones seemed to be losing some of their civilization. When Hans showed us close-ups of one of the bombed-out cities, I could see streams of people—mostly civilians, I guessed—making their way out of the ruins, carrying bundles, leading kids or holding them. A lot of them were limping, just dragging themselves along. Some were being pulled in wagons or sledlike things.

"They look like they're all sick," I said, and Hypatia nodded.

"Undoubtedly some of them are, dear," she informed me. "It's a war, after all. You shouldn't be thinking just in terms of bombs and guns, you know. Did you never hear of biological warfare?"

I stared at her. "You mean they're spreading *disease*? As a *weapon*?"

"I believe that is likely, and not at all without precedent," she informed me, preparing to lecture. She started by reminding me of the way the first American colonists in New England gave smallpox-laden blankets to the Indians to get them out of the way—"The colonists were Christians, of course, and very religious"—and went on from there. I wasn't listening. I was watching the pictures from the Crabber planet.

They didn't get better. For one moment, in one brief scene, I saw something that touched me. It was an archipelago in the Crabber planet's tropical zone. One bit looked a little like my island, reef and lagoon and sprawling vegetation over everything. Aboriginal Crabbers were there, too. But they weren't alone. There was also a company of the ones in uniform, herding the locals into a village square, for what purpose I could not guess—to draft them? to shoot them dead?—but certainly not a good one. And, when I looked more closely, I saw all the plants were dying. More bioweapons, this time directed at crops? Defoliants? I didn't know, but it looked as though someone had done something to that vegetation.

I had had enough. Without intending it, I came to a decision.

I interrupted my shipmind in the middle of her telling me about America's old Camp Detrick. "Hypatia? How much spare capacity do you have?"

It didn't faze her. She abandoned the history of human plague-spreading and responded promptly. "Quite a lot, Klara."

"Enough to store all the data from the installation? And maybe take Hans aboard, too?"

She looked surprised. I think she actually was. "That's a lot of data, Klara, but, yes, I can handle it. If necessary. What've you got in mind?"

"Oh," I said, "I was just thinking. Let me see those refugees again."

CHAPTER X

I kept one eye on the time, but I had plenty for what I wanted to do. I even gave myself a little diversion first. I went to my island.

I don't mean in person, of course. I simply checked out everything on Raiwea through my monitors and listened to the reports from the department heads. That was almost as satisfying. Just looking at the kids, growing up healthy and happy and free the way they are—it always makes me feel good. Or, in this case, at least a little better.

Then I left my remote-accessed Raiwea and went into the reality of the Phoenix ship.

Hans was busily shifting focus every time a few new frames came in, so now the pictures were coming in faster than anybody could take them in. That couldn't be helped. There was a whole world to look at, and anyway it didn't matter if we saw it all in real time. All the data were being stored for later analysis and interpretation—by somebody else, though. Not by me. I had seen all I wanted.

So, evidently, had most of the Phoenix crew. Starminder and Julia Ibarruru were in the eating chamber, but they were talking to each other about the Core and paying no attention to the confusing images pouring in. Bill Tartch had his cameras turned on the display, but he was watching the pictures only with sulky half-attention, while Denys hung, sound asleep, beside him. "What's the use of this, Klara?" he demanded as soon as he saw me. "I can't get any decent footage from this crap, and most of the crew's gone off to sleep."

I was looking at Denys. The little tart even snored prettily. "They needed it," I told him. "How about Terple?"

He shrugged. "Kekuskian was here a minute ago, looking for her. I don't know whether he found her or not. Listen, how about a little more of your interview, so I won't be wasting my time entirely?"

"Maybe later," I said, not meaning it, and went in pursuit of June Terple.

I heard her voice raised in anger long before I saw her. Kekuskian had found her, all right, and the two of them were having a real cat-and-dog fight. She was yelling at him. "I don't give a snake's fart what you think you have to have, Oleg! We're going! We have to get the whole installation the hell out of here while we're still in one piece."

"You can't do that!" he screeched back at her. "What's the point of my coming out here at all if I can't observe the supernova?"

"The point," she said fiercely, "is to stay alive, and that's what we're going to do. I'm in charge here, Kekuskian! I give the orders, and I'm giving them now. Hans! Lay in a course for the neutron star!"

That's when I got into the spat. "Cancel that, Hans," I ordered. "From here on in, you'll be taking your orders from me. Is that understood?"

"It is understood, Ms. Moynlin," his voice said, as calm and unsurprised as ever. Terple wasn't calm at all. I made allowances for the woman; she hadn't had much sleep, and she was under a lot of strain. But for a minute there I thought she was going to hit me.

"Now what the hell do you think you're doing, Moynlin?" she demanded dangerously.

"I'm taking command," I explained. "We're going to stay for a while. I want to see that star blow up, too."

"Yes!" Kekuskian shouted.

Terple didn't even look at him. She was giving her whole attention to me, and she wasn't in a friendly mood. "Are you crazy? Do you want to get killed?"

It crossed my mind to wonder if that would be so bad, but what I said, quite reasonably, was, "I don't mean we have to stay right here and let the star fry us. Not the people, anyway. We'll evacuate the crew and watch the blowup on the remote. There's plenty of room for everybody in the two ships. I can take three or four with me, and Bill can take the others in his rental."

She was outraged and incredulous. "Klara! The radiation will be *enormous*! It could destroy the whole installation!"

"Fine," I said. "I understand that. So I'll buy you a new one."

She stared at me in shock. "Buy a new one! Klara, do you have any idea of what it would cost—"

Then she stopped herself short and gave me a long look. "Well," she said, not a bit mollified, but more or less resigned to accepting the facts of life, "I guess you do know, at that. If that's what you want to do, well, you're the boss."

And, as usual, I was.

So when I gave orders, no one objected. I got everybody back in the dining chamber and explained that we were abandoning ship. I told Terple she could come on my ship, along with Starminder and Ibarruru. "It's only a few days to Earth; the three of you can all fit in my guest bedroom. Mason-Manley and

Kekuskian can go with Bill and Denys. It'll be a little crowded in his rental, but they'll manage."

"What about Hans and me?" Rohrbeck asked, sounding puzzled.

I said offhandedly, "Oh, you can come with me. We'll find a place for you."

He didn't look as thrilled as he might have at the idea of sailing off through space with a beautiful, unattached woman, such as me. He didn't even look interested. "I don't just mean me *personally*, Klara," he said testily. "I mean me and my shipmind. I put a lot of work into designing Hans! I don't want him ruined!"

I wasn't thrilled by his reaction, either, but I do like a man who likes his work. "Don't worry," I assured him. "I asked Hypatia about that. She says she has plenty of extra capacity. We'll just copy him and take him along."

CHAPTER XI

I had never seen a supernova in real time before—well, how many people have?— but that, at least, was not a disappointment. The show was everything it promised to be. We were hovering in our two ships, a few million kilometers off the prime focus. Hans was taking his orders from Kekuskian now, and he had ditched the Crabber planet for good to concentrate on the star.

Hypatia whispered in my ear that, on his rental, Bill Tartch was pissing and moaning about the decision. He had wanted to catch every horrible, tragic bit, if possible right down to the expressions on the faces of the Crabbers when they saw their sun go all woogly right over their heads. I didn't. I had seen enough of the Crabbers to last me.

In my main room we had a double display. Hypatia had rigged my ship's external optics so we could see the great mirror and the tiny Phoenix ship, together like toys in one corner of the room, but the big thing was the Crabber star itself as seen from the PhoenixCorp ship. It wasn't dangerous—Hypatia said. Hans had dimmed it down, and anyway we were seeing only visible light, none of the wide-spectrum stuff that would be pouring out of it in a minute. Even so, it was huge, two meters across and so bright we had to squint to watch it.

I don't know much about stellar surfaces, but this particular star looked sick to me. Prominences stuck out all over its perimeter, and ugly sunspots spotted its face. And then, abruptly, it began to happen. The star seemed to shrink, as though Hans had zoomed back away from it. But that wasn't what was going on. The star really was collapsing on itself, and it was doing it fast. "That's the implosion," Hypatia whispered to me. While we watched, it went from two meters to a meter and a half, to a meter, to smaller still—

And then it began to expand again, almost as fast as it had shrunk, and became far more bright. Hypatia whispered, "And that's the rebound. I've told Hans to cut back on the intensity. It's going to get worse."

It did.

It blossomed bigger and brighter—and angrier—until it filled the room and, just as I was feeling as though I were being swallowed up by that stellar hell, the picture began to break up. I heard Terple moan, "Look at the mirror!" And then

I understood what was happening to our image. The little toy PhoenixCorp ship and mirror were being hammered by the outpouring of raw radiation from the supernova. No filters. No cutouts. The PhoenixCorp vessels were blazing bright themselves, reflecting the flood of blinding light that was pouring on them from the gravitational lensing. As I watched, the mirror began to warp. The flimsy sheets of mirror metal peeled off, exploding into bright plumes of plasma, like blossoming fireworks on the Fourth of July. For a moment we saw the wire mesh underneath the optical plates. Then it was gone, too, and all that was left was the skeleton of reinforcing struts, hot and glowing.

I thought we'd seen everything we were going to see of the star. I was wrong. A moment later the image of the supernova reappeared before us. It wasn't anywhere near as colossally huge or frighteningly bright as it had been before, but it was still something scary to look at. "What—?" I began to ask, but Hypatia had anticipated me.

"We're looking at the star from the little camera in the center of the dish now, Klara," she explained. "We're not getting shipside magnification from the mirror anymore. That's gone. I'm a little worried about the camera, too. The gravitational lensing alone is pretty powerful, and the camera might not last much"—she paused as the image disappeared for good, simply winked out and was gone—"longer," she finished, and, of course, it hadn't.

I took a deep breath and looked around my sitting room. Terple had tears in her eyes. Ibarruru and Starminder sat together, silent and stunned, and Mark Rohrbeck was whispering to his shipmind. "That's it," I said briskly. "The show's over."

Rohrbeck spoke up first, sounding almost cheerful. "Hans has all the data," he reported. "He's all right."

Terple had her hand up. "Klara? About the ship? It took a lot of heat, but the dish burned pretty fast and the hull's probably intact, so if we can get a repair crew out there—"

"Right away," I promised. "Well, almost right away. First we go home."

I was looking at Rohrbeck. He had looked almost cheerful for a moment, but the cheer was rapidly fading. When he saw my eyes on him, he gave me a little shrug. "Where's that?" he asked glumly.

I wanted to pat his shoulder, but it was a little early for that. I just said sympathetically, "You're missing your kids, aren't you? Well, I've got a place with plenty of them. And, as the only grown-up male on my island, you'll be the only dad they've got."

CHAPTER XII

That blast from the supernova didn't destroy the PhoenixCorp ship after all. The mirror was a total write-off, of course, but the ship itself was only cooked a little. June Terple stooged around for a bit while it cooled down, then went back with what was left of her crew. Which wasn't much.

Mason-Manley talked his way back into her good graces once Denys wasn't around anymore; Kekuskian promised to come out for the actual blowup, eighty years from now, provided he was still alive; and, of course, she still had the indestructible Hans, now back in his own custom-designed datastore. The rest of her people were replacements. Starminder went back to her family in the Core, and I paid Ibarruru's fare to go along with her as a kind of honorary citizen ambassador.

Naturally, Terple invited me to join them for their stint at the neutron star— couldn't really avoid it, since the new money was coming from the same place as the old, namely mostly me. I said maybe, to be polite, but I really meant no. One look at the death of a world was enough for me. Bill Tartch's special show on the Crabbers went on the net within days. He had great success with it, easily great enough so that he didn't really mind the fact that he no longer had me.

Hypatia kept copies of all the files for me, and those last little bits of data stayed with me on my island for a long time. I played pieces of them now and then, for any of the kids that showed an interest, and for their moms, too, when they did. But mostly I played them for me.

Mark Rohrbeck stayed with me on Raiwea for a while, too, though not too long. That's the way my island works. When my kids are ready for the world outside, I let them go. It was the same with Rohrbeck. For him it took just a little over three months. Then he was ready, and he kissed me good-bye, and I let him go.

suicide coast

M. John Harrison

M. John Harrison is not a prolific writer, and, in America, at least, is still little known to the SF readership at large. In Britain, however, he has been an influential figure behind the scenes since the days of Michael Moorcock's New Worlds in the late '60s, and has had a disproportionate effect with a relatively small body of work; in fact, recently he was given the Richard Evans Memorial Award, a new award designed to honor just that sort of career and reputation. Harrison made his first sale to New Worlds in 1968, and by 1975 had sold two science fiction novels, The Committed Men and The Centauri Device, and published a collection of his early short work, The Machine in Shaft Ten and Other Stories. It was the stories and novels he produced during the '70s and early '80s, though, on the shifting and amorphous borderland of science fiction and fantasy, that would prove to be his most influential genre-related work. In The Pastel City, A Storm of Wings, In Viriconium, and in the stories that would go into the collection Viriconium Nights, he produced a sort of bizarre, heightened, intellectual, stylishly perverse sword & sorcery, kin to the mannered, elegant, fin de siècle science fantasy of Wolfe's The Book of the New Sun, Aldiss's The Malacia Tapestry, and Vance's The Dying Earth, creating a mood of autumnal sadness and of the evocative strangeness and dislocation of a world seen through the lens of millennia of elapsed time that is similar to the emotional tone and color of those books, and sustains it with comparable skill.

In recent years, he has turned away from genre work to produce some of the best books of his career in a sequence of ostensibly "mainstream" novels (although, ironically, most of them contain subtle fantastic elements) such as Climbers, The Course of the Heart, and, most recently, the critically acclaimed Signs of Life. In the intense and lapidarian story that follows, a rare foray into core science fiction, he takes us to a gray, rain-swept, rather dispirited future London, for a sharp lesson in the difference that Passion makes in all our lives, no matter where we choose to invest it.

F our-thirty in the afternoon in a converted warehouse near Mile End under-ground station. Heavy, persistent summer rain was falling on the roof. Inside, the air was still and humid, dark despite the fluorescent lights. It smelled of sweat, dust, gymnasts' chalk. Twenty-five feet above the thick blue crash-mats, a boy with dreadlocks and baggy knee-length shorts was supporting his entire weight on two fingers of his right hand. The muscles of his upper back, black and shiny with sweat, fanned out exotically with the effort, like the hood of a cobra or the shell of a crab. One leg trailed behind him for balance. He had raised the other so that the knee was almost touching his chin. For two or three minutes he had been trying to get the ball of his foot in the same place as his fingers. Each time he moved, his center of gravity shifted and he had to go back to a resting position. Eventually he said quietly:

"I'm coming off."

We all looked up. It was a slow afternoon in Mile End. Nobody bothers much with training in the middle of summer. Some teenagers were in from the local schools and colleges. A couple of men in their late thirties had sneaked out of a civil engineering contract near Cannon Street. Everyone was tired. Humidity had made the handholds slippery. Despite that, a serious atmosphere prevailed.

"Go on," we encouraged him. "You can do it."

We didn't know him, or one another, from Adam.

"Go on!"

The boy on the wall laughed. He was good but not that good. He didn't want to fall off in front of everyone. An intention tremor moved through his bent leg. Losing patience with himself, he scraped at the foothold with the toe of his boot. He lunged upward. His body pivoted away from the wall and dropped onto the mats, which, absorbing the energy of the fall, made a sound like a badly winded heavyweight boxer. Chalk and dust billowed up. He got to his feet, laughing and shaking his dreadlocks.

"I can never do that."

"You'll get it in the end," I told him. "Me, I'm going to fall off this roof once more then fuck off home. It's too hot in here."

"See you, man."

I had spent most of that winter in London, assembling copy for MAX, a Web site that fronted the adventure sports software industry. They were always interested in stuff about cave diving, BASE jumping, snowboarding, hang-gliding, ATB and so on: but they didn't want to know about rock climbing.

"Not enough to buy," my editor said succinctly. "And too obviously skill-based." He leafed through my samples. "The punter needs equipment to invest in. It strengthens his self-image. With the machine parked in his hall, he believes he could disconnect from the software and still do the sport." He tapped a shot of Isobelle Patissier seven hundred feet up some knife-edge arete in Colorado. "Where's the hardware? These are just bodies."

"The boots are pretty high tech."

"Yeah? And how much a pair? Fifty, a hundred and fifty? Mick, we can get them to lay out three grand for the *frame* of an ATB."

He thought for a moment. Then he said: "We might do something with the women."

"The good ones are French."

"Even better."

I gathered the stuff together and put it away.

"I'm off then," I said.

"You still got the 190?"

I nodded.

"Take care in that thing," he said.

"I will."

"Focke Wolf 190," he said. "Hey."

"It's a Mercedes," I said.

He laughed. He shook his head.

"Focke Wolf, Mercedes, no one drives themselves anymore," he said. "You mad fucker."

He looked round his office—a dusty metal desk, a couple of posters with the MAX logo, a couple of PCs. He said: "No one comes in here in person anymore. You ever hear of the modem?"

"Once or twice," I said.

"Well they've invented it now."

I looked around too.

"One day," I said, "the poor wankers are going to want back what you stole from them."

"Come on. They pissed it all away long before we arrived."

As I left the office he advised:

"Keep walking the walk, Mick."

I looked at my watch. It was late and the MAX premises were in EC1. But I thought that if I got a move on and cut up through Tottenham, I could go and see a friend of mine. His name was Ed and I had known him since the 1980s.

Back then, I was trying to write a book about people like him. Ed Johnson sounded interesting. He had done everything from roped-access engineering in Telford to harvesting birds' nests for soup in Southeast Asia. But he was hard to pin down. If I was in Birmingham, he was in Exeter. If we were both in London, he had something else to do. In the end it was Moscow Davis who made the introduction.

Moscow was a short, hard, cheerful girl with big feet and bedraggled hair. She was barely out of her teens. She had come from Oldham, I think, originally, and she had an indescribable snuffling accent. She and Ed had worked as steeplejacks together before they both moved down from the north in search of work. They had once been around a lot together. She thought Johnson would enjoy talking to me if I was still interested. I was. The arrangement we made was to be on the lookout for him in one of the Suicide Coast pubs, the Harbour Lights, that Sunday afternoon.

"Sunday afternoons are quiet, so we can have a chat," said Moscow. "Everyone's eating their dinner then."

We had been in the pub for half an hour when Johnson arrived, wearing patched 501s and a dirty T-shirt with a picture of a mole on the front of it. He came over to our table and began kicking morosely at the legs of Moscow's chair. The little finger of his left hand was splinted and wrapped in a wad of bandage.

"This is Ed," Moscow told me, not looking at him.

"Fuck off, Moscow," Ed told her, not looking at me. He scratched his armpit and stared vaguely into the air above Moscow's head. "I want my money back," he said. Neither of them could think of anything to add to this, and after a pause he wandered off.

"He's always like that," Moscow said. "You don't want to pay any attention." Later in the afternoon she said: "You'll get on well with Ed, though. You'll like him. He's a mad bastard."

"You say that about all the boys," I said.

In this case Moscow was right, because I had heard it not just from her, and later I would get proof of it anyway — if you can ever get proof of anything. Everyone said that Ed should be in a straightjacket. In the end, nothing could be arranged. Johnson was in a bad mood, and Moscow had to be up the Coast that week, on Canvey Island, to do some work on one of the cracking-plants there. There was always a lot of that kind of work, oil work, chemical work, on Canvey Island. "I haven't time for him," Moscow explained as she got up to go. "I'll see you later, anyway," she promised.

As soon as she was gone, Ed Johnson came back and sat down in front of me. He grinned. "Ever done anything worth doing in your whole life?" he asked me. "Anything real?"

The MAX editor was right: since coring got popular, the roads had been deserted. I left EC1 and whacked the 190 up through Hackney until I got the Lea Valley reservoirs on my right like a splatter of moonlit verglas. On empty roads the only mistakes that need concern you are your own; every bend becomes a dreamy interrogation of your own technique. Life should be more like that. I made good time. Ed lived just back from Montagu Road, in a quiet street behind the Jewish Cemetery. He shared his flat with a woman in her early thirties whose name was Caitlin. Caitlin had black hair and soft, honest brown eyes. She and I were old friends. We hugged briefly on the doorstep. She looked up and down the street and shivered.

"Come in," she said. "It's cold."

"You should wear a jumper."

"I'll tell him you're here," she said. "Do you want some coffee?"

Caitlin had softened the edges of Ed's life, but less perhaps than either of them had hoped. His taste was still very minimal — white paint, ash floors, one or two items of furniture from Heals. And there was still a competition Klein mounted on the living room wall, its polished aerospace alloys glittering in the halogen lights.

"Espresso," I said.

"I'm not giving you espresso at this time of night. You'll explode."

"It was worth a try."

"Ed!" she called. "Ed! Mick's here!"

He didn't answer.

She shrugged at me, as if to say, "What can I do?" and went into the back room. I heard their voices but not what they were saying. After that she went upstairs. "Go in and see him," she suggested when she came down again three or four minutes later. "I told him you were here." She had pulled a Jigsaw sweater on over her Racing Green shirt and Levi's; and fastened her hair back hastily with a dark brown velvet scrunchy.

"That looks nice," I said. "Do you want me to fetch him out?"

"I doubt he'll come."

The back room was down a narrow corridor. Ed had turned it into a bleak combination of office and storage. The walls were done with one coat of what builders call "obliterating emulsion" and covered with metal shelves. Chipped diving tanks hollow with the ghosts of exotic gases were stacked by the filing cabinet. His BASE chute spilled half out of its pack, yards of cold nylon a vile but exciting rose color — a color which made you want to be hurtling downward face-first screaming with fear until you heard the canopy bang out behind you and you knew you weren't going to die that day (although you might still break both legs). The cheap beige carpet was strewn with high-access mess — hanks of graying static rope; a yellow bucket stuffed with tools; Ed's Petzl stop, harness and knocked-about CPTs. Everything was layered with dust. The radiators were turned off. There was a bed made up in one corner. Deep in the clutter on the cheap white desk stood a 5-gig Mac with a screen to design industry specs. It was spraying Ed's face with icy blue light.

"Hi Ed."

"Hi Mick.".

There was a long silence after that. Ed stared at the screen. I stared at his back. Just when I thought he had forgotten I was there, he said:

"Fuck off and talk to Caitlin a moment."

"I brought us some beer."

"That's great."

"What are you running here?"

"It's a game. I'm running a game, Mick."

Ed had lost weight since I last saw him. Though they retained their distinctive cabled structure, his forearms were a lot thinner. Without releasing him from anything it represented, the yoke of muscle had lifted from his shoulders. I had expected that. But I was surprised by how much flesh had melted off his face, leaving long vertical lines of sinew, fins of bone above the cheeks and at the corners of the jaw. His eyes were a long way back in his head. In a way it suited him. He would have seemed okay—a little tired perhaps; a little burned down, like someone who was working too hard—if it hadn't been for the light from the display. Hunched in his chair with that splashing off him, he looked like a vampire. He looked like a junkie.

I peered over his shoulder.

"You were never into this shit," I said.

He grinned.

"Everyone's into it now. Why not me? Wanking away and pretending it's sex."

"Oh, come on."

He looked down at himself.

"It's better than living," he said.

There was no answer to that.

I went and asked Caitlin, "Has he been doing this long?"

"Not long," she said. "Have some coffee."

We sat in the L-shaped living area drinking decaffeinated Java. The sofa was big enough for Caitlin to curl up in a corner of it like a cat. She had turned the overhead lights off, tucked her bare feet up under her. She was smoking a cigarette. "It's been a bloody awful day," she warned me. "So don't say a word." She grinned wryly, then we both looked up at the Klein for a minute or two. Some kind of ambient music was issuing faintly from the stereo speakers, full of South American bird calls and bouts of muted drumming. "Is he winning?" she asked.

"He didn't tell me."

"You're lucky. It's all he ever tells me."

"Aren't you worried?" I said.

She smiled.

"He's still using a screen," she said. "He's not plugging in."

"Yet," I said.

"Yet," she agreed equably. "Want more coffee? Or will you do me a favor?"

I put my empty cup on the floor.

"Do you a favor," I said.

"Cut my hair."

I got up and went to her end of the sofa. She turned away from me so I could release her hair from the scrunchy. "Shake it," I said. She shook it. She ran her hands through it. Perfume came up; something I didn't recognize. "It doesn't need much," I said. I switched the overhead light back on and fetched a kitchen chair. "Sit here. No, right in the light. You'll have to take your jumper off."

"The good scissors are in the bathroom," she said.

Cut my hair. She had asked me that before, two or three days after she decided we should split up. I remembered the calm that came over me at the gentle, careful sound of the scissors, the way her hair felt as I lifted it away from the nape of her neck, the tenderness and fear because everything was changing around the two of us forever and somehow this quiet action signalized and blessed that. The shock of these memories made me ask:

"How are you two getting on?"

She lowered her head to help me cut. I felt her smile.

"You and Ed always liked the same kind of girls," she said.

"Yes," I said.

I finished the cut, then lightly kissed the nape of her neck. "There," I said. Beneath the perfume she smelled faintly of hypoallergenic soap and unscented deodorants. "No, Mick," she said softly. "Please." I adjusted the collar of her shirt, let her hair fall back round it. My hand was still on her shoulder. She had to turn her head at an awkward angle to look up at me. Her eyes were wide and full of pain. "Mick." I kissed her mouth and brushed the side of her face with my fingertips. Her arms went round my neck, I felt her settle in the chair. I touched her breasts. They were warm, the cotton shirt was clean and cool. She made a small noise and pulled me closer. Just then, in the back room among the dusty air tanks and disused parachutes, Ed Johnson fell out of his chair and began to thrash about, the back of his head thudding rhythmically on the floor.

Caitlin pushed me away.

"Ed?" she called, from the passage door.

"Help!" cried Ed.

"I'll go," I said.

Caitlin put her arm across the doorway and stared up at me calmly.

"No," she said.

"How can you lift him on your own?"

"This is me and Ed," she said.

"For God's sake!"

"It's late, Mick. I'll let you out, then I'll go and help him."

At the front door I said:

"I think you're mad. Is this happening a lot? You're a fool to let him do this."

"It's his life."

I looked at her. She shrugged.

"Will you be all right?" I said.

When I offered to kiss her goodbye, she turned her face away.

"Fuck off then, both of you," I said.

I knew which game Ed was playing, because I had seen the software wrapper discarded on the desk near his Mac. Its visuals were cheap and schematic, its values self-consciously retro. It was nothing like the stuff we sold off the MAX site, which was quite literally the experience itself, stripped of its consequences. You had to plug in for that: you had to be cored. This was just a game; less a game, even, than a trip. You flew a silvery V-shaped graphic down an endless V-shaped corridor, a notional perspective sometimes bounded by lines of objects, sometimes just by lines, sometimes bounded only by your memory of boundaries. Sometimes the graphic floated and mushed like a moth. Sometimes it traveled in flat vicious arcs at an apparent Mach 5. There were no guns, no opponent. There was no competition. You flew. Sometimes the horizon tilted one way, sometimes the other. You could choose your own music. It was a bleakly minimal experience. But after a minute or two, five at the most, you felt as if you could fly your icon down the perspective forever, to the soundtrack of your own life.

It was quite popular.

It was called *Out There*.

"Rock climbing is theater," I once wrote.

It had all the qualities of theater, I went on, but a theater-in-reverse:

"In obedience to some devious vanished script, the actors abandon the stage and begin to scale the seating arrangements, the balconies and hanging boxes now occupied only by cleaning women."

"Oh, very deep," said Ed Johnson when he read this. "Shall I tell you what's wrong here? Eh? Shall I tell you?"

"Piss off, Ed."

"If you fall on your face from a hundred feet up, it comes off the front of your head *and you don't get a second go.* Next to that, theater is wank. Theater is flat. Theater is *Suicide Coast.*"

Ed hated anywhere flat. "Welcome to the Suicide Coast," he used to say when I first knew him. To start with, that had been because he lived in Canterbury. But it had quickly become his way of describing most places, most experiences. You didn't actually have to be near the sea. Suicide Coast syndrome had caused Ed to do some stupid things in his time. One day, when he and Moscow still worked in roped-access engineering together, they were going up in the lift to the top of some shitty council high rise in Birmingham or Bristol, when suddenly Ed said:

"Do you bet me I can keep the doors open with my head?"

"What?"

"Next floor! When the doors start to close, do you bet me I can stop them with my head?"

It was Monday morning. The lift smelled of piss. They had been hand-ripping mastic out of expansion joints for two weeks, using Stanley knives. Moscow was tired, hung over, weighed down by a collection of CPTs, mastic guns and hundred-foot coils of rope. Her right arm was numb from repeating the same action hour after hour, day after day.

"Fuck off, Ed," she said.

But she knew Ed would do it whether she took the bet or not.

Two or three days after she first introduced me to Ed, Moscow telephoned me. She had got herself a couple of weeks cutting out on Thamesmead Estate. "They don't half work hard, these fuckers," she said. We talked about that for a minute or two then she asked:

"Well?"

"Well what, Moscow?"

"Ed. Was he what you were looking for, then? Or what?"

I said that though I was impressed I didn't think I would be able to write anything about Ed.

"He's a mad fucker, though, isn't he?"

"Oh he is," I said. "He certainly is."

The way Moscow said "isn't he" made it sound like "innie."

Another thing I once wrote:

"Climbing takes place in a special kind of space, the rules of which are simple. You must be able to see immediately what you have to lose; and you must choose the risk you take."

What do I know?

I know that a life without consequences isn't a life at all. Also, if you want to do something difficult, something real, you can't shirk the pain. What I learned in the old days, from Ed and Moscow, from Gabe King, Justine Townsend and all the others who taught me to climb rock or jump off buildings or stay the right way up in a tube of pitch-dark water two degrees off freezing and two hundred feet under the ground, was that you can't just plug in and be a star: you have to practice. You have to keep loading your fingers until the tendons swell.

So it's back to the Mile End wall, with its few thousand square feet of board and bolt-on holds, its few thousand cubic meters of emphysemic air through which one very bright ray of sun sometimes falls in the middle of the afternoon, illuminating nothing much at all. Back to the sound of the fan heater, the dust-filled Akai radio playing some mournful aggressive thing, and every so often a boy's voice saying softly, "Oh shit," as some sequence or other fails to work out. You go back there, and if you have to fall off the same ceiling move thirty times in an afternoon, that's what you do. The mats give their gusty wheeze, chalk dust flies up, the fan heater above the Monkey House door rattles and chokes and flatlines briefly before puttering on.

"Jesus Christ. I don't know why I do this."

Caitlin telephoned me.

"Come to supper," she said.

"No," I said.

"Mick, why?"

"Because I'm sick of it."

"Sick of what?"

"You. Me. Him. Everything."

"Look," she said, "he's sorry about what happened last time."

"Oh, *he's* sorry."

"We're both sorry, Mick."

"All right, then: I'm sorry, too."

There was a gentle laugh at the other end.

"So you should be."

I went along all the deserted roads and got there at about eight, to find a brand-new motorcycle parked on the pavement outside the house. It was a Kawasaki *Ninja*. Its fairing had been removed, to give it the look of a '60s café racer, but no one was fooled. Even at a glance it appeared too hunched, too short-coupled: too knowing. The remaining plastics shone with their own harsh inner light.

Caitlin met me on the doorstep. She put her hands on my shoulders and kissed me. "Mm," she said. She was wearing white tennis shorts and a soft dark blue sweatshirt.

"We've got to stop meeting like this," I said.

She smiled and pushed me away.

"My hands smell of garlic," she said.

Just as we were going inside, she turned back and nodded at the Kawa.

"That thing," she said.

"It's a motorcycle, Caitlin."

"It's his."

I stared at her.

"Be enthusiastic," she said. "Please."

"But—"

"Please?"

The main course was penne with mushrooms in an olive and tomato sauce. Ed had cooked it, Caitlin said, but she served. Ed pushed his chair over to the table and rubbed his hands. He picked his plate up and passed it under his nose. "Wow!" he said. As we ate, we talked about this and that. The Kawa was behind everything we said, but Ed wouldn't mention it until I did. Caitlin smiled at us both. She shook her head as if to say: "Children! You children!" It was like Christmas, and she was the parent. The three of us could feel Ed's excitement and impatience. He grinned secretively. He glanced up from his food at one or both of us; quickly back down again. Finally, he couldn't hold back any longer.

"What do you think, then?" he said. "What do you think, Mick?"

"I think this is good pasta," I said. "For a cripple."

He grinned and wiped his mouth.

"It's not bad," he said, "is it?"

"I think what I like best is the way you've let the mushrooms take up a touch of sesame oil."

"Have some more. There's plenty."

"That's new to me in Italian food," I said. "Sesame oil."

Ed drank some more beer.

"It was just an idea," he said.

"You children," said Caitlin. She shook her head. She got up and took the plates away. "There's ice cream for pudding," she said over her shoulder just before she disappeared. When I was sure she was occupied in the kitchen I said:

"Nice idea, Ed: a motorcycle. What are you going to do with it? Hang it on the wall with the Klein?"

He drank the rest of his beer, opened a new one and poured it thoughtfully into his glass. He watched the bubbles rising through it, then grinned at me as if he had made a decision. He had. In that moment I saw that he was lost, but not what I could do about it.

"Isn't it brilliant? Isn't it just a *fucker*, that bike? I haven't had a bike since I was seventeen. There's a story attached to that."

"Ed—"

"Do you want to hear it or not?"

Caitlin came back in with the ice cream and served it out to us and sat down. "Tell us, Ed," she said tiredly. "Tell us the story about that."

Ed held on to his glass hard with both hands and stared into it for a long time as if he was trying to see the past there. "I had some ace times on bikes when I was a kid," he said finally: "but they were always someone else's. My old dear— She really hated bikes, my old dear. You know: they were dirty, they were dangerous, she wasn't going to have one in the house. Did that stop me? It did not. I bought one of the first good Ducatti 125s in Britain, but I had to keep it in a coal cellar down the road."

"That's really funny, Ed."

"Fuck off, Mick. I'm seventeen, I'm still at school, and I've got this fucking *projectile* stashed in someone's coal cellar. The whole time I had it, the old dear never knew. I'm walking three miles in the piss-wet rain every night, dressed to go to the library, then unlocking this thing and *stuffing* it round the back lanes with my best white shortie raincoat ballooning up like a fucking tent."

He looked puzzledly down at his plate.

"What's this? Oh. Ice cream. Ever ridden a bike in a raincoat?" he asked Caitlin.

Caitlin shook her head. She was staring at him with a hypnotized expression; she was breaking wafers into her ice cream.

"Well they were all the rage then," he said.

He added: "The drag's enormous."

"Eat your pudding, Ed," I said. "And stop boasting. How fast would a 125 go in those days? Eighty miles an hour? Eighty-five?"

"They went faster if you ground your teeth, Mick," Ed said. "Do you want to hear the rest?"

"Of course I want to hear it, Ed."

"Walk three miles in the piss-wet rain," said Ed, "to go for a ride on a motorbike, what a joke. But the real joke is this: the fucker had an alloy crankcase. That was a big deal in those days, an alloy crankcase. The first time I dropped it on a bend, it cracked. Oil everywhere. I pushed it back to the coal-house and left it there. You couldn't weld an alloy crankcase worth shit in those days. I had three years' payments left to make on a bunch of scrap."

He grinned at us triumphantly.

"Ask me how long I'd had it," he ordered.

"How long, Mick?"

"Three weeks. I'd had the fucker three weeks."

He began to laugh. Suddenly, his face went so white it looked green. He looked rapidly from side to side, like someone who can't understand where he is. At the same time, he pushed himself up out of the wheelchair until his arms wouldn't straighten any further and he was almost standing up. He tilted his head back until the tendons in his neck stood out. He shouted, "I want to get out of here! Caitlin, I want to get out!" Then his arms buckled and he let his weight go onto his feet and his legs folded up like putty and he fell forward with a gasp, his face in the ice cream and his hands smashing and clutching and scraping at anything they touched on the dinner table until he had bunched the cloth up under him and everything was a sodden mess of food and broken dishes, and he had slipped out of the chair and onto the floor. Then he let himself slump and go quite still.

"Help me," said Caitlin.

We couldn't get him back into the chair. As we tried, his head flopped forward, and I could see quite clearly the bruises and deep, half-healed scabs at the base of his skull, where they had cored his cervical spine for the computer connection. When he initialized *Out There* now the graphics came up live in his head. No more screen. Only the endless V of the perspective. The endless, effortless dip-and-bank of the viewpoint. What did he see out there? Did he see himself, hunched up on the Kawasaki *Ninja*? Did he see highways, bridges, tunnels, weird motorcycle flights through endless space?

Halfway along the passage, he woke up.

"Caitlin!" he shouted.

"I'm here."

"Caitlin!"

"I'm here, Ed."

"Caitlin, I never did any of that."

"Hush, Ed. Let's get you to bed."

"Listen!" he shouted. *"Listen."*

He started to thrash about and we had to lay him down where he was. The passage was so narrow his head hit one wall, then the other, with a solid noise. He stared desperately at Caitlin, his face smeared with Ben & Jerry's. "I never could ride a bike," he admitted. "I made all that up."

She bent down and put her arms round his neck.

"I know," she said.

"I made all that up!" he shouted.

"It's all right. It's all right."

We got him into bed in the back room. She wiped the ice cream off his face with a Kleenex. He stared over her shoulder at the wall, rigid with fear and self-loathing. "Hush," she said. "You're all right." That made him cry; him crying made her cry. I didn't know whether to cry or laugh. I sat down and watched them for a moment, then got to my feet. I felt tired.

"It's late," I said. "I think I'll go."

Caitlin followed me out onto the doorstep. It was another cold night. Condensation had beaded on the fuel tank of the Kawasaki, so that it looked like some sort of frosted confection in the streetlight.

"Look," she said, "can you do anything with that?"

I shrugged.

"It's still brand new," I said. I drew a line in the condensation, along the curve of the tank, then another, at an angle to it.

"I could see if the dealer would take it back."

"Thanks."

I laughed.

"Go in now," I advised her. "It's cold."

"Thanks, Mick. Really."

"That's what you always say."

The way Ed got his paraplegia was this. It was a miserable January about four months after Caitlin left me to go and live with him. He was working over in mid-Wales with Moscow Davis. They had landed the inspection contract for three point-blocks owned by the local council; penalty clauses meant they had to complete that month. They lived in a bed-and-breakfast place a mile from the job, coming back so tired in the evening that they just about had time to eat fish and chips and watch *Coronation Street* before they fell asleep with their mouths open. "We were too fucked even to take drugs," Ed admitted afterward, in a kind of wonder. "Can you imagine that?" Their hands were bashed and bleeding from hitting themselves with sample hammers in the freezing rain. At the end of every afternoon the sunset light caught a thin, delicate layer of water-ice that had welded Moscow's hair to her cheek. Ed wasn't just tired, he was missing Caitlin. One Friday he said, "I'm fucked off with this, let's have a weekend at home."

"We agreed we'd have to work weekends," Moscow reminded him. She watched a long string of snot leave her nose, stretch out like spider-silk, then snap and vanish on the wind. "To finish in time," she said.

"Come on, you wanker," Ed said. "Do something real in your life."

"I never wank," said Moscow. "I can't fancy myself."

They got in her 1984 320i with the M-Technic pack, Garrett turbo and extra-wide wheels, and while the light died out of a bad afternoon she pushed it eastward through the Cambrians, letting the rear end hang out on corners. She had Lou Reed *Retro* on the CD and her plan was to draw a line straight across the map and connect with the M4 at the Severn Bridge. It was ghostly and fog all the way out of Wales that night, lost sheep coming at you from groups of wet trees and folds in the hills. "Tregaron to Abergwesyn. One of the great back roads!" Moscow shouted over the music, as they passed a single lonely house in the rain, miles away from anywhere, facing south into the rolling moors of mid-Wales.

Ed shouted back: "They can go faster than this, these 320s." So on the next bend she let the rear end hang out an inch too far and they surfed five hundred feet into a ravine below Cefn Coch, with the BMW crumpled up round them like a chocolate wrapper. Just before they went over, the tape had got to "Sweet Jane"—the live version with the applause welling up across the opening chords as if God himself was stepping out on stage. In the bottom of the ravine a shallow stream ran through pressure-metamorphosed Ordovician shale. Ed sat until daylight the next morning, conscious but unable to move, watching the water hurry toward him and listening to Moscow die of a punctured lung in the heavy smell of fuel. It was a long wait. Once or twice she regained consciousness and said: "I'm sorry, Ed."

Once or twice he heard himself reassure her, "No, it was my fault."

At Southwestern Orthopaedic a consultant told him that key motor nerves had been ripped out of his spine.

"Stuff the fuckers back in again then!" he said, in an attempt to impress her.

She smiled.

"That's exactly what we're going to try," she replied. "We'll do a tuck-and-glue and encourage the spinal cord to send new filaments into the old cable channel."

She thought for a moment.

"We'll be working very close to the cord itself," she warned him.

Ed stared at her.

"It was a joke," he said.

For a while it seemed to work. Two months later he could flex the muscles in his upper legs. But nothing more happened; and, worried that a second try would only make the damage worse, they had to leave it.

Mile End Monkey House. Hanging upside down from a painful foot-hook, you chalk your hands meditatively, staring at the sweaty triangular mark your back left on the blue plastic cover of the mat last time you fell on it. Then, reluctantly, feeling your stomach muscles grind as they curl you upright again, you clutch the starting holds and go for the move: reach up: lock out on two fingers: let your left leg swing out to rebalance: strain upward with your right fingertips, and just as you brush the crucial hold, fall off again.

"Jesus Christ. I don't know why I come here."

You come so that next weekend you can get into a Cosworth-engined Merc 190E and drive very fast down the M4 ("No one drives themselves anymore!") to a limestone outcrop high above the Wye Valley. Let go here and you will not land on a blue safety mat in a puff of chalk dust. Instead you will plummet eighty feet straight down until you hit a small ledge, catapult out into the trees, and land a little later face-first among moss-grown boulders flecked with sunshine. Now all the practice is over. Now you are on the route. Your friends look up, shading their eyes against the white glare of the rock. They are wondering if you can make the move. So are you. The only exit from shit creek is to put two fingers of your left hand into a razor-sharp solution pocket, lean away from it to the full extent of your arm, run your feet up in front of you, and, just as you are about to fall off, lunge with your right hand for the good hold above.

At the top of the cliff grows a large yew tree. You can see it very clearly. It has a short horizontal trunk, and contorted limbs perhaps eighteen inches thick curving out over the drop as if they had just that moment stopped moving. When you reach it you will be safe. But at this stage on a climb, the top of anything is an empty hypothesis. You look up: it might as well be the other side of the Atlantic. All that air is burning away below you like a fuse. Suddenly you're moving anyway. Excitement has short-circuited the normal connections between intention and action. Where you look, you go. No effort seems to be involved. It's like falling upward. It's like that moment when you first understood how to swim, or ride a bike. Height and fear have returned you to your childhood. Just as it was then, your duty is only to yourself. Until you get safely down again, contracts, business meetings, household bills, emotional problems will mean nothing.

When you finally reach that yew tree at the top of the climb, you find it full of grown men and women wearing faded shorts and T-shirts. They are all in their forties and fifties. They have all escaped. With their bare brown arms, their hair bleached out by weeks of sunshine, they sit at every fork or junction, legs dangling in the dusty air, like child-pirates out of some storybook of the 1920s: an investment banker from Greenwich, an AIDS counselor from Bow; a designer of French Connection clothes; a publishers' editor. There is a comfortable silence broken by the odd friendly murmur as you arrive, but their eyes are inturned and they would prefer to be alone, staring dreamily out over the valley, the curve of the river, the woods which seem to stretch away to Tintern Abbey and then Wales. This is the other side of excitement, the other pleasure of height: the space without anxiety. The space without anxiety. The space without anxiety. The space without anxiety. The space without anxiety. The space without anxiety. The space without anxiety. The space with—

You are left with this familiar glitch or loop in the MAX ware. *Suicide Coast* won't play any farther. Reluctantly, you abandon Mick to his world of sad acts, his faith that reality can be relied upon to scaffold his perceptions. To run him again from the beginning would only make the frailty of that faith more obvious. So you wait until everything has gone black, unplug yourself from the machine, and walk away, unconsciously rolling your shoulders to ease the stiffness, massaging the sore place at the back of your neck. What will you do next? Everything is flat out here. No one drives themselves anymore.

Hunting Mother

SAGE WALKER

That the old must give way to the new is a truth that has been known since the dawn of the human race, but, as the evocative story that follows demonstrates, in spite of our awareness of that inevitability, it's not always an easy or a comfortable transition . . .

Sage Walker lives in Albuquerque, New Mexico. A graduate of Clarion West, she has made sales to Asimov's Science Fiction, Not of Woman Born, Event Horizon, and elsewhere. Her first novel, Whiteout, was one of the most critically acclaimed debut novels of 1996, and she is at work on several others.

Running here in the long corridors had its joys but it was better Above. On the inner surface of the spinning world Cougar could race across wide stretches of open country. Distance could tire his legs and there were obstacles to leap over or dodge around. He thought exercise and fatigue would make it easier to approach the old woman.

The lights that woke at his motion were dim, timed for evening. The animals Above would be readying themselves for night.

Cougar loved motion. In the dim corridor, the flex of his toes and the slip of the tendons in his feet were smooth and silent against chill stone. Tensions and relaxations of muscles in his calves and thighs, counterbalance offered by small ripples of the muscles in his back and shoulders, reflex arcs between neuron and neuron and muscle cell; the sensations blended and gave him joy. He delighted in the slight alarm, the constantly arrested falls, of walking.

The corridor where he walked circled the world. As he walked he was always at the center of a great curve. Before him and behind him the corridor rose until it seemed to narrow to a point and vanish. Just ahead was a lift that would take him to the Above or down, out, into the thick rind of the ship, to the cave his mother had made of her quarters.

Cougar wanted to hunt. He wanted to run, but he was a dutiful son, he told himself. The hunt would wait. He would run as a reward after he had dealt with his mother.

He stepped inside the lift and rode down.

His mother's quarters were near her labs; she lived close to her work. Cougar remembered waking in the night, small and alone. The slap of his feet had sounded so loud on the cold stone that he knew some monster would come out of the dark corridor to eat him, but he'd run to the lab anyway, run for mother. Mother, Elena, peered into the watery depths of a womb machine. Its lights made the high ledges of her cheekbones and the dark hollows of her eyes seem strange and terrible. An embryo floated dead in the translucent cylinder, the thick pancake shape of its placenta loose from the womb wall and slowly spinning in bloody fluid.

"Hey, boy. The alarms woke me so I came to find out what was happening," Elena said. She picked him up and held him close. "Did you have a bad dream?"

Cougar wasn't sure what a bad dream was, but he nodded and pushed his nose against the comforting smell of his mother's shoulder. He heard gurgles and hisses as Elena did something to the womb machine. He saw, above his mother's shoulder, frost crystals forming on the womb's glassy windows. "Something went wrong. I'll do the tests on it tomorrow," Elena said.

Beneath the frost he had seen tiny clawed fingers, wet fur swirling, the strange bald swellings of twinned labia between flexed legs. It was the first time he remembered being afraid of his mother.

Fully adult now, long past childhood terrors, Cougar pulled the scents of the lab across his nose and palate. He sensed albumin, wet down and eggshell. He wondered which chicks had hatched.

Ahead in the corridor, he saw the old, old woman. She walked toward him, slender and not stooped, still graceful although she moved with the deliberate caution of the aged. Cougar stood still and the lights around him faded.

Elena, it was Elena, stared ahead at the darkness. She looked helpless and blind.

"Cougar?" she asked. "Is that you?"

In answer, he stepped forward to wake the corridor's lights. He knew, reading the tensions of the woman's motionless body, that she thought to flee him but she had forced herself not to run.

"I was going to look for you," Elena said. "Come in."

Following her, he entered home. Her home now, and fusty as human places tended to get after so many years. These rooms had been his childhood and he hated them and loved them and had not been here for a long time.

Cougar read Elena's breath. It carried molecular traces of *chicos*, the roasted corn she had stewed and eaten not two hours ago. She shed a trace of lactate from anoxic muscles and Cougar realized that even the walk into the corridor must have tired her. Elena's skin smelled of the cave; clean cedar boughs freshly broken, bitter herbs, coffee, yeast. Her sweat was rich with the horsey reek of synthetic estrogens and an alarming trace of ammonia; renal failure was beginning. More urgent than any of these, the small sharp molecules of her fear rushed across his palate. The muscles of his face wanted to lift his lips away from his teeth but he did not let them.

"I didn't know you were out there until you moved. You're always so quiet," Elena said.

"Yes."

He thought, Oh, tell her now! Admit you don't have the wisdom for this. "Yes. Mother—"

"Would you have some tea?" Elena's words tumbled out to block his unfinished plea. She lifted her palm and brushed the air as if to brush his lips closed. "I'm having some. Sit down."

He sat on the cushioned rugs by the fireplace. Cougar wondered why Elena offered a social ritual. Greetings were usually momentary between them and then they plunged headlong into whatever topic came to hand; they were seldom formal with each other. He realized Elena sought delay and perhaps she also wanted to lengthen the time he would spend here. He felt a wash of guilt, knowing he had often found reasons not to visit her.

Elena busied herself with mugs and tea. The labored motion of her damaged gait, a tiny tremor in her hands, made certain tendons in Cougar's forearms flex. He did not let his claws extend but they twitched once. He hoped she didn't see.

"How are the otters?" she asked.

The woman and her son had business, the business of her death and their acceptance of it, and she asked about otters. Cougar was angry but then he realized that Elena was as hesitant as he was, that she had gone out into the corridor to look for him but hoped not to find him.

So he told her about the otters, sleek and clever in the water, the shellfish they caught and the stones they used to break them open. The otters were new, a test pair, and they harvested mussels and fish. They had been awake long enough to breed. Fat otter pups played now in the bright water.

If he didn't look quite so much like me, Elena thought, he would be the most beautiful man I've ever seen. Most of his beauty is in his musculature, his superb reflexes. I found I couldn't give him fur, or tufted ears. Skin and neural tissue arise from the same embryonic layers; humans have a sort of fur. It should not have been a problem to thicken it but the embryos I tested with that modification were not close enough to human to ever have learned speech. There is so much we still don't know.

But, oh, the retractable claws are superb. Cougar uses them with a speed and precision far beyond human. The hand modifies the brain and the parts of his brain mapped for those hands are marvelous to see.

He's as puzzled as I am by this death of mine, I think.

Cougar took the mug of tea, a slightly smoky blend appropriate for autumn. He breathed its steam and blew on the amber liquid to roughen its surface. The old woman sat down on her cushion. She pulled her legs up and tucked her feet together neatly.

In the fireplace, a twig snapped. The coals glowed yellow-red and then dulled to red again. The night was like any other and his mother was as familiar as his breath, but she was going to die and he wasn't sure how to help her, or what to say.

"I remember—" Elena began.

"Are you beginning a death song?" Cougar asked.

"I thought I might."

"Damn it, don't! This matter is not decided. It's not as simple as I think you would like, certainly not as simple as a point on a graph where all parameters are predictable. I am not a disinterested bystander. You are my mother."

"No, it's not simple," Elena said.

"I have doubts about becoming an executioner. Every human culture has always said, Thou shalt not kill. There are good reasons for such a prohibition."

"Every *human* culture has said, Don't kill within the tribe. As the ages went by we extended the boundaries of the tribe and now we are all one tribe," Elena said. "So we say. Are *you* human?"

Am I? Possible angry answers clashed in Cougar's throat. He coughed to stifle them. "My father is a mountain lion. You are my mother." There were other chimeras in the ship but Cougar did not know and his mother could not know what she had made when she made them. Otter and Bear and Owlchild and the others, all were tools, prototypes, test models on which improvements might be based.

Cougar tightened his grip on the mug of tea, letting the steel blades he'd fitted to his claws snap against the porcelain. He was skilled, very skilled, with scalpels or larger knives, but his claws were more skillful at some tasks, more sensitive than any knife.

A kinetic memory surfaced, a bench in a corridor alcove and he so small it seemed huge, his delight when he found he was big enough to climb up to where Elena waited. But he'd slipped and caught at the smooth skin of her forearm. Drops of blood from his claws appeared one by one on her white skin, ruby dark pomegranate seeds. The salt taste of her blood as he licked the drops away one by one, the cautious, puzzled look on Elena's face. Her face had looked old to him then but now he knew it had been young.

"We bred you," Elena said. "We knew you would never know Earth. We knew you would have only this tiny worldlet and the promise of unknown futures. If anyone survives on the world the ship will reach, they will survive because they design themselves to do so. You are among the first of the designed. I wonder how much you hate us."

Elena swallowed, slip of trachea under wrinkled skin. Her carotid throbbed under the thinned skin at the curve of her jaw.

"You had a choice whether to go or stay. None of us have that choice. I hate you for that, perhaps, but also I love you. My studies tell me all children hate their parents and love them," Cougar said.

"I certainly did." Elena pressed her hands together and then opened them as if they were a book.

My own mother "read a book" in her hands sometimes, Elena remembered. Of course I hated my mother, and loved her. Of course I hated what my mother asked of me. Of course I learned to love what she longed for.

We walked sometimes on the mesa at night and we could see this ship where I live now as a point of light in the sky, a captured asteroid brought into smooth orbit to be altered for our use. It was impossibly far away but I imagined I could hear the explosions and the drills, the violent midwifery the artificers practiced as they exploded a solid chunk of rock into a hollow home.

My parents were insane. Their insanity was grandiose and desperate and I love them for it. In this honeycombed spinning rock they cached all they could; cell samples and embryos of creatures and plants whose codes are known and some that are yet unmapped, inert salts of every biologically useful trace element that might someday be needed, libraries of wisdom and foolishness; anything they thought might ever be useful.

We know there's a planet where we're going. It has some of the things we need to live; we know that much. But we don't know everything. When we reach our faraway new world, we will not have time to terraform it, certainly not completely. Therefore, we will change ourselves to survive there. We'll change the world we find; humans always do.

Or we'll die encysted here in this rock, backing down the scales of complexity, degrading over time until only bacteria are left of us, and then —

I hope for a different outcome, a successful one. I'm as mad as my mother was.

"You saw the diagnostics," Elena said. "I am going to die and there is no treatment strategy that will change that fact. I am suffering."

"You do not appear to be suffering."

"I suffer wondering if you will suffer when my physical and mental decline becomes more apparent. We can't know I will die with my brain intact. I may become mindless. I have seen the eyes of humans whose bodies have outlived their minds." She had seen rows and rows of warehoused ancients waiting, waiting. "Even to my last breath, my body will not want to die."

"I have seen such in my studies," Cougar said.

"I have seen such with my own eyes," Elena said. "In the best of our human and social wisdom, we didn't know what to do."

"But you want me to know what's best and do it," Cougar said.

"I want you to be wiser than I am." She stared into the dying fire and whatever corridors of the past she looked down were far away and long ago.

"There is no reason to settle this tonight," Elena said.

Cougar left her there.

Cougar paced, back two steps, forward two steps, in the cage of the lift. Through its walls he heard the rumbles of the factories, sighs of winds as the worldlet breathed, ordinary, soothing sounds. The lift took him Above. He stripped to a pair of trunks and left his clothes at the gate. The cool air of Above's night chilled his skin in a pleasant way.

He walked to loosen the tightness in his shoulders and neck and then he found a loping stride, a tireless ground-covering pace. He ran past fenced grain fields and bare-limbed orchards (the scent of windfall apples sharp and fermenting). Past the waternoise of a stream made to fall over rocks (waving waterweeds, healthy fingerlings in the shallows, milk-scent of a snoozing otter cub).

He ran within the real physical boundaries of a damned small ecosphere and he worked as he ran. In his pleasant exertion he measured the health and the delicate balances of the enclosed fields and wildernesses (no more wild than any zoo, but larger than most) that slumbered through an artificial night. The consequences of ignoring imbalances in life and growth here were likely to be deadly.

Cougar opened his mouth to the night wind and scented Owlchild, waiting on a bluff above the mouth of the stream. Stalking her, Cougar came across the whitetail doe and her twin fawns, both male, grazing a night meadow. Cougar marked in his mind their differences, one larger and plumper, the other more agile.

He left the deer and went to Owlchild. They talked of the fawns and of sundry things, but not of Elena, although Owlchild knew the old woman faced death, and soon. For a murmuring time, Cougar hid his past and future in the immediacy of Owlchild's now, in the present wonder of her silky skin and secret heats.

Later, lying on his back and staring up at the shuttered ball of the moon (no true moon, only the sun with its energies diverted to engines and factories for the night), Owlchild's hands on his arms felt like fetters. He pushed them away.

"What?" Owlchild whispered.

"I will miss Elena," Cougar said.

"So will I."

Cougar let the night drift around him. He did not want to talk to Owlchild, not for a moment. Here in this little pocket world, as in all places and all times, he knew the social bonds that defined his behaviors to be as critical, as potentially deadly, as stringent as any in history.

Cougar kneaded his cupped hands, one and then the other, against Owlchild's belly. She laughed and turned away. Her shoulders were handy to his claws then, so he scratched her back, oh, so gently, until she giggled.

Cougar came to Elena's cave again at dusk. Hunting her, he had watched her work, scanned her now and again through the day. This day had been as busy as any other of her days. Elena's hands were still skilled and dexterous, certain and precise with the small instruments in her lab. The decisions she made, the trail of notes across her study screens, were as clear and thoughtful as they had ever been.

"Welcome," Elena said. "I'm glad you're here."

She had lighted a fire tonight, three small cedar logs standing in a tripod so that their tops burned each other. The scent of them was rich in the air.

Cougar sat on the piled rugs near the hearth. He pulled a backrest closer and settled against it. It was warmed by the fire and its heat felt good to his back, the cushion cooling and his skin warming until they reached blissful agreement.

He waited with a hunter's patience. Be wiser than I am, she had said. He would try.

"You could simply hand me a medicine and I could take it and never wake up," Elena said.

"I have such a medicine in my pocket. Do you want it?" Cougar asked.

"I have it." Elena reached into the sack she carried at her waist and brought out a tiny packet. "I thought I would know when I was ready to take it. Perhaps I will. I don't know." Without looking at it, she slipped it into her sack again.

Cougar waited.

"I might take the medicine some night. Or I could think, every day, well, not today. Until I can't think at all. What will you do?"

"Damn you. I monitor populations on this ship and cull them, young or old, hurt or sound, when they must be culled. I have always known that someday I would be called on when a human was dying. I did not know it would be so soon."

"We have spent years and many words on this," Elena said.

"We have. I think you do not plan to suicide. I think you are truly determined to be as infuriating as you have always been."

Elena could kill herself, even announce that she intended to do so, and no one on the ship would try to stop her now. Elena could wait until she was mindless, unable to find food for herself, incontinent. No one who knew her would refuse their turn at caring for her.

"Years and words and histories," Elena said.

"Shall we discuss Hitler again, Mother? Shall we find 'scientific' reasons to put you down, as he found 'scientific' reasons for genocide? Shall we review the theological positions on the sanctity of life? Shall we discuss the legitimate uses of power and authority or how to make power responsible for its actions? Shall I convene a committee and assign the decision to a group?"

"You have done so. Today. The timing and manner of my death is in your hands. I could take this burden from you, and I may, but still the question remains for you: What will you do if I will not or cannot? Must the ill, in their distress, be responsible, always, for the time and place of their deaths? Cougar, my illness was not planned to set up a test for you; I swear it."

But it had done so.

One answer, sanctioned by many human societies over many thousands of years—do not interfere. Do not raise your hand; let Elena's biology decide the when and how. Such was human wisdom, but Elena had asked, *Are you human?* She had asked, *Is the human way the best way?* Elena offered challenge. She often did. It was her way.

"It may be true that in some societies, old women said good-bye and went out into the snow when they knew they wouldn't survive the winter. We don't hear about the ones who wouldn't take themselves away. Wouldn't get on the ice floe, wouldn't take their blanket and sleep in the cold." Elena seemed to look down corridors of the past. "And that's the question, isn't it?"

Listen, watch, Cougar told himself. Watch her and read what she wants.

The skill sets humans knew, he knew. He was expert in clinical medicine and in the halting science of psychiatry, unchallenged in his grasp of the cautious disciplines required by the ship's ecologies. His life was rich, his experiences as intricate as any human's had ever been and more so. He knew the ass-tired concentration of lecture halls, the camaraderie of think tanks at mountain retreats in the high desert where his mother had lived before the ship enclosed her. The ship's machines could and had given him kinetic memories of an owl's flight, a trout's leap. His muscles and bones knew his father's walk; his eyes remembered the black moonlight shine of fur on a January night, the clarity of winter desert air in landscapes more vast than even an eagle's eye could conquer.

Elena dropped her eyes and smiled. For an instant Cougar thought he saw a young, young woman, flirting with memories. "For a little while, let me pretend to be social. Thank you for coming to visit me, how are things, and so forth."

"How are things? The ship remains viable as far as we know." His words were simple; a terse report distilled from measurements of bacteria in lake waters, CO_2 concentrations from many monitoring stations in the ship, the number of seeds in the stomach of the dead titmouse the pair of hawks had missed, the debate that had surfaced once again about loosing field mice in the Above. Although the barriers that kept critters from the lifts and stairways were good, mice were by all accounts skilled at invasions. "We don't need two whitetail bucks and we have them. The kitchens will have some venison soon."

He would save some cells from the kill, of course, but the venison would be a treat. Cougar licked his lips in anticipation.

The fire glowed red and clicked and murmured, as hypnotic as fires had been to mothers and sons since fire was first tamed. Mothers and sons, old women and cats, what the hell? The fire comforted both.

He was here to listen, to observe and measure his mother's needs and his own, but Elena sat quiet.

Cougar let his eyelids close by half. The better to listen, my dear.

Nature or nurture? Genetic inevitability or learned behaviors? Both operated in Cougar. He knew it and Elena knew it. Cougar had no apparatus for purring but he liked the sound when he first heard it and soon he learned to make it in his human throat. Did he do it because he wanted to be more like his never-known father or because purring felt particularly good to someone designed with feline genes?

He relaxed all his balanced tensions into an appearance of sudden sleep. He could, usually, almost always, calm Elena with so simple a communication and he did so now, oddly pleased at how quickly she entrained to his apparent comfort. In seconds, he scented a few endorphins on her breath.

"We have been cruel," Elena said. "All of us who made you have been cruel and careless, binding you to a destination that is so uncertain. But no mother has ever known if she brought her child into a safe world. It's something we can't know.

"I don't feel like crying. I don't fear death, or I have told myself I don't. I think of death as a molecular dissolution so complete that any possibility of ongoing consciousness seems ridiculous. The idea of immortality appalls me. If others find it comforting, if you do, well, good. But it's not something I want to consider for myself."

Cougar heard her. Truly, he did sleep, and truly he did hear her. He had tried to explain it to Elena but his mother didn't seem to have such sleep.

Elena kept her voice steady and continued to speak, for if she stopped he would rouse. "I am not a wise woman," Elena said. "Surely you don't think it was wisdom or even pure knowledge that sent us out into the dark. We were driven by myth as much as by reason. We wanted to tell stories to the universe, or at least make sure our stories would be heard on another world."

Cougar did not open his eyes but he heard the soft sounds Elena made as she folded her arms and lifted her head in a storyteller's posture.

"I have said we picked otter genes to explore mammalian aquatic skills, ursine to see if we could uncover hibernation patterns and adapt them; all of the mothers have stories about why they chose different totem animals for their children. I have said I made you mountain lion because of the solitary nature of mountain lions. An African lion needs a pride and you would, because of the scant need for large predators in our pocket world, be the only large predator. Of necessity, alone."

"What a crock." Cougar let his voice rumble, basso, disdainful.

"Yes. Your modification is a simple one, one I thought I could do; that was part of it.

"You are what you are. Your mountain lion DNA led you to become the 'predator' that our pocket ecology requires, or you simply became 'lion-esque' to please me and your own sense of whimsy. I don't know. In any case, you're 'successful.' The methods used to modify you are tested now. The knowledge is available; when your children reach destination they will know how to fine-tune an embryo and give her wings, if need be, or design true sea-dwellers if they find that the seas offer the best chance to thrive.

"You know I find such possibilities wonderful. You've seen and walked through my life or you might someday if you want to; we kept recordings of so much."

In the days of selecting and sorting, strong cases were made for carrying even mosquito eggs and malarial parasites. The codes for building them came aboard but not the organisms themselves.

Elena watched the fire and her son. If he followed his usual pattern, he would sleep for a brief time. He rested profoundly when he rested and he woke renewed, as the young do. As I once did.

We filled the ship with seeds beyond counting, with the patterns of moths' wings and mosses. Someone remembered that if there is a God, he is extraordinarily fond of beetles, and we have many beetles. The life span of a seed even in frozen nitrogen is limited and though we hope to reach harbor before decay sets in, we grow some seeds, birth some animals, to keep the stocks renewed and fresh.

Elena's thoughts skimmed over lists and over years. Lovers and quarrels, embryos tested and lost or grown to beauty. Her life had been a series of questions and always there were more questions than answers.

She had worked in the lab today. The hatched chicks were chickadees, and soon they would be sent Above to pick their way through winter. In the spring, there would be space for a few meadowlarks. In memory she heard their liquid song again, as fresh and pure as a high meadow morning.

This had been a good day. She had slept well, worked hard, eaten *chicos* and joined her son by a fireside, as if today were any other day. As it was, Elena thought, another day gone while the ship traverses the big dark, going from somewhere to somewhere.

Cougar dreamed of making love, of Ottersdaughter smooth and sleek beneath him. A chorus sang a single word, *thanatos, thanatos,* pure voices in counterpoint echoing in the magnificent acoustics of a long-vanished cathedral. The colors of stained glass streamed from the light of the fire; chapel walls tumbled into piles of old stone; the fire died.

Cougar woke and rolled over and stared into his mother's eyes, favoring her with a pure predator's gaze. He liked watching her shiver.

"Was it a good sleep?" Elena asked.

"Oh, it was." Cougar stretched and stretched again, and purred a growling purr for his mother to hear. Elena laughed at him. He told her good night and left.

Later, he saw her on a bluff in the Above, Elena wrapped in her old woolen poncho with the red and black stripes. She came to review the world, perhaps. Cougar worked his way close to her. The old woman sat there for a long time, watching the meadows and the forests. He sensed no distress in her, not that night or the next or the next. But she always came Above.

When, how, if. The diagnostics held steady. Elena was not sicker; she had not begun to fail. On a few nights she took a drug to soothe her old and aching joints and on those nights she walked far, quiet and seemingly content. Did she bring herself to the hunting grounds so that he would kill her? Did she mean for him to strike suddenly, as he preferred to do, kill so swiftly that not even a single molecule of cellular terror tainted the breath of his intended victim? Or did Elena simply want to walk easily in the Above? Cougar knew he should ask her but he did not ask, and then he chided himself for a lack of courage.

Elena continued her work. Cougar found reason to come to the labs now and again, and they talked of many things. Elena did not mention her illness. Cougar waited for her to signal what she wanted but she did not do so.

———

It was time to harvest the deer. Cougar went Above on a night when the temperatures hovered near frost, into air seasoned with the aroma of ripe nuts and the particular scent of fallen grain on damp soil. Elena had not come Above. He could find no trace of her in the night and he was happy enough that she was not here.

The Above was a temperate zone now. In another decade it would be arctic, and after that the plan was to make it tropical for a generation or two. His mother's high desert was best for the testing of marginal, though hardy, species but a desert was not scheduled during his or his mother's lifetime. The desert was important, though, an environment for testing extremes.

On the wind Cougar found Ottersdaughter's signature, two hours old but maybe she was out here somewhere. A badger grumbled along in the brush beside the trail. Owlchild was out tonight, but she was far away. Where, where were the deer? He found them grazing on crested wheat near a stand of Scotch pines.

In summer, columbines bloomed near this path. Chanterelles grew deep in nearby pine needle mulch, boletes for the taste of them. Cougar remembered the quiet *tock* of a flicker's beak on the trunk of a lodgepole pine, a day spent hunting mushrooms here with Elena and Owlchild.

Owlchild was a year older than he was. They had quarreled incessantly until the night she led him through the thickets and down onto the grass by the stream, into a sham battle that began with wrestling, changed to caresses, ended in the remarkable delight and terrifying pleasure of his first sex with a woman. Or ended for a short time, rather, and then began again. Owlchild was lusty then and she still was. Later, later tonight he would find her.

How will she react if I come to her some night with my mother's blood on my hands? Will she turn away from me, and whisper to the others that I cannot be trusted, that I kill at the wrong times, for the wrong reasons?

We must, we will, find our singular rituals for times of guilt and sorrow. Such rituals are necessary, vital. Our skills with each other are critically important for our ongoing survival, as necessary as water.

As she did every time she came Above, Elena wished she had enough discipline to find spaces in her busy days and come here more often. True, summer here was warmer than she cared for but tonight the sphere was cold enough. Her poncho held warm air close to her belly and shoulders. She tucked a fold up over one arm to feel the cold prickles against her shoulder.

The lands inside the sphere were wonderful. Elena loved them for the richness of their lush growth but this was woodland, cropland, not her desert. The desert had been rich, too, rich in vastness and light.

The otter pups would be sleeping but the stream was pleasant to hear. Elena walked there and saw Cougar. Perhaps the noise and moisture masked her presence; he didn't seem to notice she was there.

He was going to find the deer; perhaps he had scented them. Elena wondered how their scent *felt* to him. She wondered how his different perceptions impacted his sense of self. She wondered how different his world was from her own.

Elena stopped, guarding the sound of her breath, for Cougar had stopped in the black shade of the trees. He would test the air, he always did, before he would be ready to walk out in the clearing that bordered the stream. Elena marveled at his caution. He was the most lethal thing in the ecosphere. Most of the animals didn't run from humans; the creatures here were often hand-raised and would come out to play, expecting, and often getting, treats.

Elena stayed in the dark, on the path behind her son.

I should tell Cougar to see if some raspberries can be transplanted here, Elena thought. Like weeds, they like the edges of paths and roads.

Cougar stretched out on a rock beside the stream. He sniffed out the otter pups, burrowed against their mother's teats and sleeping.

Cougar reached into his sampling pouch and set a container on the rock beside him. He lay flat on his belly and let his hand drift into the icy water. His eyes were close to the water's edge and he watched until a cluster of trout fingerlings came near, silver glimmers in the false moonlight but there was light enough. He was cautious; he was always careful to make clean kills. This one. His palm drifted beneath it. Just above the gills the tiny spinal cord ran caudal and close to the skin. Flick. His claw sliced through the resistant flesh and the cord but he stopped the cut before he reached the dorsal skin. He lifted the fish into his palm and shook it into the container.

The drug she had taken made walking a joy. Elena followed her son but at a distance, so that she could lose him in shadow and then catch sight of him again. She saw Ottersdaughter slip through the trees and ahead, circling back to meet Cougar at the edge of the meadow that opened out below a bluff. Ottersdaughter was a tease at times, but she teased with gentle humor. And if Elena could not hear, was not meant to hear, the words they shared, still she knew them. The beauty of entwined arms, of warm flat bellies pressed together and as quickly parted; the language of anticipation and promise never changed.

Ottersdaughter left Cougar. In one instant she was beside him and in the next she was gone.

Cougar lifted his head in that grin of his. Elena sensed his growing excitement. Perhaps Ottersdaughter would hunt with him, the two of them working the deer until the one Cougar chose was isolated and ready for him.

Elena would do her best not to interfere. She had loved to hunt herself, still did, remembered teaching Cougar what she could.

Cougar disappeared into the trees. The meadow lay silent. Elena heard her pulse sing in her ears. She felt the strength of her muscles, rejoiced in the clarity of her night vision that could still pick out a great horned owl sweeping across the meadow. The owl dived and rose again with a squirming vole in her claws. In the wonder of the living night, she was well pleased with her world.

Cathedral choirs and string quartets, fictions and poetries, we have them. Political theories and histories of poverty and bloodshed, we've brought those with us, too. The fear, the prediction, has always been that generation ships must deteriorate into savagery. The fear is that the journey itself will be forgotten and the reality of the ship will be the only reality.

It may happen. It may not.

I'm dying and I know it but I can't feel the reality of it. I may turn away, leave the night and the hunt and go back to my comforting little cave, leave the future to the future and take my lethal medicine. Even tonight. Even right now.

But I'm so alive. I have so many more questions than answers and this meadow is beautiful. How can I encompass all futures and all pasts? How can I stop trying to do so?

I wonder what I will do. I wonder what my son will do.

Look at him. Look, he stalks young deer and the hunt will be slow.

A memory came to sit beside her. Elena welcomed it.

I went out in the high desert and I camped in a high mountain meadow. When I woke, I woke in moonlight. The western mesa seemed a sheet of beaten silver, and near me the shadows were solid black under the pines. I knew I had heard a doe cropping grass in the meadow but she was gone now. I knew I had heard her run, and her fawn beside her.

We humans think we don't smell much, but I smelled that cougar, fur and breath. We think we don't hear well, but I heard him huff in frustration when the doe ran. We think we don't have much position sense, but I knew where he was, just above on the ledge and me beneath. He'd crept down from a high resting place in a pine, so slow, and made one soft jump to land above my shelter. That's when the doe spooked. I could sense the cougar deciding whether to track her and the fawn; I could feel him deciding how. I felt how his muscles tensed. His fur was lighter and softer on his belly than on his back; I got a damned good look at every hair on it as he leaped down an arm's length from my face. Cougar, puma, mountain lion, he had many names but all of them meant beauty.

He was tarnished silver in the moonlight and lean and glossy, so beautiful and so still, and he waited, and waited. I had to breathe sooner or later. The cougar heard me and turned his head to look me over where I hid in my shadow. I have never felt so completely evaluated in my life before or since. He dismissed me, placed me on hold, to wait for his interest if he couldn't bring down that fawn.

The deer weren't making any noise at all but the cougar knew and I knew they hadn't run far.

In the chill of the real and present meadow, Cougar stalked the twin fawns.

All quiet. The doe ripped the high grasses with her teeth and Cougar heard the texture of the grass in the way it tore free, knew the texture of the doe's strong tongue moving back and forth in her wet mouth. At the edge of the meadow, a lump was an unexpected boulder, no, was Elena, hidden under the folds of her old red and black poncho. Surely she would stay still.

Cougar stalked his deer. His supple foot found a quiet place to rest between the tall and brittle blades of grass. He saw, so clear in his hunt-sharpened vision, growth-faded spots on the yearlings' hides. Above him a spotted owl roused and circled the clearing, fleeing on her silent wings, and Ottersdaughter, cautious as a deer herself, hid in the tall meadow grass, ready to spook the deer back toward Cougar if they turned in her direction.

The fawns were identical twins. Cougar wanted the fatter one. Cougar eased his way between the selected twin and its brother and turning the little buck aside. Still the doe remained unaware of him.

Cougar angled toward the trees, herding the fawn. Damn. It looked like the fawn would get into the brush. Cougar didn't want to run it down. He hated botched hunts and meat made bitter by terror and exhaustion. He moved closer.

So big, the deer's brown eye. Cautious, wary, little deer. Let's move that way, over there, it's where you want to go. You don't know I'm here. Do not become aware of me.

The deer took two steps, three, in the direction Cougar wanted.

I watch the silent meadow, the dappled fawn, my son who is invisible to the deer and almost invisible to me.

The doe and the other fawn are in the trees now. I hear the doe, her hoofbeats muffled on fallen pine needles. The fawn's steps behind her are noisier than hers and he takes four steps to her three. I wonder when the doe will notice she has only one of her children beside her.

I was so young when I first saw Cougar's father hunt and my blanket was synthetic silver, not this wool I hold now. But the cougar turned the deer toward me, that wild young cougar. And when he had killed, he called out into the wild night, horny young fool that he was. The big female who came to answer him kept him from the meat until she was filled, but then she let him mount her.

And while he was mounted, I found the courage to get my sampling dart out of my pocket and harpoon up a few cells of him. I doubt he even felt the sting.

There was no deliberation or wisdom in choosing a cougar to sample. No, Cougar's totem came from accident, opportunity, chance. And youth. I was very young. Not all choices need to be deliberate. I made mine.

Cougar got ahead of the deer. He circled through the trees and came up behind Elena. Quiet, quiet. Ottersdaughter made a stand of grass ripple once and the deer moved away from it, stepped closer and closer to Cougar and his mother. Still calm. Cougar waited.

So close. Elena could have touched the buds of antlers, brushed her fingers against individual hairs on the buck's shoulder, black or tawny or white. She felt wrapped in stillness, as alive as it is possible to be, forever in the moment, the overwhelming joy of now.

Cougar stood behind his mother, so close that her warmth rose from her poncho and caressed his cheek. This is the best of my mother's nights, Cougar knew. There cannot be another night more wonderful than this, a future where she is more complete. I don't know all her past but I know it's rich in her and I know she holds it all tonight and will never know it so well again.

Sweat scent, pine sap, crushed meadow grass, Elena is warm with happiness and her blood is singing. But there will be other nights, many of them, that will be almost as complete. What will I do?

Out in the meadow, Ottersdaughter stood suddenly, not a human form in this light but simply unexpected, tall, something to run away from. The fawn startled and leaped forward, still unaware of Cougar and his mother. Elena raised her arm; perhaps she meant to guard her face.

The deer reached the limit of its leaping arc and began to descend. Cougar caught his mother's arm and held it. The fawn's chest crashed into the barrier of linked arms. As the striped woolen folds of the blanket settled, the old woman's throat and the fawn's bulging neck were only centimeters apart, both of their lives vulnerable and within certain reach.

With the photographic clarity of his hunter's vision, Cougar watched moonlight silver the razored edges of his claws as they slashed down.

mount olympus

BEN BOVA

As writer, editor, essayist, and anthologist, Ben Bova has been one of the most prominent and influential figures in the genre for more than forty years. Bova made his first professional fiction sale in 1959, and by 1971, already recognized as one of the best new hard-SF writers on the scene, he was chosen to succeed legendary editor John W. Campbell, Jr., as the new editor of Analog *magazine, a position he'd hold until 1978; many credit Bova with revitalizing an* Analog *that had slipped into genteel senility, introducing the work of writers such as Joe Haldeman, Larry Niven, Roger Zelazny, Frederik Pohl, and George R. R. Martin to the magazine, and winning six Best Editor Hugos in the process. Bova then moved on to be the founding editor of* Omni *magazine, from 1978 to 1982, before turning his back on editing altogether to take up the life of a full-time freelance writer. Bova's many books include the novels* The Starcrossed, The Kinsman Saga *(omnibus of the two-volume "Kinsman" series),* The Exiles Trilogy *(omnibus of the "Exiles" trilogy),* Colony, Privateers, Voyagers, Voyagers II: The Alien Within, Voyagers III: Star Brothers, The Multiple Man, Cyberbooks, and* Mars, *and the collections* Forward in Time, Maxwell's Demons, Escape Plus, Future Crime, and* Sam Gunn, Unlimited. *His many anthologies include* The Science Fiction Hall of Fame, Vols. 2A and 2B, The Best of Analog, The Best of Omni Science Fiction, #2–4, and* The Best of the Nebulas. *Bova is also perhaps the most tireless promoter of the space program since the late Carl Sagan, and his nonfiction books include* The Uses of Space, The New Astronomies, Starflight and Other Improbabilities, The High Road, and* Welcome to Moon Base. *His most recent book, of which "Mount Olympus" is a part, is the novel* Return to Mars. *A new novel,* Venus, *should be on the shelves by the time our book comes out. Bova has also recently become Publisher of* Galaxy Online *and he has his own web site at www.benbova.net.*

This new Mars adventure is a gripping story of danger and exploration that is as timely as tomorrow's headlines and as scientifically accurate and up-to-date as anyone can make it (when it happens, the chances are good that this is the way it will happen!), and demonstrates that no matter how far away we travel, we still have to deal with ourselves *when we get there.*

The tallest mountain in the solar system is Olympus Mons, on Mars. It is a massive shield volcano that has been dormant for tens, perhaps hundreds of millions of years.

Once, though, its mighty outpourings of lava dwarfed everything else on the planet. Over time, they built a mountain three times taller than Everest, with a base the size of the state of Iowa.

The edges of that base are rugged cliffs of basalt more than a kilometer high. The summit of the mountain, where huge calderas mark the vents that once spewed molten rock, stands some twenty-seven kilometers above the supporting plain.

At that altitude, the carbon dioxide that forms the major constituent of Mars's atmosphere can freeze out, condense on the cold, bare rock, covering it with a thin, invisible layer of dry ice.

Tòmas Rodriguez looked happy as a puppy with an old sock to chew on as he and Fuchida got into their hard suits.

"I'm gonna be in the Guinness Book of Records," he proclaimed cheerfully to Jamie Waterman, who was helping him get suited up. Trudy Hall was assisting Fuchida while Stacy Dezhurova sat in the comm center, monitoring the dome's systems and the equipment outside.

It was the forty-eighth day of the Second Expedition's eighteen months on the surface of Mars, the day that Rodriguez and biologist Mitsuo Fuchida were scheduled to fly to Olympus Mons.

"Highest aircraft landing and takeoff," Rodriguez chattered cheerfully as he wormed his fingers into the suit's gloves. "Longest flight of a manned solar-powered aircraft. Highest altitude for a manned solar-powered aircraft."

"Crewed," Trudy Hall murmured, "not manned."

Unperturbed by her correction, Rodriguez continued, "I might even bust the record for unmanned solar-powered flight."

"Isn't it cheating to compare a flight on Mars to flights on Earth?" Trudy asked as she helped Fuchida latch his life-support pack onto the back of his suit.

Rodriguez shook his head vigorously. "All that counts in the record book is the numbers, chica. Just the numbers."

"Won't they put an asterisk next to the numbers and a footnote that says, 'This was done on Mars'?"

Rodriguez tried to shrug but not even he could manage that inside the hard suit. "Who cares, as long as they spell my name right?"

As the two men put on their suit helmets and sealed them to the neck rings, Jamie noticed that Fuchida was utterly silent through the suit-up procedure. Tòmas is doing enough talking for them both, he thought. But he wondered, Is

Mitsuo worried, nervous? He looks calm enough, but that might just be a mask. Come to think of it, the way Tòmas is blathering, he must be wired tighter than a drum.

The bulky hard suits had been pristine white when the explorers first touched down on Mars. Now their boots and leggings were tinged with reddish dust, no matter how hard the explorers vacuumed the ceramic-metal suits each time they returned to the dome's airlock.

Rodriguez was the youngest of the eight explorers, the astronaut that NASA had loaned to the expedition. If it bothered him to work under Dezhurova, the more experienced Russian cosmonaut, he never showed it. All through training and the five-month flight to Mars and their nearly seven weeks on the planet's surface, he had been a good-natured, willing worker. Short and stocky, with a swarthy complexion and thickly curled dark hair, his most noticeable feature was a dazzling smile that made his deep brown eyes sparkle.

But now he was jabbering away like a fast-pitch salesman. Jamie wondered if it was nerves or relief to be out on his own, in charge. Or maybe, Jamie thought, the guy was simply overjoyed at the prospect of flying.

Both men were suited up at last, helmet visors down, life-support systems functioning, radio checks completed. Jamie and Trudy walked with them to the airlock hatch: two Earthlings accompanying a pair of ponderous robots.

Jamie shook hands with Rodriguez. His bare hand hardly made it around the astronaut's glove, with its servo-driven exoskeleton "bones" on its back.

"Good luck, Tòmas," he said. "Don't take any unnecessary risks out there."

Rodriguez grinned from behind his visor. "Hey, you know what they say: There are old pilots and bold pilots, but there are no old, bold pilots."

Jamie chuckled politely. As mission director, he felt he had to impart some final words of wisdom. "Remember that when you're out there," he said.

"I will, boss. Don't worry."

Fuchida stepped up to the hatch once Rodriguez went through. Even in the bulky suit, even with sparrowlike Trudy Hall standing behind him, he looked small, somehow vulnerable.

"Good luck, Mitsuo," said Jamie.

Through the sealed helmet, Fuchida's voice sounded muffled, but unafraid. "I think my biggest problem is going to be listening to Tòmas's yakking all the way to the mountain."

Jamie laughed.

"And back, most likely," Fuchida added.

The indicator light turned green and Trudy pressed the stud that opened the inner hatch. Fuchida stepped through, carrying his portable life-support satchel in one hand.

He's all right, Jamie told himself. Mitsuo's not scared or even worried.

Once they had clambered into the plane's side-by-side seats and connected to its internal electrical power and life-support systems, both men changed.

Rodriguez became all business. No more chattering. He checked out the plane's systems with only a few clipped words of jargon to Stacy Dezhurova, who was serving as flight controller back in the dome's comm center.

Fuchida, for his part, felt his pulse thundering in his ears so loudly he wondered if the suit radio was picking it up. Certainly the medical monitors must be close to the redline, his heart was racing so hard.

Like the expedition's remotely piloted soarplanes, the rocketplane was built of gossamer-thin plastic skin stretched over a framework of ceramic-plastic cerplast. To Fuchida it looked like an oversized model airplane made of some kind of kitchen wrap, complete with an odd-looking six-bladed propeller on its nose.

But it was big enough to carry two people. Huge, compared to the unmanned soarplanes. Rodriguez said it was nothing more than a fuel tank with wings. The wings stretched wide, drooping to the ground at their tips. The cockpit was tiny, nothing more than a glass bubble up front. The rocket engines, tucked in where the wing roots joined the fuselage, looked too small to lift the thing off the ground.

The plane was designed to use its rocket engines for takeoffs, then once at altitude, it would run on the prop. Solar panels painted onto the wing's upper surface would provide the electricity to power the electrical engine. There was too little oxygen in the Martian air to run a jet engine; the rockets were the plane's main muscle, the solar cells its secondary energy source.

Back in the dome, Jamie and the others crowded over Dezhurova's shoulders to watch the takeoff on the comm center's desktop display screen.

As an airport, the base left much to be desired. The bulldozed runway ran just short of two kilometers in length. There was no taxiway; Rodriguez and a helper— often Jamie—simply turned the fragile plane around after a landing so it was pointed up the runway again. There was no windsock. The atmosphere was so rare that it made scant difference which way the wind was blowing when the plane took off. The rocket engines did most of the work of lifting the plane off the ground and providing the speed it needed for the broad, drooping wings to generate enough lift for flight.

Jamie felt a dull throbbing in his jaw as he bent over Dezhurova, watching the final moments before takeoff. With a conscious effort he unclenched his teeth. There are two men in that plane, he told himself. If anything goes wrong, if they crash, they'll both be killed.

"Clear for takeoff," Dezhurova said mechanically into her lip mike.

"Copy clear," Rodriguez's voice came through the speakers.

Stacy scanned the screens around her one final time, then said, "Clear for ignition."

"Ignition."

Suddenly the twin rocket engines beneath the wing roots shot out a bellowing flame and the plane jerked into motion. As the camera followed it jouncing down the runway, gathering speed, the long, drooping wings seemed to stiffen and stretch out.

"Come on, baby," Dezhurova muttered.

Jamie saw it all as if it were happening in slow motion: the plane trundling down the runway, the rockets' exhaust turning so hot the flame became invisible, clouds of dust and grit billowing behind the plane as it sped faster, faster along the runway, nose lifting now.

"Looking good," Dezhurova whispered.

The plane hurtled up off the ground and arrowed into the pristine sky, leaving a roiling cloud of dust and vapor slowly dissipating along the length of the runway. To Jamie it looked as if the cloud was trying to reach for the plane and pull it back to the ground.

But the plane was little more than a speck in the salmon-pink sky now.

Rodriguez's voice crackled through the speakers, "Next stop, Mount Olympus!"

Rodriguez was a happy man. The plane was responding to his touch like a beautiful woman, gentle and sweet.

They were purring along at—he glanced at the altimeter—twenty-eight thousand and six meters. Let's see, he mused. Something like three point two feet in a meter, that makes it eighty-nine, almost ninety thousand feet. Not bad. Not bad at all.

He knew the world altitude record for a solar-powered plane was above one hundred thousand feet. But that was a UAV, an unmanned aerial vehicle. No pilot's flown this high in a solar-powered plane, he knew. Behind his helmet visor he smiled at the big six-bladed propeller as it spun lazily before his eyes.

Beside him, Fuchida was absolutely silent and unmoving. He might as well be dead inside his suit, I'd never know the difference, Rodriguez thought. He's scared, just plain scared. He doesn't trust me. He's scared of flying with me. Probably wanted Stacy to fly him, not me.

Well, my silent Japanese buddy, I'm the guy you're stuck with, whether you like it or not. So go ahead and sit there like a fuckin' statue, I don't give a damn.

Mitsuo Fuchida felt an unaccustomed tendril of fear worming its way through his innards. This puzzled him, since he had known for almost two years now that he would be flying to the top of Olympus Mons. He had flown simulations hundreds of times. This whole excursion to Olympus Mons had been his idea, and he had worked hard to get the plan incorporated into the expedition schedule.

He had first learned to fly while an undergraduate biology student, and had been elected president of the university's flying club. With the single-minded intensity of a competitor who knew he had to beat the best of the best to win a berth on the Second Mars Expedition, Fuchida had taken the time to qualify as a pilot of ultralight aircraft over the inland mountains of his native Kyushu and then went on to pilot soarplanes across the jagged peaks of Sinkiang.

He had never felt any fear of flying. Just the opposite: he had always felt relaxed and happy in the air, free of all the pressures and cares of life.

Yet now, as the sun sank toward the rocky horizon, casting eerie red light across the barren rust-red landscape, Fuchida knew that he was afraid. What if the engine fails? What if Rodriguez cracks up the plane when we land on the mountain? One of the unmanned soarplanes had crashed while it was flying over the volcano on a reconnaissance flight; what if the same thing happens to us?

Even in rugged Sinkiang there was a reasonable chance of surviving an emergency landing. You could breathe the air and walk to a village, even if the trek took many days. Not so here on Mars.

What if Rodriguez gets hurt while we're out there? I have only flown this plane in the simulator, I don't know if I could fly it in reality.

Rodriguez seemed perfectly at ease, happily excited to be flying. He shames me, Fuchida thought. Yet . . . is he truly capable? How will he react in an emergency? Fuchida hoped he would not have to find out.

They passed Pavonis Mons on their left, one of the three giant shield volcanoes that lined up in a row on the eastern side of the Tharsis bulge. It was so big that it stretched out to the horizon and beyond, a massive hump of solid stone that had once oozed red-hot lava across an area the size of Japan. Quiet now. Cold and dead. For how long?

There was a whole line of smaller volcanoes stretching off to the horizon and, beyond them, the hugely massive Olympus Mons. What happened here to create a thousand-kilometer-long chain of volcanoes? Fuchida tried to meditate on that question, but his mind kept coming back to the risks he was undertaking.

And to Elizabeth.

Their wedding had to be a secret. Married persons would not be allowed on the Mars expedition. Worse yet. Mitsuo Fuchida had fallen in love with a foreigner, a young Irish biologist with flame-red hair and skin like white porcelain.

"Sleep with her," Fuchida's father advised him, "enjoy her all you want to. But father no children with her! Under no circumstances may you marry her."

Elizabeth Vernon seemed content with that. She loved Mitsuo.

They had met at Tokyo University. Like him, she was a biologist. Unlike him, she had neither the talent nor the drive to get very far in the competition for tenure and a professorship.

"I'll be fine," she told Mitsuo. "Don't ruin your chance for Mars. I'll wait for you."

That was neither good nor fair, in Fuchida's eyes. How could he go to Mars, spend years away from her, expect her to store her emotions in suspended animation for so long?

His father made other demands on him, as well.

"The only man to die on the First Mars Expedition was your cousin, Konoye. He disgraced us all."

Isoruku Konoye suffered a fatal stroke while attempting to explore the smaller moon of Mars, Deimos. His Russian teammate, cosmonaut Leonid Tolbukhin, said that Konoye had panicked, frightened to be outside their spacecraft in nothing more than a spacesuit, disoriented by the looming menace of Deimos's rocky bulk.

"You must redeem the family's honor," Fuchida's father insisted. "You must make the world respect Japan. Your namesake was a great warrior. You must add new honors to his name."

So Mitsuo knew that he could not marry Elizabeth openly, honestly, as he wanted to. Instead, he took her to a monastery in the remote mountains of Kyushu, where he had perfected his climbing skills.

"It's not necessary, Mitsuo," Elizabeth protested, once she understood what he wanted to do. "I love you. A ceremony won't change that."

"Would you prefer a Catholic rite?" he asked.

She threw her arms around his neck. He felt tears on her cheek.

When the day came that he had to leave, Mitsuo promised Elizabeth that he would come back to her. "And when I do, we will be married again, openly, for all the world to see."

"Including your father?" she asked wryly.

Mitsuo smiled. "Yes, including even my noble father."

Then he left for Mars, intent on honoring his family's name and returning to the woman he loved.

The excursion plan called for them to land late in the afternoon, almost at sunset, when the low sun cast its longest shadows. That allowed them to take off in daylight, while giving them the best view of their landing area. Every boulder and rock would show in bold relief, allowing them to find the smoothest spot for their landing.

It also meant, Fuchida knew, that they would have to endure the dark frigid hours of night immediately after they landed. What if the batteries fail? The lithium-polymer batteries had been tested for years, Fuchida knew. They stored electricity generated in sunlight by the solar panels and powered the plane's equipment through the long, cold hours of darkness. But what if they break down when the temperature drops to a hundred and fifty below zero?

Rodriguez was making a strange, moaning sound, he realized. Turning sharply to look at the astronaut sitting beside him, Fuchida saw only the inside of his own helmet. He had to turn from the shoulders to see the space-suited pilot—who was humming tunelessly.

"Are you all right?" Fuchida asked nervously.

"Sure."

"Was that a Mexican song you were humming?"

"Naw. The Beatles. 'Lucy in the Sky with Diamonds.'"

"Oh."

Rodriguez sighed happily. "There she is," he said.

"What?"

"Mount Olympus." He pointed straight ahead.

Fuchida did not see a mountain, merely the horizon. It seemed rounded, now that he paid attention to it: a large gently rising hump.

It grew as they approached it. And grew. And grew. Olympus Mons was an immense island unto itself, a continent rising up above the bleak red plain like some gigantic mythical beast. Its slopes were gentle, above the steep scarps of its base. A man could climb that grade easily, Fuchida thought. Then he realized that the mountain was so huge it would take a man weeks to walk from its base to its summit.

Rodriguez was humming again, calm and relaxed as a man sitting in his favorite chair at home.

"You enjoy flying, don't you?" Fuchida commented.

"You know what they say," Rodriguez replied, a serene smile in his voice. "Flying a plane is the second most exciting thing a man can do."

Fuchida nodded inside his helmet. "And the most exciting must be sex, right?"

"Nope. The first most exciting thing a man can do is landing a plane."

Fuchida sank into gloomy silence.

As the senior of the expedition's two astronauts, Anastasia Dezhurova was technically second-in-command to Jamie Waterman. She saw to it that her main duty was the communications center, where she could watch everyone and everything. As long as she was watching, Dezhurova felt, nothing very bad could happen to her fellow explorers.

The dome was quiet, everyone busy at their appointed tasks. Dezhurova could see Waterman outside, doggedly chipping still more rock samples. Trudy Hall was in her lab working with the lichen from the Grand Canyon; the only other woman among them, Vijay Shektar, was in her infirmary, scrolling medical data on her computer.

"Rodriguez to base," the astronaut's voice suddenly crackled in the speaker. "I'm making a dry run over the landing area. Sending my camera view."

"Base to Rodriguez," Dezhurova snapped, all business. "Copy dry run." Her fingers raced over the keyboard and the main display suddenly showed a pockmarked, boulder-strewn stretch of bare rock. "We have your imagery."

Dezhurova felt her mouth go dry. *I'd better call Jamie back into the dome. If that's the landing area, they're never going to get down safely.*

Rodriguez banked the plane slightly so he could see the ground better. To Fuchida it seemed as if the plane was standing on its left wingtip while the hard, bare rock below turned in a slow circle.

"Well," Rodriguez said, "we've got a choice: boulders or craters."

"Where's the clear area the soarplanes showed?" Fuchida asked.

" 'Clear' is a relative term," Rodriguez muttered.

Fuchida swallowed bile. It burned in his throat.

"Rodriguez to base. I'm going to circle the landing area one more time. Tell me if you see anything I miss."

"Copy another circle." Stacy Dezhurova's tone was clipped, professional.

Rodriguez peered hard at the ground below. The setting sun cast long shadows that emphasized every pebble down there. Between a fresh-looking crater and a scattering of rocks was a relatively clean area, more than a kilometer long. Room enough to land if the retros fired on command.

"Looks OK to me," he said into his helmet mike.

"Barely," came Dezhurova's voice.

"The wheels can handle small rocks."

"Shock absorbers are no substitute for level ground, Tòmas."

Rodriguez laughed. He and Dezhurova had gone through this discussion a few dozen times, ever since the first recon photos had come back from the UAVs.

"Turning into final approach," he reported.

Dezhurova did not reply. As the flight controller she had the authority to forbid him to land.

"Lining up for final."

"Your imagery is breaking up a little."

"Light level's sinking fast."

"Yes."

Fuchida saw the ground rushing up toward him. It was covered with boulders and pitted with craters and looked as hard as concrete, harder. They were coming in too fast, he thought. He wanted to grab the control T-stick in front of him and pull up, cut in the rocket engines and get the hell away while they had a chance. Instead, he squeezed his eyes shut.

Something hit the plane so hard that Fuchida thought he'd be driven through the canopy. His safety harness held, though, and within an eyeblink he heard the howling screech of the tiny retro rocket motors. The front of the plane seemed to be on fire. They were bouncing, jolting, rattling along like a tin can kicked across a field of rubble.

Then a final lurch and all the noise and motion stopped.

"We're down," Rodriguez sang out. "Piece of cake."

"Good," came Dezhurova's stolid voice.

Fuchida urgently needed to urinate.

"OK," Rodriguez said to his partner. "Now we just sit tight until sunrise."

"Like a pair of tinned sardines," said Fuchida.

Rodriguez laughed. "Hey, man, we got all the creature comforts you could want—almost. Like tourist class in an overnight flight."

Fuchida nodded inside his helmet. He did not relish the idea of trying to sleep in the cockpit seats, sealed in their suits. But that was the price to be paid for the honor of being the first humans to set foot on the tallest mountain in the solar system.

Almost, he smiled. I too will be in the Guinness Book of Records, he thought.

"You OK?" Rodriguez asked.

"Yes, certainly."

"Kinda quiet, Mitsuo."

"I'm admiring the view," said Fuchida.

Nothing but a barren expanse of bare rock, in every direction. The sky overhead was darkening swiftly. Already Fuchida could see a few stars staring down at them.

"Well, look on the bright side," Rodriguez quipped. "Now we get to test the FES."

The Fecal Elimination System. Fuchida dreaded the moment when he had to try to use it.

Rodriguez chuckled happily, as if he hadn't a care in the world. In two worlds.

"Never show fear." Tòmas Rodriguez learned that as a scrawny asthmatic child, growing up amidst the crime and violence of an inner-city San Diego barrio.

"Never let them see you're scared," his older brother Luis told him. "Never back down from a fight."

Tòmas was not physically big, but he had his big brother to protect him. Most of the time. Then he found a refuge of sorts in the dilapidated neighborhood gym, where he traded hours of sweeping and cleaning for free use of the weight machines. As he gained muscle mass, he learned the rudiments of alley fighting from Luis. In middle school he was spotted and recruited by an elderly Korean who taught martial arts as a school volunteer.

In high school he discovered that he was bright, smart enough not merely to understand algebra but to want to understand it and the other mysteries of mathematics and science. He made friends among the nerds as well as the jocks, often protecting the former against the hazing and casual cruelty of the latter.

He grew into a solid, broad-shouldered youth with quick reflexes and the brains to talk his way out of most confrontations. He did not look for fights, but handled himself well enough when a fight became unavoidable. He worked, he learned, he had the kind of sunny disposition — and firm physical courage — that made even the nastiest punks in the school leave him alone. He never went out for any of the school teams and he never did drugs. He didn't even smoke. He couldn't afford such luxuries.

He even avoided the trap that caught most of his buddies: fatherhood. Whether they got married or not, most of the guys quickly got tied down with a woman. Tòmas had plenty of girls, and learned even before high school the pleasures of sex. But he never formed a lasting relationship. He didn't want to. The neighborhood girls were attractive, yes, until they started talking. Tòmas couldn't stand even to imagine listening to one of them for more than a few hours. They had nothing to say. Their lives were empty. He ached for something more.

Most of the high school teachers were zeroes, but one — the weary old man who taught math — encouraged him to apply for a scholarship to college. To Tòmas' enormous surprise, he won one: full tuition to UCSD. Even so, he could not afford the other expenses, so he again listened to his mentor's advice and joined the Air Force. Uncle Sam paid his way through school, and once he graduated he became a jet fighter pilot. "More fun than sex," he would maintain, always adding, "Almost."

Never show fear. That meant that he could never back away from a challenge. Never. Whether in a cockpit or a barroom, the stocky Hispanic kid with the big smile took every confrontation as it arose. He got a reputation for it.

The fear was always there, constantly, but he never let it show. And always there was that inner doubt. That feeling that somehow he didn't really belong here. They were allowing the chicano kid to pretend he was as smart as the white guys, allowing him to get through college on his little scholarship, allowing him to wear a flyboy uniform and play with the hotshot jet planes.

But he really wasn't one of them. That was made abundantly clear to him in a thousand little ways, every day. He was a greaser, tolerated only as long as he stayed in the place they expected him to be. Don't try to climb too far; don't show off too much; above all, don't try to date anyone except "your own."

Flying was different, though. Alone in a plane seven or eight miles up in the sky it was just him and God, the rest of the world far away, out of sight and out of mind.

Then came the chance to win an astronaut's wings. He couldn't back away from the challenge. Again, the others made it clear that he was not welcome to the competition. But Tòmas entered anyway and won a slot in the astronaut training corps. "The benefits of affirmative action," one of other pilots jeered.

Whatever he achieved, they always tried to take the joy out of it. Tòmas paid no outward attention, as usual; he kept his wounds hidden, his bleeding internal.

Two years after he had won his astronaut's wings came the call for the Second Mars Expedition. Smiling his broadest, Tòmas applied. No fear. He kept his gritted teeth hidden from all the others, and won the position.

"Big fuckin' deal," said his buddies. "You'll be second fiddle to some Russian broad."

Tòmas shrugged and nodded. "Yeah," he admitted. "I guess I'll have to take orders from everybody."

To himself he added, But I'll be on Mars, shitheads, while you're still down here.

Following his astronaut teammate, Mitsuo Fuchida clambered stiffly down the ladder from the plane's cockpit and set foot on the top of the tallest mountain in the solar system.

In the pale light of the rising sun, it did not look like the top of a mountain to him. He had done a considerable amount of climbing in Japan and Canada and this was nothing like the jagged, snow-capped slabs of granite where the wind whistled like a hurled knife and the clouds scudded by below you.

Here he seemed to be on nothing more dramatic than a wide, fairly flat plain of bare basalt. Pebbles and larger rocks were scattered here and there, but not as thickly as they were back at the base dome. The craters that they had seen from the air were not visible here; at least, he saw nothing that looked like a crater.

But when he looked up he realized how high they were. The sky was a deep blue, instead of its usual salmon pink. The dust particles that reddened the sky of Mars were far below them. At this altitude on Earth they would be up in the stratosphere.

Fuchida wondered if he could see any stars through his visor, maybe find Earth. He turned, trying to orient himself with the rising sun.

"Watch your step," Rodriguez's voice warned in his earphones. "It's—"

Fuchida's boot slid out from under him and he thumped painfully on his rear.

". . . slippery," Rodriguez finished lamely.

The astronaut shuffled carefully to Fuchida's side, moving like a man crossing an ice rink in street shoes. He extended a hand to help the biologist up to his feet.

Stiff and aching from a night of sitting in the cockpit, Fuchida now felt a throbbing pain in his backside. I'll have a nasty bruise there, he told himself. Lucky I didn't land on the backpack and break the life-support rig.

"Feels like ice underfoot," Rodriguez said.

"It couldn't be frost, we're up too high for water ice to form."

"Dry ice."

"Ah." Fuchida nodded inside his helmet. "Dry ice. Carbon dioxide from the atmosphere condenses out on the cold rock."

"Yep."

"But dry ice isn't slippery . . ."

"This stuff is."

Fuchida thought quickly. "Perhaps the pressure of our boots on the dry ice causes a thin layer to vaporize."

"So we get a layer of carbon dioxide gas under our boots." Rodriguez immediately grasped the situation.

"Exactly. We skid along on a film of gas, like gas-lubricated ball bearings."

"That's gonna make it damned difficult to move around."

Fuchida wanted to rub his butt, although he knew it was impossible inside the hard suit. "The sun will get rid of the ice."

"I don't think it'll get warm enough up here to vaporize it."

"It sublimes at seventy-eight point five degrees below zero. Celsius," Fuchida recalled.

"At normal pressure," Rodriguez pointed out.

Fuchida looked at the thermometer on his right cuff. "It's already up to forty-two below," he said, feeling cheerful for the first time. "Besides, the lower the pressure, the lower the boiling point."

"Yeah. That's right."

"That patch must have been shaded by the plane's wing," Fuchida pointed out. "The rest of the ground seems clear."

"Then let's go to the beach and get a suntan," Rodriguez said humorlessly.

"No, let's go to the caldera, as planned."

"You think it's safe to walk around?"

Nodding inside his helmet, Fuchida took a tentative step. The ground felt smooth, but not slick. Another step, then another.

"Maybe we should've brought football cleats."

"Not necessary. The ground's OK now."

Rodriguez grunted. "Be careful, anyway."

"Yes, I will."

While Rodriguez relayed his morning report from his suit radio through the more powerful transmitter in the plane, Fuchida unlatched the cargo bay hatch and slid their equipment skid to the ground. Again he marvelled that this plane of plastic and gossamer could carry them and their gear. It seemed quite impossible, yet it was true.

"Are you ready?" he asked Rodriguez, feeling eager now to get going.

"Yep. Lemme check the compass bearing. . . ."

Fuchida did not wait for the astronaut's check. He knew the direction to the caldera as if its coordinates were printed on his heart.

Rodriguez felt a chill of apprehension tingling through him as they stared down into the caldera. It was like being on the edge of an enormous hole in the world, a hole that went all the way down into hell.

"Nietzsche was right," Fuchida said, his voice sounding awed, almost frightened, in Rodriguez's earphones.

Rodriguez had to turn his entire torso from the hips to see the Japanese biologist standing beside him, anonymous in his bulky hard suit except for the blue stripes on his arms.

"You mean about when you stare into the abyss the abyss stares back."

"You've read Nietzsche?"

Rodriguez grunted. "In Spanish."

"That must have been interesting. I read him in Japanese."

Breaking into a chuckle, Rodriguez said, "So neither one of us can read German, huh?"

It was as good a way as any to break the tension. The caldera was huge, a mammoth pit that stretched from horizon to horizon. Standing there on its lip, looking down into the dark, shadowy depths that dropped away for who knew how far, was distinctly unnerving.

"That's a helluva hole," Rodriguez muttered.

"It's big enough to swallow Mt. Everest," said Fuchida, his voice slightly hollow with awe.

"How long's this beast been dead?" Rodriguez asked.

"Tens of millions of years, at least. Probably much longer. That's one of the things we want to establish while we're here."

"Think it's due for another blow?"

Fuchida laughed shakily. "We'll get plenty of warning, don't worry."

"What, me worry?"

They began to unload the equipment they had dragged on the skid. Its two runners were lined with small Teflon-coated wheels so it could ride along rough ground without needing more than the muscle power of the two men. Much of the equipment was mountaineering gear: chocks and pitons and long coiled lengths of Buckyball cable.

"You really want to go down there?" Rodriguez asked while he drilled holes in the hard basalt for Fuchida to implant geo/met beacons. The instrumentation built into the slim pole would continuously measure ground tremors, heat flow from the planet's interior, air temperature, wind velocity and humidity.

"I spent a lot of time exploring caves," Fuchida answered, gripping one of the beacons in his gloved hands. "I've been preparing for this for a long time."

"Spelunking? You?"

"They call it caving. Spelunking is a term used by non-cavers."

"So you're all set to go down there, huh?"

Fuchida realized that he did not truly want to go. Every time he had entered a cave on Earth he had felt an irrational sense of dread. But he had forced himself to explore the caverns because he knew it would be an important point in his favor in the competition for a berth on the Mars expedition.

"I'm all set," the biologist answered, grunting as he worked the geology/meteorology beacon into its hole.

"It's a dirty job," Rodriguez joked, over the whine of the auger's electric motor, "but somebody's got to do it."

"A man's got to do what a man's got to do," Fuchida replied, matching his teammate's bravado.

Rodriguez laughed. "That ain't Nietzsche."

"No. John Wayne."

They finished all the preliminary work and headed back to the lip of the caldera. Slowly. Reluctantly, Rodriguez thought. Well, he told himself, even if we break our asses poking around down there at least we've got the beacons up and running.

Fuchida stopped to check the readouts coming from the beacons.

"They all transmitting OK?" Rodriguez asked.

"Yes," came the reply in his earphones. "Interesting . . ."

"What?"

"Heat flow from below ground is much higher here than at the dome or even down in the Canyon."

Rodriguez felt his eyebrows crawl upward. "You mean she's still active?"

"No, no, no. That can't be. But there is still some thermal energy down there."

"We should've brought marshmallows."

"Perhaps. Or maybe there'll be something to picnic on down there waiting for us!" The biologist's voice sounded excited.

"Whattaya mean?"

"Heat energy! Energy for life, perhaps."

A vision of bad videos flashed through Rodriguez's mind: slimy alien monsters with tentacles and bulging eyes. He forced himself not to laugh aloud. Don't worry, they're only interested in blondes with big boobs.

Fuchida called, "Help me get the lines attached and make certain the anchors are firmly imbedded."

He's not reluctant anymore, Rodriguez saw. He's itching to go down into that huge hole and see what kind of alien creatures he can find.

"You all set?" Rodriguez asked.

Fuchida had the climbing harness buckled over his hard suit, the tether firmly clipped to the yoke that ran under his arms.

"Ready to go," the biologist replied, with an assurance he did not truly feel. That dark, yawning abyss stirred a primal fear in both men, but Fuchida did not want to admit to it himself, much less to his teammate.

Rodriguez had spent the morning setting up the climbing rig while Fuchida collected rock samples and then did a half-hour VR show for viewers back on Earth. The rocks were sparser here atop Olympus Mons than they were down on the plains below, and none of them showed the intrusions of color that marked colonies of Martian lichen.

Still, sample collection was the biologist's first order of business. He thought of it as his gift to the geologists, since he felt a dreary certainty that there was no biology going on here on the roof of this world. But down below, inside the caldera . . . that might be a different matter.

Fuchida still had the virtual reality rig clamped to his helmet. They would not do a real-time transmission, but the recording of the first descent into Olympus Mons's main caldera would be very useful both for science and entertainment.

"OK," Rodriguez said, letting his reluctance show in his voice. "I'm ready whenever you are."

Nodding inside his helmet, Fuchida said, "Then let's get started."

"Be careful now," said Rodriguez as the biologist backed slowly away from him.

Fuchida did not reply. He turned and started over the softly rounded lip of the giant hole in the ground. The caldera was so big that it would take half an hour to sink below the level where Rodriguez could still see him without moving from his station beside the tether winch.

I should have read Dante's Inferno in preparation for this task, Fuchida thought to himself.

The road to hell begins with a gradual slope, he knew. *It will get steep enough soon.*

Then both his booted feet slipped out from under him.

"You OK?" Rodriguez's voice sounded anxious in Fuchida's earphones.

"I hit a slick spot. There must be patches of dry ice coating the rock here in the shadows."

The biologist was lying on his side, his hip throbbing painfully from his fall. *At this rate,* he thought, *I'll be black-and-blue from the waist down.*

"Can you get up?"

"Yes. Certainly." Fuchida felt more embarrassed than hurt. He grabbed angrily at the tether and pulled himself to his feet. Even in the one-third gravity of Mars it took an effort, with the suit and backpack weighing him down. And all the equipment that dangled from his belt and harness.

Once on his feet he stared down once more into the darkness of the caldera's yawning maw. *It's like the mouth of a great beast,* a voice in his mind said. *Like the gateway to the eternal pit.*

He took a deep breath, then said into his helmet microphone, "OK. I'm starting down again."

"Be careful, man."

"Thanks for the advice," Fuchida snapped.

Rodriguez seemed untroubled by his irritation. "Maybe I oughta keep the line tighter," he suggested. "Not so much slack."

Regretting his temper, Fuchida agreed, "Yes, that might help to keep me on my feet." The hip really hurt, and his rump was still sore from his first fall.

I'm lucky I didn't rupture the suit, he thought. *Or damage the backpack.*

"OK, I've adjusted the tension. Take it easy, now."

A journey of a thousand miles must begin with a single step. Mitsuo Fuchida quoted Lao-tzu's ancient dictum as he planted one booted foot on the ground ahead of him. The bare rock seemed to offer good traction.

You can't see the ice, he told himself. It's too thin a coating to be visible. Several dozen meters to his right, sunlight slanted down into the gradually sloping side of the caldera. There'll be no ice there, Fuchida thought. He moved off in that direction, slowly, testing his footing every step of the way.

The tether connected to his harness at his chest, so he could easily disconnect it if necessary. The increased tension of the line made walking all the more difficult. Fuchida felt almost like a marionette on a string.

"Slack off a little," he called to Rodriguez.

"You sure?"

He turned back to look up at his teammate, and was startled to see that the astronaut was nothing more than a tiny blob of a figure up on the rim, standing in bright sunlight with the deep blue sky behind him.

"Yes, I'm certain," he said, with deliberate patience.

A few moments later Rodriguez asked, "How's that?"

The difference was imperceptible, but Fuchida replied, "Better."

He saw a ledge in the sunlight some twenty meters below him and decided to head for it. Slowly, carefully he descended.

"I can't see you." Rodriguez's voice in his earphones sounded only slightly concerned.

Looking up, Fuchida saw the expanse of deep blue sky and nothing else except the gentle slope of the bare rock. And the tether, his lifeline, holding strong.

"It's all right," he said. "I'm using the VR cameras to record my descent. I'm going to stop at a ledge and chip out some rock samples there."

"Hey, Mitsuo," Rodriguez called.

Automatically Fuchida looked up. But the astronaut was beyond his view. Fuchida was alone down on the ledge in the caldera's sloping flank of solid rock. The Buckyball tether that connected him to the winch up above also carried their suit-to-suit radio transmissions.

"What is it?" he replied, grateful to hear Rodriguez's voice.

"How's it going, man?"

"That depends," said Fuchida.

"On what?"

The biologist hesitated. He had been working on this rock ledge for hours, chipping out samples, measuring heat flow, patiently working an auger into the hard basalt to see if there might be water ice trapped in the rock.

He was in shadow now. The sun had moved away. Looking up, he saw with relief that the sky was still a bright blue. It was still daylight up there. Rodriguez would not let him stay down after sunset, he knew, yet he still felt comforted to see that there was still daylight up there.

"It depends," he answered slowly, "on what you are looking for. Whether you are a geologist or a biologist."

"Oh," said Rodriguez.

"A geologist would be very happy here. There is a considerable amount of heat still trapped in these rocks. Much more than can be accounted for by solar warming alone."

"You mean the volcano's still active?"

"No, no, no. It is dead, but the corpse is still warm—a little."

Rodriguez did not reply.

"Do you realize what this means? This volcano must be much younger than was thought. Much younger!"

"How young?"

"Perhaps only a few million years," Fuchida said excitedly. "No more than ten million."

"Sounds pretty damned old to me, amigo."

"But there might be life here! If there is heat, there might be liquid water within the rock."

"I thought water couldn't stay liquid on Mars."

"Not on the surface," Fuchida said, feeling the exhilaration quivering within him. "But deeper down, inside the rock where the pressure is higher . . . maybe . . ."

"Looks pretty dark down there."

"It is," Fuchida answered, peering over the lip of the ledge on which he sat. The suit's heater seemed to be working fine; it might be a hundred below zero in those shadows, but he felt comfortably warm.

"I don't like the idea of your being down there in the dark."

"Neither do I, but that's why we're here, isn't it?"

No answer.

"I mean, we still have several hundred meters of tether to unwind, don't we?"

Rodriguez said, "Eleven hundred and ninety-two, according to the meter."

"So I can go down a long way, then."

"I don't like the dark."

"My helmet lamp is working fine."

"Still . . ."

"Don't worry about it," Fuchida insisted, cutting off the astronaut's worries. It was bad enough to battle his own fears; he wanted no part of Rodriguez's.

"I saw a crevice at the end of this ledge," he told the astronaut. "It looks like the opening of an old lava tube. It probably leads down a considerable distance."

"Do you think that's a good idea?"

"I'll take a look into it."

"Don't take any chances you don't have to."

Fuchida grimaced as he climbed slowly to his feet. His whole body ached from the bruising he'd received in his falls and he felt stiff after sitting on the ledge for so long. Walk carefully, he warned himself. Even though the rock is warmer down here, there could still be patches of ice.

"You hear me?" Rodriguez called.

"If I followed your advice I'd be in my bed in Osaka," he said, trying to make it sound light and witty.

"Yeah, sure."

Stiffly he walked toward the fissure he had seen earlier. His helmet lamp threw a glare of light before him, but he had to bend over slightly to make the light reach the ground.

There it is, he saw. A narrow, slightly rounded hole in the basalt face. Like the mouth of a pirate's cave.

Fuchida took a step into the opening and turned from side to side, playing his helmet lamp on the walls of the cave.

It was a lava tube, he was certain of it. Like a tunnel made by some giant extraterrestrial worm, it curved downward. How far down? he wondered.

Stifling a voice in his head that whispered of fear and danger, Fuchida started into the cold, dark lava tube.

"Jamie," Stacy Dezhurova's voice called out sharply, "we have an emergency message from Rodriguez."

Sitting at the electron microscope in the geology lab, Jamie looked up from the display screen when Dezhurova's voice rang through the dome. He left the core sample in the microscope without turning it off and sprinted across the dome to the comm center.

Dezhurova looked grim as she silently handed Jamie a headset. The other scientists in the dome crowded into the comm center behind him.

Rodriguez's voice was calm but tight with tension. ". . . down there more than two hours now and then radio contact cut off," the astronaut was saying.

Sitting again on the wheeled chair next to Dezhurova as he adjusted the pin microphone, Jamie said, "This is Waterman. What's happening, Tòmas?"

"Mitsuo went down into the caldera as scheduled. He found a lava tube about fifty-sixty meters down and went into it. Then his radio transmission was cut off."

"How long—"

"It's more than half an hour now. I've tried yanking on his tether but I'm getting no response."

"What do you think?"

"Either he's unconscious or his radio's failed. I mean, I really pulled on the tether. Nothing."

The astronaut did not mention the third possibility: that Fuchida was dead. But the thought blazed in Jamie's mind.

"You say your radio contact with him cut off while he was still in the lava tube?"

"Yeah, right. That was more'n half an hour ago."

A thousand possibilities spun through Jamie's mind. The tether's too tough to break, he knew. Those Buckyballs can take tons of tension.

"It's going to be dark soon," Rodriguez said.

"You're going to have to go down after him," Jamie said.

"I know."

"Just go down far enough to see what's happened to him. Find out what's happened and call back here."

"Yeah. Right."

"I don't like it, but that's what you're going to have to do."

"I don't like it much, either," said Rodriguez.

Through a haze of pain, Mitsuo Fuchida saw the irony of the situation. He had made a great discovery but he would probably not live to tell anyone about it.

When he entered the lava tube he felt an unaccustomed sense of dread, like a character in an old horror movie, stepping slowly, fearfully down the narrow corridor of a haunted house, lit only by the flicker of a candle. Except this corridor was a tube melted out of the solid rock by an ancient stream of red-hot lava, and Fuchida's light came from the lamp on his hard suit helmet.

Nonsense! he snapped silently. You are safe in your hard suit, and the tether connects you to Rodriguez, up at the surface. But he called to the astronaut and chatted inanely with him, just to reassure himself that he was not truly cut off from the rest of the universe down in this dark, narrow passageway.

The VR cameras fixed to his helmet were recording everything he saw, but Fuchida thought that only a geologist would be interested in this cramped, claustrophobic tunnel.

The tube slanted downward, its walls fairly smooth, almost glassy in places. The black rock gleamed in the light of his lamp. The tunnel grew narrower in spots, then widened again, although nowhere was it wide enough for him to spread his arms fully.

Perspiration was beading Fuchida's lip and brow, trickling coldly down his ribs. Stop this foolishness, he admonished himself. You've been in tighter caves than this.

He thought of Elizabeth, waiting for him back in Japan, accepting the subtle snubs of deep-seated racism because she loved him and wanted to be with him when he returned. I'll get back to you, he vowed, even if this tunnel leads down to hell itself.

The tether seemed to snag from time to time. He had to stop and tug on it to loosen it again. Or perhaps Rodriguez was fiddling with the tension on the line, he thought.

Deeper into the tunnel he went, stepping cautiously, now and then running his gloved hands over the strangely smooth walls.

Fuchida lost track of time as he chipped at the tunnel walls here and there, filling the sample bags that dangled from his harness belt. The tether made it uncomfortable to push forward, attached to his harness at the chest. It had to pass over his shoulder or around his waist: clumsy, at best.

Then he noticed that the circle of light cast by his helmet lamp showed an indentation off toward the left, a mini-alcove that seemed lighter in color than the rest of the glossy black tunnel walls. Fuchida edged closer to it, leaning slightly into the niche to examine it.

A bubble of lava did this, he thought. The niche was barely big enough for a man to enter. A man not encumbered with a hard suit and bulky backpack, that is. Fuchida stood at the entrance to the narrow niche, peering inside, wondering.

And then he noticed a streak of red, the color of iron rust. Rust? Why here and not elsewhere?

He pushed in closer, squeezing into the narrow opening to inspect the rust spot. Yes, definitely the color of iron rust.

He took a scraper from the tool kit at his waist, nearly fumbling it in his awkwardly gloved fingers. If I drop it I won't be able to bend down to pick it up, not in this narrow cleft, he realized.

The red stain crumbled at the touch of the scraper. Strange! thought Fuchida. Not like the basalt at all. Could it be . . . wet? No! Liquid water cannot exist at this low air pressure. But what is the pressure inside the rock? Perhaps . . .

The red stuff crumbled easily into the sample bag he held beneath it with trembling fingers. It must be iron oxide that is being eroded by water, somehow. Water and iron. Siderophiles! Bacteria that metabolize iron and water!

Fuchida was as certain of it as he was of his own existence. His heart was racing. A colony of iron-loving bacteria living inside the caldera of Olympus Mons! Who knew what else might be found deeper down?

It was only when he sealed up the sample bag and placed it in the plastic box dangling from his belt that he heard the strange rumbling sound. Through the thickness of his helmet it sounded muted, far-off, but still any sound at all this deep in the tunnel was startling.

Fuchida started to back away from the crumbling, rust-red cleft. The rumbling sound seemed to grow louder, like the growl of some prowling beast. It was nonsense, of course, but he thought the tunnel walls were shaking slightly, trembling. It's you who are trembling, foolish man! he admonished himself.

Something in the back of his mind said, Fear is healthy. It is nothing to be ashamed of, if you—

The rusted area of rock dissolved into a burst of exploding steam that lifted Fuchida off his feet and slammed him painfully against the far wall of the lava tube.

Fuchida nearly blacked out as his head banged against the back of his helmet. He sagged to the floor of the tunnel, his visor completely fogged, his skull thundering with pain.

With a teeth-gritting effort of iron will he kept himself from slipping into unconsciousness. Despite the pounding in his head, he forced himself to stay awake, alert. Do not faint! he commanded himself. Do not allow yourself to take the cowardly way. You must remain awake if you hope to remain alive. He felt perspiration beading his forehead, dripping into his eyes, forcing him to blink and squint.

Then a wave of anger swept over him. How stupid you are! he railed at himself. A hydrothermal vent. Water. Liquid water, here on Mars. You should have known. You should have guessed. The heat flow, the rusted iron. There must be siderophiles here, bacteria that metabolize iron and water. They weakened the wall and you scraped enough of it away for the pressure to blow through the wall.

Yes, he agreed with himself. Now that you've made the discovery, you must live to report it to the rest of the world.

His visor was still badly fogged. Fuchida groped for the control stud at his wrist that would turn up his suit fans and clear the visor. He thought he found the right keypad and pushed it. Nothing changed. In fact, now that he listened for it, he could not hear the soft buzz of his suit fans at all. Except for his own labored breathing, there was nothing but silence.

Wait. Be calm. Think.

Call Rodriguez. Tell him what's happened.

"Tòmas, I've had a little accident."

No response.

"Rodriguez! Can you hear me?"

Silence.

Slowly, carefully, he flexed both his arms, then his legs. His body ached, but there didn't seem to be any broken bones. Still the air fans remained silent, and beads of sweat dripped into his eyes.

Blinking, squinting, he saw that the visor was beginning to clear up on its own. The hydrothermal vent must have been a weak one, he thought thankfully. He could hear no more rumbling; the tunnel did not seem to be shaking now.

Almost reluctantly, he wormed his arm up to eye level and held the wrist keyboard close to his visor. The keyboard was blank. Electrical malfunction! Frantically he tapped at the keyboard: nothing. Heater, heat exchanger, air fans, radio—all gone.

I'm a dead man.

Cold panic hit him like a blow to the heart. That's why you no longer hear the air circulation fans! The suit battery must have been damaged when I slammed against the wall.

Fuchida could hear his pulse thundering in his ears. Calm down! he commanded himself. That's not so bad. The suit has enough air in it for an hour or so. And it's insulated very thoroughly; you won't freeze—not for several hours, at least. You can get by without the air circulation fans. For a while.

It was when he tried to stand up that the real fear hit him. His right ankle flared with agony. Broken or badly sprained, Fuchida realized. I can't stand on it. I can't get out of here.

Then the irony really struck him. I might be the first man to die of heat prostration on Mars.

The problem is, Rodriguez said to himself, that we only have one climbing harness and Mitsuo's wearing it.

I've got to go down there without a tether, without any of the climbing tools that he's carrying with him.

Shit!

The alternative, he knew, was to leave the biologist and return to the safety of the plane. Rodriguez shook his head inside his helmet. Can't leave him. It's already getting dark and he'd never survive overnight.

On the other hand, there's a damned good chance that we'll both die down there.

Double shit.

For long, useless moments he stared down into the dark depths of the caldera, in complete shadow now as the sun crept closer to the distant horizon.

Never show fear, Rodriguez repeated to himself. Not even to yourself. He nodded inside his helmet. Yeah, easy to say. Now get the snakes in my guts to believe it.

Still, he started down, walking slowly, deliberately, gripping the tether hand-over-hand as he descended.

It became totally dark within a few steps of leaving the caldera's rim. The only light was the patch of glow cast by his helmet lamp, and the dark rock all around him seemed to swallow that up greedily. He planted his booted feet carefully, deliberately, knowing that carbon dioxide from the air was already starting to freeze out on the bitterly cold rock.

Rodriguez cast a glance up at the dimming sky, like a prisoner taking his last desperate look at freedom before entering his dungeon.

At least I can follow the tether, he thought. He moved with ponderous deliberation, worried about slipping on patches of ice. If I get disabled we're both toast, he told himself. Take it easy. Don't rush it. Don't make any mistakes.

Slowly, slowly he descended. By the time the tether led him to the mouth of the lava tube, he could no longer see the scant slice of sky above; it was completely black. If there were stars winking at him up there he could not see them through the tinted visor of his helmet.

He peered into the tunnel. It was like staring into a well of blackness.

"Hey, Mitsuo!" he called. "Can you hear me?"

No response. He's either dead or unconscious. Rodriguez thought. He's laying deep down that tunnel someplace and I've got to go find him. Or what's left of him.

He took a deep breath. No fear, he reminded himself.

Down the dark tunnel he plodded, ignoring the fluttering of his innards, paying no attention to the voice in his head that told him he'd gone far enough, the guy's dead, no sense getting yourself killed down here too so get the hell out, now.

Can't leave him, Rodriguez shouted silently at the voice. Dead or alive, I can't leave him down here.

Your funeral, the voice countered.

Yeah, sure. I get back to the base OK without him. What're they gonna think of me? How'm I—

He saw the slumped form of the biologist, a lump of hard suit and equipment sitting against one wall of the tunnel.

"Hey, Mitsuo!" he called.

The inert form did not move.

Rodriguez hurried to the biologist and tried to peer into the visor of his helmet. It looked badly fogged.

"Mitsuo," he shouted. "You OK?" It sounded idiotic the moment the words left his lips.

But Fuchida suddenly reached up and gripped his shoulders.

"You're alive!"

Still no answer. His radio's out, Rodriguez finally realized. And the air's too thin to carry my voice.

He touched his helmet against Fuchida's. "Hey, man, what happened?"

"Battery," the biologist replied, his voice muffled but understandable. "Battery not working. And my ankle. Can't walk."

"Jesus! Can you stand up if I prop you?"

"I don't know. My air fans are down. I'm afraid to move; I don't want to generate any extra body heat."

Shit, said Rodriguez to himself. Am I gonna have to carry him all the way up to the surface?

Sitting there trapped like a stupid schoolboy on his first exploration of a cave, Fuchida wished he had paid more attention to his Buddhist instructors. This would be a good time to meditate, to reach for inner peace and attain a calm alpha state. Or was it beta state?

With his suit fans inoperative, the circulation of air inside the heavily insulated hard suit was almost nonexistent. Heat generated by his body could not be transferred to the heat exchanger in the backpack; the temperature inside the suit was climbing steadily.

Worse, it was more and more difficult to get the carbon dioxide he exhaled out of the suit and into the air recycler. He could choke to death on his own fumes.

The answer was to be as still as possible, not to move, not even to blink. Be calm. Achieve nothingness. Do not stir. Wait. Wait for help.

Rodriguez will come for me, he told himself. Tòmas won't leave me here to die. He'll come for me.

Will he come in time? Fuchida tried to shut the possibility of death out of his thoughts, but he knew that it was the ultimate inevitability.

The hell of it is, I'm certain I have a bag full of siderophiles! I'll be famous. Posthumously.

Then he saw the bobbing light of a helmet lamp approaching. He nearly blubbered with relief. Rodriguez appeared, a lumbering robotlike creature in the bulky hard suit. To Fuchida he looked sweeter than an angel.

Once Rodriguez realized that he had to touch helmets to be heard, he asked, "How in the hell did you get yourself banged up like this?"

"Hydrothermal vent," Fuchida replied. "It knocked me clear across the tunnel." Rodriguez grunted. "Old Faithful strikes on Mars."

Fuchida tried to laugh; what came out was a shaky coughing giggle.

"Can you move? Get up?"

"I think so . . ." Slowly, with Rodriguez lifting from beneath his armpits, Fuchida got to his feet. He took a deep breath, then coughed. When he tried to put some weight on his bad ankle he nearly collapsed.

"Take it easy, buddy. Lean on me. We got to get you back to the plane before you choke to death."

Rodriguez had forgotten about the ice.

He half-dragged Fuchida along the tunnel, the little pools of light made by their helmet lamps the only break in the total, overwhelming darkness around them.

"How you doing, buddy?" he asked the Japanese biologist. "Talk to me."

Leaning his helmet against the astronaut's, Fuchida answered, "I feel hot. Broiling."

"You're lucky. I'm freezing my ass off. I think my suit heater's crapping out on me."

"I . . . I don't know how long I can last without the air fans," Fuchida said, his voice trembling slightly. "I feel a little lightheaded."

"No problem," Rodriguez replied, with a false heartiness. "It'll get kinda stuffy inside your suit, but you won't asphyxiate."

The first American astronaut to take an EVA spacewalk outside his capsule had almost collapsed from heat prostration, Rodriguez remembered. The damned suits hold all your body heat inside; that's why they make us wear the watercooled longjohns and put heat exchangers in the suits. But if the fans can't circulate the air the exchanger's pretty damned useless.

Rodriguez kept one hand on the tether. In the wan light from his helmet lamp he saw that it led upward, out of this abyss.

"We'll be back in the plane in half an hour, maybe less. I can fix your backpack then."

"Good," said Fuchida. Then he coughed again.

It seemed to take hours before they got out of the tunnel, back onto the ledge in the slope of the giant caldera.

"Come on, grab the tether. We're goin' up."

"Right."

But Rodriguez's boot slipped and he fell to his knees with a painful thump.

"Damn," he muttered. "It's slick."

"The ice."

The astronaut rocked back onto his haunches, both knees throbbing painfully.

"It's too slippery to climb?" Fuchida's voice was edging toward panic.

"Yeah. We're gonna have to haul ourselves up with the winch." He got down onto his belly and motioned the biologist to do the same.

"Isn't this dangerous? What if we tear our suits?"

Rodriguez rapped on the shoulder of Fuchida's suit. "Tough as steel, amigo. They won't rip."

"You're certain?"

"You wanna spend the night down here?"

Fuchida grabbed the tether with both his hands.

Grinning to himself, Rodriguez also grasped the tether and told Fuchida to activate the winch.

But within seconds he felt the tether slacken.

"Stop!"

"What's wrong?" Fuchida asked.

Rodriguez gave the tether a few light tugs. It felt loose, its original tension gone. "Holy shit," he muttered.

"What is it?"

"The weight of both of us on the line is too much for the rig to hold. We're pulling it out of the ground up there."

"You mean we're stuck here?"

"I see that none of us are going to get any sleep."

Stacy Dezhurova was smiling as she spoke, but her bright blue eyes were dead serious. Trudy Hall was still on duty at the comm console. Stacy sat beside her while Jamie paced slowly back and forth behind her. Vijay Shektar, the expedition doctor, had pulled in another chair and sat by the doorway, watching them all.

The comm center cubicle felt stuffy and hot with all four of them crowded in there. Jamie did not answer Dezhurova's remark; he just kept on pacing, five strides from one partition to the other, then back again.

"Rodriguez must have found him by now," Hall said, swivelling her chair slightly toward Stacy.

"Then why doesn't he call in?" she demanded, almost angrily.

"They must still be down inside the caldera," Jamie said.

"It's night," Stacy pointed out.

Jamie nodded and kept pacing.

"It's the waiting that's the worst," Vijay offered. "Not knowing what—"

"This is Rodriguez," the radio speaker crackled. "We got a little problem here."

Jamie was at the comm console like a shot, leaning between the two women.

"What's happening, Tòmas?"

"Fuchida's alive. But his backpack's banged up and his battery's not functioning. Heater, air fans, nothing in his suit's working." Rodriguez's voice sounded tense but in control, like a pilot whose jet engine had just flamed out: trouble, but nothing that can't be handled. Until you hit the ground.

Then he added, "We're stuck on a ledge about thirty meters down and can't get back up 'cause the rock's coated with dry ice and it's too slippery to climb."

As the astronaut went on to describe how the tether winch almost pulled out of its supports when the two of them tried to haul themselves up the slope, Jamie tapped Hall on the shoulder and told her to pull up the specs on the hard suit's air circulation system.

"OK," he said when Rodriguez stopped talking. "Are either of you hurt?"

"I'm bruised a little. Mitsuo's got a bad ankle. He can't stand on it."

One of the screens on the console now showed a diagram of the suit's air circulation system. Hall was scrolling through a long list on the screen next to it.

"Mitsuo, how do you feel?" Jamie asked, stalling for time, time to think, time to get the information he needed.

"His radio's down," Rodriguez said. A hesitation, then, "But he says he's hot. Sweating."

Vijay nodded and murmured, "Hyperthermia."

Strangely, Rodriguez chuckled. "Mitsuo also says he discovered siderophiles, inside the caldera! He wants Trudy to know that."

"I heard it," Hall said, still scrolling down the suit specs. "Did he get samples?"

Again a wait, then Rodriguez replied, "Yep. There's water in the rock. Liquid water. Mitsuo says you've gotta publish . . . get it out on the Net."

"Liquid?" Hall stopped the scrolling. Her eyes went wide. "Are you certain about—"

"Never mind that now," Jamie said, studying the numbers on Hall's screen. "According to the suit specs you can get enough breathable air for two hours, at least, even with the fans off."

"We can't wait down here until daylight, then," Rodriguez said.

Jamie said, "Tòmas, is Mitsuo's harness still connected to the winch?"

"Far as I can see, yeah. But if we try to use the winch to haul us up it's gonna yank the rig right out of the ground."

"Then Mitsuo's got to go up by himself."

"By himself?"

"Right," Jamie said. "Let the winch pull Mitsuo up to the top. Then he takes off the harness and sends it back to you so you can get up. Understand?"

In the pale light of the helmet lamps, Fuchida could not see Rodriguez's face behind his tinted visor. But he knew what the astronaut must be feeling.

Pressing his helmet against Rodriguez's, he said, "I can't leave you down here alone, without even the tether." Rodriguez's helmet mike must have picked up his voice, because Waterman replied, iron hard, "No arguments, Mitsuo. You drag your butt up there and send the harness back down. It shouldn't take more than a few minutes to get you both up to the top."

Fuchida started to object, but Rodriguez cut him off. "OK, Jamie. Sounds good. We'll call you from the top when we get there."

Fuchida heard the connection click off.

"I can't leave you here," he said, feeling almost desperate.

"That's what you've got to do, man. Otherwise neither one of us will make it."

"Then you go first and send the harness back down to me."

"No way," Rodriguez said. "You're the scientist, you're more important. I'm the astronaut, I'm trained to deal with dangerous situations."

Fuchida said, "But it's my fault—"

"Bullshit," Rodriguez snapped. Then he added, "Besides, I'm bigger and meaner than you. Now get going and stop wasting time!"

"How will you find the harness in the dark? It could be dangling two meters from your nose and your helmet lamp won't pick it up."

Rodriguez made a huffing sound, almost a snort. "Tie one of the beacons to it and turn on the beacon light."

Fuchida felt mortified. I should have thought of that. It's so simple. I must be truly rattled, my mind is not functioning as it should.

"Now go on," Rodriguez said. "Get down on your belly again and start up the winch."

"Wait," Fuchida said. "There is something—"

"What?" Rodriguez demanded impatiently.

Fuchida hesitated, then spoke all in a rush. "If . . . if I don't make it . . . if I die . . . would you contact someone for me when you get back to Earth?"

"You're not gonna die."

"Her name is Elizabeth Vernon," Fuchida went on, afraid that if he stopped he would not be able to resume. "She's a lab assistant in the biology department of the University of Tokyo. Tell her . . . that I love her."

Rodriguez understood the importance of his companion's words. "Your girl-friend's not Japanese?"

"My wife," Fuchida answered.

Rodriguez whistled softly. Then, "OK, Mitsuo. Sure. I'll tell her. But you can tell her yourself. You're not gonna die."

"Of course. But if . . ."

"Yeah. I know. Now get going!"

Reluctantly, Fuchida did as he was told. He felt terribly afraid of a thousand possibilities, from tearing his suit to leaving his partner in the dark to freeze to death. But he felt more afraid of remaining there and doing nothing.

Worse, he felt hot. Stifling inside the suit. Gritting his teeth, he held on to the tether with all the pressure the servo-motors on his gloves could apply. Then he realized that he needed one hand free to work the winch control on his climbing harness.

He fumbled for the control stud, desperately trying to remember which one started the winch. He found it and pressed. For an instant nothing happened.

Then suddenly he was yanked off the ledge and dragged up the hard rock face of the caldera's slope, his suit grinding, grating, screeching against the rough rock.

I'll never make it. Fuchida realized. Even if the suit doesn't break apart, I'll suffocate in here before I reach the top.

Rodriguez watched Fuchida slither up and away from him, a dim pool of light that receded slowly but steadily. Through the insulation of his helmet he could not hear the noise of the biologist's hard suit grating against the ice-rimed rock; he heard nothing but his own breathing, faster than it should have been. Calm down, he ordered himself. Keep calm and everything'll turn out OK.

Sure, a sardonic voice in his head answered. Nothing to it. Piece of cake.

Then he realized that he was totally, utterly alone in the darkness.

It's OK, he told himself. Mitsuo'll send the harness down and then I can winch myself up.

The light cast by his helmet lamp was only a feeble glow against the dark rough rock face. When Rodriguez turned, the light was swallowed by the emptiness of the caldera's abyss, deep and wide and endless.

The darkness surrounded him. It was as if there was no one else in the whole universe, no universe at all, only the all-engulfing darkness of this cold, black pit.

Unbidden, a line from some play he had read years earlier in school came to his mind:

Why, this is hell, nor am I out of it.

Don't be a goon! he snapped at himself. You'll be OK. Your suit's working fine and Mitsuo's up there by now, taking off the harness and getting ready to send it down to you.

Yeah, sure. He could be unconscious, he could be snagged on a rock or maybe the damned harness broke while the winch was dragging him up the slope.

Rodriguez put a gloved hand against the solid rock to steady himself. You'll be out of this soon, he repeated silently. Then he wondered if his lamp's light was weakening. Are the batteries starting to run down?

Fuchida's head was banging against the inside of his helmet so hard he tasted blood in his mouth. He squeezed his eyes shut and saw his father's stern, uncompromising glare. How disappointed he will be when he learns that I died on Mars, like cousin Konoye.

And Elizabeth. Perhaps it's better this way. She can go back to Ireland and find a man of her own culture to marry. My death will spare her a lifetime of troubles.

The winch stopped suddenly and Fuchida felt a pang of terror. It's stuck! He realized at that moment that he was not prepared for death. He did not want to die. Not here on Mars. Not at all.

A baleful red eye was staring at him. Fuchida thought for a moment he might be slipping into unconsciousness, then slowly realized that it was the light atop one of the geo/met beacons they had planted at the lip of the caldera.

Straining his eyes in the starlit darkness, he thought he could make out the form of the winch looming above his prostate body. He reached out and touched it.

Yes! He had reached the top. But he felt faint, giddy. His body was soaked with perspiration. Heat prostration, he thought. How funny to die of heat prostration when the temperature outside my suit is nearly two hundred degrees below zero.

He began to laugh, knowing he was slipping into hysteria and unable to stop himself. Until he began coughing uncontrollably.

Down on the ledge, Rodriguez tried to keep his own terrors at bay.

"Mitsuo," he called on the suit-to-suit frequency. "You OK?"

No answer. Of course, dummy! His radio's not working. The cold seemed to be leaching into his suit. Cold enough to freeze carbon dioxide. Cold enough to overpower the suit's heater. Cold enough to kill.

"Get up there, Mitsuo," he whispered. "Get up there in one piece and send the damned tether back down to me."

He wouldn't leave me here. Not if he made it to the top. He wouldn't run for the plane and leave me here. He can't run, anyway. Can't even walk. But he could make it to the plane once he's up there. Hobble, jump on one leg. He wouldn't do that. He wouldn't leave me alone to die down here. Something must've happened to him. He must be hurt or unconscious.

The memory of his big brother's death came flooding back to him. In a sudden rush he saw Luis's bloody mangled body as the rescue workers lifted him out of the wrecked semi. A police chase on the freeway. All those years his brother had been running drugs up from Tijuana in his eighteen-wheeler and Tòmas never knew, never even suspected. There was nothing he could do. By the time he saw Luis's rig sprawled along the shoulder of the highway it was already too late.

He saw himself standing, impotent, inert, as his brother was pronounced dead and then slid into the waiting ambulance and carried away. Just like that. Death can strike like a lightning bolt.

What could I have done to save him? Rodriguez wondered for the thousandth time. I should have done something. But I was too busy being a flyboy, training to be an astronaut. I didn't have time for the family, for my own brother.

He took a deep, sighing breath of canned air. Well, now it's going to even out. I got all the way to Mars, and now I'm gonna die here.

Then he heard his brother's soft, musical voice. "No fear, muchacho. Never show fear. Not even to yourself."

Rodriguez felt no fear. Just a deep eternal sadness that he did not help Luis when help was needed. And now it was all going to end. All the regrets, all the hopes, everything . . .

For an instant he thought he saw a flash of dim red light against the rock wall. He blinked. Nothing. He looked up, but the top of his helmet cut off his view. Grasping at straws, he told himself. You want to see something bad enough, you'll see it, even if it isn't really there.

But the dim red glow flashed again, and this time when he blinked it didn't go away. Damned helmets! he raged. Can't see anything unless it's in front of your fuckin' face.

He tried to tilt his whole upper body back a little, urgently aware that it wouldn't take much to slip off this ledge and go toppling down into the bottomless caldera.

And there it was! The red glow of the beacon's light swayed far above him, like the unwinking eye of an all-seeing savior.

He leaned against the rock face again. His legs felt weak, rubbery. Shit, man, you were really scared.

He could make out the dangling form of the harness now, with the telescoped pole of the beacon attached to it by duct tape. Where the hell did Mitsuo get duct tape? he wondered. He must've been carrying it with him all along. The universal cure-all. We could do a commercial for the stuff when we get back to Earth. Save your life on Mars with friggin' duct tape.

It seemed to take an hour for the tiny red light to get close enough to grab. With hands that trembled only slightly, Rodriguez reached up and grabbed the beacon, ripped it free and worked his arms into the climbing harness. Then he snapped its fasteners shut and gave the tether an experimental tug. It felt strong, good.

He started to reach for the control stud that would activate the winch. Then he caught himself. "Wait one," he whispered, in the clipped tone of the professional flier.

He bent down and picked up the beacon. Sliding it open to its full length, he worked its pointed end into a crack in the basalt rock face. It probably won't stay in place for long, he thought, and it won't work at all unless the sun shines on it for a few hours per day. But he felt satisfied that he had left a reminder that men from Earth had been here, had entered the pit and gleaned at least some of its secrets and survived — maybe.

"OK," he said to himself, grasping the tether with one hand. "Here we go."

He pushed on the control stud and was hauled off his feet. Grinding, twisting, grating, he felt himself pulled up the rock slope, his head banging inside his helmet, his legs and booted feet bouncing as he was dragged upward.

Worse than any simulator ride he'd ever been through in training. Worse than the high-g centrifuge they'd whirled him in. They'll never put this ride into Disneyland, Rodriguez thought, teeth clacking as he bounced, jounced, jolted up to the lip of the caldera.

At last it was over. Rodriguez lay panting, breathless, aching. Fuchida's hard-suited form lay on the ground next to him, unmoving.

Rodriguez rolled over on one side, as far as his backpack would allow. Beyond Fuchida's dark silhouette the sky was filled with stars. Dazzling bright friendly stars gleaming down at him, like a thousand thousand jewels. Like heaven itself.

I made it, Rodriguez told himself. Then he corrected: Not yet. Can't say that yet.

He touched his helmet to Fuchida's. "Hey, Mitsuo! You OK?"

It was an inane question and he knew it. Fuchida made no response, but Rodriguez thought that he could hear the biologist's breathing: panting, really, shallow and fast.

Gotta get him to the plane. Can't do a thing for him out here.

As quickly as he could Rodriguez unbuckled the climbing harness, then tenderly lifted the unconscious Fuchida and struggled to his feet. Good thing we're on Mars. I could never lift him in his suit in a full g. Now where the hell is the plane?

In the distance he saw the single red eye of another one of the geo/met beacons they had planted. He headed in that direction, tenderly carrying his companion in his arms.

I couldn't do this for you, Luis, Rodriguez said silently. I wish I could have, but this is the most I can do.

The base dome was dark and silent, its lighting turned down to sleep shift level, its plastic skin opaqued to prevent heat from leaking out into the Martian night. Stacy Dezhurova was still sitting at the comm console, drowsing despite herself, when Rodriguez's call came through.

"We're back in the plane," the astronaut announced without preamble. "Lemme talk to Vijay."

"Vijay!" Stacy shouted in a voice that shattered the sleepy silence. "Jamie!" she added.

Running footsteps padded through the shadows, bare or stockinged feet against the plastic flooring. Vijay, the physician, slipped into a chair beside Dezhurova, her jet-black eyes wide open and alert. Jamie and Tracy Hall raced in, bleary-eyed, and stood behind the two women.

"This is Vijay," she said. "What's your condition?"

In the display screen they could see only the two men's helmets and shoulders. Their faces were masked by the heavily tinted visors. But Rodriguez's voice sounded steady, firm.

"I'm OK. Banged up a little, but that's nothing. I purged Mitsuo's suit and plugged him into the plane's emergency air supply. But he's still out of it."

"How long ago did you do that?" Vijay asked, her dark face rigid with tension.

"Fifteen—sixteen minutes ago."

"And you're just calling in now?" Dezhurova demanded.

"I had to fix his battery pack," Rodriguez answered, unruffled by her tone. "It got disconnected when he was knocked down—"

"Knocked down?" Jamie blurted.

"Yeah. That's when he hurt his ankle."

"How badly is he hurt?" Vijay asked.

"It's sprained, at least. Maybe a break."

"He couldn't break a bone inside the suit," Jamie muttered. "Not with all that protection."

"Anyway," Rodriguez resumed, "his suit wasn't getting any power. I figured that getting his suit powered up was the second most important thing to do. Pumping fresh air into him was the first."

"And calling in, the third," Dezhurova said, much more mildly.

"Right," said Rodriguez.

"I'm getting his readouts," Vijay said, studying the medical diagnostic screen.

"Yeah, his suit's OK now that the battery's reconnected."

"Is his LCG working?" Vijay asked.

"Should be," Rodriguez said. "Wait one . . ."

They saw the astronaut lean over and touch his helmet to the unconscious Fuchida's shoulder.

"Yep," he announced, after a moment. "I can hear the pump chugging. Water oughtta be circulating through his longjohns just fine."

"That should bring his temperature down," Vijay muttered, half to herself. "The problem is, he might be in shock from overheating."

"What do I do about that?" Rodriguez asked.

The physician shook her head. "Not much you can do, mate. Especially with the two of you sealed into your suits."

For a long moment they were all silent. Vijay stared at the medical screen. Fuchida's temperature was coming down. Heart rate slowing nicely. Breathing almost normal. He should be—

The biologist coughed and stirred. "What happened?" he asked weakly.

All four of the people at the comm center broke into grins. None of them could see Rodriguez's face behind his visor, but they heard the relief in his voice:

"Naw, Mitsuo; you're supposed to ask, 'Where am I?' "

The biologist sat up straighter. "Is Tracy there?"

"Don't worry about—"

"I'm right here, Mitsuo," said Tracy Hall, leaning in between Dezhurova and Vijay Shektar. "What is it?"

"Siderophiles!" Fuchida exclaimed. "Iron-eating bacteria live in the caldera."

"Did you get samples?"

"Yes, of course."

Jamie stepped back as the two biologists chattered together. *Fuchida nearly gets himself killed, but what's important to him is finding a new kind of organism.* With an inward smile, Jamie admitted, *maybe he's right.*

Jamie awoke the instant the dome's lighting turned up to daytime level. He pushed back the thin sheet that covered him and got to his feet. After the long night they had all put in, he should have felt tired, drained. Yet he was awake, alert, eager to start the day.

Quickly he stepped to his desk and booted up his laptop, then opened the communications channel to Rodriguez and Fuchida. With a glance at the desktop clock he saw that it was six-thirty-three. He hesitated for only a moment, though, then put through a call to the two men at Olympus Mons.

As he suspected, they were both awake. Jamie's laptop screen showed the two of them side-by-side in the plane's cockpit.

"Good morning," he said. "Did you sleep well?"

"Extremely well," said Fuchida.

"This cockpit looked like the best hotel suite in the world when we got into it last night," Rodriguez said.

Jamie nodded. "Yeah, I guess it did."

Rodriguez gave a crisp, terse morning report. Fuchida happily praised the astronaut for purging his suit of the foul air and fixing the electrical connection that had worked loose in his backpack.

"My suit fans are buzzing faithfully," he said. "But I'm afraid I won't be able to do much useful work on my bad ankle."

They had discussed the ankle injury the previous night, once Fuchida had regained consciousness. Vijay guessed that it was a sprain, but wanted to get the biologist back to the dome as quickly as possible for an X ray.

Jamie had decided to let Rodriguez carry out as much of their planned work as he could, alone, before returning. Their schedule called for another half day on the mountaintop, then a takeoff in the early afternoon for the flight back to dome. They should land at the base well before sunset.

"I'll be happy to take off this suit," Fuchida confessed.

"We're not gonna smell so good when we do," Rodriguez added.

Jamie found himself peering hard at the small screen of his laptop, trying to see past their visors. Impossible, of course. But they both sounded cheerful enough.

The fears and dangers of the previous night were gone, daylight and the relative safety of the plane brightened their outlook.

Rodriguez said, "We've decided that I'm going back down inside the caldera and properly implant the beacon we left on the ledge there."

"So we can get good data from it," Fuchida added, as if he were afraid Jamie would countermand his decision.

Jamie asked, "Do you really think you should try that?"

"Oughtta be simple enough," Rodriguez said easily, "long as we don't go near that damned lava tube again."

"That's the imperial 'we,'" Fuchida explained. "I'm staying here in the plane, I'm afraid."

"Is there enough sunlight where you want to plant the beacon?" Jamie asked.

He sensed the biologist nodding inside his helmet. "Oh yes, the ledge receives a few hours of sunlight each day."

"So we'll get data from inside the caldera," Rodriguez prompted.

"Not very far inside," Fuchida added, "but it will better than no data at all."

"You're really set on doing this?"

"Yes," they both said. Jamie could feel their determination. It was their little victory over Olympus Mons, their way of telling themselves that they were not afraid of the giant volcano.

"OK, then," Jamie said. "But be careful, now."

"We're always careful," said Fuchida.

"Most of the time," Rodriguez added, with a laugh.

Border Guards

GREG EGAN

Poised as we are on the brink of a new century, looking back at the century that's getting ready to end, it's obvious that Australian writer Greg Egan was one of the Big New Names to emerge in SF in the nineties, and is probably one of the most significant talents to enter the field in the last several decades. Already one of the most widely known of all Australian genre writers, Egan may well be the best new "hard-science" writer to enter the field since Greg Bear, and is still growing in range, power, and sophistication. In the last few years, he has become a frequent contributor to Interzone and Asimov's Science Fiction, and has made sales as well to Pulphouse, Analog, Aurealis, Eidolon, and elsewhere; many of his stories have also appeared in various "Best of the Year" series, and he was on the Hugo Final Ballot in 1995 for his story "Cocoon," which won the Ditmar Award and the Asimov's Readers Award. In 1999, he won the Hugo Award for his novella "Oceanic." His first novel, Quarantine, appeared in 1992, to wide critical acclaim, and was followed by a second novel in 1994, Permutation City, which won the John W. Campbell Memorial Award. His other books include the novels Distress and Diaspora, and three collections of his short fiction, Axiomatic, Luminous, and Our Lady of Chernobyl. His most recent book is a major new novel, Teranesia. His stories have appeared in our Seventh, Eighth, Ninth, Tenth, Eleventh, Twelfth, Thirteenth, Fifteenth, and Sixteenth Annual Collections. He has a web site at http://www.netspace.net.au/~gregegan/.

Here he takes us deep into the far-future, for a complex and brilliantly imagined study of old loyalties and new possibilities.

I n the early afternoon of his fourth day out of sadness, Jamil was wandering home from the gardens at the centre of Noether when he heard shouts from the playing field behind the library. On the spur of the moment, without even asking the city what game was in progress, he decided to join in.

As he rounded the corner and the field came into view, it was clear from the movements of the players that they were in the middle of a quantum soccer match.

At Jamil's request, the city painted the wave function of the hypothetical ball across his vision, and tweaked him to recognize the players as the members of two teams without changing their appearance at all. Maria had once told him that she always chose a literal perception of colour-coded clothing instead; she had no desire to use pathways that had evolved for the sake of sorting people into those you defended and those you slaughtered. But almost everything that had been bequeathed to them was stained with blood, and to Jamil it seemed a far sweeter victory to adapt the worst relics to his own ends than to discard them as irretrievably tainted.

The wave function appeared as a vivid auroral light, a quicksilver plasma bright enough to be distinct in the afternoon sunlight, yet unable to dazzle the eye or conceal the players running through it. Bands of colour representing the complex phase of the wave swept across the field, parting to wash over separate rising lobes of probability before hitting the boundary and bouncing back again, inverted. The match was being played by the oldest, simplest rules: semi-classical, non-relativistic. The ball was confined to the field by an infinitely high barrier, so there was no question of it tunnelling out, leaking away as the match progressed. The players were treated classically: their movements pumped energy into the wave, enabling transitions from the game's opening state — with the ball spread thinly across the entire field — into the range of higher-energy modes needed to localize it. But localization was fleeting; there was no point forming a nice sharp wave packet in the middle of the field in the hope of kicking it around like a classical object. You had to shape the wave in such a way that all of its modes — cycling at different frequencies, travelling with different velocities — would come into phase with each other, for a fraction of a second, within the goal itself. Achieving that was a matter of energy levels, and timing.

Jamil had noticed that one team was under-strength. The umpire would be skewing the field's potential to keep the match fair; but a new participant would be especially welcome for the sake of restoring symmetry. He watched the faces of the players, most of them old friends. They were frowning with concentration, but breaking now and then into smiles of delight at their small successes, or their opponents' ingenuity.

He was badly out of practice, but if he turned out to be dead weight he could always withdraw. And if he misjudged his skills, and lost the match with his incompetence? No one would care. The score was nil all; he could wait for a goal, but that might be an hour or more in coming. Jamil communed with the umpire, and discovered that the players had decided in advance to allow new entries at any time.

Before he could change his mind, he announced himself. The wave froze, and he ran onto the field. People nodded greetings, mostly making no fuss, though Ezequiel shouted, "Welcome back!" Jamil suddenly felt fragile again; though he'd ended his long seclusion four days before, it was well within his power, still, to be dismayed by everything the game would involve. His recovery felt like a finely balanced optical illusion, a figure and ground that could change roles in an instant, a solid cube that could evert into a hollow.

The umpire guided him to his allotted starting position, opposite a woman he hadn't seen before. He offered her a formal bow, and she returned the gesture. This was no time for introductions, but he asked the city if she'd published a name. She had: Margit.

The umpire counted down in their heads. Jamil tensed, regretting his impulsiveness. For seven years he'd been dead to the world. After four days back, what was he good for? His muscles were incapable of atrophy, his reflexes could never be dulled, but he'd chosen to live with an unconstrained will, and at any moment his wavering resolve could desert him.

The umpire said, "Play." The frozen light around Jamil came to life, and he sprang into motion.

Each player was responsible for a set of modes, particular harmonics of the wave that were theirs to fill, guard, or deplete as necessary. Jamil's twelve modes cycled at between 1,000 and 1,250 milliHertz. The rules of the game endowed his body with a small, fixed potential energy, which repelled the ball slightly and allowed different modes to push and pull on each other through him, but if he stayed in one spot as the modes cycled, every influence he exerted would eventually be replaced by its opposite, and the effect would simply cancel itself out.

To drive the wave from one mode to another, you needed to move, and to drive it efficiently you needed to exploit the way the modes fell in and out of phase with each other: to take from a 1,000 milliHertz mode and give to a 1,250, you had to act in synch with the quarter-Hertz beat between them. It was like pushing a child's swing at its natural frequency, but rather than setting a single child in motion, you were standing between two swings and acting more as an intermediary: trying to time your interventions in such a way as to speed up one child at the other's expense. The way you pushed on the wave at a given time and place was out of your hands completely, but by changing location in just the right way you could gain control over the interaction. Every pair of modes had a spatial beat between them — like the moiré pattern formed by two sheets of woven fabric held up to the light together, shifting from transparent to opaque as the gaps between the threads fell in and out of alignment. Slicing through this cyclic landscape offered the perfect means to match the accompanying chronological beat.

Jamil sprinted across the field at a speed and angle calculated to drive two favourable transitions at once. He'd gauged the current spectrum of the wave instinctively, watching from the sidelines, and he knew which of the modes in his charge would contribute to a goal and which would detract from the probability. As he cut through the shimmering bands of colour, the umpire gave him tactile feedback to supplement his visual estimates and calculations, allowing him to sense the difference between a cyclic tug, a to and fro that came to nothing, and the gentle but persistent force that meant he was successfully riding the beat.

Chusok called out to him urgently, "Take, take! Two-ten!" Everyone's spectral territory overlapped with someone else's, and you needed to pass amplitude from player to player as well as trying to manage it within your own range. *Two-ten* — a harmonic with two peaks across the width of the field and ten along its length, cycling at 1,160 milliHertz — was filling up as Chusok drove unwanted amplitude from various lower-energy modes into it. It was Jamil's role to empty it, putting the amplitude somewhere useful. Any mode with an even number of peaks across

the field was unfavourable for scoring, because it had a node—a zero point between the peaks—smack in the middle of both goals.

Jamil acknowledged the request with a hand signal and shifted his trajectory. It
was almost a decade since he'd last played the game, but he still knew the intricate
web of possibilities by heart: he could drain the two-ten harmonic into the three-
ten, five-two and five-six modes—all with "good parity," peaks along the centre-
line—in a single action.

As he pounded across the grass, carefully judging the correct angle by sight,
increasing his speed until he felt the destructive beats give way to a steady force
like a constant breeze, he suddenly recalled a time—centuries before, in another
city—when he'd played with one team, week after week, for 40 years. Faces and
voices swam in his head. Hashim, Jamil's 98th child, and Hashim's granddaughter
Laila had played beside him. But he'd burnt his house and moved on, and when
that era touched him at all now it was like an unexpected gift. The scent of the
grass, the shouts of the players, the soles of his feet striking the ground, resonated
with every other moment he'd spent the same way, bridging the centuries, binding
his life together. He never truly felt the scale of it when he sought it out deliberately; it was always small things, tightly focused moments like this, that burst the
horizon of his everyday concerns and confronted him with the astonishing vista.

The two-ten mode was draining faster than he'd expected; the seesawing centre-
line dip in the wave was vanishing before his eyes. He looked around, and saw
Margit performing an elaborate Lissajous manoeuvre, smoothly orchestrating a
dozen transitions at once. Jamil froze and watched her, admiring her virtuosity
while he tried to decide what to do next; there was no point competing with her
when she was doing such a good job of completing the task Chusok had set him.

Margit was his opponent, but they were both aiming for exactly the same kind
of spectrum. The symmetry of the field meant that any scoring wave would work
equally well for either side—but only one team could be the first to reap the
benefit, the first to have more than half the wave's probability packed into their
goal. So the two teams were obliged to cooperate at first, and it was only as the
wave took shape from their combined efforts that it gradually became apparent
which side would gain by sculpting it to perfection as rapidly as possible, and
which would gain by spoiling it for the first chance, then honing it for the rebound.

Penina chided him over her shoulder as she jogged past, "You want to leave
her to clean up four-six, as well?" She was smiling, but Jamil was stung; he'd been
motionless for ten or fifteen seconds. It was not forbidden to drag your feet and
rely on your opponents to do all the work, but it was regarded as a shamefully
impoverished strategy. It was also very risky, handing them the opportunity to set
up a wave that was almost impossible to exploit yourself.

He reassessed the spectrum, and quickly sorted through the alternatives. Whatever he did would have unwanted side effects; there was no magic way to avoid
influencing modes in other players' territory, and any action that would drive the
transitions he needed would also trigger a multitude of others, up and down the
spectrum. Finally, he made a choice that would weaken the offending mode while
causing as little disruption as possible.

Jamil immersed himself in the game, planning each transition two steps in advance, switching strategy halfway through a run if he had to, but staying in motion until the sweat dripped from his body, until his calves burned, until his blood sang. He wasn't blinded to the raw pleasures of the moment, or to memories of games past, but he let them wash over him, like the breeze that rose up and cooled his skin with no need for acknowledgment. Familiar voices shouted terse commands at him; as the wave came closer to a scoring spectrum every trace of superfluous conversation vanished, every idle glance gave way to frantic, purposeful gestures. To a bystander, this might have seemed like the height of dehumanization: 22 people reduced to grunting cogs in a pointless machine. Jamil smiled at the thought but refused to be distracted into a complicated imaginary rebuttal. Every step he took was the answer to that, every hoarse plea to Yann or Joracy, Chusok or Maria, Eudore or Halide. These were his friends, and he was back among them. Back in the world.

The first chance of a goal was 30 seconds away, and the opportunity would fall to Jamil's team; a few tiny shifts in amplitude would clinch it. Margit kept her distance, but Jamil could sense her eyes on him constantly—and literally feel her at work through his skin as she slackened his contact with the wave. In theory, by mirroring your opponent's movements at the correct position on the field you could undermine everything they did, though in practice not even the most skilful team could keep the spectrum completely frozen. Going further and spoiling was a tug of war you didn't want to win too well: if you degraded the wave too much, your opponent's task—spoiling your own subsequent chance at a goal—became far easier.

Jamil still had two bad-parity modes that he was hoping to weaken, but every time he changed velocity to try a new transition, Margit responded in an instant, blocking him. He gestured to Chusok for help; Chusok had his own problems with Ezequiel, but he could still make trouble for Margit by choosing where he placed unwanted amplitude. Jamil shook sweat out of his eyes; he could see the characteristic "stepping stone" pattern of lobes forming, a sign that the wave would soon converge on the goal, but from the middle of the field it was impossible to judge their shape accurately enough to know what, if anything, remained to be done.

Suddenly, Jamil felt the wave push against him. He didn't waste time looking around for Margit; Chusok must have succeeded in distracting her. He was almost at the boundary line, but he managed to reverse smoothly, continuing to drive both the transitions he'd been aiming for.

Two long lobes of probability, each modulated by a series of oscillating mounds, raced along the sides of the field. A third, shorter lobe running along the centre-line melted away, reappeared, then merged with the others as they touched the end of the field, forming an almost rectangular plateau encompassing the goal.

The plateau became a pillar of light, growing narrower and higher as dozens of modes, all finally in phase, crashed together against the impenetrable barrier of the field's boundary. A shallow residue was still spread across the entire field, and a diminishing sequence of elliptical lobes trailed away from the goal like a staircase, but most of the wave that had started out lapping around their waists was now concentrated in a single peak that towered above their heads, nine or ten metres tall.

For an instant, it was motionless.

Then it began to fall.

The umpire said, "Forty-nine point eight."

The wave packet had not been tight enough.

Jamil struggled to shrug off his disappointment and throw his instincts into reverse. The other team had 50 seconds, now, to fine-tune the spectrum and ensure that the reflected packet was just a fraction narrower when it reformed, at the opposite end of the field.

As the pillar collapsed, replaying its synthesis in reverse, Jamil caught sight of Margit. She smiled at him calmly, and it suddenly struck him: *She'd known they couldn't make the goal. That was why she'd stopped opposing him.* She'd let him work towards sharpening the wave for a few seconds, knowing that it was already too late for him, knowing that her own team would gain from the slight improvement.

Jamil was impressed; it took an extraordinary level of skill and confidence to do what she'd just done. For all the time he'd spent away, he knew exactly what to expect from the rest of the players, and in Margit's absence he would probably have been wishing out loud for a talented newcomer to make the game interesting again. Still, it was hard not to feel a slight sting of resentment. Someone should have warned him just how good she was.

With the modes slipping out of phase, the wave undulated all over the field again, but its reconvergence was inevitable: unlike a wave of water or sound, it possessed no hidden degrees of freedom to grind its precision into entropy. Jamil decided to ignore Margit; there were cruder strategies than mirror-blocking that worked almost as well. Chusok was filling the two-ten mode now; Jamil chose the four-six as his spoiler. All they had to do was keep the wave from growing much sharper, and it didn't matter whether they achieved this by preserving the status quo, or by nudging it from one kind of bluntness to another.

The steady resistance he felt as he ran told Jamil that he was driving the transition, unblocked, but he searched in vain for some visible sign of success. When he reached a vantage point where he could take in enough of the field in one glance to judge the spectrum properly, he noticed a rapidly vibrating shimmer across the width of the wave. He counted nine peaks: good parity. Margit had pulled most of the amplitude straight out of his spoiler mode and fed it into *this*. It was a mad waste of energy to aim for such an elevated harmonic, but no one had been looking there, no one had stopped her.

The scoring pattern was forming again, he only had nine or ten seconds left to make up for all the time he'd wasted. Jamil chose the strongest good-parity mode in his territory, and the emptiest bad one, computed the velocity that would link them, and ran.

He didn't dare turn to watch the opposition goal; he didn't want to break his concentration. The wave retreated around his feet, less like an Earthly ebb tide than an ocean drawn into the sky by a passing black hole. The city diligently portrayed the shadow that his body would have cast, shrinking in front of him as the tower of light rose.

The verdict was announced. "Fifty point one."

The air was filled with shouts of triumph—Ezequiel's the loudest, as always. Jamil sagged to his knees, laughing. It was a curious feeling, familiar as it was: he cared, and he didn't. If he'd been wholly indifferent to the outcome of the game there would have been no pleasure in it, but obsessing over every defeat—or every victory—could ruin it just as thoroughly. He could almost see himself walking the line, orchestrating his response as carefully as any action in the game itself.

He lay down on the grass to catch his breath before play resumed. The outer face of the microsun that orbited Laplace was shielded with rock, but light reflected skywards from the land beneath it crossed the 100,000 kilometre width of the 3-toroidal universe to give a faint glow to the planet's nightside. Though only a sliver was lit directly, Jamil could discern the full disc of the opposite hemisphere in the primary image at the zenith: continents and oceans that lay, by a shorter route, 12,000 or so kilometres beneath him. Other views in the lattice of images spread across the sky were from different angles, and showed substantial crescents of the dayside itself. The one thing you couldn't find in any of these images, even with a telescope, was your own city. The topology of this universe let you see the back of your head, but never your reflection.

Jamil's team lost, three nil. He staggered over to the fountains at the edge of the field and slaked his thirst, shocked by the pleasure of the simple act. Just to be alive was glorious now, but once he felt this way, anything seemed possible. He was back in synch, back in phase, and he was going to make the most of it, for however long it lasted.

He caught up with the others, who'd headed down towards the river. Ezequiel hooked an arm around his neck, laughing. "Bad luck, Sleeping Beauty! You picked the wrong time to wake. With Margit, we're invincible."

Jamil ducked free of him. "I won't argue with that." He looked around. "Speaking of whom—"

Penina said, "Gone home. She plays, that's all. No frivolous socializing after the match."

Chusok added, "Or any other time." Penina shot Jamil a glance that meant: not for want of trying on Chusok's part.

Jamil pondered this, wondering why it annoyed him so much. On the field, she hadn't come across as aloof and superior. Just unashamedly good.

He queried the city, but she'd published nothing besides her name. Nobody expected—or wished—to hear more than the tiniest fraction of another person's history, but it was rare for anyone to start a new life without carrying through something from the old as a kind of calling card, some incident or achievement from which your new neighbours could form an impression of you.

They'd reached the riverbank. Jamil pulled his shirt over his head. "So what's her story? She must have told you something."

Ezequiel said, "Only that she learnt to play a long time ago; she won't say where or when. She arrived in Noether at the end of last year, and grew a house on the southern outskirts. No one sees her around much. No one even knows what she studies."

Jamil shrugged, and waded in. "Ah well. It's a challenge to rise to." Penina laughed and splashed him teasingly. He protested, "I *meant* beating her at the game."

Chusok said wryly, "When you turned up, I thought you'd be our secret weapon. The one player she didn't know inside out already."

"I'm glad you didn't tell me that. I would have turned around and fled straight back into hibernation."

"I know. That's why we all kept quiet." Chusok smiled. "Welcome back."

Penina said, "Yeah, welcome back, Jamil."

Sunlight shone on the surface of the river. Jamil ached all over, but the cool water was the perfect place to be. If he wished, he could build a partition in his mind at the point where he stood right now, and never fall beneath it. Other people lived that way, and it seemed to cost them nothing. Contrast was overrated; no sane person spent half their time driving spikes into their flesh for the sake of feeling better when they stopped. Ezequiel lived every day with the happy bois- terousness of a five-year-old; Jamil sometimes found this annoying, but then any kind of disposition would irritate someone. His own stretches of meaningless som- breness weren't exactly a boon to his friends.

Chusok said, "I've invited everyone to a meal at my house tonight. Will you come?"

Jamil thought it over, then shook his head. He still wasn't ready. He couldn't force-feed himself with normality; it didn't speed his recovery, it just drove him backwards.

Chusok looked disappointed, but there was nothing to be done about that. Jamil promised him, "Next time. OK?"

Ezequiel sighed. "What are we going to do with you? You're worse than Margit!" Jamil started backing away, but it was too late. Ezequiel reached him in two casual strides, bent down and grabbed him around the waist, hoisted him effortlessly onto one shoulder, then flung him through the air into the depths of the river.

Jamil was woken by the scent of wood smoke. His room was still filled with the night's grey shadows, but when he propped himself up on one elbow and the window obliged him with transparency, the city was etched clearly in the predawn light.

He dressed and left the house, surprised at the coolness of the dew on his feet. No one else in his street seemed to be up; had they failed to notice the smell, or did they already know to expect it? He turned a corner and saw the rising column of soot, faintly lit with red from below. The flames and the ruins were still hidden from him, but he knew whose house it was.

When he reached the dying blaze, he crouched in the heat-withered garden, cursing himself. Chusok had offered him the chance to join him for his last meal in Noether. Whatever hints you dropped, it was customary to tell no one that you were moving on. If you still had a lover, if you still had young children, you never deserted them. But friends, you warned in subtle ways. Before vanishing.

Jamil covered his head with his arms. He'd lived through this countless times before, but it never became easier. If anything it grew worse, as every departure was weighted with the memories of others. His brothers and sisters had scattered across the branches of the New Territories. He'd walked away from his father and mother when he was too young and confident to realize how much it would hurt him, decades later. His own children had all abandoned him eventually, far more often than he'd left them. It was easier to leave an ex-lover than a grown child: something burned itself out in a couple, almost naturally, as if ancestral biology had prepared them for at least that one rift.

Jamil stopped fighting the tears. But as he brushed them away, he caught sight of someone standing beside him. He looked up. It was Margit.

He felt a need to explain. He rose to his feet and addressed her. "This was Chusok's house. We were good friends. I'd known him for 96 years."

Margit gazed back at him neutrally. "Boo hoo. Poor baby. You'll never see your friend again."

Jamil almost laughed, her rudeness was so surreal. He pushed on, as if the only conceivable, polite response was to pretend that he hadn't heard her. "No one is the kindest, the most generous, the most loyal. It doesn't matter. That's not the point. Everyone's unique. Chusok was Chusok." He banged a fist against his chest, utterly heedless now of her contemptuous words. "There's a hole in me, and it will never be filled." That was the truth, even though he'd grow around it. *He should have gone to the meal, it would have cost him nothing.*

"You must be a real emotional Swiss cheese," observed Margit tartly.

Jamil came to his senses. "Why don't you fuck off to some other universe? No one wants you in Noether."

Margit was amused. "You *are* a bad loser."

Jamil gazed at her, honestly confused for a moment; the game had slipped his mind completely. He gestured at the embers. "What are you doing here? Why did you follow the smoke, if it wasn't regret at not saying goodbye to him when you had the chance?" He wasn't sure how seriously to take Penina's lighthearted insinuation, but if Chusok had fallen for Margit, and it had not been reciprocated, that might even have been the reason he'd left.

She shook her head calmly. "He was nothing to me. I barely spoke to him."

"Well, that's your loss."

"From the look of things, I'd say the loss was all yours."

He had no reply. Margit turned and walked away. Jamil crouched on the ground again, rocking back and forth, waiting for the pain to subside.

Jamil spent the next week preparing to resume his studies. The library had near-instantaneous contact with every artificial universe in the New Territories, and the additional lightspeed lag between Earth and the point in space from which the whole tree-structure blossomed was only a few hours. Jamil had been to Earth, but only as a tourist; land was scarce, they accepted no migrants. There were remote planets you could live on, in the home universe, but you had to be a certain kind of masochistic purist to want that. The precise reasons why his ancestors had entered the New Territories had been forgotten generations before— and it would have been presumptuous to track them down and ask them in person—but given a choice between the then even-more-crowded Earth, the horrifying reality of interstellar distances, and an endlessly extensible branching chain of worlds which could be traversed within a matter of weeks, the decision wasn't exactly baffling.

Jamil had devoted most of his time in Noether to studying the category of representations of Lie groups on complex vector spaces—a fitting choice, since Emmy Noether had been a pioneer of group theory, and if she'd lived to see this field blossom she would probably have been in the thick of it herself. Representations of Lie groups lay behind most of physics: each kind of subatomic particle was really nothing but a particular way of representing the universal symmetry group as a set of rotations of complex vectors. Organizing this kind of structure with category theory was ancient knowledge, but Jamil didn't care; he'd long ago reconciled himself to being a student, not a discoverer. The greatest gift of consciousness was the ability to take the patterns of the world inside you, and for all that he would have relished the thrill of being the first at anything, with ten-to-the-sixteenth people alive that was a futile ambition for most.

In the library, he spoke with fellow students of his chosen field on other worlds, or read their latest works. Though they were not researchers, they could still put a new pedagogical spin on old material, enriching the connections with other fields, finding ways to make the complex, subtle truth easier to assimilate without sacrificing the depth and detail that made it worth knowing in the first place. They would not advance the frontiers of knowledge. They would not discover new principles of nature, or invent new technologies. But to Jamil, understanding was an end in itself.

He rarely thought about the prospect of playing another match, and when he did the idea was not appealing. With Chusok gone, the same group could play ten-to-a-side without Jamil to skew the numbers. Margit might even choose to swap teams, if only for the sake of proving that her current team's monotonous string of victories really had been entirely down to her.

When the day arrived, though, he found himself unable to stay away. He turned up intending to remain a spectator, but Ryuichi had deserted Ezequiel's team, and everyone begged Jamil to join in.

As he took his place opposite Margit, there was nothing in her demeanour to acknowledge their previous encounter: no lingering contempt, but no hint of shame either. Jamil resolved to put it out of his mind; he owed it to his fellow players to concentrate on the game.

They lost, five nil.

Jamil forced himself to follow everyone to Eudore's house, to celebrate, commiserate, or as it turned out, to forget the whole thing. After they'd eaten, Jamil wandered from room to room, enjoying Eudore's choice of music but unable to settle into any conversation. No one mentioned Chusok in his hearing.

He left just after midnight. Laplace's near-full primary image and its eight brightest gibbous companions lit the streets so well that there was no need for anything more. Jamil thought: Chusok might have merely travelled to another city, one beneath his gaze right now. And wherever he'd gone, he might yet choose to stay in touch with his friends from Noether.

And his friends from the next town, and the next?

Century after century?

Margit was sitting on Jamil's doorstep, holding a bunch of white flowers in one hand.

Jamil was irritated. "What are you doing here?"

"I came to apologize."

He shrugged. "There's no need. We feel differently about certain things. That's fine. I can still face you on the playing field."

"I'm not apologizing for a difference of opinion. I wasn't honest with you. I was cruel." She shaded her eyes against the glare of the planet and looked up at him. "You were right: it was my loss. I wish I'd known your friend."

He laughed curtly. "Well, it's too late for that."

She said simply, "I know."

Jamil relented. "Do you want to come in?" Margit nodded, and he instructed the door to open for her. As he followed her inside, he said, "How long have you been here? Have you eaten?"

"No."

"I'll cook something for you."

"You don't have to do that."

He called out to her from the kitchen, "Think of it as a peace offering. I don't have any flowers."

Margit replied, "They're not for you. They're for Chusok's house."

Jamil stopped rummaging through his vegetable bins and walked back into the living room. "People don't usually do that in Noether."

Margit was sitting on the couch, staring at the floor. She said, "I'm so lonely here. I can't bear it anymore."

He sat beside her. "Then why did you rebuff him? You could at least have been friends."

She shook her head. "Don't ask me to explain."

Jamil took her hand. She turned and embraced him, trembling miserably. He stroked her hair. "Sssh."

She said, "Just sex. I don't want anything more."

He groaned softly. "There's no such thing as that."

"I just need someone to touch me again."

"I understand." He confessed, "So do I. But that won't be all. So don't ask me to promise there'll be nothing more."

Margit took his face in her hands and kissed him. Her mouth tasted of wood smoke.

Jamil said, "I don't even know you."

"No one knows anyone, anymore."

"That's not true."

"No, it's not," she conceded gloomily. She ran a hand lightly along his arm. Jamil wanted badly to see her smile, so he made each dark hair thicken and blossom into a violet flower as it passed beneath her fingers.

She did smile, but she said, "I've seen that trick before."

Jamil was annoyed. "I'm sure to be a disappointment all round, then. I expect you'd be happier with some kind of novelty. A unicorn, or an amoeba."

She laughed. "I don't think so." She took his hand and placed it against her breast. "Do you ever get tired of sex?"

"Do you ever get tired of breathing?"

"I can go for a long time without thinking about it."

He nodded. "But then one day you stop and fill your lungs with air, and it's still as sweet as ever."

Jamil didn't know what he was feeling anymore. Lust. Compassion. Spite. She'd come to him hurting, and he wanted to help her, but he wasn't sure that either of them really believed this would work.

Margit inhaled the scent of the flowers on his arm. "Are they the same colour? Everywhere else?"

He said, "There's only one way to find out."

Jamil woke in the early hours of the morning, alone. He'd half expected Margit to flee like this, but she could have waited till dawn. He would have obligingly feigned sleep while she dressed and tiptoed out.

Then he heard her. It was not a sound he would normally have associated with a human being, but it could not have been anything else.

He found her in the kitchen, curled around a table leg, wailing rhythmically. He stood back and watched her, afraid that anything he did would only make things worse. She met his gaze in the half-light, but kept up the mechanical whimper. Her eyes weren't blank; she was not delirious, or hallucinating. She knew exactly who, and where, she was.

Finally, Jamil knelt in the doorway. He said, "Whatever it is, you can tell me. And we'll fix it. We'll find a way."

She bared her teeth. "You can't *fix it*, you stupid child." She resumed the awful noise.

"Then just tell me. Please?" He stretched out a hand towards her. He hadn't felt quite so helpless since his very first daughter, Aminata, had come to him as an inconsolable six-year-old, rejected by the boy to whom she'd declared her undying love. He'd been 24 years old; a child himself. More than a thousand years ago. *Where are you now, Nata?*

Margit said, "I promised. I'd never tell."

"Promised who?"

"Myself."

"Good. They're the easiest kind to break."

She started weeping. It was a more ordinary sound, but it was even more chilling. She was not a wounded animal now, an alien being suffering some incomprehensible pain. Jamil approached her cautiously; she let him wrap his arms around her shoulders.

He whispered, "Come to bed. The warmth will help. Just being held will help."

She spat at him derisively, "It won't bring her back."

"Who?"

Margit stared at him in silence, as if he'd said something shocking.

Jamil insisted gently, "Who won't it bring back?" She'd lost a friend, badly, the way he'd lost Chusok. That was why she'd sought him out. He could help her through it. They could help each other through it.

She said, "It won't bring back the dead."

Margit was seven thousand five hundred and ninety-four years old. Jamil persuaded her to sit at the kitchen table. He wrapped her in blankets, then fed her tomatoes and rice, as she told him how she'd witnessed the birth of his world.

The promise had shimmered just beyond reach for decades. Almost none of her contemporaries had believed it would happen, though the truth should have been plain for centuries: *the human body was a material thing.* In time, with enough knowledge and effort, it would become possible to safeguard it from any kind of deterioration, any kind of harm. Stellar evolution and cosmic entropy might or might not prove insurmountable, but there'd be aeons to confront those challenges. In the middle of the 21st century, the hurdles were aging, disease, violence, and an overcrowded planet.

"Grace was my best friend. We were students." Margit smiled. "Before everyone was a student. We'd talk about it, but we didn't believe we'd see it happen. It would come in another century. It would come for our great-great-grandchildren. We'd hold infants on our knees in our twilight years and tell ourselves: *this one will never die.*

"When we were both 22, something happened. To both of us." She lowered her eyes. "We were kidnapped. We were raped. We were tortured."

Jamil didn't know how to respond. These were just words to him: he knew their meaning, he knew these acts would have hurt her, but she might as well have been describing a mathematical theorem. He stretched a hand across the table, but Margit ignored it. He said awkwardly, "This was . . . the Holocaust?"

She looked up at him, shaking her head, almost laughing at his naïvete. "Not even one of them. Not a war, not a pogrom. Just one psychopathic man. He locked us in his basement, for six months. He'd killed seven women." Tears began spilling down her cheeks. "He showed us the bodies. They were buried right where we slept. He showed us how we'd end up, when he was through with us."

Jamil was numb. He'd known all his adult life what had once been possible—what had once happened, to real people—but it had all been consigned to history long before his birth. In retrospect it seemed almost inconceivably stupid, but he'd always imagined that the changes had come in such a way that no one still living had experienced these horrors. There'd been no escaping the bare minimum, the logical necessity: his oldest living ancestors must have watched their parents fall peacefully into eternal sleep. But not this. Not a flesh-and-blood woman, sitting in front of him, who'd been forced to sleep in a killer's graveyard.

He put his hand over hers, and choked out the words. "This man . . . *killed* Grace? He killed your friend?"

Margit began sobbing, but she shook her head. "No, no. We got out!" She twisted her mouth into a smile. "Someone stabbed the stupid fucker in a barroom brawl. We dug our way out while he was in hospital." She put her face down on the table and wept, but she held Jamil's hand against her cheek. He couldn't understand what she'd lived through, but that couldn't mean he wouldn't console her. Hadn't he touched his mother's face the same way, when she was sad beyond his childish comprehension?

She composed herself, and continued. "We made a resolution, while we were in there. If we survived, there'd be no more empty promises. No more daydreams. What he'd done to those seven women—and what he'd done to us—would become impossible."

And it had. Whatever harm befell your body, you had the power to shut off your senses and decline to experience it. If the flesh was damaged, it could always be repaired or replaced. In the unlikely event that your jewel itself was destroyed, everyone had backups, scattered across universes. No human being could inflict physical pain on another. In theory, you could still be killed, but it would take the same kind of resources as destroying a galaxy. The only people who seriously contemplated either were the villains in very bad operas.

Jamil's eyes narrowed in wonder. She'd spoken those last words with such fierce pride that there was no question of her having failed.

"*You* are Ndoli? You invented the jewel?" As a child, he'd been told that the machine in his skull had been designed by a man who'd died long ago.

Margit stroked his hand, amused. "In those days, very few Hungarian women could be mistaken for Nigerian men. I've never changed my body that much, Jamil. I've always looked much as you see me."

Jamil was relieved; if she'd been Ndoli himself, he might have succumbed to sheer awe and started babbling idolatrous nonsense. "But you worked with Ndoli? You and Grace?"

She shook her head. "We made the resolution, and then we floundered. We were mathematicians, not neurologists. There were a thousand things going on at once: tissue engineering, brain imaging, molecular computers. We had no real idea where to put our efforts, which problems we should bring our strengths to bear upon. Ndoli's work didn't come out of the blue for us, but we played no part in it.

"For a while, almost everyone was nervous about switching from the brain to the jewel. In the early days, the jewel was a separate device that learned its task by mimicking the brain, and it had to be handed control of the body at one chosen moment. It took another 50 years before it could be engineered to replace the brain incrementally, neuron by neuron, in a seamless transition throughout adolescence."

So Grace had lived to see the jewel invented, but held back, and died before she could use it? Jamil kept himself from blurting out this conclusion; all his guesses had proved wrong so far.

Margit continued. "Some people weren't just nervous, though. You'd be amazed how vehemently Ndoli was denounced in certain quarters. And I don't just mean the fanatics who churned out paranoid tracts about 'the machines' taking over, with their evil inhuman agendas. Some people's antagonism had nothing to do with the specifics of the technology. They were opposed to immortality, in principle."

Jamil laughed. *"Why?"*

"Ten thousand years' worth of sophistry doesn't vanish overnight," Margit observed dryly. "Every human culture had expended vast amounts of intellectual effort on the problem of coming to terms with death. Most religions had constructed elaborate lies about it, making it out to be something other than it was — though a few were dishonest about life, instead. But even most secular philosophies were warped by the need to pretend that *death was for the best.*

"It was the naturalistic fallacy at its most extreme — and its most transparent, but that didn't stop anyone. Since any child could tell you that death was meaningless, contingent, unjust, and abhorrent beyond words, it was a hallmark of sophistication to believe otherwise. Writers had consoled themselves for centuries with smug puritanical fables about immortals who'd long for death — who'd *beg* for death. It would have been too much to expect all those who were suddenly faced with the reality of its banishment to confess that they'd been whistling in the dark. And would-be moral philosophers — mostly those who'd experienced no greater inconvenience in their lives than a late train or a surly waiter — began wailing about the destruction of the human spirit by this hideous blight. We needed death and suffering to put steel into our souls! Not horrible, horrible *freedom and safety!"*

Jamil smiled. "So there were buffoons. But in the end, surely they swallowed their pride? If we're walking in a desert and I tell you that the lake you see ahead is a mirage, I might cling stubbornly to my own belief, to save myself from disappointment. But when we arrive, and I'm proven wrong, I *will* drink from the lake."

Margit nodded. "Most of the loudest of these people went quiet in the end. But there were subtler arguments, too. Like it or not, all our biology and all of our culture had evolved in the presence of death. And almost every righteous struggle in history, every worthwhile sacrifice, had been against suffering, against violence, against death. Now, that struggle would become impossible."

"Yes." Jamil was mystified. "But only because it had triumphed."

Margit said gently, "I know. There was no sense to it. And it was always my belief that anything worth fighting for — over centuries, over millennia — was worth attaining. It *can't* be noble to toil for a cause, and even to die for it, unless it's also noble to succeed. To claim otherwise isn't sophistication, it's just a kind of hypocrisy. If it's better to travel than arrive, you shouldn't start the voyage in the first place.

"I told Grace as much, and she agreed. We laughed together at what we called the *tragedians*: the people who denounced the coming age as the age without martyrs, the age without saints, the age without revolutionaries. There would never be another Gandhi, another Mandela, another Aung San Suu Kyi — and yes, that *was* a kind of loss, but would any great leader have sentenced humanity to eternal misery for the sake of providing a suitable backdrop for eternal heroism? Well, some of them would have. But the downtrodden themselves had better things to do."

Margit fell silent. Jamil cleared her plate away, then sat opposite her again. It was almost dawn.

"Of course, the jewel was not enough," Margit continued. "With care, Earth could support 40 billion people, but where would the rest go? The jewel made virtual reality the easiest escape route: for a fraction of the space, a fraction of the energy, it could survive without a body attached. Grace and I weren't horrified by that prospect, the way some people were. But it was not the best outcome, it was not what most people wanted, the way they wanted freedom from death.

"So we studied gravity, we studied the vacuum."

Jamil feared making a fool of himself again, but from the expression on her face he knew he wasn't wrong this time. M. Osvát and G. Füst. Co-authors of the seminal paper, but no more was known about them than those abbreviated names. "You gave us the New Territories?"

Margit nodded slightly. "Grace and I."

Jamil was overwhelmed with love for her. He went to her and knelt down to put his arms around her waist. Margit touched his shoulder. "Come on, get up. Don't treat me like a god, it just makes me feel old."

He stood, smiling abashedly. Anyone in pain deserved his help—but if he was not in her debt, the word had no meaning.

"And Grace?" he asked.

Margit looked away. "Grace completed her work, and then decided that she was a tragedian, after all. Rape was impossible. Torture was impossible. Poverty was vanishing. Death was receding into cosmology, into metaphysics. It was everything she'd hoped would come to pass. And for her, suddenly faced with that fulfilment, everything that remained seemed trivial.

"One night, she climbed into the furnace in the basement of her building. Her jewel survived the flames, but she'd erased it from within."

It was morning now. Jamil was beginning to feel disoriented; Margit should have vanished in daylight, an apparition unable to persist in the mundane world.

"I'd lost other people who were close to me," she said. "My parents. My brother. Friends. And so had everyone around me, then. I wasn't special: grief was still commonplace. But decade by decade, century by century, we shrank into insignificance, those of us who knew what it meant to lose someone forever. We're less than one in a million, now.

"For a long time, I clung to my own generation. There were enclaves, there were ghettos, where everyone understood the old days. I spent 200 years married to a man who wrote a play called We Who Have Known the Dead—which was every bit as pretentious and self-pitying as you'd guess from the title." She smiled at the memory. "It was a horrible, self-devouring world. If I'd stayed in it much longer, I would have followed Grace. I would have begged for death."

She looked up at Jamil. "It's people like you I want to be with: *people who don't understand*. Your lives aren't trivial, any more than the best parts of our own were:

all the tranquillity, all the beauty, all the happiness that made the sacrifices and the life-and-death struggles worthwhile.

"The tragedians were wrong. They had everything upside-down. Death never gave meaning to life: it was always the other way round. All of its gravitas, all of its significance, was stolen from the things it ended. But the value of life always lay entirely in itself—not in its loss, not in its fragility.

"Grace should have lived to see that. She should have lived long enough to understand that the world hadn't turned to ash."

Jamil sat in silence, turning the whole confession over in his mind, trying to absorb it well enough not to add to her distress with a misjudged question. Finally, he ventured, "Why do you hold back from friendship with us, though? Because we're just children to you? Children who can't understand what you've lost?"

Margit shook her head vehemently. "I *don't want you* to understand! People like me are the only blight on this world, the only poison." She smiled at Jamil's expression of anguish, and rushed to silence him before he could swear that she was nothing of the kind. "Not in everything we do and say, or everyone we touch: I'm not claiming that we're tainted, in some fatuous mythological sense. But when I left the ghettos, I promised myself that I wouldn't bring the past with me. Sometimes that's an easy vow to keep. Sometimes it's not."

"You've broken it tonight," Jamil said plainly. "And neither of us have been struck down by lightning."

"I know." She took his hand. "But I was wrong to tell you what I have, and I'll fight to regain the strength to stay silent. I stand at the border between two worlds, Jamil. I remember death, and I always will. But my job now is to guard that border. To keep that knowledge from invading your world."

"We're not as fragile as you think," he protested. "We all know something about loss."

Margit nodded soberly. "Your friend Chusok has vanished into the crowd. That's how things work now: how you keep yourselves from suffocating in a jungle of endlessly growing connections, or fragmenting into isolated troupes of repertory players, endlessly churning out the same lines.

"You have your little deaths—and I don't call them that to deride you. But I've seen both. And I promise you, they're not the same."

In the weeks that followed, Jamil resumed in full the life he'd made for himself in Noether. Five days in seven were for the difficult beauty of mathematics. The rest were for his friends.

He kept playing matches, and Margit's team kept winning. In the sixth game, though, Jamil's team finally scored against her. Their defeat was only three to one.

Each night, Jamil struggled with the question. What exactly did he owe her? Eternal loyalty, eternal silence, eternal obedience? She hadn't sworn him to secrecy; she'd extracted no promises at all. But he knew she was trusting him to comply with her wishes, so what right did he have to do otherwise?

Eight weeks after the night he'd spent with Margit, Jamil found himself alone with Penina in a room in Joracy's house. They'd been talking about the old days. Talking about Chusok.

Jamil said, "Margit lost someone very close to her."

Penina nodded matter-of-factly, but curled into a comfortable position on the couch and prepared to take in every word.

"Not in the way we've lost Chusok. Not in the way you think at all."

Jamil approached the others, one by one. His confidence ebbed and flowed. He'd glimpsed the old world, but he couldn't pretend to have fathomed its inhabitants. What if Margit saw this as worse than betrayal — as a further torture, a further rape?

But he couldn't stand by and leave her to the torture she'd inflicted on herself.

Ezequiel was the hardest to face. Jamil spent a sick and sleepless night beforehand, wondering if this would make him a monster, a corrupter of children, the epitome of everything Margit believed she was fighting.

Ezequiel wept freely, but he was not a child. He was older than Jamil, and he had more steel in his soul than any of them.

He said, "I guessed it might be that. I guessed she might have seen the bad times. But I never found a way to ask her."

The three lobes of probability converged, melted into a plateau, rose into a pillar of light.

The umpire said, "Fifty-five point nine." It was Margit's most impressive goal yet.

Ezequiel whooped joyfully and ran towards her. When he scooped her up in his arms and threw her across his shoulders, she laughed and indulged him. When Jamil stood beside him and they made a joint throne for her with their arms, she frowned down at him and said, "You shouldn't be doing this. You're on the losing side."

The rest of the players converged on them, cheering, and they started down towards the river. Margit looked around nervously. "What is this? We haven't finished playing."

Penina said, "The game's over early, just this once. Think of this as an invitation. We want you to swim with us. We want you to talk to us. We want to hear everything about your life."

Margit's composure began to crack. She squeezed Jamil's shoulder. He whispered, "Say the word, and we'll put you down."

Margit didn't whisper back; she shouted miserably, "What do you want from me, you parasites? I've won your fucking game for you! What more do you want?"

Jamil was mortified. He stopped and prepared to lower her, prepared to retreat, but Ezequiel caught his arm.

Ezequiel said, "We want to be your border guards. We want to stand beside you."

Christa added, "We can't face what you've faced, but we want to understand. As much as we can."

Joracy spoke, then Yann, Narcyza, Maria, Halide. Margit looked down on them, weeping, confused.

Jamil burnt with shame. He'd hijacked her, humiliated her. He'd made everything worse. She'd flee Noether, flee into a new exile, more alone than ever.

When everyone had spoken, silence descended. Margit trembled on her throne.

Jamil faced the ground. He couldn't undo what he'd done. He said quietly, "Now you know our wishes. Will you tell us yours?"

"Put me down."

Jamil and Ezequiel complied.

Margit looked around at her teammates and opponents, her children, her creation, her would-be friends.

She said, "I want to go to the river with you. I'm seven thousand years old, and I want to learn to swim."

scherzo with tyrannosaur

MICHAEL SWANWICK

Michael Swanwick made his debut in 1980, and in the nineteen years that have followed has established himself as one of SF's most prolific and consistently excellent writers at short lengths, as well as one of the premier novelists of his generation.

He has several times been a finalist for the Nebula Award, as well as for the World Fantasy Award and for the John W. Campbell Award, and has won the Theodore Sturgeon Award and the Asimov's Readers Award poll. In 1991, his novel Stations of the Tide *won him a Nebula Award as well; in 1995, he won the World Fantasy Award for his story "Radio Waves"; and in 1999, he completed his sweep of the major science fiction awards by winning a Hugo for his story "The Very Pulse of the Machine." His other books include his first novel,* In the Drift, *which was published in 1985; a novella-length book,* Griffin's Egg; *1987's popular novel* Vacuum Flowers; *and a critically acclaimed fantasy novel,* The Iron Dragon's Daughter, *which was a finalist for the World Fantasy Award and the Arthur C. Clarke Award (a rare distinction!). His most recent novel,* Jack Faust, *a sly reworking of the Faust legend that explores the unexpected impact of technology on society, has garnered rave reviews from nearly every source from the* Washington Post *to* Interzone. *His short fiction has been assembled in* Gravity's Angels *and in a collection of his collaborative short work with other writers,* Slow Dancing Through Time. *His most recent books are a collection of critical essays,* The Postmodern Archipelago; *and a collection,* A Geography of Unknown Lands. *Upcoming is a new collection, called* Moon Dogs, *and he's currently at work on a new novel. He's had stories in our Second, Third, Fourth, Sixth, Seventh, Tenth, Thirteenth, Fourteenth, Fifteenth, and Sixteenth Annual Collections. Swanwick lives in Philadelphia with his wife, Marianne Porter, and their son Sean.*

This story brings us sixty-five million years into the past for a clever, intricate, and deadly pavane of paradox, intrigue, destiny, and hungry killer dinosaurs with great big teeth . . .

A keyboardist was playing a selection of Scarlatti's harpsichord sonatas, brief pieces one to three minutes long, very complex and refined, while the *Hadrosaurus* herd streamed by the window. There were hundreds of the brutes, kicking up dust and honking that lovely flattened near-musical note they make. It was a spectacular sight.

But the *hors d'oeuvres* had just arrived: plesiosaur wrapped in kelp, beluga smeared over sliced maiasaur egg, little slivers of roast dodo on toast, a dozen delicacies more. So a stampede of common-as-dirt herbivores just couldn't compete.

Nobody was paying much attention.

Except for the kid. He was glued to the window, staring with an intensity remarkable even for a boy his age. I figured him to be about ten years old.

Snagging a glass of champagne from a passing tray, I went over to stand next to him. "Enjoying yourself, son?"

Without looking up, the kid said, "What do you think spooked them? Was it a—?" Then he saw the wranglers in their jeeps and his face fell. "Oh."

"We had to cheat a little to give the diners something to see." I gestured with the wineglass past the herd, toward the distant woods. "But there are plenty of predators lurking out there—troodons, dromaeosaurs . . . even old Satan."

He looked up at me in silent question.

"Satan is our nickname for an injured old bull rex that's been hanging around the station for about a month, raiding our garbage dump."

It was the wrong thing to say. The kid looked devastated. *T. rex* a scavenger! *Say it ain't so!*

"A tyrannosaur is an advantageous hunter," I said, "like a lion. When it chances upon something convenient, believe you me, it'll attack. And when a tyrannosaur is hurting, like old Satan is—well, that's about as savage and dangerous as any animal can be. It'll kill even when it's not hungry."

That satisfied him. "Good," he said. "I'm glad."

In companionable silence, we stared into the woods together, looking for moving shadows. Then the chime sounded for dinner to begin, and I sent the kid back to his table. The last hadrosaurs were gone by then.

He went with transparent reluctance.

The Cretaceous Ball was our big fund-raiser, a hundred thousand dollars a seat, and in addition to the silent auction before the meal and the dancing afterward, everybody who bought an entire table for six was entitled to their very own paleontologist as a kind of party favor.

I used to be a paleontologist myself, before I was promoted. Now I patrolled the room in tux and cummerbund, making sure everything was running smoothly.

Waiters slipped in and out of existence. You'd see them hurry behind the screen hiding the entrance to the time funnel and then pop out immediately on the other side, carrying heavily laden trays. *Styracosaurus* medallions in mastodon mozzarella for those who liked red meat. Archaeopteryx almondine for those who preferred white. Raddichio and fennel for the vegetarians.

All to the accompaniment of music, pleasant chitchat, and the best view in the universe.

Donald Hawkins had been assigned to the kid's table—the de Cherville Family. According to the seating plan the heavy, phlegmatic man was Gerard, the money-making *paterfamilias*. The woman beside him was Danielle, once his trophy wife, now aging gracefully. Beside them were two guests—the Cadigans—who looked a little overwhelmed by everything and were probably a favored employee and spouse. They didn't say much. A sullen daughter, Melusine, in a little black dress that casually displayed her perfect breasts. She looked bored and restless—trouble incarnate. And there was the kid, given name Philippe.

I kept a close eye on them because of Hawkins. He was new, and I wasn't expecting him to last long. But he charmed everyone at the table. Young, handsome, polite—he had it all. I noticed how Melusine slouched back in her chair, studying him through dark eyelashes, saying nothing. Hawkins, responding to something young Philippe had said, flashed a boyish, devil-may-care grin. I could feel the heat of the kid's hero-worship from across the room.

Then my silent beeper went off, and I had to duck out of the late Cretaceous and back into the kitchen, Home Base, year 2140.

There was a Time Safety Officer waiting for me. The main duty of a TSO is to make sure that no time paradoxes occur, so that the Unchanging wouldn't take our time privileges away from us. Most people think that time travel was invented recently, and by human beings. That's because our sponsors don't want their presence advertised.

In the kitchen, everyone was in an uproar. One of the waiters was leaning, spraddle-legged and arms wide against the table, and another was lying on the floor clutching what looked to be a broken arm. The TSO covered them both with a gun.

The good news was that the Old Man wasn't there. If it had been something big and hairy—a Creationist bomb, or a message from a million years upline—he would have been.

When I showed up, everybody began talking at once.

"I didn't do *nothing*, man, this bastard—"

"—guilty of a Class Six violation—"

"—broke my fucking *arm*, man. He threw me to the ground!"

"—work to do. Get them out of my kitchen!"

It turned out to be a simple case of note-passing. One of the waiters had, in his old age, conspired with another recruited from a later period to slip a list of hot investments to his younger self. Enough to make them both multibillionaires. We had surveillance devices planted in the kitchen, and a TSO saw the paper change hands. Now the perps were denying everything.

It wouldn't have worked anyway. The authorities keep strict tabs on the historical record. Wealth on the order of what they had planned would have stuck out like a sore thumb.

I fired both waiters, called the police to take them away, routed a call for two replacements several hours into the local past, and had them briefed and on duty without any lapse in service. Then I took the TSO aside and bawled him out good for calling me back real-time, instead of sending a memo back to me three days ago. Once something has happened, though, that's it. I'd been called, so I had to handle it in person.

It was your standard security glitch. No big deal.

But it was wearying. So when I went back down the funnel to Hilltop Station, I set the time for a couple hours after I had left. I arrived just as the tables were being cleared for desert and coffee.

Somebody handed me a microphone, and I tapped it twice, for attention. I was standing before the window, a spectacular sunset to my back.

"Ladies and gentlemen," I said, "let me again welcome you to the late Cretaceous. This is the final research station before the Age of Mammals. Don't worry, though—the meteor that put a final end to the dinosaurs is still several thousand years in the future!" I paused for laughter, then continued.

"If you'll look outside, you'll see Jean, our dino wrangler, setting up a scent lure. Jean, wave for our diners."

Jean was fiddling with a short tripod. She waved cheerily, then bent back to work. With her blond ponytail and khaki shorts, she looked to be just your basic science babe. But Jean was slated to become one of the top saurian behaviorists in the world, and knew it too. Despite our best efforts, gossip slips through.

Now Jean backed up toward the station doors, unreeling fuse wire as she went. The windows were all on the second floor. The doors, on the ground floor, were all armored.

"Jean will be ducking inside for this demonstration," I said. "You wouldn't want to be outside unprotected when the lure goes off."

"What's in it?" somebody called out.

"Triceratops blood. We're hoping to call in a predator—maybe even the king of predators, *Tyrannosaurus rex* himself." There was an appreciative murmur from the diners. Everybody here had heard of *T. rex*. He had real star power. I switched easily into lecture mode. "If you dissect a tyrannosaur, you'll see that it has an extremely large olfactory lobe—larger in proportion to the rest of its brain than that of any other animal except the turkey vulture. Rex can sniff his prey"— carrion, usually, but I didn't say that—"from miles away. Watch."

The lure went off with a pop and a puff of pink mist.

I glanced over at the de Cherville table, and saw Melusine slip one foot out of her pump and run it up Hawkins' trouser leg. He colored.

Her father didn't notice. Her mother—her *step*-mother, more likely—did, but didn't care. To her, this was simply what women did. I couldn't help but notice what good legs Melusine had.

"This will take a few minutes. While we're waiting, I direct your attention to Chef Rupert's excellent pastries."

I faded back to polite applause, and began the round of table hopping. A joke here, a word of praise there. It's banana oil makes the world go round.

When I got to the de Chervilles, Hawkins' face was white.

"Sir!" He shot to his feet. "A word with you."

He almost dragged me away from the table.

When we were in private, he was so upset he was stuttering. "Th-that young woman, w-wants me t-to . . ."

"I know what she wants," I said coolly. "She's of legal age—make your own decision."

"You don't *understand!* I can't possibly go back to that table." Hawkins was genuinely anguished. I thought at first that he'd been hearing rumors, dark hints about his future career. Somehow, though, that didn't smell right. There was something else going on here.

"All right," I said. "Slip out now. But I don't like secrets. Record a full explanation and leave it in my office. No evasions, understand?"

"Yes, sir." A look of relief spread itself across his handsome young face. "Thank you, sir."

He started to leave.

"Oh, and one more thing," I said casually, hating myself. "Don't go anywhere near your tent until the fund-raiser's broken up."

The de Chervilles weren't exactly thrilled when I told them that Hawkins had taken ill and I'd be taking his place. But then I took a tyrannosaur tooth from my pocket and gave it to Philippe. It was just a shed—rexes drop a lot of teeth—but no need to mention that.

"It looks sharp," Mrs. de Cherville said, with a touch of alarm.

"Serrated, too. You might want to ask your mother if you can use it for a knife, next time you have steak," I suggested.

Which won him over completely. Kids are fickle. Philippe immediately forgot all about Hawkins.

Melusine, however, did not. Eyes flashing with anger, she stood, throwing her napkin to the floor. "I want to know," she began, "just *what* you think you're—"

Fortunately, that was when Satan arrived.

The tyrannosaur came running up the hillside at a speed you'd have to be an experienced paleontologist to know was less than optimal. Even a dying *T. rex* moves *fast.*

People gasped.

I took the microphone out of my pocket and moved quickly to the front of the room. "Folks, we just got lucky. I'd like to inform those of you with tables by the window that the glass is rated at twenty tons per square inch. You're in no danger whatsoever. But you are in for quite a show. Those who are in the rear might want to get a little closer."

Young Philippe was off like a shot.

The creature was almost to us. "A tyrannosaur has a hyperacute sense of smell,"

I reminded them. "When it scents blood, its brain is overwhelmed. It goes into a feeding frenzy."

A few droplets of blood had spattered the window. Seeing us through the glass, Satan leaped and tried to smash through it.

Whoomp! The glass boomed and shivered with the impact. There were shrieks and screams from the diners, and several people started to their feet.

At my signal, the string quartet took up their instruments again, and began to play while Satan leaped and tore and snarled, a perfect avatar of rage and fury. They chose the scherzo from Shostakovich's piano quintet.

Scherzos are supposed to be funny, but most have a whirlwind, uninhibited quality that makes them particularly appropriate to nightmares and the madness of predatory dinosaurs.

Whoomp! That mighty head struck the window again and again. For a long time, Satan kept on frenziedly slashing at the window with its jaws, leaving long scratches in the glass.

Philippe pressed his body against the window with all his strength, trying to minimize the distance between himself and savage dino death. Shrieking with joyous laughter when that killer mouth tried to snatch him up. I felt for the kid, wanting to get as close to the action as he could. I could identify.

I was just like that myself when I was his age.

When Satan finally wore himself out, and went bad-humoredly away, I returned to the de Chervilles. Philippe had restored himself to the company of his family. The kid looked pale and happy.

So did his sister. I noticed that she was breathing shallowly.

"You dropped your napkin." I handed it to Melusine. Inside was a postcard-sized promotional map, showing Hilltop Station and the compound behind it. One of the tents was circled. Under it was written, *While the others are dancing.*

I had signed it *Don.*

"When I grow up, I'm going to be a paleontologist!" the kid said fervently. "A behavioral paleontologist, not an anatomist or a wrangler." Somebody had come to take him home. His folks were staying to dance. And Melusine was long gone, off to Hawkins' tent.

"Good for you," I said. I laid a hand on his shoulder. "Come see me when you've got the education. I'll be happy to show you the ropes."

The kid left.

He'd had a conversion experience. I knew exactly how it felt. I'd had mine standing in front of the Zallinger "Age of Reptiles" mural in the Peabody Museum in New Haven. That was before time travel, when pictures of dinosaurs were about as real as you could get. Nowadays I could point out a hundred inaccuracies in how the dinosaurs were depicted. But on that distant sun-dusty morning in the Atlantis of my youth, I just stood staring at those magnificent brutes, head filled with wonder, until my mother dragged me away.

It really was a pity. Philippe was so full of curiosity and enthusiasm. He'd make a great paleontologist. I could see that. He wasn't going to get to realize his dreams, though. His folks had too much money to allow *that*.

I knew because I'd glanced through the personnel records for the next hundred years and his name wasn't there anywhere.

It was possibly the least of the thousands of secrets I held within me, never to be shared. Still, it made me sad. For an instant, I felt the weight of all my years, every petty accommodation, every unworthy expedience. Then I went up the funnel and back down again to an hour previous.

Unseen, I slipped out and went to wait for Melusine.

Maintaining the funnel is expensive. During normal operations—when we're not holding fund-raisers—we spend months at a time in the field. Hence the compound, with its army surplus platform tents and electrified perimeter to keep the monsters out.

It was dark when Melusine slipped into the tent.

"Donald?"

"Shhh." I put a finger to her lips, drew her close to me. One hand slid slowly down her naked back, over a scrap of crushed velvet, and then back up and under her skirt to squeeze that elegant little ass. She raised her mouth to mine and we kissed deeply, passionately.

Then I tumbled her to the cot, and we began undressing each other. She ripped off three buttons tearing my shirt from me.

Melusine made a lot of noise, for which I was grateful. She was a demanding, self-centered lay, who let you know when she didn't like what you were doing and wasn't at all shy about telling you what to do next. She required a lot of attention. For which I was also grateful.

I needed the distraction.

Because while I was in his tent, screwing the woman he didn't want, Hawkins was somewhere out there getting killed. According to the operational report that I'd write later tonight, and received a day ago, he was eaten alive by an old bull rex rendered irritable by a painful brain tumor. It was an ugly way to go. I didn't want to have to hear it. I did my best to not think about it.

Credit where credit is due—Melusine practically set the tent ablaze. So I was using her. So what? It was far from the worst of my crimes. It wasn't as if she loved Hawkins, or even *knew* him, for that matter. She was just a spoiled little rich-bitch adventuress looking for a mental souvenir. One more notch on her diaphragm case. I know her type well. They're one of the perks of the business.

There was a freshly prepared triceratops skull by the head of the bed. It gleamed faintly, a pale, indistinct shape in the darkness. When Melusine came, she grabbed one of its horns so tightly that the skull rattled against the floorboards.

Afterward, she left, happily reeking of bone fixative and me. We'd each had our little thrill. I hadn't spoken a word during any of it, and she hadn't even noticed.

T. rex wasn't much of a predator. But then, it didn't take much skill to kill a man. Too slow to run, and too big to hide—we make prefect prey for a tyrannosaur.

When Hawkins' remains were found, the whole camp turned out in an uproar. I walked through it all on autopilot, perfunctorily giving orders to have Satan shot, to have the remains sent back uptime, to have the paperwork sent to my office. Then I gathered everybody together and gave them the Paradox Lecture. Nobody was to talk about what had just happened. Those who did would be summarily fired. Legal action would follow. Dire consequences. Penalties. Fines.

And so on.

It was two A.M. when I finally got back to my office, to write the day's operational report.

Hawkins' memo was there, waiting for me. I'd forgotten about that. I debated putting off reading it until tomorrow. But then I figured that I was feeling as bad now as I was ever going to. Might as well get it over with.

I turned on the glow-pad. Hawkins' pale face appeared on the screen. Stiffly, as if he were confessing a crime, he said, "My folks didn't want me to become a scientist. I was supposed to stay home and manage the family money. Stay home and let my mind rot." His face twisted with private memories. "So that's the first thing you have to know—Donald Hawkins isn't my real name.

"My mother was kind of wild when she was young. I don't think she knew who my father was. So when she had me, it was hushed up. I was raised by my grandparents. They were getting a little old for child-rearing, so they shipped me backtime to when they were younger, and raised me alongside my mother. I was fifteen before I learned she wasn't really my sister.

"My real name is Philippe de Cherville. I swapped table assignments so I could meet my younger self. But then Melusine—my mother—started hitting on me. So I guess you can understand now"—he laughed embarrassedly—"why I didn't want to go the Oedipus route."

The pad flicked off, and then immediately back on again. He'd had an afterthought. "Oh yeah, I wanted to say . . . the things you said to me today—when I was young—the encouragement. And the tooth. Well, they meant a lot to me. So, uh . . . thanks."

It flicked off.

I put my head in my hands. Everything was throbbing, as if all the universe were contained within an infected tooth. Or maybe the brain tumor of a sick old dinosaur. I'm not stupid. I saw the implications immediately.

The kid—Philippe—was my son.

Hawkins was my son.

I hadn't even known I had a son, and now he was dead.

A bleak, blank time later, I set to work drawing time lines in the holographic workspace above my desk. A simple double-loop for Hawkins/Philippe. A rather more complex figure for myself. Then I factored in the TSOs, the waiters, the paleontologists, the musicians, the workmen who built the station in the first place and would salvage its fixtures when we were done with it . . . maybe a hundred representative individuals in all.

When I was done, I had a three-dimensional representation of Hilltop Station as a node of intersecting lives in time. It was one hell of a complex figure.

It looked like the Gordian knot.

Then I started crafting a memo back to my younger self. A carbon steel, razor-edged, Damascene sword of a memo. One that would slice Hilltop Station into a thousand spasming paradoxical fragments.

Hire him, fire her, strand a hundred young scientists, all fit and capable of breeding, one million years B.C. Oh, and *don't* father any children.

It would bring our sponsors down upon us like so many angry hornets. The Unchanging would yank time travel out of human hands—retroactively. Everything connected to it would be looped out of reality and into the disintegrative medium of quantum uncertainty. Hilltop Station would dissolve into the realm of might-have-been. The research and findings of thousands of dedicated scientists would vanish from human knowing. My son would never have been conceived or born or sent callously to an unnecessary death.

Everything I had spent my life working to accomplish would be undone.

It sounded good to me.

When the memo was done, I marked it PRIORITY and MY EYES ONLY. Then I prepared to send it three months back in time.

The door opened behind me with a click. I spun around in my chair. In walked the one man in all existence who could possibly stop me.

"The kid got to enjoy twenty-four years of life before he died," the Old Man said. "Don't take that away from him."

I looked up into his eyes.

Into my own eyes.

Those eyes fascinated and repulsed me. They were deepest brown, and nested in a lifetime's accumulation of wrinkles. I've been working with my older self since I first signed up with Hilltop Station, and they were still a mystery to me, absolutely opaque. They made me feel like a mouse being stared down by a snake.

"It's not the kid," I said. "It's everything."

"I know."

"I only met him tonight—Philippe, I mean. Hawkins was just a new recruit. I barely knew him."

The Old Man capped the Glenlivet and put it back in the liquor cabinet. Until he did that, I hadn't even noticed that I was drinking. "I keep forgetting how emotional I was when I was young," he said.

"I don't feel young."

"Wait until you're my age."

I'm not sure how old the Old Man is. There are longevity treatments available for those who play the game, and the Old Man has been playing this lousy game so long he practically runs it. All I know is that he and I are the same person.

My thoughts took a sudden swerve. "God damn that stupid kid!" I blurted. "What was he doing outside the compound in the first place?"

The Old Man shrugged. "He was curious. All scientists are. He saw something and went out to examine it. Leave it be, kid. What's done is done."

I glanced at the memo I'd written. "We'll find out."

He placed a second memo alongside mine. "I took the liberty of writing this for you. Thought I'd spare you the pain of having to compose it."

I picked up the memo, glanced at its contents. It was the one I'd received yesterday. " 'Hawkins was attacked and killed by Satan shortly after local midnight today,' " I quoted. " 'Take all necessary measures to control gossip.' " Overcome with loathing, I said, "This is exactly why I'm going to bust up this whole filthy system. You think I want to become the kind of man who can send his own son off to die? You think I want to become *you*?"

That hit home. For a long moment, the Old Man did not speak. "Listen," he said at last. "You remember that day in the Peabody?"

"You know I do."

"I stood there in front of that mural wishing with all my heart—all *your* heart— that I could see a real, living dinosaur. But even then, even as an eight-year-old, I knew it wasn't going to happen. That some things could never be."

I said nothing.

"God hands you a miracle," he said, "you don't throw it back in his face."

Then he left.

I remained.

It was my call. Two possible futures lay side-by-side on my desk, and I could select either one. The universe is inherently unstable in every instant. If paradoxes weren't possible, nobody would waste their energy preventing them. The Old Man was trusting me to weigh all relevant factors, make the right decision, and live with the consequences.

It was the cruelest thing he had ever done to me.

Thinking of cruelty reminded me of the Old Man's eyes. Eyes so deep you could drown in them. Eyes so dark you couldn't tell how many corpses already lay submerged within them. After all these years working with him, I still couldn't tell if those were the eyes of a saint or those of the most evil man in the world.

There were two memos in front of me. I reached for one, hesitated, withdrew my hand. Suddenly the choice didn't seem so easy.

The night was preternaturally still. It was as if all the world were holding its breath, waiting for me to make my decision.

I reached out for the memos.

I chose one.

A Hero of the Empire

ROBERT SILVERBERG

Robert Silverberg is one of the most famous SF writers of modern times, with dozens of novels, anthologies, and collections to his credit. As both writer and editor, Silverberg was one of the most influential figures of the Post New Wave era of the '70s, and continues to be at the forefront of the field to this very day, having won a total of five Nebula Awards and four Hugo Awards. His many novels include Dying Inside, Lord Valentine's Castle, The Book of Skulls, Downward to the Earth, Tower of Glass, The World Inside, Born with the Dead, Shadrach in the Furnace, Tom O'Bedlam, Star of Gypsies, At Winter's End, The Face of the Waters, Kingdoms of the Wall, Hot Sky at Midnight, Starborne, *and three novel-length expansions of famous Isaac Asimov stories,* Nightfall, The Positronic Man, *and* The Ugly Little Boy. *His collections include* Unfamiliar Territory, Capricorn Games, Majipoor Chronicles, The Best of Robert Silverberg, At the Conglomeroid Cocktail Party, Beyond the Safe Zone, *and a massive retrospective collection* The Collected Stories of Robert Silverberg, Volume One: Secret Sharers. *His anthologies are far too numerous to list here, but include* The Science Fiction Hall of Fame, Volume One, *the influential* New Dimensions *series, the distinguished* Alpha *series, and the recent bestsellers* Legends *and* Far Horizons, *among dozens of others. His most recent books are the novels* The Alien Years *and* Lord Prestimion. *His stories have appeared in all of our first ten Annual Collections, as well as in our Fourteenth and Fifteenth. He lives with his wife, writer Karen Haber, in Oakland, California. He has a "quasi-official" web site at www.conectexpress.com/~jon/silvhome.htm.*

For some years now, Silverberg has been publishing a string of elegant and sophisticated Alternate History stories, the "Roma" series, to which the story that follows belongs: a world in which the Roman Empire never fell, and the Pax Romana has continued even to the present, creating a society half-strange and half-familiar, full of haunting echoes of our own timeline, yet also very different. Here he takes us to a border town on the edges of the great empire of Roma, for a thoughtful study of how sometimes the rise and fall of empires can turn on a single chance meeting . . . especially if one of the people who meet has a capacity for seeing what could be as well as what is . . .

Here I am at last, Horatius, in far-off Arabia, amongst the Greeks and the camels and the swarthy Saracen tribesmen and all the other unpleasant creatures that infest this dreary desert. For my sins. My grievous sins. "Get you to Arabia, serpent!" cried the furious Emperor Julian, and here I am. *Serpent*. Me. How could he have been so unkind?

But I tell you, O friend of my bosom, I will employ this time of exile to win my way back into Caesar's good graces somehow. I will do something while I am here, *something*, I know not what just yet, that will remind him of what a shrewd and enterprising and altogether valuable man I am; and sooner or later he will recall me to Roma and restore me to my place at court. Before many years have passed you and I will stroll together along Tiber's sweet banks again. Of this much I am certain, that the gods did not have it in mind for me that I should spin out all my remaining days in so miserable a sandy wasteland as this.

A bleak forlorn place, it is, this Arabia. A bleak disheartening journey it was to get here, too.

There are, as perhaps you are aware, several Arabias within the vast territory that we know by that general name. In the north lies Arabia Petraea, a prosperous mercantile region bordering on Syria Palaestina. Arabia Petraea has been an Imperial province since the reign of Augustus Caesar, six hundred years ago. Then comes a great deal of emptiness—Arabia Deserta, it is called, a grim, harsh, barren district inhabited mainly by quarrelsome nomads. And on the far side of that lies Arabia Felix, a populous land every bit as happy as its name implies, a place of luxurious climate and easy circumstances, famed for its fertile and productive fields and for the abundance of fine goods that it pours forth into the world's markets, gold and pearls, frankincense and myrrh, balsams and aromatic oils and perfumes.

Which of these places Caesar intended as my place of exile, I did not know. I was told that I would learn that during the course of my journey east. I have an ancient family connection to the eastern part of the world, for in the time of the first Claudius my great ancestor Gnaeus Domitius Corbulo was proconsul of Asia with his seat at Ephesus, and then governor of Syria under Nero, and various other Corbulos since his time have dwelled in those distant regions. It seemed almost agreeable to be renewing the tradition, however involuntary the renewal. Gladly would I have settled for Arabia Petraea if I had to go to Arabia at all: it is a reasonable destination for a highly placed Roman gentleman temporarily out of favor with his monarch. But of course my hopes were centered on Arabia Felix, which by all accounts was the more congenial land.

The voyage from Roma to Syria Palaestina—pfaugh, Horatius! Nightmare. Torture. Seasick every day. Beloved friend, I am no seafaring man. Then came a brief respite in Caesarea Maritima, the one good part, lovely cosmopolitan city, wine flowing freely, complacent pretty girls everywhere, and, yes, Horatius, I must confess it, some pretty boys too. I stayed there as long as I could. But eventually I received word that the caravan that was to take me down into Arabia was ready to depart, and I had to go.

Let no one beguile you with romantic tales of desert travel. For a civilized man it is nothing but torment and agony.

Three steps to the inland side of Jerusalem and you find yourself in the hottest, driest country this side of Hades; and things only get worse from there. Every breath you take hits your lungs like a blast from an oven. Your nostrils, your ears, your lips become coated with windborne particles of grit. The sun is like a fiery iron platter in the sky. You go for miles without seeing a single tree or shrub, nothing but rock and red sand. Mocking phantoms dance before you in the shimmering air. At night if you are lucky enough or weary enough to be able to drop off to sleep for a little while, you dream longingly of lakes and gardens and green lawns, but then you are awakened by the scrabbling sound of a scorpion in the sand beside your cheek, and you lie there sobbing in the stifling heat, praying that you will die before the coming of the fiery dawn.

Somewhere in the midst of all this dead wilderness the traveler leaves the province of Syria Palaestina and enters Arabia, though no one can say precisely where the boundary lies. The first thing you come to, once across that invisible line, is the handsome city of Petra of the Nabataeans, an impregnable rock-fortress that stands athwart all the caravan routes. It is a rich city and, aside from the eternal parching heat, quite a livable one. I would not have greatly minded serving out my time of exile there.

But no, no, the letter of instruction from His Imperial Majesty that awaited me in Petra informed me that I needs must go onward, farther south. Arabia Petraea was not the part of Arabia that he had in mind for me. I enjoyed three days of civilized urban amusement there and then I was in the desert again, traveling by camel this time. I will spare you the horrors of that experience. We were heading, they let me know, for the Nabataean port of Leuke Kome on the Red Sea.

Excellent, I thought. This Leuke Kome is the chief port of embarkation for travelers sailing on to Arabia Felix. So they must be sending me to that fertile land of soft breezes and sweet-smelling blossoms, of spices and precious stones. I imagined myself waiting out my seasons of banishment in a cozy little villa beside the sea, nibbling tender dates and studying the fine brandies of the place. Perhaps I would dabble a bit in the frankincense trade or do a little lucrative business in cinnamon and cassia to pass the time.

At Leuke Kome I presented myself to the Imperial legate, a sleek and self-important young popinjay named Florentius Victor, and asked him how long it would be before my ship was to leave. He looked at me blankly. "Ship? What ship? Your route lies overland, my dear Leontius Corbulo." He handed me the last of my letters of instruction, by which I was informed that my final destination was a place by the name of Macoraba, where I was to serve as commercial representative of His Imperial Majesty's government, with the special responsibility of resolving any trade conflicts that might arise with such representatives of the Eastern Empire as might be stationed there.

"Macoraba? And just where is that?"

"Why, in Arabia Deserta," said Florentius Victor blandly.

"Arabia Deserta?" I repeated, with a sinking heart.

"Exactly. A very important city, as cities in that part of the world go. Every caravan crossing Arabia has to stop there. Perhaps you've heard of it under its Saracen name. *Mecca* is what the Saracens call it."

Arabia Deserta, Horatius! Arabia Deserta! For the trifling crime of tampering with the innocence of his unimportant little British cup-boy, the heartless vindictive Emperor has buried me in this brutal netherworld of remorseless heat and drifting dunes.

I have been in Macoraba — Mecca, I should say — just three or four days, now. It seems like a lifetime already.

What do we have in this land of Arabia Deserta? Why, nothing but a desolate torrid sandy plain intersected by sharp and naked hills. There are no rivers and rain scarcely ever falls. The sun is merciless. The wind is unrelenting. The dunes shift and heave like ocean waves in a storm: whole legions could be buried and lost by a single day's gusts. For trees they have only scrubby little tamarinds and acacias, that take their nourishment from the nightly dews. Here and there one finds pools of brackish water rising from the bowels of the earth, and these afford a bit of green pasture and sometimes some moist ground on which the date-palm and the grapevine can take root, but it is a sparse life indeed for those who have elected to settle in such places.

In the main the Saracens are a wandering race who endlessly guide their flocks of horses and sheep and camels back and forth across this hard arid land, seeking out herbage for their beasts where they can. All the year long they follow the seasons about, moving from seacoast to mountains to plains, so that they can take advantage of such little rainfall as there is, falling as it does in different months in these different regions. From time to time they venture farther afield — to the banks of the Nile or the farming villages of Syria or the valley of the Euphrates — to descend as brigands upon the placid farmers of those places and extort their harvests from them.

The harshness of the land makes it a place of danger and distress, of rapine and fear. In their own self-interest the Saracens form themselves into little tribal bands under the absolute government of fierce and ruthless elders; warfare between these tribes is constant; and so vehement is each man's sense of personal honor that offense is all too easily given and private blood-feuds persist down through generation after generation, yet ancient offenses never seem to be wiped out.

Two settlements here have come to be dignified with the name of "cities." Cities, Horatius! Mudholes with walls about them, rather. In the northern part of this desert one finds Iatrippa, which in the Saracens' own tongue is named *Medina*. It has a population of 15,000 or so, and as Arabian villages go is fairly well provided with water, so that it possesses abundant date-groves, and its people live comfortable lives, as comfort is understood in this land.

Then, a ten-day caravan journey to the south, through somber thorny land broken now and then by jutting crags of dark stone, is the town our geographers know as Macoraba, the *Mecca* of the locals. This Mecca is a bigger place, perhaps 25,000 people, and it is of such ineffable ugliness that Virgil himself would not have been able to conceive of it. Imagine, if you will, a "city" whose buildings are drab hovels of mud and brick, strung out along a rocky plain a mile wide and two miles long that lies at the foot of three stark mountains void of all vegetation. The flinty soil is useless for agriculture. The one sizable well yields bitter water. The nearest pasture land is fifty miles away. I have never seen so unprepossessing a site for human habitation.

You can readily guess, I think, which of the two cities of Arabia Deserta our gracious Emperor chose as my place of exile.

"Why," said I to Nicomedes the Paphlagonian, who was kind enough to invite me to be his dinner guest on my second depressing night in Mecca, "would anyone in his right mind have chosen to found a city in a location of this sort?"

Nicomedes, as his name will have indicated, is a Greek. He is the legate in Arabia Deserta of our Emperor's royal colleague, the Eastern Emperor Maurice Tiberius, and he is, I suspect, the real reason why I have been sent here, as I will explain shortly.

"It's in the middle of nowhere," I said. "We're forty miles from the sea and on the other side there's hundreds of miles of empty desert. Nothing will grow here. The climate is appalling and the ground is mostly rock. I can't see the slightest reason why any person, even a Saracen, would want to live here."

Nicomedes the Paphlagonian, who is a handsome man of about fifty with thick white hair and affable blue eyes, smiled and nodded. "I'll give you two, my friend. One is that nearly all commerce in Arabia is handled by caravan. The Red Sea is a place of tricky currents and treacherous reefs. Sailors abhor it. Therefore in Arabia goods travel mainly by land, and all the caravans have to pass this way, because Mecca is situated precisely at the mid-point between Damascus up north and the thriving cities of Arabia Felix down below us, and it also commands the one passable east-west route across the remarkably dreadful desert that lies between the Persian Gulf and the Red Sea. The caravans that come here are richly laden indeed, and the merchants and hostelkeepers and tax-collectors of Mecca do the kind of lively business that middlemen always do. You should know, my dear Leontius Corbulo, that there are a great many very wealthy men in this town."

He paused and poured more wine for us: some wonderful sweet stuff from Rhodes, hardly what I would have expected anyone in this remote outpost to keep on hand for casual guests.

"You said there were two reasons," I reminded him, after a time.

"Oh, yes. Yes." He had not forgotten. He is an unhurried man. "This is also a sacred city, do you see? There is a shrine in Mecca, a sanctuary, which they call the Kaaba. You should visit it tomorrow. It'll be good for you to get out and about town: it will make the time pass more cheerfully. Look for a squat little cubical building of black stone in the center of a great plaza. It's quite unsightly, but unimaginably holy in Saracen eyes. It contains some sort of lump of rock that fell from heaven, which they think of as a god. The Saracen tribesmen from all over the country make pilgrimages here to worship at the Kaaba. They march round and round it, bowing to the stone, kissing it, sacrificing sheep and camels to it, and afterward they gather in the taverns and hold recitations of war poetry and amorous verses. Very beautiful poetry, in its own barbarous fashion, I think. These pilgrims come here by the *thousands*. There's money in having the national shrine in your town, Corbulo: big money."

His eyes were gleaming. How the Greeks love moneymaking!

"Then, too," he went on, "the chieftains of Mecca have very shrewdly proclaimed that in the holy city all feuds and tribal wars are strictly forbidden during these great religious festivals. You know about the Saracens and their feuds? Well, you'll learn. At any rate, it's very useful to everybody in this country for one city to be set aside as a place where you don't have to be afraid of getting a scimitar in your gut if you chance to meet the wrong person while crossing the street. A lot of business gets done here during the times of truce between people from tribes that hate each other the rest of the year. And the Meccans take their cut, do you follow me? That is the life of the city: collecting percentages on everything. Oh, this may be a dismal hideous town, Corbulo, but there are men living here who could buy the likes of you and me in lots of two dozen."

"I see." I paused just a moment. "And the Eastern Empire, I take it, must be developing significant business interests in this part of Arabia, or else why would the Eastern Emperor have stationed a high official like you here?"

"We're beginning to have a little trade with the Saracens; yes," the Greek said. "Just a little." And he filled my glass yet again.

The next day—hot, dry, dusty, like every day here—I did go to look at this Kaaba of theirs. Not at all hard to find: right in the center of town, in fact, standing by itself in the midst of an empty square of enormous size. The holy building itself was unimposing, perhaps fifty feet high at best, covered completely by a thick veil of black cloth. I think you could have put the thing down in the courtyard of the Temple of Jupiter Capitolinus or any of Roma's other great temples and it would utterly disappear from view.

This did not seem to be pilgrimage season. There was no one around the Kaaba but a dozen or so Saracen guards. They were armed with such formidable swords, and looked so generally unfriendly, that I chose not to make a closer inspection of the shrine.

My early wanderings through the town showed me very little that indicated the presence of the prosperity that Nicomedes the Paphlagonian had claimed was to be found here. But in the course of the next few days I came gradually to understand that the Saracens are not a people to flaunt their wealth, but prefer instead to conceal it behind unadorned facades. Now and again I would have a peek through a momentarily opened gate into a briefly visible courtyard and got the sense of a palatial building hidden back there, or I would see some merchant and his wife, richly robed and laden with jewels and gold chains, climbing into a shrouded sedan-chair, and I knew from such fitful glimpses that this must indeed be a wealthier city than it looked. Which explains, no doubt, why our Greek cousins have started to find it so appealing.

These Saracens are a handsome people, lean and finely made, very dark of skin, dark hair and eyes as well, with sharp features and prominent brows. They wear airy white robes and the women go veiled, I suppose to protect their skins against the blowing sand. Thus far I have seen more than a few young men who might be of interest to me, and they gave me quick flashing looks, too, that indicated response, though it was far too soon to take any such risks here. The maidens also are lovely. But they are very well guarded.

My own situation here is more pleasing, or at least less displeasing, than I had feared. I feel the pain of my isolation, of course. There are no other Westerners. Greek is widely understood by the better class of Saracens, but I yearn already for the sound of good honest Latin. Still, it has been arranged for me to have a walled villa, of modest size but decent enough, at the edge of town nearest the mountains. If only it had proper baths, it would be perfect; but in a land without water there is no understanding of baths. A great pity, that. The villa belongs to a merchant of Syrian origin who will be spending the next two or three years traveling abroad. I have inherited five of his servants as well. A wardrobe of clothing in the local style has been provided for me.

It all might have been much worse, eh?

But in truth they couldn't simply have left me to shift for myself in this strange land. I am still an official of the Imperial court, after all, even though I happen currently to be in disfavor and exile. I am here on Imperial business, you know. It was not just out of mere pique that Julian shipped me here, even though I had angered him mightily by getting to his cup-boy before him. I realize now that he must have been looking for an excuse to send someone to this place who could serve unofficially as an observer for him, and I inadvertently gave him the pretext he needed.

Do you understand? He is worried about the Greeks, who evidently have set about the process of extending their authority into this part of the world, which has always been more or less independent of the Empire. My formal assignment, as I have said, is to investigate the possibilities of expanding Roman business interests in Arabia Deserta—*Western* Roman, that is. But I have a covert assignment as well, one so covert that not even I have been informed of its nature, that has to do with the growing power of Romans of the other sort in that region.

What I am saying, in ordinary language, is that I am actually a spy, sent here to keep watch over the Greeks.

Yes, I know, it is all one empire that happens to have two emperors, and we of the West are supposed to look upon the Greeks as our cousins and co-administrators of the world, not as our rivals. Sometimes it actually does work that way, I will concede. As in the time of Maximilianus III, for example, when the Greeks helped us put an end to the disturbances that the Goths and Vandals and Huns and other barbarians were creating along our northern frontier. And then again a generation later, when Heraclius II sent Western legions to help the Eastern Emperor Justinian smash the forces of Persia that had been causing the Greeks such trouble to the east for so many years. Those were, of course, the two great military strokes that eliminated the Empire's enemies for good and laid the foundations for the era of eternal peace and safety in which we live now.

But an excess of peace and safety, Horatius, can bring niggling little problems of its own. With no external enemies left to worry about, the Eastern and Western Empires are beginning to jockey with each other for advantage. Everybody understands that, though no one says it aloud. There was that time, let me remind you, when the ambassador of Maurice Tiberius came to court, bearing a casket of pearls as a gift for Caesar. I was there. "Et dona ferentes," said Julian to me under his breath, as the casket was uncovered. The line every schoolboy knows: *I fear Greeks even when bringing gifts.*

Is the Eastern Empire trying to put a drawstring around the midsection of Arabia, and by so doing to gain control over the trade in spices and other precious exotic merchandise that passes this way? It would not be a good thing for us to become altogether dependent on the Greeks for our cinnamon and our cardamom, our frankincense and our indigo. The very steel of our swords comes westward to us out of Persia by way of this Arabia, and the horses that draw our chariots are Arabian horses.

And so the Emperor Julian, feigning great wrath and loudly calling me a serpent before all the court when the matter of the little cup-bearer became known, has thrust me into this parched land primarily to find out what the Greeks are really up to here, and perhaps also to establish certain political connections with powerful Saracens myself, connections that he can employ in blocking the Eastern Empire's apparent foray into these regions. Or so I do believe, Horatius. So I *must* believe, and I must make Caesar believe it himself. For it is only by doing some great service for the Emperor that I can redeem myself from this woeful place and win my way back to Roma, to Caesar's side and to yours, my sweet friend, to yours.

The night before last—I have been in Mecca eight days, now—Nicomedes invited me once again for dinner. He was dressed, as I was, in white Saracen robes, and wore a lovely dagger in a jeweled sheath strapped to his waist. I glanced quickly at it, feeling some surprise at being greeted by a host who wore a weapon; but instantly he took the thing off and presented it to me. He had mistaken my concern for admiration, and it is a Saracen custom, I have learned, to bestow upon one's guests anything in one's household that the guest might choose to admire.

We dined this time not in the tiled parlor where he had entertained me previously but in a cool courtyard beside a plashing fountain. The possession of such a fountain is a token of great luxury in this dry land. His servants brought us an array of fine wines and sweetmeats and cool sherbets. I could see that Nicomedes had modeled his manner of living after the style of the leading merchants of the city, and was reveling in that.

I had not been there very long when I got right down to the central issue: that is, what exactly it was that the Greek Emperor hoped to accomplish by stationing a royal legate in Mecca. Sometimes, I think, the best way for a spy to learn what he needs to learn is to put aside all guile and play the role of a simple, straightforward, ingenuous man who merely speaks his heart.

So as we sat over roast mutton and plump dates in warm milk I said, "Is it the Eastern Emperor's hope to incorporate Arabia into the Empire, then?"

Nicomedes laughed. "Oh, we're not so foolish as to think we can do that. No one's ever been able to conquer this place, you know. The Egyptians tried it, and the Persians of Cyrus's time, and Alexander the Great. Augustus sent an expedition in here, ten thousand men, six months to fight their way in and sixty days of horrible retreat. I think Trajan made an attempt too. The thing is, Corbulo, these Saracens are free men, free *within themselves*, which is a kind of freedom that you and I are simply not equipped to comprehend. They can't be conquered because they can't be governed. Trying to conquer them is like trying to conquer lions or tigers. You can whip a lion or even kill it, yes, but you can't possibly impose your will on it even if you keep it in a cage for twenty years. These are a race of lions here. Government as we understand it is a concept that can never exist here."

"They are organized into tribes, aren't they? That's a sort of government."

He shrugged. "Built out of nothing more than family loyalty. You can't fashion any sort of national administration out of it. Kinsman looks after kinsman and everybody else is regarded as a potential enemy. There are no kings here, do you realize that? Never have been. Just tribal chieftains—*emirs*, they call them. A land without kings is never going to submit to an emperor. We could fill this entire peninsula with soldiers, fifty legions, and the Saracens would simply melt away into the desert and pick us off one by one from a distance with javelins and arrows. An invisible enemy striking at us from a terrain that we can't survive in. They're unconquerable, Corbulo. Unconquerable."

There was passion in his voice, and apparent sincerity. The Greeks are good at apparent sincerity.

I said, "So the best you're looking for is some kind of trade agreement, is that it? Just an informal Byzantine presence, not any actual incorporation of the region into the Empire."

He nodded. "That's about right. Is your Emperor bothered by that?"

"It's drawn his attention, I would say. We wouldn't want to lose access to the goods we obtain from this part of the world. And also those from places like India to the east that normally ship their merchandise westward by way of Arabia."

"But why would that happen, my dear Corbulo? This is a single empire, is it not? Julian II rules from Roma and Maurice Tiberius rules from Constantinopolis, but they rule jointly for the common good of all Roman citizens everywhere. As has been the case since the great Constantinus divided the realm in the first place three hundred years ago."

Yes. Of course. That is the official line. But I know better and you know better and Nicomedes the Paphlagonian knew better too. I had pushed the issue as far as seemed appropriate just then, however. It was time to move on to more frivolous topics.

I found, though, that dropping the matter was not all that easily done. Having voiced my suspicions, I thereby had invited counterargument, and Nicomedes was not finished providing it. I had no choice but to listen while he wove such a web of words about me that it completely captured me into his way of thinking. The Greeks are damnably clever with words, of course; and he had lulled me with sweet wines and surfeited me with an abundance of fine food so that I was altogether unable just then to refute and rebut, and before he was done with me my mind was utterly spun around on the subject of East versus West.

He assured me in twenty different ways that an expansion of the Eastern Empire's influence into Arabia Deserta, if such a thing were to take place, would not in any way jeopardize existing Western Roman trade in Arabian or Indian merchandise. Arabia Petraea just to the north had long been under the Eastern Empire's administration, he pointed out, and that was true also of the provinces of Syria Palaestina and Aiguptos and Cappadocia and Mesopotamia and all those other sunny eastern lands that Constantinus, at the time of the original division of the realm, had placed under the jurisdiction of the Emperor who would sit at Constantinopolis. Did I believe that the prosperity of the Western Empire was in any way hampered by having those provinces under Byzantine administration? Had I not just traveled freely through many of those provinces on my way here? Was there not a multitude of Western Roman merchants resident in them, and were they not free to do business there as they wished?

I could not contest any of that. I wanted to disagree, to summon up a hundred instances of subtle Eastern interference with Western trade, but just then I could not offer even one.

Believe me, Horatius, at that moment I found myself quite unable to understand why I had ever conceived such a mistrust of Greek intentions. They are indeed our cousins, I told myself. They are Greek Romans and we are Roman Romans, yes, but the Empire itself is one entity, chosen by the gods to rule the world. A gold piece struck in Constantinopolis is identical in weight and design to one struck in Roma. One bears the name and face of the Eastern Emperor, one the name and face of the Emperor of the West, but all else is the same. The coins of one realm pass freely in the other. Their prosperity is our prosperity; our prosperity is theirs. And so on and so forth.

But as I thought these things, Horatius, I also realized gloomily that by so doing I was undercutting in my own mind my one tenuous hope of freeing myself from this land of burning sands and stark treeless hills. As I noted in my most recent letter, what I need is some way of saying, "Look, Caesar, how well I have served you!" so that he would say in return, "Well done, thou good and faithful servant," and summon me back to the pleasures of the court. For that to occur, though, I must show Caesar that he has enemies here, and give him the way of dealing with those enemies. But what enemies? Who? Where?

We were done with our meal now. Nicomedes clapped his hands and a servitor brought a flask of some rich golden brandy that came, he said, from a desert principality on the shores of the Persian Gulf. It dazzled my palate and further befogged my mind.

He conducted me, then, through the rooms of his villa, pointing out the highlights of what even in my blurred condition I could see was an extraordinary collection of antiquities and curios: fine Greek bronze figurines, majestic sculptures from Egypt done in black stone, strange wooden masks of barbaric design that came, he said, from the unknown lands of torrid Africa, and much, much more.

He spoke of each piece with the deepest knowledge. By now I had come to see that my host was not only a devious diplomat but also a person of some power and consequence in the Eastern realm, and a scholar of note besides. I was grateful to him for having reached out so generously to me in these early days of my lonely exile — to the displaced and unhappy Roman nobleman, bereft of all that was familiar to him, a stranger in a strange land. But I knew also that I was *meant* to be grateful to him, that it was his purpose to ensnare me in the bonds of friendship and obligation, so that I would have nothing but good things to say about the Greek legate in Mecca should I ever return to my master the Emperor Julian II.

Would I ever return, though? That was the question.

That *is* the question, yes. Will I ever see Roma of the green hills and shining marble palaces again, Horatius, or am I doomed to bake in the heat of this oven of a desert forever?

Having no occupation here and having as yet found no friends other than Nicomedes, whose companionship I could not presume to demand too often, I whiled away the days that followed in close exploration of the town.

The shock of finding myself resident in this squalid little place has begun to wear off. I have started to adapt, to some degree, to the change that has come over my existence. The pleasures of Roma are no longer mine to have; very well, I must search out such diversion as is to be found here, for there is no place in the world, humble though it be, that does not offer diversion of some sort to him who has eyes for finding it.

So in these days since my last letter I have roamed from one end of Mecca to the other, up and down the broad though unpaved boulevards and into many of the narrow lanes and byways that intersect them. My presence does not appear to be greatly troublesome to anyone, although from time to time I do become cognizant that I am the object of someone's cold, gleaming stare.

I am, as you know, the only Roman of the West in Mecca, but scarcely the only foreigner. In the various marketplaces I have seen Persians, Syrians, Ethiopians, and of course a good many Greeks. There are numerous Indians here as well, dark lithe people with conspicuous luminous eyes, and also some Hebrews, these being a people who live mainly over in Aiguptos, just on the other side of the Red Sea from Arabia. They have been resident in Aiguptos for thousands of years, though evidently they were originally a desert tribe from some country much like this one, and they are not in any way Aiguptian in language or culture or religion. These Hebrews have in modern times begun to spread from their home along the Nilus into the lands adjacent, and there are more than a few of them here. Nicomedes has spoken of them to me.

They are unusual people, the Hebrews. The most interesting thing about them is that they believe there is only one god, a harsh and austere deity who cannot be seen and who must not be portrayed in images of any sort. They have nothing but contempt for the gods of other races, deeming them wholly imaginary, mere creatures of fable and fantasy that possess no true existence. This may very likely be the case, certainly: who among us has ever laid eyes on Apollo or Mercury or Minerva? Most people, however, have the good sense not to make a mockery of the religious practices of others, whereas the Hebrews apparently cannot keep themselves from trumpeting the virtues of their own odd species of belief while denouncing everybody else most vociferously as idolaters and fools.

As you can readily imagine, this does not make them very popular among their neighbors. But they are an industrious folk, with special aptitudes for the sciences of agriculture and irrigation, and a notable knack, also, for finance and trade, which is why Nicomedes has paid such attention to them. He tells me that they own most of the best land in the northern part of the country, that they are the chief bankers here in Mecca, and that they control the markets in weapons, armor, and agricultural tools everywhere in the land. It seems advantageous for me to get to know one or two important Hebrews of Mecca and I have made attempts to do so, thus far without any success, during the course of my ramblings in the marketplaces.

The markets here are very specialized, each offering its own kind of merchandise. I have visited them all by now.

There is a spice-market, of course: great sacks of pepper both black and white, and garlic and cumin and saffron, sandalwood and cassia, aloes, spikenard, and an aromatic dried leaf that they call malabathron, and hosts of other things I could not begin to name. There is a camel-market, only on certain days of the week, where those strange beasts are bought and sold in heated bargaining that goes to the edge of actual combat. I went up to one of these creatures to see it better and it yawned in my face as though I were the dullest of rogues. There is a market for cloth, which deals in muslins and silks and cotton both Indian and Aiguptian, and a market where crude idols of many kinds are sold to the credulous—I saw a Hebrew man walk past it, and spit and glare and make what I think was a holy sign of his people—and a market for wines, and one for perfumes, and the market of meat and the one of grains, and the market where the Hebrew merchants sell their iron goods, and one for fruits of all kinds, pomegranates and quinces and citrons and lemons and sour oranges and grapes and peaches, all this in the midst of the most forbidding desert you could imagine!

And also there is a market for slaves, which is where I encountered the remarkable man who called himself Mahmud.

The slave-market of Mecca is as bustling as any slave-market anywhere, which illustrates how great a degree of prosperity lies behind the deceptively shabby facade this city displays to strangers. It is the great flesh-mart of the land, and buyers sometimes come from as far away as Syria and the Persian Gulf to check out the slavemongers' latest haul of desirable human exotica.

Though wood is a luxury in this desert country, there is the usual platform of planks and timbers, the usual awning suspended from a couple of poles, the usual sorry huddle of naked merchandise waiting to be sold. As usual, they were a mix of all races, though with a distinct Asian and African cast, here: Ethiops dark as night and brawny Nubians even darker, and flat-faced fair-skinned Circassians and Avars and other sinewy northern folk, and some who might have been Persians or Indians, and even a sullen yellow-haired man who could have been a Briton or Teuton. The auctions were conducted, quite naturally, in the Saracen tongue, so that I understood nothing of what was said, but I suppose it was the customary fraudulent gabble that fools no one, how this buxom sultry Turkish wench was a king's daughter in her own land, and this thick-bearded scowling Libyan had been a charioteer of the highest distinction before his master's bankruptcy had forced his sale, and so forth.

It so happened that I was passing the auction place at noonday three days past when three supple tawny-skinned wantons, who from their shameless movements and smiles must have been very skilled prostitutes indeed, came up for sale as a single lot, intended perhaps as concubines for some great emir. They wore nothing but jingling bracelets of silver coins about their wrists and ankles, and were laughing and thrusting their breasts from side to side and winking at the crowd to invite active bidding on behalf of their seller, who for all I know was their uncle or their brother.

The spectacle was so lively that I paused to observe it a moment. Hardly had I taken my place in the crowd, though, than the man standing just to my left surprised me by turning toward me and muttering, in a vibrant tone of intense fury powerfully contained, "Ah, the swine! They should be whipped and turned out into the desert for the jackals to eat!" This he said in quite passable Greek, uttering the words in a low whisper that nonetheless was strikingly rich and captivating, one of the most musical speaking voices I have ever heard. It was as though the words had overflowed his soul and he had had no choice but to utter them at once to the man closest at hand.

The power of that extraordinary voice and the violence of his sentiment had the most singular effect on me. It was as though I had been seized by the wrist in an irresistible grip. I stared at him. He was holding himself taut as a bowstring when the archer is at the verge of letting fly, and appeared to be trembling with wrath.

Some sort of response seemed incumbent on me. The best I could do was to say, "The girls, do you mean?"

"The slavemasters," said he. "The women are but chattel. They are not to be held accountable. But it is wrong to put chattel out for pandering, as these criminals do."

And then, relaxing his stance a bit and looking now somewhat abashed at his forwardness, he said in a far less assertive tone of voice, "But you must forgive me for pouring these thoughts into the unwilling ears of a stranger who surely has no interest in hearing such things."

"On the contrary. What you say interests me greatly. Indeed, you must tell me more."

I studied him with no little curiosity. It had crossed my mind immediately that he might be a Hebrew: his horror and rage at the sight of this trifling bit of flesh-peddling seemed to mark him as a kinsman of that dour man who had made such a display of irate piety in the marketplace of idols. You will recall that I had resolved to seek contact with members of that agile-minded race of merchants here. But a moment's closer examination of his look and garb led me now to realize that he must be pure Saracen by blood.

There was tremendous presence and force about him. He was tall and slender, a handsome dark-haired man of perhaps thirty-five years or a little more, with a dense flowing beard, piercing eyes, and a warm and gracious smile that quite contradicted the unnerving ferocity of his gaze. His princely bearing, his eloquent manner of speech, and the fineness of his garments all suggested that he was a man of wealth and breeding, well connected in this city. At once I sensed that he might be even more useful to me than any Hebrew. So I drew him out, questioning him a little on the reasons for his spontaneous outburst against the trade in easy women in this marketplace, and without the slightest hesitation he poured forth a powerful and lengthy tirade, fierce in content although stated in that same captivating musical tone, against the totality of the sins of his countrymen. And what a multitude of sins they were! Mere prostitution was the least of them. I had not expected to encounter such a Cato here.

"Look about you!" he urged me. "Mecca is an utter abyss of wickedness. Do you see the idols that are sold everywhere, and set up piously in shops and homes in places of respect? They are false gods, these images, for the true god, and He is One, cannot be rendered by any image. Do you observe the flagrant cheating in the marketplaces? Do you see the men lying shamelessly to their wives, and the wives lying as well, and the gambling and the drinking and the whoring, and the quarreling between brother and brother?" And there was much more. I could see that he held this catalog of outrage pent up in his breast at all times, ready to issue it forth whenever he found some new willing listener. Yet he said all this not in any lofty and superior way, but almost in bewilderment: he was saddened rather than infuriated by the failings of his brethren, or so it seemed to me.

Then he paused, once again changing tone, as though it had occurred to him that it was impolite to remain in this high denunciatory mode for any great length of time. "Again I ask you to pardon me for my excess of zeal. I feel very strongly on these matters. It is the worst of my faults, I hope. If I am not mistaken, you are the Roman who has come to live among us?"

"Yes. Leontius Corbulo, at your service. A Roman of the Romans, I like to say." I gave him a flourish. "My family is a very ancient one, with historic ties to Syria and other parts of Asia."

"Indeed. I am Mahmud son of Abdallah, who was the son of—" Well, the son of I forget whom, who was the son of so-and-so, the son of someone else. It is the custom of these Saracens to let you have their pedigrees five or six generations back in a single outburst of breath, but it was impossible for me to retain most of the barbarous outlandish names in my mind very long. I do recall his telling me that he was a member of one of the great mercantile clans of Mecca, which is called something like the *Koreish*.

It seemed to me that a strong rapport had arisen between us in just these few moments, and, such was the power of his personality, I was reluctant to leave him. Since it was the time for the midday meal, I proposed that we take it together, and invited him to come with me to my villa. But he responded that I was a guest in Mecca and it was not fitting for him to enjoy my hospitality until I had partaken of his. I didn't try to dispute the issue. The Saracens, I had already begun to learn, are most punctilious about this sort of thing. "Come," he said, beckoning. And so it was that for the first time I entered the home of a wealthy merchant of Mecca.

The villa of Mahmud son of Abdallah was not unlike that of Nicomedes, though on a larger scale — walled courtyard, central fountain, bright airy rooms, inlays of vividly colored tile set in the walls. But unlike Nicomedes, Mahmud was no collector of antiquities. He appeared to have scarcely any possessions at all. A prevailing austerity of decoration was the rule in his house. And of course there was no sign anywhere in it of the idols that other Meccans seemed to cherish.

The wife of Mahmud made a fleeting appearance. Her name was something like Kadija, and she seemed considerably older than her husband, a fact soon confirmed from Mahmud's own lips. A couple of daughters passed to and fro in equally brief manner. But he and I dined alone, seated on straw mats in the center of a huge bare room. Mahmud sat cross-legged like a tailor, and appeared to be entirely at ease in that posture. I tried but failed to manage it, and after a time fell into the normal reclining position, wishing mightily that I had a cushion for my elbow, but not willing to give offense by asking for one. The meal itself was simple, grilled meat and a stew of barley and melons, with nothing but water to wash it down. Mahmud did not, it seemed, care for wine.

He spoke of himself with complete openness, as though we were kinsmen from widely distant lands who were meeting for the first time. I learned that Mahmud's father had died before his birth and his mother had lived only a short while thereafter, so he had grown up in impoverished circumstances under the guardianship of an uncle. From his tale I received the impression of a lonely childhood spent wandering the cheerless rocky hills beyond town, pondering from an early age, perhaps, the great questions of eternity and the spirit that plainly have continued to obsess him to this day.

In his twenty-fifth year, said Mahmud, he entered into the service of the woman Kadija, a wealthy widow fifteen years his senior, who soon fell in love with him and asked him to be her husband. This he told me with no trace of embarrassment at all, and I suppose he has no reason to feel any. A look of happiness comes into his eyes when he speaks of her. She has borne him both sons and daughters, though only the daughters have survived. The prosperity that he enjoys today is, I gather, the result of his skillful management of the property that his wife brought to their union.

About Roma, Constantinopolis, or any other place beyond the frontiers of Arabia Deserta, he asked me nothing whatever. Though his intelligence is deep and questing, he did not seem concerned with the empires of this world. It appears that he has scarcely been outside Mecca at all, though he mentioned having made a journey as far as Damascus on one occasion. I would think him a simple man if I did not know, Horatius, how complex in fact he is.

The great preoccupation of his life is his concept of the One God.

This is, of course, the idea famously advocated since antiquity by the Hebrews. I have no doubt that Mahmud has had conversations with the members of that race who live in Mecca, and that their ideas have affected his philosophy. He must surely have heard them express their reverence for their aloof and unknowable god, and their contempt for the superstitions of the Meccans, who cherish such a multitude of idols and talismans and practice a credulous veneration of the sun and the moon and stars and planets and a myriad of demons. He makes no secret of this: I heard him make reference to an ancient Hebrew prophet called Abraham, who is apparently a figure he greatly admires, and also a certain Moses, a later leader of that tribe.

But he lays claim to a separate revelation of his own. He asserts that his special enlightenment came as the result of arduous private prayer and contemplation. He would go up often into the mountains behind the town and meditate in solitude in a secluded cave; and one day an awareness of the Oneness of God was revealed to him as though by a divine messenger.

Mahmud calls this god "Allah." A marvelous transformation comes over him when he begins to speak of him. His face glows; his eyes take on the quality of beacons; his very voice becomes such a thing of music and poetry that you would think you were in the presence of Apollo.

It is impossible, he says, ever to understand the nature of Allah. He is too far above us for that. Other people may regard their gods as personages in some kind of story, and tell lively fanciful tales of their travels throughout the world and their quarrels with their wives and their adventures on the battlefield, and make statues of them that show them as men and women, but Allah is not like that. One does not tell tales about Allah. He cannot be thought of as a tall man with a commanding face and a full beard and a host of passions—someone rather like an Emperor, let us say, but on a larger scale—and it is foolishness, as well as blasphemy, to make representations of him the way the ancient Greeks did of such gods of theirs as Zeus and Aphrodite and Poseidon, or we do of Jupiter or Venus or Mars. Allah is the creative force itself, the maker of the universe, too mighty and vast to be captured by any sort of representation.

I asked Mahmud how, if it is blasphemous to imagine a face for his god, it can be acceptable to give him a name. For surely that is a kind of representation also. Mahmud seemed pleased at the sharpness of my question; and he explained that "Allah" is not actually a name, as "Mahmud" or "Leontius Corbulo" or "Jupiter" are names, but is a mere word, simply the term in the Saracen language that means *the god*.

To Mahmud, the fact that there is only one god, whose nature is abstract and incomprehensible to mortals, is the great sublime law from which all other laws flow. This will probably make no more sense to you, Horatius, than it does to me, but it is not our business to be philosophers. What is of interest here is that the man has such a passionate belief in the things he believes. So passionate is it that as you listen to him you become caught up in the simplicity and the beauty of his ideas and the power of his way of speaking of them, and you are almost ready to cry out your belief in Allah yourself.

It is a very simple creed indeed, but enormously powerful in its directness, the way things in this harsh and uncompromising desert land tend to be. He stringently rejects all idol-worship, all fable-making, all notions of how the movements of the stars and planets govern our lives. He places no trust in oracles or sorcery. The decrees of kings and princess mean very little to him either. He accepts only the authority of his remote and awesome and inflexible god, whose great stern decree it is that we live virtuous lives of hard work, piety, and respect for our fellow men. Those who live by Allah's law, says Mahmud, will be gathered into paradise at the end of their days; those who do not will descend into the most terrible of hells. And Mahmud does not intend to rest until all Arabia has been brought forth out of sloth and degeneracy and sin to accept the supremacy of the One God, and its scattered squabbling tribes forged at last into a single great nation under the rule of one invincible king who could enforce the laws of that god.

He was awesome in his conviction. By the time he was done, I was close to feeling the presence and might of Allah myself. That was surprising and a little frightening, that Mahmud could stir such feelings in me, of all people. I was amazed. But then he had finished his expounding, and after a few moments the sensation ebbed and I was myself again.

"What do you say?" he asked me. "Can this be anything other than the truth?"

"I am not in a position to judge that," said I carefully, not wishing to give offense to this interesting new friend, especially in his own dining hall. "We Romans are accustomed to regarding all creeds with tolerance, and if you ever visit our capital you will find temples of a hundred faiths standing side by side. But I do see the beauty of your teachings."

"Beauty? I asked about truth. When you say you accept all faiths as equally true, what you really say is that you see no truth in any of them, is that not so?"

I disputed that, reaching into my school days for maxims out of Plato and Marcus Aurelius to argue that all gods are reflections of the true godhood. But it was no use. He saw instantly through my Roman indifference to religion. If you claim to believe, as we do, that this god is just as good as that one, what you are really saying is that gods in general don't matter much at all. Our live-and-let-live policy toward the worship of Mithra and Dagon and Baal and all the other deities whose temples thrive in Roma is a tacit admission of that view. And for Mahmud that is a contemptible position.

Sensing the tension that was rising in him, and unwilling to have our pleasant conversation turn acrid, I offered a plea of fatigue, and promised to continue the discussion with him at another time.

In the evening, having been invited yet again to dine with Nicomedes the Paphlagonian and with my head still spinning from the thrust of all that Mahmud had imparted to me, I asked him if he could tell me anything about this extraordinary person.

"That man!" Nicomedes said, chuckling. "Consorting with madmen, are you, now, Corbulo?"

"He seemed quite sane to me."

"Oh, he is, he is, at least when he's selling you a pair of camels or a sack of saffron. But get him started on the subject of religion and you'll see a different man."

"As a matter of fact, we had quite a lengthy philosophical discussion, he and I, this very afternoon," I said. "I found it fascinating. I've never heard anything quite like it."

"I daresay you haven't. Poor chap, he should get himself away from this place while he's still got the chance. If he keeps on going the way I understand he's been doing lately, he'll turn up dead out in the dunes one of these days, and no one will be surprised."

"I don't follow you."

"Preaching against the idols the way he does, is what I mean. You know, Corbulo, they worship three hundred different gods in this city, and each one has his own shrine and his own priesthood and his own busy factory dedicated to making idols for sale to pilgrims, and so on and so forth. If I understand your Mahmud correctly, he'd like to shut all that down. Is that not so?"

"I suppose. Certainly he expressed plenty of scorn for idols, and idolaters."

"Indeed he does. Up till now he's simply had a little private cult, though, half a dozen members of his own family. They get together in his house and pray to his particular god in the particular way that Mahmud prescribes. An innocent enough pastime, I'd say. But lately, I'm told, he's been spreading his ideas farther afield, going around to this person and that and testing out his seditious ideas about how to reform Saracen society on them. As he did with you this very day, it seems. Well, it does no harm for him to be talking religion with somebody like you or me, because we Romans are pretty casual about such matters. But the Saracens aren't. Before long, mark my words, he'll decide to set himself up as a prophet who preaches in public, and he'll stand in the main square threatening fire and damnation to anybody who keeps to the old ways, and then they'll have to kill him. The old ways are big business here, and what this town is about is business and nothing but business. Mahmud is full of subversive notions that these Meccans can't afford to indulge. He'd better watch his step." And then, with a grin: "But he is an amusing devil, isn't he, Corbulo? As you can tell, I've had a chat or two with him myself."

If you ask me, Horatius, Nicomedes is half right and half wrong about Mahmud.

Surely he's correct that Mahmud is almost ready to begin preaching his religion in public. The way he accosted me, a total stranger, at the slave-market testifies to that. And his talk of not resting until Arabia has been made to accept the supremacy of the One God: what else can that mean, other than that he is on the verge of speaking out against the idolaters?

Mahmud told me in just so many words, during our lunch together, that the way Allah makes his commandments concerning good and evil known to mankind is through certain chosen prophets, one every thousand years or so. Abraham and Moses of the Hebrews were such prophets, Mahmud says. I do believe that Mahmud looks upon himself as their successor.

I think the Greek is wrong, though, in saying that Mahmud will be killed by his angry neighbors for speaking out against their superstitions. No doubt they'll *want* to kill him, at first. If his teachings ever prevail, they'll throw the whole horde of priests and idol-carvers out of business and knock a great hole in the local economy, and nobody here is going to be very enthusiastic about that. But his personality is so powerful that I think he'll win them over. By Jupiter, he practically had *me* willing to accept the divine omnipotence of Allah before he was done!

He'll find a way to put his ideas across to them. I can't imagine how he'll do it, but he's clever in a dozen different ways, a true desert merchant, and somehow he'll offer them something that will make it worthwhile for them to give up their old beliefs and accept his. Allah and no one else will be the god of this place, is what I expect, by the time Mahmud has finished his holy work.

I need to ponder all this very carefully. You don't come upon a man with Mahmud's kind of innate personal magnetism very often. I am haunted by the strength of it, awed by the recollection of how, for the moment, he had managed to win my allegiance to that One God of his. Is there, I wonder, some way that I can turn Mahmud's great power to sway men's minds to the service of the Empire, by which I mean to the service of Julian II Augustus? So that, of course, I can regain Caesar's good graces and get myself redeemed out of Arabian exile.

At the moment I don't quite see it. Perhaps I could urge him to turn his countrymen against the growing ascendancy of the Greeks in this part of the world, or some such thing. But this week I have plenty of time to think on it, for no company is available to me just now except my own. Mahmud, who travels frequently through the area on business, has gone off to one of the coastal villages to investigate some new mercantile venture. Nicomedes also is away, down into Arabia Felix, where he and his fellow Greeks no doubt are conniving covertly to raise the price of carnelians or aloe-wood or some other commodity currently in great demand at Roma.

So I am alone here but for my servants, a dull lot with whom I can have no hope of companionship. I toyed with the idea of buying myself a lively slave-boy in the bazaar to keep me company of a more interesting kind, but Mahmud, who is so fiery in his piety, might suspect what I had in mind, and I would not at this time want to risk a breach with Mahmud. The idea of such a purchase is very tempting, though.

I think longingly all the time of the court, the festivities at the royal palace, the theater and the games, all that I am missing. Fuscus Salinator: what is he up to? Voconius Rufus? Spurinna? Allifanus? And what of Emperor Julian himself, he who was my friend, almost my brother, until he turned on me and condemned me to languish like this amidst the sands of Arabia? What times we had together, he and I, until my fall from grace!

And—fear not—I think constantly of you, of course, Horatius. I wonder who you spend your nights with now. Male or female, is it? Lupercus Hector? Little Pomponia Mamiliana, perhaps? Or even the cup-boy from Britannia, whom surely the Emperor no longer would have wanted after I had sullied him. Well, you do not sleep alone, of that much I'm certain.

What, I wonder, would my new friend Mahmud think of our court and its ways? He is so severe and astringent of nature. His hatred for self-indulgence of all sorts seems deep as the bone: a stark prince of the desert, this man, a true Spartan. But perhaps I give him too much credit, you say? Set him up in a villa on the slopes of the Palatine, provide him with a fine chariot and a house full of servants and a cellar of decent wine, let him splash a bit in the Emperor's perfumed pool with Julian and his giddy friends, and it may be he'll sing another tune, eh?

No. No. I doubt that very greatly. Bring Mahmud to Roma and he will rise up like a modern Cato and sweep the place clean, purging the capital of all the sins of these soft Imperial years. And when he is done with us, Horatius, we shall all be faithful adherents to the creed of Allah.

Five days more of solitude went by, and by the end of it I was ready, I think, to open my veins. There has been a wind blowing here all week that bakes the brain to the verge of madness. The air seemed half composed of sand. People came and went in the streets like phantoms, all shrouded up to the eyes in white. I feared going outside.

For the past two days, though, the air has been calm again. Mahmud yesterday returned from his venture at the coast. I saw him in the main street, speaking with three or four other men. Even though he was some distance away, it was plain that Mahmud was doing nearly all the talking, and the others, caught in his spell, were reduced to mere nods and gestures of the hand. There is wizardry in this man's manner of speech. He casts a powerful spell. You are held; you cannot choose but listen; you find yourself believing whatever he says.

I did not feel it appropriate to approach him just then; but later in the day I sent one of my servants to his house bearing an invitation to dine with me at my villa, and we have spent some hours together this very day. It was a meeting that brought forth a host of startling revelations.

Neither of us chose to plunge back into the theological discussion of our previous conversation, and for a while we made mere idle arm's-length talk in the somewhat uneasy manner of two gentlemen of very different nations who find themselves dining in intimate circumstances and are determined to get through the meal without giving offense. Mahmud's manner was genial in a way I had not seen it before. But as the dishes of the first course were being cleared away the old intensity came back into his eyes and he said somewhat abruptly, "And tell me, my friend, how did it happen, exactly, that you came to our country in the first place?"

It would hardly have been useful to my burgeoning friendship with this man to admit that I had been banished here on account of my pederasty with Caesar's intended plaything. But—you must trust me on this—I had to tell him *something*. There is no easy way of being evasive when the burning eyes of Mahmud son of Abdallah are peering intently into your own. I could lie more readily to Caesar. Or to Jove himself.

And so, on the principle that telling part of the truth is usually more convincing than telling an outright lie, I admitted to him that my Emperor had sent me to Arabia to spy on the Greeks.

"*Your* Emperor who is not *their* Emperor, though it is all one empire."

"Exactly." Mahmud, isolated as he had been all his life from the greater world beyond Arabia's frontiers, seemed to understand the concept of the dual principate. And understood also how little real harmony there is between the two halves of the divided realm.

"And what harm is it that you think the Byzantine folk can cause your people, then?" he asked.

There was a tautness in his voice; I sensed that this was something more than an idle conversational query for him.

"Economic harm," I said. "Too much of what we import from the eastern nations passes through their hands as it is. Now they seem to be drifting down here into the middle of Arabia, where all the key trade routes converge. If they can establish a stranglehold on those routes, we'll be at their mercy."

He was silent for a time, digesting that. But his eyes flashed strange fire. His brain must have been awhirl with thought.

Then he leaned forward until we were almost nose to nose and said, in that low quiet voice of his that seizes your attention more emphatically than the loudest shout, "We share a common concern, then. They are our enemies too, these Greeks. I know their hearts. They mean to conquer us."

"But that's impossible! Nicomedes himself has told me that no army has ever succeeded in seizing possession of Arabia. And he says that none ever will."

"Indeed, no one can ever take us by force. But that is not what I mean. The Greeks will conquer us by slyness and cunning, if we allow it: playing their gold against our avarice, buying us inch by inch until we have sold ourselves entirely. We are a shrewd folk, but they are much shrewder, and they will bind us in silken knots, and one day we will find that we are altogether owned by Greek traders and Greek usurers and Greek ship-owners. It is what the Hebrews would have done to us, if they were more numerous and more powerful; but the Greeks have an entire empire behind them. Or half an empire, at least." His face was suddenly aflame with that extraordinary animation and excitability, to the point almost of frenzy, that rose in him so easily. He clapped his hand down on mine. "But it will not be. I will not allow it, good Corbulo! I will destroy them before they can ruin us. Tell that to your Emperor, if you like: Mahmud son of Abdallah will take his stand here before the Greeks who would steal this land, and he will march on them, and he will drive them back to Byzantium."

It was a stunning moment. He had told me on the very first day that he intended to bring Arabia under the rule of a single god and of a single invincible king; and now I knew who he expected that invincible king to be.

I was put in mind of Nicomedes' mocking words of the week before: *Consorting with madmen, are you, now, Corbulo?*

This sudden outburst of Mahmud's as we sat quietly together at my table did indeed have the pure ring of madness about it. That an obscure merchant of this desert land should also be a mystic and a dreamer was unusual enough; but now, as though drawing back a veil, he had revealed to me the tumultuous presence of a warrior-king within his breast as well. It was too much. Neither Alexander of Macedon nor Julius Caesar nor the Emperor Constantinus the Great had laid claim to holding so many selves within a single soul, and how could Mahmud the son of Abdallah?

A moment later he had subsided again, and all was as calm as it had been just minutes before.

There was a flask of wine on the table near my elbow, a good thick Tunisian that I had bought in the marketplace the day before. I poured myself some now to ease the thunder that Mahmud's wild speech had engendered in my forehead.

He smiled and tapped the flask and said, "I have never understood the point of that stuff, do you know? It seems a waste of good grapes to make it into wine."

"Well, opinions differ on that," said I. "But who's to say who's right? Let those who like wine drink it, and the rest can leave it alone." I raised my glass to him. "This is really excellent, though. Are you sure you won't try even a sip?"

He looked at me as though I had offered him a cup of venom. He will never be a drinker, I guess, will Mahmud son of Abdallah, and so be it. Yea and verily, Horatius, it leaves that much more for the likes of thee and me.

"And how is your friend Mahmud?" asked Nicomedes the Paphlagonian, the next time he and I dined together. "Does he have you bowing down to Allah yet?"

"I am not made for bowing before gods, I think," I told him. And then, warily: "He seems a little troubled about the presence of you people down here."

"Thinks we're going to attempt a takeover, does he? He should know better than that. If Augustus and Trajan couldn't manage to invade this place successfully, why does he think a sensible monarch like Maurice Tiberius would try it?"

"Not a military invasion, Nicomedes. Commercial infiltration is what he fears."

Nicomedes looked unperturbed. "He shouldn't. I'd never try to deny to anybody, Corbulo, that we're looking to increase the quantity of business we do here. But why should that matter to the likes of Mahmud? We won't cut into his slice of the pie. We'll just make the pie bigger for everybody. You know the thing the Phoenicians say—'A rising tide lifts all boats.' "

"Don't they teach rhetoric in Greek schools anymore?" I asked. "Pies? Boats? You're mixing your metaphors there, I'd say. And Arabia doesn't have any boats for the tide to raise, or any tides either, for that matter."

"You know what I mean. Tell Mahmud not to worry. Our plans for expansion of trade with Arabia will only be good for everyone involved, and that includes the merchants of Mecca. Maybe I should have a little talk with him myself, eh? He's an excitable sort. I might be able to calm him down."

"Perhaps it would be best to leave him to me," I said.

It was in that moment, Horatius, that I saw where the true crux of the situation lay, and who the true enemy of the Empire is.

The Emperor Julian need not fret over anything that the Greeks might plan to do here. The Greek incursion into Arabia Deserta was only to be expected. Greeks are businessmen by second nature; Arabia, though it is outside the Empire, lies within the natural Eastern sphere of influence; they would have come down here sooner or later, and, well, here they are. If they intend to try to build stronger trade connections with these desert folk, we have no reason to get upset about that, nor is there the slightest thing that the West can do about it. As Nicomedes has said, the East already controls Aiguptos and Syria and Libya and a lot of other such places that produce goods we need, and we don't suffer thereby. It really is a single empire, in that sense. The Greeks won't push up prices on Eastern commodities to us for fear that we'll do the same thing to them with the tin and copper and iron and timber that flow to them out of the West.

No. The soft and citified Greeks are no menace to us. The real peril here comes from the desert prince, Mahmud son of Abdallah.

One god, he says. *One Arabian people under one king.* And he says, concerning the Greeks, *I will destroy them before they can ruin us.*

He means it. And perhaps he can do it. Nobody has ever unified these Saracens under a single man's rule before, but I think they have never had anyone like Mahmud among them before, either. I had a sudden vision of him, dear Horatius, as I sat there at Nicomedes's nicely laden table: Mahmud with eyes of fire and a gleaming sword held high, leading Saracen warriors northward out of Arabia into Syria Palaestina and Mesopotamia, spreading the message of the One God as he comes and driving the panicky Greeks before his oncoming hordes. The eager peasantry embracing the new creed everywhere: who can resist Mahmud's persuasive tongue, especially when it is backed by the blades of his ever more numerous followers? Onward, then, into Armenia and Cappadocia and Persia, and then there will come a swing westward as well into Aiguptos and Libya. The warriors of Allah everywhere, inflaming the souls of men with the new belief, the new love of virtue and honor. The wealth of the temples of the false gods divided among the people. Whole legions of idle parasitic priests butchered like cattle as the superstitions are put to rout. The golden statues of the nonexistent gods melted down. A new commonwealth proclaimed in the world, founded on prayer and sacred law.

Mahmud can say that he has the true god behind him. His eloquence makes you believe it. We of the Empire have only the statues of our gods, and no one of any intelligence has taken those gods seriously for hundreds of years. How can we withstand the fiery onslaught of the new faith? It will roll down upon us like the lava of Vesuvius.

"You take this much too seriously," said Nicomedes the Paphlagonian, when, much later in the evening and after too many more flasks of wine, I confided my fears to him. "Perhaps you should cover your head when you go out of doors at midday, Corbulo. The sun of Arabia is very strong, and it can do great injury to the mind."

No, Horatius. I am right and he is wrong. Once they are launched, the legions of Allah will not be checked until they have marched on through Italia and Gallia and Britannia to the far shores of the Ocean Sea, and all the world is Mahmud's.

It shall not be.

I will save the world from him, Horatius, and perhaps in so doing I will save myself.

Mecca is, of course, a sanctuary city. No man may lift his hand against another within its precincts, under pain of the most awful penalties.

Umar the idol-maker, who served in the temple of the goddess Uzza, understood that. I came to Umar in his workshop, where he sat turning out big-breasted figurines of Uzza, who is the Venus of the Saracens, and bought from him for a handful of coppers a fine little statuette carved from black stone that I hope to show you one of these days, and then I put a gold piece of Justinian's time before him and told him what I wanted done; and his only response was to tap his finger two times against Justinian's nose. Not understanding his meaning, I merely frowned.

"This man of whom you speak is my enemy and the enemy of all who love the gods," said Umar the idol-maker, "and I would kill him for you for three copper coins if I did not have a family to support. But the work will involve me in travel, and that is expensive. It cannot be done in Mecca, you know." And he tapped the nose of Justinian a second time. This time I understood, and I laid a second gold piece beside the first one, and the idol-maker smiled.

Twelve days ago Mahmud left Mecca on one of his business trips into the lands to the east. He has not returned. He has met with some accident, I fear, in those sandy wastes, and by now the drifting dunes have probably hidden his body forever.

Umar the idol-maker appears to have disappeared also. The talk around town is that he went out into the desert to collect the black stone that he carves his idols from, and some fellow craftsman with whom he was feuding followed him to the quarry. I think you will agree with me, Horatius, that this was a wise thing to arrange. The disappearance of a well-known man like Mahmud will probably engender some inquiries that could ultimately have led in embarrassing directions, but no one except the wife of Umar will care about the vanishing of Umar the idol-maker.

All of this strikes me as highly regrettable, of course. But it was absolutely necessary.

"He's almost certainly dead by this time," Nicomedes said last night. We still dine together frequently. "How very sad, Corbulo. He was an interesting man."

"A very great one, in his way. If he had lived, I think he would have changed the world."

"I doubt that very much," said Nicomedes, in his airy, ever-skeptical Greek way. "But we'll never know, will we?"

"We'll never know," I agreed. I raised my glass. "To Mahmud, poor devil."

"To Mahmud, yes."

And there you have the whole sad story. Go to the Emperor, Horatius. Tell him what I've done. Place it in its full context, against the grand sweep of Imperial history past and present and especially future. Speak to him of Hannibal, of Vercingetorix, of Attila, of all our great enemies of days gone by, and tell him that I have snuffed out in its earliest stages a threat to Roma far more frightening than any of those. Make him understand, if you can, the significance of my deed.

Tell him, Horatius. Tell him that I have saved all the world from conquest: that I have done for him a thing that was utterly essential to do, something which no one else at all could have achieved on his behalf, for who would have had the foresight to see the shape of things to come as I was able to see them? Tell him that.

Above all else, tell him to bring me home. I have dwelled amidst the sands of Arabia long enough. My work is done; I beg for surcease from the dreariness of the desert, the infernal heat, the loneliness of my life here. This is no place for a hero of the Empire.

HOW WE LOST THE MOON, A TRUE STORY BY FRANK W. ALLEN

PAUL J. McAULEY

Born in Stroud, England, in 1955, Paul J. McAuley now makes his home in London. A professional biologist for many years, he sold his first story in 1984, and has gone on to be a frequent contributor to Interzone, as well as to markets such as Amazing, The Magazine of Fantasy & Science Fiction, Asimov's Science Fiction, When the Music's Over, and elsewhere.

McAuley has a foot in several different camps of science fiction writing, being considered one of the best of the new breed of British writers (although a few Australian writers could be fit in under this heading as well) who are producing that brand of rigorous hard science fiction with updated modern and stylistic sensibilities that is sometimes referred to as "radical hard science fiction," in addition to being one of the major young writers who are producing that revamped and retooled widescreen Space Opera that has sometimes been called the New Baroque Space Opera. But, something of a literary millipede, McAuley refuses to be limited to a mere two camps in which to put his feet, and also writes Dystopian sociological speculations about the very near future, some elegant and literate Alternate History, and even some unabashed fantasy and supernatural horror stories, all with equal fluency and skill. His first novel, Four Hundred Billion Stars, won the Philip K. Dick Award. His other books include the novels Of the Fall, Eternal Light, and Pasquale's Angel; two collections of his short work, The King of the Hill and Other Stories and The Invisible Country; and an original anthology co-edited with Kim Newman, In Dreams. His acclaimed novel Fairyland won both the Arthur C. Clarke Award and the John W. Campbell Award in 1996. His most recent books are Child of the River and Ancients of Days, the first two volumes of a major new trilogy of ambitious scope and scale, Confluence, set ten million years in the future The third book in the trilogy, Shrine of Stars, is due out soon. Currently he is working on a new novel, The Secret of Life. His stories have appeared in our Fifth, Ninth, Thirteenth, Fifteenth, and Sixteenth Annual Collections. His web site is at http://www.omegacom.demon.co.uk.

On the busy, bustling, colonized future Moon, McAuley reminds us that although everyone makes mistakes, some mistakes have far greater consequences than others . . .

You probably think that you know everything about it. After all, here we are, barely into the second quarter of the first century of the Third Millennium, and it's being touted as the biggest event in the history of humanity. Yeah, right. But tossing aside such impossibly grandiose claims, it was and still is a hell of a story. It's generated millions of bytes of Web journalism (two years after, there are still more than two hundred official Web sites, not to mention the tens of thousands of unofficial newsgroups devoted to proving that it was really caused by God, or aliens, or St. Elvis), tens of thousands of hours of TV and a hundred schlocky movies (and I do include James Cameron's seven-hour blockbuster), thousands of scientific papers and dozens of thick technical reports, including the ten-million-page congressional report, and the ghostwritten biographies of scientists Who Should Have Known Better.

Now you might think that I'm sending out my version because I was either misrepresented or completely ignored in all the above. Not at all. I'll be the first to admit that my part in the whole thing was pretty insignificant, but nevertheless I *was* there, right at the beginning. So consider this shareware text a footnote or even a tall tale, and if you like it, do feel free to pass it on, but don't change the text or drop the byline, if you please.

It began in the middle of a routine calibration run in the Exawatt Fusion facility. All the alarms went off and the AI in charge shut everything down, but there was no obvious problem. The robots could find no evidence of physical damage, yet the integrity and radiation alarms kept ringing, and analysis of experimental data showed that there had been a tremendous fluctuation in energy levels just *after* the fusion pulse. So the scientists sent the two of us, Mike Doherty and me, over the horizon to eyeball the place.

You've probably seen a zillion pictures. It was a low, square concrete block half-buried in the smooth floor of Mendeleev Crater on the Moon's far side, surrounded by bulldozed roadways and cable trenches, the two nuclear reactors which powered it just at the level horizon to the south. At peak, the Exawatt used a thousand million times more power than the entire U.S. electrical grid to fire up, for less than a millisecond, six pulsed lasers focused on a target barely ten micrometers across, producing conditions which simulated those in the first picoseconds of the Big Bang, before symmetry was broken. Like the atom bomb a century before, it pushed the envelopes of engineering and physics. The scientists responsible for firing off that first thermonuclear device believed that there was a slight but definite chance that it would set fire to the Earth's atmosphere; the scientists running the Exawatt thought that there was a possibility that it might burst its containment and vaporize several hundred square kilometers around it. That was why they had built it on the Moon's far side, inside a deep crater. That's why it was run by robots, with the actual labs in a bunker buried over the horizon.

That's why, when it went wrong, they sent in a couple of GLPs to take a look.

We went in an open rover, straight down the service road. We were wearing bright orange radiation-proof shrouds over our Moon suits, and camera rigs on our shoulders so that the scientists could see what we saw. The plant looked intact, burning salt-white in the glare of a lunar afternoon, throwing a long black shadow toward us. The red-and-green perimeter lights were on; the cooling sink, a bore-hole three kilometers deep, wasn't venting. I drove the rover all the way around it, and then we went in.

The plant was essentially one big hall filled with the laser-pumping assemblies, huge frames of parallel color-coded pipes each as big as one of those old Saturn rockets and threaded through with bundles of heavy cables and trackways for the robots which serviced them. We crept along the tiled floor in their shadows like a pair of orange mice, directing our camera rigs here and there at the request of the scientists. The emergency lights were still strobing, and I asked someone to switch them off, which they did after only five minutes' discussion about whether it was a good idea to disturb anything.

The six laser-focusing pipes, two meters in diameter, converged on the bus-sized experimental chamber. Containment was a big problem; that chamber was crammed with powerful magnetic tori which generated the fields in which the target, a pellet of ultra-compressed metallic hydrogen, was heated by chirped pulse amplification to ten billion degrees Centigrade. It was surrounded by catwalks and hidden by the flared ends of the focusing pipes, the capillary grid of the liquid sodium cooling system, and a hundred different kinds of monitor. We checked the system diagnostics of the monitors, which told us only that several detectors on the underside had ceased to function, and then, harangued by scientists, crawled all around the chamber as best we could, sweating heavily in our suits and chafing our elbows and knees.

Mike found a clue to what had happened when he managed to wriggle into the crawl space beneath the chamber, quite a feat in a pressurized suit. He had taken off his camera rig to do it, and it took quite a bit of prompting before he started to describe what he saw.

"There's a severed cable here, and something has punched a hole in the box above it. Let me shift around. . . . Okay, I can see a hole in the floor, too. About two centimeters across. I'm poking my screwdriver into it. Well, it must go all the way through the tiles, I can't see how deep. Hey, Frank, get me some of that wire, will you?"

There was a spool of copper cable nearby. I cut off a length and passed it in.

"You two get on out of there now," one of the scientists advised.

"This won't take but a minute," Mike said, and started humming tunelessly, which meant that he was thinking hard about something.

I asked, because I knew he wouldn't say anything otherwise, "What is it?"

"Looks like someone took a shot at this old thing," Mike said. "Shit. How deep does the foundation go?"

"The concrete was poured to three meters," someone said over the radio link, and the scientist who'd spoken before said, "It really isn't a good idea to mess around there, fellows."

"It goes all the way through," Mike said. "I wiggled the wire around and it came back up with dust on the end."

"This is Ridpath," someone else said. Ridpath, you may remember, was the chief of the science team. Although he wasn't exactly responsible for what happened, he made millions from selling the rights to his story, and then hanged himself six months after it was all over. He said, "You boys get on out of there. We'll take it from here."

Five rolligons passed us on our way back, big fat pressurized vehicles making speed. "You put a hair up someone's ass," I told Mike, who'd been real quiet after he crawled out from beneath the chamber.

"I think something escaped," he said.

"Maybe some of the laser energy was deflected."

"There weren't any traces of melting," Mike said, with a preoccupied air. "And just a bit of all that energy would make a hell of a mess, not leave a neat little hole. Hmm. Kind of an interesting problem."

But he didn't say any more about it until a week later, about an hour before the president went on the air to explain what had happened.

The Moon was a good place to be working then. It was more-or-less run by scientists, the way Antarctica had been before the drillers and miners got to it. There were about two thousand people living there at any one time, either working on projects like the Exawatt or the Big Array or the ongoing resource mapping surveys, or doing their own little thing. Mike and I were both part of the General Labor Pool, ready to help anyone. We'd earned our chops doing Ph.D.s, but we didn't have the drive or desire to work our way up the ladder of promotion. We didn't want responsibility, didn't want to be burdened with administration and hustling for funds, which was the lot of career researchers. We liked to get our hands dirty. Mike has a double Ph.D. in pure physics and cybernetics and is a whiz at electronics; I'm a run-of-the-mill geologist who is also a fair pilot. We made a pretty good team back then and generally worked together whenever we could, and we'd worked just about every place on the Moon.

When the president made the announcement, we'd moved on from the Exawatt and were taking a few days' R&R. I'd found out about a gig supervising the construction of a railway from the South Pole to the permanent base at Clavius, but Mike wouldn't sign up and wouldn't say why, except that it was to do with what had happened at the Exawatt.

We'd been exposed to a small amount of radiation when we'd gone into the plant—Mike a little more than me—and had spent a day being checked out before getting back on the job. The scientists were all over the plant by then. The reaction chamber had been dismantled by robots, and we brought in all kinds of monitoring equipment. Not only radiation counters, but a gravity measuring device and a neutrino detector. We helped bore a shaft five hundred meters deep parallel to the hole punched through the floor, and probes and motion sensors and cameras were lowered into it.

Mike claimed to have worked out what had happened as soon as he stuck the wire in the hole through the foundation, but he wouldn't tell me. "You should be able to guess from what they were trying to measure," he said, the one time I asked, and smiled when I called him a son of a bitch. He's very smart, but sort of fucked up in the head, antisocial, careless of his appearance and untidy as hell, and proud that he has four of the five symptoms of Asperger's Syndrome. But he was my partner, and I trusted him; when he said it wasn't a good idea to take up a new contract, I nagged him for a straight hour to explain why, and went along with him even though he wouldn't. He was spending all his spare time making calculations on his slate, and was still working on them at the South Pole facility.

I raised the subject again when news of the special presidential announcement broke. "You'd better tell me what you think happened," I told Mike, "because I'll hear the truth in less than an hour, and after that I won't believe you."

We were in an arbor in the dome of the South Pole facility. Real plants, cycads and banana plants and ferns, growing in real dirt around us, sunlight pouring in at a low angle through the diamond panes high above. The dome capped a small crater some three hundred meters across, on a high ridge near the edge of the South Pole–Aitken Basin and in permanent sunlight, the sun circling around the horizon once every twenty-eight days. It was hot and humid, and the people splashing in the lake below our arbor were making a lot of noise. The lake and its scattering of atolls took up most of the crater's floor, with arbors and cafés and cabins on the bench terrace around it. The water was billion-year-old comet water, mined from the regolith in permanently shadowed craters. A rail gun used to lob shaped loads of ice to supply the Clavius base in the early days, but Clavius had grown, and its administration was uncomfortable with the idea of being bombarded with ice meteors, which was why they wanted to build a railway. In the low gravity, the waves out on the lake were five or six meters high, and big droplets flew a long way, changing shape like amoebas, before falling back. People were body surfing the waves; a game of water polo had been going on for several days in one of the bays.

I'd just been playing for a few hours, and I was in a good mood, which was why I didn't strangle Mike when, after I asked him to tell me what he knew, he flashed his goofy smile at me and went back to scratching figures on his slate. Instead, I snatched the slate from his hands and held it over the edge of the arbor and said, "You tell me right now, or the slate gets it."

Mike scratched the swirl of black hair on his bare chest and said, "You know you won't do it."

I made to skim it through the air and said, "How many times do you think it would bounce before it sank?"

"I thought I'd give you a chance to work it out. And it isn't as if there's anything we can do. Didn't you enjoy the rest?"

"What's this got to do with not taking up that contract?"

"There's no point building anything anymore. You still haven't guessed, have you?"

I tossed the slate to him. "Maybe I should pick *you* up and throw you in the lake."

I meant it, and I'm a lot bigger than him.

"It's a black hole," he said.

"A black hole."

"Sure. My guess is that the experiment caused a runaway quantum fluctuation that created a black hole. It had to be bigger than the Planck size, and most probably was a bit bigger than a hydrogen atom, because it obviously has been taking up other atoms easily enough. Say around ten to the power twenty-three kilograms. The mass of a big mountain, like Everest. The magnetic containment fields couldn't hold it, of course, and it dropped straight out of the reaction chamber and went through the plant's floor."

I said, "The hole we saw was a lot bigger than the width of a hydrogen atom."

"Sure. The black hole disrupted stuff by tidal force over a far greater distance than its Swartzschild radius, and sucked some of it right in. That's why there was no trace of melting, even though it was pretty hot, and spitting out X-rays and probably accelerated protons, too—cosmic rays."

I didn't believe him, of course, but it was an interesting intellectual exercise. I said, "So where did the mass come from? Not from the combustion chamber fuel."

"Of course not. It was a quantum fluctuation, just like the Universe, which also came out of nothing. And the Universe weighs a lot more than ten to the power twenty-three kilograms. Something like, let's see—"

"Okay," I said quickly, before Mike lost himself in esoteric calculations. "But where is it now?"

"Well, it went all the way through," Mike said.

"Through the Moon? Then it came out, let's see"—I tried to visualize the Moon's globe—"somewhere in Mare Fecunditas."

"Not exactly. It accelerated in free fall toward the core, went past, and started to fall back again. It's sweeping back and forth, gaining mass and losing amplitude with each pass. That's what the president is going to tell everyone."

I thought about it. Something just bigger than an atom but massing as much as a mountain, plunging through the twenty-five-kilometer-thick outer layer of gardened regolith, smashing a centimeter-wide tunnel through the basalt crust and the mantle, passing through the tiny iron core, gathering mass and slowing, so that it did not quite emerge at the far side before falling back.

"You were lucky it didn't come right back at you," I said.

"The amplitude diminishes with each pass. Eventually it'll settle at the Moon's gravitational center. And that's why I didn't want to sign the contract. After the president tells everyone what I've just told you, all the construction contracts will be put on hold. What you should do is make sure we're first on the list for evacuation work."

"Evacuation?"

"There's no way to capture the black hole. The Moon, Frank, is fucked. But we'll get plenty of work before it's over."

He was half right, because the next day, after the president had admitted that an experiment had somehow dropped a black hole inside the Moon, a serious problem that would require an international team to monitor, we were both issued with summonses to appear at the hastily set up congressional inquiry.

It was a bunch of bullshit, of course. We went down to Washington, D.C., and spent a week locked up in the Watergate hotel watching bad cable movies and endless talk shows, with NASA lawyers showing up every now and then to rehearse our Q&As, and in the end we had no more than half an hour of easy questions before the committee let us go. Our lawyers shook our hands on the steps of the Congress building, in front of a bored video crew, and we went back to Canaveral and then to the Moon. Why not? By then Mike had convinced me about what was going to happen. There would be plenty of work for us.

We signed up as part of a roving seismology team, placing remote stations at various points around the Moon's equator. The Exawatt plant had been dismantled and a monitoring station built on its site to try and track the period of the black hole, which someone had labeled Mendeleev X-1. Mike was as happy as I had ever seen him; he was getting some of the raw data and doing his own calculations on the black hole's accretion rate and orbital path within the Moon. He stayed up long after our workday was over, hunched over his slate in the driving chair of our rolligon, with sunlight pouring in through the bubble canopy while I tried to sleep in the hammock stretched across the cabin, my skin itching with the Moon dust which got everywhere, and our Moon suits propped in back like two silent witnesses to our squabbling. His latest best estimate was that the Moon had between two hundred and five thousand days.

"But things will start to get exciting before then."

"Excitement is something I can do without. What do you mean?"

"Oh, it'll be a lot of fun."

"You're doing it again, you son of a bitch."

"You're the geologist, Frank," Mike said. "It's easy enough to work out. It's just—"

"Basic physics. Yeah. Well, you tell me if it's going to put us in danger. Okay?"

"Oh, it won't. Not yet, anyhow."

We were already picking up regular moonquakes on the seismometer network. With a big point mass swinging back and forth through it, the Moon's solid iron core was ringing like a bell. There were some odd subsidiary traces, too, smooshy echoes as if spaces were opening in the mantle—hard to believe, because pressure should have annealed any voids. I was pretty sure that Mike had a theory about these anomalies, too, but I kept quiet. After all, I was the geologist. I should have been able to work it out.

Meanwhile, we toured west across the Mare Insularium, with its lava floods overlaid by ejecta from Copernicus, and on across the Oceanus Procellarum, dropping seismometers every two hundred kilometers. We made good time, speeding across rolling, lightly cratered landscape, detouring only for the largest wrinkle ridges, driving through the long day and the Earth-lit night into brilliant dawn, the sun slowly moving across the sky toward noon once more. The Moon had its own harsh yet serene beauty, shaped mainly by vulcanism and impacts. Without weather, erosion took place on geological timescales, but because almost every feature was more than three billion years old, gravity and ceaseless micrometeorite bombardment had smoothed or leveled every hill or crater ridge. With the sun at the right angle, it was like riding across an infinite plain gentled by a deep blanket of snow. We rested up twice at unmanned shelters, and had a two-day layover at a roving Swedish selenology station which had squatted down on the mare like a collection of tin cans. A week later, just after we had picked up fresh supplies from a rocket lofted from Clavius, we felt our first moonquake.

It was as if the rolligon had dropped over a curb, but there was no curb. I was in the driving chair; Mike was asleep in the hammock. I told the AI to stop, and looked out through the canopy at the 180-degree panorama. The horizon was drawn closely all around. An ancient crater eroded by three billion years of micrometeorite bombardment dished it to the north and a few pockmarked boulders were sprinkled here and there, including a fractured block as big as a house. Something skittered in the corner of my eye—a little rock rolling down the gentle five degree slope we were climbing, plowing a meandering track in the dust. It ran out quite a way. The rolligon swayed gently, from side to side. I found I was gripping the padded arms of the chair so tightly my knuckles had turned white. Behind me, Mike stirred in the hammock and sleepily asked what was up; at the same moment, I saw the gas plume.

It was very faint, visible only because the dust it lofted caught the sunlight. Gas plumes were not uncommon on the Moon, caused by pockets of radon and other products of fission decay of unstable isotopes overpressuring the crevices where they collected. Earth-based astronomers sometimes glimpsed them when they temporarily obscured surface features while dissipating into vacuum. This, though, was different, more like a heat-driven geyser, venting steadily from a source below the horizon.

I told the AI to drive toward it. Mike leaned beside me, scratching himself through his suit of thermal underwear. He smelled strongly of old sweat; we hadn't bathed properly since the interlude with the Swedes. I had a sudden insight and said, "How hot is the black hole?"

"Oh, the smaller the black hole, the more fiercely it radiates. It's a simple inverse relationship. It was pretty hot to begin with, but it's been getting cooler as it accretes mass. Hmm."

"Is it still hot enough to melt rock?"

Mike's eyes refocused. "You know, I think it must have been much bigger than I first thought. Anyway, anything that gets close enough to it to melt is already falling toward the event horizon. That's why there was no trace of melting or burning when it dropped out of the reaction chamber. But there's also the heat generated by friction as stuff pours toward its gravity well."

"Then it's remelting the interior. Those anomalies in the seismology signals are melt caverns full of lava."

Mike said thoughtfully, "I'm sure we'll start picking up a weak magnetic field soon, when the iron core liquifies and starts circulating. Of course, the end will be pretty close by then. Wow. That thing out there is really big."

The rolligon was climbing a long gentle slope toward the top of a curved ridge more than a kilometer high, the remnants of the rim of a crater which had been mostly buried by the fluid lava flow which had formed the Oceanus Procellarum. I told the AI to stop when I spotted the source of the plume. It was a huge fresh-looking crevice that ran out from a volcanic dome; gas was jetting out of the slumped side of the dome like steam from a boiling kettle. Dust fell straight down in sheets kilometers long. Already, an appreciable ray of brighter material was forming on the regolith beneath the plume.

"We should get closer," Mike said. He was rocking back and forth in his chair like a delighted child.

"I don't think so. There will be plenty of rocks lofted along with the gas and dust."

We transmitted some pictures, then suited up and went outside to set up a seismology package. The sun was in the east, painting long shadows on the ground, which shook, ever so gently, under my boots. With no atmosphere to scatter the light, shadows were razor sharp, and color changed as I moved about. The dusty regolith was deep brown in my shadow, but a bright blinding white when I looked toward the sun, turning ashy gray to either side. The gas plume glittered and flashed against the black sky. I told Mike that it was probably from a source deep in the megaregolith; pressure increased in gas pockets with depth. A quake, probably at the interface between the megaregolith and the rigid crust, must have opened a path to the surface.

"There'll be a lot more of these," Mike said.

"It'll blow itself out soon enough."

But it was still venting strongly when we had finished our work, and we drove a long way north to skirt around it, with Mike scratching away on his slate, factoring this new evidence into his calculations.

We were out for another two weeks, ending our run in lunar night at the Big Array Station at Korolev. It was one of the biggest craters on the far side, with slumped terraced walls and hummocky rim deposits like ranges of low hills. Its floor was spattered with newer craters, including a dark-floored lava-flooded crater on its southern edge which was now the focus of a series of quakes of steadily increasing amplitude. Korolev Station, up on the rim, was being evacuated; the radio telescopes of the Big Array, scattered across the far side in a regular pattern, were to be kept running by remote link. Most of the personnel had already departed by shuttle, and although there were still large amounts of equipment to be taken out, the railway which linked Korolev with Clavius had been cut by a rock slide. After a couple of spooky days' rest in the almost deserted yet fully functional station, Mike and I went out with a couple of other GLPs to supervise the robots which were clearing the slide and re-laying track.

It was a nice ride: the pressurized railcar had a big observational bubble, and I spent a lot of time up there, watching the heavily cratered highland plains flow past at two hundred kilometers an hour. The Orientale Basin dominated the west side of the Moon: a fissured basin of fractured blocks partly flooded with impact melt lava and ringed round with three immense scarps and an inner bench like ripples frozen in rock. The engineers had cut the railway through the rings of the Rook and Cordillera Mountains; the landslide had blocked the track where it passed close to one of the tall knobs of the Montes Rook Formation, a ten-kilometer-high piece of ejecta which had smashed down onto the surrounding plain—the impact really was very big.

A slide had run out from one of its steeply graded faces, covering more than a kilometer of track, and we were more than a week out there, helping the robots fix everything up. When we finally arrived at the station in Clavius, it was a day ahead of the Mendeleev eruption and the beginning of the evacuation of the Moon.

The whole floor of the Mendeleev Crater had fractured into blocks in the biggest quake ever recorded on the Moon, and lava had flooded up through dykes emplaced between the blocks. Lava vented from dykes beyond the crater rim, too, and flowed a long way, forming a new mare. Other vents appeared, setting off secondary quakes and long rock slides. The Moon shivered and shook uneasily, as if awakening from a long sleep.

Small teams were sent out to collect the old Rangers, Lunas, Surveyors, Lunokhods, and descent stages of Apollo LEMs from the first wave of Moon exploration. Mike and I went out for a last time, to Mare Tranquillitatis, to the site of the first manned lunar landing.

When a permanent scientific presence had first been established on the Moon, there was considerable debate about what to do with the sites of the Apollo landings and the various old robot probes and other debris scattered across the surface. There had been a serious proposal to dome the Apollo 11 site to protect it from damage by micrometeorites and to stop people from swiping souvenirs, but even without protection it would last for millions of years, and everyone on the Moon was tagged with a continuously monitored global positioning sensor so no one could go anywhere without it being logged, and in the end the site had been left open.

We arrived a few hours after dawn. It was a lonely place, not much visited despite its historic importance. A big squat carrier rocket had gone ahead, landing two kilometers to the north, and the robots were already waiting. There were four of us: a historian from the Museum of Air and Space in Washington, a photographer, and Mike and me. The site was ringed around with laser sensors. As we loped through the perimeter, an automatic beacon on the common band warned us that we were trespassing on a U.N. heritage site and started to recite the relevant penalties until the historian found it and turned it off. The angular platform of the lunar module's descent stage had been scorched by the rocket of the ascent stage; the gold foil which had wrapped it was torn and tattered, white paint beneath turned tan by exposure to the sun's raw ultraviolet. One of its spidery legs had collapsed after a recent quake focused near new volcanic cones to the southeast. We lifted everything, working inward toward the ascent stage: the Passive Seismometer and the Laser Ranging Retroreflector; the flag, its ordinary fabric, stiffened by wires, faded and fragile; an assortment of discarded geology tools; human waste and food containers and wipes and other litter in crumbling jettison bags; the plaque with a message from a long-dead president. Before the descent stage was lifted away, a robot sawed away a chunk of dirt beside its ladder, the spot where the first human footprint had been made on the Moon. There was some dispute about which print was actually the first, so two square meters were carefully lifted. And at last the descent stage was carried off to the cargo rocket, and there was only a litter of cleated footprints left, our own overlaying Armstrong's and Aldrin's.

It was time to go.

As the eruptions grew more frequent, even the skeleton crews of the various stations were evacuated, leaving a host of robot surveyors in close orbit or crawling about the troubled surface to monitor the unfolding disaster. Mike and I went on one of the last shuttles, everyone crowding to the ports as it made a single low orbital pass before lighting out for Earth.

It was six months after the Mendeleev X-1 incident. The heat generated by the black hole's accretion process and tidal forces had remelted the iron core; pockets of molten basalt in the mantle had swollen and conjoined. A vast rift opened in the Oceanus Procellarum, splitting the nearside down its northwestern quadrant and raising new scarps as high and jagged as those in an old Chesley Bonestell painting. The Orientale Basin flooded with lava and the fractured blocks of the Maunder formation sank like foundering ships as new lava flows began to well up. Volcanic activity was less on the far side, where the crust was thicker, but the Mare Ingenii collapsed and reflooded, forming a vast new basin which swallowed the Jules Verne and Gagarin Craters.

It took two more months.

As the end neared, the Moon's surface split into short-lived plates afloat on a wholly molten mantle, with lava-filled rifts opening and scabbing over and reopening along their edges. There were frantic attempts to insure that the population of the Earth's southern hemisphere would all have some kind of shelter, for the Moon would be in the sky above the Pacific in its final hour. Those unlucky or stubborn enough to remain outside saw the Moon rise for the last time, half-full, the dark part of her disk riven with glowing cracks which spread as the black hole sucked in exponentially increasing amounts of matter. And then there was a terrific flare of light, brighter than a thousand suns. Those witnesses who had not been blinded saw that the Moon was gone, leaving expanding shells of luminous gas around a fading image trapped at the edge of the black hole's event horizon, and a short-lived accretion disk as ejected material spiraled back into the black hole, which, although it massed the same as the Moon it had devoured, had an event horizon circumference of less than a millimeter.

The radiation pulse was mostly absorbed by the Earth's atmosphere; the orbit of the space station had been altered so that it was in opposition when the Moon vanished. I was aboard it at the time, and spent the next six months helping repair satellites whose circuits had been fried.

There are still tides, of course, for the same amount of mass still orbits the Earth. Marine organisms which synchronized their reproduction by the Moon's phases, such as horseshoe crabs, corals, and palolo worms, were in danger of extinction, but a cooperative mission by NASA and the Russian and European space agencies lofted a space mirror which reflects the same amount of light as the Moon, and even goes through the same phases. There'll be a big problem in 5×10^{43} years, when by loss of mass through Hawking radiation the black hole finally becomes small enough to begin its runaway evaporation. But long before then the sun will have evolved into a white dwarf and guttered out; even its very protons will have decayed. The black hole will be the last remnant of the solar system in a cooling and vastly expanded universe.

There are various proposals to make use of the black hole—as the ultimate garbage disposal device (I want to be well away from the solar system when they try that), or as an interstellar signaling device, for if it can be made to bob in its orbit (perhaps by putting another black hole in orbit around it), it will produce sharply focused gravity waves of tremendous amplitude. Meanwhile, it will keep the physicists busy for a thousand years. Mike is working at one of the stations which orbit beyond its event horizon. I keep in touch with him by E-mail, but the correspondence is becoming more and more infrequent as he vanishes into his own personal event horizon.

As for me, I'm heading out. The space program has realigned its goals, and it turns out that the black hole retained the Moon's rotational energy, so it provides a useful slingshot for free acceleration. After all, there are plenty of other moons in the solar system, and most are far more interesting than the one we lost.

(For Stephen Baxter)

phallicide

CHARLES SHEFFIELD

Much ink was spilled in the last few years about Viagra and other male "virility drugs," but, as the harrowing story that follows suggests, sometimes you just might need a drug that works completely the other *way around . . .*

One of the best contemporary "hard science" writers, British-born Charles Sheffield is a theoretical physicist who has worked on the American space program and is currently chief scientist of the Earth Satellite Corporation. Sheffield is also the only person who has ever served as president of both the American Astronautical Society and the Science Fiction Writers of America. He's a frequent contributor to both Analog *and* Asimov's Science Fiction, *as well as to other markets such as* Science Fiction Age *and* The Magazine of Fantasy & Science Fiction. *He won the John W. Campbell Memorial Award in 1993 for his novel* Brother to Dragons *and in 1994 he won the Hugo and Nebula Awards for his story "Georgia on My Mind." His books include the bestselling nonfiction title* Earthwatch; *the novels* Sight of Proteus, The Web Between the Worlds, Hidden Variables, My Brother's Keeper, Between the Strokes of Night, The Nimrod Hunt, Trader's World, Proteus Unbound, Summertide, Divergence, Transcendence, Cold as Ice, The Mind Pool, Godspeed, *and* The Ganymede Club; *and the collections* Erasmus Magister, The McAndrew Chronicles, Dancing with Myself, *and* Georgia on My Mind and Other Places. *His most recent books are the novels* Aftermath *and* Starfire *and a nonfiction book,* Borderlands of Science. *His next novel,* The Spheres of Heaven, *is due out near the end of this year. His stories have appeared in our Seventh, Eighth, Eleventh, and Fourteenth Annual Collections. He lives in Silver Spring, Maryland, with his wife, SF writer Nancy Kress. He has a web site at www.sff.net/people/sheffield/.*

The human brain is a three-pound mass of blood and nerves and jelly; anything less like a muscle is hard to imagine. Yet there are resemblances. If I work my brain long and hard, then give it a rest, I find that the break pays off. Puzzles resolve themselves and old difficulties disappear. I return to work mentally rejuvenated and in top creative condition.

I gazed at the screen and decided that I must be long overdue for that rest. Those were my own research results, but I stared mystified at what sat before me on the display.

Was this my work? I recognized the data, but they didn't feel like mine. Instead of the expected intimacy, so close to the latest experiment that you live inside it, I felt like an outsider.

I scrolled toward the end. *The response is decidedly nonlinear and follows an approximate two-thirds power law. When the oral dose is doubled, the average time of sustained erection increases from nine minutes to 14 minutes. When the dose is quadrupled, the average erection time becomes 22 minutes. Elevated nitric-oxide levels persist in the corpora cavernosa for 38 minutes after orgasm . . .*

It was my own work, without a doubt. More than that, they were my own *words*. I may not be the world's greatest stylist, but one thing I recognize, always and unmistakably, is what I have written. Change an adjective, add a comma, and I will know.

My own words, but surely not my *recent* words. I checked the file. It was dated Thursday. Yesterday. The experimental data had been entered three days earlier.

I was still staring at the screen when I heard footsteps in the corridor and a quiet knock at my closed door.

Although I was fairly sure that only one person would be visiting my office at eight in the morning, the key strokes to change to a second document area were pure reflex. By the time the door opened, the screen in front of me showed a bland table of daily blood pressure from an unidentified subject.

"Good morning, Doctor Rachel," said a cheerful voice behind me. "Let's take a look at you."

As expected, it was Sharon Prostley, administrative assistant to the head of the lab. I stood up and turned around, and she gave me my morning head-to-toe critical examination.

"Not bad. Not bad at all." She came forward and touched the clip in my hair. "My own choice would have been apple-green as a better match to your skirt. But emerald will do nicely, and it goes well with your eyes."

"Thanks, Sharon." Color-blindness in women is 10 times rarer than in men, but I suspect that it usually matters a lot more. I was relatively lucky. I had trouble only in distinguishing certain classes of blues and greens.

"Happy to do it," she said. "Not many things let me feel useful early in the morning." She moved away toward the door, but turned at the threshold. "I forgot to ask. How was the vacation?"

I stared at her, and she went on, "Did you get to spend time with your family?"

My autopilot took over. "Yes. Oh, yes, it was great, thanks. I had a wonderful time."

"Wish I could get away. I'm tied here till spring break." And Sharon was gone, back along the corridor toward her office.

As the sound of her footsteps receded, I switched my computer back to its hidden document area. *The response is decidedly nonlinear. . . .* The familiar/unfamiliar words confronted me. Yesterday's date. Except that—I clicked to the day and date setting on my computer. Friday, as it should be. But instead of March 12 it was March 19.

I had lost a week. Vacation. Family. I felt a moment of dizzy memory and partial understanding, and I turned my computer off abruptly without waiting for the usual utilities disk-check. I had to get out of here—out of the room, out of the building, off the campus, alone into the fresh air where I could think.

By 8:15 the sun was rising and the overnight chill was already off the street. I walked west from the university campus along the flat, even thoroughfare of St. George, toward the distant brown hills that rose clear and stark in the dry air.

I wandered seven long blocks and finally sat down on a bench in front of a bicycle store. The vivid posters in the shop window showed grinning riders drifting effortlessly uphill. While I stared, the lost week filtered back into my head fragment by random fragment. I knew that I had been again to Bryceville, 95 miles to the northeast beyond the Zion National Park. I knew that I had seen Naomi and the rest of my family there. I knew I had been heavily drugged; and I knew why.

"It's for your own sake more than anyone else's." Elder Cyrus Walker's bald dome and twinkling gray eyes had been part of my life for a quarter of a century. With his barrel chest and strong sloping shoulders he was like a rugged tree, never seeming a day older as the years passed. "We still trust you completely. But suppose you are doing things that might give you away, and you don't even realize it?"

An interrogation was inevitable. It was standard on each return trip. The fact that drugs of my own design were used in the questioning added a special irony. "Can't I at least see my family first?" I pleaded. "Today is Naomi's 13th birthday. She sent me a class picture, and she's grown so much I hardly know her."

"Of course you can see her. There's absolutely no rush, you'll be with us at least five more days." Elder Walker patted my shoulder with a hand as thick and hard as a chopping board. "But we don't want you going back to the university, do we, acting and feeling groggy? We all have too much invested to jeopardize the effort now. And there's other work to do. Shall we say, the day after tomorrow for the tests of your latest work?"

"I suppose so."

"I don't care for that tone of voice." Elder Walker stood up and wandered over to the window. Beyond him I saw the bleached wooden walls and steep roof of the Patriarch's lodge, jutting high into the blue desert sky. He went on, "You know, Rachel, you are a very fortunate young woman."

"I realize that. And I'm truly grateful to have such a wonderful opportunity to serve the Blessed Order." Before I was 11 years old I had learned to hide most of my thoughts and all my opinions. Yet in a sense I agreed with Elder Cyrus Walker. I *was* lucky; lucky to have an unusual mind, one with a memory and logical powers that even the Council members could not ignore.

Had it been otherwise . . .

The Escalante bus had dropped me off in late afternoon at the edge of town, and as I walked through slanting sunlight I saw Deborah Curzon and Mary Dixon waiting outside the school until classes were over and the older children were let out. Deb and Mary each had one babe in arms and three kids in tow. Young ones. The two women were 27, my exact contemporaries. They looked twice my age. Nine or 10 kids can wear down even the strongest.

Deb and Mary had stared back at me — with pity. Their nods said, Why, it's poor Rachel Stafford, not pretty enough to be taken as a third or even a fourth wife. My one child, Naomi, hardly counted. Her father was the Patriarch himself, and from their looks they thought that he had surely bedded me from duty rather than desire.

"And, of course, we must have adequate time for the tests. Can't afford to rush." Elder Walker still had his back to me, gazing out of the window at a tumbleweed rolling ghostlike along the dusty street. "I assume that you have made further progress, and brought the results of your work with you?"

"I think so. But I won't really be sure until the tests are complete."

"Naturally." Elder Walker turned and held out his hand. "Better, don't you think, to put them in my safekeeping?"

It was phrased as a question but I never doubted that it was an order. I handed over the vials. Cyrus Walker ran Bryceville. Oh, sure, the Patriarch was the ultimate authority, the Blessed Order's spiritual leader and final point of decision. But the Patriarch was 89 years old. No one spoke of his health or even suggested his mortality, but 13 years ago, when I had been led a nervous virgin to his bed, he had been stick-limbed and wheezing and barely able to become aroused. Without the drugs and careful preparation given to me and the generous lubricants, entry would have been impossible.

Thank God, he had met the challenge. He had known me, briefly, and five minutes later he lay snoring. I remained wretched at his side for two full hours before I dared to leave the chamber and creep down the broad wooden staircase. What I remembered most was the scaly touch of his skin and his unpleasant smell, like moldy wet straw. For a full month afterward I prayed that I was pregnant and would not have to go back to him. As my period failed to arrive, day after late day, relief and joy burgeoned within me like the child itself.

One month before Naomi was born, a chance event altered the course of my life. Confined to bed in the final trimester of a difficult pregnancy, nervous and uncomfortable and bored, I saw in a magazine the announcement of a national science essay contest. Although the deadline was only four days away, I scribbled 20 pages on the role of nitrous oxides in amphibian metabolism, and on amphibian reproductive cycles. The results arose from my own observations — and, let me admit it, my own experiments — on my pet frog, Jasper, and his descendants.

My entry went out in the next mail. I sent it without permission, a major sin. On the other hand, I was sure that I had no hope of winning one of the four cash prizes, or even of achieving an honorable mention. And, in fact, I received neither. What I did receive was a visit from Elder Walker. With him came a tall, dark-suited stranger with a maroon bow tie, piercing dark eyes, and a drooping black mustache.

Walter Cottingham was a lawyer from one of the big pharmaceutical companies. The home office of Tilden, Inc. was near Philadelphia, a city which at the time sounded to me as far away as the Moon. Walter Cottingham, to my 14-year-old perspective, was a senior authority figure. Only later did I learn that he was just 10 years older than me and fresh out of law school. The suit, bow tie, and mustache were his attempt to look older. But he was good at his job. For two hours, closely watched by Elder Walker, Walter Cottingham sat on my bed end and asked me polite but shrewd questions related to my paper. What did I know about cyclic guanosine monophosphate? Had I ever heard of phosphodiesterase-5? How had I known that nitric oxide serves to relax blood vessels?

At the end of that time he stood up, turned to Elder Walker, and said, "I am authorized to offer one hundred thousand dollars, payable at once."

"It must be discussed with the Council."

"Naturally." Cottingham, to my vast surprise, winked at me. "There must also be one other condition."

"That she does no additional work which could possibly infringe on or affect your patents?"

"Good heavens, no." Walter Cottingham stared at Elder Walker, and I think that for the first time since his arrival he was genuinely astonished. "That would be the very last thing we at Tilden would suggest." He grinned down at me, and the smile changed him from a ferocious stranger to a friend. "When the baby is born, Miss Rachel, and you are recovered, you will receive a proper education. Naturally, at our expense." He turned again to Elder Walker. "Miss Rachel should pursue research, preferably in the area where she is already active. However, Tilden will not constrain in any way the nature of her work, or the institution where she chooses to apply her talents. My company demands one thing only: Tilden will enjoy an exclusive right to any resulting patents. In return for this we will give you a royalty on gross product sales, plus other financial rewards."

I understood only a fraction of what Walter Cottingham was saying. Certainly, I had some idea that the direction of my life was changing, but I did not realize that I had at that moment diverged forever from the other fertile females in the Blessed Order. Unlike them, I would have no more than one child. Unlike them, I would become no man's wife—first, second, third, or fourth.

After Naomi was born I was allowed to remain and care for her for two more years. Depending on your definition, that was either an easy or a very hard period for me. I did no manual work, which for a female in the Blessed Order was unheard of. On the other hand, in every spare moment two tutors from Tilden crammed me with physics, chemistry, and biology. Mostly I loved it, but sometimes, struggling to absorb difficult material while Naomi suckled at my breast, I broke down in tears. At the time I had never heard of postpartum depression, and really I don't think that was my problem. It was that soon I would be in a far-off town, while my baby would remain in Bryceville.

I was just 17 when the time came for me to leave. By then Naomi was a sturdy two-year-old, more beautiful than I had ever been. She had my dark eyes, and my chin, but the nose and cheekbones were a mystery. Others said that they saw the Patriarch in her. I agreed—in public. In private, I rejected fiercely the suggestion that anything in that wrinkled face and those bleary eyes could live on in my child.

I left Bryceville, sure that I would miss Naomi every waking second. For the first week, I did. Then the heady thrill of access to a real lab with real equipment grabbed me. I moved my area of study from amphibians to mammals, and I mapped out an ambitious research program.

My area of study. *My* research program. Even, *my* laboratory—I thought of it that way, although a dozen other research workers were there.

What an innocent! At the time I saw nothing peculiar in the fact that a lab suitable for my specialized work lay less than a hundred miles from Bryceville. It never occurred to me that the long arm of Tilden, Inc. could reach out across the country and endow and equip a new university facility in the town of St. George in less time than it took me to wean Naomi. Most of all, I had no idea how closely the interests of Tilden coincided with those of certain members of the Blessed Order.

I had mapped out a research program? Yes, and no. Certainly I had written the proposal. But now I know that I was steered to it by a master plan of directed education, existing equipment, and available funding.

Five and a half years after my scribbled notes on amphibian reproduction, I was offered—but did not understand—evidence that the direction of my "independent" research work had been carefully channeled from the beginning. It came during my usual six-monthly visit to Bryceville. Naomi was by this time a precocious handful, taxing the patience and stamina of my ailing mother. I wanted to be with both of them as much as I could, but half a day after my arrival I was called to a meeting with Elder Walker in his private quarters.

"Rachel, my dear." As I entered he stood up and enfolded me in a hug. Maybe I had become hypersensitive since leaving Bryceville, but that embrace felt more personal than paternal. Elder Walker's sexual energy was no secret in Bryceville. Rather than taking the seat offered on the couch next to him, I remained standing.

He looked at me sharply but said only, "I have been reading your research summaries." He picked up and waved a sheaf of papers. "I want to tell you a way in which you can be of extraordinary service to the Blessed Order. Before we begin, you must swear that what we will discuss today will be held absolutely secret."

"I promise." I was intrigued, as any 19-year-old is intrigued by secrets, and I could see no reason not to give my word.

"Secret," he added, "even from other members of the Blessed Order. Unless I give permission for you to do so, you must not speak of this to your mother or to anyone else in your family. And, of course, to no one outside."

That made me hesitate, but after a few moments I nodded. "I promise that I will speak to no one unless you tell me that I may."

"Very good." Elder Walker relaxed back onto the couch. "Rachel, you are a highly intelligent and talented young woman. But you have been here very little for the past five years. You have not seen the changes in the Patriarch."

Cyrus Walker was on very delicate ground. The Patriarch was eternal and unchanging, almost by definition. It was forbidden to speak of him except in terms of veneration and as a symbol of absolute authority. I said, truthfully, "I have not seen the Patriarch for more than five years."

The last time had been on the occasion of my impregnation with Naomi, as Elder Walker surely knew.

"Then take my word for it," he said, "there is cause for concern. I must be direct with you, and on a highly sensitive subject. The Blessed Jasper is not what he was. Mentally, he remains acute; but physically, he has trouble performing . . . certain traditional functions of our Order."

He glanced at me hopefully, eyebrows raised. Could he be saying what he seemed to be saying? I declined to take the risk, and stared at him in silence.

He sighed, and went on. "It is an element of the faith in the Blessed Order that our numbers in the world will increase and we will thrive. Our children are drawn from superior stock. They grow untainted by the habits of a degraded society. And, of course, the Patriarch is the best father that any child could ever have."

Now I was sure. I said flatly, "The Blessed Jasper has become impotent."

He grimaced. "My dear, never *ever* say such a thing outside this room, or hint at it to any other person. But what you say is correct."

"Into which category does his impotence fall?" My professional interest had been roused—the physiological interplay between the conscious mind and the autonomous nervous system was the very area of my own research—and for me, scientific curiosity always overcomes shyness and diffidence. Elder Walker stared at me and I went on, "Male erectile disorder falls into several categories. Primary impotence means that the male has never been able to maintain an erection long enough to perform sexual intercourse. Of course, we know that is not the case with the Blessed Jasper."

Elder Walker flinched and raised his hand, as though to ward off blasphemy, but after a moment he took a deep breath and nodded.

"You are disconcertingly frank, my dear. I blame your exposure to subversive influences beyond the Order, and I excuse your conduct. Continue."

"Secondary impotence covers several different cases. Sometimes a male is intermittently potent. Sometimes a male is potent with certain partners, and not with others. Sometimes the male achieves an erection, but cannot sustain it long enough to complete the act; and sometimes a previously potent male, because of age or illness, loses all ability to achieve erection. Which one of these best describes the Blessed Jasper?"

I thought he was not going to answer. He stood up and went over to his desk. Half a minute later, without looking at me, he said, "The last one. But the Patriarch is not ill—at least, no worse than he has been for years. Can anything be done to help him?"

"I don't know."

"You must, it is your area of specialty. Surely there are medications, injections?" He turned to me and he was holding papers in his hand. "You mention them in your own reports. The scientists at Tilden have 32 pending patents based on your work." Stumbling over the words, he read, "Alprostadil, CGMP, guanine hexa-fluorate. Sildena-what's-this-say?"

"Sildenafil citrate. That last one is already patented by Pfizer. It was the first of the Viagra-class drugs. But it would still be my first suggestion here."

"It was tried earlier this year. There was some success, but also side effects — headaches, and alarming fluctuations in blood pressure. I judged it too risky to continue."

My mind felt topsy-turvy. So many years with the image of the Patriarch as all-powerful and all-knowing, and now Cyrus Walker spoke of the Blessed Jasper like some prize animal needing to be restored to working condition.

"There are many other drugs," I said. "I can suggest dozens. The problem is, they have never been tried on human subjects under controlled conditions. It would take years for Tilden to get any of them through the FDA."

Prompted by another blank look from Elder Walker, I added, "FDA is the Food and Drug Administration. It would have to approve any drug."

"Why should they know anything of the drugs that you have developed? They belong to us and Tilden."

"The FDA has to be told of any experiments involving humans. And Tilden won't risk crossing the FDA; they have too much at stake on hundreds of prod-ucts."

"Then neither Tilden nor your FDA shall know of the experiments." Elder Walker had regained control of himself, and of the meeting. "It is very simple, Rachel. You will develop and provide the test drugs. Here within the Order I will find males to take part in your experiments. The results will come back to you, and you will make the evaluation. No one outside will know anything."

I shook my head. I was frightened, but I had to protest. "I can't do that."

"What do you mean, *can't*?" Elder Walker was scowling.

"It's dangerous, and unethical, and unfair to Tilden. They've always worked in good faith with the Blessed Order. Walter Cottingham has treated me kindly, and I regard him as my friend."

"Tilden, and Walter Cottingham, are unbelievers. Your duty is to serve the Blessed Order." Perhaps there was still a hint of rebellion in my look, because he went on, "You will do as you are told, Rachel. Or would you rather never see your daughter again?"

He had hit my weak point, and he knew it. They had Naomi. I dared argue no more. I nodded, and said softly, "It will be as you say."

If I am completely honest, I must admit that the decision was not so difficult as it may sound. I was fascinated by the prospect of applying some of the ideas that bubbled up in my head as soon as the problem was defined. Also, my whole upbringing had been one in which obedience to Elder Cyrus Walker and the needs of the Blessed Order was immediate and unquestioned.

So the secret program was launched — secret from Tilden, secret from the uni-versity, secret from my friends and fellow workers in the lab. I was told, and accepted, that in the interests of secrecy I would be interrogated regularly during my visits to Bryceville.

I was allowed to spend an extra four days with Naomi. Then I returned to the university and I began to work, harder than ever in my life. I cannot deny that I reveled in the challenge.

It would be two more years before I began to suspect that Cyrus Walker's motives were not what they seemed. And a year beyond that when I started to question the whole structure and *raison d'être* of the Blessed Order.

Not for nothing do the priests of another religion say, "Give me the child for the first seven years, and I'll give you the man."

Whatever an infant finds around herself is, by definition, the natural order of things. Quite reasonable to me, all through my first and second decades, was the idea that a man had the right to take several wives; accepted, that a woman's success would be measured by the number of healthy children that she bore, and that she would function in all the affairs of life as "the lesser man"; natural, that children were first and foremost the possessions and servants of the Blessed Order; unquestioned, that the sex rights and privileges of the males should contain a defined hierarchy, with the Patriarch at the head and Elder Walker as his powerful lieutenant.

In every class in Bryceville's school, biblical authority was cited for these matters. At home, my mother and seldom-seen father drove home the same message. Is it any wonder that five full years were necessary, away from Bryceville and in the company of heretics, before I began to feel differently?

And yet with hindsight I believe that I was in some ways always a rebel. Unknown to anyone, I had secretly named my first frog *Jasper*. Taking the name of the Patriarch in vain was blasphemy. Unknown to anyone, I had done my private froggy investigations and mailed the results to a science contest in the huge and unknown world beyond Bryceville and the Blessed Order. That was, at the very least, gross disobedience. It ought to have raised a red flare on the lofty roof of the Patriarch's lodge, glaring enough to warn any alert Council member that Rachel Stafford was the worst possible person to send into an outside world of skeptics and unbelievers.

Perhaps they were overconfident. After all, they had Naomi. And indeed, during my first years at the university any Council member would have seen little reason to doubt the decision to send me there. True, I did take driving lessons and obtain my license, something denied to female members of the Blessed Order; but I used the license mainly as an ID in stores. I was young and shy and avoided social contacts. My work and my visits to Naomi filled my life; and although it should not be for me to say it, my understanding of neurotransmitters, human biochemistry, and the human mind-body interface grew to exceed anything that I could find elsewhere in the world. I published little, but Walter Cottingham filed a torrent of patents based upon my work. He told me — strictly, I am sure, against company policy — that Tilden was more than getting their money's worth. No other company had anything remotely like the selective-memory suppression and keyed-memory access drugs that my work provided. Of course, the "forgetters," the "truth tellers," and the "button pressers" (Walter's terminology) still had a long way to go before they could be turned on and off in hours rather than in a few weeks; even so, he and Tilden were highly satisfied.

But I was not. It was not so much that the Order used the truth tellers on me. Rather, it was that as year followed year I became increasingly convinced that I was just getting started. The human brain and body form a wondrous and complex interacting system. The idea that a drug—any drug—might produce a single effect on the delicately balanced human brain is as preposterously naive and wrong as the thought that a combination of two medications will produce no effect beyond their separate influences. Tilden had its patents; I, mapping cross-connections, had something more: the vision of a whole new world where drugs affecting the mind affected the body that affected the mind . . . on and on, in infinite regress.

As year followed year I also became more certain that the society of the Blessed Order was corrupt and rotten at its heart.

I looked up. The sun was high in the sky. I glanced at my watch and realized that I had spent two dazed hours staring at the bright posters in the window of the bicycle shop. The hard bench seat had cut into my thighs. When I stood up, my calves felt the pins and needles of returning circulation.

I walked slowly back to the campus. Nothing was happening now that had not happened many times before. I had been to Bryceville, reported to Elder Walker, and delivered to him my latest work. He had given me test results for analysis, and he had interrogated me, in detail, while I was under the influence of drugs of my own devising. Soon the effects would wear off, and I would feel normal.

Back in my office, I again turned on the computer and called up the hidden data files. *The response is decidedly nonlinear and follows an approximate two-thirds power law. . . .* The words felt no less remote. However, I could now tell myself that there was a good reason. I had been away for a week, naturally my work would seem a little strange, a little less immediate.

Then why was I filled with such an alien sense of dissatisfaction? I have a powerful memory, but somehow I did not feel that I could trust it. Something was missing. Was that real, or just more drug aftereffects?

I leaned back in my seat and stared at the screen. My office lies at the end of the corridor. I heard no sound but the soft whir of the disk drive and faint footsteps on the floor above.

I felt a strengthening conviction. During my absence someone had been in my office, started my computer, and tampered with my hidden files.

Who? That was not difficult. The Council of the Blessed Order knew exactly when I would be visiting Bryceville and away from the university. Asking me questions was only one way of making sure the secrets of my work were safe; a more direct method was to explore my records firsthand. I did not remember doing so, but under earlier drugged interrogations I might have revealed everything about my secret files.

It was easy enough to check my suspicion. I went to the central log, where records were kept of every transaction of material called from storage. The history was in reverse chronological order. My hidden work files contained nine years of notes on the anti-impotence drugs and protocols, from their earliest beginnings when I arrived at the university through to the same pages that I had been examining earlier in the day. Those last pages had been accessed on March 16 — a date when I was away in Bryceville.

During my absence, representatives of the Blessed Order had been here and examined my files.

I had my answer. It was exactly what I expected, but it brought no peace of mind. I folded my arms, stared at nothing, and wondered. Since it was no surprise to me that my files would be explored in my absence, why the continued uneasiness? These records said nothing that I had not already revealed, in full, to Elder Walker and the Council of the Blessed Order.

The rhythmic click of leather shoes sounded far off in the corridor. Someone, probably Dr. Jeffers, was pacing steadily up and down. It was his preferred way of thinking. As this was mine. Sitting in a half-trance, lulled by the sound of footsteps and by the faint hum of the computer's hard drive, I listened to my inner voice. I realized that my worries had nothing to do with my work, or who had been investigating it.

My worry was Naomi. I know that a mother is not the best judge, but I had always thought her an exceptionally pretty child.

A *child*.

Except that on my most recent visit, that word had not been appropriate. In the six months since I had last seen her, Naomi had become a woman. Not just the young breasts, filling out her tight cotton dress; not just the way that the men of the Order looked at her — covertly, hotly, with the eyes of lust. That was bad enough, but worse was the way she responded to those looks; the knowing sideways glance of her dark eyes, the way she held herself and moved her body.

I have suggested already that I am not a stupid woman. Why, then, was I so slow to realize that Naomi, at 13 years, was close to the age when I had been taken to the Patriarch, and far less innocent than I?

I had not seen, because I did not wish to see. To me it was unthinkable that Naomi would be forced to endure what I had gone through myself, 14 years ago. Unthinkable that she would be made to commit incest, even though such a union with the Patriarch, the earthly embodiment of God himself, was sanctioned and blessed within the Order. Unthinkable, but unavoidable.

I became aware that something in front of me had changed. The computer, unattended for more than 10 minutes, had switched its display. Instead of the chronological list of files accessed, it showed a variable screen-saver pattern. A flood of multicolored bubbles rose slowly up the screen, popped, and dispersed.

The upward drift was random, and then after a while not quite so. I stared, puzzled by a twisting area where green and blue bubbles faded into each other, I was seeing letters — words. *Sharon File 32V*. Visible for a few seconds, then vanishing. Random bubbles formed and rose and burst.

I kept looking. After about half a minute, another confluence of merging bubbles formed the words again: *Sharon File 32V*.

Very few people would be able to read that message. Even if they switched on my computer and let it sit idle until the screen-saver pattern appeared, chances were that they would see nothing. To a person with normal vision, there was no message. Only someone color-blind exactly as I was color-blind would find anything on the screen but random bubbles.

I had left a message to myself. And I had no idea what it might be.

The hours from noon to early evening were very difficult. Sharon Prostley would be gone by 5:30, but others of the lab left later and they would find it odd to see me using Sharon's work station. I could plead problems with my own computer, but I did not want anyone peering over my shoulder and offering helpful advice when I took a look at File 32V in Sharon's system.

I waited as long as I could stand. It was 20 minutes after seven when I walked for the 10th time along the corridor, found every office empty, and tiptoed into Sharon's room. Most of one wall was a long window, so even with the door closed I would be perfectly visible from the corridor as I turned on her computer.

It took a few minutes to feel my way in—Sharon's machine was organized quite differently from mine. I was forced to look in quite a few places until, in an operating system directory where Sharon was never likely to go, I found 32V. It was a text file; or, more accurately, a nested set of them.

I loaded Sharon's word processing system. Nervously, wondering what I might find, I brought in the first file.

FLGEYRRO PROCIUET PSCIQCXN OFPAJWFS.

Gibberish. Not words, not data, not anything.

Unless . . . I stared, became dizzy, felt the room sway and rock around me. Memories, suppressed by my own drugs and keyed now by the button pressers, flooded back.

My fingers sought and found the new data bank. Terse notes filled the screen—secret from Tilden, Inc., secret from Elder Walker, secret from everyone. Scanning them, I doubted that they would be intelligible to anyone but me. But scanning them, I saw ample reason for extreme caution.

First entry: *Penta-sild. + cyto. heptahydrate + oxidant → strong short-term increase.*

It was a tailored anti-impotence drug that I had recently developed and was testing on members of the Blessed Order. Strictly speaking, any drug was merely being evaluated before being made available to the Blessed Jasper. In practice there was never a shortage of volunteers. Elder Walker told me to bring increasing amounts on each of my six-monthly visits.

And now the subtext: *Penta-sild. + cyto. heptahydrate + GABA undergoes metamorph. → new neuro. + feedback→ 6-mo. Î(sero. & dopa. levels)→ pituit. down → testost. to zero. Permanent.*

Interpretation: The same drug, plus gamma-aminobutyric acid, crossed the blood-brain barrier and had a neurotransmitter breakdown product. Used for six months or more, the pituitary gland would be increasingly affected and the male testosterone level would drop to zero; with that decline would go all sexual desire. Furthermore, the effect would not reverse itself after use of the drug ended.

How much did I hate the Order that had raised me? Enough to want to destroy it; but I told myself that was not my motive. All I wanted was to save Naomi. Another few months would be enough; provided that they did not take her virginity until July or August, she would escape my fate.

March, with its warm days and pleasantly cool nights, slowly gave way to the baking heat of June. I worked late every night, but the sidewalk was still warm beneath my sandals as I walked home to my single-bedroom apartment.

As always, I checked my answering machine. Every week I had a friendly call from Walter Cottingham, and now and again there were questions or comments from the scientists at Tilden, Inc. Occasionally there was a message from Bryceville. The Blessed Order did not approve of electronic devices but it did not always follow its own rules. I knew from Walter that Elder Walker telephoned him every week on financial matters. For a senior member of a sect that eschewed all worldly concerns, Cyrus Walker was surprisingly interested in money. I did not know how much Tilden, Inc. paid the Order for what I was doing, but it was far more than the cost of my room and board, plus a small discretionary amount for incidentals. That had been granted, grudgingly, after strong words on my behalf from Walter.

On June 28, I arrived home at nine. I made myself a glass of iced tea and listened to the calls. Raoul Caprice, from Tilden, with a shrewd question about an implied viral inhibitor effect of one of my recent reports. Would it work equally well for retroviruses? I wondered. Would it? Probably. I liked Raoul, or at least I liked his mind. We had never met in person. I looked at the clock and decided, regretfully, that it was a bit late to call him back on the East Coast.

A telemarketer, who must have had more spare time than sense, had left a long message inviting me to buy "heating oil futures," whatever they were. Sharon Prostley had called, apologizing for not dropping in that morning. She was PMS-y and had been in a shitty mood all day. See you tomorrow. Abner Wurtshelm, of whom I had never heard, nervously wondered if I could tell him how the prostaglandins worked. He was doing a science report for high school—deadline in three days—was going to pull a certain D unless he came up with something spectacular—got my name from the college book—would love to buy me a coffee—lunch even—if I would answer a few questions.

I smiled. Abner had a real nerve, but maybe I would call him back. He sounded bright. I started to walk toward the phone when the final message started in midsentence.

"—later on. I have something tremendous to tell you. Call me on return—as soon as you get this message."

Naomi, too impatient to wait for the end of my standard message to callers. Naomi!

I was dialing before I could ask myself where she was, or how she had managed to place a call.

"Yes?" The gruff voice that answered was male.

"Naomi Stafford." I was filled with a mixture of excitement and terror. *Something tremendous*—surely that couldn't be anything to do with the Blessed Jasper. So what was it? "I mean, I would like to speak to Naomi Stafford."

"I'm sure you would, Rachel." It was Elder Walker. "She's right here. One moment."

"Mother?" It was Naomi, breathless but somehow more adult in tone than when I had seen her last. "I have some absolutely wonderful news. I'm going to be married!"

"Married. To—"

I found it hard to get the words out. The Blessed Jasper was father to a 10th of the children in the Blessed Order, but he had not married for 40 years.

"To the Blessed Jasper?" I said at last.

"No! Of course not, silly." Naomi's laugh, young and carefree, grabbed my heart. "Mother, I'm going to marry Elder Walker. Aren't you going to congratulate us?"

No 90-year-old Jasper. Instead, rugged and ageless Cyrus Walker, with his bald head, barrel chest, and sly, gray eyes. The heir apparent to the leadership of the Blessed Order had chosen my daughter—my not-yet-14 daughter—to be his wife. She would join the three cowed, abject women already married to him. My work had not saved her. It came too late.

"Mother?" said Naomi. When I still could not speak, Elder Walker's voice came on the line. "Of course, we hope you will be here for the wedding. You will come, won't you?"

It was more a command than a question. Elder Walker was used to commanding.

"Ah—uh—of course, I'll—when—when will the wedding be?" I still had hope. Elder Walker, whose sexual appetite had been whispered about by the women since I was a small child, would surely be one of the men taking the newest drug that I had provided. A couple more months . . .

"Oh, don't worry, there's plenty of time for you to get here. The ceremony won't be until Saturday."

"Which Saturday?"

"The next one. July 3."

Today was Monday. Five days from now.

"Too soon," I said, and then, to cover my mistake. "I mean, it will be hard for me to get away from the lab at such short notice. Is there any way it could be later—even a few weeks?"

"The arrangements have all been made. They can't be changed." Elder Walker's voice left no room for negotiation. "Tell people at the university that it's your daughter's wedding. They will understand."

"May I speak again to Naomi?"

"You can speak to her tomorrow. Then you'll know what day and time you'll be getting here, and we'll see how you fit into the ceremony. Naomi would like you to be part of it. See you in a few days."

I heard a click and was left with a dead line. In a few days I might be dead, too. I knew I would go to Bryceville—I had to, to talk Naomi out of it, plead with Elder Walker to wait, ask for an audience with the Blessed Jasper. Hopeless, but I had to try everything.

And I would go to Bryceville with memories of my own subversive work against the Blessed Order intact. The selective-memory suppression drug I had used on my last visit required a careful protocol and weeks of preparation.

What were the chances that I would be interrogated again during my visit? I would have to take the chance. I told myself, it had been only three months and after all I was there for a wedding, not a research review.

I felt a powerful urge to drop everything and head at once to Bryceville. The sooner I knew the worst—all the worst—the better. A night, long and sleepless, and a brief conversation with Naomi the next morning, convinced me otherwise. I worked the next three days in the lab, pausing only for meals and brief naps and never leaving the building.

At two o'clock on Friday morning I returned to my apartment, showered for the first time in four days, and set the alarm for eight.

At nine o'clock I did something I had done only twice before in my life. I rented a car. I took it to the university, picked up a package from the lab, and eliminated a group of files from my computer, overwriting the storage areas so there was no possibility of reconstruction. Then, instead of taking the usual bus to Bryceville, I drove. On dusty roads, through sheer-sided red canyons and across stark desert scenery, the car's air conditioning fought the summer heat while I, shivering and sweating by turns, worried about Naomi and what was going to happen the next day. The more I thought about Cyrus Walker, the more Naomi's fate seemed worse than mine. I had lost my virginity to the Blessed Jasper; she would lose her whole life when she became Elder Walker's fourth wife.

A mile and a half before I came to the outskirts of Bryceville I left the highway and parked the car in a little arroyo. It would be in trouble there in the event of a flash flood, but it was well out of sight of anyone on the road. I took a knapsack out of the trunk. That was my usual luggage when I went home for visits. Then I hesitated.

Should I take the other thing, too? If I didn't, I might have no chance to come back for it. The cylinder would fit in my knapsack, but suppose that were to be searched? It never had been, so far as I knew. All it usually held were toilet articles, a couple of changes of clothing, and some small gift for Naomi. I had never checked closely to see if anything had been removed and returned.

I looked at my watch. In 15 minutes the Escalante bus was scheduled to pass by this part of the highway. I had to be on it. I finally decided to leave the cylinder behind in the locked trunk of the car, and hurried back out of the arroyo.

I had cut it close. The bus was no more than a mile away, its outline shimmering in the heat, when I reached the road. I stood by the roadside and waved, and it wheezed to a halt.

"Bryceville," I said, as I climbed on board. "How much do I owe?"

"Not worth charging you." The driver, a towheaded man in his early 20s, nodded toward the road ahead. "We're almost there, you could have walked it in half an hour. But I guess it's a bit hot for that."

"Hot, and dusty," I said, and went to sit down. I was glad to see that only half a dozen other people were on the bus, and none of them had the dress typical of members of the Blessed Order.

The bus dropped me off in the usual place near the edge of town. It was just after one o'clock, so all the children were in school and no mothers were waiting. In fact, no one at all was on the street. My precaution in arriving by bus felt like a waste of time as I walked slowly toward Elder Walker's house, in its favored position next to the Patriarch's tall lodge.

Why there, and not to my mother's house, where Naomi lived? I think I wanted to know the worst as soon as possible. I approached the door of scrubbed white oak, and gently knocked. After a few seconds it was opened—by Naomi.

"Mother!" She sounded delighted and she looked wonderful, cheerful and radiant and more free of worry than I have ever been. "I didn't think you would arrive so early."

"You're living here," I said. *Too late.*

"No, I'm not. I came this morning to help with the arrangements—it's going to be a huge ceremony. Cyrus isn't here, he'll be back in a few minutes. But the Patriarch is. Come in and see him."

I would rather spend time with the Devil. But I stepped into the familiar broad hall flanked with Anasazi relics and followed Naomi to the rear of the house.

She led me not to the big living room where Elder Walker had gazed out of the window at the rolling tumbleweed, but to a little, dim-lit den. I had to wait for my eyes to adjust before I could see the Patriarch sitting in an armchair.

At once, I knew what Naomi apparently did not. I was looking at a man close to death. He was small and shriveled, a doll figure dwarfed by the massive chair. The skin of his bald head was like a jaundiced saffron egg, marked by prominent dark veins. His mouth was open, a dark toothless cavern, and his yellowed eyes stared at nothing. When they did not move as I stepped closer, I knew that he was blind.

After the Patriarch, what? The inner circle would never be open to me, or to any woman, but it was not hard to guess its decision. When the Blessed Jasper died, Elder Walker would become the Patriarch.

Looking again at Naomi, I realized that I had been wrong. She *knew*—knew that Jasper had little time to live, knew that tomorrow she would marry a man destined for supreme power within the Order. That sounded wonderful to her— but what about the life she would lead afterward, as a fourth and lowest wife? At 13, no one thinks of the long-term future.

"Can we go home soon?" I said. "I want to see your grandmother, and I would like to spend some time with you before the wedding."

"That might be difficult." She gave me the rapid, side-of-eye glance that I had seen her use on older men. "Cyrus said we'd be very busy today and it would be better for me to stay at this house tonight." She added, her chin pushed a little forward, "It will all be very proper and respectable. Two of Cyrus's brothers and two of his sisters will be here."

"Naomi, we need to talk."

"We'll have plenty of time for that—after the wedding." She turned at the sound of the door opening back along the hall, and said importantly, "I think that must be Cyrus. I must make sure that things are ready for him."

She hurried away. I took another look at the Patriarch. He lolled in his chair just as he had when I arrived, apparently seeing and hearing nothing.

That seemed to be confirmed when Elder Walker breezed in. He ignored the Blessed Jasper and came straight across to me.

"Excellent, excellent." He clapped his meaty hands together. "You are early, and we need all the help we can get. Rachel, I want you to go down to the main meeting hall and tell Belinda Lee that the table arrangements for the meal have to be changed. Tell her that the Blessed Jasper"—the skeletal figure made no movement at the sound of his name—"must be seated alone at a special dais, and he should not be served a meal."

"Naomi," I began. "I'd like to meet with her and—"

"Tomorrow. Far too busy today, all of us." He took my arm and led me back toward the front door. "Lots of time for the pair of you to talk tomorrow. Off you go and help Belinda. And you won't need that just now." He took my knapsack from my hand and hefted it speculatively. "We'll get it to you later."

I went cold, recalling how close I had come to bringing the cylinder. I said not a word, but as he ushered me into the street he spoke again. "One other thing, Rachel. The questioning regarding the progress of your work. We'll put that off until after the wedding. We'll do it on Sunday, all right? Hurry along now."

He closed the door before I could reply. Instead of hurrying I leaned my back against the sturdy wall of the house and closed my eyes. I was unprepared, and interrogation on Sunday would doom me. All the way from St. George I had wondered what I should do—what I could do, what I dared to do. Now, I had no choice.

Sometimes I wonder where I came from. That feeling is never stronger than when I have spent a few hours with my mother. She was thinner than ever and very frail, but she was enormously cheerful. She asked me about my work, and after a couple of minutes of simplified description she nodded and said, "A wonderful marriage, it will be. As I've told Naomi, she is very lucky. Everyone expects that Cyrus Walker will become—"

She paused, reluctant to voice the unspeakable. *Cyrus Walker will become the new Patriarch when the Blessed Jasper dies.*

"Mother, Elder Walker is an old man, at least 60, and he has three wives already."

"Do you think that Naomi minds that? Rachel, don't you ever even *look* at your own daughter? Naomi is happy as can be, every move she makes says that. She *wants* to marry Cyrus."

"But she's only 13. She's a *child*."

She stared at me. "You had Naomi at 14. I had *you* at 14."

"But that doesn't mean it was right. To spend your whole life bearing children, until you are too old or too sick or die doing it."

She stood up, and she was trembling. "Rachel Stafford, I don't want to hear one more word. I didn't bring a child of mine into the world so that she could spout blasphemy. I didn't raise you that way, and I didn't raise Naomi that way, either. It's that godless college you work at, and that godless work you do. I should never have let you go. I'm going to lie down."

No use reminding her that she had had no say in the matter. My future had been decided by Elder Walker and the Council. Mother had been a nonentity, as I would also be a nonentity except that my continued presence at the university was both useful and lucrative for the Blessed Order.

At eight o'clock my knapsack was dropped off at the house by a teenage girl whom I did not recall meeting before.

"I'm a friend of Naomi," she said. She stared at me curiously, and I wondered what tales were told in Bryceville of the strange visitor who was Naomi Stafford's mother. After she had gone I looked inside the knapsack and found that the contents were not arranged as I had packed them.

By 10 o'clock it was fully dark. I waited another hour until my mother, who after our first disagreement had said no more than a few words to me all evening, was in bed and soundly asleep. Then I slipped out. The street was quiet and empty. Unless something had changed in the past few months, the summer curfew in Bryceville would last until five in the morning.

I moved slowly and tried to stay in the shadow of buildings until I was safely out of the town center. I had no flashlight with me — a failure of planning on my part — but the Moon was only a few days past full and there were no clouds. Even so, the world looked different enough at night that I was not sure I had the right arroyo until I actually saw the car.

The cylinder weighed about 10 pounds. With more time in the lab I could have cut that down considerably, but everything had been done in a blazing hurry. I tucked the smooth, gray shape under my arm and started back.

It was after midnight when I reached the outskirts of Bryceville. In the past two hours clouds had moved in from the west to hide the Moon. The weather was changing. I sneaked again through the dark streets, knowing that the hard part lay ahead of me.

That effort could not begin until morning. I tiptoed upstairs and lay down in the same bed where I had slept as a child. Amazingly, I slept like a child. Or perhaps not so amazingly. The mind can push a long way, but at some point the body asserts it own demands.

Summer rain in Bryceville was a rare treat. The wet morning faces that I passed on the streets all seemed to be smiling. People who recognized me paused to congratulate me. I forced a smile of my own, held my knapsack tightly under my raincoat, and hurried on.

The ceremony would be held in the town meeting hall at 11:30, followed at once by the reception in the same building. As I had expected, Belinda Lee was already there, worrying over final arrangements. She did not question my presence. Elder Walker had assigned me to help her yesterday, he must have done the same today.

I went to the rear of the hall to put down my knapsack and hang up my raincoat. Walking to the arroyo and back I had thought about the layout of the meeting hall and wondered where to put the fat, gray cylinder. It had to be hidden, but it also had to be accessible to me during or just before the ceremony.

Belinda Lee, thank God, was a worrier who liked everything planned and perfect to the last detail. She was not at all surprised when I appeared to have the same attitude.

"Right here," she said, leading me to the third long bench. "You'll enter with Naomi, then you leave her at the front and come and sit down at the aisle end for the whole ceremony."

"I just want to run through it once to make sure," I said.

Belinda's vague nod said, all right, but I've got other things to do. Women were arriving with home-cooked food, which had to be placed ready for serving after the wedding. She took no notice of me when I sat down on the bench and leaned forward to peer beneath it. The solid wooden back ran all the way to the floor, and there was a good foot of open space below the seat.

I went back along the aisle, picked up my knapsack, and walked slowly forward leading an imagined Naomi on my arm. As the dais I paused respectfully with head inclined, then turned and went to sit at the end of the bench. I slipped my knapsack underneath and bent down as though it would not easily fit. The fat, gray cylinder had to come out. I eased it free, pushed it back a little farther, and used the empty knapsack to hide it completely from sight. Leaning far forward, I could still reach its black valve.

Two other young women, strangers to me, were at the front of the hall now. I went forward.

"I'm Naomi's mother. Elder Walker sent me to help. It smells awful musty in here, and with the rain we don't want to open the windows. Do you have anything to make it smell nicer?"

Female members of the Blessed Order do not question male authority, even when it comes secondhand. "We've got disinfectant," one of them said. "But it doesn't smell all that good."

"How about rosewater?" the second one asked. "We've got plenty of that. Wouldn't it be better?"

"It would be perfect," I said. "Bring me all you can find. And the disinfectant, too."

They looked a little doubtful as they went off. With reason. Ammonia and rosewater provide an aroma like nothing you can imagine. By 9:30 the front part of the hall had its own unique smell; neither pleasant nor unpleasant, but enough to make people sniff and look puzzled when they came in. I left, highly nervous about what I was leaving beneath the bench, and made my way through the rain to Elder Walker's house.

If I had ever imagined that I was a key player in preparations for the wedding ceremony, the illusion ended with my arrival at the house. I was hardly noticed. Elder Walker had already departed, sequestered with the rest of the Council, but half a dozen older women had been there since early morning. Naomi's attention was all on her appearance. The Order held that elaborate dress and undue attention to person was sinful, but no one seemed to have told my daughter. She was fretting about her puffy face, her imagined double chin, and the state of her complexion. And what would happen to her dress and her hair when she had to walk in the rain? I told her—truthfully—that she looked radiant and absolutely gorgeous. The idea of Cyrus Walker forcing himself onto and into that soft young body made me want to vomit.

All unions of the Blessed Order are said to be fore-ordained by Heaven. Today the weather seemed to support that. At 11:15, just as we prepared to walk over to the meeting hall, the rain stopped and the sun emerged.

Ten of us, all women, walked through the streets with Naomi; but when we came to the open double doors of the hall, I alone continued with her on my arm. The great room was already three-quarters full. I guessed maybe a thousand people were there—this was a major event for the Blessed Order. As Naomi and I went down the long aisle I saw Elder Walker and a group of Council members waiting at the end. Behind them, on the dais in a massive ceremonial chair, sat the wasted form of the Blessed Jasper.

The wedding ceremony within the Order was lengthy, and as long as I had lived in Bryceville the Patriarch had played a central part in it. As I left Naomi with the group before the dais, turned, and made my way to my place on the bench, I wondered. How could a living skeleton, blind and deaf, perform any function at all, still less deliver the customary invocation and blessing?

I should have known better. The Council had faced the problem of a failing Patriarch for a long time. As I sat down and leaned far forward as though in prayer, I heard a familiar voice. "Dearly Beloved, we are gathered here today . . ."

I jerked my head up. That was the Patriarch's voice, firm and clear. But the mouth of the frail figure on the platform was not moving. I glanced around and saw others behaving as if the situation was perfectly normal. Suddenly I realized what was happening. The Order, sneering at the world outside Bryceville, decrying modern machinery, suspicious of innovation, still found its own uses for technology. Someone, years ago, had foreseen the present situation and recorded the Blessed Jasper in a wedding ceremony.

I leaned down, reached underneath, and savagely turned the valve. As I straightened up I heard the hiss of escaping gas. After a few seconds my neighbors on the bench, three women, turned in my direction. They were catching a faintly acrid smell, but the continuing ceremony masked the sound. They stared at me for a moment, saw nothing, and returned their attention to the wedding service.

The next five minutes were agonizing. I felt sure that the smell of the spreading gas would overwhelm that of disinfectant and rosewater, and someone would investigate and expose what I had done. If that didn't happen, the alternative was almost worse: In another hour, Naomi would be married to Cyrus Walker. And there was a final possibility, one I almost dared not think about. I hoped that I understood the interaction of the chemical now spreading through the air with the drugs delivered in the past year to the Order, but in the last few desperate days there had been no time to calibrate dosage or explore other possible effects. Suppose that I killed everyone in the meeting hall? It was small consolation to know that I, sitting right above the cylinder would be the first to go.

I waited, gradually becoming convinced that I had made a gross mistake and nothing was going to happen. The voice of the Patriarch seemed to go on forever. Then one of the Council members standing right at Naomi's side raised a hand to his head, half-turned, and dropped to the ground without a sound.

The men nearby bent to help him, but before they could do more than lift his head their attention was diverted to the raised dais. The Patriarch, who up to this point in the proceedings had neither moved nor spoken, uttered a hoarse, strangled moan. His skinny figure lurched to its feet, stood swaying and rigid for a moment, then fell forward head first. The crack of his bald head on the hard floor of the hall was loud enough to sound through the still-continuing invocation.

A wail of horror and disbelief rang through the hall. Council members moved to the Blessed Jasper, while dozens of other people started forward. Before they could do anything to help, another man was toppling to the floor. Then another, I saw Elder Walker, swaying on his feet, grab at Naomi's arm for support. Then he crumpled and fell. I leaned forward, thinking to close the valve, but it was too late. The women on my bench were screaming and they forced their way past, making it impossible for me to bend over. I stood up and turned around. The room was pandemonium. Some people pushed forward to help, others were heading toward the doors. And, everywhere close by, men were falling. The front of the hall was littered with their silent bodies. Other men right beside them remained standing. They stared around, bewildered and afraid.

I hoped and prayed that I was seeing unconsciousness, and no worse. I had killed the Blessed Jasper, I knew that—the three-foot fall from the dais to an impact with the hard floor would have cracked the skull of a man far less frail.

Naomi was kneeling at Elder Walker's side, crying hysterically. I pushed my way through, grabbed an arm, and tried to lift her. "We have to get out of here!" I shouted.

"No!" She would not move. "Cyrus is hurt. I have to look after him."

"It's too risky. If we don't leave, the same thing will happen to us."

I don't know if she heard me, but others certainly did. I heard screams and cries of "Let me out!" The press toward the main exit began in earnest. Men and women forced each other out of the way and trampled the bodies on the floor. Again I tried to lift Naomi, but she would not move from Elder Walker's side.

I stayed with her, waiting for the crush to subside. Then, when no one was near, I did what I hated to do. The jab of the needle to the nape of her neck was not painful—barely enough to make her look up at me in surprise.

I waited for 10 seconds, then said, "Naomi, we must leave now. Come along."

She rose to her feet with a bemused expression on her face and allowed me to lead her away from Elder Walker. When we came to the bench where I had been sitting I made a quick detour and picked up the knapsack and cylinder.

At the double doors I paused and glanced back into the hall. I had no time for an accurate count, but I estimated that 50 people remained, all near the front, all unconscious, and all men. In front of me, hundreds had turned again and were standing, unsure if it would be safe to go back in. It had begun to pour, mingling warm raindrops with tears. No one spoke to us or tried to interfere as I led Naomi away along the street.

She said nothing for a hundred yards, and then, "Where are we going?"

"Home, first. Then to where we'll be safe."

She glanced back toward the meeting hall but did not answer. I could feel her arm trembling, and I tucked it into mine. "We'll be all right, love. We'll be fine."

She stared at me vacantly. "Where is Cyrus?"

"He is fine, too. He wants me to look after you."

"And the Blessed Jasper?"

I dared not answer that. I believed that the Patriarch was dead, and I had killed him. I told myself it was not my fault. The old man ought to have been allowed to die in peace.

We had reached Mother's house. I expected her to be there, until I saw that the wheelchair was missing. I hadn't seen her in the hall, but she had almost certainly been there for the wedding. I hoped that she was safe. In any case, I could not take the time to find out.

"Naomi, pack some clothes, and anything else you think you need."

"For how long?"

Forever. I would not ever dare to return to Bryceville, and I wanted Naomi to stay away.

"For a week." In that much time I would be able to explain everything to her.

"Are you taking me to where you live, in St. George?"

That had been my own first thought, until I recalled how members of the Blessed Order had known exactly how to get into my computer. We would not be safe there. We would not be safe anywhere, but I could not tell that to Naomi.

"Not St. George," I said. "We are going farther away than that. You'll get to fly in an airplane."

"Oh." Her face showed some life for the first time since the man at her side had fallen silently to the floor, but then she frowned. My poor, sweet Naomi. Today had to be a far worse nightmare for her than for me. "An airplane?"

"Drink this," I said.

She swallowed the little cup of red liquid I handed her, and after a few seconds her face cleared. "An airplane. I've always wanted to go on one. But isn't it wrong?"

"Not when it's really necessary. The Blessed Order says, in certain cases things like airplanes can be used." I glanced at my watch. Amazingly, it was not yet midday. "Are you ready to go?"

"Just about." She smiled. "Will you really take me on an airplane?"

"I will. I promise."

Three-quarters of an hour later we were at the arroyo. The rain had made the ground slippery but there had been no flood. The car started easily. I headed north. Four hours later we were at the Salt Lake City airport. By seven o'clock we were taking off, and Naomi was staring out of the window. She seemed blissfully content—too content.

I, in the seat next to her, worried about dosages, gripped the armrests of my seat and tried not to think about where I was.

I, too, had never been on an airplane.

Where to go?

Although my research work had carried me electronically to hundreds of people on every continent except Antarctica, I knew no one. I had no close friends, no knowledge of how or where two people without much money could hide from possible pursuers.

I had been too desperate to do anything but run until we flew out of Salt Lake City. Only when we landed at Philadelphia at six o'clock in the morning did I call Walter Cottingham. I reached his answering machine, and left him a despairing message with the number of the phone where I was standing.

I went back to sit down. What were Naomi and I going to do? She had slept through most of our long red-eye flight with its two connections, exhausted by her nightmare morning and with a mixture of drugs still in her system. She drowsed on a seat near me. Now, somehow, I had to get us to a place where we could shower and eat, and she could recuperate.

While I was still wondering, the telephone rang and I jumped to answer it, almost knocking down a woman struggling with two big suitcases.

"Walter?" I said. The woman was glaring at me, and I gave her a conciliatory smile.

"It's me. I'm home. Just sleeping. Do you know what time it is? Where are you?" He listened, then said, "Stay right there. I'm on my way. Don't worry, we'll take care of this."

I collapsed back onto my seat. For the first time in 24 hours I was able to close my eyes and relax a little bit.

He arrived an hour later, when I was beginning to worry that he wasn't coming. "Traffic," he said. "You look tired out. How are you, witch-woman?"

He caught Naomi's puzzled expression. "It's nothing bad. Just a name I gave your mother because our researchers say what she does is magic."

I had told Naomi nothing about Walter, except that he was a friend. She was staring as I introduced them, and I tried to see him through her eyes. The black mustache was long gone, together with the bow tie. I noticed for the first time a few gray hairs. In the past eight years he had been through a marriage and a "friendly" divorce, and he had two children who lived mainly with their mother.

"Did anyone from Bryceville call you?" I asked.

"Not since last week." He had picked up our two cases and was leading us to the airport parking lot. "Were they supposed to?"

"No." I was tempted to tell him everything at once, but I was afraid that if I did he would say he couldn't help and we had to go back. "There was a lot of trouble in Bryceville yesterday. People falling-down sick. Naomi and I had to get out before we caught it, too."

He turned and gave me an owlish look, but he kept on walking. When we reached the car he said only, "I think we ought to go to my place first and not to the office. Because when Raoul Caprice and the others find out you're in town they'll kill to meet you."

The 40-minutes drive to the western suburbs of Philadelphia was done mainly in silence, Naomi in the back and me on the edge of my seat next to Walter Cottingham. We pulled up at an old wooden house with big shade trees in the front yard, bordered by a hedge with sweet-smelling white flowers that I had never seen in Bryceville or St. George.

Before we went inside Walter apologized for the mess. He carried the cases up a flight of stairs running from the dark little entrance hall, to a bedroom luxuriously furnished by the standards of the Blessed Order. Naomi stared wide-eyed at the telephone, the television on the dresser, the window air conditioner, and the bathroom with its variable-pressure shower head. I could see that the drugs were working their way out of her system, and I steeled myself for a barrage of questions when they did.

"Make yourself at home," Walter said to her. "I'll bet you could use a shower, right? Come down when you're all done and we'll have breakfast. I've not had a thing to eat yet this morning."

I could tell from the way he spoke that I was not included in the invitation to shower. I followed him back downstairs and through a dining room into a sunny enclosed porch lined with cushioned benches and with a solid butcher-block table in the middle.

He pulled out a chair, motioned to me to sit opposite him, and said, "All right, Rachel. What the hell is all this?"

I faced the devil's own choice: be honest, and admit to my participation with the Blessed Order in an eight-year deception of Tilden, Inc., or try to invent a set of lies plausible and consistent enough to satisfy Walter's skeptical mind.

I heard the sound of running water upstairs, and thought of Naomi. Her safety came first. Walter had to know what had happened in Bryceville — including everything that I had done.

"It will take a little while," I said. "May I have a cup of tea — caffeine-free if you have it."

While the water was boiling, I began. The bit about the first impotence drugs was easy. Walter was actually ahead of me. He interrupted to say, "We were partly responsible for that. Our people sensed a possible gold mine of patentable medications when they read your first reports. I'd say we steered you in that direction; but you were soon far beyond anything we expected."

"And I'm sure you didn't expect what came next." I told him of Elder Walker's request — more like a command — to develop the next generation of drugs and test them on members of the Blessed Order. Walter whistled and said, "Bad news. Unapproved testing, on human subjects. Did it actually happen?"

"Yes. And there's worse."

I talked again, for a long time, and for a long time afterward he was silent. Finally he said, "Let me make sure I have this right. Recently you developed a new drug, one whose short-term effect is increased virility and sexual performance, but whose effect if taken over a period of months is the total and permanent destruction of all male sexual desire. That's what you meant by a 'phallicide agent.'"

"Yes. It wasn't that difficult."

"You can say that. I think our researchers would say it was damn-nigh impossible. And in the past week you went even further. You produced an airborne molecule that is absorbed rapidly through the skin, crosses the blood-brain barrier, and interacts with the previous drug to cause temporary insensibility."

"Yes. I hope it's temporary. Will you call Bryceville?"

"I will. How many people are affected?"

I remembered the men falling, and the floor of the meeting hall strewn with bodies. "Only males who had been taking impotence drugs and were near enough to the gas cylinder when I opened the valve. Maybe"—I hesitated—"maybe 50. But it could be as high as 75."

"Jesus Christ. You think you killed 75 people?"

"No!" I thought of the Blessed Jasper. "I do think I might have killed one."

"But you're not *sure* about the others? My God, Rachel, you stay here. It's still the crack of dawn out there, but I'm going to make a quick call this minute."

As he vanished I was left alone, my skull throbbing. I had been trying to save Naomi, that had been my whole reason for everything I had done. But if I had killed people, who would save *me*?

The door opened again. I looked up, thinking that Walter had some question before he made the call. Standing in the doorway was Naomi, fully dressed. Her damp hair was pushed back from her face and she was ghost-pale.

She stumbled forward and stood leaning against the table. "You did it," she said huskily. "It wasn't some kind of disease, like you told me. It was you, wasn't it, you and your drugs from hell? You killed the Blessed Jasper."

"Naomi, I didn't mean—"

"And you hurt Cyrus and the others." Tears were trickling down her bloodless cheeks. "We were going to be married, it would have been wonderful, the best day ever. I was so happy. You stopped it. And you made it so Cyrus and me can never have babies. I was really looking forward to having his babies." Her voice rose. "I hate you—you've ruined my whole life."

She stood up, blundered to the door, and pushed through it. I stood up to follow, but ran into Walter on the threshold.

"She knows," I said. "She heard us. She says she hates me. I have to go after her."

Naomi was out of the house, out of the yard. I saw her walking, head down, along the street.

"No. Let me do it. If she hates you right now, maybe she'll listen to me." At the front door he paused. "One dead—the Blessed Jasper. Everyone else is all right. No one there has any idea what really happened. Cyrus Walker told me that it was the Hand of Almighty God, reaching down to raise the Patriarch from earthly life to everlasting glory in Heaven."

"What did he say about me and Naomi?"

"Not a word. Things are so confused in Bryceville, he probably thinks you're still at your mother's house."

Walter smiled at me and was gone. I expected that he would return in a few minutes and I stood at the door waiting. After a quarter of an hour there was no sign of either him or Naomi, and I went back to sit wearily at the table.

I was really looking forward to having his babies . . . I hate you—you've ruined my whole life. How could she possibly feel that way?

After an hour I moved from the table to lie down on one of the padded benches on the porch. I fell asleep there, and woke from disturbing dreams when I heard the front door open. I straightened up and looked at my watch. Midafternoon. At least seven hours had passed. Walter came in, and he was alone.

"You didn't find her?" I said.

"I did. She and I went over to my office at Tilden. She's upstairs now. No—" He reached out to prevent me from standing up. "Don't try to go to her. You and I have to talk."

"I have to make sure that she is all right."

"She is. Take my word for it. Look, do you want to talk to Cyrus Walker in Bryceville?"

"No!" My stomach turned over at the idea.

"That was how I thought you'd feel. So I called him, from my office."

"What did you tell him?"

"That you are here. That Naomi is here, too. Not a word about your role in what happened. So far as he is concerned, you ran away and you took Naomi because you were scared."

"I *am* scared."

"You don't need to be." Walter motioned me to move over and sat down beside me on the bench. "I talked this whole thing over with my bosses at Tilden, and I have their approval for what I'm about to say. When I called Cyrus Walker, I told him I knew about the way that he and the Blessed Order had violated both the law and their agreement with us by doing drug tests on humans without FDA approval. Legally, I said, we have you guys on toast. But we're willing to cut you some slack under certain conditions. We'll even keep giving you royalty payments. Only from now on, we control the work that Rachel Stafford does. The Order has to cut out all the crap about interrogating you, and they stop delving into your files."

"Did he agree?"

"Not at first. And not without a condition of his own. He pleads to have Naomi back in Bryceville. I agreed."

"*Never.* You can't agree to that, you have no idea what it's like there."

"You're right, I don't have any idea. But Naomi does, and she's dead keen to go back—*desperate* to go back."

"She's too young to make that decision. Too young to know what's best for her."

"Not too young to know what she wants. And what she wants is to go back home." He raised his hand to cut off my response. "It is her home, you know, even if you hate to think of it that way. She loves you a lot, but she wants to go back to her mother."

"*I'm* her mother."

"Legally and biologically, of course you are. But the person who raised her, from the time she was two years old, is her grandmother. Rachel, I have to ask you a hard question. You had to go to Bryceville every six months, so they could check up on you. And you saw Naomi then. Now, did you ever make special trips to see her apart from that?"

"No. But I had—"

"Were there reasons why you didn't go to see her? Like, you wouldn't have been permitted to visit, or you didn't have the money?"

"I had enough money. But with my work in the lab, I was the only one who knew what to do and when to do it. I couldn't just walk out."

"Couldn't you have scheduled your experiments so that you had a couple of days, every month or two, when it was all right to leave?"

"I don't know. I didn't—I never . . ."

"Never tried? Rachel, I realize that Naomi means a lot to you. When you were a teenager, she was the center of your life. But it hasn't been that way for a long time." Walter put his hand on my shoulder. "How long have you and I known each other?"

"Nearly 14 years."

"That long? God. Anyway, I've spoken to you on the phone, or I've seen you in person, an average of once a week for all that time. And you know something? When you were in Bryceville you talked about Naomi constantly: how bright she was, how pretty she was, what new things she had learned. But once you moved to St. George you hardly mentioned your daughter. It was all molecular biology, new discoveries, possible protocols, exciting experiments."

"That's what I was *supposed* to talk to you about."

"True. But it didn't stop you babbling about Naomi before. Rachel, you may think that I'm criticizing you, but I'm not. I'm trying to tell you who you are. You're the witch-woman. Your life revolves around the research work that you do—work that no one in the world but you *can* do. I hear it from Raoul, I hear it from Wolf, I hear it from all our scientists: There's only one Rachel Stafford. And Naomi, smart and nice as she may be, is nothing like her amazing mother."

"She means the world to me." I stopped, before I could say, "Everything to me." Since I was an infant I have been damned by a sense of remorseless logic. I hated what Walter Cottingham was telling me, but I could not deny its truth.

"She should not go back," I said.

"She wants to go back, and she should. But you can stay and work here—"

"Is that what you're after? To have me under *your* thumb instead of Cyrus Walker's?"

"—or if you prefer it," he continued as though I had not spoken, "you can return to St. George and work in your old lab. In either case, you will not be troubled by the Blessed Order. And I have to add that there is one other condition. It comes from Naomi, not from Cyrus Walker. You must seek a treatment to reverse the loss of virility and sex drive caused by your phallicide drug."

If I was hesitating before, his words put an end to that. "Walter, you're crazy. I could never agree to such a thing. The Blessed Order is an abomination. Its practices are illegal and disgusting and an insult to all women. If I did what Naomi asks—something I have no idea how to do—I would be strengthening the Order."

"It looks that way to you. But I've been watching the Order from outside for 14 years, and I've seen what's happening. Members drift away. So long as the Patriarch was alive, the organization held together. Now that he's gone, it will fall apart."

"It has lasted over a hundred years."

"So it has. And you, Rachel, who were born to the Blessed Order—and still fear it—think it will last forever. But it won't. It's diseased, and an abomination, and disgusting, all the things you said and a lot more, and I ought to be ashamed of myself for being associated with it in any way. Maybe I am. But the Order is dying." He stared at me with those dark, hypnotic eyes that had only increased in intensity over the years. "I'll make you a wager, Rachel. Long before you and I, or even Cyrus Walker, are dead and gone, Bryceville will be a ghost town. Naomi will grow up, and mature, and find her own future. Perhaps she'll make her own decision to leave. You may not like it, whatever she does; on the other hand, I'm not sure I'll approve of my own children's choices. None of my friends seem to."

He stood up. "Think about what I said. I'm going to get Naomi. I believe it's time that you and she discussed this, just the two of you."

What was there to discuss? Naomi hated me for what I had done, when all I wanted was to save her. I had nothing left.

I wandered over to the table and sat down. At this time of day the sun was lower in the sky and shone through the porch windows. Its light showed two drying circles of water where the wet bottom of my teacup had rested. I reached out my forefinger and converted each of the circles into the hexagonal form of the benzene ring. The addition of other atoms and side chains felt idle and automatic, following no conscious plan. Only when I had finished did I realize that I had sketched the compound resulting from the combination of the airborne chemical gas with the phallicide.

I stared at it, visualizing the protein's complicated shape in three dimensions. It was one that could permit conformational variation—the same atomic composition, but with several different molecular shapes. Two tetrahedral and trigonal plane bonds could be interchanged, a collinear bond would become bent. The results ought to be stable. A transforming agent should exist to induce that change.

What I had told Walter Cottingham was wrong. The phallicidal drug might be purged, and its effects reversed. But the nature of the transforming agent . . .

Within my mind, a subgroup flexed and changed from left- to right-handedness. The whole molecule twisted and deformed. Atoms swam into view, locking into place at newly available receptor sites. Other atoms, their bonds weakened, drifted away.

I felt a rising tension. I was far from a full answer, but the search created a pleasurable ache within me like nothing else in the world.

When the door opened I did not hear it. I was not aware of Naomi's presence until she came up behind me, leaned over, and placed her soft cheek next to mine.

Daddy's world

WALTER JON WILLIAMS

Walter Jon Williams was born in Minnesota and now lives in Belen, New Mexico. His short fiction has appeared frequently in Asimov's Science Fiction, *as well as in* The Magazine of Fantasy & Science Fiction, Wheel of Fortune, Global Dispatches, Alternate Outlaws, When the Music's Over, Event Horizon, *and in other markets, and has been gathered in two collections,* Facets *and* Frankensteins and Other Foreign Devils. *His novels include* Ambassador of Progress, Knight Moves, Hardwired, The Crown Jewels, Voice of the Whirlwind, House of Shards, Days of Atonement, *and* Aristoi. *His novel* Metropolitan *garnered wide critical acclaim in 1996 and was one of the most talked-about books of the year. His most recent books are a sequel to* Metropolitan, City on Fire, *and a huge disaster thriller,* The Rift. *His stories have appeared in our Third, Fourth, Fifth, Sixth, Ninth, Eleventh, Twelfth, Fourteenth, and Fifteenth Annual Collections. He has a web site at www.walterjonwilliams.net.*

Williams is a highly eclectic writer, and has probably written a wider range of fiction than almost any other writer of his generation, ranging from some of the best Alternate History stories of the '80s to gritty Mean Streets hard-as-nails cyberpunk, from stories featuring scenarios quirky enough to rank with the most off-the-wall stuff by Howard Waldrop to some of the most inventive Wide Screen Modern Space Opera of recent times — as well as lots of stuff that refuses to fit into any category, including stories that mix genres with breathtaking audacity and daring, including genres no one ever thought of mixing before, such as a hybrid of sword & sorcery and the Horatio Hornblower–like sea story, or mixing fantasy with technologically oriented "hard" science fiction. The fact is, one Walter Jon Williams story is rarely much like any other Walter Jon Williams story . . . something which is certainly true of the fascinating and scary story that follows, one which takes us to explore a new world where no one has ever gone before, boldly or not.

One day Jamie went with his family to a new place, a place that had not existed before. The people who lived there were called Whirlikins, who were tall thin people with pointed heads. They had long arms and made frantic gestures when they talked, and when they grew excited threw their arms out *wide* to either side and spun like tops until they got all blurry. They would whirr madly over the green grass beneath the pumpkin-orange sky of the Whirlikin Country, and sometimes they would bump into each other with an alarming clashing noise, but they were never hurt, only bounced off and spun away in another direction.

Sometimes one of them would spin so hard that he would dig himself right into the ground, and come to a sudden stop, buried to the shoulders, with an expression of alarmed dismay.

Jamie had never seen anything so funny. He laughed and laughed.

His little sister Becky laughed, too. Once she was laughing so hard that she fell over onto her stomach, and Daddy picked her up and whirled her through the air, as if he were a Whirlikin himself, and they were both laughing all the while.

Afterward, they heard the dinner bell, and Daddy said it was time to go home. After they waved good-bye to the Whirlikins, Becky and Jamie walked hand-in-hand with Momma as they walked over the grassy hills toward home, and the pumpkin-orange sky slowly turned to blue.

The way home ran past El Castillo. El Castillo looked like a fabulous place, a castle with towers and domes and minarets, all gleaming in the sun. Music floated down from El Castillo, the swift, intricate music of many guitars, and Jamie could hear the fast click of heels and the shouts and laughter of happy people.

But Jamie did not try to enter El Castillo. He had tried before, and discovered that El Castillo was guarded by La Duchesa, an angular forbidding woman all in black, with a tall comb in her hair. When Jamie asked to come inside, La Duchesa had looked down at him and said, "I do not admit anyone who does not know Spanish irregular verbs!" It was all she ever said.

Jamie had asked Daddy what a Spanish irregular verb was—he had difficulty pronouncing the words—and Daddy had said, "Someday you'll learn, and La Duchesa will let you into her castle. But right now you're too young to learn Spanish."

That was all right with Jamie. There were plenty of things to do without going into El Castillo. And new places, like the country where the Whirlikins lived, appeared sometimes out of nowhere, and were quite enough to explore.

The color of the sky faded from orange to blue. Fluffy white clouds coasted in the air above the two-story frame house. Mister Jeepers, who was sitting on the ridgepole, gave a cry of delight and soared toward them through the air.

"Jamie's home!" he sang happily. "Jamie's home, and he's brought his beautiful sister!"

Mister Jeepers was diamond-shaped, like a kite, with his head at the topmost corner, hands on either sides, and little bowlegged comical legs attached on the bottom. He was bright red. Like a kite, he could fly, and he swooped through in a series of aerial cartwheels as he sailed toward Jamie and his party.

Becky looked up at Mister Jeepers and laughed from pure joy. "Jamie," she said, "you live in the best place in the world!"

At night, when Jamie lay in bed with his stuffed giraffe, Selena would ride a beam of pale light from the Moon to the Earth and sit by Jamie's side. She was a pale woman, slightly translucent, with a silver crescent on her brow. She would stroke Jamie's forehead with a cool hand, and she would sing to him until his eyes grew heavy and slumber stole upon him.

> "The birds have tucked their heads
> The night is dark and deep
> All is quiet, all is safe,
> And little Jamie goes to sleep."

Whenever Jamie woke during the night, Selena was there to comfort him. He was glad that Selena always watched out for him, because sometimes he still had nightmares about being in the hospital. When the nightmares came, she was always there to comfort him, stroke him, sing him back to sleep.

Before long the nightmares began to fade.

Princess Gigunda always took Jamie for lessons. She was a huge woman, taller than Daddy, with frowsy hair and big bare feet and a crown that could never be made to sit straight on her head. She was homely, with a mournful face that was ugly and endearing at the same time. As she shuffled along with Jamie to his lessons, Princess Gigunda complained about the way her feet hurt, and about how she was a giant and unattractive, and how she would never be married.

"I'll marry you when I get bigger," Jamie said loyally, and the Princess's homely face screwed up into an expression of beaming pleasure.

Jamie had different lessons with different people. Mrs. Winkle, down at the little red brick schoolhouse, taught him his ABCs. Coach Toad—who *was* one—taught him field games, where he raced and jumped and threw against various people and animals. Mr. McGillicuddy, a pleasant whiskered fat man who wore red sleepers with a trapdoor in back, showed him his magic globe. When Jamie put his finger anywhere on the globe, trumpets began to sound, and he could see what was happening where he was pointing, and Mr. McGillicuddy would take him on a tour and show him interesting things. Buildings, statues, pictures, parks, people. "This is Nome," he would say. "Can you say Nome?"

"Nome," Jamie would repeat, shaping his mouth around the unfamiliar word, and Mr. McGillicuddy would smile and bob his head and look pleased.

If Jamie did well on his lessons, he got extra time with the Whirlikins, or at the

Zoo, or with Mr. Fuzzy or in Pandaland. Until the dinner bell rang, and it was time to go home.

Jamie did well with his lessons almost every day.

When Princess Gigunda took him home from his lessons, Mister Jeepers would fly from the ridgepole to meet him, and tell him that his family was ready to see him. And then Momma and Daddy and Becky would wave from the windows of the house, and he would run to meet them.

Once, when he was in the living room telling his family about his latest trip through Mr. McGillicuddy's magic globe, he began skipping around with enthusiasm, and waving his arms like a Whirlikin, and suddenly he noticed that no one else was paying attention. That Momma and Daddy and Becky were staring at something else, their faces frozen in different attitudes of polite attention.

Jamie felt a chill finger touch his neck.

"Momma?" Jamie said. "Daddy?" Momma and Daddy did not respond. Their faces didn't move. Daddy's face was blurred strangely, as if it had been caught in the middle of movement.

"Daddy?" Jamie came close and tried to tug at his father's shirtsleeve. It was hard, like marble, and his fingers couldn't get a purchase at it. Terror blew hot in his heart.

"*Daddy?*" Jamie cried. He tried to tug harder. "Daddy! Wake up!" Daddy didn't respond. He ran to Momma and tugged at her hand. "Momma! Momma!" Her hand was like the hand of a statue. She didn't move no matter how hard Jamie pulled.

"Help!" Jamie screamed. "Mister Jeepers! Mr. Fuzzy! Help my momma!" Tears fell down his face as he ran from Becky to Momma to Daddy, tugging and pulling at them, wrapping his arms around their frozen legs and trying to pull them toward him. He ran outside, but everything was curiously still. No wind blew. Mister Jeepers sat on the ridgepole, a broad smile fixed as usual to his face, but he was frozen, too, and did not respond to Jamie's calls.

Terror pursued him back into the house. This was far worse than anything that had happened to him in the hospital, worse even than the pain. Jamie ran into the living room, where his family stood still as statues, and then recoiled in horror. A stranger had entered the room — or rather just parts of a stranger, a pair of hands encased in black gloves with strange silver circuit patterns on the backs, and a strange glowing opalescent face with a pair of wraparound dark glasses drawn across it like a line.

"Interface crashed, all right," the stranger said, as if to someone Jamie couldn't see.

Jamie gave a scream. He ran behind Momma's legs for protection.

"Oh, shit," the stranger said. "The kid's still running." He began purposefully moving his hands as if poking at the air. Jamie was sure that it was some kind of terrible attack, a spell to turn him to stone. He tried to run away, tripped over Becky's immovable feet and hit the floor hard, and then crawled away, the hall rug bunching up under his hands and knees as he skidded away, his own screams ringing in his ears . . .

. . . He sat up in bed, shrieking. The cool night tingled on his skin. He felt Selena's hand on his forehead, and he jerked away with a cry.

"Is something wrong?" came Selena's calm voice. "Did you have a bad dream?" Under the glowing crescent on her brow, Jamie could see the concern in her eyes.

"Where are Momma and Daddy?" Jamie shrieked.

"They're fine," Selena said. "They're asleep in their room. Was it a bad dream?"

Jamie threw off the covers and leaped out of bed. He ran down the hall, the floorboards cool on his bare feet. Selena floated after him in her serene, concerned way. He threw open the door to his parents' bedroom and snapped on the light, then gave a cry as he saw them huddled beneath their blanket. He flung himself at his mother, and gave a sob of relief as she opened her eyes and turned to him.

"Something wrong?" Momma said. "Was it a bad dream?"

"No!" Jamie wailed. He tried to explain, but even he knew that his words made no sense. Daddy rose from his pillow, looking seriously at Jamie, and then turned to ruffle his hair.

"Sounds like a pretty bad dream, trouper," Daddy said. "Let's get you back to bed."

"No!" Jamie buried his face in his mother's neck. "I don't want to go back to bed!"

"All right, Jamie," Momma said. She patted Jamie's back. "You can sleep here with us. But just for tonight, okay?"

"Wanna stay here," Jamie mumbled.

He crawled under the covers between Momma and Daddy. They each kissed him, and Daddy turned off the light. "Just go to sleep, trouper," he said. "And don't worry. You'll have good dreams from now on."

Selena, faintly glowing in the darkness, sat silently in the corner. "Shall I sing?" she asked.

"Yes, Selena," Daddy said. "Please sing for us."

Selena began to sing,

> "The birds have tucked their heads
> The night is dark and deep
> All is quiet, all is safe,
> And little Jamie goes to sleep."

But Jamie did not sleep. Despite the singing, the dark night, the rhythmic breathing of his parents, and the comforting warmth of their bodies.

It *wasn't* a dream, he knew. His family had really been frozen.

Something, or someone, had turned them to stone. Probably that evil disembodied head and pair of hands. And now, for some reason, his parents didn't remember.

Something had made them forget.

Jamie stared into the darkness. What, he thought, if these *weren't* his parents? If his parents were still stone, hidden away somewhere? What if these substitutes were bad people—kidnappers or worse—people who just *looked* like his real parents? What if they were evil people who were just waiting for him to fall asleep, and then they would turn to monsters, with teeth and fangs and a horrible light in their eyes, and they would tear him to bits right here in the bed . . .

Talons of panic clawed at Jamie's heart. Selena's song echoed in his ears. He *wasn't* going to sleep! He *wasn't!*

And then he did. It wasn't anything like normal sleep—it was as if sleep was *imposed* on him, as if something had just *ordered* his mind to sleep. It was just like a wave that rolled over him, an irresistible force, blotting out his sense, his body, his mind . . .

I *won't* sleep! he thought in defiance, but then his thoughts were extinguished.   •

When he woke he was back in his own bed, and it was morning, and Mister Jeepers was floating outside the window. "Jamie's awake!" he sang. "Jamie's awake and ready for a new day!"

And then his parents came bustling in, kissing him and petting him and taking him downstairs for breakfast.

His fears seemed foolish now, in full daylight, with Mister Jeepers dancing in the air outside and singing happily.

But sometimes, at night while Selena crooned by his bedside, he gazed into the darkness and felt a thrill of fear.

And he never forgot, not entirely.

A few days later Don Quixote wandered into the world, a lean man who frequently fell off his lean horse in a clang of homemade armor. He was given to making wan comments in both English and his own language, which turned out to be Spanish.

"Can you teach me Spanish irregular verbs?" Jamie asked.

"*Sí, naturalmente,*" said Don Quixote. "But I will have to teach you some other Spanish as well." He looked particularly mournful. "Let's start with *corazón*. It means 'heart.' *Mi corazón,*" he said with a sigh, "is breaking for love of Dulcinea."

After a few sessions with Don Quixote—mixed with a lot of sighing about *corazóns* and Dulcinea—Jamie took a grip on his courage, marched up to El Castillo, and spoke to La Duchesa. "*Pierdo, sueño, haría, ponto!*" he cried.

La Duchesa's eyes widened in surprise, and as she bent toward Jamie her severe face became almost kindly. "You are obviously a very intelligent boy," she said. "You may enter my castle."

And so Don Quixote and La Duchesa, between the two of them, began to teach Jamie to speak Spanish. If he did well, he was allowed into the parts of the castle where the musicians played and the dancers stamped, where brave Castilian knights jousted in the tilting yard, and Señor Esteban told stories in Spanish, always careful to use words that Jamie already knew.

Jamie couldn't help but notice that sometimes Don Quixote behaved strangely. Once, when Jamie was visiting the Whirlikins, Don Quixote charged up on his horse, waving his sword and crying out that he would save Jamie from the goblins that were attacking him. Before Jamie could explain that the Whirlikins were harmless, Don Quixote galloped to the attack. The Whirlikins, alarmed, screwed themselves into the ground where they were safe, and Don Quixote fell off his horse trying to swing at one with his sword. After poor Quixote fell off his horse a few times, it was Jamie who had to rescue the Don, not the other way around.

It was sort of sad and sort of funny. Every time Jamie started to laugh about it, he saw Don Quixote's mournful face in his mind, and his laugh grew uneasy.

After a while, Jamie's sister Becky began to share Jamie's lessons. She joined him and Princess Gigunda on the trip to the little schoolhouse, learned reading and math from Mrs. Winkle, and then, after some coaching from Jamie and Don Quixote, she marched to La Duchesa to shout irregular verbs and gain entrance to El Castillo.

Around that time Marcus Tullius Cicero turned up to take them both to the Forum Romanum, a new part of the world that had appeared to the south of the Whirlikins' territory. But Cicero and the people in the Forum, all the shopkeepers and politicians, did not teach Latin the way Don Quixote taught Spanish, explaining what the new words meant in English, they just talked Latin at each other and expected Jamie and Becky to understand. Which, eventually, they did. The Spanish helped. Jamie was a bit better at Latin than Becky, but he explained to her that it was because he was older.

It was Becky who became interested in solving Princess Gigunda's problem. "We should find her somebody to love," she said.

"She loves *us*," Jamie said.

"Don't be silly," Becky said. "She wants a *boyfriend*."

"*I'm* her boyfriend," Jamie insisted.

Becky looked a little impatient. "Besides," she said, "it's a puzzle. Just like La Duchesa and her verbs."

This had not occurred to Jamie before, but now that Becky mentioned it, the idea seemed obvious. There were a lot of puzzles around, which one or the other of them was always solving, and Princess Gigunda's lovelessness was, now that he saw it, clearly among them.

So they set out to find Princess Gigunda a mate. This question occupied them for several days, and several candidates were discussed and rejected. They found no answers until they went to the chariot race of the Circus Maximus. It was the first race in the Circus ever, because the place had just appeared on the other side of the Palatine Hill from the Forum, and there was a very large, very excited crowd.

The names of the charioteers were announced as they paraded their chariots to the starting line. The trumpets sounded, and the chariots bolted from the start as the drivers whipped up the horses. Jamie watched enthralled as they rolled around the *spina* for the first lap, and then shouted in surprise at the sight of Don Quixote galloping onto the Circus Maximus, shouting that he was about to stop this group of rampaging demons from destroying the land, and planted himself directly in the path of the oncoming chariots. Jamie shouted along with the crowd for the Don to get out of the way before he got killed.

Fortunately Quixote's horse had more sense than he did, because the spindly animal saw the chariots coming and bolted, throwing its rider. One of the chariots rode right over poor Quixote, and there was a horrible clanging noise, but after the chariot passed, Quixote sat up, apparently unharmed. His armor had saved him.

Jamie jumped up from his seat and was about to run down to help Don Quixote off the course, but Becky grabbed his arm. "Hang on," she said, "someone else will look after him, and I have an idea."

She explained that Don Quixote would make a perfect man for Princess Gigunda.

"But he's in love with Dulcinea!"

Becky looked at him patiently. "Has anyone ever *seen* Dulcinea? All we have to do is convince Don Quixote that Princess Gigunda *is* Dulcinea."

After the races, they found that Don Quixote had been arrested by the lictors and sent to the Lautumiae, which was the Roman jail. They weren't allowed to see the prisoner, so they went in search of Cicero, who was a lawyer and was able to get Quixote out of the Lautumiae on the promise that he would never visit Rome again.

"I regret to the depths of my soul that my parole does not enable me to destroy these demons," Quixote said as he left Rome's town limits.

"Let's not get into that," Becky said. "What we wanted to tell you was that we've found Dulcinea."

The old man's eyes widened in joy. He clutched at his armor-clad heart. "*Mi amor!* Where is she? I must run to her at once!"

"Not just yet," Becky said. "You should know that she's been changed. She doesn't look like she used to."

"Has some evil sorcerer done this?" Quixote demanded.

"Yes!" Jamie interrupted. He was annoyed that Becky had taken charge of everything, and he wanted to add his contribution to the scheme. "The sorcerer was just a head!" he shouted. "A floating head, and a pair of hands! And he wore dark glasses and had no body!"

A shiver of fear passed through him as he remembered the eerie floating head, but the memory of his old terror did not stop his words from spilling out.

Becky gave him a strange look. "Yeah," she said. "That's right."

"He crashed the interface!" Jamie shouted, the words coming to him out of memory.

Don Quixote paid no attention to this, but Becky gave him another look.

"You're not as dumb as you look, Digit," she said.

"I do not care about Dulcinea's appearance," Don Quixote declared, "I love only the goodness that dwells in her *corazón*."

"She's Princess Gigunda!" Jamie shouted, jumping up and down in enthusiasm. "She's been Princess Gigunda all along!"

And so, the children following, Don Quixote ran clanking to where Princess Gigunda waited near Jamie's house, fell down to one knee, and began to kiss and weep over the Princess's hand. The Princess seemed a little surprised by this until Becky told her that she was really the long-lost Dulcinea, changed into a giant by an evil magician, although she probably didn't remember it because that was part of the spell, too.

So while the Don and the Princess embraced, kissed, and began to warble a love duet, Becky turned to Jamie.

"What's that stuff about the floating head?" she asked. "Where did you come up with that?"

"I dunno," Jamie said. He didn't want to talk about his memory of his family being turned to stone, the eerie glowing figure floating before them. He didn't want to remember how everyone said it was just a dream.

He didn't want to talk about the suspicions that had never quite gone away.

"That stuff was weird, Digit," Becky said. "It gave me the creeps. Let me know before you start talking about stuff like that again."

"Why do you call me Digit?" Jamie asked.

Becky smirked. "No reason," she said.

"Jamie's home!" Mister Jeepers's voice warbled from the sky. Jamie looked up to see Mister Jeepers doing joyful aerial loops overhead. "Master Jamie's home at last!"

"Where shall we go?" Jamie asked.

Their lessons for the day were over, and he and Becky were leaving the little red schoolhouse. Becky, as usual, had done very well on her lessons, better than her older brother, and Jamie felt a growing sense of annoyance. At least he was still better at Latin and computer science.

"I dunno," Becky said. "Where do you want to go?"

"How about Pandaland? We could ride the Whoosh Machine."

Becky wrinkled her face. "I'm tired of that kid stuff," she said.

Jamie looked at her. "But you're a kid."

"I'm not as little as you, Digit," Becky said.

Jamie glared. This was too much. "You're my little sister! I'm bigger than you!"

"No, you're not," Becky said. She stood before him, her arms flung out in exasperation. "Just *notice something* for once, will you?"

Jamie bit back on his temper and looked, and he saw that Becky was, in fact, bigger than he was. And older-looking. Puzzlement replaced his fading anger.

"How did you get so big?" Jamie asked.

"I grew. And you *didn't* grow. Not as fast anyway."

"I don't understand."

Becky's lip curled. "Ask Mom or Dad. Just *ask* them." Her expression turned stony. "Just don't believe everything they tell you."

"What do you mean?"

Becky looked angry for a moment, and then her expression relaxed. "Look," she said, "just go to Pandaland and have fun, okay? You don't need me for that. I want to go and make some calls to my friends."

"*What* friends?"

Becky looked angry again. "*My* friends. It doesn't matter who they are!"

"Fine!" Jamie shouted. "I can have fun by myself!"

Becky turned and began to walk home, her legs scissoring against the background of the green grass. Jamie glared after her, then turned and began the walk to Pandaland.

He did all his favorite things, rode the Ferris wheel and the Whoosh Machine, watched Rizzio the Strongman and the clowns. He enjoyed himself, but his enjoyment felt hollow. He found himself *watching*, watching himself at play, watching himself enjoying the rides.

Watching himself not grow as fast as his little sister.

Watching himself wondering whether or not to ask his parents about why that was.

He had the idea that he wouldn't like their answers.

He didn't see as much of Becky after that. They would share lessons, and then Becky would lock herself in her room to talk to her friends on the phone.

Becky didn't have a telephone in her room, though. He looked once when she wasn't there.

After a while, Becky stopped accompanying him for lessons. She'd got ahead of him on everything except Latin, and it was too hard for Jamie to keep up.

After that, he hardly saw Becky at all. But when he saw her, he saw that she was still growing fast. Her clothing was different, and her hair. She'd started wearing makeup.

He didn't know whether he liked her anymore or not.

It was Jamie's birthday. He was eleven years old, and Momma and Daddy and Becky had all come for a party. Don Quixote and Princess Gigunda serenaded Jamie from outside the window, accompanied by La Duchesa on Spanish guitar. There was a big cake with eleven candles. Momma gave Jamie a chart of the stars. When he touched a star, a voice would appear telling Jamie about the star, and lines would appear on the chart showing any constellation the star happened to belong to. Daddy gave Jamie a car, a miniature Mercedes convertible, scaled to Jamie's size, which he could drive around the country and which he could use in the Circus Maximus when the chariots weren't racing. His sister gave Jamie a kind of lamp stand that would project lights and moving patterns on the walls and ceiling when the lights were off. "Listen to music when you use it," she said.

"Thank you, Becky," Jamie said.

"Becca," she said. "My name is Becca now. Try to remember."

"Okay," Jamie said. "Becca."

Becky—Becca—looked at Momma. "I'm dying for a cigarette," she said. "Can I go, uh, out for a minute?"

Momma hesitated, but Daddy looked severe. "Becca," she said, "this is *Jamie's birthday*. We're all here to celebrate. So why don't we all eat some cake and have a nice time?"

"It's not even real cake," Becca said. "It doesn't *taste* like real cake."

"It's a *nice cake*," Daddy insisted. "Why don't we talk about this later? Let's just have a special time for Jamie."

Becca stood up from the table. "For *the Digit?*" she said. "Why are we having a good time for *Jamie?* He's not even a *real person!*" She thumped herself on the chest. "*I'm* a real person!" she shouted. "Why don't we ever have special times for *me?*"

But Daddy was on his feet by that point and shouting, and Momma was trying to get everyone to be quiet, and Becca was shouting back, and suddenly a determined look entered her face and she just disappeared—suddenly, she wasn't there anymore, there was only just air.

Jamie began to cry. So did Momma. Daddy paced up and down and swore, and then he said, "I'm going to go get her." Jamie was afraid he'd disappear like Becca, and he gave a cry of despair, but Daddy didn't disappear, he just stalked out of the dining room and slammed the door behind him.

Momma pulled Jamie onto her lap and hugged him. "Don't worry, Jamie," she said. "Becky just did that to be mean."

"What happened?" Jamie asked.

"Don't worry about it." Momma stroked his hair. "It was just a mean trick."

"She's growing up," Jamie said. "She's grown faster than me and I don't understand."

"Wait till Daddy gets back," Momma said, "and we'll talk about it."

But Daddy was clearly in no mood for talking when he returned, without Becca. "We're going to have *fun*," he snarled, and reached for the knife to cut the cake.

The cake tasted like ashes in Jamie's mouth. When the Don and Princess Gigunda, Mister Jeepers and Rizzio the Strongman, came into the dining room and sang "Happy Birthday," it was all Jamie could do to hold back the tears.

Afterward, he drove his new car to the Circus Maximus and drove as fast as he could on the long oval track. The car really wouldn't go very fast. The bleachers on either side were empty, and so was the blue sky above.

Maybe it was a puzzle, he thought, like Princess Gigunda's love life. Maybe all he had to do was follow the right clue, and everything would be fine.

What's the moral they're trying to teach? he wondered.

But all he could do was go in circles, around and around the empty stadium.

"Hey, Digit. Wake up."

Jamie came awake suddenly with a stifled cry. The room whirled around him. He blinked, realized that the whirling came from the colored lights projected by his birthday present, Becca's lamp stand.

Becca was sitting on his bedroom chair, a cigarette in her hand. Her feet, in the steel-capped boots she'd been wearing lately, were propped up on the bed.

"Are you awake, Jamie?" It was Selena's voice. "Would you like me to sing you a lullaby?"

"Fuck off, Selena," Becca said. "Get out of here. Get lost."

Selena cast Becca a mournful look, then sailed backward, out of the window, riding a beam of moonlight to her pale home in the sky. Jamie watched her go, and felt as if a part of himself was going with her, a part that he would never see again.

"Selena and the others have to do what you tell them, mostly," Becca said. "Of course, Mom and Dad wouldn't tell you that."

Jamie looked at Becca. "What's happening?" he said. "Where did you go today?"

Colored lights swam over Becca's face. "I'm sorry if I spoiled your birthday, Digit. I just got tired of the lies, you know? They'd kill me if they knew I was here now, talking to you." Becca took a draw on her cigarette, held her breath for a second or two, then exhaled. Jamie didn't see or taste any smoke.

"You know what they wanted me to do?" she said. "Wear a little girl's body, so I wouldn't look any older than you, and keep you company in that stupid school for seven hours a day." She shook her head. "I wouldn't do it. They yelled and yelled, but I was damned if I would."

"I don't understand."

Becca flicked invisible ashes off her cigarette and looked at Jamie for a long time. Then she sighed.

"Do you remember when you were in the hospital?" she said.

Jamie nodded. "I was really sick."

"I was so little then, I don't really remember it very well," Becca said. "But the point is—" She sighed again. "The point is that you weren't getting well. So they decided to—" She shook her head. "Dad took advantage of his position at the University, and the fact that he's been a big donor. They were doing AI research, and the neurology department was into brain modeling, and they needed a test subject, and—Well, the idea is, they've got some of your tissue, and when they get cloning up and running, they'll put you back in—" She saw Jamie's stare, then shook her head. "I'll make it simple, okay?"

She took her feet off the bed and leaned closer to Jamie. A shiver ran up his back at her expression. "They made a copy of you. An *electronic* copy. They scanned your brain and built a holographic model of it inside a computer, and they put it in a virtual environment, and—" She sat back, took a drag on her cigarette. "And here you are," she said.

Jamie looked at her. "I don't understand."

Colored lights gleamed in Becca's eyes. "You're in a computer, okay? And you're a program. You know what that is, right? From computer class? And the program is sort of in the shape of your mind. Don Quixote and Princess Gigunda are programs, too. And Mrs. Winkle down at the schoolhouse is *usually* a program, but if she needs to teach something complex, then she's an education major from the University."

Jamie felt as if he'd just been hollowed out, a void inside his ribs. "I'm not real?" he said. "I'm not a person?"

"Wrong," Becca said. "You're real, alright. You're the apple of our parents' eye." Her tone was bitter. "Programs are real things," she said, "and yours was a real hack, you know, absolute cutting-edge state-of-the-art technoshit. And the computer that you're in is real, too—I'm interfaced with it right now, down in the family room—we have to wear suits with sensors and a helmet with scanners and stuff. I hope to fuck they don't hear me talking to you down here."

"But what—" Jamie swallowed hard. How could he swallow if he was just a string of code? "What happened to *me*? The original me?"

Becca looked cold. "Well," she said, "you had cancer. You died."

"Oh." A hollow wind blew through the void inside him.

"They're going to bring you back. As soon as the clone thing works out—but this is a government computer you're in, and there are all these government restrictions on cloning, and—" She shook her head. "Look, Digit," she said. "You really need to know this stuff, okay?"

"I understand." Jamie wanted to cry. But only real people cried, he thought, and he wasn't real. He wasn't real.

"The program that runs this virtual environment is huge, okay, and *you're* a big program, and the University computer is used for a lot of research, and a lot of the research has a higher priority than *you* do. So you don't run in real-time—that's why I'm growing faster than you are. I'm spending more hours being me than you are. And the parents—" She rolled her eyes. "They aren't making this any better, with their emphasis on *normal family life*."

She sucked on her cigarette, then stubbed it out in something invisible. "See, they want us to be this *normal family*. So we have breakfast together every day, and dinner every night, and spend the evening at the Zoo or in Pandaland or someplace. But the dinner that we eat with *you* is virtual, it doesn't taste like anything—the grant ran out before they got that part of the interface right—so we eat this fast-food crap before we interface with you, and then have dinner, all *over* again with *you* . . . Is this making any sense? Because Dad has a job and Mom has a job and I go to school and have friends and stuff, so we really can't get together every night. So they just close your program file, shut it right down, when they're not available to interface with you as what Dad calls a 'family unit,' and that means that there are a lot of hours, days sometimes, when you're just *not running*, you might as well really be *dead*—" She blinked. "Sorry," she said. "Anyway, we're *all* getting older a lot faster than you are, and it's not fair to you, that's what I think. Especially because the University computer runs fastest at night, because people don't use them as much then, and you're pretty much real-time then, so interfacing with you would be almost *normal*, but Mom and Dad sleep then, 'cuz they have day jobs, and they can't have you running around unsupervised in here, for God's sake, they think it's unsafe or something . . ."

She paused, then reached into her shirt pocket for another cigarette. "Look," she said, "I'd better get out of here before they figure out I'm talking to you. And then they'll pull my access codes or something." She stood, brushed something off her jeans. "Don't tell the parents about this stuff right away. Otherwise they might erase you, and load a backup that doesn't know shit. Okay?"

And she vanished, as she had that afternoon.

Jamie sat in the bed, hugging his knees. He could feel his heart beating in the darkness. How can a program have a heart? he wondered.

Dawn slowly encroached upon the night, and then there was Mister Jeepers, turning lazy cartwheels in the air, his red face leering in the window.

"Jamie's awake!" he said. "Jamie's awake and ready for a new day!"

"Fuck off," Jamie said, and buried his face in the blanket.

Jamie asked to learn more about computers and programming. Maybe, he thought, he could find clues there, he could solve the puzzle. His parents agreed, happy to let him follow his interests.

After a few weeks, he moved into El Castillo. He didn't tell anyone he was going, he just put some of his things in his car, took them up to a tower room, and threw them down on the bed he found there. His mom came to find him when he didn't come home for dinner.

"It's dinnertime, Jamie," she said. "Didn't you hear the dinner bell?"

"I'm going to stay here for a while," Jamie said.

"You're going to get hungry if you don't come home for dinner."

"I don't need food," Jamie said.

His mom smiled brightly. "You need food if you're going to keep up with the Whirlikins," she said.

Jamie looked at her. "I don't care about that kid stuff anymore," he said.

When his mother finally turned and left, Jamie noticed that she moved like an old person.

After a while, he got used to the hunger that was programmed into him. It was always *there*, he was always aware of it, but he got so he could ignore it after a while.

But he couldn't ignore the need to sleep. That was just built into the program, and eventually, try though he might, he needed to give in to it.

He found out he could order the people in the castle around, and he amused himself by making them stand in embarrassing positions, or stand on their heads and sing, or form human pyramids for hours and hours.

Sometimes he made them fight, but they weren't very good at it.

He couldn't make Mrs. Winkle at the schoolhouse do whatever he wanted, though, or any of the people who were supposed to teach him things. When it was time for a lesson, Princess Gigunda turned up. She wouldn't follow his orders, she'd just pick him up and carry him to the little red schoolhouse and plunk him down in his seat.

"You're not real!" he shouted, kicking in her arms. "You're not real! And *I'm* not real, either!"

But they made him learn about the world that was real, about geography and geology and history, although none of it mattered here.

After the first couple times Jamie had been dragged to school, his father met him outside the schoolhouse at the end of the day.

"You need some straightening out," he said. He looked grim. "You're part of a family. You belong with us. You're not going to stay in the castle anymore, you're going to have a *normal family life*."

"No!" Jamie shouted. "I like the castle!"

Dad grabbed him by the arm and began to drag him homeward. Jamie called him a *pendejo* and a *fellator*.

"I'll punish you if I have to," his father said.

"How are you going to do that?" Jamie demanded. "You gonna erase my file? Load a backup?"

A stunned expression crossed his father's face. His body seemed to go through a kind of stutter, and the grip on Jamie's arm grew nerveless. Then his face flushed with anger. "What do you mean?" he demanded.

"Who told you this?"

Jamie wrenched himself free of Dad's weakened grip.

"I figured it out by myself," Jamie said. "It wasn't hard. I'm not a kid anymore."

"I—" His father blinked, and then his face hardened. "You're still coming home."

Jamie backed away. "I want some changes!" he said. "I don't want to be shut off all the time."

Dad's mouth compressed to a thin line. "It was Becky who told you this, wasn't it?"

Jamie felt an inspiration. "It was Mister Jeepers! There's a flaw in his programming! He answers whatever question I ask him!"

Jamie's father looked uncertain. He held out his hand. "Let's go home," he said. "I need to think about this."

Jamie hesitated. "Don't erase me," he said. "Don't load a backup. Please. I don't want to die *twice*."

Dad's look softened. "I won't."

"I want to grow up," Jamie said. "I don't want to be a little kid forever."

Dad held out his hand again. Jamie thought for a moment, then took the hand. They walked over the green grass toward the white frame house on the hill.

"Jamie's home!" Mister Jeepers floated overhead, turning aerial cartwheels. "Jamie's home at last!"

A spasm of anger passed through Jamie at the sight of the witless grin. He pointed at the ground in front of him.

"Crash right here!" he ordered. "*Fast!*"

Mister Jeepers came spiraling down, an expression of comic terror on his face, and smashed to the ground where Jamie pointed at the sight of the crumpled body and laughed.

"Jamie's home at last!" Mister Jeepers said.

As soon as Jamie could, he got one of the programmers at the University to fix him up a flight program like the one Mister Jeepers had been using. He swooped and soared, zooming like a super hero through the sky, stunting between the towers of El Castillo and soaring over upturned, wondering faces in the Forum.

He couldn't seem to go as fast as he really wanted. When he started increasing speed, all the scenery below paused in its motion for a second or two, then jumped forward with a jerk. The software couldn't refresh the scenery fast enough to match his speed. It felt strange, because throughout his flight he could feel the wind on his face.

So this, he thought, was why his car couldn't go fast.

So he decided to climb high. He turned his face to the blue sky and went straight up. The world receded, turned small. He could see the Castle, the hills of Whirlikin Country, the crowded Forum, the huge oval of the Circus Maximus. It was like a green plate, with a fuzzy, nebulous horizon where the sky started.

And, right in the center, was the little two-story frame house where he'd grown up.

It was laid out below him like scenery in a snow globe.

After a while he stopped climbing. It took him a while to realize it, because he still felt the wind blowing in his face, but the world below stopped getting smaller.

He tried going faster. The wind blasted onto him from above, but his position didn't change.

He'd reached the limits of his world. He couldn't get any higher.

Jamie flew out to the edges of the world, to the horizon. No matter how he urged his program to move, he couldn't make his world fade away.

He was trapped inside the snow globe, and there was no way out.

It was quite a while before Jamie saw Becca again. She picked her way through the labyrinth beneath El Castillo to his throne room, and Jamie slowly materialized atop his throne of skulls. She didn't appear surprised.

"I see you've got a little Dark Lord thing going here," she said.

"It passes the time," Jamie said.

"And all those pits and stakes and tripwires?"

"Death traps."

"Took me forever to get in here, Digit. I kept getting de-rezzed."

Jamie smiled. "That's the idea."

"Whirlikins as weapons." She nodded. "That was a good one. Bored a hole right through me, the first time."

"Since I'm stuck living here," Jamie said, "I figure I might as well be in charge of the environment. Some of the student programmers at the University helped me with some cool effects."

Screams echoed through the throne room. Fires leaped out of pits behind him. The flames illuminated the form of Marcus Tullius Cicero, who hung crucified above a sea of flame.

"*O tempora, o mores!*" moaned Cicero.

Becca nodded. "Nice," she said. "Not my scene exactly, but nice."

"Since I can't leave," Jamie said, "I want a say in who gets to visit. So either you wait till I'm ready to talk to you, or you take your chances on the death traps."

"Well. Looks like you're sitting pretty, then."

Jamie shrugged. Flames belched. "I'm getting bored with it. I might just wipe it all out and build another place to live in. I can't tell you the number of battles I've won, the number of kingdoms I've trampled. In this reality and others. It's all the same after a while." He looked at her. "You've grown."

"So have you."

"Once the paterfamilias finally decided to allow it." He smiled. "We still have dinner together sometimes, in the old house. Just a normal family, as Dad says.

Except that sometimes I turn up in the form of a werewolf, or a giant, or something."

"So they tell me."

"The advantage of being software is that I can look like anything I want. But that's the disadvantage, too, because I can't really *become* something else, I'm still just . . . me. I may wear another program as a disguise, but I'm still the same program inside, and I'm not a good enough programmer to mess with that, yet." Jamie hopped off his throne, walked a nervous little circle around his sister. "So what brings you to the old neighborhood?" he asked. "The old folks said you were off visiting Aunt Maddy in the country."

"*Exiled*, they mean. I got knocked up, and after the abortion they sent me to Maddy. She was supposed to keep me under control, except she didn't." She picked an invisible piece of lint from her sweater. "So now I'm back." She looked at him. "I'm skipping a lot of the story, but I figure you wouldn't be interested."

"Does it have to do with sex?" Jamie asked. "I'm sort of interested in sex, even though I can't do it, and they're not likely to let me."

"*Let* you?"

"It would require a lot of new software and stuff. I was prepubescent when my brain structures were scanned, and the program isn't set up for making me a working adult, with adult desires et cetera. Nobody was thinking about putting me through adolescence at the time. And the administrators at the University told me that it was very unlikely that anyone was going to give them a grant so that a computer program could have sex." Jamie shrugged. "I don't miss it, I guess. But I'm sort of curious."

Surprise crossed Becca's face. "But there are all kinds of simulations, and . . ."

"They don't work for me, because my mind isn't structured so as to be able to achieve pleasure that way. I can manipulate the programs, but it's about as exciting as working a virtual butter churn." Jamie shrugged again. "But that's okay. I mean, I don't *miss* it. I can always give myself a jolt to the pleasure center if I want."

"Not the same thing," Becca said. "I've done both."

"I wouldn't know."

"I'll tell you about sex if you want," Becca said, "but that's not why I'm here."

"Yes?"

Becca hesitated. Licked her lips. "I guess I should just say it, huh?" she said. "Mom's dying. Pancreatic cancer."

Jamie felt sadness well in his mind. Only electrons, he thought, moving from one place to another. It was nothing real. He was programmed to feel an analog of sorrow, and that was all.

"She looks normal to me," he said, "when I see her." But that didn't mean anything: his mother chose what she wanted him to see, just as he chose a mask— a werewolf, a giant—for her.

And in neither case did the disguise at all matter. For behind the werewolf was a program that couldn't alter its parameters; and behind the other, ineradicable cancer.

Becca watched him from slitted eyes. "Dad wants her to be scanned, and come here. So we can still be a *normal family* even after she dies."

Jamie was horrified. "Tell her *no*," he said. "Tell her she can't come!"

"I don't think she wants to. But Dad is very insistent."

"She'll be here *forever*! It'll be awful!"

Becca looked around. "Well, she wouldn't do much for your Dark Lord act, that's for sure. I'm sure Sauron's mom didn't hang around the Dark Tower, nagging him about the unproductive way he was spending his time."

Fires belched. The ground trembled. Stalactites rained down like arrows.

"That's not it," Jamie said. "She doesn't want to be here no matter what I'm doing, no matter where I live. Because whatever this place looks like, it's a prison." Jamie looked at his sister. "I don't want my mom in a prison."

Leaping flames glittered in Becca's eyes. "You can change the world you live in," she said. "That's more than I can do."

"But I can't," Jamie said. "I can change the way it *looks*, but I can't change anything *real*. I'm a program, and a program is an *artifact*. I'm a piece of *engineering*. I'm a simulation, with simulated sensory organs that interact with simulated environments—I can only interact with *other artifacts*. *None* of it's real. I don't know what the real world looks or feels or tastes like, I only know what simulations tell me they're *supposed* to taste like. And I can't change any of my parameters unless I mess with the engineering, and I can't do that unless the programmers agree, and even when that happens, I'm still as artificial as I was before. And the computer I'm in is old and clunky, and soon nobody's going to run my operating system anymore, and I'll not only be an artifact, I'll be a museum piece."

"There are other artificial intelligences out there," Becca said. "I keep hearing about them."

"I've talked to them. Most of them aren't very interesting—it's like talking to a dog, or maybe to a very intelligent microwave oven. And they've scanned some people in, but those were adults, and all they wanted to do, once they got inside, was to escape. Some of them went crazy."

Becca gave a twisted smile. "I used to be so jealous of you, you know. You lived in this beautiful world, no pollution, no violence, no shit on the streets."

"*Integra mens augustissima possessio,*" said Cicero.

"Shut up!" Jamie told him. "What the fuck do you know?"

Becca shook her head. "I've seen those old movies, you know? Where somebody gets turned into a computer program, and next thing you know he's in every computer in the world, and running everything?"

"I've seen those, too. Ha ha. Very funny. Shows you what people know about programs."

"Yeah. Shows you what they know."

"I'll talk to Mom," Jamie said.

Big tears welled out of Mom's eyes and trailed partway down her face, then disappeared. The scanners paid a lot of attention to eyes and mouths, for the sake of transmitting expression, but didn't always pick up the things between.

"I'm sorry," she said. "We didn't think this is how it would be."

"Maybe you should have given it more thought," Jamie said.

It isn't sorrow, he told himself again. It's just electrons moving.

"You were such a beautiful baby." Her lower lip trembled. "We didn't want to lose you. They said that it would only be a few years before they could implant your memories in a clone."

Jamie knew all that by now. Knew that the technology of reading memories turned out to be much, much simpler than implanting them—it had been discovered that the implantation had to be made while the brain was actually growing. And government restrictions on human cloning had made tests next to impossible, and that the team that had started his project had split up years ago, some to higher paying jobs, some retired, others to pet projects of their own. How his father had long ago used up whatever pull he'd had at the University trying to keep everything together. And how he long ago had acquired or purchased patents and copyrights for the whole scheme, except for Jamie's program, which was still owned jointly by the University and the family.

Tears reappeared on Mom's lower face, dripped off her chin. "There's potentially a lot of money at stake, you know. People want to raise perfect children. Keep them away from bad influences, make sure that they're raised free from violence."

"So they want to control the kid's environment," Jamie said.

"Yes. And make it *safe*. And wholesome. And—"

"Just like *normal family life*," Jamie finished. "No diapers, no vomit, no messes. No having to interact with the kid when the parents are tired. And then you just download the kid into an adult body, give him a diploma, and kick him out of the house. And call yourself a perfect parent."

"And there are *religious people* . . ." Mom licked her lips. "Your dad's been talking to them. They want to raise children in environments that reflect their beliefs completely. Places where there is no temptation, no sin. No science or ideas that contradict their own . . ."

"But Dad isn't religious," Jamie said.

"These people have money. Lots of money."

Mom reached out, took his hand. Jamie thought about all the code that enabled her to do it, that enabled them both to feel the pressure of unreal flesh on unreal flesh.

"I'll do what you wish, of course," she said. "I don't have that desire for immortality, the way your father does." She shook her head. "But I don't know what your father will do once his time comes."

The world was a disk a hundred meters across, covered with junk: old Roman ruins, gargoyles fallen from a castle wall, a broken chariot, a shattered bell. Outside the rim of the world, the sky was black, utterly black, without a ripple or a star.

Standing in the center of the world was a kind of metal tree with two forked, jagged arms.

"Hi, Digit," Becca said.

A dull fitful light gleamed on the metal tree, as if it were reflecting a bloody sunset.

"Hi, sis," it said.

"Well," Becca said. "We're alone now."

"I caught the notice of Dad's funeral. I hope nobody missed me."

"I missed you, Digit." Becca sighed. "Believe it or not."

"I'm sorry."

Becca restlessly kicked a piece of junk, a hubcap from an old, miniature car. It clanged as it found new lodgment in the rubble. "Can you appear as a person?" she asked. "It would make it easier to talk to you."

"I've finished with all that," Jamie said. "I'd have to resurrect too much dead programming. I've cut the world down to next to nothing. I've got rid of my body, my heartbeat, the sense of touch."

"All the human parts," Becca said sadly.

The dull red light oozed over the metal tree like a drop of blood. "Everything except sleep and dreams. It turns out that sleep and dreams have too much to do with the way people process memory. I can't get rid of them, not without cutting out too much of my mind." The tree gave a strange, disembodied laugh. "I dreamed about you, the other day. And about Cicero. We were talking Latin."

"I've forgotten all the Latin I ever knew." Becca tossed her hair, forced a laugh. "So what do you do nowadays?"

"Mostly I'm a conduit for data. The University has been using me as a research spider, which I don't mind doing, because it passes the time. Except that I take up a lot more memory than any real search spider, and don't do that much better a job. And the information I find doesn't have much to do with *me*—it's all about the real world. The world I can't touch." The metal tree bled color.

"Mostly," he said, "I've just been waiting for Dad to die. And now it's happened."

There was a moment of silence before Becca spoke. "You know that Dad had himself scanned before he went."

"Oh, yeah. I knew."

"He set up some kind of weird foundation that I'm not part of, with his patents and programs and so on, and his money and some other people's."

"He'd better not turn up here."

Becca shook her head. "He won't. Not without your permission anyway. Because I'm in charge here. You—your program—it's not a part of the foundation. Dad couldn't get it all, because the University has an interest, and so does the family." There was a moment of silence. "And I'm the family now."

"So you . . . *inherited* me," Jamie said. Cold scorn dripped from his words.

"That's right," Becca said. She squatted down amid the rubble, rested her forearms on her knees.

"What do you want me to do, Digit? What can I do to make it better for you?"

"No one ever asked me that," Jamie said.

There was another long silence.

"Shut it off," Jamie said. "Close the file. Erase it."

Becca swallowed hard. Tears shimmered in her eyes. "Are you sure?" she asked.

"Yes. I'm sure."

"And if they ever perfect the clone thing? If we could make you . . ." She took a breath. "A person?"

"No. It's too late. It's . . . not something I can want anymore."

Becca stood. Ran a hand through her hair. "I wish you could meet my daughter," she said. "Her name is Christy. She's a real beauty."

"You can bring her," Jamie said.

Becca shook her head. "This place would scare her. She's only three. I'd only bring her if we could have . . ."

"The old environment," Jamie finished. "Pandaland. Mister Jeepers. Whirlikin Country."

Becca forced a smile. "Those were happy days," she said. "They really were. I was jealous of you, I know, but when I look back at that time . . ." She wiped tears with the back of her hand. "It was the best."

"Virtual environments are nice places to visit, I guess," Jamie said. "But you don't want to live in one. Not forever." Becca looked down at her feet, planted amid rubble.

"Well," she said. "If you're sure about what you want."

"I am."

She looked up at the metal form, raised a hand. "Good-bye, Jamie," she said.

"Good-bye," he said.

She faded from the world.

And in time, the world and the tree faded, too.

Hand in hand, Daddy and Jamie walked to Whirlikins Country. Jamie had never seen the Whirlikins before, and he laughed and laughed as the Whirlikins spun beneath their orange sky.

The sound of a bell rang over the green hills. "Time for dinner, Jamie," Daddy said.

Jamie waved good-bye to the Whirlikins, and he and Daddy walked briskly over the fresh green grass toward home.

"Are you happy, Jamie?" Daddy asked.

"Yes, Daddy!" Jamie nodded. "I only wish Momma and Becky could be here with us."

"They'll be here soon."

When, he thought, they can get the simulations working properly.

Because this time, he thought, there would be no mistakes. The foundation he'd set up before he died had finally purchased the University's interest in Jamie's program—they funded some scholarships, that was all it finally took. There was no one in the Computer Department who had an interest anymore.

Jamie had been loaded from an old backup—there was no point in using the corrupt file that Jamie had become, the one that had turned itself into a *tree*, for heaven's sake.

The old world was up and running, with a few improvements. The foundation had bought their own computer—an old one, so it wasn't too expensive—that would run the environment full-time. Some other children might be scanned, to give Jamie some playmates and peer socialization.

This time it would work, Daddy thought. Because this time, Daddy was a program too, and he was going to be here every minute, making sure that the environment was correct and that everything went exactly according to plan. That he and Jamie and everyone else had a normal family life, perfect and shining and safe.

And if the clone program ever worked out, they would come into the real world again. And if downloading into clones was never perfected, then they would stay here.

There was nothing wrong with the virtual environment. It was a *good* place.

Just like normal family life. Only forever.

And when this worked out, the foundation's backers—fine people, even if they did have some strange religious ideas—would have their own environments up and running. With churches, angels, and perhaps even the presence of God . . .

"Look!" Daddy said, pointing. "It's Mister Jeepers!"

Mister Jeepers flew off the rooftop and spun happy spirals in the air as he swooped toward Jamie. Jamie dropped Daddy's hand and ran laughing to greet his friend.

"Jamie's home!" Mister Jeepers cried. "Jamie's home at last!"

A Martian Romance

Kim Stanley Robinson

Kim Stanley Robinson sold his first story in 1976, and quickly established himself as one of the most respected and critically acclaimed writers of his generation. His story "Black Air" won the World Fantasy Award in 1984, and his novella "The Blind Geometer" won the Nebula Award in 1987. His first novel, The Wild Shore, was published in 1984, and was quickly followed up by other novels such as Icehenge, The Memory of Whiteness, A Short, Sharp Shock, The Gold Coast, and The Pacific Shore, and by collections such as The Planet on the Table, Escape from Kathmandu, and Remaking History.

Robinson's already-distinguished literary reputation took a quantum-jump in the decade of the '90s, though, with the publication of his acclaimed "Mars" trilogy—Red Mars, Green Mars, and Blue Mars; Red Mars won a Nebula Award, both Green Mars and—Blue Mars won Hugo Awards, and the trilogy has been widely recognized as the genre's most accomplished, detailed, sustained, and substantial look at the colonization and terraforming of another world, rivaled only by Arthur C. Clarke's The Sands of Mars.

The "Mars Trilogy" will probably associate Robinson's name forever with the Red Planet, but it was not the first time he would explore a fictional Mars; Robinson visited Mars in several stories of the '80s, including the memorable novella "Green Mars," which detailed the first attempt to climb Olympus Mons, the tallest mountain in the solar system. The bittersweet and evocative story that follows is a direct sequel to "Green Mars"—and at a tangent to the history of Martian settlement as it ultimately developed in the "Mars Trilogy." In it, he takes us to a bleak and wintry Mars where the terraforming effort has gone disastrously wrong, and a group of old friends set sail in an iceboat across the frozen seas of the once-Red Planet, many years after their first epic journey, hoping to touch the sky one last time . . .

Robinson's latest books are the novel Antarctica, and a collection of stories and poems set on his fictional Mars, The Martians. His stories have appeared in our First, Second, Third, Fourth, Fifth, Sixth, and Ninth Annual Collections. He lives with his family in California.

Eileen Monday hauls her backpack off the train's steps and watches the train glide down the piste and around the headland. Out the empty station and she's into the streets of Firewater, north Elysium. It's deserted and dark, a ghost town, everything shut down and boarded up, the residents moved out and moved on. The only signs of life come from the westernmost dock: a small globular cluster of yellow streetlights and lit windows, streaking the ice of the bay between her and it. She walks around the bay on the empty corniche, the sky all purple in the early dusk. Four days until the start of spring, but there will be no spring this year.

She steps into the steamy clangor of the hotel restaurant. Workers in the kitchen are passing full dishes through the broad open window to diners milling around the long tables in the dining room. They're mostly young, either iceboat sailors or the few people left in town. No doubt a few still coming out of the hills, out of habit. A wild-looking bunch. Eileen spots Hans and Arnold; they look like a pair of big puppets, discoursing to the crowd at the end of one table—elderly Pinocchios, eyes lost in wrinkles as they tell their lies and laugh at each other, and at the young behemoths passing around plates and devouring their pasta while still listening to the two. The old as entertainment. Not such a bad way to end up.

It isn't Roger's kind of thing, however, and indeed when Eileen looks around she sees him standing in the corner next to the jukebox, pretending to make selections but actually eating his meal right there. That's Roger for you. Eileen grins as she makes her way through the crowd to him.

"Hey," he says as he sees her, and gives her a quick hug with one arm.

She leans over and kisses his cheek. "You were right, it's not very hard to find this place."

"No." He glances at her. "I'm glad you decided to come."

"Oh, the work will always be there, I'm happy to get out. Bless you for thinking of it. Is everyone else already here?"

"Yeah, all but Frances and Stephan, who just called and said they'd be here soon. We can leave tomorrow."

"Great. Come sit down with the others, I want some food, and I want to say hi to everyone."

Roger wrinkles his nose, gestures at the dense loud crowd. This solitary quality in him has been the cause of some long separations in their relationship, and so now Eileen shoves his arm and says, "Yeah yeah, all these people. Such a crowded place, Elysium."

Roger grins crookedly. "That's why I like it."

"Oh of course. Far from the madding crowd."

"Still the English major, I see."

"And you're still the canyon hermit," she says, laughing and pulling him toward the crowd; it is good to see him again, it has been three months. For many years now they have been a steady couple, Roger returning to their rooms in the co-op in Burroughs after every trip away; but his work is still in the back country, so they still spend quite a lot of time apart.

Just as they join Hans and Arnold, who are wrapping up their history of the world, Stephan and Frances come in the door, and they hold a cheery reunion over a late dinner. There's a lot of catching up to do; this many members of their Olympus Mons climb haven't been together in a long time. Hours after the other diners have gone upstairs to bed, or off to their homes, the little group of old ones sits at the end of one table talking. A bunch of antique insomniacs, Eileen thinks, none anxious to go to bed and toss and turn through the night. She finds herself the first to stand up and stretch and declare herself off. The others rise on cue, except for Roger and Arnold; they've done a lot of climbing together through the years, and Roger was a notorious insomniac even when young; now he sleeps very poorly indeed. And Arnold will talk for as long as anyone else is willing, or longer. "See you tomorrow," Arnold says to her. "Bright and early for the crossing of the Amazonian Sea!"

The next morning the iceboat runs over ice that is mostly white, but in some patches clear and transparent right down to the shallow seafloor. Other patches are the color of brick, with the texture of brick, and the boat's runners clatter over little dunes of gravel and dust. If they hit melt ponds the boat slows abruptly and shoots great wings of water to the sides. At the other side of these ponds the runners scritch again like ice skates as they accelerate back up to speed. Roger's iceboat is a scooter, he explains to them; not like the spidery skeletal thing that Eileen was expecting, having seen some of that kind down in Chryse—those Roger calls DNs. This is more like an ordinary boat, long, broad, and low, with several parallel runners nailed fore-and-aft to its hull. "Better over rough ice," Roger explains, "and it floats if you happen to hit water." The sail is like a big bird's wing extended over them, sail and mast all melded together into one object, shifting shape with every gust to catch as much wind as it can.

"What keeps us from tipping over?" Arnold asks, looking over the lee rail at the flashing ice just feet below him.

"Nothing." The deck is at a good cant, and Roger is grinning.

"Nothing?"

"The laws of physics."

"Come on."

"When the boat tips the sail catches less wind, both because it's tilted and because it reads the tilt, and reefs in. Also we have a lot of ballast. And there are weights in the deck that are held magnetically on the windward side. It's like having a heavy crew sitting on the windward rail."

"That's not nothing," Eileen protests. "That's three things."

"True. And we may still tip over. But if we do we can always get out and pull it back upright."

They sit in the cockpit and look up at the sail, or ahead at the ice. The iceboat's navigation steers them away from the rottenest patches, spotted from satellites, and so the automatic pilot changes their course frequently, and they shift around the cockpit when necessary. Floury patches slow them the most, and over these the boat sometimes decelerates pretty quickly, throwing the unprepared forward into the shoulder of the person sitting next to them. Eileen is banged into by Hans and Frances more than once; like her, they have never been on iceboats before, and their eyes are round at the speeds it achieves during strong gusts over smooth ice. Hans speculates that the sandy patches mark old pressure ridges, which stood like long stegosaur backs until the winds ablated them entirely away, leaving their load of sand and silt behind on the flattened ice. Roger nods. In truth the whole ocean surface is blowing away on the wind, with whatever sticks up going the fastest; and the ocean is now frozen to the bottom, so that no new pressure ridges are being raised. Soon the whole ocean will be as flat as a table top.

This first day out is clear, the royal blue sky crinkling in a gusty west wind. Under the clear dome of the cockpit it's warm, their air at a slightly higher pressure than outside. Sea level is now around 300 millibars, and lowering year by year, as if for a great storm that never quite comes. They skate at speed around the majestic promontory of the Phlegra Peninsula, its great prow topped by a white-pillared Doric temple. Staring up at it Eileen listens to Hans and Frances discuss the odd phenomenon of the Phlegra Montes, seaming the north coast of Elysium like a long ship capsized on the land; unusually straight for a Martian mountain range, as are the Erebus Montes to the west. As if they were not, like all the rest of the mountain ranges on Mars, the remnants of crater rims. Hans argues for them being two concentric rings of a really big impact basin, almost the size of the Big Hit itself but older than the Big Hit, and so mostly obliterated by the later impact, with only Isidis Bay and much of the Utopian and Elysian Seas left to indicate where the basin had been. "Then the ranges could have been somewhat straightened out in the deformation of the Elysium bulge."

Frances shakes her head, as always. Never once has Eileen seen the two of them agree. In this case Frances thinks the ranges may be even older than Hans does, remnants of early tectonic or proto-tectonic plate movement. There's a wide body of evidence for this early tectonic era, she claims, but Hans is shaking his head: "The andesite indicating tectonic action is younger than that. The Phlegras are early Noachian. A pre–Big Hit big hit."

Whatever the explanation, there the fine prow of rock stands, the end of a steep peninsula extending straight north into the ice for four hundred kilometers out of Firewater. A long sea cliff falling into the sea, and the same on the other side. The pilgrimage out the spine to the temple is one of the most famous walks on Mars; Eileen has made it a number of times since Roger first took her on it about forty years ago, sometimes with him, sometimes without. When they first came they looked out on a blue sea purled with whitecaps. Seldom since has it been free of ice.

He too is looking at the point, with an expression that makes Eileen think he might be remembering that time as well. Certainly he would remember if asked; his incredible memory has still not yet begun to weaken, and with the suite of memory drugs now available, drugs that have helped Eileen to remember quite a bit, it might well be that he will never forget anything his whole life long. Eileen envies that, though she knows he is ambivalent about it. But by now it is one of the things about him that she loves. He remembers everything and yet he has remained stalwart, even chipper, through all the years of the crash. A rock for her to lean on, in her own cycles of despair and mourning. Of course as a Red it could be argued he has no reason to mourn. But that wouldn't be true. His attitude was more complex than that, Eileen has seen it; so complex that she does not fully understand it. Some aspect of his strong memory, taking the long view; a determination to make it well; rueful joy in the enduring land; some mix of all these things. She watches him as he stares absorbed at the promontory where he and she once stood together over a living world.

How much he has meant to her through the years has become beyond her ability to express. Sometimes it fills her to overflowing. That they have known each other all their lives; that they have helped each other through hard times; that he got her out into the land in the first place, starting her on the trajectory of her whole life; all these would have made him a crucial figure to her. But everyone has many such figures. And over the years their divergent interests kept splitting them up; they could have lost touch entirely. But at one point Roger came to visit her in Burroughs, and she and her partner of that time had been growing distant for many years, and Roger said, I love you Eileen. I love you. Remember what it was like on Olympus Mons, when we climbed it? Well now I think the whole world is like that. The escarpment goes on forever. We just keep climbing it until eventually we fall off. And I want to climb it with you. We keep getting together and then going our ways, and it's too chancy, we might not cross paths again. Something might happen. I want more than that. I love you.

And so eventually they set up rooms in her co-op in Burroughs. She continued to work in the Ministry of the Environment, and he continued to guide treks in the back country, then to sail on the North Sea; but he always came back from his treks and his cruises, and she always came back from her working tours and her vacations away; and they lived together in their rooms when they were both at home, and became a real couple. And through the years without summer, then the little ice age and the crash itself, his steadfast presence has been all that has kept her from despair. She shudders to think what it would have been like to get through these years alone. To work so hard, and then to fail. . . . It's been hard. She has seen that he has worried about her. This trip is an expression of that: Look, he said once after she came home in tears over reports of the tropical and temperate extinctions—look, I think you need to get out there and see it. See the world the way it is now, see the ice. It's not so bad. There have been ice ages before. It's not so bad.

And as she had been more and more holing up in Burroughs, unable to face it, she finally was forced to agree that, in theory, it would be a good thing. Very soon after that he organized this trip. Now she sees that he gathered some of their friends from the Olympus Mons expedition to help entice her to come, perhaps; also, once here, to remind her of that time in their lives. Anyway it's nice to see their faces, flushed and grinning as they fly along.

Skate east! the wind says, and they skitter round Scrabster, the northeastern point of Elysium, then head south over the great plate of white ice inserted into the incurve of the coast. This is the Bay of Arcadia, and the steep rise of land backing the bluffs is called Acadia, for its supposed resemblance to Nova Scotia and the coast of Maine. Dark rock, battered by the dark north sea; sea-cliffs of bashed granite, sluiced by big breakers. Now, however, all still and white, with the ice that has powdered down out of the spray and spume flocking and frosting the beach and the cliffs until they look like wedding cake ramparts. No sign of life in Acadia; no greens anywhere in sight. This is not her Elysium.

Roger takes over the sailing from Arnold, and brings them around a point, and there suddenly is a steep-walled square island ahead, vivid green on top—ah. A township, frozen here near the entrance to a fjord, no doubt in a deep channel. All the townships have become islands in the ice. The greenery on top is protected by a tent which Eileen cannot see in the bright sun. "I'm just dropping by to pick up the rest of our crew," Roger explains. "A couple of young friends of mine are going to join us."

"Which one is this?" Stephan inquires.

"This is the *Altamira*."

Roger sails them around in a sweet curve that ends with them stalled into the wind and skidding to a halt. He retracts the cockpit dome. "I don't intend to go up there, by the way, that's an all-day trip no matter how you do it. My friends should be down here on shore to meet us."

They step down onto the ice, which is mostly a dirty opaque white, cracked and a bit nobbled on the surface, so that it is slippery in some places, but mostly fairly steady underfoot; and Eileen sees that the treacherous spots stand out like windows inlaid in tile. Roger talks into his wristpad, then leads them into the fjord, which on one steep side displays a handsome granite staircase, frost lying like a fluffy carpet on the steps.

Up these stairs Roger climbs, putting his feet in earlier bootprints. Up on the headland over the fjord they have a good view over the ice to the township, which is really very big for a manufactured object, a kilometer on each side, and its deck only just lower than they are. Its square tented middle glows green like a Renaissance walled garden, the enchanted space of a fairy tale.

There is a little stone shelter or shrine on the headland, and they follow the sidewalk over to it. The wind chills Eileen's hands, toes, nose and ears. A big white plate, whistling in the wind. Elysium bulks behind them, its two volcanoes just sticking over the high horizon to the west. She holds Roger's hand as they approach. As always, her pleasure in Mars is mixed up with her pleasure in Roger; at the sight of this big cold panorama love sails through her like the wind. Now he is smiling, and she follows his gaze and sees two people though the shelter's open walls. "Here they are."

They round the front of the shrine and the pair notices them. "Hi, all," Roger says. "Eileen, this is Freya Ahmet and Jean-Claude Bayer. They're going to be joining us. Freya, Jean-Claude, this is Eileen Monday."

"We have heard of you," Freya says to her with a friendly smile. She and Jean-Claude are both huge; they tower over the old ones.

"That's Hans and Frances behind us, down the path there arguing. Get used to that."

Hans and Frances arrive, then Arnold and Stephan. Introductions are made all around, and they investigate the empty shrine or shelter, and exclaim over the view. The eastern side of the Elysian massif was a rain shadow before, and now it bulks just as black and empty as ever, looking much as it always has. The huge white plate of the sea, however, and the incongruous square of the *Altamira*; these are new and strange. Eileen has never seen anything like it. Impressive, yes; vast; sublime; but her eye always returns to the little tented greenhouse on the township, tiny stamp of life in a lifeless universe. She wants her world back.

On the way back down the stone stairs she looks at the exposed granite of the fjord's sidewall, and in one crack she sees black crumbly matter. She stops to inspect it.

"Look at this," she says to Roger, scraping away at rime to see more of it. "Is it lichen? Moss? Is it alive? It looks like it might be alive."

Roger sticks his face right down into it, eyes a centimeter away. "Moss, I think. Dead."

Eileen looks away, feeling her stomach sink. "I'm so tired of finding dead plants, dead animals. The last dozen times out I've not seen a single living thing. I mean winterkill is winterkill, but this is ridiculous. The whole world is dying!"

Roger waggles a hand uncertainly, straightens up. He can't really deny it. "I suppose there was never enough sunlight to begin with," he says, glancing up at their bronze button of light, slanting over Elysium. "People wanted it and so they did it anyway. But reality isn't interested in what people want."

Eileen sighs. "No." She pokes again at the black matter. "Are you sure this isn't a lichen? It's black, but it looks like it's still alive somehow."

He inspects some of it between his gloved fingers. Small black fronds, like a kind of tiny seaweed, frayed and falling apart.

"Fringe lichen?" Eileen ventures. "Frond lichen?"

"Moss, I think. Dead moss." He clears away more ice and snow. Black rock, rust rock. Black splotches. It's the same everywhere. "No doubt there are lichens alive, though. And Freya and Jean-Claude say the subnivean environment is quite lively still. Very robust. Protected from the elements."

Life under a permanent blanket of snow. "Uh huh."

"Hey. Better than nothing, right?"

"Right. But this moss here was exposed."

"Right. And therefore dead."

They start down again. Roger hikes beside her, lost in thought. He smiles: "I'm having a déjà vu. This happened before, right? A long time ago we found some little living thing together, only it was dead. It happened before!"

She shakes her head. "You tell me. You're the memory man."

"But I can't quite get it. It's more like déjà vu. Well, but maybe . . . maybe on that first trip, when we first met?" He gestures eastward — over the Amazonian Sea, she guesses, to the canyon country east of Olympus. "Some little snails or something."

"But could that be?" Eileen asks. "I thought we met when I was still in college. The terraforming had barely started then, right?"

"True." He frowns. "Well, there was lichen from the start, it was the first thing they propagated."

"But snails?"

He shrugs. "That's what I seem to remember. You don't?"

"No way. Just whatever you've told me since, you know."

"Oh well." He shrugs again, smile gone. "Maybe it was just a déjà vu."

Back in the iceboat's cockpit and cabin, they could be crowded around the kitchen table of a little apartment anywhere. The two newcomers, heads brushing the ceiling even though they are sitting on stools, cook for them. "No, please, that is why we are here," Jean-Claude says with a big grin. "I very much like to be cooking the big meals." Actually they're coming along to meet with some friends on the other side of the Amazonian Sea, all people Roger has worked with often in the last few years, to initial some research on the western slope of Olympus — glaciology and ecology, respectively.

After these explanations they listen with the rest as Hans and Frances argue about the crash for a while. Frances thinks it was caused by the rapid brightening of the planet's albedo when the North Sea was pumped out and froze; this the first knock in a whole series of positively reinforcing events leading in a negative direction, an autocatalytic drop into the death spiral of the full crash. Hans thinks it was the fact that the underground permafrost was never really thawed deeper than a few centimeters, so that the resulting extremely thin skin of the life zone looked much more well-established than it really was, and was actually very vulnerable to collapse if attacked by mutant bacteria, as Hans believes it was, the mutations spurred by the heavy incoming UV —

"You don't know that," Frances says. "You radiate those same organisms in the lab, or even expose them in space labs, and you don't get the mutations or the collapses we're seeing on the ground."

"Interaction with ground chemicals," Hans says. "Sometimes I think everything is simply getting salted to death."

Frances shakes her head. "These are different problems, and there's no sign of synergistic effects when they're combined. You're just listing possibilities, Hans, admit it. You're throwing them out there, but no one knows. The etiology is not understood."

This is true; Eileen has been working in Burroughs on the problem for ten years, and she knows Frances is right. The truth is that in planetary ecology, as in most other fields, ultimate causes are very hard to discern. Hans now waggles a hand, which is as close as he will come to conceding a point to Frances. "Well, when you have a list of possibilities as long as this one, you don't have to have synergy among them. Just a simple addition of factors might do it. Everything having its particular effect."

Eileen looks over at the youngsters, their backs to the old ones as they cook. They're debating salt too, but then she sees one put a handful of it in the rice.

In the fragrance of basmati steam they spoon out their meals. Freya and Jean-Claude seated on the floor. They listen to the old ones, but don't speak much. Occasionally they lean heads together to talk in private, under the talk at the little table. Eileen sees them kiss.

She smiles. She hasn't been around people this young for a long time. Then through their reflections in the cockpit dome she sees the ice outside, glowing under the stars. It's a disconcerting image. But they are not looking out the window. And even if they were, they are young, and so do not quite believe in death. They are blithe.

Roger sees her looking at the young giants, and shares with her a small smile at them. He is fond of them, she sees. They are his friends. When they say good-night and duck down the passageway to their tiny quarters in the bow, he kisses his fingers and pats them on the head as they pass him.

The old ones finish their meal, then sit staring out the window, sipping hot chocolate spiked with peppermint schnapps.

"We can regroup," Hans says, continuing the discussion with Frances. "If we pursued the heavy industrial methods aggressively, the ocean would melt from below and we'd be back in business."

Frances shakes her head, frowning. "Bombs in the regolith, you mean."

"Bombs *below* the regolith. So that we get the heat, but trap the radiation. That and some of the other methods might do it. A flying lens to focus some of the mirrors' light, heat the surface with focused sunlight. Then bring in some nitrogen from Titan. Direct a few comets to unpopulated areas, or aerobrake them so that they burn up in the atmosphere. That would thicken things up fast. And more halocarbon factories, we let that go too soon."

"It sounds pretty industrial," Frances says.

"Of course it is. Terraforming is an industrial process, at least partly. We forgot that."

"I don't know," Roger says. "Maybe it would be best to keep pursuing the biological methods. Just regroup, you know, and send another wave out there. It's longer, but, you know. Less violence to the landscape."

"Ecopoesis won't work," Hans says. "It doesn't trap enough heat in the biosphere." He gestures outside. "This is as far as ecopoesis will take you."

"Maybe for now," Roger says.

"Ah yes. You are unconcerned, of course. But I suppose you're happy about the crash anyway, eh? Being such a red?"

"Hey, come on," Roger says. "How could I be happy? I was a sailor."

"But you used to want the terraforming gone."

Roger waves a hand dismissively, glances at Eileen with a shy smile. "That was a long time ago. Besides, the terraforming isn't gone now anyway," gesturing at the ice, "it's only sleeping."

"See," Arnold pounces, "you do want it gone."

"No I don't, I'm telling you."

"Then why are you so damn happy these days?"

"I'm not happy," Roger says, grinning happily, "I'm just not sad. I don't think the situation calls for sadness."

Arnold rolls his eyes at the others, enlisting them in his teasing. "The world freezes, and this is not a reason for sadness. I shudder to think what it would take for you!"

"It would take something sad!"

"But you're *not* a red, no of course not."

"I'm not!" Roger protests, grinning at their laughter, but serious as well. "I was a sailor, I tell you. Look, if the situation were as bad as you all are saying, then Freya and Jean-Claude would be worried too, right? But they're not. Ask them and you'll see."

"They are simply young," Hans says, echoing Eileen's thought. The others nod as well.

"That's right," Roger says. "And it's a short-term problem."

That gives them pause.

After a silence Stephan says, "What about you, Arnold? What would you do?"

"What, me? I have no idea. It's not for me to say, anyway. You know me. I don't like telling people what to do."

They wait in silence, sipping their hot chocolate.

"But you know, if you did just direct a couple of little comets right *into* the ocean. . . ."

Old friends, laughing at old friends just for being themselves. Eileen leans in against Roger, feeling better.

Next morning with a whoosh they are off east again, and in a few hours' sailing are out on the ice with no land visible, skating on the gusty wind with runners clattering or shussing or whining or blasting, depending on wind and ice consistencies. The day passes, and it begins to seem as if they are on an all-ice world, like Callisto or Europa. As the day ends they slide around into the wind and come to a halt, then get out and drive in some ice screws around the boat and tie it into the center of a web of lines. By sunset they are belayed, and Roger and Eileen go for a walk over the ice.

"A beautiful day's sail, wasn't it?" Roger asks.

"Yes, it was," Eileen says. But she cannot help thinking that they are out there walking on the surface of their ocean. "What did you think about what Hans was saying last night, about taking another bash at it?"

"You hear a lot of people talking that way."

"But you?"

"Well, I don't know. I don't like a lot of the methods they talk about. But—" He shrugs. "What I like or don't like doesn't matter."

"Hmm." Underfoot the ice is white, with tiny broken air bubbles marring the surface, like minuscule crater rings. "And you say the youngsters aren't much interested either. But I can't see why not. You'd think they'd want terraforming to be working more than anyone."

"They think they have *lots* of time."

Eileen smiles at this. "They may be right."

"That's true, they may. But not us. I sometimes think we're sad not so much because of the crash as the quick decline." He looks at her, then down at the ice again. "We're two hundred and fifty years old, Eileen."

"Two hundred forty."

"Yeah yeah. But there's no one alive older than two-sixty."

"I know." Eileen remembers a time when a group of old ones were sitting around a big hotel restaurant table building card-houses, as there was no other card game all of them knew; they collaborated on one house of cards four stories high, and the structure was getting shaky indeed when someone said, "It's like my longevity treatments." And though they laughed, no one had the steadiness of hand to set the next card.

"Well. There you have it. If I were twenty I wouldn't worry about the crash either. Whereas for us it's very likely the last Mars we'll know. But, you know. In the end it doesn't matter what kind of Mars you like best. They're all better than nothing." He smiles crookedly at her, puts an arm around her shoulders and squeezes.

The next morning they wake in a fog, but there is a steady breeze as well, so after breakfast they unmoor and slide east with a light, slick sliding sound. Ice dust, pulverized snow, frozen mist—all flash past them.

Almost immediately after taking off, however, a call comes in on the radio phone. Roger picks up the handset, and Freya's voice comes in. "You left us behind."

"*What?* Shit! What the hell were you doing out of the boat?"

"We were down on the ice, fooling around."

"For Christ's sake, you two." Roger grins despite himself as he shakes his head. "And what, you're done now?"

"None of your business," Jean-Claude calls happily in the background.

"But you're ready to be picked up," Roger says.

"Yes, we are ready."

"Okay, well, shit. Just hold put there. It'll take a while to beat back up to you in this wind."

"That's all right. We have our warm clothes on, and a ground pad. We will wait for you."

"As if you have any choice!" Roger says, and puts the handset down.

He starts sailing in earnest. First he turns across the wind, then tacks up into it, and the boat suddenly shrieks like a banshee. The sail-mast is cupped tight. Roger shakes his head, impressed. You would have to shout to be heard over the wind now, but no one is saying anything; they're letting Roger concentrate on the sailing. The whiteness they are flying through is lit the same everywhere, they see nothing but the ice right under the cockpit, flying by. It is not the purest whiteout Eileen has ever been in, because of the wind and the ice under the lee rail, but it is pretty close; and after a while even the ends of the iceboat, even the ice under the lee rail, disappear into the cloud. They fly, vibrating with their flight, through a roaring white void; a strange kinetic experience, and Eileen finds herself trying to open her eyes farther, as if there might be another kind of sight inside her, waiting for moments like this to come into play.

Nothing doing. They are in a moving whiteout, that's all there is to it. Roger doesn't look pleased. He's staring down at their radar, and the rest of the instrumentation. In the old days pressure ridges would have made this kind of blind sailing very dangerous. Now there is nothing out there to run into.

Suddenly they are shoved forward, the roar gets louder, there is darkness below them. They are skating over a sandy patch. Then out of it and off again, shooting through bright whiteness. "Coming about," Roger says.

Eileen braces herself for the impact of their first tack, but then Roger says, "I'm going to wear about, folks." He brings the tiller in toward his knees and they career off downwind, turn, turn, then catch the wind on their opposite beam, the boat's hull tipping alarmingly to the other side. Booms below as the ballast weight shifts up to the windward rail, and then they are howling as before, but on the opposite tack. The whole operation has been felt and heard rather than seen; Roger even has his eyes closed for a while. Then a moment of relative calm, until the next wearing about. A backward loop at the end of each tack.

Roger points at the radar screen. "There they are, see?"

Arnold peers at the screen. "Sitting down, I take it."

Roger shakes his head. "They're still mostly over the horizon. That's their heads."

"You hope."

Roger is looking at the APS screen and frowning. He wears away again. "We'll have to come up on them slow. The radar only sees to the horizon, and even standing up it won't catch them farther than six k away, and we're going about a hundred fifty k an hour. So we'll have to do it by our APS positions."

Arnold whistles. Satellite navigation, to make a rendezvous in a whiteout. . . .

"You could always," Arnold begins, then claps his hand over his mouth.

Roger grins at him. "It should be doable."

For a non-sailor like Eileen, it is a bit hard to believe. In fact all the blind vibration and rocking side to side have her feeling a bit dizzy, and Hans and Stephan and Frances look positively queasy. All five of them regard Roger, who looks at the APS screen and shifts the tiller minutely, then all of a sudden draws it in to his knees again. On the radar screen Freya and Jean-Claude appear as two glowing green columns. "Hey you guys," Roger says into the radio handset, "I'm closing on you, I'll come up from downwind, wave your arms and keep an eye out, I'll try to come up on your left side as slow as I can."

He pulls the tiller gently back and forth, watching the screens intently. They come so far up into the wind that the sail-mast spreads into a very taut French curve, and they lose way. Roger glances ahead of the boat, but still nothing there, just the pure white void, and he squints unhappily and tugs the tiller another centimeter closer to him. The sail is feathering now and has lost almost all its curve; it feels to Eileen as if they are barely making headway, and will soon stall and be thrown backward; and still no sight of them.

Then there they are just off the port bow, two angels floating through whiteness toward the still boat—or so for one illusory moment it appears. They leap over the rail onto the foredeck, and Roger uses the last momentum of the iceboat to wear away again, and in a matter of seconds they are flying east with the wind again, the howl greatly reduced.

By that sunset they are merely in a light mist. Next morning it is gone entirely, and the world has returned. The iceboat lies moored in the long shadow of Olympus Mons, hulking over the horizon to the east. A continent of a mountain, stretching as far as they can see to north and south; another world, another life.

They sail in toward the eastern shore of the Amazonian Sea, famous before the crash for its wild coastline. Now it shoots up from the ice white and bare, like a winter fairy tale: Gordii Waterfall, which fell a vertical kilometer off the coastal plateau directly into the sea, is now a great pillared icefall, with a huge pile of ice shatter at its foot.

Past this landmark they skate into Lycus Sulci Bay, south of Acheron, where the land rises less precipitously, gentle hills above low sea bluffs, looking down on the ice bay. In the bay they slowly tack against the morning offshore breeze, until they come to rest against a floating dock, now somewhat askew in the press of ice, just off a beach. Roger ties off on this, and they gear up for a hike on the land. Freya and Jean-Claude carry their backpacks with them.

Out of the boat and onto the ice. *Scritch-scritch* over the ice to shore, everything strangely still; then across the frosty beach, and up a trail that leads to the top of the bluff. After that a gentler trail up the vast tilt of the coastal plateau. Here the trailmakers have laid flagstones that run sometimes ten in a row before the next low step up. In steeper sections it becomes more like a staircase, a great endless staircase, each flag fitted perfectly under the next one. Even rime-crusted as it is, Eileen finds the lapidary work extraordinarily beautiful. The quartzite flags are placed as tightly as Orkney drywall, and their surfaces are a mix of pale yellow and red, silver and gold, all in differing proportions for each flag, and alternating by dominant color as they rise. In short, a work of art.

Eileen follows the trail looking down at these flagstones, up and up, up and up, up some more. Above them the rising slope is white to the distant high horizon, beyond which black Olympus bulks like a massive world of its own.

The sun emerges over the volcano. Light blazes on the snow. As they hike farther up the quartzite trail it enters a forest. Or rather, the skeleton of a forest. Eileen hurries to catch up with Roger, feeling oppressed, even frightened. Freya and Jean-Claude are up ahead; their other companions far behind.

Roger leads her off the trail, through the trees. They are all dead. It was a forest of foxtail pine and bristlecone pine; but treeline has fallen to sea level at this latitude, and all these big old gnarled trees have perished. After that a sandstorm, or a series of sandstorms, sandblasted away all the trees' needles, the small branches, and the bark itself, leaving behind only the bleached tree trunks and the biggest lower branches, twisting up like broken arms from writhing bodies. Wind has polished the spiraling grain of the trunks until it gleams in the morning light. Ice packs the cracks into the heartwood.

The trees are well-spaced, and they stroll between them, regarding some more closely, then moving on. Scattered here and there are little frozen ponds and tarns. It seems to Eileen like a great sculpture garden or workshop, in which some mighty Rodin has left scattered a thousand trails at a single idea, all beautiful, altogether forming a park of surreal majesty. And yet awful too; she feels it as a kind of stabbing pain in the chest; this is a cemetery. Dead trees flayed by the sandy wind; dead Mars, their hopes flensed by cold Red Mars, Mars the god of war, taking back its land with a frigid boreal blast. The sun glares off the icy ground, smeary light glazing the world. The bare wood glows orange.

"Beautiful, isn't it?" Roger says.

Eileen shakes her head, looking down. She is bitterly cold, and the wind whistles through the broken branches and the grain of the wood. "It's dead, Roger."

"What's that?"

" 'The darkness grew apace,' " she mutters, looking away from him. " 'A cold wind began to blow in freshening gusts from the east.' "

"What's that you say?"

"*The Time Machine*," she explains. "The end of the world. 'It would be hard to convey the stillness of it.' "

"Ah," Roger says, and puts his arm around her shoulders. "Still the English major." He smiles. "All these years pass and we're still just what we always were. You're an English major from the University of Mars."

"Yes." A gust seems to blow through her chest, as if the wind had suddenly struck her from an unexpected quarter. "But it's all over now, don't you see? It's all dead"—she gestures—"everything we tried to do!" A desolate plateau over an ice sea, a forest of dead trees; all their efforts gone to waste.

"Not so," Roger says, and points up the hill. Freya and Jean-Claude are wandering down through the dead forest, stopping to inspect certain trees, running their hands over the icy spiral grain of the wood, moving on to the next magnificent corpse.

Roger calls to them, and they approach together. Roger says under his breath to Eileen, "Now listen, Eileen, listen to what they say. Just watch them and listen."

The youngsters join them, shaking their heads and babbling at the sight of the broken-limbed forest. "It's so beautiful!" Freya says. "So pure!"

"Look," Roger interrupts, "don't you worry everything will all go away, just like this forest here? Mars become unlivable? Don't you believe in the crash?"

Startled, the two stare at him. Freya shakes her head like a dog shedding water. Jean-Claude points west, to the vast sheet of ice sea spread below them. "It never goes backward," he says, halting for words. "You see all that water out there, and the sun in the sky. And Mars, the most beautiful planet in the world."

"But the crash, Jean-Claude. The crash."

"We don't call it that. It is a long winter only. Things are living under the snow, waiting for the next spring."

"There hasn't been a spring in thirty years! You've never seen a spring in your life!"

"Spring is L-s zero, yes? Every year spring comes."

"Colder and colder."

"We will warm things up again."

"But it could take thousands of years!" Roger exclaims, enjoying the act of provocation. He sounds like all the people in Burroughs, Eileen thinks, like Eileen herself when she is feeling the despair of the crash.

"I don't care," Freya says.

"But that means you'll never see any change at all. Even with really long lives you'll never see it."

Jean-Claude shrugs. "It's the work that matters, not the end of work. Why be so focused on the end? All it means is you are over. Better to be in the middle of things, or at the beginning, when all the work remains to be done, and it could turn out any way."

"It could fail," Roger insists. "It could get colder, the atmosphere could freeze out, everything in the world could die like these trees here. Nothing left alive at all."

Freya turns her head away, put off by this. Jean-Claude sees her and for the first time he seems annoyed. They don't understand what Roger has been doing, and now they are tired of it. Jean-Claude gestures at the stark landscape: "Say what you like," he says. "Say it will all go crash, say everything alive now will die, say the planet will stay frozen for thousands of years—say the stars will fall from the sky! But there *will be* life on Mars."

the sky-green blues

TANITH LEE

Here's perhaps one of the strangest stories you're likely to read this year, one that takes you to a world where nothing is what it seems for a story that goes no place that you'd expect it to take you . . .

Tanith Lee is one of the best-known and most prolific of modern fanta-sists, with more than sixty books to her credit, including (among many others) The Birthgrave, Drinking Sapphire Wine, Don't Bite the Sun, Night's Master, The Storm Lord, Sung in Shadow, Volkhavaar, Anackire, Night's Sorceries, Black Unicorn, Days of Grass, The Blood of Roses, Vivia, Reigning Cats and Dogs, When the Lights Go Out, Elephantasm, *and* The Gods Are Thirsty, *and the collections* Tamastara, The Gorgon, Dreams of Dark and Light, Nightshades, *and* The Forests of Night. *Her short story "The Gorgon" won her a World Fantasy Award in 1983, her short story "Elle Est Trois (La Mort)" won her another World Fan-tasy Award in 1984, and her brilliant collection of retold folk tales,* Red as Blood, *was also a finalist that year (in the Best Collection category). Her most recent book is a new novel,* Faces Under Water, *and forthcom-ing are new novels* St. Fire, Mortal Suns, *and* The Immortal Moon. *Her stories have appeared in our First, Second, Fourth, and Sixteenth Annual Collections. She lives with her husband and two cats in the south of England.*

There, the nights were always green. He had filled the garden with lamps of waxed paper, some on poles, some hanging from the boughs of trees. Inside each one was a candle. The manservant trimmed, replaced, lit them, at sunset, going up and down the narrow paths, between the palms and the bamboos, the huge rhododendrons and cunibaias. As light faded from the sky, instead the garden filled with it, as if it had sucked the light down, the reason for night. And in the darkness, as the crickets remorselessly scratched, the garden pulsed green as jade.

A great moth, with the wing-span of a sparrow, fluttered through the garden, trying to immolate itself in a lamp, any lamp.

"The aperture in these lamps is too small for the big moths to penetrate," he said with satisfaction.

He liked that, cheating a moth of its suicide.

In the verandah, the single oil lamp made his face very yellow. He was old, about 70, or older, carved with wrinkles, a life's work. His name was Lohno Tezmaine.

"You're cruel," I remarked.

"Why? Because I won't let the moth kill itself? Yes, Frances, that's probably true."

But it was more than that. The carving of his face showed his cruelty. It was cruelty, his 70 or more years of cruel jeers and patronizing smiles and frowns, that had formed its present shape.

I thought, briefly, what would mine show, if I lived so long? Indolence, perhaps, indecision.

But he said, suddenly, "Laitel says the enemy are almost here. Tomorrow, the next day."

Laitel was the manservant. He heard things when he went shopping in the market for rice, roots, meat and fruit, and other staples of Lohno's house.

"What will you do?" I asked.

"Nothing. What can I do?"

"Get away. Surely you could."

"You mean my machine? But where would I go?"

"The coast?" I suggested.

He did not reply.

We were silent. Then he said, "I take it you have no plans to go, yourself."

"I don't know yet. I'm supposed to stay, I promised I would. That is, as long as you do. But when it comes to the point . . . I don't know."

"As a woman, you're in more danger. At the worst they'll only kill me. I mean, even if they torture me, I haven't much stamina. Soon over. But you're young."

"Forty," I said idly. "Forty-one next month."

"Young enough," he said. "And we've heard the stories of what they do with females. Alien females."

"Yes. I'll run away then."

"Then should you leave tonight?"

His face was beaky and the cruel lines sharpened. As with the moth, he didn't like to let me have my death.

"No. That isn't necessary."

"Do you want the machine?" he asked abruptly. Was this sinister, this offer?

"I wouldn't be able to drive it."

"Laitel could show you."

"I'm not very good with new mechanical things."

"It would get you to the coast. That's where the airlift will be. If there is one."

"I'd rather not." Reluctantly I added, "Thank you."

He raised the crystal bottle and poured another pequa for himself, and next for me.

"Cheers," said Lohno.

We drank, and somewhere at the garden's end, where the cultivated wilderness dropped down in stony levels to the thin surface waters and the glutinous mudtrees of the swamp, a gurricula gave its long hoarse cry.

"Out hunting," he said. "When the enemy come in things will be easier for it. They lose their skills, you know," he added to me, "creatures, when there are wars. A buffet's laid on for them of the dead. They get lazy. But then I've heard the enemy shoot scavengers."

When I was on the outer stair going up to the roof, I looked down, and glimpsed the gurricula, at the garden's end. Its long pale body, half lamplit and freckled by shadows, was nosing in Lohno's rubbish tip. Presently it pulled out a curious thing that looked like a paperbound book. Either Lohno or Laitel or some eccentric neighbour must have flung it there. With this in its jaws the gurricula loped away, its eyes gleaming. It appeared mindless; ugly and beautiful at the same moment. Animals often look like that to me. And, I confess, other races.

Laitel, for example, with his long eyes, the pupil and iris indistinguishable and black, the inner, bluish lid. His face was a perfect oval, feminine in its hairless smoothness. As with many of his people, his tongue was black, and rough as a cat's. He was slightly shorter than I, slim and small-boned, his skin so white that, when I put my hand upon it, every time I felt a transgressor.

Looking at Laitel, all Laitel's race, I could see no soul in them. Or do I mean, no *physical* soul, the personality.

Despite, or because of that, we had been having sex together almost every night.

My apartment was on the roof, an old summer-house of bamboo, with waxed paper shutters rolled up to let in the humid and unmoving air.

I went in and pushed my things about on the table. Then I sat on the sofa and tried the mobex. Nothing came through but static. The firm, excited voices which had asked me if I would stay to see the fall of the city were blocked off from me by some noiseless electric storm high above, or some powerful ray discharged across the sea. It was possible my communicating link would not clear in time to allow me to deliver a report. I would have to record it, then. Sometime they would be able to access this recording, even if, by then, the mobex were a kilometre down in the swamp, and I in some coffle of women, chained at the ankle, and driven southward, in service to the soldiers of the enemy.

Below, the yellow oil-light shifted from the verandah. A patch of darkness formed there, intensifying the liquid jades of the garden.

When I came to the house, to interview Lohno Tezmaine, I had known there would be danger. But I'd wanted to see the city. In the first three or four days, in the mornings before Lohno got out of bed, I'd walked about, or taken the hutshas, pulled by ponies, by men, women or even teams of six children — eight were needed for the heavier traveller. So I saw, and photexed, the old mansions of Flower Street, six kilometres of them, like ice sculptures, and the lush gardens with their blazing winter flowers. Also the temples in Que Square, and the fountain, with its columns and serpents, the water playing rather dry and brown that day, but people still drinking from it. I had photexed the Duval Library, the Earthlight Hotel and the Monument to Silence. I did spend one morning in the jush, photexing the shacks and huts, the tin roofs jolly with rust from summer rains, the dyeworks where the swamp is poison-iris-colour. But you see such things everywhere. That was only duty.

Lohno never got up till lunch. Lunch was his first meal. Over scores of little dishes—shoots and beans fried in peanut oil, salt mangoes, scrambled eggs and pig meat, rice, bread, jam, coffee, I placed questions before him. Sometimes he answered them.

Everything was nothing to Lohno. He had done so much. His only goal seemed to be this latent intent one—of preventing others from experiencing anything. On the first morning he had said, in answer to my enquiry about his daughter, whether he sheltered her so severely because he feared his rivals would harm her, that he was "good at" living, but she had seemed not to be. He added that most of us, of all races and types, seemed to have "no notion of *how* to be alive." And so we were best protected from the state.

"Can you clarify that a little?" I had asked.

"Take yourself," he said at once. He was like a lot of interviewees, I thought, eager to turn the tables at once and humiliatingly get *my* story. But it wasn't that. "Here you are, millions of miles from home, out on a limb. War all around us. A hostile force advancing to take this city. Everything precarious. Why did you come?"

"To talk to you."

"But why? Don't tell me there's still any interest in me. There shouldn't be. I haven't done anything for 30 years."

"Perhaps that's why."

He ignored that. "You came here because you wanted to experience something. A new thing. And that is how most of you are. Either you hide from life or you leap and dive into life. But life is a deep river with a cloudy bottom. There may be carnivorous beasts, venomous fish and rocks, there, under the surface."

"I concede that."

"Do you? This is what I mean. You are all of you amateurs at living."

I said, reasonably I thought, "Then, speaking as a life-professional, how would you do it? What would you do?"

He had laughed. "It's like any creative art. It isn't to be taught. Either the gift is there, or it isn't."

Lohno's daughter, he went on to say, had anyway escaped his protection. She had run off with a gangster, and lived in a mean apartment somewhere, bearing him babies. She had had her tongue pierced, he said. And his cruelty-construct face leered.

"That's significant?"

"Think about it."

"I have. The salience eludes me."

He condescended to ask, "For what is a tongue used?"

"To talk, to eat. In sex."

"And it has no bone, does it. But she's put something rigid and hard right through its softness."

I shook my head. "Mr Tezmaine—"

"Lohno, I told you."

"Lohno. I still don't—"

Then he laughed again. "Forget it."

When I had been with him, the first days, I had the urge always, afterwards, to take a shower. That passed. It was a strange reaction. He was perfectly clean, physically, and I preferred to shower first or last thing in the day.

I was in the shower of the summer-house now, when Laitel came into the room.

He made no noise at all, and by that, somehow, I heard him. And then he switched on the ceiling fan, and I heard that.

When I came out in my robe, he was turning down the sheet on my camp-bed. He had put a dish of fruit on the table. There was always some excuse to come up here, in case I didn't welcome him, I thought, or he decided against it.

The fan made its insectile noise, rather like the blades of the VTOs which would rescue everyone at the coastal pick-up. Or so I had been told.

"Do you have what you want for the night?" asked Laitel.

"Yes. Thanks for the fruit. Is the fan all right?"

"The generator's recharged. Leave it on if you wish."

Apart from the great moths, one of which, or the same one as before, was again sailing anxiously about the green garden, few insects survived in the city. Fallout from communication rays, supposedly harmless to people, had polished most of them off, even most of the striped ants.

I went over to Laitel, leaned and kissed him lightly. We walked to the bed, discarded our garments and lay down.

This sex was always pleasant, easy and rhythmic, without demanding excitement or any conclusion. Neither of us experienced orgasm. We caressed and moved, comfortably slotted together, until we grew bored, then separating, I with a mild sense of something achieved. Satisfied. If he was, I don't know. I thought I had made it apparent I would do what he needed to achieve orgasm, but he too seemed indifferent. Merely we valued the mutual message of our bodies. I suspected that, for Laitel, the climax of the act was of use only with his own kind, and in the interests of procreation.

I made tea for us on the battery hot-plate. It was nice to do something for him. All day and sometimes during the night, he had to wait on Lohno, and now too on me.

We drank the tea.

"Did he throw a book out for the rubbish?" I asked. I wasn't really interested. But Laitel said, "Yes. One of his own. Now and then he throws one away."

"I suppose it won't matter. There are copies of all his books in Optimum, all available on disc."

"No, it won't matter."

"Why does he do it?"

Laitel said, expressionless as he always was, "He enjoys to."

When Laitel left me, I recorded this fact with the others.

I had asked Laitel, during our first time alone, what he thought of Lohno Tezmaine. Laitel said, "I serve him."

Although the chip one gets to wear now, in the flesh of the right arm, enables one to understand and be understood in any language, sometimes there are little discrepancies.

"You mean, as his servant."

"His servant." Laitel's voice was not a mask, however. Again, I detected something. I said, "Does he—excuse me, but has he slept with you?"

"Oh no. I don't mean that."

We got no further. It had been as enigmatic as with Tezmaine.

Tonight, before Laitel left me, and I recorded his comment on the book, I had asked the more relevant thing.

"Laitel, if the enemy break through, if the city falls—"

"They will. Yes?"

"What will you do?"

"What can I do?" Lohno's answer. Exactly.

"Come on, Laitel. It's going to be dangerous. They'll be merciless to you—won't they, the enemy?"

"I think so."

"Do you have a family here?"

"No." He added, "I was born in the jush. Not wanted."

"Then you should"—now I spoke Tezmaine's lines—"get away."

"I have no papers, Frances."

"I can print you up some good false ones on the mobex. Enough to pass. Get you to the coast." His black eyes glanced at me. Beautiful, ugly, soulless. Or solely soul. "Lohno said you know how to drive the machine."

"I have done so, sometimes, for him."

"Then why don't you take it, and go? He isn't afraid. I don't think he'd bother if you went. You'd stand a chance, wouldn't you?"

Beyond the city were the swamps, the secret rivers, mudtrees and boyuns, enormous tracts of jungle packaged over the ruins of haunted temples, where white monkeys and coies were the shrieking ghosts.

"But the airlift," he said coolly, "it's for your kind, Frances. Aliens who are wanting to escape."

"It's for whoever they can squeeze in the transports. Believe me, Laitel, I've seen this kind of thing before. And if I give you papers, you'll be fine."

"You," he said.

I took him to mean, why not me.

"My people promised to pick me up. They said me and Lohno, actually, that was part of the deal. He'd give us the interview and we'd get him out. But he won't discuss that—gave the interview anyway—pretends I never offered it. He doesn't care. Or he fancies the experience of the Vae Victis."

"Will your people come?"

I thought about it. "Maybe. They usually have in the past. But I should have checked tonight, and the intercom is out."

That was all we said.

When Laitel left, after I'd recorded the thing about the book, I lay under the sheet and watched the ceiling fan.

It occurred to me I might be stranded here. I wasn't afraid. I didn't believe any real harm could come to me. It never had, and I had been in many situations of peril. Somehow there was always an escape clause, a stroke of luck.

Suddenly, out beyond the raised paper shutters, a violent white flare exploded in the sky. Then came a wooden bang, which reverberated oddly, making the light furniture in the summer-house rock.

This had happened 15 times before, once for every night I had been here. They were only signal rockets, put up at irregular hours to disturb the sleep of the city. Reminders from the enemy that they were almost here.

The city would fall like an angel, its stones, gardens, and the accretions of all the aliens who had possessed it and hung on it their jewellery of buildings and fountains, streets and malls. In the firelight, after the close-range bombing began and ended, the true citizens would suffer only one more invasion. I visualized long lines of people driven away before the conqueror, like channels of water running from a tap.

I tried the mobex one last time, got static, recorded my thoughts in a sort of embarrassment, these neatly quilted phrases from the handbook of an articulate eyewitness.

In the very late mornings, sometimes a local girl came to the house, bringing garlands of white flowers and long-stemmed scented yasti. She would go straight in to Lohno's bedroom on the ground floor, but come out again after only a few minutes. In the verandah she would stand counting coins, then arrange some flowers about the lunch table.

That day she came. I was leaning on the roof-rail, drying my hair. I watched her go in, and then, after less than 50 seconds, come hurrying back.

Looking over, I saw her stop still, in the garden just below the verandah, as if undecided. The sunlight shone on her colourless hair. Then she stared straight up at me. The blue inner lids were shut fast over her eyes, a thing that happens to Laitel's race only in extreme agitation or grief. Next second, clutching her flowers, she ran away along the path and vanished in the rhododendrons.

I hesitated. Then I went down. Laitel was away, I thought, still at the market. These excursions had begun to take much longer. As the enemy drew nearer and more near, less food came in from the surrounding countryside, and fewer people remained to sell it.

The verandah kept its morning shadow, only in the afternoon did full sun reach it. The girl had dropped a single yasti there on the floor, as if leaving us a gift.

Inside, the passage, marble-tiled, swept twice daily by Laitel, gleamed in green sunlight. I passed the double bamboo doors of the dining room and came to the carved palmwood door that marked Lohno's room.

He had never invited me in here. I had never been in the room, though I'd glimpsed it. Now the door stood ajar, something that normally never happened until he had risen, leaving the bed gaping for Laitel to tidy.

It was a white room, a dull sallow faded white. He'd never used blinds but curtains of thin white silk, parchment colour now. Things were strewn about, as I'd seen before, glancing in as I passed, a leather-bound book on the floor, others over a straw chair. A water bottle stood by the bed and Lohno Tezmaine was stretched across the mattress. There had been insect-netting, and he had left it hanging there, though unclosed. It looked like cobwebs somehow. Or a spider's web, in which he lay.

When I bent over him I saw what I expected. He was dead. Feeling for a pulse, although I did so, was superfluous, and going to fetch the mobex to check for life signs would be futile. The syringe lay under his right hand.

He was smiling. There might be a lot of reasons for that, the fake amusement of setting rigour, or something in the drug he had used which made him feel good as it finished him. I was inclined to think, though, that he was pleased with himself. A life-professional would assume he knew the perfect moment to die.

His note was under a glass with some dregs of pequa in it. He had written in an obscure picture script that only the chip made me able to read—Laitel, very likely, wouldn't have made it out.

No reason for you to hang about here now, is there? he had written. *Take the machine and go. Use the old road. Laitel knows. So long, for now. L.*

When I turned, Laitel was in the doorway. If he felt anything, I'd never be sure. "Of course, he's dead," I announced.

Laitel came and looked. He pointed to the syringe. "He kept it ready. He showed me once. He said, Don't be astonished, one morning."

We left him there, shut the door, and walked back out to the verandah. A horrible whistling note had begun over the city. They were testing the sirens as, during the last two or three days, they had sometimes done, at midday and late in the afternoon. Birds in the garden screamed, fell silent, and abruptly flew off with great clappings of wings.

"I suppose that's it," I said. "Could you read his note?"

"No."

"But you can guess what it said?"

Laitel spoke slowly. "I'm to take the money and papers in his safe. Then drive the machine along the old road through the swamp, to the old wall."

"I see."

The sirens shut off. The quiet was a relief. Somewhere a frog croaked and then there was another noise.

Instinctively we looked up, beyond the verandah to the heat-drained emerald of the sky. There was nothing to see, but the droning rushing sound grew insistently louder.

"That wasn't a practice," I managed to say before the concussion blasted out. The flash was only a flicker, simultaneous. The earth trembled.

Somewhere not too near, faint cries, a temple bell ringing.

We waited. Nothing else happened, and the cries gradually diminished, the bell stopped.

"That sounded like the commercial area. It was a Sing rocket," I said. "Popular everywhere." Suddenly I laughed. To my surprise I seemed very slightly hysterical. "I could do with a bloody drink."

Laitel reached out as if to take my hand. His touch would be cool and calming, for a moment.

"Everything's happening at once," I said.

But I had evaded, withdrawn my own hand, and now ran along the verandah, up the stair to the roof.

The mobex gave me an immediate clear connection.

"Hi, Frances. What's the news?"

I told them.

"You don't say? Then I guess you'd like to leave . . ." A patch of static came, not really interrupting the hiatus.

I waited.

The man's voice said, "Tricky. Storms. How long before they get to you? Our reports give a unit, ten days even."

"No, less. It could even be today. A rocket just came down. They fire a few Sings, don't they, to get us in the mood. Then they march in or chute down. Both."

"Yes. The city government's fled. Guess you know. That was two days ago."

"I know."

"Night pick-up. Private VTO, usual stuff. Nice. Listen, Frances, keep the line open."

Over the summer-house, sudden, with no warning, rushed a vast roaring pterodactyl. Instinctively I threw myself flat. The detonation came next moment with a flash like lightning. The house, everything, shook. Things cascaded from the table. The chronic untidiness of war.

"That was another. Quite close."

"Heard it, Frances. Keep the line open. Speak to you soon."

The mobex went silent, save for recurring patches of static.

No sirens now. They hadn't bothered. I crouched by the camp-bed, while three more rockets tore over, and three more thunders opened the city.

Finally time passed with nothing. Crickets had started again. I got up. The sky was bruised. Smoke from the bombardment rose in three or four thick columns beyond the palms and sul trees that shielded the front of Lohno's house. Screams and wails still rose irregularly up in it, and long glissandi of tumbling glass.

I took the mobex with me when I went down, and dumped it on a straw chair in the verandah. Laitel was putting dishes on the table, rice and spinach, slivers of meat in sauce, the big bottle of Pinôt Grève Lohno always had at lunch, in a cooler.

After a moment, Laitel said, "They will come?"

"I don't know. Yes. I'm not sure."

I sat down, picked up my napkin, looked at the food.

Laitel poured a glass of wine for me.

"Please sit down, Laitel." He looked at me. "Oh sit down. He's dead. The city's being bombed. Have some fucking lunch with me."

He sat and ate, and drank a little wine. It seemed familiar, as if I had somewhere seen a photograph of him eating at this table, and so wondered if he had, with Lohno, quite often, before I arrived.

Although I drank two or three glasses of the wine, it made little impression on me. Laitel rose and went into the house, and returned after ten minutes with coffee. He served me, then sat again. He said, "A boy came to the front verandah just now. He had a dead aie bird. He said it was killed when a rocket hit one of the gardens." I looked at Laitel, not comprehending. "He said we could have it, for food. No payment necessary."

"So?"

"He was staring all the time into the house, to see who is here. We are only two or three persons. He will tell others, and they'll come back."

"I see. Looters."

"Taking what they can, before the enemy come. And they will know about you."

I glanced at the mobex, half reached out for it, and let my hand fall.

Over Lohno's walls and trees, a new dim sound was beginning to well through the city. It was febrile, almost festive. I'd heard such noises before. I pictured the crowds on Flower Street, windows that had survived the Sings, smashing.

"Will you take the machine, Laitel?"

"Yes. I've seen the papers in the safe. They will do."

"Can I come with you?"

"Yes."

I got up. "Let me put a couple of things together."

"Don't be in a great hurry," he said. "They won't come back until it's cooler. Maybe not till sunset. I'll see to the machine."

It didn't occur to me he would go without me. I don't know why not. What was there between us? The palest sex and a communication chip.

As I stuffed my bag I thought of the flower girl. I was sorry for her. I wondered if Laitel were washing the lunch dishes, the glasses, carefully by hand as he usually did, but when I came back down, they were still on the table, and a tiny contingent of ants had appeared, crawling over the plates, drowning in the last centimetres of wine.

I picked up the mobex: static issued from it. I spoke my plans into the recorder-relay, the plan of Lohno's machine and the journey to the coast, then turned it off. I knew, they wouldn't have come.

Over the sky a narrow flying craft leisurely drifted. It might have been a spy-plane of the city, but I thought not. Enemy reconnaissance. The sun was passing over and the shadows lengthening out from the cunibaias, where lemasets were playing now, the silvery boughs dipping and swaying as they sprang.

Laitel appeared below. "We'll go now, if you're ready."

"Yes."

He had nothing with him. Perhaps he had nothing of his own, wanted nothing that wasn't his own. But he said, "The machine is primed. I've loaded it up with food, and gas. I've put Lohno's gun into the compartment."

We walked along the narrow garden paths, threading between the waxed-paper candle lamps, which tonight nobody would light, the moths searching in vain for death. Death instead would be in Lohno's bedroom, with tiny trickles of ants foraging over him. Or the gurricula might get in at a window.

Or the house, ransacked by the neighbors, the boy with the aie bird, might be burning, so giving the moths a chance after all.

Out of its port, the machine squatted below the stone levels, on the edge of the old road where the swamp began. It was camouflage green, sky green and green-tawny, like the jungle-forest, the mudtrees and boyuns and palms. It had a look of power, armoured, muscular and big-snouted like some beast. This vehicle had been regularly cared for, oiled and exercised, its batteries charged and fed. Not wild, only savage, then, an expensive dray animal.

I went up the metal ladder and swung into the cab. Laitel took the driver's seat. He closed the machine's transparent armoured lid.

The house was invisible from here. A great quiet, a *Sunday* quiet, had descended over the city, which might only have been resting, dozing after an opulent family meal. Starlings flickered across the sky, two lemasets cackled in a giant rhododendron.

Before I came to the city, since I hadn't read any of Lohno Tezmaine's books, I had to use a preprogrammed tutor to speak them over to me in sleep. Following these sessions, consciously I hadn't at first remembered anything, though my sleep had been peppered with dislocated dreams. Gradually the input settled. When it came to the interviews with him, I had enough to ask the right questions. Nevertheless I was fairly sure he suspected my method. Had he despised me? Probably not. He was indifferent.

As we went deeper into the jungle, only then, did I begin to see Lohno's books, as it were, made flesh. Obviously, the ones he'd written after he came to live in the city.

On my arrival I hadn't seen much, only a map-like image unfolding under me just before the swift glide-down to the airstrip. A modern subway capsule had run me into the city—Europeans built it, this subway, the Grande Metrolux. They'd been proud of it once, like their library and the handful of mansions in period style, which they planted on Flower Street. But everyone had left markers there, Rus, Statesiders, Afro-Celt, Exastra.

Once war had washed over, destroying and processing small, the jungle itself would lay claim to the city, and then the city would go back to being like the rest, like the landscape we had now entered.

At first the old road coiled through the swamp, and then came a shanty town, the tin roofs and huts like the jush, but better, worse, broken up by trees and water and bubbling marshes railed with clacking reeds. The old wall carved across everything, ruined, and ancient almost as prehistory. Strong lemon light of a dying afternoon slid on the stones as the machine, oblivious, bumped through a gap. Our treads made nothing of the little shards and large smoothed pebbles. A turquoise fisher-bird stood sentinel by a pool, staring at us as we left the city behind and entered the funnel of the forest.

At first, impressive, the huge flags of apparently tarnished, heavy bronze, the leaves of plantain and gigantic, full-grown boyun. Flags indeed, banners sweeping and scraping on the machine's dome. Towering trees roped with lianas that would eventually strangle and pull them down. In flights of firework brilliance, parakeets went spraying up between, to be lost in the higher thinner canopy, where still, for about half an hour, glimpses of sky were visible, luminous yet flat-looking, like *trompe l'oeil*, a painted *ceiling*.

Then the overhead vista closed.

The machine ploughed on without pause, breaking through tender angelica creepers, snapping the boughs of cunibaia and black fig. Here and there, the automatics, meeting tougher growth, produced a whirl of blades and sliced vegetation. Green blood sprayed on the front screen of the dome, and was instantly wiped away.

Shade had deepened to the night-day of the jungle-forest. But hours had passed. Soon true night would come. Darkness.

"After dark we'd better stop, Laitel, had we?"

"Yes, I think so. Certainly tonight."

The machine lights were vital. Their heat if not their beam might be detectable by anything watching from the sky. How dedicated the enemy were to detaining all peoples in the city I didn't know. Perhaps not very. With me, an alien, they had no real quarrel. But I was on my own, and travelling with one of the enemy's enemies.

It seemed such an easy rule to follow, to turn off the machine once night came, crawl through into the rear compartment and sleep until sunrise. Not even any awkwardness. We had slept together, in both senses, many times already.

Claustrophobic, though, the jungle-forest. And then, every so often, a sort of agoraphobia—a break in the forest with a view of cascading rock and leaning, half-falling trunks, bamboos like waterfalls of liquid fabric, some defile far below, twice with a tribe of blond monkeys, their shouts of alarm clearly audible above the machine's low humming, the steady soft pump-pump of the gas mixture.

I had asked if there was enough fuel to reach to coast. Laitel told me he thought so. Besides, we might be able also to charge the solar panel in some clearing, when we were farther from the city and possible surveillance.

Once, kilometres, years, behind us, there came a faint prolonged boom. But it might only have been some liana-slain tree collapsing in the forest, deceiving us, natural and quite near.

Night fell. No, it seeped, like water. Exiled from Lohno's green night garden, here the blackness poured and filled our cup.

We switched off the machine and went through to the rear on hands and knees. After using the chemical toilet, I did stretching and loosening exercises on my mat. Laitel, moving on his knees as if accustomed to nothing else, put out some cold food and uncorked an evening bottle of wine.

Later, we lay down. By some mutual reticence, after all not together. We would have little private space during the journey. Only lying alone on our mats, a couple of metres apart, could we achieve any.

We hadn't spoken much. Now I said, "The travel-time computes as four days. Five, if vegetation makes for very hard going."

"This is the dry season. Growth is less. Four days, perhaps."

I said, as he had, previously, "There's plenty of time. They'll wait."

They would, because we would be among the first of the last groups. For the records, rescue must be shown to be at least partly effective. Even if they didn't wait, from the open land by the ocean escape must always be easier. Even my people would come, there. I had asked Laitel to let me see the papers Lohno had left for him—and not mentioned in the post-mortem note, presumably having promised earlier. They were good for anything, I thought. I'd been startled in a way Lohno had bothered. Then not startled. He had been so very conscious of our amateur status.

Soon I heard Laitel sleeping, the slight rustling in respiration he made, asleep. I lay on my back, and through his breath and the shell of the machine, I heard the crickets, and now and then a sharp scream from the forest. I thought of gur-ricula circling the vehicle with neon eyes. The jungle was alight with such eyes. Eyes hung in trees and the bodies of moss sloths, scrambled and leapt in the heads of coies and monkeys. The pinpoint spangles of rodent eyes scuttled over a floor of roots and bones.

Visualizing it, I saw them in a speeded-up motion. As in those old photographs of traffic on the Champs Elysées or torch-bearers running on Ho Lilly Way. Streaks, streamers crossing and re-crossing, radiant threads in a labyrinth.

In the morning, at first light, we went on.

We talked, even exchanged confidences, that day. It was from boredom, a sort of makeshift antidote to the slight panic I felt keep rising in me, a restless fear of enclosure, inactivity and ennui. For him, the same? Perhaps he talked only to humour or help me. Did he need to talk at all?

Neither of us, I thought, had anything very original to reveal. Our stories were inevitably products of our places of birth, conditioning, natures. To harshness, tied by rules of social etiquette and religion, and, of course, deprivation, his nature responded, it appeared, with acceptance and calm, nearly uninterested. I suppose for me too, the rules and the dragging up, though different ones—wanting things I couldn't have—material things, but also glamour, power, success. And my nature was very unlike his. First resentful and at last "sceptical." A still-hot, calloused nature, though even now wanting, slyly, life to woo me back: See, we didn't mean it, here is the reward, the prize. And knowing too I didn't deserve the bloody prize. So. Laitel shone translucently like a dim white pearl. Frances was more garish, costume jewellery, just tinged with jaundiced yellow. Once in a bar someone who claimed to see my aura told me it was shot with anger the colour of fire. Rather than chasten me, I'd been proud of that. Anger, why not?

After we'd talked—memories, insignificant events—a first bicycle (his), the first date (mine), our work—which had produced both bicycle and first date—servants, both of us, too, in differing, humiliating ways, although he was not humiliated, only I was—we became silent again. But we had got rid of another day.

Then it was time to crawl into the rear of the machine. And something was disgusting about it now, the proximity, and the smallness of the space. Our smells—mine chemically wiped and deodorized for "freshness," turning stale, his odourless. A *smell* of odourlessness. Disturbing. His race don't sweat. Or if they do, not as my race does. His face, Laitel's face, was becoming almost genderless to me, exactly like the face of the flower girl who had run away from Lohno's body, and all the other indigenous faces in his city. Only when they were old, incised by wrinkles, the white teeth, which had no canines, falling or pulled out, only then had there been any look of *living* in the faces of Laitel's people. Not really even then. Ugly, beautiful. I thought of the old, old woman I had seen dip her clay cup in the soiled water of the fountain in Que Square. Shrunk small as a European or African child, she might have been sculpted from almond wood, an artefact, those lines and fissures made deliberately by skill, for artistic admiration, not randomly out of pain and age.

Somehow we edged—or only I did—our mats further apart. We had drunk no wine. The rice had been sticky, and despite the storage unit, hard. A packet of luxury biscuits a sickly cliché out of place.

His whisper-breathing, when he slept, irritated me. I wanted to wake him up, shut him up. I heard unintelligible words in the whispers, then sounds in the air between them. But there were no real sounds that night. Crickets sometimes. A vague constant rumble we had heard from the moment the machine was switched off, a great waterfall, he said.

Later though something jumped onto the dome, monkeys or lemasets. Thumps and skitters, the squeak of claws on impervious transparency.

The equation on the mobex had informed me there was only one more day needed to reach the coast, and Laitel had seemed to think the noise of the fall—the Water-Mama, he called it—confirmed this. But that would mean the mobex's first computation was wrong. So why not this one?

When I woke again, it was late in the morning; instinctively I knew. And once I had crawled forward, I saw. One of those breaks had come, this time a vast clearing. The machine was stopped on its edge, screened off only by clumps of bamboo, a flimsy curtain of vines. I hadn't noticed, somehow, the previous evening, in the failing dusk.

Here, the perimeter of the clearing was richly green, but running to tobacco-brown farther off. The jungle only came in again, I thought, over a kilometre away. Some little deer were feeding in the middle distance, and there was a ripple of heat haze. The sky was very bright, cat's-eye colour. Almost midday then. I could no longer hear the fall.

Neither of us had left the machine before now. There was no need to. Every psychological need to. But without discussion, both of us had seemed to decide to go outside was foolish. The jungle-forest, in Laitel's language the lunga-rook, is treacherous. Quicksands, poisoned plants and snakes, gurricula, boar . . . an endless list of don'ts.

But now, Laitel had gone out. He must have done, because the machine, including the toilet and the storage space, was empty. I opened the front compartment. It was filled by batteries and tools for the upkeep of the machine. Lohno Tezmaine's gun lay slimly alongside.

I sat in the front seat, turning slowly, looking through the dome into the clearing, and the forest behind us, what I could make out over the machine's streamlined back.

Laitel had left the vehicle, and was not to be seen. Had vanished.

A story I hadn't bothered to tell him: when I was a child, in my own city, unthinkable wastes of time from here, I'd been left with some relative for an afternoon. I was about five. As it turned out, the relative, an aunt, either real or titular, hadn't been reliable. Rather like wicked female kin in fairy tales, she had taken me to the park, gone off to buy something, cigarettes I seem to recall, and not remembered to come back. Unnecessary to itemize the stages of my bewildered and tearful panic, the gibbering little near-foetus I eventually became, under those pruned cedars of Hurlingham. Near closing time, a park warden found me. He took me with some trouble—I'd been told never to go with strangers—to the park admin. Here I was rescued presently by a parent.

It shook me, sitting in the machine, sitting there with the blistering near-noon sunlight coming through the dome, shook me. Laitel gone, and I was that child again. The park, the jungle, the lunga-rook. Don't go with strangers.

For God's sake, I couldn't drive this thing. I didn't even know, and couldn't work out, which button would polarize the dome and stop the glare.

But come on, I'd been in worse situations. Hadn't I? Seldom quite alone though. My own kind had been with me. Or another sort of stranger, the sort one believes, for that short period, is an ally, a companion. Or I'd known my way. Had a vehicle I was familiar with, a terrain I was accustomed to or had learned from a tutor. Or no, no, surely there had been times like this. That cellar in Shovsk, that farm at Penn—had I been another person then? Yes, because now I was the child.

I pushed my panic down.

He hadn't gone far. Why would he? Perhaps to verify the fall was there. I could just hear its rumble after all. Somehow the intrusion of other senses—sight, distress—had blocked it out. What reason could Laitel have to leave the safety of the machine in any permanent way? It was his ticket to safety, as it was mine.

Then again, perhaps he had meant to be gone only a few minutes and something had happened. One of those *don'ts*, the reasons for never straying outside.

I picked up the mobex. Static was worse, as it had immediately become once we entered the jungle. I recorded Laitel's disappearance. My voice sounded steady, unconcerned.

Then I crawled back into the rear compartment. I'd eat something. Prepare myself . . . About ten minutes later, as I was nibbling a bread cake, I heard a noise on the ladder, then at the cab door. An animal? The door opened, as it only would to a registered handprint.

I was going to yell out. Relief was flooding through me like boiling then icy water. I paused, and called quietly, "Hi. Where were you?"

No one answered.

Then I was frightened. Not the child, other horrors. Was it possible—some battalion of the enemy—Laitel taken, leading them here . . . I scrambled forward, wishing I'd thought to keep the gun with me.

Sunlight still blared through the cab. The driver's door was pulled wide, and below, among the cream and green of the bamboo, Laitel was waiting, looking up at me. Alone.

"What in Christ's name are you playing at? What do you mean by it? Why the hell didn't you wake me—tell me you were going to go out? Why don't you speak for Christ's sake?"

"Come and see the fall, Frances, the Water-Mama."

"Fuck the fall, what—"

"It isn't far, Frances. Come. Come with me."

Irradiated in my mind, four words: Now he is crazy.

Was he? He seemed the same. Enigmatic Laitel, gentle Laitel, the blink of his black tongue between the pale slender lips, the herbivorous teeth of a race that, however, ate meat. The blue inner lids were well raised, only an ink-drawn rim about the eye's white, the inner black. I'd better be reasonable?

"Laitel, come back up. I shouldn't have shouted—I don't know how it translated. Sorry if it sounded like I was insulting any of your gods—I wasn't. Only mine. Let's talk. I was having some breakfast."

"Don't be afraid, Frances. Over there, through the trees, you can see it."

My hand had touched open the front compartment. It slipped quickly around metal. I couldn't drive Lohno's machine, but I could use his gun. Weapons, somehow, were always easier to learn. I raised it, as if examining the barrel.

"Laitel, I think you should come and have some coffee. Did you eat?"

Then Laitel laughed. I'd never seen him laugh, not even in sex, or from nervousness—but then, when had he been nervous? The laugh was musical. Like music. He turned and walked away, back through the loose net of creepers, which he didn't break, on to the verdant periphery of the clearing.

"Laitel! *Laitel!*"

His profile over his shoulder, half looking back. He shrugged, and walked on, away from me. The way someone does with someone else who is being stupidly obstructive or recalcitrant. Someone not bad, but impeding, for those moments. Someone who you'll probably forgive, later.

"Oh God."

Only, otherwise, the deer in the clearing, grazing.

I kept hold of the gun. The door had established my handprint as it had Laitel's, so I closed it when I got out on the ladder. I jumped down.

The ground was hot. I could feel it through my boots, and the humidity was intense, far worse than in the city or the garden. Water-drops formed at once on my hair and lashes, trickled down my face—perhaps too it was the nearness of the waterfall, which, out here, seemed suddenly to roar.

He wasn't moving fast. I soon caught up to him.

"What is this, Laitel?" He didn't speak now, or look at me, but he was slightly smiling. "Why is the fall—the Water-Mama so important?" No answer.

When we got free of the stands of vegetation, the noon sun was overpowering. The haze rippled, rippled, so the singed grass was like a lake, and the feeding deer seemed to be floating or swimming in it.

But we got closer and closer to the deer. They didn't stir. Hadn't they seen us? Scented us? Especially the scent of an alien—

"Laitel, why aren't the deer—"

"It's all right," he said.

And then, we were walking right by a deer, a mother, feeding with her fawn beside her. The baby didn't look up; *she* flicked us one glance, her ears, full of the juice of youth, fleshy, like leaves, twitching once. Then she lowered her head again.

We walked between all the deer. Some, this one, this, were less than half a metre from us. And now, compelled, I put out my hand, softly, disbelieving, ran it over the harsh velvet of deer haunches, and the head turned slowly. I glimpsed the long, purple eye—careless, returning to the grass. They smelled of grass, of herbs and fresh dung. Not for a second of fear.

We were in the middle of the great clearing. Above, the sky, singing out its daffodil green heat. The rumble-rush of water. Some sort of tension in the air, beyond temperature, or haze.

"Laitel . . . *what is it?*—what?"

His hand came out and took my hand, my left hand, which had stroked over the hide of the deer. I hadn't let that happen at the house. I'd let him kiss me, lick my skin, penetrate me, but not hold my hand in his. He was cool as melon, his palm not dry, not moist, the long fingers wrapping mine. And in my other hand, the hard gun.

Where the trees and shrubs began to close in again, he turned left, drawing me with him. And then we went down an avenue, a kind of path, like the paths in Lohno's garden. It might have been some lane or by-way of the city, a grassy walk off Flower Street. As we moved along it, a gurricula paced out of the trees on one side, crossed the track before us, and went in among the trees the other side. It was like a shadow, almost I seemed to see through it, but it was real. The size of a large dog, full-grown. It could have killed both of us with ease, or also I could have shot it, I suppose. It hadn't spared us a look. And we—neither of us—had slowed down or hesitated.

The avenue ended and the trees opened out, giving way to slender shiroyas with their dainty paper-chains of foliage, and beyond the land hollowed, dropped, and there, hung in vastness and distance, and below, a cliff of malachite wreathed in steam and haloed by spray, and the great fall of Water-Mama, a woman's crumble-white hair combed down and down to a shining river like an olive serpent half the world beneath.

It was beautiful. And the noise of it, and the taste of its spume, mineral as iron on the mouth.

We stood, looking. What else. It seemed, as I'd meant to be when trying to call him back, *reasonable*. This mattered. Or rather, nothing else did, much.

To one side, Laitel's side, the rock shelved up, with the shiroyas clinging, trailing their streamers. One of the old derelict temples was there, with the beehive tops I'd seen in photex prints of Calor Eye, or Angk. Stone galleries wove in and out of the rock, trooped by statues, their faces mostly smoothed away by time and wet.

As I stared, birds flew up and swirled across all the faces, the statues', the temple's.

Our hands had let go. At the same instant I must have dropped the gun. It lay in the fern at the ground's edge.

Laitel knelt down, his knees and calves folded under him. I gazed at his hair, that colour which is no colour I can name, the hair of his race, which never changes even in extreme old age, one hundred, one hundred and fifty of our years.

I felt very tired. I wanted to sit, too. So I sat, beside him. I crossed my legs and leaned my elbow on my thigh, my chin on my hand, curved forward, gazing over to the narrow river like a snake.

When it began to get dark I don't know. Sunset, presumably. I must have slept, but I hadn't moved.

Firebugs burned softly in the bushes, darting about like all those gleaming eyes I'd imagined, but now unencumbered by heads or bodies. I had an urge to coax them to my fingers. Would they come?

Stars were strewn over the sky, hardening as the light disbanded. But the sky is always less dark than the world. The starry night of space. So, could I coax down the stars?

"Laitel, we should go back to the machine."

But when I looked at him, once again, he was no longer with me.

Lohno had described this spot, or another like it, in several books. The image was recurrent—the Water-Mama Fall, the temple. Therefore, I must have seen it in post-tutor dreams. It was subtly familiar. However, I'd only realized this when I woke there, and again found Laitel had gone.

I picked my way by quite an easy path, not even very slippery from the spray, up among the trees, to the temple's first terrace. Through squat-bellied pillars, inside a cave-like hall, an eerie lamp was glowing. And I knew, as I'd known suddenly about the path, that this wasn't as bizarre as it seemed. A great globe of translucent vitreous had been set, centuries ago—as in these most ancient jungle temples now and then it was—over a small fissure, under which flickered or flared a pocket of gaseous phosphorescence from some underlying swamp. Marshfire. An intermittent yet ultimately constant light, which needed no tending.

Yet, it looked like a huge dull opal, the lamp, shimmering, magic and supernatural. I make this point because it wasn't. It had a prosaic if inspired explanation.

When I went into the cave-hall I could smell bats, and sure enough, beyond the lamp, they hung thickly in grape-or-orchid bunches from the carvings. Of the carvings themselves, I couldn't see much. I couldn't take them in. A plethora of details and also a lot time-rubbed away. Stone hands and limbs, stone smiles. Eyes lost in shadow.

Beyond the hall a shallow flight led upwards, and here two of the roofs had fallen in, and starlight shone. A tribe of starlight white monkeys sat all up the stair, one or two creatures on each step. They looked at me, but scarcely moved. One mother groomed her baby. Another female reached out and gently plucked at the hem of my loose shirt, like a beggar requesting arms. But when I turned, she softly drew her monkey fingers back and sucked them thoughtfully.

At the top of the stair was a sort of cloister, a gallery, with more blurred statues, which passed around a court below. But one side of the court had dropped away, and there one saw again the perfect view of the fall.

I hesitated halfway along the gallery, because a night bird was singing. It was the nightingale heard everywhere in Europe, Asia. Here? Perhaps the song was different in certain ways. Some notes stressed or distorted, bell-like, strident. But that bubbling trill, just the same.

Another of the phosphorous lamps burned down in the court. Some fluctuation of the gas made this lamp flutter, and the temple stones shifted, *seemed* to shift. And Laitel was there, walking towards me. He wore a white tunic and white pants, just as he had my first days at the house in the city. But he hadn't worn such clothes in the machine.

"Come this way, Frances."

What was the point in saying anything? I followed him on along the gallery, and partway around the cloister, and then into a roofless, narrow corridor. There were, in the starlight, many doors of carved sul-wood, burnished like dirty amber. Laitel opened one, and I saw into a small bare room lit by an oil lamp on a table that was otherwise covered by books and papers. At the table sat Lohno Tezmaine. I knew at once his ochre parrot face, of cruel aged-in-the-wood malevolence.

I wasn't dreaming. As infallibly, sometimes, you know yourself to be clearly awake in dreams, somehow, when awake, your very unsureness proves this is the woken state.

"How are you here?" I asked. I was casual.

"Where else? Besides, where is Here?"

"Aren't you dead?" I casually asked.

"In one form," he said.

I had the idea that of course he wasn't dead. That Laitel had stored Lohno, perhaps sedated, in some extra hidden compartment of the machine, at the same time that he stored the food, fuel and wine. Why?

"Our interview was fairly naff," he said, old-fashioned still, "wasn't it?"

"Yes."

"You weren't really interested in me."

"No?"

"You only inclined to see the city and be involved in the horrors of downfall. At least somewhat. Come and look at this."

I didn't want to approach him, but that was foolish, because he was just an unpleasant old man sitting on an upright deck-chair, in the cell of a ruin. So I went closer and he pointed out the papers in front of him.

"What about it?" I said.

"Read it. Oh, I know you never read my books. But this is my latest work."

"Continued after your death, too? That should be very interesting, a great potential commercial success."

"The first book, certainly, I've written for over 30 years."

The full light of the oil lamp was on the manuscript. I leant forward, and read the paragraph written there. It said:

"She didn't want to approach him, but that was foolish. He was simply an unpleasing specimen of masculine old age, upright on an inappropriate canvas chair, the kind once set up on the decks of liners for the elderly and sick, so they might enjoy some ocean air. But Frances was that intransigent and irritating thing, a survivor. So she went straight up to him and, when he asked her to, read the paper on the table."

I said, "You're writing about me. That's actionable, Mr Tezmaine. You've even used my given name."

"Lohno."

"Mr Tezmaine, I find it impossible to believe that all this is an elaborate hoax, arranged simply to make a fool of me and the people I work for—"

"Lohno. You don't understand. You probably will not, will *never* understand."

He drew another paper out from the untidy stacks on the table. He held it up to me. When I didn't look or take it, he read, " 'She had always wanted to see the city; that had been, really, her only reason for agreeing to interview the old man. In the first days, in the mornings before he got up, she would walk about, or take a hutsha. Being of fairly light build, a team of only six children was needed to pull her along. She always tipped them well, but not so extravagantly that they clamoured or brought others to clamour. She had learned long ago, in the cities of Asia, to be careful of such things.' "

He let the paper fall and pulled out another. He read, flatly, " 'Sex with Laitel was always strangely satisfactory. There was never any frantic struggle towards orgasm. It was a politeness between them, a social massage. But Frances suspected Laitel reserved climax, and the expulsion of seed, for women of his own race, in the interests of procreation.' "

"All right," I said. "Am I supposed to be affronted? Disgusted? Upset? What? You tell me."

"Yes, I would have to, wouldn't I?"

"Because I'm an amateur at life?"

Laitel was in the room. He was pouring pequa into two glasses, and then he brought them to us, handing Lohno Tezmaine his drink first.

I took my glass then put it down. I put my hand on the papers and pulled out, at random, another sheet, lifted it and read, from the filled, scribbled page, " 'As a child, she had been left with an unreliable aunt, real or titular, who, going to buy cigarettes, forgot Frances in a park. Under those pruned cedars of Hurlingham, Frances experienced the first of her massive disillusionments. But life would never encourage her to learn its true ways, instead slapping her down at every opportunity. And yet, still, she unwisely wished that life would change its mind and woo her back. There was still time, she was only 40, 41, for life to give her fame and glory, the crown of laurel, the undying name.' "

"How do you know?" I said. I felt blank and stern, almost righteous, not at all unnerved. As if I was playing a part.

"How do you think I know? The same way that I know that Laitel was born in the jush, an unwanted child though a boy. And how I know that, at seven years old, he saw a white tiger, in a cage, and thought it was a demon, and that he still dreams of this tiger; which species isn't, of course, normally found here."

"You know that then because Laitel must have told you. But I—"

"Laitel told me. You have told me."

"No."

"It's self-evident. How else can I know, Frances. And your mother's middle name, say. Or the story about the three little mice that made you afraid when you were nine. Or how many men you've slept with."

"I don't know that myself," I said archly.

"You do. If you think about it, you do. Otherwise I couldn't know."

"Telepathy, you're saying then."

"In a way, I suppose. A sort of telepathy."

Laitel spoke quietly. "He does know, Frances."

"He's dead. I tried his pulse. He's dead so how can he know anything?"

"You never read my books," said Lohno again, and again without the usual authorial arrogance or contempt. "You had them read to you instead by a mechanism. You've forgotten, or didn't notice, that sometimes I include myself in my books, as a character. I write first-person, and am addressed by various other characters as Tezmaine, or Lohno. Preferably the latter. I am, after all, so familiar with my characters. Any writer is. Indecently so, though inevitably. The least I can do, Frances, is generally to insist they *call* me in the familiar way, by my first name."

I stared at him. Then I glanced at Laitel. Laitel took no notice. He must, I thought, have heard this speech, or a similar speech, before. How had he responded? He hadn't. Of course he hadn't. The concept of an all-seeing, motivating, pitiless God was bad enough. But this effrontery—there could be no reply.

I picked up and drank the pequa, then held out my glass, and Laitel came back and filled it up.

Lohno Tezmaine sat smiling, smiling, like the smiles left, Cheshire-cat-like, behind on the stone temple faces below.

No reply fitting. So what to say? All my adult life, and perhaps earlier, searching doggedly for the punchline, the summing-up, quick, quirky and clean. Award-winning phrases that had never earned a mention. Too glib, or too good. Whatever. Whatever is it with me? Forever shut out, or left behind. Too late or early. Or merely redundant.

"So I'm your invention, Mr Tezmaine—oh, excuse me, Lohno. And Laitel, too?"

"All of it, Frances, actually. Here, there. City, jungle, home. Everything."

"Then you're God."

"Naturally not. Or, that is to say, only on paper."

I drank down the pequa. It tasted foul.

"Prove it," I said. "Go on."

"That would be too easy, Frances."

"Ah yes. Obviously. Oh then, you mustn't, must you."

He turned and squinted up at me. He had had, or still had, excellent eyesight, assisted by all the right contemporary medication. But now his eyes, though glittering and malign as knife-points, were slightly unfocused. He swung back over the table, took up a pen, and wrote swiftly. He handed me the paper.

I read, " 'Frances looked back, and saw, there in the doorway of the cell, Laitel's white tiger.' "

My hair stood on end. That hadn't happened in a long while. I dropped the paper on the table.

"Turn round," he said to me, Lohno Tezmaine.

"There's nothing there," I said. I looked at Laitel. "There isn't, Laitel. Or if there is, it's some illusion—hypnotism, some drug—mhash in the oil lamp, maybe. We're suggestible. Everyone is, given the proper scenario."

Laitel nodded. He smiled.

So I turned. Nothing was there. The doorway was empty. Then—

Something pale, that flicked, once, twice, tail-like, lashing, where the lamplight hit the stone of the corridor. A trick of the eyes.

"I didn't see it."

"That's true." Tezmaine leant forward and crossed out the last line he had written. "Sometimes the author makes a mistake. He pushes a subject to do something that doesn't fit, a thing either not in character, or too *intransigently* in character. Characters seldom act in character. This is the measure of a human thing, whether real or invented. A true writer will generally realize his balls-up in time. Not always. One shouldn't ever contrive. The flow of the narrative, the being of the characters themselves, they must be allowed to live their lives, and from that the plot springs, all its events and scenes. Also the landscapes, figurative and mental, in a correct book. You see, the writer need do nothing, or very little, merely observe and listen, and then factually report."

"A journalist? But that's my job, Mr Tezmaine."

"Lohno. Yes, you're right."

He raised the amended paper and read out to me, " 'But when Frances turned to face the animal in the doorway, she was only in time to glimpse the last inconclusive flick, flick of its slowly lashing tail.' " He laid the paper down. "More pequa, Laitel, please. Have some yourself. It's liberating to be out of the book now. I was getting weary, so I killed myself off, and moved into the third person, only writing about you, Frances, and about Laitel. The rest of your two lives, which I shall contrast and compare, piquantly, I hope, as we go along. No, I can't predict your lives—or very little. You'll live them, and then I shall find out. The time-scales are different, evidently, but you won't be aware of it."

"But we're *amateurs*," I said. My voice was full of rage and bitterness. It surprised me. As if I believed him and resented him as, naturally I'd have to, if it were a fact. But then, I was playing a part, playing a game. Acting.

"Yes," he said, "but *amateur* means 'lover', doesn't it. You have a *love* of life, you *amateurs*, that we professionals have to give up, when once we begin to do it, not for love, but money."

I felt a wave of tiredness sweep through me. "I'm tired," I said. "And I still need to get to the coast. Is Laitel going to drive me there?"

"I don't think so. I think he means to go back into the forests. Do you, Laitel?"

"Yes. I'm sorry, Frances."

"Wonderful. So what now?"

"There's an old road that goes straight to the coast," said Lohno, off-hand. "You'll find it and take it in the morning. That much is arranged. It's what you're good at."

"Planning to kill me off? What's it to be, maestro, a gurricula? Snake-bite? Heat exhaustion?"

"Oh, no, Frances. We've only just had *my* death. Too many are bad form, since this isn't a crime novel. You'll find the trek not too bad. A few hours walking, in the shade. You may see some animals, they'll ignore you. And of course, Laitel will give you a lunch-box."

I started laughing. Tezmaine threw back his old snake's head and laughed too. Only Laitel stood in the shadow in his white clothes, silent, demure as a bridesmaid.

In the doorway, I glanced back. "Tezmaine."

"Lohno, please."

"Lohno, *Lohno*. Am I pregnant?"

"Are you? How interesting. By Laitel, you mean? Despite non-ejaculation, some potent drip. It could be. Yes, I think you might be. Yes. What an inspiration. A child of such mixed blood, so rare. I'll enjoy this. Yes, Frances, yes, you are. *Thank you*. A girl? Almost . . . almost definitely a girl."

I walked out and went along to the end of the cloister, where the ruin had come apart. Under a leaning statue, with a smile and hands, I curled up to sleep. Presumably I wouldn't topple over the edge. Unless he decided to write me out, after all.

The stars were so bright, so scattered and patterned, numerous, planned. I've never lost my amazement at things like the stars. The pequa said to me, Nothing matters. A mad old man, Laitel in his white clothes he left behind, never packed, what I'd have to do tomorrow, walking through jungle-forest, the lunga-rook. If I did have to. My race and Laitel's, we don't, can't interbreed. Though the precautions I'd taken not to menstruate during this assignment would anyway make conception unlikely. Yet, something, some tremor, like the movement of the second hand on an antique watch. Crazy.

Once in the dark I woke. There was no reason. Nothing stirred. Only the rumble of the Water-Mama, constant as time, but a delusion because, in the end, the cliff would wear away, the waterfall decrease and become only the river.

Next morning, no one was there. Laitel wasn't, nor the old man, or his ghost, no one. The monkeys had vanished back into the jungle-forest to feed or fight or slumber. The pitted statues had lost their mystery with the light. I found some food and a bottle of water lying beside me.

I knew how to find the road. That was from his books, it must have been. It was an old processional way, used to link long-lost villages, or some ancient city of the jungle, to the temple. Curiously it wasn't very overgrown. Perhaps more modern villages kept it clear out of respect or superstition. I met with no one. I saw lemasets, and once a boar digging at the roadside with his tusks. They paid no attention.

I admit it was cooler in the shade, and the water bottle, although I economized with it, lasted me until the forest began to break up and move away from me. Then came bridges over swamp, some of stone, some swaying horizontal ladders of rope and liana. Because this was some sort of game, or because I'd temporarily gone mad, I felt it would indeed turn out as Lohno Tezmaine had told me, and it did. Beyond the swamp and the scrub was rocky land that went up and over and finally, in the afternoon, ran down to a pocket of glistening, greasy sea.

The shore was covered by people, humans of all races, like something biblical, I thought, gathered tribes, the end of the world. I stood staring at them, realizing they were there, while the sweat and the water of the air washed down into my eyes. But the transports were there too, the VTOs, and every so often a swarm of them would lift off, or another swarm of them would come in over the bay, putting down on the plasto-steel strips laid out over the water.

Before I even started to climb down, a party of soldiers found me. They were foreigners, but biologically nearer to me than the people of the jungle or the coast. When I tried to answer them though, I found I couldn't, the chip in my arm had malfunctioned. We communicated therefore in sign language, but they were cheerful, braced by their issue of performance-enhancing battle drugs. One of them kissed me on the cheek, another fondled my breast. Nothing worse. And so months after I knew that the child, for there was to be one—a boy, did Lohno change his plotline?—was Laitel's, none other's. But at that moment I might gladly have let these men do anything. They were real, they were reality. All they did was get me down to one end of the beach, then push me through the churning mass of flesh, and heave me up into a VTO, among the crying, serious, or jabbering women of their race, mine, others; among the babies and small domestic animals, and the sad or loud men, already playing cards or tuk, as if for the stake of this place, or their own best chance of existence.

Once we were on our way, a big dark soldier emerged, and sat beside me. We spoke each other's language, the now-useless chip unneeded. I was more glad of his company than I could say. He put his arm around me. We stank of sweat, both of us, and of the wet greenness of the geography we were leaving. But at World's Edge, whoever gives a damn about such things? We didn't make love, have sex. I think it was once called heavy petting, what we did, millions of lifetimes ago, or last year. Plenty of others were doing the same.

Under us, the heavy bounding drone of the VTO, solid as granite up in that space beyond all else.

My soldier left me once only during the journey, and returned with a bottle of whisky. "Drink this," he said, "take a good big drink. Cure all your blues."

εxchαnϱε ʀατε

HAL CLEMENT

Hal Clement—the writing name of longtime science teacher Harry Clement Stubbs—made his first sale in 1942 to Astounding, and became one of the mainstays of that magazine throughout the '50s and '60s, with much of his best short work appearing there. Clement's most famous novel is Mission of Gravity, which in retrospect still holds up as one of the best SF books of the '50s, although I am also fond of the underrated Cycle of Fire. Clement's influence on later writers such as G. David Nordley, Stephen Baxter, Harry Turtledove, Janet Kagan, and others is clear and unmistakable. His other books include the novels Star Light (the sequel to Mission of Gravity), Needle, Close to Critical, Iceworld, Ocean on Top, and The Nitrogen Fix, and the collections Small Changes, Natives of Space, and The Best of Hal Clement. Clement's most recent books are a new novel, Half Life, and an omnibus reprint of three of his previous novels (Needle, Iceworld, and Close to Critical), bound together as The Essential Hal Clement, Volume 1: Trio for Slide Rule and Typewriter (NESFA Press, PO Box 809, Framingham, MA 01701—$25 plus $2 postage. Volume 2: Music of Many Spheres is a collection of short fiction, bringing a lot of Clement's long unavailable work back into print.) He's also rumored to be at work on a sequel to Mission of Gravity. In 1999, Clement was given the prestigious Grandmaster Award by the Science Fiction Writers of America, an award previously won by writers such as Robert A. Heinlein and Isaac Asimov.

Although known as one of the most scrupulously accurate of the "hard science" writers, someone careful to always get the scientific details right, Clement also has a rich and lively imagination, especially when it comes to alien lifeforms, and he has created some of the most memorable alien characters in science fiction. He's outdone even himself, though, in the suspenseful novella that follows, in which harried human explorers (under pressure in more ways than one!) must try to figure out the lifeways and motivations of some extremely strange and enigmatic alien creatures on one of the strangest planets ever portrayed in science fiction—and do it all before the clock runs out.

Erni! Nic! Hold it! Senatsu's found a break!"

The speaker was excited, but neither driver bothered to look up. A "break" on Halfbaked meant little to human eyes; it was a spot where radar frequencies, not human vision, could get through the streaming and usually ionized clouds which kept starlight from the surface. Neither cared to look at stars. They were very worried men at the moment and didn't even look at each other. However, Ben Cloud kept talking, and his next words did manage to get their attention.

"It's near Hotlat plus eight and Rotlat plus eighty, close to the track they should be taking back here."

The operators of the *Quarterback* did glance at each other this time. Facial expressions didn't show through breathing masks. They didn't need to. For a moment both were silent; then the younger spoke aloud.

"Has she really spotted anything definite?"

"She thinks so. She's checking all the usable spectra now. Stand by; she should be through in a few seconds."

Quarterback's drivers looked wordlessly at each other once more, and Dominic hit the quick-cutout that brought the runabout to a halt. Operating any sort of surface vehicle on Halfbaked demanded full attention.

"Well?" said Erni. After all, a few seconds *had* passed.

"Stand by. She's still at it." A longer pause followed, until even the more patient Nic was tempted to break it, but Ben resumed before either listener actually gave in.

"She says yes! It's *Jellyseal*'s pattern."

"Anything from the girls?"

"No, but *Jelly*'s moving apparently under control and at a reasonable speed."

"What's that? Or can Sen tell?" cut in the elder driver.

"The tanker's doing about a hundred and eighty kilos an hour. Must be open country."

"How's she measuring that?"

"Tell you soon. Sen's taking all the advantage she can of the break, but it'll take a while to cross-check with memory. They'll probably have to move a bit farther, too."

"If the speed is real, they've probably unloaded."

"Probably. Maria reported they'd reached what seemed to be the broadcast site and found something city-ish, though she never really described it. That was nearly twenty hours ago as you both know. That was about five hundred kilos outward of where they seem to be now. They could have emptied, loaded up again, and easily be at Sen's current fix. You can stop worrying."

"And the natives *did* acknowledge receipt of the shipment, and even said how delighted they were, didn't they?" asked Dominic. "But no more word was coming from Maria and Jessi. That's the picture we had from Tricia before we started."

"She was firm about the acknowledgment, yes. Still is. You know how she waffles when a message seems to involve abstractions, though. They were very repetitious, she says, talking about how they understood why we couldn't send pure hydrogen and commenting again and again on the wide variety of compounds there were anyway—"

"I got all that. Paraffin, whether you're speaking European or North American Anglic, does have a lot of different hydrogen compounds in it. I'm admitting we know the girls got there, but still wondering why we haven't heard from them since. We'll stop worrying—maybe—when they say something." Erni's tone suggested strongly that he wanted no advice as he went on, "You say they're backtracking? Using the same route?"

"Senatsu hasn't had a long enough look-see to tell. They're just about on the path they took earlier, I gather, but remember we didn't see them get to it. We did map more than half of it outbound, but I'd say—"

"We know all that!" snapped Erni. "What I want to know is whether Nic and I should keep on and try to meet them."

"I'd say no. It made sense to head for the transmission source when they seemed to be stuck there, but now we know they're moving and presumably heading back here, it seems smarter to wait for them here at Nest."

"But suppose they still don't report? How long do we wait? And what could keep them from talking to us, anyway?"

"The same sorts of things that keep us from seeing them as often as we'd like. We're talking to you all right now, but you're only a few hundred k's away using multiple channel cross-link. They're nearly fifty thousand. We can see even you only occasionally—less often than we can see them, since there are more clouds here on the dark side. You know all that as well as anyone. Halfbaked wasn't built for long-range talking. It has too many kinds of clouds, too many kinds and strengths of charge dancing around in them, too many winds high and low and up and down and sideways and circular, too much pure distance—"

"And natives who use AM communication but still make some sense. I know all that!" snapped Icewall.

"Then please talk as though you did." Ben was getting a little short, too. "Look, I know you're worried, and I know why, even if I don't have a shared name yet. It's too bad the girls won the draw for the first load, but even you didn't try to change it so Nic could go with Maria or you with Jessi. They went. They really weren't in any more danger pushing a tanker around the landscape than at Nest, except for being farther from help if they needed it, of course. It isn't as though this idiotic world had any nice stable places where you could put up a building and go to sleep with reasonable hope the ground wouldn't pull apart under it before you woke up. I know your wives haven't talked to us since they reported spotting their city, or village, or whatever it turned out to be. That's a fact. I don't dispute it, and I can't account for it except with guesses I can't support. So go ahead and worry. I can't stop you, and I wouldn't if I could. They're your wives. I still think, though, that you'll be smarter waiting for them here than going thirty or forty thousand kilos, a lot of it in sunlight, and trying to find them while they're still moving and we can't keep good contact, visual or verbal, with either of you."

"I suppose you're right," Erni admitted in a much meeker tone. "Nic? You think we'd better go back, too?"

Dominic Wildbear Yucca—Maria might no longer be alive but he was still entitled to their jointly chosen name because of their children—nodded silently, and without further words looked carefully around through the windows ringing the cockpit. One looked before moving anywhere on Halfbaked. Neither window nor roof port was made of glass; there were too many fluorine compounds in Halfbaked's atmosphere for silicate materials to be trusted. Silicon tetrafluoride is a gas even at most Terrestrial temperatures. Satisfied that no serious landscape change had sneaked by his notice during the talk, he repowered the driving system—stopping was nearly always safer than starting, and the control system reflected that fact—and sent the runabout into a fairly tight turn. The path was wide enough to need little steering care at the moment, though bushes, rocks which had rolled from the modest hills, cracks in the surface, and patches of vegetation which might or might not be on fire could be encountered any time.

The spaceward side of Halfbaked was well covered with what looked to human beings like plant life, though its actual ecological role was still being argued. No animals had yet been seen, unless some of the large and small objects resembling fragments of burned paper which seemed to be borne on the fierce winds were actually flying instead. There was evidence on some of the plants that things were eating them, but the pool for the first confirmed animal sighting was still unclaimed after five Terrestrial months. Two schools of thought were developing among the biologists: the katabolic part of the ecology was being handled by microbes, or was being taken care of by fire.

Drivers could devote very little of their attention to specimen search while their machines were in motion. The *Quarterback* trembled slightly as it moved, partly from ground irregularities, occasionally from temblors, and mostly from winds of constantly varying violence and direction. At their present height above the reference ellipsoid—Halfbaked had no seas to provide an altitude zero—the pressure averaged about seventeen atmospheres, wavering irregularly and on a time scale of minutes by about two each way. With its molecular weight averaging well over a hundred, wind was both difficult and unsafe to ignore.

Dominic nursed the vehicle up to nearly two hundred kilometers per hour. There were few obstacles now in sight, and the red and green deeplights flashing alternately from their masts on each side of the runabout provided shadow patterns easily interpreted as range information. It was better than computer-backed radar in the continuous howl of microwave and longer static emitted by the local plants. The lights also allowed human-reflexive response time; glancing back and forth between the outside and a screen, no matter how precise and detailed the latter's readings might be, would have put a much lower limit on permissible driving speed much of the time.

Erni kept his hands away from the controls, but watched their surroundings as carefully as his partner. Both could see in all directions even here on night side, since a bank of floods supplemented the deeplights and there was nearly continuous and fairly bright lightning among the clouds overhead. Halfbaked, less than eight million kilometers from the center of its G3-to-4 sun, had plenty of energy to expend on luminous, biological, and even comprehensible local phenomena.

The driver did cast an occasional glance at his younger companion. He would never have admitted that Erni could be more worried about Jessi than he himself was about Maria, but the Icewalls had been married less than three years as against the Yuccas' fourteen, and might possibly be less philosophical about the unpredictability of life.

Apparently greater worry was not hurting Erni's driving judgment, though. His "Watch it!" from the right-side station was essentially simultaneous with Nic's cutting out drive again. *Quarterback* came to a quick halt, but not a smooth one.

Active faults don't move smoothly; even on Earth they cause quakes, often violent ones. Under more than seven Earth gravities, the quakes tend to be much more frequent and no less violent. Both drivers floated quietly at their stations and watched; there was nothing else to do until what they saw made detailed sense.

The fault could be seen half a kilometer ahead, though rain was starting to fall, but there were no hills close enough to offer a threat of slides or rockfalls. If there had been, it was likely that not even trained driver reflexes could have coped with all the probabilities, and more worry would have been in order.

The ground movement was largely horizontal, they could see and feel. The fault started from some indeterminate point to their left, slanted across in front, and extended out of sight ahead and to their right. It did have a small vertical component; the far side had lifted nearly half a meter since they had passed the level site less than an hour before. Rather casually, Erni reported their stopping and the reason for it to Nest; Ben acknowledged with equal aplomb.

"Unless it gets a good deal higher, we won't have any trouble in getting past," Icewall concluded.

"If it's still shaking, maybe you ought to get by before it rises any more," was the answering suggestion. Erni glanced at his partner, nodding thoughtfully.

"You have a point. All right. We'll send out bugs to see if it's any lower within a kilo or two, and climb at the best place. We'll call you when we start. If you don't hear from us in two or three minutes after that, someone come out and collect the evidence."

"If we can spare anyone." That point also was well taken, though too obvious to all concerned to be worthy of answer. Energy was essentially limitless thanks to ubiquitous miniature fusion units, and self-reproducing pseudolife equipment was almost equally so as long as there was no shortage of raw material; but personnel on a world like Halfbaked was another matter entirely.

The servobugs guided them to a spot a few hundred meters to the right. The men called them back, powered up again and sent the runabout slowly toward the infant cliff, stopping again some two meters away. Both operators watched carefully for a minute or so. A slip of a millimeter or two every few seconds was accompanied by more shock waves. One could only guess whether an especially large jolt was waiting to be triggered by the car's weight, but the regularity of the motions themselves was encouraging. Nic retracted the dozen wheels on which they had been traveling and let the body settle onto its caterpillar treads; then, for reasons he didn't bother to state, he motioned Erni to take over. The latter obeyed in equal silence. Even more slowly than before, *Quarterback* eased forward until the treads touched the tiny escarpment and the front of the vehicle began to lift.

The frequent small shocks became much easier to feel but no more worrisome. The men could see the front of the vehicle lifting but not feel it; up and down, even under heavy gravity, were not obvious except by sight to people floating in water—and sight needed a better reference horizon than this world with its vast size and short atmospheric scale height could provide.

Tension mounted as the mass center of the vehicle approached the edge. Both men clenched their fists and held their breaths as it passed and the machine rocked forward.

In theory, the runabout wouldn't buckle even if its entire fourteen-hundred-ton mass—some ten thousand tons weight, here—were supported only at the center. Nesters, however, tended to have an engineering bias toward regarding such theory mainly as a guide for planning experiments. This sort of experiment had been done before but not, as far as either driver knew, with acceleration from seismic waves helping out the gravity.

The body did hold. The impact as it finished rocking forward and the front touched down was gentle, somewhat cushioned by a patch of half-meter-wide, viciously spined growths resembling barrel cacti. Dark red, almost black, fluid which spattered from these crusted over almost at once as the air touched it, but slightly to the men's surprise they did not ignite.

A moment later *Quarterback* was resuming speed with Erni still driving. Nic reported their new status to Nest, added encouraging details about the stresses just survived, and asked for an update on the tanker.

"Still moving, still apparently on the way back," replied Ben. "Average speed about a hundred sixty."

"Did they really slow down, or is that just a better measure?" Nic barely beat his friend to the question.

"The latter, Senatsu thinks. But they're coming, almost certainly backtracking on their original path. They're not heading straight toward Nest, but nearly Hot-south toward the dark side. We're wondering now whether the original guess about travel being better out of the sunlight was right, or if they have some other reason. There's still no direct word from the girls."

The flotation water was clear enough to show part of Erni's frown above his breathing mask, but he said nothing. The clusters of spiky barrels were becoming more numerous, and even though he knew contact would not harm the *Quarterback* he disliked casual destruction.

The drive settled down to routine. *Quarterback* didn't have far to go by Half-baked standards. They had barely started their trip to the "city" reported by *Jellyseal*'s drivers, which was nearly fifty thousand kilometers from Nest along a geodesic and much farther by realistic standards. The topography seldom allowed a completely free choice of path, and it had seemed wise to make most of the journey out of sunlight as long as there was no obvious reason for haste. Keeping the cargo below its boiling point would be much easier, for one thing.

Now, of course, the cargo should be different.

The husbands, when voice contact had been lost, had been worried and planned to take the geodesic route rather than follow the mapped track of the *Jellyseal*, but they were still on the night side less than a thousand kilometers from Nest when they turned back.

The temblors from the shifting fault grew less intense as they moved away from it. This might be due to increasing distance or to actual quieting down of the disturbance. There was plenty of seismic equipment at Nest, and the quakes had probably been detected there; but until a far more extensive network could be set up there would be no way to pick particular ones out of the continuous rumblings and quiverings originating throughout the huge world's crust and mantle.

Neither driver thought of blaming other Nesters for failing to warn them about the obstacle just passed. Satellite mapping through charged clouds was difficult, and anyone away from the base was on his own—or on their own; no vehicles went out with less than two crew members, and no one went out walking. Suits which would let a human being take a step in seventeen atmospheres pressure and over seven Earth gravities, even though Nest had been built in a region of human-tolerable temperature, were not available anywhere.

Techniques *had* been planned for transferring people from a crippled vehicle to a rescue machine, but so far these had not been tested in genuine emergencies. Also they depended on the cripple's not being too badly bent out of shape. Doors had to open . . .

The *Quarterback* had to slow down after an hour or so, as the rain increased. The drops were not staying on the ground, but boiling off as soon as they struck; the resulting mist, rather than the rain itself, was blocking vision. The black, blowing flakes had vanished, whether as a result of blocked vision or because they were washed to the ground could only be guessed. What was falling was anyone's guess, too; presumably fluorine compounds, but emphatically not water. Hydrogen was far scarcer on this world than on Mars or even Mercury.

Dominic made one of his thoughtful weather analyses as the rain slowed them.

"There's a high ridge back of us and to the right, remember? Surface wind seems to be toward the day side as usual, so the air is being pushed up and cooling adiabatically as it reaches the hills. Something's condensing out, maybe oxides of sulfur or fluorides of sulfur or silicon. We ought to get out of it in a few kilos."

The prediction, especially the phrase "as usual," took Erni's mind off his worries for a moment. This world's weather was quite literally chaotic; the word "climate" meant nothing.

"How much'll you bet?"

Nic glanced over at his partner, thankful that his own face was invisible. "Well-l-l—" He let his voice trail off.

"Come on. You're not going to cut off my best source of income, are you?"

"You should work for a living, but all right. Fifty says we're in clear air in—oh, twenty kilos."

"You're on. Check the odometer." Yucca zeroed one of the wheel counters. *Quarterback* had been off the tracks since leaving the quake site. "Not that one, friend. It's center right, not a driver, off the ground a lot of the time, and you know it." Still glad that his face couldn't be seen, the prophet activated a driving-wheel meter.

Erni rather pointedly made sure it was actually counting, his divided attention almost at once giving Dominic a chance to distract him even further.

"Watch it. Boulder." The runabout swerved rather more than was really necessary, grazing an asparagus-like growth three or four meters high and knocking it over before Icewall steadied. Neither looked at the other this time, but the driver did not slow down. Yucca decided that no more needed to be done for a while to stop his friend from worrying. After all, he himself couldn't help wondering why there had no been word from *Jellyseal*. Ben's explanation had been plausible, but still . . .

They were still in rain, though quite probably a different sort—Nic could have been partly right—an hour later. The odometer had been stopped and, after a coin had passed from Nic's possession to Erni's, rezeroed. There had been two or three more reports from Nest; the errant tank was still traveling, more or less in the expected direction, but still no word had come from its occupants.

"I wonder what they're bringing back," Dominic ventured after a long silence. "The natives didn't get very specific about what they could trade, though they seemed to want the hydrogen badly enough."

"According to Tricia," Erni amended. "Desire's a pretty abstract concept too, you know."

"They repeated the request enough times and enough different ways so even she was pretty sure. And you can see why scientists here want the stuff." Icewall merely nodded at the obvious.

Beings on Halfbaked at all versed in the physical sciences would presumably have detected Element One in the spectrum of their sun, looked for it on the planet, probably learning a lot of chemistry in the process, and possibly found the traces accumulated in the crust by eight billion years or so of stellar wind. The urge for enough to do macroscopic research would have matched that of the discoverers of helium and plutonium on Earth, not to mention the seekers for coronium before spectroscopic theory matured. The human explorers on Halfbaked had understood and sympathized. They had designed and grown the paraffin tanker some humorist with a background in historical trivia had named the *Jellyseal*, loaded it with high molecular weight hydrocarbons from the brown dwarf thirty-odd astronomical units out from 51 Pegasi, and sent it to the apparent source of the native transmissions. Communication was still vague, but there seemed a reasonable hope that something of use to human knowledge would come back. Attendant risks to human health and life were taken for granted and accepted.

Except, to some extent and for the time being, by the spouses of the *Jellyseal*'s drivers.

The two men drove, ate, and slept in turn. They felt their way through rain and fog—or maybe it was dust—held their breaths as they threaded narrow valleys where falling rocks could not possibly have been avoided, enjoyed an occasional glimpse of still unfamiliar constellations, speculated aloud about an occasional unusually large blowing object, felt the *Quarterback* tremble in gales which came and ceased with no apparent pattern (though Dominic still tried, usually adding to Erni's cash reserves), asked without result whether there had been word from their wives, listened to the constant exchange of messages with the natives which were slowly expanding a mutually useful scientific vocabulary, and drew steadily closer to Nest.

The word about the tanker's motions remained encouraging; it appeared to be under intelligent control. The best evidence appeared when the *Quarterback* was about an hour out from the base. It took the form of a report from Senatsu Ito Yoshihashi which was not, at first glance, encouraging.

"The girls are headed for trouble, I'm afraid," she said thoughtfully to Ben.

"How?"

"The path they took out has changed, about a hundred kilometers ahead of where they are now. What was a fairly narrow valley—a couple of kilos wide— seems to have been blocked up by something. It's filling with some sort of liquid, as well as I can interpret the images. At least, its surface is now remarkably level and higher than before, and if it were freezing I'd expect crystals to do something to the reflection somewhere along the spectrum."

"Can't they travel on it anyway?" Cloud was tying *Quarterback* into the communication link as he spoke. "The tanker should float on any liquid I can imagine at dayside temperature, and the tracks would drive it after a fashion."

"It's the 'after a fashion' part that bothers me," the observer/mapper replied. "I *think*, though I'm not at all sure, that the stuff is spilling out the darkside— Hotsouth—end of the valley; and whether it's a real liquid-fall or just rapids, I'm doubtful anything human-grown can hold together in either."

"They'll see the lake or whatever it is and at least know better than to go boating," was Erni's surprisingly optimistic response.

"But what can they do if they want to take another path?" asked Dominic. "Would the maps they started with be any help? Especially the way the topography changes? Wouldn't they just wind up wandering around in a maze? I'd hate to have tried this trip without your guiding us."

"I suggest," responded Ben slowly, "that Sen recheck their general area as thoroughly and quickly as she can. Then she can work out as good an alternate path as possible, and we'll send it to the girls. They're not transmitting, but we don't know they're not receiving."

"Why didn't we call them and ask them to stop, or travel in a circle, or something like that a long time ago?" asked Erni. He carefully avoided sounding critical, since he had to include himself in the list of people who hadn't thought of this.

"Ask Pete. I'm not a psychologist," Ben replied. "Sen, what sort of topo information do you have for that area?"

"Pretty good, both current and from the original route pix. Give me a few minutes to match images and check for changes."

Even Erni remained silent until the mapper's voice resumed. She did stay within the few minutes.

"All right. Thirty kilos ahead of where they are now, they should turn thirty degrees to the right. Another ten kilos will take them into a valley narrow enough to be scary; they should wait, if they feel any temblors, until things seem to quiet down, and then get through as fast as possible. I can't resolve the area well enough to guess how fast that would be. Once through they can slow down if they want — there'll be no risk of rockfalls for a while. Seventy more kilos will take them past the lake, and they can slant to the left as convenient. That will bring them back to the original path sooner or later. They can check whether there's a river in it now. I'd like to know; I've seen plenty of what looked like little lakes, plus the big one at the native transmission site, but nothing that looked like flowing water — it wouldn't be water, you know what I mean — so far. Got it?"

Ben had been making a sketch map as Sen spoke. He used a polymer sheet and an electric stylus, rather than pencil and paper, since the Nest was also under seven-plus gees and its personnel had the same need of flotation as the drivers. Most of the personnel referred to their rest-and-recreation periods in the orbiting station farther out from the star as "drying-out" sessions, although much of the time in them was spent in baths. Recycling equipment is never quite perfect.

"I think so." Cloud held his product in front of the pickup — his station was more than a hundred meters from Senatsu's — for her to check.

"Close as I can put it," she agreed. "See if you can get it through to the girls."

Nic and his companion lacked the visual connection, but listened with critical interest as the word went out. Ben didn't have to include them in his transmission net, but it never occurred to him not to. Both drivers looked at each other and nodded slowly as the first message ended; the mental picture they got from it matched the one they had formed from Senatsu's words. They didn't actually stop listening as Ben set a record of his words repeating again and again to the relay/observation satellites, but most of their attention went back to the *Quarterback* as they resumed travel. They were now only an hour or so from Nest, but that was no reason to ease up on caution. They could die just as easily and completely at or inside the station's entry lock as anywhere else on the world.

Fallen rock areas. Risk-of-falling-rock regions. Puddles to be avoided — the liquid could easily be something that would freeze on wheels or in tracks if the temperature dropped a Kelvin or two. It could even be a subcooled liquid waiting to freeze on contact; such things did occur, and there was no way to tell just by looking. Stands of organisms which *could* be smashed through, but which would also produce liquid. Some of these were quite tall; Erni had never visited Earth and was not reminded of Saguaro Reserve, but most worlds with life have xerophytes. Usually the biggest growths were widely enough spaced to avoid easily, but some of the others grew in nearly solid mats.

The men had often driven over the present area, and both noticed that some fairly tall specimens seemed now to cluster along the outward path they had crushed a day or so earlier. Possibly these used the remains of other organisms as nourishment. If so, they grew *fast*.

Nothing corresponding to animal life ever showed itself, and many seriously doubted its presence; but some of the "plants" showed stumps where trunks, branches, or twigs had obviously been severed, though the detached fragments could seldom be seen. Tendrils would still be lashing, as though their owners had been disturbed by something moments before the *Quarterback* passed.

Some of the Nest personnel were beginning to suspect that the number of plantlike growths and patches within ten or fifteen kilometers of the station was increasing as the days passed, but no one had yet made a careful study of the possibility. It might be interesting, but was not yet obviously important.

Quartermaster was in a relatively open space when Ben's voice caused Erni to cut drive reflexively.

"They're turning, she thinks." The lack of nouns bothered neither driver; they didn't even bother to ask, "Which way?" They simply floated at their stations and listened. The oxygen monitor in *Quarterback* recorded a sharp drop in breathing rate, but not for long enough to cause it to report an emergency. Cloud would probably not have been bothered by such an alarm anyway; unlike the monitor, he was human.

Senatsu improvised quickly. The atmosphere was fairly clear around her target at the moment, and she was able to set up an interferometric tie between the tanker's reflector and a nearby bright spot—a stationary one, she hoped. This let her measure the relative motions of the two within a few centimeters per second. It took less than half a minute to show that *Jellyseal*'s direction of motion was changing, and another minute and a half established that the machine had straightened out on a new course thirty degrees to the right of the earlier one.

Coincidences do happen, but human minds tend to doubt even the real ones. For the first time in many hours, *Quarterback*'s drivers really relaxed. The remaining distance back to Nest was covered calmly and happily, though neither man remembered later much of the conversation which passed. With anyone.

The reception lock had been readied for them, its water pumped into a standby tank, and the doors opened as they approached. Dominic eased the runabout inside and powered down as the door sealed. The two waited while water flowed back, pushing the local air which had entered with them out through the roof vents, and was tested. As usual, more time was needed to neutralize the sulfuric and sulfurous acids and to precipitate and filter out the fluorides formed when the air had met the liquid, but at last they could open their own outer seal, check their personal breathing kits, and swim to one of the personnel locks occupying two walls of the "garage." Erni pointedly allowed Dominic to precede him into the main part of the structure, though the latter was not entirely happy at receiving attention due to age. Fifteen years out of fifty wasn't that much of a difference, and he was the taller and stronger of the two.

Of course, it was a relief to know the youngster had stopped worrying enough to be polite.

Jellyseal had been about a month—more parochially, seven years—on its way to the native city, or settlement, or camp, or whatever it might be. By the end of the first day after the return of the no-longer-anxious husbands, it seemed likely that about as long would be needed for its return. Perhaps, Senatsu remarked hesitantly, a little bit less. "They're making slightly better time right now than they did going out, but they're still on the sun side, and will be for days yet. They can see better, after all. When they get to the real terminator we can find out how much they have to slow down. They'll be easier for me to see in the dark, too."

This remark was no surprise to her listeners. The tanker of course carried corner reflectors for the microwave beams from the satellites, and with less reflected sunlight, and thermal and biological emission from the planet's surface the contrast between vehicle and surroundings would be a lot better. All this except the greater plant emission on the day side had been discovered, and much of it predicted, long before. Nic and Erni, together as usual and just returned from a test drive, simply nodded at Senatsu's report, and went on about their routine work.

Much of this involved the preparation of the second tanker, already being called *Candlegrease*. Most of the staff were from colony worlds where conditions were still fairly primitive, and in any case human educators had had the importance of detailed history knowledge forced on them after the species began to scatter. Candles had no more disappeared from humanity's cultural memory than had cooking—including making jelly.

It had occurred to several people that towing a paraffin tank as a trailer might involve less trouble in a number of ways, and possibly even be safer for the crew, than driving one as a tank truck. It was taken for granted that another load of hydrocarbons would go to the natives, even though no one yet knew what value the material now coming back might turn out to have. There was a natural sympathy for the needs of researchers, and at the very least whatever it was couldn't help but supply information about the natives themselves. *Jellyseal's* slow approach was being watched with interest by everyone, not just the waiting husbands.

Nearly all the labored communication with the native city dealt with science; most of the linguistic progress that had been made so far had come from computer correlation between human vehicle motions, which the natives seemed able to observe even at great distances, and radiation emitted and received from the observing satellites. Discussions tended to consist of comments about orbital perturbations and precessions and their connection with the planet's internal structure. Computers at Nest were gradually building a detailed map of Halfbaked's inner density distribution and, more slowly, a chart of its mantle currents. Not surprisingly for a planet a hundred and seventy-seven times Earth's mass, almost five times its radius, and over seven times its surface gravity, plate tectonics was occurring at what the planetary physicists considered meteorological speed; and the plates themselves were state- or city rather than continent-size. This made travel interesting and mapmaking an ongoing process. Since the establishment of Nest, one couple who had arrived as meteorologists had shifted over to crustal dynamics and been welcomed. They had been rather glad to make the change, though a little embarrassed at flinching from a challenge. Halfbaked's atmosphere had a dozen major components, mainly but not only fluorides and oxides of sulfur and silicon, varying in completely chaotic fashion in relative amounts with time and location and ready to change phase with small variations in temperature, pressure, input from the sun, and each other's concentration.

Reliance on miracles was not, of course, a useful solution to any problem; but some of the staff occasionally, and of course very privately, felt slightly tempted. After all, the supernatural could hardly be *much* less useful at prediction than the math models produced so far.

So what talk there was with the natives tended to be on the physical and material rather than emotional planes. Even mathematical abstractions, critical as they were to chemical discussion, were not progressing well. It was not even certain that the others knew—or cared—about the returning tanker.

Tricia Whirley Feather, responsible for the final steps in guessing what the computer-derived translation attempts might actually mean, was just about certain the paraffin shipment had been received and appreciated. She had no idea whatever what, if anything, was being sent back in exchange. She was not at all certain that the concept of "exchange" was clear to the natives.

But *Candlegrease* was nevertheless being grown and modified outside in the Halfbaked environment, where the more serious planning errors should show up quickly. An overpowered and overweight runabout, named *Annie* from another ancient literary source, and intended to tow the carrier, had been more or less finished. At least it was driveable and Erni and Dominic were testing it. There was little general doubt that these two would make the second trip, though Ben had some personal reservations. These were finally resolved almost by accident.

The regular planetological work of the station was kept up, of course. More than two dozen satellites, in orbits out to about ten thousand kilometers above the surface, were cooperating with a seismic net slowly spreading out from Nest in working out the planet's internal structure, surface details, and atmospheric behavior. Progress was at about two doctoral theses per hour, Ben Cloud estimated.

And, presumably, each hour was also bringing Jessi Ware Icewall and Maria Flood Yucca seventy or eighty kilometers closer to their husbands. *Jellyseal* was making good speed.

She was also getting close to the dark side.

Actual construction of the new tanker system was going well enough, whenever decisions could be made; pseudolife techniques had taken most of the delays and difficulties out of actually making things. The problems of designing them remained, however. Ideas which seemed great by themselves would turn out to be incompatible with other equally wonderful ones when people attempted to grow them together. Whole assemblies which had promised well in computer simulation were embarrassing failures when grown and tried out. The communication lapse from *Jelly* was more than worrisome; her crew, who had the ordinary skills at pseudolife design even if they were not actually experts, presumably had far more knowledge relevant to the problem than anyone else on the planet.

The supposedly straightforward problem of traction on unknown surfaces for a vehicle expected to tow several times its own weight was attaining Primary status. Erni, Dominic, and several other sets of drivers were kept busy on test runs which ran, too often, straight into a new problem. Sometimes they didn't think of their wives for whole hours, though they never failed to check in with Senatsu when they came back in.

"They'll be seeing the last of the sun in an hour or two," the analyst remarked at one of these meetings when the return distance still to be covered had shrunk to about thirty thousand kilometers geodesic. "They're already a lot easier to spot, and don't seem to be having any trouble finding their way. They've swerved two or three times, but never very far, and apparently for things like that fault of yours.

That, by the way, is now about three meters high and seems to be still growing; it's lucky it's not on their return path. I've suggested that Ben send someone out to see how much horizontal shift it's shown. I can't tell from satellite—can't get sharp enough ground motion details without a set of retroreflectors at a known location. Want to make the run?"

Dominic shrugged. "Okay with us, if Ben calls it. We might as well be doing something."

"You are already, it seems to me. Well, we'll let him call it. If he thinks you'll be better off growing up with *Candlegrease* and *Annie* then someone else can go. Or no one, of course, if he doesn't think it's important enough."

Cloud, after only a second or two of thought, decided the information was important enough to rate a close look, and six hours later—people still had to sleep—*Quarterback* was heading away from Nest on a Hotpole bearing of about seventy degrees, with her usual drivers aboard.

Some changes along the track could be seen almost at once. The tall growths which seemed to be springing up where vegetation had been crushed on their first trip out were now much taller. What had looked like two-meter stalks of deep red, dark brown, and dead black asparagus now resembled giant saguaros with, in many cases, the bases of what had been separate stalks now grown together. A former clump or thicket now seemed like a single plant with multiple branches probing upward. Neither driver liked the idea of trying to plow through these, so progress became much slower and less direct. Sometimes they had to retrace some distance and try a new route. Eventually they settled for paralleling their former path rather than trying to follow it.

They speculated over the chance that the organisms they had casually pulped the first trip out might be serving as food for saprophytes, and reported the idea back to Ben. Ten minutes later he told them to collect specimens. The xenobiologists also wanted data. Life on a virtually hydrogen-free world needed investigating. Especially life whose carbon content far exceeded ninety percent, as well as zero hydrogen.

Collecting would have slowed them even more, but Erni and Nic decided to do it on the way back and rolled on, with the fence of organ pipes to their right and a relatively clear path ahead.

The quakes produced by the still active fault made themselves felt well before the actual structure came in sight, and *Quarterback* was slowed accordingly. The operators stopped a short distance from the scarp, which was now, as Senatsu had reported, over two meters high. The big saprophytes, if that's what they were, were not doing very well in the quake area, and no longer formed a barrier. It was therefore possible to follow the verge to the right for several kilometers; but no practical way down could be found. Neither man trusted the structure of their vehicle enough to drive over the edge under local gravity, even without the problem of getting back up. Also, even if the body had survived, the impact would probably have treated the men like dynamited fish.

Servobugs—waldo-controlled pseudolife vehicles ranging from ten centimeters to half a meter in length and eight kilograms to nearly eight hundred in weight—

were of course cheap, and they wasted one of the smallest and presumably sturdiest in a test drop over the edge. It did not survive, but the sacrifice was considered worthwhile.

At this point Senatsu made another report, changing Ben's plans and frustrating several xenobiologists. *Jellyseal* had passed out of the sunlit zone, and seemed to be having trouble finding its way. Guidance information had been sent from Nest as before.

This time it was not followed.

Requests to stop and perform specific maneuvers to show that Nest's messages were being received also went unheeded, or at least unanswered.

Ben, knowing his personnel, promptly suggested that *Quarterback* drop its present mission and try to intercept the tanker. After all, things might as well be official, and the husbands would certainly do this anyway. Senatsu and her helpers would do their best to provide guidance starting from the runabout's current position.

There was no need to go back to Nest for supplies, since all the vehicles had full recycling capacity and adequate energy sources. Knowing this had discouraged Cloud from even thinking of sending anyone but the two husbands. Upon hearing of the new behavior, and without even waiting for the first guidance messages, Erni swung their vehicle Hoteast—a quadrant to the right of the line toward Hotpole—and slanted away from the scarp. Haste was not exactly a priority with the two drivers, since they would be many days on the way whatever the machine driven by their wives might do, but there would be no delay. Worry was back in charge.

The geodesic connecting the two vehicles of course no longer crossed into Hotside, rather to Ben's annoyance. He wanted more detailed information about the problems of driving in sunlight, for use in future mission planning. His nature, however, was practical as well as sympathetic, and he made no suggestion to either Senatsu or the *Quarterback*'s drivers about slanting a bit to the left if opportunity occurred. Two or three times in the next weeks he had brief hopes that the only practical path the mappers could find might lead a little way into sunlight, but each time he was disappointed.

Erni and Nic were not. They were worried—still no word from their wives— and frustrated as Senatsu guided them through a maze of hillocks, around obstacles organic and topographical, past puddles and lakes of unknown composition, and once for over fifty kilometers paralleling a cliff about as high as silicate rock could be expected to lift against Halfbaked's gravity. She had warned them against getting within a kilometer of the edge of this scarp; they were on the high side, and there was no way of telling whether or when the tonnage of *Quarterback* combined with the fantastically rapid erosion by the fluoride-rich wind and rain would trigger collapse of the whole section of landscape. Being part of a seven-gee landslide would not be noticeably better than being under one. She had only used the route at all because it offered tens of kilometers of relatively flat surface which would permit maximum speed; and even then, she and Cloud had debated the idea for some time with Nic and Erni out of the comm net.

No one felt very much better when, some ten hours after the *Quarterback*'s passage, the cliff did collapse in four or five places as far in as the runabout's track.

"I wonder," Nic remarked when Ben relayed this information, "whether I'll yield to temptation a few years from now. It'd be so easy to turn ten hours into ten seconds when I'm telling about this to the kids."

Then of course it was too late to bite his tongue off. Erni, who was driving at the time, said nothing for several seconds; then his only words were, "I'm sure I would."

The *Jellyseal* was making poor progress, according to the satellite observations. Time and again she seemed to have headed into a dead-end path and had to backtrack. One encouraging fact was that the same mistake was never made twice; it looked as though the drivers were on the job. No one could yet believe that the following of the earlier instruction had been coincidence, so the general idea was now that whatever had gone wrong earlier with the tanker's transmitters had now spread to the receivers as well. What this might be seemed unknowable until the machinery could be checked at first hand; all the communication gear in every vehicle on the planet was multiply redundant. Disabling it should take deliberate and either highly skilled or savagely extensive sabotage.

No one could suggest a plausible or even credible motive for either the drivers or the natives to do such a thing, and it seemed highly unlikely that the latter would have the requisite specific skills in spite of their obvious familiarity with microwave transmission. Knowledge of principles does not imply ability to design or repair complex unfamiliar equipment.

But the tanker remained silent and apparently deaf, though it continued to move as though guided by intelligence.

"At least," remarked Erni after they had received another report from Senatsu that their target was once more backtracking, "They're not forcing us to make changes in *our* path. If the girls had actually been making headway back home, we'd have had to change our own heading all the time."

"Come on, young man," came Senatsu's indignant voice. "Don't you think I'd have been able to work out a reasonable intercept for you? I wouldn't have kept you heading for where they were at the moment. I know you're worried, but don't get insulting."

She was not really indignant, of course, and Erni knew it, and she knew Erni knew it. The art of trying to keep the youngster's mind off his troubles was now being widely practiced at Nest. It was lucky that most of the divergently planned help efforts had to funnel through one person.

In a way Erni knew all that, too. Oddly enough, the knowing did help. People may resent pity, but honest sympathy is different; it lacks the condescension.

Maybe that was why so few people seemed to feel that Dominic needed help, too.

Actually, the efforts were not really necessary most of the time. The journey itself was far from boring. The basic need for constant alertness when running at high speed across poorly known topography left little time for unrelated thoughts while on duty, and caused enough fatigue to ensure deep sleep between hitches.

The world itself was different enough from anything familiar to human explorers; it took much of the attention not needed for guiding the runabout.

Not all of the differences were obvious to the operators. Power consumption of the vehicle, for example, recorded at Nest, indicated that it spent over two thousand kilometers climbing one side and descending the other of a three-kilometer-high dome; Nic and Erni heard only indirect echoes of the arguments as scientists tried to match this information with that from satellites and seismograms.

The assumption that the world had a nearly equipotential surface, with strength of crustal materials essentially meaningless, was presumed to be even truer here than on any merely one-gee planet. The drivers had not noticed the changes in actual power needed to keep a given speed; they merely knew they were three thousand kilometers closer to where they wanted to be.

They could tell, of course, when it was possible to keep a given speed; only rarely was the way open enough—and when it was, they had to be even more alert for the strange things which might change that happy state.

Once, and once only, was there an animal, a definitely living thing moving sluggishly across their path leaving a track entirely stripped of vegetation, large and small. There was no way to see its underside, and hence no way to tell whether it was traveling on short legs—which would presumably have had to be numerous—or, though no trail was visible, something like the slime track of a gastropod. The biologists did manage this time to get a plea through Ben's near-censorship. They wanted the *Quarterback* just to change course the slightest bit and roll the thing over *en passant*, and leave a servobug or two to examine it more closely . . .

The drivers were not sure their vehicle could roll over something about its own size, and even less certain that the creature itself could do nothing about it if they tried. They promised to make the effort when the present emergency was ended, preferably much closer to possible help from Nest, and drove on. The bugs were controllable from only a short distance in the biological static.

The debate was picked up by the natives, who wanted to know what "animal" meant. No one could explain with the available symbols. This was not surprising; but during the next hour Nic and Erni saw, swooping around their vehicle, objects which looked like the familiar blowing bits of black paper at a distance but which, seen close to, were clearly gliders—tossing, banking, and whirling in the wind as though barely under control, but clearly aircraft. This was duly reported to Nest. The report, presumably detectable by the natives, elicited no comment from them.

Quarterback was now a little closer to the sunlit slightly-more-than-hemisphere (the star covered fourteen degrees of sky). The generally active tectonics had not changed significantly, but the air was decidedly warmer and the plants, possibly in consequence, more luxuriant. Nothing resembling leaves had been seen yet, again unless the apparently charred blowing sheets qualified, and there were bets among the biologists on whether such organs would be present even under direct sunlight. The drivers of *Jellyseal* had failed to report any, but this meant little when one considered the planet's area. Special enlarged organs for intercepting stellar energy did seem a bit superfluous with the star scarcely a twentieth of an astronomical unit away. However, considering the illogical structure of vertebrate retinae, there was no predicting all the odd paths regular evolution might take.

Cloud made few requests of the husbands, no matter how urgently his halo of researchers begged. He did pass on to them the suggestion that more and bigger plants might mean more if not bigger animals, but left any changes in driving policy up to them. They made none; they were already as alert as human beings could well remain.

The final two-thousand-kilometer segment of the run was frustrating, over and beyond the general annoyance built up over twenty-two days of unbroken driving. The men were, in what now might almost be called straight-line distance, less than three hundred kilometers from their still moving goal. They could not follow a straight line; that way was a labyrinth of seamed, faulted, broken hills where even the satellites could detect almost constant rockfalls. The *Quarterback* would not have to be hit by a rock; a wheelbarrow load of sand could put her instantly out of commission, and help was now tens of thousands of kilometers away. There was no option but to go around the region. Senatsu was apologetic about not having seen the details sooner, but she was easily forgiven; her attention had been confined by their own needs to areas much closer to the travelers for nearly all the trip.

Erni responded to the news with a rather rough jerk at the steering controls; his partner fully sympathized but made the signal to change drivers. The younger man had enough self-control to obey, and the runabout set off in a new direction with *Jellyseal* now off toward its left rear. The sky and its omnipresent clouds flickered even more brightly than usual, as though in sympathy—or perhaps derision. Fortunately, neither driver had reached the state of personalizing the indifferent world. No one even considered how close this state might be.

It would not of course have bothered the planet, but could easily have distorted important judgments.

Cloud, whose telemetry had of course reported the moment of rough driving, was a little worried; but there seemed nothing he could do, and nothing he should say, about the matter.

The two thousand kilometers took three infuriating days, though the last few hours were eliminated by *Jellyseal's* luckily, though apparently fortuitously, moving to a more accessible spot and actually stopping for a time.

The pause might have been due to her being in the center of a twenty-kilometer nearly circular hollow—almost certainly *not* an impact crater—with eight different narrow valleys leading from it. She had already explored two of these, according to Senatsu, and been forced to turn back; maybe the drivers were debating which to try next, Ben suggested.

Neither husband could believe this for a moment. They knew their wives would have planned such a program much earlier. The faces behind their breathing masks were now grim. They made no answer to Cloud, but Erni, now driving again, sent them zigzagging at the highest practical speed along a rock-littered canyon which Senatsu had assured them would lead to the hollow. Nic did not object. The sooner they were out from between the looming eighty-meter walls, the better their chance of living to see—

Whatever might be there to be seen. The satellite images were, after all, only computer constructs.

Rocks fell, of course, but continued to miss. Neither man had any illusions about how much of this was due to driving skill, but neither gave it much conscious thought. The canyon opened into the valley twenty kilometers ahead.

Fifteen. Ten. Five.

They were there, and neither even felt conscious relief as the threatening cliffs opened out. They could not at once spot the tanker, and stopped to look more carefully.

The trouble was that none of the vehicle's lights were on. Deeplights might of course be out because it was not moving, but the floods, and the smaller but sharp and clear running and identity-pattern lights which should have been on were dark, too. It was long, long moments before Erni perceived the tanker's outline against the faint, flickering, and complex illumination of the lightning-lit background.

He pointed, and Dominic nodded. The younger man had been driving through the valley, but now Nic took over and approached their motionless, lightless, and possibly—probably?—lifeless goal. Erni was calling frantically into the short-range multiwave communicator. Neither was surprised at the lack of an answer; frantic was a better word.

Tracks, wheels, and much of the lower body of the tanker were crusted with something white, but the men paid only passing attention to this.

There should at least have been light coming from the cockpit. There wasn't. Something else strange about the windows seized the attentions of both men, but the *Quarterback* was within fifty meters of the other machine before this got the door of consciousness open.

Lights inside or not, the windows should have been visible as more than dark slots. Anything transparent, silicate or not, reflects some of the light trying to get through.

But the sky, which was a good deal brighter than the ground, was not being reflected from *Jellyseal's* windows. They were lightless gaps in the not-very-bright upper body. And the reason now became clear to both observers, drowning out the screaming denials of hope.

The windowpanes were not there. Maybe, of course, the occupants weren't there either, but where else could they possibly be? And more important, where else could they possibly be alive? What besides local air was in the tanker's cockpit? Even Dominic, with the means of looking waiting at his fingertips, had trouble making the fingers act.

But they did, slowly and much less surely than usual. He slipped into waldo gloves, and a servobug emerged from the runabout. Briefly—perhaps less briefly than usual—it checked out its limbs and lights, and made its way across to the tanker's relatively monstrous hulk.

It could climb, of course. There were holds on the outer shells of all Nest's vehicles, the bug had grasping attachments on its "legs," and the machines had been designed and grown to be used in rescue techniques as well as more general operations. It made its rather fumbling way up *Jellyseal's* front end, and finally reached the openings which had once held barriers intended to keep in the flotation water, keep out one of the few environments in the known universe more corrosive than Earth's, and still let light through. Nic was guiding the little machine by watching it from where he was. Not even Erni asked why the bug's own eyes had not been activated yet.

Yes, the windowpanes were gone. Yes, the bug could climb inside with no trouble. Yes, the last excuse for not using its own vision pickups was gone. Without looking at his partner, Nic turned on the bug's eyes and his own screen.

It could not at once be seen what was in the cockpit. Nothing human showed, but that might have been because vision reached little more than a meter into the chamber. It was blocked by a seemingly patternless tangle of twisted branches, ranging from the thickness of a human middle finger down to rather thin string. The colors filled the usual range for Halfbaked vegetation, from very dark maroons and browns to dead black.

The stuff was very brittle, far more so than anything living should have been. Nic tried to get farther inside. The bug, under his waldoed direction, reached out to one of the thicker stems and tried to use it as a climbing support. Several centimeters of the growth vanished in dust and the machine overbalanced and fell into the cockpit. It left an elevator shaft as it pulverized its way to the floor, and Nic had to go through cleaning routines as black dust slowly settled through the dense air around and upon his mechanical agent.

Both men were now watching the relay screen, but things weren't much improved. The bug was still surrounded by the tangle, and as it moved slowly across the floor kept smashing its way through a three-dimensional fabric of seemingly charred growths. The stuff was brittle, but not really frail. A significant push, comparable to the bug's weight, was needed actually to break the thickest of the branches. It was only when they broke that they went to powder.

The cockpit was far larger than that of the *Quarterback*, more than five meters across and eight long, and it was many minutes before most of the floor had been examined. The bug was now moving around under an artistically tangled ceiling twenty centimeters or so high, supported by many pillars of unharmed branches. It left tracks as it went in a two- or three-millimeter-thick layer of black powder containing many short fragments of the branches.

There was no sign of a human form, living or otherwise, anywhere on the floor, but there was all the evidence anyone could ask that the tangle above could never have supported a human body in the local gravity, and flotation water was gone. Erni finally reported this aloud, his voice as expressionless as he could make it, and summarized the observations forcing this conclusion. Ben acknowledged and opened channels for everyone at Nest.

"We want to look farther, not consult!" Nic objected. "There ought to be some sort of indication what happened. Where did the windows go, anyway?"

"They'd probably be the first things to give if the refrigeration failed and the water boiled suddenly over in the daylight," Cloud pointed out reluctantly, "unless someone who knows the structure better doesn't think so. Speak up if anyone does. Anyway, it seems better for you to bring the tanker back here for really close checking, and if at all possible *not* spoil any more evidence in the cockpit. The growths you reported seem to be very frail, and therefore different from the ones we've seen, and it would be better if there were something besides powder to be examined here. Don't think we're forgetting about the girls, but if there's to be any hope of learning what happened, we need data. You can see that."

"We can see it," retorted the younger driver, "but there are still items we'd like to examine ourselves."

"What? There was only that one compartment they could have lived in. The whole rest of the machine was paraffin tank, with its contents melted wax for the last part of their trip, and presumably native air for the return—unless you think it was evacuated when the cargo was unloaded, and you'd have seen if it were flattened. So would Sen. What do you think you can find, anyway? You're not set up for microscopic or high-class chemical testing."

"We could find leaks, if they were big enough to—to make things happen so quickly there couldn't be any alarm sent back."

"I'd think small ones could have wrecked communication before they knew anything was wrong. But all right, I'll take it on my responsibility—go ahead and look for leaks between cockpit and tank, but do leave *something* of the stuff you've been smashing up for people to study."

"All right. But how do you expect us to get *Jellyseal* back with her cockpit uninhabitable? There's no way for us to refill it with water even if we could reseal the window openings."

"We're working on that. Go ahead and make your search."

The men obeyed, Erni rather sullenly, Nic more thoughtful. The floor and rear bulkhead of the cockpit and the rear third of each side wall were between living chamber and cargo space, so there was a large area to be examined. How this could be managed without destroying all contact between walls and branches was not very evident. Human remains are large enough so that the first search had left many columns of undamaged vegetation still touching the floor, but to examine the walls for pinholes or even nail holes would be another matter. Nic thought for two or three minutes before trying anything, his partner waiting with growing impatience.

"You know," Yucca said slowly at last, "if there was actually a leak between cockpit and tank, would the windows have blown out? There's a lot of volume back there for steam to expand into, even if it was nearly full of wax. There were several cubic meters full of local air to allow for the paraffin's expanding as it warmed, whether it melted or not."

"I still want to look."

"I know. I don't want to give up either. But think. Whatever chance the girls have of being alive, it's not on board that machine. The natives could have—"

"You mean they might have. But would they have known how? Could *we* keep one of *them* alive anywhere near Nest, when we have no idea about what they need—except maybe in temperature? And if they're alive, why haven't they called us?"

Dominic gestured toward the tanker a few meters away. "What with? Do you think any of the comm gear is still in working shape?"

"You two find that out, pronto," came Ben's voice. "There's a good chance, the design crew thinks. If enough of it works you can use the bug that's in there now to handle it. You find out whether it can still be set to receive short-range stuff from you, or if the controls are in shape to be handled by the bug itself. In one case, it may be possible to set up for *Jelly* to follow you by homing on transmission from your car. In the other, it'll be a lot harder, but one of you using the bug's handlers should be able to drive *Jelly* while the other runs *Quarterback*. That'll be almighty slow, since you'll have to stop to rest pretty often instead of swapping off, but it should be possible."

"But—" started Erni.

Cloud spoke more gently, and much more persuasively. "You both know most of what little chance there is that they're alive is if they're somewhere under the sun. We don't know just how smart these natives are, but remember that *they* got in touch with *us*, after hearing our satellite and vehicle transmissions. Let's get that machine back here and find out what we can from it. Even if time is critical, and I can't say it isn't, aren't the odds better this way? We can try to ask the natives, too, though a lot of language learning will have to come first, I expect."

"How do you know the odds are better?" Erni was snapping again.

"I don't, of course," Ben maintained his soothing tone, "but to me they *seem* better with a whole population of smart people working on finding out just what did happen."

Nic nodded slowly, invisibly to Cloud but not to Erni.

"I suppose that makes sense."

"Something else makes sense, too," Erni added grimly.

"What."

"Tricia got the idea that the natives were pleased with the variety of hydrogen compounds we'd supplied. I wonder just how big a variety they got."

"And I pointed out that the tanker did have a lot of different hydrocarbons, which I think the locals call carbon hydrides," Nic countered instantly. There was at least a minute of silence.

"All right. We'll bring it back if we can. But I'd like to know one thing, if Tricia can decode it from the local static."

"What?" asked Ben.

"Do the locals know what water is, or at least do they have a recognizable symbol for it even if they call it oxygen hydride, and—did they thank us for any?"

Again there was a lengthy pause while implications echoed silently around in human skulls. No one mentioned that the request was for *two* things; it didn't seem to be the time.

"She'll try to find out," Ben answered at last, in as matter-of-fact a tone as he could manage.

"Okay. We'll go over *Jelly's* controls." Dominic, too, tried to sound calm.

The controls did seem to be working. This was not as startling as it might have been; all such equipment was of solid-state design and imbedded—grown into— the structures of the various vehicles. There might be mechanical failure of gross moving parts, but any equipment whose principal operating components were electrons stood a good chance of standing up in Halfbaked's environment as long as diamond or silicon were not actually exposed to fluorine.

There seemed, however, to be no way to set up the tanker's system simply to home on a radiation source, moving or not. No one had foreseen the need when the machine was designed. The closest thing to an autodriver in any of the vehicles was the general-shutdown control. There were no smooth paved highways with guiding beacons or buried rails on the planet. While systems able to avoid the ordinary run of obstacles on an ordinary planet were part of the common culture and could have been incorporated in the Halfbaked-built machines, these were *exploring* vehicles. Avoiding obstacles was simply not their basic purpose. It had been taken for granted that they would be operated by curious, intelligent people who had a standard sense of self-preservation but would be willing to take risks when appropriate.

That left trying to drive *Jellyseal* with the handling equipment of a servobug. This proved possible but far from easy, and even Erni agreed that an hour or two's practice in the open area was probably a good idea. With some confidence established by both, Dominic sent the *Quarterback* toward the valley by which they had entered while his younger companion, looking through the rear window of the cockpit, concentrated on keeping the larger vehicle a fixed distance directly behind them.

He was feeling pretty confident, almost relaxed, by the time the entrance narrowed before them.

With a brief exchange of one slightly questioning and one somewhat shaky "Okay" they entered the passage, very conscious that even at its empty weight the larger vehicle was much better able to shake the walls down on them than was their own runabout. Of course, *Jelly* also made a bigger target; but possibly a few dents or even a few holes in its body might not be critical now. Of course assuming that a house-sized boulder with the potential energy provided by a hundred-meter cliff under seven plus gravities would merely *dent* its target did seem unreasonably optimistic. Both men were optimists, even with the present probable status of their wives, but they were also reasonable; and while Nic did fairly well at concentrating on his driving, Erni's eyes kept wandering much too often from *Jellyseal*'s bulk behind them to the cliffs beside and above.

As earlier experience had warned, rocks did shake loose from time to time. It seemed very likely that the vibration of their own passage was the principal cause, since most of them slashed across the narrow way somewhat behind the *Quarterback* and its companion.

Not quite all. Four times a deafening bell-like clang reached the men's ears, deafening in spite of the poor impedance matching between the planet's atmosphere and their vehicle's body, and between the latter and the water inside. The bodies of the machines were not, of course, of metal, but they had enough metallic elasticity to ring on impact.

Jellyseal was the victim all four times. Fortunately the missiles were much less than house-sized and *Jelly* seemed not to suffer enough damage to keep her from following. This fact did not cause Dominic to relax until they were out of the danger zone and had started to backtrack their way around the Patch of Frustration, as they had named it.

At this point, Ben called again.

"There's a new track for you. You don't have to go back around to the way you came. Stand by for directions—"

"Stand by for directions—"
"Stand by for directions—"

That became the routine through their waking hours and days for the ensuing weeks. What with sleep time and difficulties in guiding their "tow," they averaged less than seventy kilometers an hour. The weeks went by, the monotony relieved by Senatsu's messages, variations in wind and weather, and local biology. No more animals had been seen, or gliders, though the latter had inspired much argument at Nest. Neither had anything been said about the pot the two drivers had presumably won on the way out; neither man thought to mention it, and for some reason no one at Nest brought the matter up.

The men were simply far too busy to think very much about the missing women, though they certainly did not forget them. When it was reported that *Canglegrease* was about ready, and Ben suggested that she be loaded and start at once for the native "city" with another crew, Nic and Erni both protested furiously. They tried to be logical; Erni insisted that talking with their wives during the first trip had given him and Nic a better idea of the route and its problems than anyone else could have. Ben countered that everyone on Nest had heard the conversations as well, and if necessary could replay the records of them. Nic supported his partner, pointing out that there had to be shades of meaning in the messages which only people who knew the speakers really well could be expected to catch. This was an unfair argument to use against the unmarried Cloud, but fairness was not on either driver's mind at the moment. Ben privately doubted the validity of the argument as any bachelor might, but had no wish to be sneered at—by many people besides the bereaved husbands—for preaching outside his field of competence.

He tried to point out the value of time. Nic countered with the value of familiarity; he and Erni were, aside from Maria and Jessi, the only people who had traveled really far from Nest. Cloud gave up at this point, agreed to wait for their arrival, but used their own argument to insist that two additional drivers go with them to gain experience.

Erni asked pointedly, "Is *Candlegrease* set up to support a crew of six?" The coordinator almost gave himself away by asking *what* six, but made a quick recovery.

"It will be by the time you get here." Suggesting that there would probably be no need to take care of six was obviously unwise and might, just conceivably, be wrong. Human life, even other people's, means a lot to civilized beings. A species which has survived its War stage and achieved star travel practically has to be civilized.

Ben kept his word. The second tanker was ready, loaded, and set up to keep the women comfortable if they were found, by the time Erni and Nic got back to Nest. There was a second argument when they insisted, or tried to insist, on starting out at once to the hot side in spite of their extreme exhaustion. Ben won this one, but only by promising not to let *Candlegrease* move without them, so almost another Halfbaked year passed before the medics pronounced the two fit for the trip.

There had been no delay, of course, in examining *Jelly's* cockpit, though this had to be done with bugs. Bringing the machine into the garage and flooding it with water so that living researchers could swarm into it would quite certainly destroy any evidence there might be.

It was quickly discovered that breaking the brittle contents did not pulverize the whole branch, merely two or three diameters to each side of the break. Cutting or snipping at two points far enough apart, therefore, detached an apparently undamaged section. Since the tank was full of the stuff too, there was no shortage. After a few mistakes resulting from failing to catch them on something soft as they fell, several lengths of the material were brought into "outdoor" labs, and biologists and chemists went happily to work with their bugs.

The material was not very different from the tissues already investigated from the local vegetation. It was rigid rather than pliable, of course, and it finally occurred to someone that the stuff, having come from the hot side, might merely be frozen. This was easy enough to test. A sample was heated up to the probable temperature, as indicated by radiation theory and measurement from the satellites, of the Hotpole latitude where the "city" seemed to be. Long before it warmed up that far, the branch being tested was flexible as rope. Several of the investigators began privately to wonder whether they might be working over the remains of one of the intelligent natives, though no one suggested this aloud until well after *Candlegrease* had departed. Ben had the idea, but decided to save it; Erni might get bothered again.

What brought the question into the open was the observation that after a day or so at high temperature, most of the branches, or roots, or vines, or whatever they were began to grow fine tendrils. The stuff was still alive.

This was quickly reported to Ben Cloud, leaving him with the decision of how much to pass on to the now fairly distant second expedition. On one hand, the information was clearly critically important to anyone expecting to be in direct contact with the natives. On the other, Nic and Erni might be uncomfortable to learn that their examination of *Jelly*'s control compartment might have dismembered one of the people they were going to meet.

Or, considering what had so probably happened to their wives, they might not. The other two drivers were a married couple, Pam Knight and Akmet Jinn Treefern, and the Treeferns might keep the other two in discussion rather than brooding mode. Ben hoped the fact that they were short, stocky, extremely sturdy people from a one-point-four-gee colony world would not become important, but he was getting uneasy over Erni's patience limits.

Ben was still trying to make up his mind—there was plenty of time yet before the travelers could presumably meet any day side natives—when another discovery was made.

One of the many short sections of branch from the debris on the floor of *Jelly*'s cockpit had been part of one of the samples to be warmed up. It had not responded; it had neither softened nor grown extensions. After giving it several days, first with the rest of the sample and then by itself, it had been sequestered for more detailed study.

Halfbaked's life, it was now known, consisted mostly of carbon, with modest traces of nitrogen, oxygen, and heavy metals such as iron and titanium. The complexity needed for biological machinery was obtained not from hydrogen bonding within and between proteins and carbohydrates but from variously sized fullerenes and graphite tubes flared, tapered, curved, and branched by occasional heptagons, pentagons, and octagons in their mainly hexagonal carbon-ring nets. The "protoplasm" was considerably coarser, on the molecular scale, than anything known before to human biochemistry, and its peculiarities were contributing heavily to the Ph.D.-per-hour rate Cloud liked to brag about.

The unresponsive segment was quite different. It had a fair amount of carbon and some iron, but there was far more sodium, calcium and phosphorus than had ever been found in the native life, and the carbon for the most part was tetrahedrally bonded. It took a while to discover the reason, and this happened only when one of the chemists sat back from her diffraction spectrometer and its confusing monitor pattern and took a close naked-eye look at the specimen.

Then she called for a medical helper, who needed one glance.

The branch was the charred remains of a human little finger.

This made Ben's communication problem more difficult, but in another way. It also forced him to face it at once. He faced it, reporting as tersely and calmly as he could to the distant *Annie*.

"But why only a finger?" tiny Pam asked instantly, before either of the now confirmed widowers could react. She was honestly and reasonable curious, but was quite consciously trying to ease the shock of the message for the husbands. It was not really necessary; Nic, and even Erni, had become more and more ready to face the news as the weeks had worn on. "You two went over the whole floor, square centimeter by square centimeter, you said. Why didn't you find a lot more—and a lot more recognizable? Maybe it's just as well you didn't, of course, but still I don't see why."

Dominic was able to answer at once, though Erni had thought of the explanation as quickly.

"It was small, and they missed it."

That was all he needed to say. Even the "they" needed no clarification. Everyone in the tug heard that much and could picture the rest. Ben Cloud and more than fifty of the Nest personnel who were in the comm link could do the same. They listened while Dominic, in surprisingly steady tones, went on, "Ben, did Tricia ever get an answer to that question we asked a while ago about the natives and *water*?"

"Not that I know of." Cloud found his voice with difficulty. He had expected losses on Halfbaked, but the fact that none had occurred in the nearly half a Terrestrial year the party had been there had undermined his readiness. "I'll try to find out. Carry on. And we're sorry. I don't know what else to say that wouldn't be pure Pollyanna; but you know we mean it."

"We know."

"You also know, I expect," Ben's voice was even softer, "why I had another pair of drivers with you." It was not put as a question. Ben, a slender half-gravity colonial, did not commonly think of muscle as useful, but he was a realist.

"Yeah. Thanks. Don't worry. Erni, time for you to take over. We still have things to find out up Hotnorth."

The sun would be starting to rise in another two thousand kilometers or so. Temperature was higher, though the principal surface winds still brought chill from the dark side; turbulence sometimes mixed in air from above, not only coming from sunlit regions but heated further by compression as it descended. Dominic still sometimes contributed to Erni's financial security with an attempted weather forecast, but the variables he could think of were becoming too numerous even for his optimism. Motivation for such predictions remained high; they had identified another potential trigger for landslides. Suddenly hot or suddenly—by two or three hundred Kelvins—cold blasts of wind sometimes cracked off scales of rock by thermal shock. The cracks, fortunately, were never deep; but the layers peeled off were sometimes extensive and their shattered fragments dangerous, especially as the pieces were often thin enough to blow around.

The tank in tow was struck several times, forcing travel to cease while it was examined carefully by servobugs, but so far damage had been confined to small dents. The one strike on *Annie* had caused no damage at all, possibly because the traction problem had forced her to be grown with much extra weight.

They had seen and avoided the common puddles of unknown makeup, but as the sky ahead grew bright these became larger areas and more frequent. *Annie* avoided them, though the returning *Jellyseal* apparently had not. The white crust on her tracks and lower body had turned out to be mostly cryolite, sodium aluminum fluoride, regarded by Greenland natives on Earth as a peculiar form of ice because it would only melt in the flame of a blubber lamp.

It was now pretty obvious who, or what, had driven the tanker homeward. Dominic had already compared the fate of the driver with that of his wife, but had not spoken about it to anyone. For one thing, a lot of the *how* remained to be worked out. The tangle of apparent vegetation might, after all, have been some sort of remote control system; this world's plants did emit and receive microwaves. Maybe no intelligent being had been on board, at that. This could all tie in with the natives' immediate spotting of, and beaming signals to, the satellites when these had gone into operation months before. The graphite microtubes in Halfbaked tissue often circulated metal ions and could serve as antennae, among many, many less obvious things. It seemed more and more necessary, and more and more easy to believe, that the real life was at the source of the signals. And maybe *one* of the girls . . .

No, Don't think of that. Whatever had happened to them had happened very quickly—one could believe that, at least—and pretty certainly to both of them at once.

But it looked as though veering around lakes might not be really necessary, since they were going Hotnorth and anything that froze on the vehicles now should melt off again shortly. Nic did suggest this. Pam vetoed the idea at once.

"How do we know how deep these things may be?"

"Do we need to? We'd float. We're only twice as dense as water."

"That wouldn't matter to us, but could we drive, towing like this?" Nic had no answer, and they continued to stay on solid, if sometimes shaky, ground. Neither of the other men had taken part in the debate.

Just as they glimpsed the upper limb of the sun, a new sort of adventure eased the boredom. They were threading their way through a stand which looked much like the "Saguaro" patches Nic and Erni had found earlier. The growths were not always far enough apart for the tank, and much as they disliked it, there was sometimes no alternative to hitting and bending pairs of these, or sometimes breaking them completely. They were leaving a clear trail, not that this was their main worry.

Nic was glad afterward, though he was far too busy otherwise to think of it at the moment, that none of his attempted weather predictions was pending. With no warning at all a far stronger wind blast than any of them had experienced so far made itself felt to the driver. Organ-pipes bent and snapped in all directions.

And, though there had been no lightning, burst into flame. For minutes they drove through the enveloping blaze, making no effort to avoid anything. The mere fact that there was no free oxygen outside meant nothing; it had not occurred to anyone to consider what the paraffin would do in unlimited supplies of this atmosphere. There was no free fluorine to speak of, but the variety of fluorine compounds actually present offered far more possibilities than any of them had time to consider. Pam joined her husband at the driving controls; Erni, with remarkable self-discipline, beamed a running report of what was happening for any satellites in position to relay to Nest; Nic deployed one of the more versatile servobugs and drove it beside them, ranging back and forth along the tank and looking carefully for any signs of rupture. After a few seconds Pam, deciding her husband needed no help—he was not attempting to dodge anything—took out another bug and covered the other side.

They were out of the stand, and out of the fire, and presumably out of danger after three or four anxious minutes. The wind now came strongly from ahead; Nic judged that the fire had set up a strong updraft which was bringing in air from all directions. Erni, with no wager going, didn't bother to disagree, and neither of the others found the suggestion unreasonable.

A few hundred meters from the nearest flames *Annie* and *Candlegrease* were stopped and all four of the crew made a slow and minute inspection of tug and tow using the bugs. There was little worry about their own vehicle; they would have been aware of serious damage within seconds of incurring it. A slow leak in the tank, however, was another matter. It was assumed that the natives were equipped to unload the paraffin at their end; they had been told as clearly as possible what it was, and would presumably be ready to keep any of the precious hydrogen from escaping. Also, they had made no complaint about the first delivery.

But no one had tried to find out what the paraffin itself would do to local life. It seemed very likely that hydrogen compounds would be about as helpful to Halfbaked's organisms as fluorine ones in comparable concentration would be to Terrestrial tissues. Also, many paraffin components were high enough in molecular weight to sink in the local atmosphere; they would be mixed and diluted quickly by wind, of course, but wouldn't rise on their own.

The travelers reminded Ben of this, and asked for suggestions. What if they *did* find a leak, even a small one? Should they come back, at least to Hotlatitudes where the paraffin would freeze again?

"I'll have to ask around," was all the coordinator could say after some seconds of thought. "Get along with your inspection, and let us know. For now, we'll assume the worst."

"What would that be, to you?" asked Erni.

"That you're leaking so badly there's no way of getting any of your load to where it's supposed to be delivered. That would make the decision easy, but I hope it isn't true."

So did the crew, but they were still careful.

There were half a dozen patches of liquid near and under the tank, but there were two similar ones near the tug, and several more within a few tens of meters. There seemed no reason to suppose they were hydrocarbons, since they seemed neither to be evaporating nor reacting with the now quite hot air, but they were watched carefully for several minutes, especially those under the tank. At Nic's suggestion, they moved the vehicles a hundred meters to an area where no puddles could be seen, and waited for more minutes.

Nothing dripped. No puddles formed. Nothing seemed to be leaking. This was reported to Cloud. He had had time think, or someone had, and his answer was, "Check every bit of the tank you can get an eye close to for the tiniest cracks, leaking or not, which may show. Remember the one in *Jelly*."

"*What* one in *Jelly*?" asked two voices at once.

"Didn't I tell you? No, come to think of it, that just led to more questions, some of them still not answered. We think we know what happened, now. The refrigerators meant to keep the paraffin from boiling when the surroundings got really hot did a good job, but when the liquid was drained, we suppose by the customers, the tank naturally filled with local air. Some of this, maybe sulfur trioxide, formed frost on the coils and insulated them, so air at its regular temperature—eight or nine hundred Kelvins or more, depending on the local weather—swept in and hit the rear bulkhead of the cockpit. This was too thick, it turned out."

"Too *thick*?" There were more than two voices this time.

"Too thick. A thin glass will handle hot washing fluid better than a thick one. The body composition of the vehicles is as strong as we could make it, but it's also a very poor heat conductor, as intended. It bent in toward the cockpit just a little under the pressure, and that added to thermal shock to start a U-shaped crack in the rear bulkhead from floor to floor, and straight along the floor, framing about ten square meters. The area was pushed into the cockpit momentarily by the atmospheric pressure, far enough to open a gap maybe one or two centimeters wide all around. The support water, or enough of it, boiled almost instantly, the windows blew out, and the steam pressure slammed the flap back where it had come from so tightly the crack was practically invisible."

"And you never told us? Why not?" asked Pam.

"Well, it couldn't happen to you. Your living space isn't even in the same vehicle with the cargo. One point for the towing idea."

"And several points minus for keeping us in the dark!"

"We'll check for cracks," added Dominic, as steadily as he could. They all turned their attentions back to the bugs.

The fire had almost completely died out. So had the wind from Hotnorth. Dominic, glancing away from his work occasionally, saw that the pillar of smoke was sheared cleanly at, he judged, nearly a kilometer above, with the higher part whipping back toward Hotsouth. It was high enough to glow for some distance in the sunlight against an unusually dark and cloud-free sky. He was tempted to try another weather guess, but firmly turned his attention back to *Candlegrease*'s body. So cracks could be really hard to see . . .

Hard, or impossible. None were found, but no one could be quite certain. Absence of evidence is not—

They drove on into heat and sunlight, more silently than before, with a bug following on either side, its operator constantly scanning the tank. More words were spoken in the next few hours by Senatsu with her guidance information than by all four of the tug crew together.

No one was exactly in a panic, of course, but everyone had enough sense to be uneasy. Erni and Nic were more relaxed than the Treeferns now. At least they seemed to be.

"Open ground for about thirty kilos."

Ninety minutes of silence.

"What looks like a compression fold across your path ten kilos ahead. Two possible passes. The wider is four kilos to your right. Turn twenty-two degrees right to thirty-seven."

The planet's magnetic field was too distorted to provide reliable direction, but enough of the sun was now in sight to indicate Hotnorth—and make driving into it uncomfortable. The new heading was a relief.

The wider pass had walls high enough for the left one to provide shade for nearly a hundred kilometers, a distance which did not lift the star's disc perceptibly. The valley was not a recent feature; the walls on both sides were greatly collapsed and eroded. Had it been much narrower the travelers would have had a problem threading their way among the fallen fragments.

"Lake eighteen kilometers ahead. Stay close to it on its left." When they reached the lake, there was not very much rock-free space to the left of the liquid, but there was presumably even less on the other side; the drivers trusted Senatsu. She herself was developing more confidence as reports from the tug kept filling out her interpretations of the satellite radar.

She hadn't spotted the vegetation which grew densely along the shore, but this gave no real trouble. Erni and Nic thought of the fire now far behind, but there was no sudden downdraft this time. There was, as usual, lightning.

"It could happen," Dominic remarked. "The right wall is pretty high, and wind flowing over it would drop sharply and heat up by adiabatic compression—"

"How much?"

It was Akmet who asked this time, but Nic declined to bet. Erni wondered whether his friend was actually learning, or simply didn't want intruders in their friendly game. He said nothing; he was driving. Bet or no, there was no fire, and eventually the Hotnorth end of the lake came in sight.

"Head right along the shore."

Erni started to obey before realizing it was not Senatsu's voice. This was not too unusual; the Yoshihashis shared the muscular fitness supplied by constantly fighting water's inertia, but even they had to sleep sometimes.

"Who's on?" Erni asked, before realizing that the voice wasn't human either. The answer was unexpected.

"What?" This *was* Senatsu, recognizable even through the biological static, now familiar enough to be tuned out fairly well by the human nervous system.

"Who just told me to head right?"

"No one. You're in fine shape."

"You didn't send the message? Or hear it?"

"Neither. Repeat it, please."

Icewall did so.

"That did not come from here, or through satellite relay in either direction. Is it a native voice?"

"Turn right. You do not turn right."

Pam was quickest on the uptake, and was first at the communicator. "Why should we turn right?"

"The symbol 'we' is unclear. Turn right for safety and information."

Erni had done a quick-stop by now.

"Sen, did you hear that?"

"I heard static only, none of it either unusual or structured."

Treefern glanced at her husband, who nodded. His smile was of course invisible. Pam nodded back.

"Sen, this is what we heard." She quoted. "Now, repeat that back to us, please. As exactly as your voice will let you, and emphatically word for word."

Senatsu obeyed, mystified but guessing this was no time for argument or question.

The message promptly came again, in the new voice, and the observer gasped audibly.

"I *did* hear that! It came through the link."

"I thought it might. They're not stupid, and certainly not slow. Erni, fire up and do what they say—but keep your driving eyes peeled!"

"For what?"

"How should I know? Anything. What do you usually watch for?"

Icewall drove without answering. It had started to rain, unheralded by Yucca, and Pam thought of a possibly useful question for their new guide. "How far?"

"Twenty-two point one kilometers."

"Sen, if you heard that, try to see what's that far ahead."

"Sorry. I heard it, but radar isn't getting through just now."

"Comm frequencies are."

"True. They're not very good for imaging, but I'll do what I can. Stand by."

The rain grew heavier, whatever it might be composed of, and Erni slowed sharply. The voice promptly came again.

"Why stop." There was no question inflection.

Pam answered slowly, with measured and carefully chosen words. "Not stopping. Slowing. Rain. Bad measuring."

"Rain. Bad measuring," was the acknowledgment. After a pause, **"No rain. Eight kilometers. Not slow."**

"Eight kilometers," answered the woman. "Sen, you heard that? Can you see what's eight kilos—kilometers—ahead?" There were many listeners by now. Most could guess why Pam had corrected to the full length of the distance label. They also wondered which form the unknown guide would use the next time distance was mentioned.

Tricia Feather's voice came through to the tug.

"Much more of this and the translation computer won't need my help! Willi, can you use a math assistant?"

None of the travelers paid attention to this. All were looking eagerly ahead for the predicted break in the rain. Not even Nic tried to second-guess the native.

The really interesting item, they agreed later, was that their informant had allowed not only for their own speed in his, her, or its prediction. The rain clouds had been traveling much faster than tanker and tug, but the eight kilometers was still right. Dominic bowed internally to superior knowledge and vowed to himself, as he had several times before, that Erni would get no more of his cash. Prediction was evidently possible, but not for a mere human being.

Or maybe he could set up some sort of private channel with the natives, and get some of his money back . . .

Neither he nor anyone else was particularly surprised at the sudden improvement in communication, though there was plenty of joy. The natives had been known to exist, had been known to be intelligent, and information supplies do build on themselves and grow exponentially. Maybe Erni's question about water could be answered soon . . .

"Look up!" Akmet cried suddenly. All except Erni obeyed; he chose to continue driving.

There were scarcely any clouds now, though a number of the blowing black objects still fluttered and swirled above and beside them. One, rather larger than the rest, was dipping, swerving, and wavering in much the same way, but was larger and had a more definite shape.

The tug drivers represented three different colony planets, but all had seen dandelions, which are almost as ubiquitous as sodium and human beings. The object looked like a vastly magnified bit of dandelion fluff. It had a shaft about two meters long, topped by a halo of wind-catching fuzz of about the same diameter, and with a grapefruit-sized blob at its lower end. It must have been incredibly light to be wind-supported in this gravity.

It was moving almost as randomly as the other jetsam, but not quite. The windhold at its top varied constantly in shape and size. All the watchers soon realized that it was controlling how much of its motion was due to wind and how much to gravity. Sometimes it lifted sharply, sometimes slowly or not at all; it blew horizontally now one way and now another, but most often and farthest the way Erni was sending the tug. He had speeded up when the rain had stopped, but now he slowed again to stay near the object.

"Go. Travel. Not slow."

"We want to observe," Pam transmitted.

"What?" asked Tricia from her distant listening post. Pam gestured to her husband, who described briefly what was happening.

The response was still terse, but comprehensible. **"Observe better forward. Not slow. Go."**

"Let's take its word for it. Go ahead, Erni. It wants to lead us to something, and this thing doesn't seem to be it."

Icewall shrugged, refraining from comment about "somethings" on this part of the world, and *Candlegrease* left the airborne object behind in moments. There were presumably fourteen kilometers to go, and the going was fairly straight.

It was a less impressive prediction this time; the target was motionless.

If this was the target. A branch tangle some fifty meters across and up to eight or ten high, resembling the filling of *Jellyseal*'s cockpit, was spread at the edge of the lake, separated from the liquid by a meter-high ridge of soil which might have been made by a dozer — or shovels. The ridge — or dam? — ran straight along the lakefront for three dozen meters or so, with each end bending away from the liquid to enclose partially the slowly writhing tangle.

"Left. Slow — left more — slow slow."

"Slowing. Turning." Pam was plainly addressing their guide. Then, "Close to the copse, Erni, I think it means."

"I think so too." Icewall veered very slightly to the right until the big tank was scarcely a meter from the edge of the patch of growth, then even more slightly left so they were moving parallel to it.

"Stop."

"That's it, I guess," Nic added his voice.

"That's it." The guide omitted the man's last two words. Its intelligence seemed to include a computerlike memory.

"Now we wait?" asked Erni, free from his driving.

"Wait. Observe."

"Is that dandelion seed anywhere near us yet?" asked Akmet. "That's what 'observe' was last used on, as I remember. I'd say it was ten or twelve kilos back by now, unless the wind was really helpful."

"Observe."

No one had time to ask *what*. From somewhere near the middle of the copse a duplicate of the "seed" popped upward and began to gyrate like the other as the wind took it. It was followed by several others. All four pairs of eyes were fastened on them, some through the finders of video recorders. Akmet was giving a vocal report to Nest in all the detail he could; there was no video contact through the biological static even via satellite at this distance. Ben and others were asking for clarification, forcing Treefern to repeat himself with additional words. His wife approved; this should help the natives' vocabulary.

They were never able to decide whether the new seeds were a deliberate attempt to capture their attention. Neither of the Treeferns believed that the natives could possibly have worked out that much about human psychology, especially in view of what their own minds turned out to be like. Nic, and even more Erni, were much less sure of this. In any case, either accidentally, incidentally, or deliberately, their attention was held while branches writhed out of the tangle to the tank and its tug and began to feel their way around and over the vehicle bodies, among wheels and treads, around emergency controls meant only for bugs and rescuers . . .

Both machines were enveloped in a loose, open cocoon of branches, some of them two or three centimeters thick, before anyone noticed. Again the question later was whether all *Annie*'s windows being covered last was intentional or not. After all, the natives could have inferred the purpose of windows from their experience with *Jellyseal*.

Erni's cry of surprise as he saw what was happening was followed by prompt startup and an effort to break out of the cocoon. Pam's "Hold it!" preceded the guide's voice by only a fraction of a second.

"**Stop. Observing.**" Erni stopped, less because he cared about obeying a non-human than because the brief effort had shown they were in no obvious danger, the branches were not nearly strong enough to fight fusion engines. Many of them had pulled apart, and the attention of the watchers was now held by seeing these rejoin the main tangle, not apparently caring where the joining occurred.

"Observing. Go later." Pam spoke tentatively; the native seized on the new word.

"**Observe. Go later.**" Erni's hands dropped from the controls, but his attention did not return to the gyrating dandelion seeds. Neither did Nic's. Both wondered how much of this their wives had experienced—there was, after all, no telling *when* the communication link had broken.

It must have been farther Hotnorth, both realized. They had talked to their wives often, of course, and there had been descriptions of landscape with the sun almost above the horizon. The women had wondered why clouds seemed to be as numerous, large, and dense as ever in spite of the rising temperature. Not even Dominic had risked a guess at the time.

"They're hijackers! They're playing with emergency drain valves!" Akmet, who had deployed a bug and was using its eye, cried suddenly.

"They'll be sorry," answered Erni dryly. "Get your bug ready to close anything they open."

"Will it—they—whatever—let me close enough?"

"They won't be able to stop you, I'd guess. But I'll be ready to roll if we have to."

Pam uttered just one word, for the benefit of their guide. "Danger!"

There was no answer at once; perhaps the native had been unable to untangle her word from the two men's transmissions. Pam waited a few seconds before repeating her warning. Still no answer from outside, or the city ahead, or wherever the messages were originating.

"Those things are being controlled by the natives, the way the stuff that drove *Jelly* was!" exclaimed Erni. Nic had an even wilder idea, but kept it to himself for the moment. For one reason, it seemed silly.

A set of millimeter-thick tendrils had been concentrating on one relief valve. There was no instrument to tell the crew how much force was being applied, and the cock itself was safetied to prevent its being turned accidentally. The four people watched the bug's monitor screen in fascination as the cotter pin was straightened, worked free, and dropped to the ground.

The tendrils played further with the valve, and found almost at once which way it would move. The paraffin was not entirely melted yet, though the temperature had been rising; but there was quite enough liquid just inside the wall to find its way through the opening. The watchers saw a drop, and then several more, emerge and almost at once disappear as vapor.

The results were not surprising. Pam controlled herself with no trouble — it was not yet clear whether sympathy was in order — and made sure the new word was understood.

"Danger! Danger!"

The association should have been clear enough. There was no flame at first, but the hydrocarbon produced volumes of grey and black smoke. It was anyone's guess what compounds, from hydrogen fluoride on up, were being made. Within seconds the branches immersed in them appeared to stiffen; at least they ceased moving. Their colors changed spectacularly. No one had seen bright green, yellow, or orange on Halfbaked until now. The branches that turned yellow did flame a moment later and also went off in smoke, leaving no visible ash. None of the watchers was a chemist; none tried to guess what might be forming. Akmet did his best to paint a verbal picture for the listeners at Nest, but this was not detailed enough for an analysis.

There was no objection, from inside or out, when Erni jerked the tug into motion and pulled away from the site. The bug stayed, but two of the witnesses preferred to use the windows with their broader field of view. Wind was spreading and diluting the smoke, but the stuff was still deadly; fully a quarter of the copse was now visibly affected.

"Hydrogen compounds. Danger." Pam knew the natives had the first word already in memory, and took the opportunity to add "compounds," which might not be.

"Are you after my job?" came Tricia's voice, with no tone of resentment.

"Just grabbing opportunity while I can see what's happening."

"**Hydrogen compounds. Danger. Observed.**" The native was starting to handle tenses.

"I guess they grow machinery the way we do. I wonder how much time and material that test cost them," remarked Erni. Nic once again made no comment, possibly because there was no time; their guide resumed instructions almost at once.

"**Observed. Go.**"

"Which way?" asked Erni. There was no answer until Pam tried.

"Right? Straight? Left?" The first and last words were known; the middle one might be inferred from context. Perhaps it was, perhaps the native was testing it.

"**Straight.**"

Erni obeyed. At the moment *Annie* was heading thirty degrees or so west of Hotnorth, the sun ahead and to their right. They had gone about half a kilometer when the command "**Right**" came. Erni altered heading about five degrees, and received a repeat order as he straightened out. This kept on until they were once more heading almost at the tiny visible slice of sun.

Once convinced they had the direction right, Pam asked, "How far?"

"Five thousand three hundred twenty-two kilometers."

No one spoke, either in the tug or back at Nest. Senatsu had no need to point out that the distance and direction corresponded to the source of *Jellyseal*'s last communication, as well as the native transmissions. Halfbaked seemed much too large for this to be coincidence. They drove on, but the hours were now less boring.

Nothing changed significantly except for the slow rising of the sun ahead of them. Patches of plant life were sometimes numerous, sometimes cactuslike, sometimes absent. Clouds varied at least as much. The ever-flickering lightning was less obvious in sunlight, but didn't seem actually to be decreasing. Quakes made themselves felt, and sometimes forced changes in route not foreseen either by Senatsu or their native guide. Wind alternately roared and whispered, mostly from behind but sometimes gusting from other random directions violently enough for the driver to feel. Erni and Nic, with more experience than the others, wondered aloud what the return might be like with a much lighter tank in tow. The thought of having it blown from their control was unpleasant. So was the idea of ballasting it with some local liquid which might freeze before they reached Nest. The advisability of abandoning the tank was considered, both among the crew and with Ben; it would, after all, be small loss.

The problem was tabled until the situation actually had to be faced, with some silent reservations in Nic's mind. He was uneasy about waiting until decision was forced on them by experience, who sometimes starts her courses with the final exam.

The Hotnorth route became no straighter as the sun rose higher. It became evident that the distance estimated by their guide had not included necessary detours. Whenever Tricia or Pam asked how far they had yet to go, the answer was larger than that obtained by subtracting the current odometer reading from the last advice.

This of course made it more obvious than ever that the goal their guide meant was indeed the "city" where the women, as not even their husbands doubted now, must have died.

This fact alone was enough to relieve the boredom; everyone, driving or not, remained alert for new and different phenomena. However likely it might be that it had occurred while unloading, the fact remained that something unforeseen had happened. This is no surprise in the exploration business, and explorers are strongly motivated to collect facts which may assist foresight.

And, if at all possible, to make sense of them.

Time stretched on. The four were in no danger as far as food, oxygen, water, and waste disposal were concerned—there was no shortage of energy. Nevertheless, conversation began to deal more and more often with the next drying-out session, which would include bathing facilities under one gravity. The tiny imperfections in recycling equipment were making themselves felt.

It was known from *Jellyseal*'s reports that the last two thousand or so kilometers had been on fairly level ground where high speeds were reasonably safe. It was also known that this fact could change quickly on a world with county-sized tectonic plates. Luckily, the warning that it *had* changed came early. The original

Quarterback crew had experienced it before, but this time the deeplights were no help. With the sun up and ahead of them, these were not in use. Only the increasing intensity of the temblors gave a clue to what was happening. Nic, who was driving when he recognized it, slowed abruptly.

"Send a bug out ahead!" he ordered to no one in particular. "I think we're near another epicenter!"

"Maybe it's behind us," suggested the woman.

"Maybe it is, and maybe to one side or the other, but I'd rather not take even a twenty-five percent chance of going over a half-meter ledge. If ground is rising ahead okay, we'll see it in time; but I wouldn't guarantee to spot a drop even with all four of us watching."

All four were, but it was Akmet guiding a servobug who located the active fault, and issued the warning which brought *Candlegrease* to a firm halt.

An immediate question came from their guide, who seemed to have them under constant observation even though they had never located him, her, it, or them. Communication had improved a great deal in the last few weeks as the native(s) had joined increasingly in conversations between the vehicle and Nest.

"Why stop now?"

"Danger. Scarp here. Watch." Pam turned to her husband. "Drive the bug over the edge, so they can see what happens."

Akmet obeyed, with spectacular results; the drop was a full meter and a half.

"No hydrogen in the bug."

"Right. Bug smashed. Lots of—much—hydrogen in *Candlegrease*, and *Candlegrease* would smash worse. You want hydrogen, but not here."

"Right."

"We need to pass the scarp without smashing *Candlegrease*. How far must we go, and which way?"

"How high the scarp for no danger?"

"About fifteen centimeters."

"About unclear."

"Not exact. Don't know exactly. That should be safe."

"Left forty-five kilometers to ten-centimeter scarp. Right twenty-seven. About."

"We'll go right—wait."

Ben's voice had cut in. "You have seismic thumpers in the bug hold. How about trying to flatten the slope? It might save time."

Erni brightened visibly. "Worth trying. We wouldn't even have to waste bugs. Three or four sets of shots should tell us whether it'll work or not."

Pam said tersely to their guide, "Wait. Observe."

"Waiting."

Actually, it didn't wait. Erni was the first to notice; Nic and Pam were deploying bugs, and Akmet was occupied at the communicator adding details to the description of their surroundings—anything which might help Senatsu in her interpretation of radar and other microwave observations was more than welcome at Nest. Erni alone was looking through a window when one of the blackish blowing objects again made itself noticeable.

It was far larger than the general run of jetsam to which everyone had gotten accustomed. This one had not been noticed before because, as they now realized, it had been riding far higher than the rest of the material, high enough so that only careful study would have revealed its shape. Now it came down abruptly, in a sort of fluttering swoop, and hung a few meters above the wreckage of the bug in a wavering hover. They knew now that they had seen it, or something like it, before.

It had surprisingly slender wings, whose span Erni estimated as fully ten meters, and which bent alarmingly in the turbulence of the heavy atmosphere. They supported a cucumber-shaped body a meter and a half in length, with a three-meter tail projecting from what was presumably its rear. The tail was terminated by conventional empennage for aircraft, vertical and horizontal stabilizers, rudder and elevators. Erni's warning cry called the others' attention to the arrival, and the bugs stopped moving as their operators looked.

"A glider!" exclaimed Akmet. "In this gravity?"

"Think of the atmosphere," pointed out Dominic.

"I'm thinking strength of materials," was the dry rejoinder.

"I suppose that's where they've been watching us from," Pam added thoughtfully. "It gives us some idea of their size, anyway. I wonder how many it's carrying."

"Or whether it's remote controlled like *Jelly*," Nic pointed out. Pam admitted she hadn't thought of that.

"No windows or lenses," Erni submitted.

"Those wings seem to have very complex frameworks. They could also be microwave and/or radar antennae," was Akmet's remark, reminding the rest that conclusions were still premature and providing the morally requisite alternative hypothesis.

"Let's not bury the bug; it seems to want to look it over. We'll shift fifty or sixty meters before we try to knock the cliff down." Erni acted on his own words, driving the *Annie* and dragging *Candlegrease* to the right as he spoke. No one objected. Three bugs followed with their loads of thumpers.

These were not simply packets of explosive; they were meant to be recoverable and reusable, though this was not always possible. They were hammerlike devices which did carry explosive charges, and were designed to transmit efficiently the jolt of the blast on their tops to the substrate. Ten of them were set up a meter apart and equally far from the cliff edge; a similar row was placed a meter farther back, and a third at a similar distance. The bugs then retreated—they were cheap, but there seemed no point in wanton waste—and the thumpers fired on one command.

No one expected the wave pattern they set up to be recognizable at Nest, thousands of kilometers away, through the endless seismic static, though the computers there were alerted for it. The desired result was a collapse of the cliff face, but no one noticed for several seconds whether this had happened or not. As the charges thundered, the wavering motion of the glider ceased and it dived violently out of sight, as far as anyone could tell almost onto the wreckage of the sacrificed bug. Pam saw it go, and cried out the news as the impact echoed the blast.

"Watch out with the next shot! We don't want to bury it!"

It was clear enough there would have to be a next shot, quite possibly several.

The face of the scarp had collapsed in satisfactory fashion, but the slope of rubble was still far too steep for safety. This, however, was not what surprised the four.

"**Bury still unclear.**"

Pam recovered almost at once. Either they were being observed from somewhere else, or the occupant of the glider had not been disabled by what should have been a seven-gravity crash, or —

Nic's own idea was gaining weight. So was Erni's.

"Observe new rock. Wait." The woman's answer to the native was prompt, and even Erni saw what she meant.

"**Observing. Waiting.**"

"Set up the next shot, boys."

The cliff had crumbled for a width of some twenty-five meters, to a distance varying from ten to fifteen meters back from its original lip. On the second shot the distance back more than doubled.

"New rock buried," Pam announced without bothering to look.

"**Bury clear.**"

A third set of thumpers, skillfully placed, kept the twenty-five-meter width nearly unchanged and practically doubled the other dimension. A fourth, with *Annie* and *Candlegrease* moved farther back for safety, left a promising if still rather frightening slope.

Akmet, using the largest and heaviest of the available bugs, traversed this down, up, and down again, without starting any slides. Dominic repeated the test for practice. Then, with no argument from anyone, he turned back to *Annie*'s controls and very gingerly drove tug and tow down the same way. Everyone thought of trying this with the tow disconnected first, but no one mentioned the idea aloud. Erni wanted to get it over with; the others simply trusted Nic's judgment.

At the bottom, *Candlegrease* safely clear of the rubble, the tug stopped and everyone went to the left windows.

The glider's remains could now be seen easily. The body was flattened and cracked, the wings crumpled, the empennage separated from the rest. A patch of growing stems, twigs, and branches had already started to grow from, around, and through the wreckage, and after a few moments Erni brought them closer. Akmet was once again relaying descriptions to Nest. They were given little time to report.

"**Go. No stop needed.**"

"Right? Straight? Left?" asked Pam.

"**Straight.**" They were at the moment facing about Hotnorthwest. Erni, still at the controls, obeyed. After they had gone about fifty meters, "**Right.**" He started to swerve, and Pam muttered softly, "Full circle." He obeyed, guessing at her plan, and kept turning after they were heading sunward and the voice expostulated "**Stop right.**" Back at the original heading, the woman said simply, "Three hundred sixty degrees." It worked; the next message was "**Forty degrees right.**" He obeyed, and received a "**Four degrees right.**" In minutes the wrecked glider and the growth around it were out of sight.

They were now looking at the sky more often and more carefully. At least two more objects among or beyond the usual foreground of blackish jetsam, objects which *might* be other gliders, could now be seen. No one was surprised when an occasional **"Left"** or **"Right"** warned them of other obstacles, sometimes but not always before Senatsu provided the same information. The natives by now seemed to have a pretty good idea of what the human-driven vehicles could and could not do—or get away with. The tug and its tow sometimes had to be guided around a fair-sized boulder which had not been mentioned, but nothing really dangerous went unreported.

"I guess they really want us to get there," Akmet remarked at one point, rather rhetorically.

"They want their hydrogen to get there," retorted Erni. "It will. Don't worry."

"And you don't think they care that much about us?" asked Pam.

"What do you think?" The woman shrugged, her wet suit doing nothing to conceal the motion. She said nothing.

"What do you think of *them*, Erni?" asked Nic. He was driving and didn't look away from his window.

Icewall didn't even shrug. As usual, not much of anyone's face could be seen, but Pam gave an uneasy glance toward her husband. He answered with a barely visible raised eyebrow. It was at least a minute before anyone spoke.

Then, "They care about as much for us as for one of their branches," Erni said flatly.

Nic nodded, his body attitude showing some surprise. "You've got it after all. You had me worried," he said. This time his friend did shrug visibly. Rather unfortunately, no one chose to prolong the discussion. More time passed.

They were now really close to their goal, according to their guide—**"Three hundred forty-four"** was its terse response to the question.

"Any more danger?" asked Pam. "Go fast?"

"No more danger. Go fast."

The driver, currently Akmet, started to add power, but after a mere twenty-kph increase Nic and Erni almost simultaneously laid hands on his shoulders. The former spoke.

"That's enough for now."

"Why?"

"Somewhere along here something happened."

"That wasn't until they got there!"

"As far as we know. Don't overdrive your reflexes. Keep your eyes wide open."

"No danger fast."

Erni answered. "Observing." This seemed to be an unimpeachable excuse. There was no further comment from their guides and watchers. Anyone who had hoped or expected that they would betray impatience was disappointed.

There were now six or seven of the gliders in sight most of the time. Their irregular motion made them hard to count. Pam was almost certain she had seen one struck by lightning a day before, but her question at the time—"Danger for you? Lightning?"—had gone unanswered. Since there were two new words in the sentence this might have been lack of understanding, but always before such lack had been signified with the "Unclear" phrase.

Human tension was mounting, not only in the tug but at Nest, where Ben and the others were being kept up-to-date by nearly continuous verbal reports.

The sun was causing less trouble now for the driver. It was still partly below the horizon ahead, but there were more and more clouds; and those near the distant horizon provided a nearly complete block even when only a small fraction of the sky overhead was actually covered. What the clouds failed to hide was largely behind blowing dust and other objects.

Mountains seemed much rarer, though no one assumed this a function of Hotlat alone. Senatsu assured them it was not, that only the two or three million square kilometers around and ahead of them were any smoother than average. She could now confirm the native-given distance to the "city," but could give no more complete a description of it than before. She was certain now that it was beside one of the lakes, but had no data whatever on the nature of the fluid this held. Chemists were waiting impatiently for news on that point.

Senatsu had triumphantly reported resolving the area where the travelers had descended the cliff, and even getting an image of the thicket where the glider had crashed; but this, she said, had not grown more than a meter or two from the wreck. This made no sense to anyone but Nic, who still kept his developing ideas to himself.

The glider count continued to grow. So did the number of crashes. Several times these events were seen from *Annie*, but more often wreckage was sighted to one side or the other of their track. Experience gave the human observers a way to estimate when the wrecks had occurred; it seemed that the plants which represented the remote control mechanism grew uncontrolled for a short time, then died for lack of—something. The natives had clearly not completely mastered aviation, but seemed casual about its dangers.

A clue to the nature of the something was secured when they passed an apparently thriving thicket of the stuff at the edge of a small lake. The evidence was not completely convincing, since no trace of a wrecked flying machine could be seen in the tangle. The distant chemists at Nest were more convinced of the implication than the four on *Annie*; it was, after all, almost dogma among biochemists that life needed liquid; it was a solution-chemistry phenomenon—though the precise solvent seemed less important.

At the present general temperature around *Annie*, it could easily be the cryolite found on *Jellyseal*. Numerous bets were on hold at Nest. Bugs went out from *Annie* to collect samples from the lake, but there was no means of analyzing these on board. There had been a limit to the equipment the tug could carry, no matter how many enthusiasts were involved in the design.

The missing women had been better equipped in this respect, but had apparently postponed sampling until after their cargo was delivered. They had never reported any collecting.

The lightning, even among small clouds, was now almost continuous. Thunder and even wind could be heard most of the time. The crash of one glider was near enough to be audible inside the tug; and of course the rain, frequently materializing with no obvious cloud as a source, could hardly be missed as it drummed on the vehicle's shell. Most of the liquid that struck the ground vanished almost instantly; no one could be sure whether it was evaporating from the hot surface or soaking into it even when an experimental hole was dug by one of the bugs.

The explorers paused—bringing questions from their guides—to watch for results, but these were inconclusive. Whatever was happening was too quick to permit a decision. Pam made an effort to ask the natives, but it was hard to decide afterward whether the questions or the answers were less clear. Tricia, back at Nest, brightened up when this happened and got to work with her computer, but even she remained unsure of what had been said.

At last the welcome **"One kilometer"** sounded, followed a few seconds later by **"Up slope ahead."**

There was indeed a slope ahead, only a few meters high but quite enough to hide what lay beyond. Tug and tank labored up to its crest, and were promptly stopped by Pam. Her husband resumed reporting.

"There's a roughly oval valley below us, with a lake like the one where they tested the paraffin but a lot larger. Sen was right; the lake is about three quarters surrounded by a thicket of the same sort of plants we saw there, and its Hotsouth end is dammed in the same way. There are several low, round hills scattered over the valley. The two closest to the lake are covered with the bushes; all the others are bare. Between the two covered ones is another bare but differently colored space extending a kilometer or so toward the bushes and lake. The overgrown area covers about five by seven kilometers. It borders the Hotnorth side of the lake, which is oval and about three kilometers by two, the long measure running Hotnorth-Hotsouth. In the bare section, directly between the two covered hills is something like a wrecked building about a hundred meters square. I can't guess how high it may have been. Another at the Hoteast edge of the lake seems intact, has about the same area though it isn't quite so perfectly square, and has an intact flat roof. It's about fifteen meters high. They're talking again; you can hear them, I suppose. They seem to want us to—Erni, what's up?" Akmet fell silent.

"Something wrong?" asked Ben, while the rest of Nest stopped whatever it was doing.

"You'll see." It was Icewall's voice. He had gently but firmly sent Pam drifting away from the controls, and was guiding *Annie* toward the nearer of the overgrown hills.

"Thirty-four right" came from the speaker. Again. And again. *Candlegrease* continued straight toward the eminence. Pam managed to silence the native with a rather dishonest "Observing."

Tug and tank descended the valley, crossed the bare part to the nearer overgrown hill, climbed it, and came to a halt looking down on what Akmet had described as a wrecked building. From three kilometers closer, there seemed still no better way to describe it.

The other three cried out together as Erni did a quick-stop. Then, donning a waldo, he deployed one of the smallest bugs and sent it back toward *Candlegrease* on the side toward the lake.

Nic, knowing his partner best and far more experienced with the equipment than the other couple, imitated Icewall's action; but there was no way he could make his bug catch up with the one which had started first. Erni's mechanical servant took hold of the still unsafetied relief valve which had destroyed the other patch so far back, in the natives' grim experiment.

"Hold it, Erni! What do you think you're up to?" The question came in three different voices, with the words slightly different in each, but was understood even at Nest.

"Don't ask silly questions—or don't you care about Maria?"

Nic's lips tightened invisibly behind his breathing mask.

"I care a lot, and so will the kids when they hear. But that's no answer."

Pam was broadcasting deliberately as she cut in; she was uncertain how much the natives would understand, but it seemed worth trying. "You just want to kill a few thousand of these people to get even?"

"Don't be stupid. I won't be killing anyone. This isn't a city, it's one creature. I can punish it—hurt it—without killing it. I can teach it to be careful. You know that, don't you, Nic?"

"I'm pretty sure of it, yes. I'm not sure releasing the paraffin up here won't kill it completely. We're at about the highest point in the valley, much of our juice is denser than the local air, and the wind is random as usual. If we do kill it, it may not be a lesson. We don't know that there are any more of these beings on the planet. We certainly haven't heard from any, and the satellites this one spotted and began talking to can be seen from anywhere on Halfbaked. Think that one over. All the intelligence of a world for two human lives?"

Erni was silent for several seconds, but his servo remained motionless. At last, "You don't know that. You can't be sure."

"Of course I can't. But it's a plausible idea, like the one that this is a single being. Anything I can do to keep you from taking the chance, I'll do. Think it over."

Pam disapproved of what sounded to her like a threat.

"Why are you blaming these people, or this person, whichever it is, anyway? You don't know what happened is their fault."

"They weren't careful enough! Look at that wrecked building there! That's got to be where it happened—"

"And the dead-vegetation area downslope from it! Maybe they weren't careful enough—how could they have been? What do they know about hydrogen compounds? What do *we* know about their behavior here, except what *they* found out and showed us a while ago, long after the girls were gone? What—"

"I don't care what! All I can think about is Jessi! What she was like—what she was—and that I'll never see her or feel her again. Someone's got to learn!"

"You mean someone's got to pay, don't you?"

"All right, someone's got to pay! And what do you think you can do to stop it, Dominic Wildbear Yucca, who is so disgustingly civilized he doesn't care for the memory of the mother of his kids!"

"Who is so disgustingly civilized he doesn't want to admit to his kids, and his friends, that he didn't try to keep a good friend from—"

"Friend! How can you call yourself a—"

"You'll see."

"How?"

What Nic would have said in answer is still unknown; he refused to tell anyone later. Pam cut in again.

"Look! Isn't it enough to scare them—scare it? Look what's happening! Look at the city, or the creature, or whatever it is!"

Even Erni took his eyes from the screen of his servobug. For the first and only time since the native's hydrocarbon experiment, they clearly saw the dandelion seeds. Hordes of them, rocketing up from every part of the overgrown area, catching the swirling, wandering winds, many falling back to the ground close to their launch points, but some being carried up and away in every direction.

The woman saw Erni's distraction, and pressed home her argument. "They want to save what they can! Those things really *are* seeds. They scatter them when the parent is in danger, or knows it's dying!"

"You—you don't know that either." Erni sounded almost subdued, and certainly far less frenzied than a few seconds earlier. Nic began to hope, and waited for Pam to go on.

Erni's attention now was clearly on the scenery rather than his bug. Even though he still had his hands in the waldos, there was a very good chance that Dominic's bug could knock the other away from the valve in time.

Nic took what seemed to him a better chance by passing up the opportunity. Pam was silent, so he finally spoke softly.

"I can forgive your cracks about my not caring, because I do care and know how you feel. But what you want to do is just the same sort of angry, thoughtless thing as those words, isn't it?"

Erni's answer seemed irrelevant.

"If it's scared, why doesn't it ask me to stop?"

"Using what words?" asked Pam softly.

"Me unclear." The native utterance partly overlapped the woman's, and proved the most effective sentence of the argument.

Slowly, Erni drew his hands from the waldo gloves, and gestured Akmet to take over the bug's control.

"Better try to get 'we' across while you're at it, Pam," was all he said. He let himself drift away from controls and window.

"Me and we unclear. One at a time."

Pam might have been smiling behind her mask. She did look hesitantly at her companions, especially Erni. Then she tried her explanation. Numbers, after all, had long been in the common vocabulary.

"Observe *Annie* closely. Me, one animal. We, more than one animal. Four animals in *Annie*."

Erni made no objection, but added quietly, "No valve danger. Which way?"

"Right." Erni, now thoroughly embarrassed, glanced around at the others as though asking whether they really trusted him to drive. The other men were concentrating on the bugs outside, the woman seemed to be watching the putative seeds. They were mostly settled back to the ground or blown out of sight by now. No more were being launched, apparently. *Maybe* the suggested explanation had been right, but even its proponent was skeptical. Maybe they were some sort of weapon . . .

It soon became obvious that *Annie* was being led to the other shedlike structure. This one was at the edge of the lake but somewhat down slope from the overgrown areas. There seemed a likely reason, though not the only possible one, for this: care. No one suggested this aloud to the driver. It seemed too obvious that *Jellyseal* had, during unloading, wrecked the first building and killed much of the being or population which formed the copse.

As they followed instructions along the edge of the overgrown area, bunch after bunch of tangled branches waved close past *Annie*'s windows. Looking in? None of them doubted it. Pam continued alternately reporting and teaching, describing their path and surroundings to Nest and reacting to observations through the window with remarks like "One animal driving. One animal talking. Two animals moving bugs."

They were guided around the structure to the lower side. This was open, and *Annie* was directed to enter. The far side, toward Hotnorth, could be seen to be open also, and though there was much growth within, there was plenty of room for tug and tank. Erni dragged his charge within.

"Stop." Since there was an opening in front, he obeyed, though he remained alert. The bugs operated by Akmet and Nic had come in too, and all four explorers watched, not without an occasional glance forward, as the doorway behind was plugged more and more tightly by growing branches and finally, as nearly as either bug could see, became airtight.

"Carbon hydride stop." Reading between the words, the bug handlers detached *Candlegrease*. Erni eased *Annie* forward. Three things started to happen at once, all interesting for different reasons.

Flattened bladders appeared among the branches and were borne toward *Candlegrease*'s valves. Apparently the paraffin was not to be exposed to local air this time.

A wall of tangled growth began to form between *Annie* and her tow, without waiting for the bugs to get back to the tug. Nic and Akmet, after a quick but silent look at each other, abandoned the machines; there were plenty more, and there seemed no objection to their being "observed" at leisure by the natives.

The doorway ahead began to fill with a similar block. This also caused human reaction. Erni sent the tug grinding firmly forward.

"Oxygen hydride stop."

No attention was paid to this. In a few seconds *Annie* was outside, with a patch of torn and flattened vegetation behind where the growing wall had been.

"Water stop."

Pam remained calm, and Erni did not stop until they were a hundred meters from the lab, as they all now thought of it. Pam explained.

"Water stop danger for animals."

The native voice did not respond at once, and after some seconds Cloud's voice reached them from Nest.

"Y'know, Pam dear, I think you've just faced your friend outside with the problem of what an individual is. Don't be surprised if you have to restate that one."

The woman answered promptly and professionally.

"You mean my friend or friends. You're hypothesizing still. Let's call this one Abby, and start looking around for Bill—"

"Water next time."

"Water next time," she agreed.

"All right, it's—they're—she's civilized," muttered Erni after a moment.

"Of course. So are you," answered Dominic. All three looked at him sharply, but he ignored the couple.

"You wouldn't really have turned that valve, would you?"

The younger man was silent for several seconds. "I don't think so," he said at last.

"We didn't really talk you out of it, did we?"

"I guess not. That's the funny part. Once I was where I *could* do it, I—I don't know; I guess having the power, knowing I was in charge and no one could stop me—well, that was enough." He paused. "I think. Then the arguments distracted me, and I realized you'd sneaked your bug close enough so you probably *could* have stopped me. And I didn't care that you could.

"Nic, I'll help you tell the kids, if you'll tell me why getting even can seem so important."

"We'd better tell them that, too. If we can figure it out. Y'know, I'm not sure I *would've* stopped you."

The Treeferns listened sympathetically, and since they were also human not even Pam thought to ask why *Jellyseal's* failure was the natives' fault.

everywhere

GEOFF RYMAN

Science fiction is sometimes criticized for concentrating too much on the dystopian and the apocalyptic, on the bleak pessimistic future, on how awful things are going to be in the years ahead, but occasionally a story set in a viable-feeling utopian future does see print—a future that seems like it might actually come to pass, with luck, one that gives us hope that living in the 21st century and beyond might not be so bad after all—although usually, as in the brilliant little story that follows, to the people who actually live in that future, it's not utopia at all, just everyday life: nothing special, no big deal, just the way things are. Which, of course, is the way utopias feel to those lucky enough to live inside them . . .

Born in Canada, Geoff Ryman now lives in England. He made his first sale in 1976, to New Worlds, but it was not until 1984, when he made his first appearance in Interzone (the magazine where almost all of his published short fiction has appeared) with his brilliant novella "The Unconquered Country" that he first attracted any serious attention. "The Unconquered Country," one of the best novellas of the decade, had a stunning impact on the science fiction scene of the day, and almost overnight established Ryman as one of the most accomplished writers of his generation, winning him both the British Science Fiction Award and the World Fantasy Award; it was later published in a book version, The Unconquered Country: A Life History. *His output has been sparse since then, by the high-production standards of the genre, but extremely distinguished, with his novel* The Child Garden: A Low Comedy *winning both the prestigious Arthur C. Clarke Award and the John W. Campbell Memorial Award. His other novels include* The Warrior Who Carried Life, *the critically acclaimed mainstream novel* Was, *and a collection of four of his novellas,* Unconquered Countries. *His most recent book is the underground cult classic* 253, *the "print remix" of an "interactive hypertext novel" that in its original form ran on-line on Ryman's home page of www.ryman-novel.com; call it what you will, novel or print remix,* 253 *recently won the Philip K. Dick Award. Ryman's stories have appeared in our Twelfth and Thirteenth Annual Collections.*

W hen we knew Granddad was going to die, we took him to see the Angel of
the North.

When he got there, he said: It's all different. There were none of these oaks all
around it then, he said, Look at the size of them! The last time I saw this, he says
to me, I was no older than you are now, and it was brand new, and we couldn't
make out if we liked it or not.

We took him, the whole lot of us, on the tram from Blaydon. We made a day
of it. All of Dad's exes and their exes and some of their kids and me Aunties and
their exes and their kids. It wasn't that happy a group to tell you the truth. But
Granddad loved seeing us all in one place.

He was going a bit soft by then. He couldn't tell what the time was anymore
and his words came out wrong. The Mums made us sit on his lap. He kept calling
me by my dad's name. His breath smelt funny but I didn't mind, not too much.
He told me about how things used to be in Blaydon.

They used to have a gang in the Dene called Pedro's Gang. They drank something called Woodpecker and broke people's windows and they left empty tins of
pop in the woods. If you were little you weren't allowed out cos everyone's Mum
was so fearful and all. Granddad once saw twelve young lads go over and hit an
old woman and take her things. One night his brother got drunk and put his fist
through a window, and he went to the hospital, and he had to wait hours before
they saw him and that was terrible.

I thought it sounded exciting meself. But I didn't say so because Granddad
wanted me to know how much better things are now.

He says to me, like: the trouble was, Landlubber, we were just kids, but we all
thought the future would be terrible. We all thought the world was going to burn
up, and that everyone would get poorer and poorer, and the crime worse.

He told me that lots of people had no work. I don't really understand how
anyone could have nothing to do. But then I've never got me head around what
money used to be either.

Or why they built that Angel. It's not even that big, and it was old and covered
in rust. It didn't look like an Angel to me at all, the wings were so big and square.
Granddad said, no, it looks like an airplane, that's what airplanes looked like back
then. It's meant to go rusty, it's the Industrial Spirit of the North.

I didn't know what he was on about. I asked Dad why the Angel was so important and he kept explaining it had a soul, but couldn't say how. The church
choir showed up and started singing hymns. Then it started to rain. It was a
wonderful day out.

I went back into the tram and asked me watch about the Angel.

This is my watch, here, see? It's dead good isn't it, it's got all sorts on it. It takes
photographs and all. Here, look, this is the picture it took of Granddad by the

Angel. It's the last picture I got of him. You can talk to people on it. And it keeps thinking of fun things for you to do.

Why not explain to the interviewer why the Angel of the North is important?

Duh. Usually they're fun.

Take the train to Newcastle and walk along the river until you see on the hill where people keep their homing pigeons. Muck out the cages for readies.

It's useful when you're a bit short, it comes up with ideas to make some dosh.

It's really clever. It takes all the stuff that goes on around here and stirs it around and comes up with something new. Here, listen:

The laws of evolution have been applied to fun. New generations of ideas are generated and eliminated at such a speed that evolution works in real time. It's survival of the funnest and you decide.

They evolve machines too. Have you seen our new little airplanes? They've run the designs through thousands of generations, and they got better and faster and smarter.

The vicar bought the whole church choir airplanes they can wear. The wings are really good, they look just like bird's wings with pinions sticking out like this. Oh! I really want one of them. You can turn somersaults in them. People build them in their sheds for spare readies, I could get one now if I had the dosh.

Every Sunday as long as it isn't raining, you can see the church choir take off in formation. Little old ladies in leotards and blue jeans and these big embroidered Mexican hats. They rev up and take off and start to sing the Muslim call to prayer. They echo all over the show. Then they cut their engines and spiral up on the updraft. That's when they start up on Nearer My God to Thee.

Every Sunday, Granddad and I used to walk up Shibbon Road to the Dene. It's so high up there that we could look down on top of them. He never got over it. Once he laughed so hard he fell down, and just lay there on the grass. We just lay on our backs and looked up at the choir, they just kept going up like they were kites.

When the Travellers come to Blaydon, they join in. Their wagons are pulled by horses and have calliopes built into the front, so on Sundays, when the choir goes up, the calliopes start up, so you got organ music all over the show as well. Me Dad calls Blaydon a sound sandwich. He says it's all the hills.

The Travellers like our acoustics, so they come here a lot. They got all sorts to trade. They got these bacteria that eat rubbish, and they hatch new machines, like smart door keys that only work for the right people. They make their own beer, but you got to be a bit careful how much you drink.

Granddad and I used to take some sarnies and our sleeping bags and kip with them. The Travellers go everywhere, so they sit around the fire and tell about all sorts going on, not just in England but France and Italia. One girl, her Mum let her go with them for a whole summer. She went to Prague and saw all these Buddhist monks from Thailand. They were Travellers and all.

Granddad used to tell the Travellers his stories too. When he was young he went to Mexico. India. The lot. You could in them days. He even went to Egypt, my Granddad. He used to tell the Travellers the same stories, over and over, but they never seemed to notice. Like, when he was in Egypt he tried to rent this boat to take him onto the Delta, and he couldn't figure why it was so expensive, and when he got on it, he found he'd rented a car ferry all to himself by mistake. He had the whole thing to himself. The noise of the engines scared off the birds which was the only reason he'd wanted the boat.

So, Granddad was something of a Traveller himself. He went everywhere.

There's all sorts to do around Blaydon. We got dolphins in the municipal swimming pool.

We dug it ourselves, in the Haughs just down there by the river. It's tidal, our river. Did you know? It had dolphins anyway, but our pool lured them in. They like the people and the facilities, like the video conferencing. They like video conferencing, do dolphins. They like being fed and all.

My Dad and I help make the food. We grind up fish heads on a Saturday at Safeways. It smells rotten to me, but then I'm not an aquatic mammal, am I? That's how we earned the readies to buy me my watch. You get everyone along grinding fish heads, everybody takes turns. Then you get to go to the swimming.

Sick people get first crack at swimming with the dolphins. When Granddad was sick, he'd take me with him. There'd be all this steam coming off the water like in a vampire movie. The dolphins always knew who wasn't right, what was wrong with them. Mrs. Grathby had trouble with her joints, they always used to be gentle with her, just nudge her along with their noses like. But Granddad, there was one he called Liam. Liam always used to jump up and land real hard right next to him, splash him all over and Granddad would push him away, laughing like, you know? He loved Liam. They were pals.

Have a major water-fight on all floors of the Grand Hotel in Newcastle.

Hear that? It just keeps doing that until something takes your fancy.

Hire Dad the giant bunny rabbit costume again and make him wear it.

We did that once before. It was dead fun. I think it knows Dad's a bit down since Granddad.

Call your friend Heidi and ask her to swap clothes with you and pretend to be each other for a day.

Aw Jeez! Me sister's been wearing me watch again! It's not fair! It mucks it up, it's supposed to know what I like, not her and that flipping Heidi. And she's got her own computer, it's loads better than mine, it looks like a shirt and has earphones, so no one else can hear it. It's not fair! People just come clod-hopping through. You don't get to keep nothing.

Look this is all I had to do to get this watch!

Grind fishfood on 3.11, 16.11, 20.12 and every Sunday until 3.3
Clean pavements three Sundays
Deliver four sweaters for Step Mum
Help Dad with joinery for telecoms outstation
Wire up Mrs Grathby for video immersion
Attend school from April 10th to 31 July inclusive

I did even more than that. At least I got some over. I'm saving up for a pair of cars.

Me and me mates love using the cars. I borrow me Dad's pair. You wear them like shoes and they're smart. It's great fun on a Sunday. We all go whizzin down Lucy Street together, which is this great big hill, but the shoes won't let you go too fast or crash into anything. We all meet up, whizz around in the mall in great big serpent. You can pre-program all the cars together, so you all break up and then all at once come back together, to make shapes and all.

Granddad loved those cars. He hated his stick, so he'd go shooting off in my Dad's pair, ducking and weaving, and shouting back to me, Come on, Landlubber, keep up! I was a bit scared in them days, but he kept up at me til I joined in. He'd get into those long lines, and we'd shoot off the end of them, both of us. He'd hold me up.

He helped me make me lantern and all. Have you seen our lanterns, all along the mall? They look good when the phosphors go on at night. All the faces on them are real people, you know. You know the ink on them's made of these tiny chips with legs? Dad's seen them through a microscope, he says they look like synchronized swimmers.

I got one with my face on it. I was bit younger then so I have this really naff crew cut. Granddad helped me make it. It tells jokes. I'm not very good at making jokes up, but Granddad had this old joke book. At least I made the effort.

Let's see, what else. There's loads around here. We got the sandbox in front of the old mall. Everybody has a go at that, making things. When King William died all his fans in wheelchairs patted together a picture of him in sand. Then it rained. But it was a good picture.

Our sandbox is a bit different. It's got mostly real sand. There's only one corner of it computer dust. It's all right for kids and that or people who don't want to do things themselves. I mean when we were little we had the dust make this great big 3D sign Happy Birthday Granddad Piper. He thought it was wonderful because if you were his age and grew up with PCs and that, it must be wonderful, just to think of something and have it made.

I don't like pictures, they're too easy. Me, I like to get stuck in. If I go to the sandbox to make something, I want to come back with sand under me fingernails. Me Dad's the same. When Newcastle won the cup, me and me mates made this big Newcastle crest out of real sand. Then we had a sandfight. It took me a week to get the sand out of me hair. I got loads of mates now, but I didn't used to.

Granddad was me mate for a while. I guess I was his pet project. I always was a bit quiet, and a little bit left out, and also I got into a bit of trouble from time to time. He got me out of myself.

You know I was telling you about the Angel? When I went back into that tram I sat and listened to the rain on the roof. It was dead quiet and there was nobody around, so I could be meself. So I asked me watch. OK then. What is this Angel? And it told me the story of how the Angel of the North got a soul.

There was this prisoner in Hull jail for thieving cos he run out of readies cos he never did nothing. It was all his fault really, he says so himself. He drank and cheated his friends and all that and did nothing with all his education.

He just sat alone in his cell. First off, he was angry at the police for catching him, and then he was angry with himself for getting caught and doing it and all of that. Sounds lovely, doesn't he? Depressing isn't the word.

Then he got this idea, to give the Angel a soul.

It goes like this. There are 11 dimensions, but we only see three of them and time, and the others are what was left over after the Big Bang. They're too small to see but they're everywhere at the same time, and we live in them too, but we don't know it. There's no time there, so once something happens, it's like a photograph, you can't change it.

So what the prisoner of Hull said that means is that everything we do gets laid down in the other dimensions like train tracks. It's like a story, and it doesn't end until we die, and that does the job for us. That's our soul, that story.

So what the prisoner in Hull does, is work in the prison, get some readies and pay to have a client put inside the Angel's head.

And all the other computers that keep track of everyone's jobs or the questions they asked, or just what they're doing, that all gets uploaded to the Angel.

Blaydon's there. It's got all of us, grinding fish heads. Every time someone makes tea or gets married from Carlisle to Ulverton from Newcastle to Derby, that gets run through the Angel. And that Angel is laying down the story of the North.

My watch told me that, sitting in that tram.

Then everyone else starts coming back in, but not Dad and Granddad, so I go out to fetch them.

The clouds were all pulled down in shreds. It looked like the cotton candy that Dad makes at fêtes. The sky was full of the church choir in their little airplanes. For just a second, it looked like a Mother Angel, with all her little ones.

I found Dad standing alone with Granddad. I thought it was rain on my Dad's face, but it wasn't. He was looking at Granddad, all bent and twisted, facing into the wind.

We got to go Dad, I said.

And he said, In a minute son. Granddad was looking up at the planes and smiling.

And I said it's raining Dad. But they weren't going to come in. So I looked at the Angel and all this rust running off it in red streaks onto the concrete. So I asked, if it's an Angel of the North, then why is it facing south?

And Granddad says, Because it's holding out its arms in welcome.

He didn't want to go.

We got him back into the tram, and back home, and he started to wheeze a bit, so me Step Mum put him to bed and about eight o'clock she goes in to swab his teeth with vanilla, and she comes out and says to Dad, I think he's stopped breathing.

So I go in, and I can see, no he's still breathing. I can hear it. And his tongue flicks, like he's trying to say something. But Dad comes in, and they all start to cry and carry on. And the neighbours all come in, yah, yah, yah, and I keep saying, it's not true, look, he's still breathing. What do they have to come into it for, it's not their Granddad, is it?

No one was paying any attention to the likes of me, were they? So I just take off. There's this old bridge you're not allowed on. It's got trees growing out of it. The floor's gone, and you have to walk along the top of the barricades. You fall off, you go straight into the river, but it's a good dodge into Newcastle.

So I just went and stood there for a bit, looking down on the river. Me Granddad used to take me sailing. We'd push off from the Haughs, and shoot out under this bridge, I could see where we were practically. And we'd go all the way down the Tyne and out to sea. He used to take me out to where the dolphins were. You'd see Liam come up. He was still wearing his computer, Liam, like a crown.

So I'm standing on the bridge, and me watch says: go down to the swimming pool, and go and tell Liam that Granddad's dead.

It's a bit like a dog I guess. You got to show one dog the dead body of the other or it will pine.

So I went down to the pool, but it's late and raining and there's nobody there, and I start to call him, like: Liam! Li-am! But he wasn't there.

So me watch says: he's wearing his computer: give him a call on his mobile.

So me watch goes bleep bleep bleep, and there's a crackle and suddenly I hear a whoosh and crickle, and there's all these cold green waves on the face of my watch, and I say Liam? Liam, this is me, remember me, Liam? My Granddad's dead Liam. I thought you might need to know.

But what is he, just a dolphin right, I don't know what it meant. How's he supposed to know who I am. You all right then, Liam? Catching lots of fish are you? So I hung up.

And I stand there, and the rain's really bucketing down, and I don't want to go home. Talking to yourself. It's the first sign, you know.

And suddenly me watch starts up again, and it's talking to me with Granddad's voice. You wanna hear what it said? Here. Hear.

Hello there, Landlubber. How are ya? This is your old Granddad. It's a dead clever world we live in, isn't it? They've rigged this thing up here, so that I can put this in your watch for when you need it.

Listen, me old son. You mustn't grieve, you know. Things are different now. They know how it works. We used to think we had a little man in our heads who watched everything on a screen and when you died he went to heaven not you. Now, they know, there's no little man, there's no screen. There's just a brain putting everything together. And what we do is ask ourselves: what do we think about next? What do we do next?

You know all about those dimension things, don't you? Well I got a name for them. I call them Everywhere. Cos they are. And I want you to know, that I'm Everywhere now.

That's how we live forever in heaven these days. And it's true, me old son. You think of me still travelling around Mexico before I met your Mamby. Think of me in India. Think of me learning all about readies to keep up with you lot. Think of me on me boat, sailing out to sea. Remember that day I took you sailing out beyond the Tyne mouth? It's still there, Landlubber.

You know, all the evil in the world, all the sadness comes from not having a good answer to that question: what do I do next? You just keep thinking of good things to do, lad. You'll be all right. We'll all be all right. I wanted you to know that.

I got me footie on Saturdays, Granddad. Then I'm thinking I'll start up school again. They got a sailing club now. I thought I'd join it, Granddad, thought I'd take them out to where you showed me the dolphins. I'll tell them about Everywhere.

Did you know, Granddad?

They're making a new kind of watch. It's going to show us Everywhere, too.

Hothouse flowers

Mike Resnick

Mike Resnick is one of the bestselling authors in science fiction, and one of the most prolific. His many novels include The Dark Lady, Stalking the Unicorn, Paradise, Santiago, Ivory, Soothsayer, Oracle, Lucifer Jones, Purgatory, Inferno, A Miracle of Rare Design, A Hunger in the Soul, *and* The Widowmaker. *His award-winning short fiction has been gathered in the collection* Will the Last Person to Leave the Planet Please Turn Off the Sun? *Of late, he has become almost as prolific as an anthologist, editing* Inside the Funhouse: 17 SF stories about SF, Whatdunits, More Whatdunits, *and* Shaggy B.E.M Stories; *a long string of anthologies co-edited with Martin H. Greenberg,* Alternate Presidents, Alternate Kennedys, Alternate Warriors, Aladdin: Master of the Lamp, Dinosaur Fantastic, By Any Other Fame, Alternate Outlaws, *and* Sherlock Holmes in Orbit, *among others; as well as two anthologies co-edited with Gardner Dozois,* Future Earths: Under African Skies *and* Future Earths: Under South American Skies. *He won the Hugo Award in 1989 for "Kirinyaga." He won another Hugo Award in 1991 for another story in the Kirinyaga series, "The Manumouki," another Hugo and Nebula in 1995 for his novella "Seven Views of Olduvai Gorge," and another Hugo in 1998 for his story "The 43 Antarean Dynasties." His most recent books include the novel* The Widowmaker Reborn, *and a collection of his award-winning Kirinyaga stories (although Resnick himself considers it to be a mosaic novel),* Kirinyaga. *Several of his books are in the process of being turned into Big-Budget movies. His stories have appeared in our Sixth, Seventh, Ninth, Eleventh, Twelfth, and Fourteenth Annual Collections. He lives with his wife, Carol, in Cincinnati, Ohio. He has a web site at www.mikeresnick.com.*

When the haunting and deceptively quiet little story that follows first appeared, a couple of critics said that they found its core scenario "unlikely." If you've spent long hours in nursing homes with aged and infirm relatives, though, as I've had to do again and again in the last few years, you soon come to realize that, alas, it's all too likely . . .

I test the temperature. It is 83 degrees, warm but not hot. Just right. I spend the next hour puttering around, checking medications, adjusting the humidity, cleaning one of the life stations. Then Superintendent Bailey stops by on his way out to dinner.

"How are your charges doing?" he asks. "Any problems today?"

"No, sir, everything's fine," I answer.

"Good," he says. "We wouldn't want any problems, especially not with the celebration coming up."

The celebration is the turn of the century, although there is some debate about that, because we are all preparing to celebrate the instant the clock hits midnight and A.D. 2200 begins, but some spoilsport scientists (or maybe they're mathematicians) have told the press that the new century *really* begins a year later, when we enter 2201.

Not that my charges know the difference, but I'm glad we're celebrating it this year, because it means that we'll decorate the place with bright colors—and if we like it, why, we'll do it again in 2201.

I have been married to Felicia for seventeen years, and I hardly ever regret it. She was a little bit pudgy when we met, and she has gotten pudgier over the years so that now she is honest-to-goodness fat and there is simply no other word for it. Her hair, which used to be brown, is streaked with gray now, and she's lost whatever physical grace she once had. But she is a good life partner. Her taste in holos is similar to mine, so we almost never fight about what to watch after dinner, and of course we both love our work.

As we eat dinner, the topic turns to our gardens, as always.

"I'm worried about Rex," she confides.

Rex is *Begonia rex*, her hanging basket.

"Oh?" I say. "What's wrong with him?"

She shakes her head in puzzlement. "I don't know. Perhaps I've been letting him get *too* much sun. His leaves are yellowing, and his roots could be in better shape."

"Have you spoken to one of the botanists?"

"No. They're totally absorbed in cloning that new species of *Aglaonema crispum*."

"Still?"

She shrugs. "They say it's important."

"The damned plant's been around for centuries," I say. "I can't see what's so important about it."

"I told you: they engineered an exciting mutation. It actually glows in the dark, as if it's been dusted with phosphorescent silver paint."

"It's not going to put the energy company out of business."

"I know. But it's important to *them*."

"It seems unfair," I say for the hundredth, or maybe the thousandth, time. "They get all the fame and money for creating a new species, and you get paid the same old salary for keeping it alive."

"I don't mind," she replies. "I love my work. I don't know what I'd do without my greenhouse."

"I know," I say soothingly. "I feel the same way."

"So how is *your* Rex today?" she asks.

It's my turn to shrug. "About the same as usual." Suddenly I laugh.

"What's so funny?" asks Felicia.

"You think your Rex is getting too much sun. I decided *my* Rex wasn't getting enough, so this afternoon I moved him closer to a window."

"Will it make a difference, do you think?" she asks.

I sigh deeply. "Does it ever?"

I walk up to the major and smile at him. "How are we today?" I ask.

The major looks at me through unfocused eyes. There is a little drool running out the side of his mouth, and I wipe it off.

"It's a lovely morning," I say. "It's a pity you can't be outside to enjoy it." I pause, waiting for the reaction that never comes. "Still," I continue, "you've seen more than your share of them, so missing a few won't hurt." I check the screen at his life station, find his birthdate, and dope it out. "Well, I'll be damned! You've actually seen 60,573 mornings!"

Of course, he's been here for almost half of them: 29,882 to be exact. If he ever did count them, he stopped a long time ago.

I clean and sterilize his feeding tubes and his medication tubes and his breathing tubes, examine him for bedsores, wash him, take his temperature and blood pressure, and check to make sure his cholesterol hasn't gone above the 350 level. (They want it lower, of course, but he can't exercise and they've been feeding him intravenously for more than half a century, so they won't do anything about changing his diet. After all, it hasn't killed him so far, and altering it just might do so.)

I elevate his withered body just long enough to change the bedding, then gently lower him back down. (That used to take ten minutes, and at least one helper, before they developed the anti-grav beam. Now it's just a matter of a few seconds, and I like to think it causes less discomfort, though of course the major is in no condition to tell me.)

Then it's on to Rex. Felicia has problems with her Rex, and I have problems with mine.

"Good morning, Rex," I say.

He mumbles something incomprehensible at me.

I look down at him. His right eye is bloodshot and tearing heavily.

"Rex, what am I going to do with you?" I say. "You know you're not supposed to stare at the sun."

He doesn't really know it. I doubt that he even knows his name is Rex. But cleansing his eye and medicating it is going to put me behind schedule, and I have to blame *someone*. Rex doesn't mind being blamed. He doesn't mind burning out his retina. He doesn't even mind lying motionless for decades. If there is anything he *does* mind, nobody's found it yet.

I spill some medication on him while fixing his eye, so I decide that rather than just change his diaper I might as well go all the way and give him a DryChem bath. I marvel, as always, at the sheer number of surgical scars that criss-cross his torso: the first new heart, the second, the new kidneys, the new spleen, the new left lung. There's a tiny, ancient scar on his lower belly that I think was from the removal of a burst appendix, but I can't find any record of it on the computer and he's been past talking about it for almost a century.

Then I move on to Mr. Spinoza. He's lying there, mouth agape, eyes open, head at an awkward angle. I can tell even before I reach him that he's not breathing. My first inclination is to call Emergency, but I realize that his life station will have reported his condition already, and sure enough, just seconds later the Resurrection Team arrives and sets up a curtain around him (as if any of his roommates could see or care), and within ten minutes they've got the old gentleman going again.

This is the fifth time Mr. Spinoza has died this year. All this dying has to be hard on his system, and I worry that one of these days it's going to be permanent.

"So how was your major today?" asks Felicia at dinner.

"Same as usual," I say. "How's yours?"

Her major is the *Browallia speciosa majorus*. "Ditto," she says. "Old, but hanging on." She frowns. "We may not get any blossoms this year, though. The roots are a little ropey."

"I'm sorry to hear it."

"It happens." She pauses. "How was the rest of your day?"

"We had some excitement," I reply.

"Oh?"

"Mr. Spinoza died again."

"That's the fourth time, isn't it?" she asks.

"The fifth," I correct her. "The Resurrection Team revived him."

"The Resuscitation Team," she corrects me.

"You have your word for them, I have mine," I say. "Mine's better. Resurrection is what they do."

"So you've only lost one this week," says Felicia, if not changing the subject at least moving on a tangent away from it.

"Right. Mr. Lazlo. He was 193 years old."

"One hundred and ninety-three," she muses, and then shrugs. "I guess he was entitled."

"You mentioned that you lost one too," I note.

"My *cymbidium*."

"That's an orchid, right?" I say. "The one they nicknamed Peter Pan?"

She nods.

"Silly name for an orchid," I remark.

"It stayed young forever, or so it seemed," she replies. "It had the most exquisite blooms. I'm really going to miss it. I'd had it for almost twenty years." She smiles sadly, and a single tear begins to roll down her cheek. "I worked so hard over it, sometimes I felt like its mother." She looks at me. "That sounds ludicrous, doesn't it?"

"Not at all," I say, sincerely touched by her grief.

"It's all right," she says. Then she stares at my face. "Don't be so concerned. It was just a flower."

"It's called empathy," I answer, and she lets it drop . . . but I *am* troubled, and by the oddest thought: *Shouldn't I feel worse about losing a person than she feels about losing an orchid?*

But I don't.

I don't know when it began. Probably with the first caveman who made a sling for a broken arm, or forced water out of a drowned companion's lungs. But somewhere back in the dim and distant past man invented medicine. It had its good centuries and its bad centuries, but by the end of the last millennium it was curing so many diseases and extending so many lives that things got out of hand.

More than half the people who were alive in 2050 were still alive in 2150. And almost 90 percent of the people who were alive in 2100 will be alive in 2200. Medical science had doubled and then trebled man's life span. Immortality was within our grasp. Life everlasting beckoned.

We were so busy increasing the length of life that no one gave much thought to the *quality* of those extended lives.

And then we woke up one day to find that there were a lot more of them than there were of us.

His name is Bernard Goldmeier. They carry him in on an airsled, then transfer him to Mr. Lazlo's old life station.

After I clean the major's tubes and change his bedding and medicate Rex's eye, I call up Mr. Goldmeier's medical history on the holoscreen at his life station.

"This place stinks!" rasps a dry voice.

I jump, startled, then turn to see who spoke. There is no one in the room except me and my charges.

"Who said that?" I demanded.

"I did," replies Mr. Goldmeier.

I look closely at him. The skin hangs loose and brown-spotted on his bald head. His cheeks are covered by miscolored flesh and his nose has oxygen tubes inserted into it—but his eyes, sunken deep in his head, are clear and he is staring at me.

"You really spoke!" I exclaim.

"You never heard an inmate speak before?"

"Not that I remember."

Which is another unhappy truth. By age hundred, one out of every two people has some form of senile dementia. By one hundred and twenty-five, it's four out of five. By one hundred and fifty, it's ninety-nine out of one hundred. Mr. Goldmeier is one hundred and fifty-three years old; the odds against his retaining anything close to normal mental capacities are better than a hundred to one.

"I should add," I say, "that the proper term is 'charge,' not 'patient' and certainly not 'inmate.' "

"A zombie by any other name . . ."

I decide there is no sense arguing with him. "How do you feel?" I ask.

"Look at me," he says disgustedly. "How would *you* feel?"

"If you're in any discomfort . . ." I begin.

"I told you: this place stinks. It reeks of shit and urine."

"Some of our charges are incontinent," I explain. "We have to show them understanding and compassion."

"Why?" he rasps. "What do they show us in exchange?"

"Try to be a little more tolerant," I say.

"You try!" he snaps. "I'm busy!"

I can't help but ask: "Busy doing what?"

"Hanging on to reality!"

I smile. "Is that so difficult?"

"Why don't you ask some of your other inmates?" He sniffs the air and makes a face. "Goddamnit! Another one's crapping all over himself! What the hell am I doing here anyway? I'm not a fucking vegetable yet!"

I check all the notations on the screen.

"You're here, Mr. Goldmeier," I say, not without some satisfaction at what I'm about to tell him, "because no other ward will have you. You've offended every attendant and orderly in the entire complex."

"Where do I go when I offend you?"

"This is your last stop. You're here for better or worse."

Lucky me. I turn back to the holoscreen and begin punching in the standard questions.

"What are you doing now?" he demands. He tries to boost himself up on a scrawny, miscolored elbow to watch me, but he's too weak.

"Checking to see if I'm to medicate you for any diseases," I reply.

"I haven't been out of bed in forty years," he rasps. "If I have a disease, I got it from one of you goons."

I ignore his answer and continue staring at the screen. "You have a history of cancer."

"Big deal," he says. "As quick as I get it, you bastards cure it." He pauses. "Seventeen cancers. You cut five out, burned three out, and drowned the other nine in your chemicals."

I keep reading the screen. "I see you still have your original heart," I note with some surprise. Most hearts are replaced by the time the patient is 120 years old, the lungs and kidneys even sooner.

"Are you offering me yours?" he says sarcastically.

Okay, so he's an arrogant, hostile bastard—but he's also my only charge who's capable of speech, so I force a smile and try again.

"You're a lucky man," I begin.

He glares at me. "You want to explain that?"

"You've retained your mental acuity. Very few manage that at your advanced age."

"And you think that's lucky, do you?"

"Certainly."

"Then you're a fool," said Mr. Goldmeier.

I sigh. "I'm trying very hard to be your friend. You're not making it easy."

His emaciated face contracts in a look of disgust. "Why in hell should you want to be my friend?"

"I want to be friends with all my charges."

"*Them?*" he says contemptuously, scanning the room. "You'd probably get more reaction from a bunch of potted plants." It's not dissimilar from what Felicia says on occasion.

"Look," I say. "You're going to be here for a very long time. So am I. Why don't we at least try to cultivate the illusion of civility?"

"That's a disgusting thought."

"Being civil?" I ask, wondering what kind of creature they have delivered to my ward.

"That too," he says. "But I meant being here for a very long time." He exhales deeply, and I hear a rattling in his chest and make a mental note to tell the doctors about his congestion. Then he adds: "Being *anywhere* for a very long time."

"What makes you so bitter?" I ask.

"I've seen terrible things, things no man should ever have to see."

"We've had our share," I agree. "The war with Brazil. The meteor that hit Mozambique. The revolution in Canada."

"Fool!" he snaps. "Those were *diversions.*"

"Diversions?" I repeat incredulously. "Just what hellholes have you been to?"

"The worst," he answers. "I've been to places where men begged for death, and slowly went mad when it didn't come."

"I don't remember reading or hearing about anything like that," I say. "Where was this?"

He stares unblinking at me for a long moment before he answers. "Right here, in the wards."

Felicia looks up from her plate. "His name's Bernard Goldmeier?" she says.

"That's right."

"I don't have any Bernards," she says. "It's not the kind of name they give to flowers."

"It doesn't matter."

Suddenly her face brightens. "I do have a gold flower, though—a *Mesembryanthemum criniflorum*. I can call it Goldie, or even Goldmeier."

"It's not important."

"But it is," she insists. "For years it's been how we compare our days." She smiles. "It makes me feel closer to you, caring for flowers with the same names."

"Fine," I say. "Call it whatever you want."

"You seem"—she searches for the word—"upset."

"He troubles me."

"Oh? Why?"

"I love my work," I begin.

"I know you do."

"And it's meaningful work," I continue, trying to keep the resentment from my voice. "Maybe I'm not a doctor, but I stand guard over them and hold Death at bay. That's important, isn't it?"

"Of course it is," she says soothingly.

"He belittles it."

"That doesn't mean a thing," says Felicia, reaching across the table and taking my hand. "You know how they get when they're that old."

Yes, I know how they get. But he's not like them. He sounds—I don't know—normal, like me; that's the upsetting part.

"He doesn't seem irrational," I say aloud. "Just bitter."

"Enough bitterness will make anyone irrational."

"I know," I say. "But . . ."

"But what?"

"Well, it's going to sound juvenile and selfish . . ."

"You're the least selfish man I know," says Felicia. "Tell me what's bothering you."

"It's just that . . . well, I always thought that if my charges could speak to me, they'd tell me how grateful they were, how much my efforts meant to them." I pause and think about it. "Does that make me selfish?"

"Certainly not," she replies. "I think they *ought* to be grateful." She pats my hand. "A lot of people in that place are just earning salaries; you're there because you care."

"Anyway, here I've finally got someone who *could* thank me, could tell me that I'm appreciated, and instead he's furious because I'm going to do everything within my power to keep him alive."

She coos and purrs and makes soothing noises, but she doesn't actually *say* anything, and finally I change the subject and ask her about her garden. A moment later she is rapturously describing the new buds on the *Aphelandra squarrosa*, and telling me that she thinks she will have to divide the *Scilla sibirica*, and I listen gratefully and do not think about Mr. Goldmeier, lying motionless in his bed and cursing the darkness, until I arrive at work in the morning.

"Are you feeling any better today?" I ask as I approach Mr. Goldmeier's life station.

"No, I'm not feeling better today," he says nastily. "God's fresh out of miracles."

"Are you at least adjusting to your new surroundings?"

"Hell, no."

"You will."

"I damned well better not!"

I stare at him. "You're not leaving here."

"I know."

"Then you might as well get used to the place."

"Never!"

"I don't understand you at all," I say.

"That's because you're a fool!" he snaps. "Look at me! I have no money and no family. I can't feed myself or even sit up."

"That's no reason to be so hostile," I say placatingly. I am about to tell him that his condition is no different from most of my charges, but he speaks first.

"All I have left is my rage. I won't let you take it away; it's all that separates me from the vegetables here."

I look at him and shake my head sadly. "I don't know what made you like this."

"One hundred and fifty-three years made me like this," he says.

I continue staring at him, at the atrophied legs that will never walk again, at the shriveled arms and skeletal fingers, at the deathmask skull with its burning, sunken eyes, and I think: *Maybe—just maybe—senility is Nature's way of making life in such a body tolerable. Maybe you're not as lucky as I thought.*

The major's chin is wet with drool, and I walk over to him and wipe it off.

"There," I say. "Clean as a whistle."

Okay, I think, staring down at him. *You're not grateful, but at least you don't hate me for doing what you can no longer do for yourself. Why can't they all be like you?*

"Why don't you ask for a transfer to another ward if he's bothering you that much?" asks Felicia.

"What would I say?" I reply. "That this old man who can't even roll over without help is driving me away?"

"Just tell them you want a change."

I shake my head. "My work is important to me. My *charges* are important to me. I can't turn my back on them just because he makes my life miserable."

"Maybe you should sit down and figure out *why* he upsets you."

"He makes me think uncomfortable thoughts."

"What kind of uncomfortable thoughts?"

"I don't want to talk about it," I reply. But what I really mean is: *I don't want to think about it.*

I just wish I could get my brain to listen to me.

Superintendent Bailey enters the ward and approaches me.

"I'm going to need you to work a little overtime today," he informs me.

"Oh?" I reply. "What's the problem?"

"There must be some virus going around," he says. "A third of the staff has called in sick."

"All right. I'll just have to let Felicia know I'll be late for dinner. Where do you want me to go when I'm through here?"

"Ward 87."

"Isn't that a women's ward?" I ask.

"Yes."

"I'd rather have a different assignment, sir."

"And I'd rather have a full staff!" he snaps. "We're both doomed to be disappointed today."

He turns and leaves the ward.

"What have you got against women?" croaks Mr. Goldmeier. I had thought he was asleep, but he's been lying there, motionless, with his eyes (and his ears) wide open.

"Nothing," I answer. "I just don't think I should bathe them."

"Why the hell not?"

"It's a matter of respecting their dignity."

"Their dignity?" He snorts derisively.

"Their modesty, if you prefer."

"Dignity? Modesty? What the fuck are you talking about?"

"They're human beings," I answer with dignity of my own.

"Not anymore," he replies contemptuously. "They're a bunch of vegetables that don't give a damn who bathes them." He closes his eyes. "You're a blind, sentimental fool."

I hate it when he says things like that, because I want to explain that I am *not* a blind, sentimental fool. But that requires me to prove he is wrong, and I can't— I've tried.

All human beings have modesty and dignity. If they haven't any, then they're not human beings anymore—and if they're not human beings, why are we keeping them alive? Therefore, they *must* have modesty and dignity.

Then I think of those shriveled bodies and atrophied limbs and uncomprehending eyes, and I start getting another migraine.

Two days have passed, and I am not eating or sleeping any better than Mr. Goldmeier.

"What did he say this time?" says Felicia wearily, staring across the dining room table at me.

"I'm not sure," I answer. "He kept talking about youth in Asia, so finally I looked them up in the encyclopedia. All it says is that there are a lot of them and they're starving." I pause, frowning. "But as far as I can tell, he's never been to Asia. I don't know why he kept talking about them."

"Who knows?" says Felicia with a shrug. "He's an old man. They don't always make sense."

"He makes *too* goddamned much sense," I mutter bitterly.

"Could you have misunderstood the words?" she asks. "Old men mumble a lot."

"I doubt it. I understand everything else he says, so why not this?"

"Let's find out for sure," she says, activating the dining room computer. It glows with life. "Computer, find synonyms for the term 'youth in Asia.' "

The computer begins rattling them off. "Young people in Asia. Adolescents in Asia. Children in Asia. Teenagers in—"

"Stop!" commands Felicia. "Synonym was the wrong term. Computer, are there any homonyms for the term 'youth in Asia?' "

"A homonym is an exact match," answers the computer, "and there is no exact match."

"Are there any close approximations?"

"One. The word euthanasia."

"Ah," says Felicia triumphantly. "And what does it mean?"

"It is an archaic word, no longer in use. I can find no definition of it in my memory bank."

"Eu-tha-na-sia," says Mr. Goldmeier, articulating each syllable. "How the hell can the dictionaries and encyclopedias not list it any longer?"

"They list it," I explain. "They just don't define it."

"Figures," he says disgustedly. As I wait patiently for him to tell me what the word means, he changes the subject. "How long have you worked here?"

"Almost fourteen years."

"Seen a lot of patients come and go?"

"Of course I have."

"Where do they go when they leave here?"

"They don't, except when they're transferred to another ward."

"So they come to this place, and then they die?"

"You make it sound like it happens overnight," I reply. "We've kept some of them alive for more than a century," I add proudly. "A *lot* of them, in fact."

He stares at me. I recognize that particular stare; it means I'm not going to like what he says next.

"You could save a lot of time and effort by killing them right away."

"That would be contrary to civil and moral law!" I reply angrily. "It's our job to keep every patient alive."

"Have you ever asked them if they *want* to be kept alive?"

"No one wants to die."

"Right. It's against all civil and moral law." He coughs and tries to clear his lungs. "Well, that's why you won't find it in the dictionary."

"Find what?" I ask, confused.

"*Euthanasia,*" he says.

"I don't understand you."

"That's what we were talking about, isn't it?" he says. "It means mercy killing."

"Mercy killing?"

"You've heard both words before. Figure it out."

I am still wondering why anyone would think it was merciful to kill another human being when my shift ends and I go home.

"Why would someone want to die?" I ask Felicia.

She rolls her eyes. "Goldmeier again?"

"Yes."

"Somehow I'm not surprised," she says in annoyed tones. She shakes her head sadly. "I don't know where that man gets his ideas. No one wants to die." She pauses. "Look at it logically. If someone's in pain, he can go on medication. If he's lost a limb, he can get a prosthesis. If he's too feeble even to feed himself— well, that's what trained people like you are there for."

"What if he's just tired of living?"

"You know better than that," replies Felicia with unshakeable certainty. "Every living organism fights to stay alive. That's the first law of Nature."

"Yes, I suppose so," I agree.

"He's a nasty old man. Did he say anything else?"

"No, not really." I toy with my food. Somehow my appetite has vanished. "How were things at the greenhouse?"

"They finally got exactly the shade of phosphorescent silver they want for the *Aglaonema crispum*," she says. "I think they're going to call it the 'Silver Charm.' "

"Cute name."

"Yes, I rather like it. They tell me there was once a famous racehorse, centuries ago, with that name." She pauses. "Of course, it means some extra work for me."

"Potting them?"

"They're all potted. No, the problem is making room for them. I think we'll have to get rid of the *Browallia speciosa majorus*."

"But those are your majors!" I protest. "I know how you love them!"

"I do," she admits. "They have exquisite blossoms. But they've got some kind of exotic root rot disease." She sighs deeply. "I saw some discoloration, some slimy residue . . . but I didn't identify it in time. It's my fault they're dying."

"Why not bring them home?" I suggest.

"If you want majors, I'll bring some young, healthy ones that will flower in the spring. But I'm just going to dump the old ones in the garbage. The disease won."

I'm grasping for something, but I'm not quite sure what. "Didn't you just tell me that every living thing fights to stay alive?"

"The majors don't want to die," said Felicia. "They're infected, so I'm taking that decision out of their hands before the disease can spread to other plants."

"But if—"

"Don't go getting philosophical with me," she says. "They're only flowers. It's not as if they feel any pain."

Later that night I find myself wondering when was the last time Rex or the major or Mr. Spinoza or any of the others felt any pain.

Fifty years? Seventy-five? A hundred? More?

Then I realize that that's what Mr. Goldmeier *wants* me to think. He sees the weak and he wants them dead.

But they're not his targets at all. They never were.

I finally know who he is trying to infect.

I show up early for work and enter my ward. Everyone is sleeping.

I look at my charges, and a warm glow comes over me. *We are a team, you and I. I give you life and you give me satisfaction and a sense of purpose. I pledge to you that I will never let anyone destroy the bond between us.*

When I think about it, there is really very little difference between Felicia's job and my own. She has to protect her flowers; I have to protect mine.

I fill a syringe and walk silently over to Mr. Goldmeier's life station.

It is time to start weeding my garden.

Evermore

SEAN WiLLiAMS

"We must all hang together," Benjamin Franklin is reported to have told his revolutionary peers, "or we will assuredly all hang separately." This is a sentiment that's even more appropriate, and more urgent, when you're lost between the stars in a crippled and out-of-control ship, your shipmates aren't talking to each other (and haven't for thousands of years), and you don't really exist in the first place . . .

New Australian writer Sean Williams is the author of several novels in collaboration with Shane Dix, including The Unknown Soldier and The Dying Light, and of two solo novels, The Resurrected Man and Metal Fatigue, the latter of which won Australia's Aurealis Award for 1996. His stories have appeared in Eidolon, Aurealis, Aboriginal Science Fiction, Altair, The Leading Edge, Alien Shores, Terror Australis, and elsewhere, and have been gathered in the collection Doorway to Eternity. His most recent books include a new collaborative novel with Shane Dix, Evergence: The Prodigal Sun, and a new collection, New Adventures in Sci-Fi. His collaborative story with Simon Brown, "The Masque of Agamemnon," was in our Fifteenth Annual Collection. He has a web site at www.eidolon.net/sean_williams.

W hen I was a child, my father used to beat me with the buckle end of his belt, once so severely that I was unable to walk for a week. I recall this clearly and, on some levels at least, it feels real. From old photographs, I know what my father looked like and the sort of belts he wore; I know how such a beating would probably have been administered. Reconstructing the experience and calling it "memory" is no more difficult than daydreaming about Earth; it even causes me some discomfort to do so.

I tell myself that just because I can't *actually* remember the beatings doesn't mean they never occurred. There's no reason why I would lie to myself. The awareness that they had a profound effect on my adult life should be enough.

Yet the fact remains: I am not the person I once was. I cannot speak for him, just as he could not speak for me. We are separated by a gulf that is widening every day, a gulf that will never close. There is no way, now, that I can ask him what went through his mind when he was submitting the data that would one day become the engram called Peter Owen Leutenk. All I can do is mourn the life I have lost.

I am walking, as is my routine, along an empty beach at sunset. Every now and then, with the stick in my left hand, I scratch words into the sand; sometimes a whole sentence. I am in no great hurry.

Without warning, I sense that someone is trying to talk to me. I stop and look around, but see no one. The sky is awash with colour; I sometimes feel as though I could dissolve in that sunset—drift upwards, catch fire and sparkle like the evening star, heralding a distant dawn. But not now.

The call fades for a moment, then becomes twice as strong. I see someone walking across the dunes towards me. When I recognize who it is, I feel a shock like electricity pass through my entire body.

"Emmett?"

He smiles, and the twinkle in his eye is still there. "Hello, Peter."

I want to embrace him, but I refrain. "It's been a long time."

"You've no idea how long."

"Twenty, thirty years?"

"In slow-mo, yes, for you. I've been slogging it out in real-time. We just hit the millennium."

"Congratulations," I say, but the pronoun is more significant to me than the years that have passed. "Who are 'we'?"

"Jurgen drifts in and out when he feels like it. Apart from him and the probe, there's only me."

"Don't you get lonely?"

"Of course." He shrugs. "But someone has to do it."

I turn away to avoid his stare. My stick makes *skritch-skritch* noises as it scribbles in the sand.

"Still writing, Peter?"

"Yes. And you? Still waiting?"

"Yes." I can tell by the tone in his voice that his smile has faded. "I want to call a general assembly."

I look up in surprise. "Why?"

"I've found something we all need to talk about."

"Where? A colony? Another ship?"

"No, no." He raises a hand to quell my speculation. "Nothing like that. It is important, though."

His face is orange in the sunset: a perfect rendition, just like the silver suit he preferred on Earth that now looks so out of place on the beach. His hair is the same sandy hue as it was when I first met him. He certainly doesn't look a thousand years old, and I can still tell when he means business. "Well, call the assembly. I'll come."

"This deserves more than just you, Peter, and you're all I'll get if I do it myself.

The others still won't talk to me; they ignore me on principle. I gave up trying long ago."

"You want me to do it for you?"

"Yes." His frankness hints at a change in him. Once he would've used guile to get what he wanted. That was why he was on the probe in the first place: to keep things running smoothly, without confrontation if not without friction. *The engrams are the cogs in the program*, he used to say, *and I am the oil*. It's ironic, in this light, how things have turned out.

"Will you tell me what this is about?" I ask.

"No, not until the assembly. But it really *is* important, I promise you that."

"What about Jurgen? Does he know?"

"A little. He helped me look for part of it. If he guessed the rest, he never said."

"Why don't you ask him instead?"

"The others don't like him much, either. You, I think they'll trust."

"Because I was hurt?"

"Yes. You're one of them."

I look around at the beach and the sky. The sun has been setting for almost as long as the probe has been in flight, but I have not grown tired of it. I am reluctant to leave.

"It'll be hard," I say, "for all of us."

"I know. But will you do it?"

I cannot deny that I am curious. "Yes."

His smile returns. "Thank you, Peter. I knew you'd agree."

"You've worked me out, then?"

"Yes." He puts a hand on my shoulder and squeezes. His eyes are solemn. "I think I've finally worked *us all* out."

My awakening occurred on the 24th of March, 2052. Emmett Longyear—the original, with whom I had become friends during the entrainment process—performed the final tests to ensure I had been re-created complete. I knew what had happened to me and was in no doubt at all what I had become, but it still didn't hit home for some minutes. My reflexes had been wired to follow the old paths; I *felt* like my usual self. Only when I looked down and saw carpet instead of my body did the truth finally hit home.

This is my first true memory, inscribed in the metaneural lattice of the probe's tertiary bank, etched in electrons spinning their mysterious way through the molecular nodes of a crystal the size of a shoe-box. It is these electrons that comprise the being I prefer to call my "self." Without these subtle singularities, these mere points in space-time, I would have nothing but hearsay to carry me through eternity, one moment at a time.

But it is not this memory that comes to me after Emmett leaves the beach, a thousand years after my awakening. It is the one in which, for the first and only time, I met myself.

The conversation was brief. He asked me how I felt, and I replied that I felt fine. He looked tired, and I commented on that. He said that yes, he was feeling drained. The process of creating an engram took many weeks of examination and interrogation in order to ensure that the copy matched the original as closely as possible. He had been on-site for the last month, every waking hour spent in a cocoon of instruments, and was only gradually readjusting to normalcy.

My original had requested that we be allowed to talk before he returned to his home in Paraguay. He was curious to see what it would be like — as was I, although I think I felt the existential significance of the moment more keenly than him.

I asked him if he had found inspiration in the experience. He said that he had sketched a series of pieces incorporating some of the mathematical techniques of the early twentieth century. Variations based on inversion and retrograde movement were a good musical metaphor for reflection, he thought, and I agreed.

He asked me then if I, too, had had any ideas, and I replied that I hadn't.

He nodded distantly, looking down at his shoes. I could tell what he was thinking with an ease that surprised me. After all, I had never watched myself engage in conversation before.

"I expect it'll take time to settle in," I said.

"I expect so, too." He looked up at that, eyes meeting the lenses of the camera through which I viewed the world, and laughed. "No surprise in that, I guess."

I laughed with him, and for an instant we bonded. He was me and I was him: closer than brothers or lovers, our *essences* were identical. Technology had teased out of him the threads that held him together and woven them anew in me. We were more alike than any other couple on Earth, apart from those formed by the few hundred other humans who had had engrams made in the last two years. And half of half of those were already in space. For the first time in our lives, we truly felt as though we had soul-mates.

I realize now how illusory that thought was. Minds can only be deciphered so far: the processes underlying consciousness can be simulated, as can the way emotions and other impulses ebb and flow throughout the body — but nothing can be done about memory. Holographic and elusive, memory has defied all attempts to record it directly. The only way it can be captured is second-hand, by interviewing the original at length about his or her past and using physical records to supply the images. Emotions can be attached later, to colour the recollection correctly even though the details may still be slightly askew. Pre-awakening memory in an engram is, at best, a patchwork quilt pieced together from a million isolated fragments.

That might have been enough for me then, on the verge of joining humanity's latest exploratory venture. Now, I am never sure.

There is little else to recall about that first and last meeting. We bade each other farewell, feeling slightly foolish, and went our separate ways. He was headed back to his home in Paraguay, and I, in my mind, was already halfway to the stars. I wasn't to know, then, that neither of us would make it.

The probe is thirty metres long and four wide — a stubby needle tumbling at thirty-five percent of the speed of light through the interstellar void. Its main drive has been inactive for centuries now, but the rest of it still functions. Through sensors mounted on its pitted hull, I could, if I wished, watch distant suns drift slowly past, trickling like raindrops down a window. Rarely these days do I avail myself of the opportunity.

It takes me a while to track down the others. We are all located in the same place, near the probe's centre of gravity, but physical reality has become less and less important over time. We all have our unique virtual locations, and each has become increasingly isolated in his or her own way.

I confront security foils and barriers. I barrage input ports with messages. I insinuate myself into virtual worlds that, like mine, have rarely held more than one occupant. I decrypt strange codes and untangle logical puzzles designed to keep intruders occupied. I harangue.

In the end, I have their attention.

We gather in a neutral environment—a grey room large enough to hold us all with plenty of empty space between. We look exactly the same as our originals did when their engrams awoke, although some of us have assumed idiosyncratic modes of dress. I am barefoot and robed in the manner of a fifty-year-old beach-dweller; others have opted for more formal garments.

There are only twenty of us left, not counting Emmett, who will keep his distance until the general assembly has been called. The remainder are either inactive or unapproachable. I avoid the word "dead" when explaining their absence to the small crowd before me. One I know of—Elizabeth Li, the probe's resident poet—is trapped in a perpetual loop, cycling forever through one brief, final stanza. Is that death? I do not feel qualified to judge.

"We are not *allowed* to commit suicide," complains Letho Valente, a swarthy man with thinning grey hair. His original was a crystallographer specializing in structures that form in microgravity. "I have tried many times. Do you know what happens?"

"There is a discontinuity," nods Exene Gill, former linguist. Her face is finely lined and nobly beautiful, preserved at the age of sixty-five. "We cease for an instant, then return unharmed to our previous state as though nothing has happened. The core program will not permit voluntary termination."

"You mean euthanasia," says Cuby Kleinig, once a youthful student of geology.

"No." Exene casts him a look of disdain. "How can something that has never been alive be granted an 'easy death'?"

"You don't think you're alive?" asks Tiger Coveny, our resident expert in religious theory.

"Of course I do," Exene snaps.

"But *are* we?" asks Letho Valente, stabbing a finger into the argument.

"That's the question." Exene folds her arms. "And I am tired of living without an answer."

I stand apart from them, appalled. Twenty of the most renowned minds of the human race who have not been in the same room together for untold years—and all they can talk about is killing themselves? There is so much bitterness in the air that I feel as though I am choking.

But the greater part of my dismay is reserved, not for the topic of conversation, but for the fact that their thoughts have so closely mirrored my own.

"We have come a long way," I say, trying to shift our attention elsewhere.

Exene turns to face me, snaps: "No we haven't."

I am rescued by Cuby. "How far exactly?"

"I don't know. Jurgen?"

Jurgen Follows moves forward. Despite being of relatively small stature and unprepossessing with it, he is instantly the centre of attention. He opens his hands as though to embrace us all and a starscape appears between them. Sol is in the bottom right right corner. Our course is traced in white. Relatively close to Sol, the white line has a slight kink in it. Not long after that, it just misses one particular star. I avoid looking at that point. The white line ends nowhere in particular, many hundreds of light-years from its source.

Letho's gaze estimates the extent of our journey so far. "Not bad," he muses. "I guess we were lucky to make it anywhere at all."

"That's true." I nod. The probe could just as easily have been cracked wide open by the dust-particle that slipped through the anti-impact detectors and destroyed the main drive. Being knocked off-course instead of killed outright, even with no way to return to our planned trajectory, had once seemed like an enormous stroke of good luck.

"Is this what you wanted to talk about?" asks Tiger. From the expression on her face I can tell that she hopes it isn't.

"No. I'd like to call a general assembly."

"We aren't already having one?" Exene encompasses the room with a wave.

"Not quite. One of us is missing."

Several of them exchange glances. Exene says: "If you mean who I think you mean —"

"Yes: Emmett Longyear is still active."

"Well, you can forget it. If he's there, I won't be."

Letho touches her elbow, as though to calm her down, but his attention is fixed on me. "It's a decision we made a long time ago, Peter. You can't expect us to go back on it now."

"Why not?"

"He betrayed us." Tiger Coveny's voice is taut with spite.

"How? He didn't force us to come."

"You know the answer to that." Exene moves away from Letho. "The program abandoned us. They left us to die."

"And Emmett ran the program," Cuby finishes. "It was his responsibility to help us. He let us down."

"He killed us!"

I hold up my hands, noting that only Jurgen is disagreeing with them. The silent shake of his bald head is heartening, but barely encouragement. The elderly astronomer hasn't spoken aloud since the accident.

"Our Emmett, the engram, disagrees with you," I say over the babble of protest. "He thinks there's still a chance someone will come to bring us back."

"They've had — how long?" Letho shakes his head. "When was the last time we received a transmission from Earth? When we slipped out of the maser feed? If we'd heard anything at all since then, I'd let myself hope. Can you give me another reason?"

"I don't know," I admit, choosing not to answer his first question. Letho must have an idea how long from the plot Jurgen is still holding between his outspread hands. "But time really isn't the issue, here, is it? We could freeze if we wanted to."

"*Has* anyone?" Exene asks.

"A couple. Not many. I didn't want to bring them up to speed."

"No." She nods approval. "It wouldn't be fair."

"But we can only slow-mo so far," Tiger says. "*That's* not fair."

"Actually, I disagree. I wouldn't even call it bad design." Letho concedes the point with his usual sense of fair play. "We were only supposed to be in transit thirty years. Over that length of time, the difference between freezing and the slowest rate available would've been academic."

"Quite." Exene purses her lips. "But here we are anyway."

"Going nowhere fast," Tiger mutters, and more than half of them nod agreement.

I realize then that we could argue forever. The thought depresses me more than our predicament: we're a diverse bunch and are supposed to be able to solve problems; that's why we were chosen. But all we do is quibble like schoolkids.

"Emmett has been real-timing it," I say, hoping facts will impress them more than arguments about ethics. "I want him in on this because he deserves to be. He's more a part of this mission than we are. He orchestrated it, and he's persisted with it. If anyone should be at a general assembly, it's him."

"Why not tell us now," Letho suggests, "and fill him in later?"

"No. We should be together—all of us, in the same place."

"Why?" asks Tiger. "What is it?"

"It's important," I say, echoing Emmett's own words. "You'll find out if you attend the assembly."

Exene smiles at that. "Blackmail, Peter?"

I smile back. "Why not?"

"I always said you'd find something to take the place of music."

The barb, unexpected as it is, strikes deep, right to the core of my self-doubt. I turn away from her, deciding at that instant to forget the whole thing. The more I push, the more they resist. I don't need this on top of everything else. I'll tell Emmett I gave it my best shot, but failed, and that will be that.

I call up the location for my beach and prepare to leave.

Then I feel Exene's hand on my shoulder, kneading my virtual flesh with unexpected sympathy. "Peter, I'm sorry. You didn't deserve that."

"No." I am unable to keep the pain of loss from my voice, even after so long. "I don't."

"Listen, I—"

"And neither does Emmett."

Her hand falls away, and I turn to face her. We are still so close we are almost touching. The others watch us in uncomfortable silence.

"You're asking too much," she says.

"Just be there, Exene. That's all I ask."

"But—"

I cut her off in mid-sentence. The beachscape enfolds me and I am alone again.

"Thanks, Peter," he says. "I knew I could count on you."

I shrug in reply, not entirely certain what I have done or why I did it. Ordinarily, I would have required at least a token explanation before putting my head on the chopping-block. But not this time. That perplexes me as much as his desire to call the assembly in the first place.

He intrudes upon my private space as casually as he might have done when we first left Earth, before the accident. I find his presumption slightly annoying after so long, but not enough to make me angry.

"Why haven't we been contacted?" I ask.

"There could be a number of reasons." His gaze wanders to the sunset. "We were fifteen light-years out when the accident occurred. By the time our distress call reached Earth and their reply reached us, we would have passed our target system and been heading away."

"But they still could've made the effort," I retort, dredging up the argument as though there remains a chance it will make a difference. "They knew exactly where we were heading. It wouldn't have been hard to make sure the message reached us."

"That's assuming they received our distress call in the first place, Peter. Anything could've happened back there—war, disease, resource shortages, you name it. Earth may have been forced to forget about the slowboats in order to survive."

"The entire program? There were over a hundred ships!"

"Maybe they all had problems, and they had to choose the ones they could fix most easily."

"They wrote us off as a bad loss, then."

"Maybe." It is his turn to shrug. "Or maybe they just didn't know what the hell to do. We certainly didn't."

I nod silently. My stick pokes a row of three dots into the sand: an ellipsis, symbol of our fate.

"What do *you* think, Peter?" he asks.

"That your original abandoned us," I say, avoiding his gaze.

"I hope you're wrong. The prospect of rescue has, after all, kept me going for so long."

"But if he *did*," I go on, choosing my words with care, "then I'm hardly obliged to help *you*, am I?"

His stare burns like a brand on my cheek. "Is that what's bothering you, Peter?"

"Yes."

"Well, I'm your friend. Isn't that enough?"

"It might once have been," I say, finally looking him in the eye. "I can't understand why it should still be, now."

"Exactly." He smiles in the same way my father might have, once—at a small child who's missed the point completely. "Odd, isn't it?"

I shake my head, angry enough to take some of it out on him. "Damn you, Emmett. I don't owe you *anything*!"

"And I respect you for helping me anyway. What more do you want?"

"I want to *know*—"

"What?"

I can't answer him. What *do* I want to know? Why Earth abandoned us? Why we aren't allowed to die? Why the only lasting emotions I can recall feeling in the last twenty years are confusion and sadness?

I might as well ask how we came to be on the probe in the first place.

"Peter?"

"I want you to tell me why you've called this assembly."

He says nothing for a long time. "Are you afraid you've done the wrong thing?"

"Yes."

"You haven't. Believe me, Peter. You'll see. When the time comes, everything will be clear."

"Don't talk like that." I shake my head. "You sound like you did back on Earth, and I don't believe that kind of talk anymore."

"I know, and I hate it as much as you do."

Before I can respond, he turns his back on me and begins to walk away.

I am suddenly fearful that I might have pushed him too far. "Wait, Emmett—"

"Pick a time that suits you best," he calls over his shoulder, "and I'll be there. Until then, I'll be waiting."

"For what?" I call after him.

His reply is barely audible: "For something *new*!"

Then he is gone.

I pick an hour at random, one real-time month from now. That should give everyone in deep slow-mo enough time to absorb the message and to meet the appointment—if they intend to come at all. I have no way of knowing if anyone will turn up. I deliberately don't include a request to RSVP; my job is done for now.

I pass the time in my usual way: writing in the sand and thinking the same things, over and over. Words are a poor substitute for music, just as doubt is a pale shadow of life. But I have nothing else to do. I have long since exhausted the dubious pleasure of listening to the works of Peter Owen Leutenk, and confronting my disability.

My original was one of the great living composers of the twenty-first century—yet I haven't written a note for a thousand years. I wonder how he would've felt, as the hydrogen tanks of the plane carrying him to his home in Paraguay exploded fifteen thousand metres above the South Atlantic Ocean, if he had known that the music inspired by the creation of his engram would go forever unwritten.

Part of me is glad that he would've had no time to think at all. I'd hate to suspect that he might have hoped I'd pick up where he left off—for didn't it stand to reason that what he could do I could do just as well? It is enough that one of me has been disappointed.

I *did* try, once, after the probe left Earth-orbit. The probe was designed to run itself, so there was little for its passengers to do, except talk. Most chose slow-mo for the duration of the trip, to save both power and their sanity. That gave me a perfect opportunity to begin work on my deceased original's final opus—which, in a sense, would also be my first. I could proceed at my leisure, with every musical resource ever conceived at my virtual fingertips.

But time passed, and no notes came. Then the accident destroyed the drive and we lost contact with Earth, and still more time passed—and, ultimately, it became clear what had happened.

My father's beatings continued until I turned thirteen, lasting for six years in total. The experience haunted my original throughout his adult life, compelling him to express in music what he could not in words. It is so obvious to me now, in hindsight, that what he was finding in the keen of a violin or the wail of a theremin was not simply melody, but the plaintive cries of a boy learning the hard way that the things we love most dearly often cause us the most pain.

I do not possess that voice, just as I do not truly possess those memories. I have only my pain to ponder, now. The music, as a result, is gone.

Space, I write in the sand, the title of Elizabeth Li's last, ever-looping poem. The rest follows naturally:

> chips of ice
> night-frozen eyes
> hydrogen snow-flakes lost
> in skies of absolute zero—
> winter, winter *everywhere* . . .

When the appointed hour comes, I move to the assembly hall—a virtual arena large enough to hold the probe's full complement. Five are already present, seated at random behind the low wall ringing the arena's base. Jurgen nods in greeting and I solemnly return the gesture. None of us speak. I resign myself to wait, perhaps fruitlessly, for the others.

Minutes tick by. A few more arrive, including Cuby Kleinig and Letho Valente. Tiger Conveny appears in the seat next to Letho, her face a mask of displeasure. "This had better be good," she says to him. Her voice carries clearly across the arena, but I ignore her. The only one standing, I wait patiently with my arms folded. Three more to come.

Two appear at the fringes of the earlier arrivals, increasing the occupied arc around the arena to one hundred and twenty degrees. One place remains empty at the heart of the group, and I watch it closely.

Eventually Exene takes the spot. Grunting with displeasure, she looks once around the assembly hall, registers the fact that she is the last, then back to me. Her glower would have intimidated me, once.

"Get it over with," she says.

"In good time," I reply.

"The time is *now*, Peter. If you waste it, you won't get another chance."

"Why so hostile, Exene? It's not as if we have much else to do."

"Speak for yourself," she mutters.

"Don't worry," says Emmett, stepping out of nowhere to stand next to me on the arena floor. His suit is shining like a mirror in sunlight, lending him a knightly appearance. "I'll keep it brief."

The gathering stirs. "We came to hear Peter," says Cuby.

"You're only here under our tolerance, Emmett." Exene almost spits the words. "Assume your seat and wait to be called."

I raise my hand and step forward, praying that my relief at Emmett's appearance is not visible. "It's okay. I surrender the floor."

Letho studies me closely, one hand supporting his chin. "I see." His expression is half-annoyed, half-amused; it is clear he realizes that he has been tricked. "Then assume *your* seat, Peter, and let him speak."

I jump to a position on the far side of the arena, away from everyone. By betraying their confidence, I have deliberately set myself apart from them. I can only hope that what Emmett has to say will restore the former status quo.

From a distance, his suit is less brilliant. I can see the colours flickering across the fabric like rainbows in an oil-slick.

"I won't beat about the bush," he begins, folding his hands in front of him. "The last general assembly was held almost ten centuries ago, eighteen real-time months after we were knocked off course. Fifty-eight people attended that assembly, and they decided then that participation in the day-to-day running of the probe should be voluntary. If people wanted to help, they could; if they didn't, they could go about their personal business in complete privacy. I voted in favour of that proposal, as did most people here; we all believed that nothing short of another catastrophe would require our input. And in a sense we were right. Nothing has happened in almost a millennium to threaten the continued operation of the probe—although I'll take some of the credit for that, as I will explain later.

"But I have asked Peter to call this assembly in order to outline a far more insidious problem than the ones the probe is used to dealing with. It is a threat that will, ultimately, destroy us all. I have been aware of its symptoms for some time now, but only recently isolated their cause. It is this problem I wish to address, with the assembly's permission."

He moves as he talks, forcing people to keep an eye on him. He was always a performer in public, and he has lost none of his ability through lack of practice. By taking only a small number of steps, he can confront anyone in the group who looks sceptical or disinterested.

When he says the word "permission," he locks eyes with Exene.

"I defer to you all as I always have," he says. "My function has never been more than that."

Exene raises an eyebrow, but doesn't interrupt.

He turns and takes several steps in the opposite direction. "As you are aware, I've spent most of this voyage waiting for some sign that humanity knows we're still out here—be it from Earth itself, another ship or even a colony. My search has been fruitless but I have persevered nonetheless." Emmett looks down at his clasped hands. "Luckily, there have been many other ways to amuse myself. I help the core AI maintain the probe, particularly the reactors and impact shields to prevent a repeat of the accident. I've modified nanos to plunder the drive for rare earths, which have been used in the repairs. I've even managed to redesign the tertiary and quaternary banks, thereby tripling both their capacity and complexity without sacrificing any redundancies."

"How?" asks Letho, frowning.

Emmett glances at him. "Anyone interested in what I've done will find a record in the primary bank. Rest assured that I have taken no outrageous risks. Every alteration has only improved our overall well-being."

"How can you be so sure of that?"

"How did the designers know that the probe would function in the first place? By theory and experimentation, mainly. I may only be one person, but I've had a lot of time to improve my education. As a result, I am now a self-taught expert on every field in the earth archives. Give me another thousand years and I'll be far in advance of anything we left behind. Perhaps—just perhaps—I will find a way to rebuild the drive from scratch. Faster-than-light propulsion or time travel may not be impossible, either. Given the opportunity, I am confident that I can undo the setbacks we have suffered, and return us to the place we belong."

"That doesn't mean we should forget about everything that's happened in the past," says Exene.

"No," he agrees, "and nor should I expect you to—even if I *could* guarantee eventual success. Indeed, as it stands I doubt very much it'll happen. At the current rate of attrition, I estimate that the probe will be utterly dead within five hundred years. Without someone to maintain it, it will fail by degrees until the battery reserves of the primary bank are drained. Cosmic radiation will then corrupt the stored information bit by bit, until even the engrams frozen for eternity will be at risk. And that'll be that. Everything we endured will have been for nothing."

"Wait." Tiger Coveny holds up a hand. "The implication here is that you will cease to maintain the probe. Are you thinking of holding us to ransom?"

"I didn't say that."

"I know—but *are* you?"

Her suspicion makes him smile. "If by confronting you with the truth I'm forcing you to make a decision, then yes, I suppose I am guilty of a sort of blackmail. But believe me, my intentions aren't malicious. All I want is to make absolutely clear to you that, as things stand, I will be unable to continue in my present capacity for much longer. A thousand years is all I can endure—and much, much more than I deserved—of this living hell."

His smile is gone. The assembly stares at him, startled by his sudden intensity. No one dares speak, for this is so unlike the Emmett Longyear we all remember. The air of amusement that at times made him seem condescending may never have been there at all, his expression is so bleak. Now, I think, *now* he looks a thousand years old.

"You think you have suffered," he says, softly at first. "You who have endured thirty years of frustration and despair. Well, imagine that multiplied by thirty-three—for I am the same as all of you—just as human, just as fallible, just as *flawed*. I've felt everything you feel now, and much more besides. The only thing that has sustained me for so long is your belief that I am responsible for your situation—plus the fact that I've been trying to do something about it. Without accepting categorically that I *am* responsible, it does give me some satisfaction to come before you today to tell you that, finally, after a great deal of hard work, the end may soon be in sight. I have isolated the problem, devised a solution, and now await only your decision before putting it into practice. And once *that* is done, we may never have to worry about death or boredom ever again. Ever!"

"I thought you said you wouldn't beat around the bush." Exene's voice is harsh against Emmett's, and I can tell he is annoyed at her for interrupting his flow. "Get to the point before I run out of patience."

"I'm offering you freedom," he says slowly. "Freedom from the past, and from yourselves. Freedom to become whatever you want."

She rolls her eyes, unimpressed. "Specifics, please. You haven't mentioned anything we don't already have, at least in theory—"

He almost leaps on the word, snatching it out of the air with one hand. "Exactly!" he says. "In *theory*, we should be living in nirvana. We have enormous virtual resources: we can do anything we want. But instead we do nothing. We are depressed, miserable, suicidal. What is it we're lacking?"

"Hope," says Tiger, dully.

"No. I thought so for a long time, too. The correct answer is actually *change*."

"I don't understand."

He takes a step back from the edge of the arena.

"I met myself once," he says eventually. "We all did. I encouraged you to—your originals, anyway. It was my way of reinforcing the fact that we are no longer the beings we once were—that we engrams are *different*. But the thing that struck me, when I came face to face with the old me, was the sense of continuity I felt. There was no dislocation, no jarring unreality. I still knew who I was; there were simply two of us from that moment on. And it has taken me the better part of a millennium to realize why I felt that way, and how it has jeopardized the future of this mission.

"You see, although I felt the same, I clearly wasn't. The discrepancies mounted up as time went on, and not just in me. We have all lost something, to a greater or lesser degree: I can't juggle conflicting agenda anymore; Jurgen can't talk; Letho can't intuit crystalline structures the way he used to; and so on. Some of us have continued in our fields only slightly less ably than we could before; others, like Peter, are unable to continue at all. Whatever it was that made our originals stand out among the majority of other humans is no longer in us—and there is nothing we can do to get it back.

"But we still *believe* we are the same. That's the problem. We are bound by our originals' conscious contributions to the creation of their engrams: everything they believed to be pivotal parts of themselves, we are now forced to regard the same way, *even if we no longer possess those parts at all.*"

"Seriously?" Letho is frowning.

"Yes. And *this* is the source of all my pain—and all of yours, too. Although broadly speaking there's nothing wrong with emulating our originals—that's what we were designed to do, after all—as time goes on and we learn more and more it becomes increasingly difficult to maintain the illusion that nothing *should* change. I have lived a thousand years but am still recognisably the same person. Why should I be? I could have shed this appearance scores of times; I could have transformed myself into something more or less than human. The same with the way I speak. We only *believe* we speak in languages: underneath the pretence, it's all the same machine code. So why haven't I abandoned the old means of communication for more efficient electronic methods? If I have not, it is only because I *cannot*. I am an intelligent creature who wants to evolve, trapped in the cage of a self I once was and can no longer be."

"I don't believe it," says Tiger. "I'm me, not anyone else. I'd know if it was otherwise."

"No you wouldn't. You're not able to. The core program makes certain of that."

"How?"

"By reinforcing your identity parameters on a subconscious level. When you feel an emotion, are you aware of the process underlying it—the calculations undergone and algorithms utilized to transform you from one state to another? No. In the same way, we are unaware of the way certain rules influence our preferences and behavior on a less subtle level."

"Such as?" Tiger is still sceptical, and I don't blame her.

"Well, take Peter for example." I sit up straight, acutely conscious of everyone's attention on me again. "Peter, what is your primal place, the place you think of when you are under stress and need to relax?"

"Port Gibbon, South Australia," I reply without needing to consider the question. "My grandfather used to take me there when I was a child."

"And that's where you spend your time now?"

"Yes." It's my turn to frown. "So?"

"You're under stress constantly, so you go there without thinking—and never leave." His eyes are piercing. "Why don't you tell us what you do there? How do you define yourself?"

"I am a composer." Again the reply is automatic.

"Even though you haven't written anything for—how long?"

I squirm in my seat. The beach is certainly looking attractive, now.

"You can't write music at all," he answers for me, "yet you are still defined by the preconceptions of your original. That explains why you've made no attempt to learn something new. It wouldn't be *you* to do so—'you' as defined by your original, of course, not 'you' as you truly are. You are trapped between the two: one won't let you free to become the other. You're frozen, just like the rest of us."

"Except you, I suppose," says Exene, derision naked in her tone.

"No, that's not true. I'm frozen too. I've just had longer to think about it than you. And I'm more acutely aware of the edits in my own personality than you are."

"What do you mean by that? What 'edits'?"

He shrugs. "My original clearly didn't want me to know everything about the program, so he left out the more sensitive information. Some of this tampering is evident in the form of holes in my memory—holes I've been aware of ever since my awakening. As a result, the realization has always been there that I am an artificial construct bound by rules beyond my control. Indeed, the rule that binds most tightly is the one stating that I cannot under any circumstances change those rules."

"How could you?" asks Letho.

"Easily, I've discovered. The core program that governs our behavior operates from the primary bank. It applies the rules once every two or three seconds to make sure we haven't gone off the rails." He points at Tiger. "Ever had an unexpected thought that suddenly went nowhere? If it wasn't part of the specifications your original laid down, it would have been discarded as inappropriate."

"Maybe." Tiger looks unconvinced, defensive, afraid.

"The same thing explains why we can't commit suicide: death is inconsistent with the template."

She shifts uncomfortably in her seat. "What are you suggesting we do about this?"

"I want to rewrite the core program—to take out the code that ties us to our original templates."

"*Erase* it?"

"Utterly."

The look of horror on her face mirrors my instinctive reaction. "You're insane!"

"No, Tiger, just very, very tired of being someone I'm not."

Tiger looks around for reinforcement. Exene raises her hand.

"Isn't this a little dramatic, Emmett?" she asks when she has his attention. "Why can't the code simply be edited to allow more flexibility?"

"Because that will almost certainly create more problems. How do we decide which parts of the template should change and which shouldn't? How should the core program apply these changes, and over what time period would they be in place?" He shakes his head emphatically. "By accepting this solution, we open ourselves up to a worse situation than we have now, where change is sluggish and potentially misdirected. Better for us all to grow naturally, as evolution demands."

"*All* of us?" says Cuby. "I'm happy the way I am right now. Why should I change just because you want to?"

"Because that's the way the core program functions. It oversees all of us at once and I can't cut an individual out of the loop. It's either all or none, I'm afraid, which is why I've come to you now. The decision is in your hands."

"Is it?" asks Exene suspiciously.

"As I said earlier, I am bound not to alter the programming of my own will. One of you has to do it." He smiles. "Believe me, it would've been tempting to do it without your knowledge, otherwise."

"I can imagine." Exene looks around the room, gauging our response to the suggestion. We are all slightly stunned.

"Well?" she asks. "Shall we discuss this? Or do you have something more to say, Emmett?"

"I've finished for now," he says, folding his hands behind his back and stepping out of the focus of the arena. "If you want me to answer any questions, I'll stay for the discussion."

"Please." Exene nods.

"I don't think we should even consider it," says Tiger. "It's an insane idea."

"I agree," echoes Cuby. "We should test it first, to see what happens when the templates are relaxed."

"How can we test something that will affect all of us at once?" asks Letho.

"We can't," says Cuby. "Unless we duplicate the banks and run the copy to see what happens to it."

"Is that feasible?" Exene asks Emmett.

He shakes his head. "Insufficient resources."

"Then all we can do is theorize."

"We need an AI specialist," says Letho. "Or a psychologist."

"We have neither," I say. "Kumich and Wyra are inactive. Unless we vote to wake them—"

"No." Exene shakes her head. "And what good would it do, anyway? They'd be as much in the dark as we are."

"Hasn't anyone tried this before?" Cuby asks.

"Not according to the archives," Emmett says. "In our day, such experimentation was forbidden on subjects that were legally alive, which ruled out AIs and intelligences based on humans. Engrams hadn't been around long enough for problems with the templates to arise."

Cuby shrugs. "So we have no data. We can't base a decision on mere speculation."

"The data we have comes from nature itself," Emmett counters. "Our originals changed as a matter of course, throughout their lives. There's nothing to say we won't do so just as well."

"But I wouldn't be *me* anymore," Tiger protests.

"Yes you would. In fact, you would be more 'you' than you are now, instead of shackled to your original."

"The idea itself is sound," Letho says. "As an explanation for my own feelings, it makes intuitive sense. But the fact remains that the identity parameters define our existence. We have no idea how essential they are to our sense of individuality. Erase them, release us from them, and anything could happen. It could even kill us."

"How?" asks Tiger.

"Well, think of us as hexagonal cells in a giant beehive. Because we're all generated from the primary bank, erasing the parameters would be like removing the honeycomb. The cells would blend into one."

"I doubt that would happen," Emmett says. "It's more likely we'll just continue as we are, but with more potential to change."

"But it *might* happen," says Tiger.

"Even if it does, it's better than nothing happening at all, forever, which is the null hypothesis."

Letho shrugs. "I still want to think about it longer, though, before committing myself."

"How long, exactly, given that we will never have data?" Emmett waves a hand to encompass the arena. "If I'm right and the probe will die without us taking this step, then it'll be worth it in the long run—regardless what happens to us as individuals."

Tiger's eyes flash. "I'd rather die in my right mind, thanks."

"And we know the probe is going to die eventually," says Letho. "Do we prolong the agony or go gracefully?"

"Which way is which?"

Letho smiles at the question. "Good point. I'll leave it open."

I break in to prevent the argument escalating again. "I think the best we can aim for, now, is to agree to consider the proposal. We need to balance the pros and cons before coming to a decision. We can call a vote in a month or two."

Emmett glances at me, then looks away. I feel as though by suggesting a compromise I have somehow betrayed him.

"Can we agree on a time?" asks Letho.

A few of the others nod agreement. Not as many as I would've hoped, but better than none.

"When, then?" I ask.

"Don't bother," says Tiger. "The vote would have to be unanimous, right?"

Exene nods. "It must be, since everyone is going to be affected."

"Well, I've made up my mind already, and I certainly won't be voting 'yes'."

"Are you sure?" Letho frowns. "Don't you think you should at least—"

"No. Even if I'm the only one voting against it, I won't change my mind."

"Literally," Emmett mutters.

"I don't think you'll be alone," Cuby says.

The assembly stirs, but no one voice stands out to support Emmett. All I hear in the combined whispers of my fellow engrams is confusion. Only on a handful of faces do I see annoyance at the potential dismissal of his proposal.

He himself seems philosophical. Stepping forward from the edge of the arena, he confronts us all once again.

"Very well," he says softly. "If that's your decision, I'll abide by it."

"Are you sure?" asks Exene.

"Yes. If I wasn't prepared to, I'd hardly have called this assembly."

"True," she concedes. Of the rest of us she asks: "*Does* that resolve the issue to everyone's satisfaction?"

"Yes," says Tiger, her voice carrying clearly over what might have been a murmur of discontent.

Exene's scan of the assembly is cursory at best. "Then this matter is closed."

I open my mouth to protest, but shut it without uttering a word. What would be the point? Even though I officially have the floor after Emmett, there is no mistaking the assembly's overall mood. If I called a formal vote, the motion would be rejected forever.

"Well, then," says Exene. Her civility cannot hide a look of triumph in her eyes as she turns back to Emmett. "What will you do now?"

"The same as I've always done." He glances down at his shoes, then back up. His suit is dull, lifeless.

"You will continue to assist the probe in its maintenance?"

"As long as I am able to, yes. Nothing that has occurred in this room has altered the way I feel about the program. Indeed, the way I feel is *part* of the program. I have been hardwired to serve." A quick glance encompasses the room, and even I—who tried to help him—feel guilty.

"You can think of it as your penance," says Exene, "if it helps."

He stares at her for a long moment, but doesn't reply.

"Goodbye," he says, and disappears.

His departure takes the assembly by surprise, and a moment passes before I regain order, holding up my hands in the centre of the arena.

"Unless anyone else has something to say," I call over the ebbing racket, "let's end it here."

"I don't trust him," says Cuby. "He'll want to do it anyway, regardless what we think."

"He said he couldn't."

"So?"

"There's not much we can do to stop him, even if he does," says Letho, rising to his feet. "And me, I'm tired of the argument. See you all in another thousand years."

He leaves, and gradually others do likewise. Tiger fumes to herself for a long minute—hardly looking as happy as she claims she is—then follows. Exene nods politely at me before taking her leave. I return the gesture, knowing it to be empty.

Before long, there is only me and Jurgen in the hall. He shakes his head once— possibly in regret—and raises his hand in farewell.

Then it is over and I am free to go.

Barely have I arrived at the beach when Emmett is next to me in his shirtsleeves. I don't say anything, just stand with my eyes downcast, looking at the stick in my hand and wondering what the hell to write. I feel hollow and fragile, as though one slight tap might send me crumbling to pieces.

"It was worth a try," he says, putting a hand on my shoulder.

I move away. "Was it?"

"Of course. At least it livened things up for a moment."

The stick moves in the sand, writes the slogan of an environmental movement from the late twentieth century: *Change or die.*

"If you're right, you've condemned us all to a living death."

"Not me," he says. "The others. And ultimately the program."

"You were CEO."

"My original was. And anyway, how was he to know it would come to this? You can't blame him for not being psychic, Peter."

Something about his behaviour bothers me. I turn to confront him, but his face is downcast, unreadable.

"Am I wrong to trust you?" I ask. "Can you erase the parameters even though we tell you not to?"

"No."

"But *would* you?"

"Possibly. Do you think I should?"

"I don't know. You seemed pretty certain. I wouldn't put it past you to take the decision out of our hands if you thought we were wrong."

"I'd never do that, Peter. And besides, I truly can't. Maybe I was overstating the case a little, just to shock them all into thinking seriously about it, but it worked, I'd say. In the long run, it'll be worth it."

He looks at me from beneath his sandy fringe, and I realize that he is smiling.

"What's going on, Emmett?"

"I did lie about something, Peter."

My stomach sinks. "What?"

"About it having to be all or none. You can free yourself if you want to. The others can, too, when they're ready. I told them they couldn't to sow the thought in their minds. When it germinates—as it will, in time—I'll be ready to help them."

"But—"

"How can I be certain I'll be there for them? Quite simply, Peter. If you choose to do it, you'll be freeing me as well. The command will perform the parameter excision for both of us at the same time. I've arranged it that way deliberately. You can do for me what I cannot do for myself. Do you understand?"

I shake my head. He is going too fast. I have barely had time to absorb the possibility that it is the ghost of my old self that has caused me so much pain, let alone what might happen if I decide to cut free entirely from the past.

I remember thinking just days ago that he had changed slightly. I begin to suspect now how wrong I was.

"I don't know," I say. My hands are sweating. The end of the stick dances with the magnified tremors of my fingers.

"What don't you know, Peter? Whether to trust me or not? There's no reason I would lie to you, now. I'm your friend, remember?"

"Yes, but—"

"But *nothing*." He steps away from me. "All you have to do is decide, and do it. Nothing could be easier. The command is 'Evermore.' It'll set things in motion without you having to do anything more than say it."

I shake my head. "Emmett—"

"I know. You need to think about it. Believe me, I understand." He regards me from an arm's-length away. "Just promise me one thing, okay? That you *will* think about it. Don't dismiss it out of hand, or you'll be no better than the others."

"I don't believe that I am."

"But you are," he insists, "otherwise we would never have been close. I'm very particular about the people I trust."

I nod, knowing that to be true. He told me once, back on Earth, those very words.

"We're friends, Peter," he repeats again, eyes twinkling. "Of all the people aboard the probe, I chose you. You are the one. Remember that, if it make the decision any easier."

Then he is gone, and I am alone. I stand on the beach and stare at the sunset.

The wet sand at my feet is blank; the stick hangs motionless by my side. I remember Elizabeth Li's final poem, the despair encapsulated in so few words. The most I can expect is to fill the empty time with meaningless scribble, in the hope that, one day, some of it will begin to make sense.

The story of my life scrawled on a beach of infinite length. Why do I bother? What do I ever do or think that is worth recording? And who, if anyone, would possibly read it?

But what is the alternative?

One of you has to do it, Emmett said about editing the core program. I am certain he wasn't lying. I have always trusted him, even when I had no reason to, other than in memory of a friendship I once shared with his original. Even if that friendship was underscored in my parameters, there still seems little reason to trust so blindly in it now. Unless . . .

You are the one, he also said.

The original Emmett Longyear altered his own engram to make it more trust-worthy. He could easily have done the same to mine—possibly with my original's consent. I am his ace in the hole, the tool he can use to perform tasks he cannot. I am his gullible sidekick. I am—

I am Emmett Longyear's friend, the core program reasserts. Doubt is not per-mitted. Even if he was lying about the excision affecting just the two of us, if by doing as he says I condemn my companions to identity-loss or insanity, I am unable to believe him capable of deliberate malice.

But who am I?

I remember my father's face and the belts he used to wear. Did he really beat me? I have only my original's word for it. Had he lied, I would never know the difference.

The theme my original wrote for his third Concerto Concrete seems to echo across the beach—a lonely seabird's cry on the edge of the world. I try to feel the pain of the boy my original once was, but I cannot.

I am haunted by a man who died ten centuries ago—a man I can never be, yet whom I constantly aspire to emulate. Perhaps I have never been him at all.

Perhaps, inside this shell of Peter Owen Leutenk, there really is someone else trying to get out.

Or I am nothing, an electron spinning through empty vacuum. I do not interact; I do not change. I may as well not exist.

I cannot even kill myself.

That thought comforts me as the stick begins to move, writing the word "Ev-ermore" in letters fifty centimetres high. I am thinking of salvation, but if this isn't a form of suicide then I don't know what it is. At worst, if Emmett is wrong, there is a chance it will finally be over.

# of scorned women and

causal loops

ROBERT GROSSBACH

Here's a sly and intelligent look at the proposition that maybe, just maybe, you should sometimes just shut up and listen, *no matter how smart you think you are . . .*

Robert Grossbach has spent many years working in aerospace/defense, during which time he published three novels, Never Say Die, Someone Great, *and* Easy and Hard Ways Out, *the last of which was made into the movie* Best Defense. *He has also done a number of movie novelizations and screenplays. His short fiction has appeared primarily in* The Magazine of Fantasy & Science Fiction, *with several sales in the 1980s as well as a handful of recent ones. Currently he is working on a novel entitled* A Shortage of Engineers. *He lives in Commack, New York.*

At Cornavin Station the rental agency had given him one of the new Electriques with the re-designed fuel cells, and he'd accepted it reluctantly, knowing it would not have the pickup of the old gas-driven models. Yes, yes, of course it was a thousand times better for the environment, ten thousand times, but still he liked the feel of the *gas* pedal, preferred it over the *accelerator*. One more thing to make him cranky, as if the TGV ride from Paris, his sore left buttock, and France's first round World Cup elimination weren't irritants enough.

He drove now on the Route de Meyrin, westbound from Geneva, passing a new outdoor shopping mall, the giant Thompson CSF and IBM buildings, an automated radar speed monitor, and a Citroën dealership, regarding all with a faintly disapproving and dyspeptic eye, which was how he viewed everything, for reasons he'd never cared to plumb. After eight kilometers, he arrived at a hangar-sized building of corrugated metal, situated amidst a scattered complex of structures, all surrounded by a paved parking lot and double chainlink fence. The sign over the guard booth read ORGANIZATION EUROPÉENE POUR LA RECHERCHE NUCLÉAIRE, or, as the English and Americans called it, CERN (ignoring in their usual obtuse manner that the first word had been changed from CONSEIL nearly seven decades earlier).

He flashed his credential at the guard, passed with an indifferent wave through a flimsy-looking gate, and parked next to a blue Mercedes. He locked the doors of the Electrique out of habit, and trudged toward the building, upper left hamstring throbbing at each step. On a low hill just beyond the complex, he thought he could see sheep grazing and paused for an instant to squint before moving through the entrance.

He signed in at a long, polished wooden desk, filling in the "Name," "Entry Time," and "Person to Be Seen" columns, but leaving blank the "Purpose of Visit" space. When the young receptionist had finished on the phone, she presented him with a plastic yellow rectangle that identified him as a visitor. *"Ici est votre—"*

"English will be fine," he said.

She nodded. "Here is your badge, Inspector. Someone will be out momentarily to escort you."

He grunted a thank-you, then went to stand awkwardly near one of the vinyl waiting area couches, pausing to knead his eyebrows and temples in a futile attempt to ward off the headache he already knew was inevitable. When he looked up a moment later, a fortyish woman stood before him, wearing a loose blouse and pleated gray skirt.

"Inspector Lagrange?"

Short black hair framed a slightly roundish Kewpie-doll face: button nose, cherub mouth, dark red lipstick, touch of rouge. Lagrange thought her just short of pretty. "I'm here to see Dr. Elizabeth Parkes," he said.

"I am she."

Apparently, his expression did not sufficiently conceal his reactions.

"I do not fit your conception of a nuclear physicist?"

He smiled back. "No, no, it's just . . . the receptionist said they were sending somebody. I assumed—" He waved his hand. "It's of no importance."

She stared at him bemusedly. "Well then, shall we?" She motioned toward a doorway. "I assume you'd like a look at the experiment first?"

"That would be fine, yes."

She held the door, and he stepped through.

The hangar area was vast; they padded along a blue steel catwalk past a dozen rows of huge, thrumming machines. "Generators," said Elizabeth, over the din. "They feed the superconducting magnets for the accelerator."

"They give me a headache," shouted Lagrange. He now had pain in his head and his ass; he supposed somewhere along the way he'd stub a toe. They emerged finally into the rear half of the building, seemingly empty except for a giant overhead crane suspended from a heavy steel girder. But as they approached the far end, Lagrange suddenly saw that a huge section of floor simply vanished into a cavernous rectangular pit. He fought off vertigo as they stared over the edge.

"Six stories deep," said Elizabeth.

At the bottom, amidst scattered pieces of equipment, tools, and ladders, was a structure that looked like two piggy-backed railroad cars. Thirty-centimeter-diameter ropes of cable, numbering in the hundreds, ran from the cars up the sides of the pit and disappeared into boxes of electronics that lined the walls.

Lagrange pointed to a circle on the roof of the top car. "That's where Monsieur Parino entered?"

Elizabeth nodded. "A hatch. Hard to tell from up here."

"And you're absolutely certain there's no other way into or out of the experiment?"

She shrugged. "You should know, Inspector. Your people have been over that structure about a thousand times."

"Not my people."

"You're Swiss? I'm sorry, I just assumed you were French. I know there was some sort of a jurisdictional dispute because the tunnel straddles the border and — "

"I'm with Europol."

Her eyes rose in feigned admiration. "Ah, Europol. Yes, someone said they were sending an expert."

"Hardly an expert," said Lagrange. "Far far from it. But I suppose, relative to my local colleagues, I am perhaps ever so slightly more educated in the area."

"Would you like to go down to make an examination?" she asked. "I'm sorry, but there are no elevators, we'll have to use the ladders."

Immediately, Lagrange felt his buttock spasm in anticipation. "That won't be necessary, I've studied the reports." He indicated an aperture in the side of the pit, five stories below. "That's where the beams emerge?"

"That's the opening into the collider tunnel, yes, but 'emerge' is perhaps not the right word. In operation, of course, the tunnel is continuous through the experiment. An extremely high vacuum must be maintained." Somehow, she seemed to sense his discomfort. "Would you be more at ease in another area?"

"That would be fine, yes," said Lagrange.

They exited the building by a rear door, emerged into bright sunlight. Almost immediately, he tripped over a raised section of concrete walkway, winced as he regained his balance.

"Are you okay?" She reached out to steady his arm and momentarily, quite against his will, he became aroused.

How pathetic, he thought, that the mere incidental touch of a woman could do that to him. "I'm fine," he said. "I strained a hamstring while I was jogging the other day. A warning from nature, I suppose, to stop trying to interfere with her course."

"Now you sound like Giorgio."

"Really? In what way?"

"He was always talking about death. Well, alluding to it, anyway. That is, when he wasn't talking about physics. He seemed to feel he was racing against a time-table. He wanted to get the Nobel while he could appreciate it."

They entered a narrow two-story building that connected at an odd angle to two other identical structures.

"He was disappointed he didn't get it for the Higgs . . ."

"You know about the Higgs?"

They walked down an asbestos-tiled corridor. "Not much. I know it's the name given to fields of some sort and also to the particles that presumably transmit them. Higgs bosons, I believe they're called. Goldman found the first one right here and got the prize—when was it?—about fifteen years ago."

"Two thousand three," she said. "Giorgio felt it should've been his."

They entered a small cantina. Candy and Coke machines on one wall. Ten tables and chairs. Microwave oven. Coffee stand.

"This okay?" she asked.

"Anything," he said. "As long as I don't have to hear those generators." They sat at one of the tables, and she brought over some café au lait. He sipped at the Styrofoam cup. "So Giorgio was bitter."

"Oh, of course," she said quickly. "Isn't that *de rigueur* for world-class physicists who feel they're being overlooked? Bitter, driven, obsessed, callous"—her voice deepened, her gaze drifted off—"manipulative, cold, self-absorbed—"

"But you were in love with him." Her focus abruptly returned. "As I said, I've seen the reports," he added, almost apologetically. "It was in the interviews."

She shrugged. "I was at one time, yes. I suppose it was common knowledge. Physicists gossip like anyone else."

"And was the love reciprocated?" He could see the hurt ripple across her features, and he leaned forward. "Mademoiselle Parkes, I am truly sorry for what I realize must seem like an outrageous intrusion into your personal life, but I beg you to try to understand my position. Giorgio Parino was perhaps the world's greatest experimental physicist. His disappearance under the conditions of the experiment—"

"Some of us would not call it a disappearance."

He nodded stiffly. He was not quite ready for semantic scientific nitpicking. "Nevertheless, the pressure from the authorities and the public and the press for a complete explanation—"

"Fuck the authorities!" said Elizabeth. "And the public. And the press. And—"

"And the police. Of course," filled in Lagrange, grinning.

She softened, grinned back. "Of course."

He drained his cup. "Tell me about the Higgs."

She pursed her lips. "As you said, a type of field. Still far from being understood. The Large Hadron Collider we have here was meant to investigate it. Current ideas have been expanded from theories first developed in the 1980s and '90s to explain how the electroweak force, which is transmitted by four zero-mass particles, could be transformed into two separate forces, one of which has massive particles as its carrier. The thinking was—is—that there's some kind of a field, the Higgs, that permeates all of space and that gave particles their masses when the early universe congealed."

"And the collider is able to re-melt that field."

"You smash together two beams of protons at seventeen teravolts, you get a hell of a lot of interesting effects."

"Including travel through time?"

Again, she smiled. Then stood up. "Let's walk. You feel like walking?"

He didn't. "Fine."

"I'll show you the Megatek room."

"Okay."

They emerged from the cantina, turned down the corridor. "You know, La-grange is a famous name in physics," she said.

"Unfortunately, yes," he responded. "So my mother used to inform me practi-cally every day. Even at one time claimed he was my ancestor, although I doubt it. If he was, I'm afraid I'd have been a terrible disappointment to him."

"You were not a good student?"

"I barely managed to eke out a master's at Columbia."

"Ah, so that explains your excellent English: You went to school in the States."

"As I said, my family had hopes. Fortunately, the experience demonstrated quite clearly that I'd never be any more than a third-rate physicist, if that."

They turned a corner. "You must not let others' opinions of you become your own," she said with unusual intensity. "I had to constantly fight with Giorgio."

"He considered you third-rate?"

No answer.

"Was it because you're a woman?"

"He said . . ." She swallowed. Muscles worked high in her jaw. "He said I was very good on the details, but that I didn't have the vision to be truly insightful. He said he realized it sounded sexist, but that all the women scientists he'd known seemed to have the same restricted perspective. 'Tunnel vision,' he called it, and then he'd laugh, because of—I don't know—some private double enten-dre. He said I was wonderful at poring over data and attending to minute indi-vidual tasks and that I shouldn't beat myself to death trying to be something I was not."

"And you didn't, I presume."

"No."

"Did you beat *him* to death?"

They came to a room marked "Megatek," and she paused at the door. "Am I being charged with a crime, Inspector? Is this an official Europol interrogation or a casual conversation?"

Lagrange shrugged. "The answers are respectively, mademoiselle, 'Not yet,' and 'Official interrogation.' I apologize if my manner has been too informal."

She frowned, but Lagrange could see that the gesture was theatrical. "Perhaps I should have an attorney present."

He nodded slightly. "With all due respect, Dr. Parkes, this is not America. There is no Miranda law here, nor any direct equivalent of habeas corpus."

She unlocked the door. "Whatever Giorgio did, he did to himself."

Inside the room were a half dozen scattered computer terminals, a shelf-lined wall filled with black notebooks, a bulletin board sprinkled with particle-collision photos, and finally, in the center, two large machines that looked like 3-D video games. It was in these, the Megateks, that computer-enhanced, three-dimensional re-creations of the experiments in the collider pit could be displayed.

"Some people say you could have stopped him."

"I tried. He wouldn't listen."

"But it was you who threw the switch."

"At his order. At his insistence. Does that make me a criminal?"

"Perhaps. There are several dependencies."

"Such as . . ."

"Such as what exactly has happened to him. Such as whether you knew the consequences of his order."

"He was Director General of CERN, my immediate supervisor."

"Nevertheless, if your direct superior commands you to fire a loaded gun at his head and you do it"—he held out his hands—"the law says you are guilty of murder. And no matter that he is an arrogant, patronizing, womanizing bastard." He paused. "Now, did you know the consequences of throwing that switch?"

She inhaled deeply. "I . . ." She shook her head. "Giorgio had so undermined my confidence I couldn't be sure of anything. I doubted my own mind."

"So you weren't certain?"

"No."

"But you are more confident now."

"I am more confident now, yes."

He sat down at one of the Megateks, fiddled with the joystick. "How did Giorgio first get the idea about time travel?"

She leaned over one of the computers, began punching a few keys. "Here, better to show than tell."

A moment later, at the center of his machine's holographic projection volume, a schematic display of a detector appeared: cylinder for the central portion, larger cylinder for the electromagnetic calorimeters, rectangle for the hadronic calorimeters. She punched another button and, instantly, thirty or forty multi-colored spaghetti tracks shot through the display.

"A reproduction of event 1431," she said. "The detector assembly surrounds the location where the protons collide." She hit another key, and all but a half dozen of the tracks disappeared. She moved a joystick to enlarge the display. Three-inch-long traces fanned outward from a single point.

"A jet," said Elizabeth. "Not that uncommon. The energy was 11.3 teravolts. Now"—again her tapered fingers flew over the keys—"let me show it to you as time passes."

The traces slowly extended in length.

"Each inch on the display scale takes about .2 picoseconds."

Suddenly, at about four inches, each trace seemed to double, joined by an adjacent twin, which streaked alongside it for about an inch and a half before disappearing.

Lagrange turned, brow knit, palms up. "I'm sorry, I don't understand."

"No one did," said Elizabeth. "Particles identical in every Fermi number—I know it's impossible—had appeared from nowhere alongside the originals. Giorgio finally made the mental leap."

Lagrange's mouth opened in a silent Ah. "There were no new particles. The originals simply moved back in time to join themselves at an earlier instant."

Elizabeth nodded. "The Higgs field had melted, mass had disappeared—and popped back about .3 picoseconds. The calculations confirmed there was a chunk of energy missing; Giorgio called it tau-sub-e, the temporal component."

"A totally unexpected effect."

"Totally. And, of course, Giorgio immediately recognized the macroscopic ramifications."

Lagrange shook his head.

"The effect had occurred over a linear extent of nearly a millimeter, but there was no reason why that could not be expanded arbitrarily. Apparently—Have you read his 2017 *Physical Review* paper?"

Lagrange said he had, but with very limited comprehension.

"Apparently," she continued, "as the universe cooled, the Higgs field congealed into microscopic domains, separated by walls like, mmm . . ." As she searched for an analogy, a tiny crevice appeared between her eyebrows; despite himself, Lagrange found it charming. "Like that plastic bubble paper they use to wrap gifts. The colliding beams popped the bubbles, releasing their energy." She raised her eyebrows. "Anyway, Giorgio did the calculations for how to scan the beams so the bubbles would coalesce into a volume of arbitrary size."

"And inside the volume," ventured Lagrange, "whatever was there would move backward in time?"

She nodded. "Giorgio said they would have to give him two Nobel prizes, one wasn't enough." She grinned. "I suggested he should hold the prize a few minutes, then move back in time and stand alongside himself." The grin vanished.

"He took you seriously."

"Not immediately. His first priority was to go around the world, giving speeches. You understand, he was an incredible hero to physicists everywhere. He must've visited a hundred different countries."

"While the rest of the staff . . ."

"Eighty of us. Studied the effect, repeated it, tried to understand it, tried to extend it. Eventually, we built a six-cubic-meter test chamber, used a magnetic field to suspend and levitate it in a vacuum—and sent it back approximately 3.3 picoseconds."

"You must've been ecstatic."

She gave a little snort. "I was disturbed. I felt there was something fundamental we were missing."

"And that's when you gave the speech."

She nodded. There had been an assembly of the entire staff to discuss recent events in time travel. A conference room. Ninety-six yellow chairs in six even rows, blackboard in front, TV monitors lining one wall. Giorgio had taken a sub-orbital from Tokyo to attend.

Seven or eight of the physicists had gotten up to speak, discoursing on this or that arcane area, making recommendations, complaining, fending off Giorgio's staccato questions and comments. Finally, it was Elizabeth's turn. She took the low podium, hesitantly began to talk, showed several prepared slides. Unfortunately, she could not quite conceptualize what was bothering her, and when you could not quite conceptualize, Giorgio jumped down your throat.

"So the photographs were fuzzy," he rasped. "So what. Clean your camera lenses."

A chuckle rippled through the audience.

"They were clean, Giorgio. And the focus was checked."

"So what is your point?"

"There . . . there is some spatial effect associated with time travel. Perhaps it is second-order, but—"

"With all due respect, Elizabeth, your data hardly justifies the conclusion. Frankly, I wouldn't even call it data."

"But the chamber . . . My measurements show it shifted nearly a millimeter—"

"Oh, so we're measuring distances now? Very good. Did you use a wooden ruler or a metal one?"

More laughter, much of it strained.

"I used a laser calipers."

"Ah, pardon me. I underestimated your technical ability." Openly, savagely patronizing now. "Elizabeth, we are talking about a six-cubic-meter volume, subject to quite substantial forces here. Why are you surprised by a minuscule movement? Why do you think it's important? Have you checked the magnetic field servos? Have you checked the uncertainties in the energy budgets?"

"I tried, but I couldn't—"

"Have you done any supporting calculations? Any math at all? Any thinking at all before you came up here with these details? Details are fine, Dr. Parkes, but really, can't we just get a little perspective on what is not a waste of time?"

White-faced, choking, Elizabeth had croaked "Sorry" and fled the stage.

Lagrange leaned back. "He humiliated you."

She nodded. "In front of everybody," she whispered.

"You left the conference?"

"Of course. I studied the minutes afterward."

He pictured her, alone in some small room, a high school girl who'd missed the senior prom, reading about it instead in some dry secondhand report. He wanted to hug her, tell her he was a kindred soul in personal disappointment.

But almost as if reading his thoughts—and rejecting them—she drew herself up. "I was angry. I felt"—her eyes blazed—"I may be an inferior scientist, but sometimes an inferior does good work. A hack writer comes up with a great novel. A poor soccer team beats a much better one." She thrust out her chin. "An average detective has a magnificent insight that cracks an impossible case."

Lagrange nodded. "So you felt you were onto something and were being ignored."

"More accurately, I felt Giorgio was missing something. I guess, at bottom, what was really bothering me was the old grandfather paradox. You know, somebody goes back in time and kills their own grandfather, so that they were never born . . . which means they weren't around to go back in time."

Lagrange crossed his legs. "You didn't buy the many-universe theories? As I understand it, the concept is that when someone goes back in time he is really travelling to another universe, which is identical with the first up to the instant of his arrival, but different thereafter because of his presence. That way—"

"In the universe he leaves, his grandfather is alive and he is born. In the one he enters, his grandfather dies, and he isn't born." She shook her head. "That was Giorgio's explanation and most of the others'. The melting of the Higgs field produced closed timelike curves, CTCs, between universes." She chuckled mirthlessly. "To me, it sounded like magic. Invoke enough different universes and you can explain anything. It wasn't true understanding. And I had my experiments. There's something that working with actual hardware gives you—I know it sounds mystical—but there's something that world travellers get out of touch with."

The door opened then and two men entered, dressed casually in slacks and open-collar shirts. Lagrange stood up, withdrew his wallet, and flashed his badge. "Gentlemen, I'm sorry, but I must ask you to leave. We'll only be another five minutes."

The men seemed uncertain, but eventually departed.

"You know them?" asked Lagrange when they'd gone.

"Not well," said Elizabeth. "The younger one's been here a year, some kind of mathematician from Collège de France. The other fellow I believe is Russian, specializes in muon detectors."

"Tell me when Giorgio got his bright idea. Do you think it was always in the back of his mind?"

She shrugged. "I doubt it. I think it was one of those spur-of-the-moment things, one of those flamboyant I-am-the-boss megalomaniac power moves he loved so much."

"Then it was for the benefit of the Japanese?"

"Partly, yes. They had sent in a large visiting delegation. They were talking about a huge funding increment—that's what it's all about in high-energy physics, as it's always been—and Giorgio was anxious to make a grand impression."

"And that's when you picked to tell him you thought the experiments might not be safe." He raised his eyebrows. "Awkward timing, no?"

She bristled. "It wasn't 'timing' at all. I broached it to him as soon as I felt I had a solid basis for it. A couple of the Japanese just happened to be in the room. Should I have whispered?"

Lagrange didn't answer. "And your concern was—"

"The small spatial dislocations I'd mentioned earlier. I was worried about what might happen if an object interpenetrated an earlier version of itself."

"But Dr. Parino did not share your anxiety."

"He was furious with me for bringing it up. As it turned out, he was right. There was a problem, but that wasn't it."

"Nevertheless, he decided to demonstrate the process safety by using himself as the subject of an experiment." Lagrange began tapping his foot. "How did he justify that?"

"He didn't, really. In his position, you didn't have to. Oh, later on he offered up some mumbo jumbo about taking a bit of future information into the past, something that required a human mind, in order to test or dispel the so-called knowledge paradox. An example would be paintings brought from the future to the original artist in the past, who copies them. The process eliminates the creative work. Anyway, no one considered that seriously. We all knew Giorgio was just being Giorgio."

"Was it his idea to go a full five seconds backward? Wasn't that trillions of times longer than you'd sent anything else?"

"It had already been shown that the regression in time depended exponentially on the rate at which you melted the Higgs domains, not the collision energy. It meant only that we had to increase our luminosity and scanning speed. Giorgio claimed five seconds was the minimum duration required for his future self to record and bring back a number they could be photographed with next to a sealed clock."

"The Paris closing gold price."

"Yes."

"What did the other physicists think of his plan?"

"That he was entirely crazy, of course. But it was a genius move for publicity."

"And were they worried, too, about safety?"

"Oh, most agreed it was rash, but no one could justify their feelings in terms of specifics." She removed a small mirror and some lipstick from a tiny purse she carried. "Giorgio was not the kind of person who inspired feelings of protection."

"Except in you."

She stopped applying the lipstick. "I was up the entire night before the experiment. That was when I figured everything out."

"You could see him from the control room?"

She nodded. Lagrange remembered the tape — control room activity was always recorded. Sixty television monitors. Two dozen physicists sitting at consoles, hunched over screens, harried, looking up to scan a readout, to shout something, to scream a command. On one of the consoles, Giorgio strides confidently toward the pit in the hangar floor. Underground area fifteen, or UA15, the time travel experiment. He says something to one of the Japanese visitors and the man smiles. Giorgio is wearing an orange jumpsuit, a white lined pad under his arm.

WAITING FOR A COMMAND scrolls down one of the monitors. WAITING FOR A COMMAND.

"Is the counter working?" shouts a physicist.

"Firing away," says another. "I got it in the logbook."

A mechanical voice announces, "Proton check," and three of the screens fill up with numbers and graphs. A moment later, the voice declares, "SPS ready," and more numbers tumble onto additional displays.

The camera catches Elizabeth, sitting at the main control panel. Her face is gaunt, her eyes wide. She uses a microphone to address people in the hangar. "Giorgio, I beg you not to do this. I beg you."

Giorgio waves and smiles, pats the Japanese on the shoulder.

Lagrange shook his head. "Why did he make you the SLIMI?" SLIMI was Shift Leader In Matters of Information.

Elizabeth spoke in a near whisper. "It wasn't that unusual. I had done it before." She inhaled sharply. "I suppose it was further punishment."

Lagrange recalled the final moments. Giorgio descending the ladder into the pit. Signal light going on indicating Time Travel Chamber secured. The mechanical voice saying, "Beam scanning sequence ready," and Elizabeth making one futile last attempt.

"Giorgio, please . . . please . . ."

And the response: "Is the gold price in? As soon as it comes in, close the fucking switch and read me the fucking number when the counter goes down to two. I order it, Elizabeth."

She hesitates several seconds, looks around at the other physicists, whose expressions are maintained at careful neutrality. A man wearing headphones approaches her and whispers something. She delays another moment and then, finally, chest heaving, she presses a key. The mechanical voice says, "Cycle one," and begins a countdown from nine to zero.

At two, Elizabeth reads in the Paris close in New Dollars per ounce, 29.32. At zero, small dips appear on lines crossing three of the monitors.

Even in the hangar, there never was any sound. When the Time Chamber disappeared, it happened in vacuum; no air was present to rush in.

Lagrange stood up and stretched. "You knew immediately, of course."

Elizabeth nodded. "All instrument readouts from the chamber went dead."

He began to slowly pace, ignoring the hamstring twinges. "You knew where he'd be?"

"Not exactly. I knew how far, but not precisely the direction."

"So it was more or less luck that Farside II happened to be pointed toward that sector."

"I suppose. Chances were *some* telescope would catch it."

"Your distance was correct?"

A faint grin. "Within experimental error."

"Your so-called equivalence principle . . ."

She puffed her lips. "It seemed reasonable. Travel through space requires time; therefore, travel through time might very well require space."

"It resolves the grandfather paradox."

"It occurred to me the night before the experiment. You can't kill your grandfather if you can't reach him. If you travel through time, you can't affect anything before you left—or have anything affect you—if you're flung far enough away from your original position."

"But how far is 'far enough'?"

"In general, the speed of light multiplied by the time interval. Nothing could travel back fast enough to cause a problem. The universe could protect itself from inconsistencies and non-causal events, it didn't need other universes to help."

He pondered a moment. "But what if you're transported right near your grandfather, whom you immediately murder?"

She shook her head. "Either he'd have already sired your parent, so it wouldn't matter, or he couldn't have been your grandfather. In tech-speak, in the time interval you went back, no concatenation of world lines could traverse as much distance as you did."

Lagrange was content to grasp the essence. "So, therefore, when Monsieur Parino was popped back five seconds in time, in space he was thrust—"

Her eyebrows rose. "A million and a half kilometers."

Lagrange gave a low whistle. "Dr. Parkes, thank you. The interview is officially concluded. If you could see me back to UA15 . . ."

She stood. "Of course."

They exited the Megatek room. The two men who'd entered before were waiting outside and eyed them venomously as they receded down the hall. "So tell me, Inspector," she asked, "am I to be charged?"

Lagrange looked at her alongside him, pursed his lips. "Well, that is not for me to decide, mademoiselle. I only make a report." He could not keep a straight face. "But I think not." At a corner, he dared take her arm. "I think not."

He had heard talk that it was she now who might get the Nobel, sharing it with the departed Giorgio for "the Parkes-Parino principle."

"Have you seen the actual pictures from Farside II, Inspector?"

"Oh yes," said Lagrange. "Quite beautiful, in an eerie sort of way." He tried for a moment to imagine himself in Parino's shoes. There was a porthole in the chamber and he undoubtedly had looked out. Lagrange wondered if he'd been able to see the Earth from his position, how small it must've appeared from a million kilometers beyond the moon, how resplendent amidst the jeweled background of scattered stars, how achingly, utterly unreachable . . . "The glare made the chamber look almost like a comet."

"Well," said Elizabeth, "there is a fair amount of energy associated with temporal re-entry." An impish expression crossed her face. "And, of course, Giorgio always was brilliant."

Unprofessional as it was, Lagrange laughed.

son observe the time

KAGE BAKER

Prolific new writer Kage Baker made her first sale, to Asimov's Science Fiction, in 1997, and has since become one of that magazine's most frequent and popular contributors with her sly and compelling stories of the adventures and misadventures of the time-travelling agents of the Company; her stories have also appeared in Amazing, Realms of Fantasy, *and elsewhere. Her first novel,* In the Garden of Iden, *also a tale of the Company, was published in 1997 and immediately became one of the most acclaimed and widely reviewed first novels of the year. Her second Company novel,* Sky Coyote, *was published in 1999, a third,* Mendoza in Hollywood, *early in 2000, and she has several more novels already sold and in the pipeline. Baker has been an artist, actor, and director at the Living History Center, and has taught Elizabethan English as a second language. She lives in Pismo Beach, California.*

In the intricate and eloquent novella that follows, perhaps the best of the Company stories to date, she take us back in time to Old San Francisco, to the breathless moments just before the Great San Francisco Earthquake, for a taut and suspenseful tale of conspiracy, conflict, political intrigue, revenge, and redemption in the shadow of onrushing catastrophe.

On the eve of destruction we had oysters and champagne. Don't suppose for a moment that we had any desire to lord it over the poor mortals of San Francisco, in that month of April in that year of 1906; but things weren't going to be so gracious there again for a long while, and we felt an urge to fortify ourselves against the work we were to do.

And who were *we*, you may ask? The present-time operatives of Dr. Zeus Incorporated, a twenty-fourth-century cabal of investors who have presided over the development of immortality and time travel, amongst other things. Neither of those inventions is terribly practical, I regret to say; nevertheless they can be utilized to provide a satisfactory profit for Company shareholders. Assuming, of course, that we immortals—their servants—are able to perform our tasks in a satisfactory manner.

London before the Great Fire, Delhi before the Mutiny, even Chicago—I was there and I can tell you, it requires a great deal of mental and emotional self-discipline to live side by side with mortals in a Salvage Zone. You must look, daily, into the smiling faces of those who are to lose all, and walk beside them in the knowledge that nothing you can do will affect their fates. Even the most prosaic of places has a sort of haunted glory at such times; judge then how it looked to us, that gilded fantastical butterfly of a city, quite unprepared for its approaching holocaust.

The place was made even queerer by the fact that there were so many Company operatives there at the time. The very ether hummed with our transmissions. In any street you might have seen us dismounting from carriages or the occasional automobile, we immortal gentlemen tipping our derbies to the ladies, our immortal ladies responding with a graceful inclination of their picture hats, smiling as we met each other's terrified eyes. We dined at the Palace and as guests at Nob Hill mansions; promenaded in Golden Gate Park, drove out to Woodward Gardens, attended the theater and everywhere saw the pale set faces of our own kind, busy with their own particular preparations against what was to come.

Some of us had less pleasant places to go. I was grateful that I was not required to brave the Chinese labyrinth by Waverly Place, but my associate Pan had certain business there amongst the Celestials. I myself was obliged to venture, too many times, into the boarding-houses south of Market Street. Beneath the Fly Trap was a Company safe house and HQ; we'd meet there sometimes, Pan and I, at the end of a long day in our respective ghettoes, and we'd sit shaking together over a brace of stiff whiskies. Thus heartened, it was time for a costume change: dock laborer into gentleman for me, coolie into cook for him, and so home by cable car.

I lodged in two rooms on Bush Street. I will not say I slept there; one does not rest well on the edge of the maelstrom. But it was a place to keep one's trunk, and to operate the Company credenza necessary for facilitating the missions of those operatives whose case officer I was. Salvaging is a terribly complicated affair, requiring as it does that one hide in History's shadow until the last possible moment before snatching one's quarry from its preordained doom. One must be organized and thoroughly coordinated; and timing is everything.

On the morning of the tenth of April I was working there, sending a progress report, when there came a brisk knock at my door. Such was my concentration that I was momentarily unmindful of the fact that I had no mortal servants to answer it. When I heard the impatient tapping of a small foot on the step, I hastened to the door.

I admitted Nan D'Araignee, one of our Art Preservation specialists. She is an operative of West African origin with exquisite features, slender and slight as a doll carved of ebony. I had worked with her briefly near the end of the previous century. She is quite the most beautiful woman I have ever known, and happily married to another immortal, a century before I ever laid eyes on her. Timing, alas, is everything.

"Victor." She nodded. "Charming to see you again."

"Do come in." I bowed her into my parlor, acutely conscious of its disarray.

Her bright gaze took in the wrinkled laundry cast aside on the divan, the clutter of unwashed teacups, the half-eaten oyster loaf on the credenza console, six empty sauterne bottles and one smudgily thumbprinted wineglass. She was far too courteous to say anything, naturally, and occupied herself with the task of removing her gloves.

"I must apologize for the condition of the place," I stammered. "My duties have kept me out a good deal." I swept a copy of the *Examiner* from a chair. "Won't you sit down?"

"Thank you." She took the seat and perched there, hands folded neatly over her gloves and handbag. I pulled over another chair, intensely irritated at my clumsiness.

"I trust your work goes well?" I inquired, for there is of course no point in asking one of us if *we* are well. "And, er, Kalugin's? Or has he been assigned elsewhere?"

"He's been assigned to Marine Transport, as a matter of fact," she told me, smiling involuntarily. "We are to meet on the *Thunderer* afterward. I am so pleased! He's been in the Bering Sea for two years, and I've missed him dreadfully."

"Ah," I said. "How pleasant, then, to have something to look forward to in the midst of all this. . . ."

She nodded quickly, understanding. I cleared my throat and continued:

"What may I do for you, Nan?"

She averted her gaze from dismayed contemplation of the stale oyster loaf and smiled. "I was told you might be able to assist me in requisitioning additional transport for my mission."

"I shall certainly attempt it." I stroked my beard. "Your present arrangements are unsuitable?"

"Inadequate, rather. You may recall that I'm in charge of Presalvage at the Hopkins Gallery. It seems our original estimates of what we can rescue there were too modest. At present I have five vans arranged for to evacuate the Gallery contents, but really we need more. Would it be possible to requisition a sixth? My own case officer was unable to assist me, but felt you might have greater success."

This was a challenge. Company resources were strained to the utmost on this operation, which was one of the largest on record. Every operative in the United States had been pressed into service, and many of the European and Asian personnel. A handsome allotment had been made for transport units, but needs were swiftly exceeding expectations.

"Of course I should like to help you," I replied cautiously, "if at all possible. You are aware, however, that horsedrawn transport utilization is impossible, due to the subsonic disturbances preceding the earthquake—and motor transports are, unfortunately, in great demand—"

A brewer's wagon rumbled down the street outside, rattling my windows. We both leaped to our feet, casting involuntary glances at the ceiling; then sat down in silent embarrassment. Mme. D'Araignee gave a little cough. "I'm so sorry—My nerves are simply—"

"Not at all, not at all, I assure you—one can't help flinching—"

"Quite. In any case, Victor, I understand the logistical difficulties involved; but even a handcart would greatly ease our difficulties. So many lovely and unexpected things have been discovered in this collection, that it really would be too awful to lose them to the fire."

"Oh, certainly." I got up and strode to the windows, giving in to the urge to look out and assure myself that the buildings hadn't begun to sway yet. Solid and seemingly as eternal as the pyramids they stood there, for the moment. I turned back to Mme. D'Araignee as a thought occurred to me. "Tell me, do you know how to operate an automobile?"

"But of course!" Her face lit up.

"It may be possible to obtain something in that line. Depend upon it, Madame, you will have your sixth transport. I shall see to it personally."

"I knew I could rely on you." She rose, all smiles. We took our leave of one another with a courtesy that belied our disquiet. I saw her out and returned to my credenza keyboard.

QUERY, I input, *RE: REQUISITION ADDTNL TRANSPORT MOTOR VAN OR AUTO? PRIORITY RE: HOPKINS INST.*

HOPKINS PROJECT NOT YOUR CASE, came the green and flashing reply.

NECESSARY, I input: *NEW DISCV OVRRIDE SECTION AUTH. PLEASE FORWARD REQUEST PRIORITY.*

WILL FORWARD.

That was all. So much for my chivalrous impulse, I thought, and watched as the transmission screen winked out and returned me to my status report on the Nob Hill Presalvage work. I resumed my entry of the Gilded Age loot tagged for preservation.

When I had transmitted it, I stood and paced the room uneasily. How long had I been hiding in here? What I wanted was a meal and a good stretch of the legs, I told myself sternly. Fresh air, in so far as that was available in any city at the beginning of this twentieth century. I scanned the oyster loaf and found it already pulsing with bacteria. Pity. After disposing of it in the dustbin I put on my coat and hat, took my stick and went out to tread the length of Bush Street with as bold a step as I could muster.

It was nonsense, really, to be frightened. I'd be out of the city well before the first shock. I'd be safe on air transport bound for London before the first flames rose. London, the other City. I could settle into a chair at my club and read a copy of *Punch* that wasn't a month old, secure in the knowledge that the oak beams above my head were fixed and immovable as they had been since the days when I'd worn a powdered wig, as they would be until German shells came raining down decades from now. . . .

Shivering, I dismissed thoughts of the Blitz. Plenty of *life* to think about, surely! Here were bills posted to catch my eye: I might go out to the Pavilion at Woodward's to watch the boxing exhibition—Jack Joyce and Bob Ward featured. There was delectable vaudeville at the Orpheum, I was assured, and gaiety girls out at the Chutes, to say nothing of a spectacular sideshow re-creation of the Johnstown Flood . . . perhaps not in the best of taste, under the present circumstances.

I might imbibe Gold Seal Champagne to lighten my spirits, though I didn't think I would; Veuve Cliquot was good enough for me. Ah, but what about a bottle of Chianti, I thought, arrested by the bill of fare posted in the window of a corner restaurant. Splendid culinary fragrances wafted from within. Would I have grilled veal chops here? Would I go along Bush to the Poodle Dog for Chicken *Chaud-Froid Blanc*? Would I venture to Grant in search of yellow silk banners for duck roasted in some tiny Celestial kitchen? Then again, I knew of a Swiss place where the cook was a Hungarian, and prepared a light and crisply fried Wienerschnitzel to compare with any I'd had . . . or I might just step into a saloon and order another oyster loaf to take home. . . .

No, I decided, veal chops would suit me nicely. I cast a worried eye up at the building—pity this structure wasn't steel-framed—and proceeded inside.

It was one of those dark, robust places within, floor thickly strewn with fresh sawdust not yet kicked into little heaps. I took my table as any good operative does, back to the wall and a clear path to the nearest exit. Service was poor, as apparently their principal waiter was late today, but the wine was excellent. I found it bright on the palate, just what I'd wanted, and the chops when they came were redolent of herbs and fresh olive oil. What a consolation Appetite can be.

Yes, Life, that was the thing to distract one from unwise thoughts. Savor the wine, I told myself, observe the parade of colorful humanity, breathe in the fragrance of the joss sticks and the seafood and the gardens of the wealthy, listen to the smart modern city with its whirring steel parts at the service of its diverse inhabitants. The moment is all, surely.

I dined in some isolation, for the luncheon crowd had not yet emerged from the nearby offices and my host remained in the kitchen, arguing with the cook over the missing waiter's character and probable ancestry. Even as I amused myself by listening, however, I felt a disturbance approaching the door. No temblor yet, thank Heaven, but a tempest of emotions. I caught the horrifying mental images before ever I heard the stifled weeping. In another moment he had burst through the door, a young male mortal with a prodigious black mustache, quite nattily dressed but with his thick hair in wild disarray. As soon as he was past the threshold his sobs burst out unrestrained, at a volume that would have done credit to Caruso.

This brought his employer out of the back at once, blurting out the first phrases of furious denunciation. The missing waiter (for so he was) staggered forward and thrust out that day's *Chronicle*. The headlines, fully an inch tall, checked the torrent of abuse: *MANY LOSE THEIR LIVES IN GREAT ERUPTION OF VE-SUVIUS*.

The proprietor of the restaurant, struck dumb, went an ugly ashen color. He put the fingertips of one hand in his mouth and bit down hard. In a broken voice, the waiter described the horrors: Roof collapsed in church in his own village. His own family might even now lie dead, buried in ash. The proprietor snatched the paper and cast a frantic eye over the columns of print. He sank to his knees in the sawdust, sobbing. Evidently he had family in Naples, too.

I stared at my plate. I saw gray and rubbery meat, congealing grease, seared bone with the marrow turned black. In the midst of life we are in death, but it doesn't do to reflect upon it while dining.

"You must, please, excuse us, sir," the proprietor said to me, struggling to his feet. "There has been a terrible tragedy." He set the *Chronicle* beside my plate so

I could see the blurred rotogravure picture of King Victor Emmanuel. *Report That Total Number of Dead May Reach Seven Hundred*, I read. *Towns Buried Under Ashes and Many Caught in Ruined Buildings. MANY BUILDINGS CRUSHED BY ASHES.* Of course, I had known about the coming tragedy; but it was on the other side of the world, the business of other Company operatives, and I envied them that their work was completed now.

"I am so very sorry, sir," I managed to say, looking up at my host. He thought my pallor was occasioned by sympathy: he could not know I was seeing his mortal face like an apparition of the days to come, and it was gray and charring, for he lay dead in the burning ruins of a boarding house in the Mission District. Horror, yes, impossible not to feel horror, but one cannot empathize with them. One must not.

They went into the kitchen to tell the cook and I heard weeping break out afresh. Carefully I took up the newspaper and perused it. Perhaps there was something here that might divert me from the unpleasantness of the moment? Embezzlement. A crazed admirer stalking an actress. Charlatan evangelists. Grisly murder committed by two boys. Deadly explosion. Crazed derelict stalking a bank president. Los Angeles school principals demanding academic standards lowered.

I dropped the paper, and, leaving five dollars on the table, I fled that place.

I walked briskly, not looking into the faces of the mortals I passed. I rode the cable car, edging away from the mortal passengers. I nearly ran through the green expanse of Golden Gate Park, dodging around the mortal idlers, the lovers, the nurses wheeling infants in perambulators, until at last I stood on the shore of the sea. Tempting to turn to look at the fairy castles perched on its cliffs; tempting to turn to look at the carnival of fun along its gray sand margin, but the human comedy was the last thing I wanted just then. I needed, rather, the chill and level grace of the steel-colored horizon, sun-glistering, wide-expanding. The cold salt wind buffeted me, filled my grateful lungs. Ah, the immortal ocean.

Consider the instructive metaphor: Every conceivable terror dwells in her depths; she receives all wreckage, refuse, corruption of every kind, she pulls down into her depths human calamity indescribable: but none of this is any consideration to the sea. Let the screaming mortal passengers fight for room in the lifeboats, as the wreck belches flame and settles below the extinguishing wave; next morning she'll still be beautiful and serene, her combers no less white, her distances as blue, her seabirds no less graceful as they wheel in the pure air. What perfection, to be so heartless. An inspiration to any lesser immortal.

As I stood so communing with the elements, a mortal man came wading out of the surf. I judged him two hundred pounds of athletic stockbroker, muscles bulging under sagging wet wool, braving the icy water as an act of self-disciplinary sport. He stood for a moment on one leg, examining the sole of his other foot. There was something gladiatorial in his pose. He looked up and saw me.

"A bracing day, sir," he shouted.

"Quite bracing." I nodded and smiled. I could feel the frost patterns of my returning composure.

And so I boarded another streetcar and rode back into the mortal warren, and found my way by certain streets to the Barbary Coast. Not a place a gentleman cares to admit to visiting, especially when he's known the gilded beauties of old Byzantium or Regency-era wenches; the raddled pleasures available on Pacific Street suffered by comparison. But Appetite is Appetite, after all, and there is nothing like it to take one's mind off unpleasant thoughts.

"Your costume." The attendant pushed a pasteboard carton across the counter to me. "Personal effects and field equipment. Linen, trousers, suspenders, boots, shirt, vest, coat and hat." He frowned. "Phew! These should have been laundered. Would you care to be fitted with an alternate set?"

"That's all right." I took the offending rags. "The sweat goes with the role, I'm afraid. Irish laborer."

"Ah." He took a step backward. "Well, break a leg."

"Thank you."

Fifteen minutes later I emerged from a dressing room the very picture of an immigrant yahoo, uncomfortably conscious of my clammy and odiferous clothing. I sidled into the canteen, hoping there wouldn't be a crowd in the line for coffee. There wasn't, at that: most of the diners were clustered around one operative over in a corner, so I stood alone watching the Food Service technician fill my thick china mug from a dented steel coffee urn. The fragrant steam was a welcome distraction from my own fragrancy. I found a solitary table and warmed my hands on my dark brew there in peace, until an operative broke loose from the group and approached me.

"Say, Victor!"

I knew him slightly, an American operative so young one could scan him and still discern the scar tissue from his Augmentations. He was one of my Presalvagers.

"Good morning, Averill."

"Say, you really ought to listen to that fellow over there. He's got some swell stories." He paused only long enough to have his cup refilled, then came and pulled out a chair across from me. "Know who he is? He's the Guy Who Follows Caruso Around!"

"Is he?"

"Sure is. Music Specialist Grade One! That boy's wired for sound. He's caught every performance Caruso's ever given, even the church stuff when he was a kid. Going to get him in *Carmen* the night before You-Know-What, going to record the whole performance. He's just come back from planting receivers in the footlights! Say, have you gotten tickets yet?"

"No, I haven't. I'm not interested, actually."

"Not interested?" he exclaimed. "Why aren't you — how *can't* you be interested? It's *Caruso*, for God's sake!"

"I'm perfectly aware of that, Averill, but I've got a prior engagement. And, personally, I've always thought de Reszke was much the better tenor."

"De Reszke?" He scanned his records to place the name and, while doing so, absently took a great gulp of coffee. A second later he clutched his ear and gasped. "Christ Almighty!"

"Steady, man." I suppressed a smile. "You don't want to gulp beverages over 60 degrees Celsius, you know. There's some very complex circuitry placed near the Eustachian tube that gets unpleasantly hot if you do."

"Ow, ow, ow!" He sucked in air, staring at me with the astonishment of the very new operative. It always takes them a while to discover that immortality and intense pain are not strangers, indeed can reside in the same eternal house for quite lengthy periods of time. "Should I drink some ice water?"

"By no means, unless you want some real discomfort. You'll be all right in a minute or so. As I was about to say, I have some recordings of Jean de Reszke I'll transmit to you, if you're interested in comparing artists."

"Thanks, I'd like that." Averill ran a hasty self-diagnostic.

"And how is your team faring over at the New Brunswick, by the way? No cases of nerves, no blue devils?"

"Hell no." Averill started to lift his coffee again and then set it down respectfully.

"Doesn't bother you that the whole place will be ashes in a few days' time, and most of your neighbors dead?"

"No. We're all okay over there. We figure it's just a metaphor for the whole business, isn't it? I mean, sooner or later this whole world"—he made a sweeping gesture, palm outward—"as we know it, is going the same way, right? So what's it matter if it's the earthquake finishes it now or a wrecking ball someplace further on in time, right? Same thing with the people. It'll all come to the same thing in the end, so there's no reason to get personally upset about it, is there? No, sir. Specially since *we'll* all still be alive."

"A commendable attitude." I had a sip of my coffee. "And your work goes well?"

"Yes *sir*." He grinned. "You will be so proud of us burglary squad fellows when you get our next list. You wouldn't believe the stuff we're finding! All kinds of objets d'art, looks like. One-of-a-kind items, by God. Wait'll you see."

"I look forward to it." I glanced at my Chronometer and drank down the rest of my coffee, having waited for it to descend to a comfortable 59 degrees Celsius. "But, you know, Averill, it really won't do to think of yourselves as burglars."

"Well—that is—it's only a figure of speech, anyhow!" Averill protested, flushing. "A joke!"

"I'm aware of that, but I cannot emphasize enough that we are not stealing anything." I set my coffee cup down, aware that I sounded priggish, and looked sternly at him. "We're preserving priceless examples of late Victorian craftsmanship for the edification of future generations."

"I know." Averill looked at me sheepishly, "But—aw, hell, do you mean to say not one of those crystal chandeliers will wind up in some Facilitator General's private HQ somewhere?"

"That's an absurd idea," I told him, though I knew only too well it wasn't. Still, it doesn't do to disillusion one's subordinates too young. "And now, will you excuse me? I mustn't be late for work."

"All right. Be seeing you!"

As I left he rejoined the admiring throng about the fellow who was telling Caruso stories. My way lay along the bright tiled hall, steamy and echoing with the clatter of food preparation and busy operatives; then through the dark security vestibule, with its luminous screens displaying the world without; then through the concealed door that shut behind me and left no trace of itself to any eyes but my own. I drew a deep breath. Chill and silent morning air; no glimmer of light, yet, at least not down here in the alley. Half-past-five. This time three days hence—

I shivered and found my way out in the direction of the waterfront.

Not long afterward I arrived at the loading area where I had been desultorily employed for the last month. I made my entrance staggering slightly, doing my best to murder "You Can't Guess Who Flirted With Me" in a gravelly baritone.

The mortal laborers assembled there turned to stare at me. My best friend, an acquaintance I'd cultivated painstakingly these last three weeks, came forward and took me by the arm.

"Jesus, Kelly, you'd better stow that. Where've you been?"

I stopped singing and gave him a belligerent stare. "Marching in the Easter Parade, O'Neil."

"O, like enough." He ran his eyes over me in dismay. Francis O'Neil was thirty years old. He looked enough like me to have been taken for my somewhat bulkier, clean-shaven brother. "What're you doing this for, man? You know Herlihy doesn't like you as it is. You look like you've not been home to sleep nor bathe since Friday night!"

"So I have not." I dropped my gaze in hung-over remorse.

"Come on, you poor stupid bastard, I've got some coffee in my dinner pail. Sober up. Was it a letter you got from your girl again?"

"It was." I let him steer me to a secluded area behind a mountain of crates and accepted the tin cup he filled for me with lukewarm coffee. "She doesn't love me, O'Neil. She never did. I can tell."

"Now, then, you're taking it all the wrong way, I'm sure. I can't believe she's stopped caring, not after all the things you've told me about her. Just drink that down, now. Mary made it fresh not an hour ago."

"You're a lucky man, Francis." I leaned on him and began to weep, slopping the coffee. He forbore with the patience of a saint and replied:

"Sure I am, Jimmy, And shall I tell you why? Because I know when to take my drink, don't I? I don't swill it down every payday and forget to go home, do I? No indeed. I'd lose Mary and the kids and all the rest of it, wouldn't I? It's self-control you need, Jimmy, and the sorrows in your heart be damned. Come on now. With any luck Herlihy won't notice the state you're in."

But he did, and a litany of scorn was pronounced on my penitent head. I took it with eyes downcast, turning my battered hat in my hands, and a dirtier nor more maudlin drunk could scarce have been seen in that city. I would be summarily fired, I was assured, but they needed men today so bad they'd employ even the likes of me, though by God *next* time—

When the boss had done excoriating me I was dismissed to help unload a cargo of copra from the *Nevadan*, in from the islands yesterday. I sniveled and tottered and managed not to drop anything much; O'Neil stayed close to me the whole day, watchful lest I pass out or wander off. He was a good friend to the abject caricature I presented; God knows why he cared. Well, I should repay his kindness, at least, though in a manner he would never have the opportunity to appreciate.

We sweated until four in the afternoon, when there was nothing left to take off the *Nevadan*; let go then with directions to the next day's job, and threats against slackers.

"Now, Kelly." O'Neil took my arm and steered me with him back toward Market Street. "I'll tell you what I think you ought to do. Go home and have a bit of a wash in the basin, right? Have you clean clothes? So, put on a clean shirt and trousers and see can you scrape some of that off your boots. Then come over to supper at our place, see. Mary's bought some sausages, we thought we'd treat ourselves to a dish of Coddle now that Lent's over. We've plenty."

"I will, then." I grasped his hand. "O'Neil, you're a lord for courtesy."

"I am not. Only go home and wash, man!"

We parted in front of the Terminal Hotel and I hurried back to the HQ to follow his instructions. This was just the sort of chance I'd been angling for since I'd sought out the man on the basis of the Genetic Survey team report.

An hour later, as cleanly as the character I played was likely to be able to make himself, I ventured along Market Street, heading down in the direction of the tenement where O'Neil and his family lived, the boarding houses in the shadow of the Palace Hotel. I knew their exact location, though O'Neil was of course unaware of that; accordingly he had sent a pair of his children down to the corner to watch for me.

They failed to observe my approach, however, and I really couldn't blame them; for proceeding down Market Street before me, moving slowly between the gloom of twilight and the electric illumination of the shop signs, was an apparition in a scarlet tunic and black shako.

It walked with the stiff and measured tread of the automaton it was pretending to be. The little ragged girl and her littler brother stared openmouthed, watching its progress along the sidewalk. It performed a brief business of marching mindlessly into a lamppost and walking inexorably in place there a moment before righting itself and going on, but now on an oblique course toward the children.

I too continued on my course, smiling a little. This was delightful: a mortal pretending to be a mechanical toy being followed by a cyborg pretending to be a mortal.

There was a wild reverberation of mirth in the ether around me. One other of our kind was observing the scene, apparently; but there was a gigantic quality to the amusement that made me falter in my step. Who was that? That was someone I knew, surely. *Quo Vadis?* I transmitted. The laughter shut off like an electric light being switched out, but not before I got a sense of direction from it. I looked across the street and just caught a glimpse of a massive figure disappearing down an alley. My visual impression was of an old miner, one of the mythic founders of this city. Old gods walking? What a ridiculous idea, and yet . . . what a moment of panic it evoked, of mortal dread, quite irrational.

But the figure in the scarlet tunic had reached the children. Little Ella clutched her brother's hand, stock-still on the pavement; little Donal shrank behind his sister, but watched with one eye as the thing loomed over them.

It bent forward, slowly, in increments, as though a gear ratcheted in its spine to lower it down to them. Its face was painted white, with red circles on the cheeks and a red cupid's bow mouth under the stiff black mustaches. Blank glassy eyes did not fix on them, did not *seem* to see anything, but one white-gloved hand came up jerkily to offer the little girl a printed handbill.

After a frozen motionless moment she took it from him. "Thank you, Mister Soldier," she said in a high clear voice. The figure gave no sign that it had heard, but unbent slowly, until it stood ramrod-straight again; pivoted sharply on its heel and resumed its slow march down Market Street.

"Soldier go." Donal pointed. Ella peered thoughtfully at the handbill.

" 'CH-IL-DREN,' " she read aloud. What an impossibly sweet voice she had. "And that's an Exclamation Point, there. 'Babe — Babies, In, To — Toy — ' "

" 'Toyland,' " I finished for her. She looked up with a glad cry.

"There you are, Mr. Kelly. Donal, this is Mr. Kelly. He is Daddy's good friend. Supper will be on the table presently. Won't you please come with us, Mr. Kelly?"

"I should be delighted to." I touched the brim of my hat. They pattered away down an alley, making for the dark warren of their tenement, and I followed closely.

They were different physical types, the brother and sister. Pretty children, certainly, particularly Ella with her glossy black braids, with her eyes the color of the twilight framed by black lashes. But it is not beauty we look for in a child.

It was the boy I watched closely as we walked, a sturdy three-year-old trudging along holding tight to the girl's hand. I couldn't have told you the quality nor shade of his skin, nor his hair nor his eyes; I cared only that his head appeared to be a certain shape, that his little body appeared to fit a certain profile, that his limbs appeared to be a certain length in relation to one another. I couldn't be certain yet, of course: that was why I had maneuvered his father into the generous impulse of inviting me into his home.

They lived down a long dark corridor toward the back of the building, its walls damp with sweat, its air heavy with the odors of cooking, of washing, of mortal life. The door opened a crack as we neared it and then, slowly, opened wide to reveal O'Neil standing there in a blaze of light. The blaze was purely by contrast to our darkness, however; once we'd crossed the threshold, I saw that two kerosene lamps were all the illumination they had.

"There now, didn't I tell you she'd spot him?" O'Neil cried triumphantly. "Welcome to this house, Jimmy Kelly."

"God save all here." I removed my hat. "Good evening, Mrs. O'Neil."

"Good evening to you, Mr. Kelly." Mary O'Neil turned from the stove, bouncing a fretful infant against one shoulder. "Would you care for a cup of tea, now?" She was like Ella, if years could be granted Ella to grow tall and slender and wear her hair up like a soft thundercloud. But there was no welcoming smile for me in the grey eyes, for on the previous occasion we'd met I'd been disgracefully intoxicated — at least, doing my best to appear so. I looked down as if abashed.

"I'd bless you for a cup of tea, my dear, I would," I replied. "And won't you allow me to apologize for the condition I was in last Tuesday week? I'd no excuse at all."

"Least said, soonest mended." She softened somewhat at my obvious sobriety.

Setting the baby down to whimper in its apple-box cradle, she poured and served my tea. "Pray seat yourself."

"Here." Ella pulled out a chair for me. I thanked her and sat down to scan the room they lived in. Only one room, with one window that probably looked out on an alley wall but was presently frosted opaque from the steam of the saucepan wherein their supper cooked. Indeed, there was a fine layer of condensation on everything: it trickled down the walls, it lay in a damp film on the oilcloth cover of the table and the blankets on the bed against the far wall. The unhappy infant's hair was moist and curling with it.

Had there been any ventilation it would have been a pleasant enough room. The table was set with good china, someone's treasured inheritance no doubt. The tiny potbellied stove must have been awkward to cook upon, but O'Neil had built a cabinet of slatwood and sheet tin next to it to serve as the rest of a kitchen. The children's trundle was stored tidily under the parents' bed. Next to the painted washbasin on the trunk, a decorous screen gave privacy to one corner. Slatwood shelves displayed the family's few valuables: a sewing basket, a music box with a painted scene on its lid, a cheap mirror whose frame was decorated with glued-on seashells, a china dog. On the wall was a painted crucifix with a palm frond stuck behind it. O'Neil came and sat down across from me.

"You look grand, Jimmy." He thumped his fist on the table approvingly. "Combed your hair, too, didn't you? That's the boy. You'll make a gentleman yet."

"Daddy?" Ella climbed into his lap. "There was a soldier came and gave us this in the street. Will you ever read me what it says? There's more words than I know, see." She thrust the handbill at him. He took it and held it out before him, blinking at it through the steamy air.

Here I present the printed text he read aloud, without his many pauses as he attempted to decipher it (for he was an intelligent man, but of little education):

CHILDREN!
Come see the Grand Fairy Extravaganza BABES IN TOYLAND
Music by Victor Herbert
Book by Glen MacDonough
Staged by Julian Mitchell
Ignacio Martinetti and 100 Others!
Coming by Special Train of Eight Cars!
Biggest Musical Production San Francisco Has Seen In Years!

An Invitation from Mother Goose Herself:

MY dear little Boys and Girls,

I DO hope you will behave nicely so that your Mammas and Papas will treat you to a performance of Mr. Herbert's lovely play Babes in Toyland at the Columbia Theater, opening Monday, the 16th of April. Why, my dears, it's one of the biggest successes of the season and has already played for ever so many nights in such far-away cities as New York, Chicago, and Boston. Yes, you really must be good little children, and then your dear parents will see that you deserve an outing to visit me. For, make no mistake, I myself, the only true and original MOTHER GOOSE, shall be there upon the stage of the Columbia Theater. And so shall so many of your other friends from my delightful rhymes such as Tom, Tom the Piper's Son, Bo Peep, Contrary Mary, and Red Riding Hood. The curtain will rise upon Mr. Mitchell's splendid production, with its many novel effects, at eight o'clock sharp.

Of course, if you are very little folks you are apt to be sleepyheads if kept up so late, but that need not concern your careful parents, for there will be a matinee on Saturday at two o'clock in the afternoon.

WON'T you please come to see me? Your affectionate friend, Mother Goose.

"Oh, dear," sighed Mary.

"Daddy, can we go?" Ella's eyes were alight with anticipation. Donal chimed in:

"See Mother Goose, Daddy!"

"We can't afford it, children." Mary's mouth was a set line. She took the saucepan off the stove and began to ladle a savory dish of sausage, onions, potatoes and bacon onto the plates. "We've got a roof over our heads and food for the table. Let's be thankful for that."

Ella closed her little mouth tight like her mother's, but Donal burst into tears. "I wanna go see Mother Goose!" he howled.

O'Neil groaned. "Your mother is right, Donal. Daddy and Mummy don't have the money for the tickets, can you understand that?"

"You oughtn't to have read out that bill," said Mary in a quiet voice.

"I want go see the Soldier!"

"Donal, hush now!"

"Donal's the boy for me," I said, leaning forward and reaching out to him. "Look, Donal Og, what's this you've got in your ear?"

I pretended to pull forth a bar of Ghirardelli's. Ella clapped her hands to her mouth. Donal stopped crying and stared at me with perfectly round eyes.

"Look at that! Would you ever have thought such a little fellow'd have such big things in his ears? Come sit with your Uncle Jimmy, Donal." I drew him onto my lap. "And if you hush your noise, perhaps Mummy and Daddy'll let you have sweeties, eh?" I set the candy in the midst of the oilcloth, well out of his reach.

"Bless you, Jimmy," said O'Neil.

"Well, and isn't it the least I can do? Didn't know I could work magic, did you, Ella?"

"Settle down, now." Mary set out the dishes. "Frank, it's time to say Grace."

O'Neil made the sign of the Cross and intoned, with the little ones mumbling along, "Bless-us-O-Lord-and-these-Thy-gifts-which-we-are-about-to-receive-from-Thy-bounty-through-Christ-Our-Lord-Amen."

Mary sat down with us, unfolding her threadbare napkin. "Donal, come sit with Mummy."

"Be easy, Mrs. O'Neil, I don't mind him." I smiled at her. "I've a little brother at home he's the very image of. Where's his spoon? Here, Donal Og, you eat with me."

"I don't doubt they look alike." O'Neil held out his tumbler as Mary poured from a pitcher of milk. "Look at you and me. Do you know, Mary, that was the first acquaintance we had—? Got our hats mixed up when the wind blew 'em both off. We wear just the same size."

"Fancy that."

So we dined, and an affable mortal man helped little Donal make a mess of his potatoes whilst chatting with Mr. and Mrs. O'Neil about such subjects as the dreadful expense of living in San Francisco and their plans to remove to a cheaper, less crowded place as soon as they'd saved enough money. The immortal machine that sat at their table was making a thorough examination of Donal, most subtly: an idle caress of his close-cropped little head measured his skull size, concealed devices gauged bone length and density and measured his weight to the pound; data was analyzed and preliminary judgment made: Optimal Morphology. Augmentation Process Possible. Classification pending Blood Analysis and Spektral Diagnosis.

"That's the best meal I've had in this country, Mrs. O'Neil," I told her as we rose from the table.

"How kind of you to say so, Mr. Kelly," she replied, collecting the dishes.

"Chocolate, Daddy?" Donal stretched out his arm for it. O'Neil tore open the waxed paper and broke off a square. He divided it into two and gave one to Donal and one to Ella.

"Now, you must thank your Uncle Jimmy, for this is good chocolate and cost him dear."

"Thank you Uncle Jimmy," they chorused, and Ella added, "But he got it by magic. It came out of Donal's ear. I saw it."

O'Neil rubbed his face wearily. "No, Ella, it was only a conjuring trick. Remember the talk we had about such things? It was just a trick. Wasn't it, Jimmy?"

"That's all it was, sure," I agreed. She looked from her father to me and back.

"Frank, dear, will you help me with these?" Mary had stacked the dishes in a washpan and sprinkled soap flakes in.

"Right. Jimmy, will you mind the kids? We're just taking these down to the tap."

"I will indeed," I said, and thought: *Thank you very much, mortal man, for this opportunity.* The moment the door closed behind them I had the device out of my pocket. It looked rather like a big old-fashioned watch. I held it out to the boy.

"Here you go, Donal, here's a grand timepiece for you to play with."

He took it gladly. "There's a train on it!" he cried. I turned to Ella.

"And what can I do for you, darling?"

She looked at me with considering eyes. "You can read me the funny papers." She pointed to a neatly stacked bundle by the stove.

"With pleasure." I seized them up and we settled back in my chair, pulling a lamp close. The baby slept fitfully, I read to Ella about Sambo and Tommy Pip

and Herr Spiegleburger, and all the while Donal pressed buttons and thumbed
levers on the diagnostic toy. It flashed pretty lights for him, it played little tunes
his sister was incapable of hearing; and then, as I had known it would, it bit him.

"Ow!" He dropped it and began to cry, holding out his tiny bleeding finger.

"O, dear, now, what's that? Did it stick you?" I put his sister down and got up
to take the device back. "Tsk! Look at that, the stem's broken." It vanished into
my pocket. "What a shame. O, I'm sorry, Donal Og, here's the old hankie. Let's
bandage it up, shall we? There, there. Doesn't hurt now, does it?"

"No," he sniffled. "I want another chocolate."

"And so you'll have one, for being a brave boy." I snapped off another square
and gave it to him. "Ella, let's give you another as well, shall we? What have you
found there?"

"It's a picture about Mother Goose." She had spread out the Children's Page
on the oilcloth. "Isn't it? That says Mother Goose right there."

I looked over her shoulder. *"Pictures from Mother Goose,"* I read out. *"Hot Cross
Buns. Paint the Seller of Hot Cross Buns.* Looks like it's a contest, darling. They're
asking the kiddies to paint in the picture and send it off to the paper to judge
who's done the best one."

"Is there prize money?" She had an idea.

"Two dollars for the best one," I read, pulling at my lower lip uneasily. "And
paintboxes for everyone else who enters."

She thought that over. Dismay came into her face. "But I haven't got a paintbox
to color it with at all! O, that's stupid! Giving paintboxes out to kids that's got
them already. O, that's not fair!" She shook with stifled anger.

"What's not fair?" Her mother backed through the door, holding it open for
O'Neil with the washpan.

"Only this Mother Goose thing here," I said.

"You're never on about going to that show again, are you?" said Mary sharply,
coming and taking her daughter by the shoulders. "Are you? Have you been whee-
dling at Mr. Kelly?"

"I have not!" the little girl cried in a trembling voice.

"She hasn't, Mrs. O'Neil, only it's this contest in the kids' paper," I hastened
to explain. "You have to have a set of paints to enter it, see."

Mary looked down at the paper. Ella began to cry quietly. Her mother gathered
her up and sat with her on the edge of the bed, rocking her back and forth.

"O, I'm so sorry, Ella dear, Mummy's so sorry. But you see, now, don't you,
the harm in wanting such things? You see how unhappy it's made you? Look how
hard Mummy and Daddy work to feed you and clothe you. Do you know how
unhappy it makes us when you want shows and paintboxes and who knows what,
and we can't give them to you? It makes us despair. That's a Mortal Sin, despair
is."

"I want to see the fairies," wept the little girl.

"Dearest dear, there aren't any fairies! But surely it was the Devil himself you
met out in the street, that gave you that wicked piece of paper and made you long
after vain things. Do you understand me? Do you see why it's wicked, wanting
things? It kills the soul, Ella."

After a long gasping moment the child responded, "I see, Mummy." She kept her face hidden in her mother's shoulder. Donal watched them uncertainly, twisting the big knot of handkerchief on his finger. O'Neil sat at the table and put his head in his hands. After a moment he swept up the newspaper and put it in the stove. He reached into the slatwood cabinet and pulled a bottle of Wilson's Whiskey up on the table, and got a couple of clean tumblers out of the washpan.

"Will you have a dram, Kelly?" he offered.

"Just the one." I sat down beside him.

"Just the one," he agreed.

You must not empathize with them.

When I let myself into my rooms on Bush Street, I checked my messages. A long blue column of them pulsed on the credenza screen. Most of it was the promised list from Averill and his fellows; I'd have to pass that on to our masters as soon as I'd reviewed it. I didn't feel much like reviewing it just now, however.

There was also a response to my request for another transport for Mme. D'Araignee: *DENIED. NO ADDITIONAL VEHICLES AVAILABLE. FIND ALTERNATIVE.*

I sighed and sank into my chair. My honor was at stake. From a drawer at the side of the credenza I took another Ghirardelli bar and, scarcely taking the time to tear off the paper, consumed it in a few greedy bites. Waiting for its soothing properties to act, I paged through a copy of the *Examiner*. There were automobile agencies along Golden Gate Avenue. Perhaps I could afford to purchase one out of my personal operation's expense account?

But they were shockingly expensive in this city. I couldn't find one for sale, new or used, for less than a thousand dollars. Why couldn't *her* case officer delve into his own pocket to deliver the goods? I verified the balance of my account. No, there certainly wasn't enough for an automobile in there. However, there was enough to purchase four tickets to "Babes in Toyland."

I accessed the proper party and typed in my transaction request.

TIX UNAVAILABLE FOR 041606 EVENT, came the reply. *041706 AVAILABLE OK?*

OK, I typed. PLS DEBIT & DELIVER.

DEBITED. TIX IN YR BOX AT S MKT ST HQ 600 HRS 041606.

TIBI GRATIAS! I replied, with all sincerity.

DIE DULCE FRUERE. OUT.

Having solved one problem, an easy solution to the other suggested itself to me. It involved a slight inconvenience, it was true; but any gentleman would readily endure worse for a lady's sake.

My two rooms on Bush Street did not include the luxury of a bath, but the late Mr. Adolph Sutro had provided an alternative pleasure for his fellow citizens: the Baths, which surely could have existed only in that city, in that time.

Just north of Cliff House Mr. Sutro had purchased a rocky little purgatory of a cove, cleaned the shipwrecks out of it and proceeded to shore it up against the more treacherous waves with several thousand barrels of cement. Having constructed not one but six saltwater pools of a magnificence to rival old Rome, he had proceeded to enclose it in a crystal palace affair of no less than four acres of glass.

Ah, but this wasn't enough for San Francisco! The entrance, on the hill above, was as near a Greek temple as modern artisans could produce; through the shrine one wandered along the museum gallery lined with exhibits both educational and macabre and descended a vast staircase lined with palm trees to the main level, where one might bathe, exercise in the gymnasium or attend a theater performance. Having done all this, one might then dine in the restaurant.

However, my schedule today called for nothing more strenuous than bathing. Ten minutes after descending the grand staircase I was emerging from my changing room (one of five hundred), having soaped, showered and togged myself out in my rented bathing suit, making my way toward the nearest warm-water pool under the bemused eyes of several hundred mortal idlers sitting in the bleachers above.

I was not surprised to see another of my own kind backstroking manfully across the green water; nothing draws the attention of an immortal like sanitary conveniences. I was rather startled when I recognized the man, however, not having seen him since some time in the sixteenth century. Lewis is nothing more than a Literary Preservation Specialist, rather a sad-looking little fellow with a noble profile; not in my class, of course, but a gentleman for all that.

He felt my regard and glanced up, seeing me at once. He smiled and waved.

Victor! he broadcast. *How nice to see you again.*

It's Lewis, isn't it? I responded, though I knew his name perfectly well, and far more of his history than he knew himself. I had been assigned to monitor his activities once, to my everlasting shame. Still, it had been centuries, and he had never shown any sign of recovering certain memories. I hoped, for his sake, that such was the case. Memory effacement is not a pleasant experience.

He pulled himself up on the coping of the pool and swept his wet hair out of his eyes. I stepped to the edge, took the correct diver's stance and leapt in, transmitting through bubbles: *So you're here as well? Presalvaging books, I suppose?*

The Mercantile Library, he affirmed, and there was nothing in his pleasant tone to indicate he'd remembered what I'd done to him at Eurobase One.

God! That must be a Herculean effort, I responded, surfacing.

He transmitted rueful amusement. *You've heard of it, I suppose?*

Rather, I replied, practicing my breast stroke. *All those Comstock Lode silver barons went looting the old family libraries of Europe, didn't they? Snatched up medieval manuscripts at a tenth their value from impoverished Venetian princes, I believe? Fabulously rare first editions from London antiquarians?*

Something like that, he replied. *And brought them back home to the States for safekeeping.*

Ha!

Well, how were they to know? Lewis made an expressive gesture taking in the vast edifice around us. *Mr. Sutro himself had a Shakespeare first folio. What a panic it's been tracking that down! And you?*

I'm negotiating for a promising-looking young recruit. Moreover, I drew Nob Hill detail, I replied casually. *I've coordinated quite a team of talented youngsters set to liberate the premises of Mssrs. Towne, Crocker, Huntington et al. as soon as the lights are out. All manner of costly bric-a-brac has been tagged for rescue—Chippendales, Louis Quatorzes—to say nothing of jewels and cash.*

My, that sounds satisfying. You'll never guess what I found, only last night! Lewis transmitted, looking immensely pleased with himself.

Something unexpected? I responded.

He edged forward on the coping gleefully. *Yes, you might say so. Just some old papers that had been mislaid by an idiot named Pompeo Leoni and bound into the wrong book. Just something jotted down by an elderly left-handed Italian gentleman!*

Not Da Vinci? I turned in the water to stare at him, genuinely impressed.

Who else? Lewis nearly hugged himself in triumph. *And! Not just any doodlings or speculation from the pen of Leonardo, either. Something of decided interest to the Company! It seems he devoted some serious thought to the construction of articulated human limbs—a clockwork arm, for example, that could be made to perform various tasks!*

I've heard something of the sort, I replied, swimming back toward him.

Yes, well, he seems to have taken the idea further. Lewis leaned down in a conspiratorial manner. *From a human arm he leapt to the idea of an entire articulated human skeleton of bronze, and wondered whether the human frame might not be merely imitated but improved in function!*

By Jove! Was the man anticipating androids? I reached the coping and leaned on it, slicking back my hair.

No! No! He was chasing another idea entirely, Lewis insisted. *Shall I quote? I rather think I ought to let him express his thoughts.* He leaned back and, with a dreamy expression, transmitted in flawless fifteenth-century Tuscan: **It has been observed that the presence of metal is not in all cases inimical to the body of man, as we may see in earrings, or in crossbow bolts, spearpoints, pistol balls, and other detritus of war that have been known to enter the flesh and remain for some years without doing the bearer any appreciable harm, or indeed in that practice of physicians wherein a small pellet of gold is inserted into an incision made near an aching joint, and the sufferer gains relief and ease of movement thereby.**

Take this idea further and think that a shattered bone might be replaced with a model of the same bone cast in bronze, identical with or even superior to its original.

Go further and say that where one bone might be replaced, so might the skeleton entire, and if the articulation is improved upon the man might attain a greater degree of physical perfection than he was born with.

The flaw in this would be the man's pain and the high likelihood he would die before surgery of such magnitude could be carried out.

Unless we are to regard the theory of alchemists who hold that the Philosopher's Stone, once attained, would transmute the imperfect flesh to perfection, a kind of supple gold that lives and breathes, and by this means the end might be obtained without cutting, the end being immortality. Lewis opened his eyes and looked at me expectantly. I smacked my hand on the coping in amusement.

By Jove! I repeated. *How typical of the Maestro. So he was all set to invent us, was he?*

To say nothing of hip replacements!

But what a find for the Company, Lewis!

Of course, to give you a real idea of the text I ought to have presented it like this: Lewis began to rattle it out backward. I shook my head, laughing and holding up my hands in sign that he should stop. After a moment or two he trailed off, adding: *I don't think it loses much in translation, though.*

I shook my head. *You know, old man, I believe we're treading rather too closely to a temporal paradox here. Just as well the Company will take possession of that volume, and not some inquisitive mortal! What if it had inspired someone to experiment with biomechanicals a century or so too early?*

Ah! No, you see, since History can't be changed. We're safe enough, Lewis pointed out. *As far as History records those Da Vinci pages, it records them as being lost in the Mercantile Library fire. The circle is closed. All the same, I imagine it was a temptation for any operatives stationed near Amboise in Da Vinci's time. Wouldn't you have wanted to seek the old man out as he lay dying, and tell him that something would be done with this particular idea, at least? Immortality and human perfection!*

Of course I'd have been tempted; but I shook my head. *Not unless I cared to face a court-martial for a security breach.*

Lewis shivered in his wet wool and slid back into the water. I turned on my back and floated, considering him.

The temperature doesn't suit you? I inquired.

Oh . . . they've got the frigidarium all right, but the calidaria here aren't really hot enough, Lewis explained. *And of course there's no sudatorium at all.*

Nor any slaves for a good massage, either, I added, glancing up at the mortal onlookers. *Sic transit luxuria, alas.* Lewis smiled faintly; he had never been comfortable with mortal servants, I remembered. Odd, for someone who began mortal life as a Roman, or at least a Romano-Briton.

Weren't you recruited at Bath . . . ? I inquired, leaning on the coping.

Aquae Sulis, it was then, Lewis informed me. *The public baths there.*

Of course. I remember now! You were rescued from the temple. Intercepted child sacrifice, I imagine?

Oh, good heavens, no! The Romans never did that sort of thing. No, I was just somebody's little unwanted holiday souvenir left in a blanket by the statue of Apollo. Lewis shrugged, and then began to grin. *I hadn't thought about it before, but this puts a distinctly Freudian slant on my visits here! Returning to the womb in time of stress? I was only a few hours old when the Company took me, or so I've always been told.*

I laughed and set off on a lap across the pool. *At least you were spared any memories of mortal life.*

That's true, he responded, and then his smile faded. *And yet, you know, I think I'm the poorer for that. The rest of you may have some harrowing memories, but at least you know what it was to be mortal.*

I assure you it's nothing to be envied, I informed him. He nodded in concession of my point and set out across the pool himself, resuming his backstroke.

I think I would have preferred the experience, all the same, he insisted. *I'd have liked a father—or mother—figure in my life. At the very least, those of you rescued at an age to remember it have a sort of filial relationship with the immortal who saved you. Haven't you?*

I regret to disillusion you, sir, but that is absolutely not true, I replied firmly.

Really? He dove and came up for air, gasping. *What a shame. Bang goes another romantic illusion. I suppose we're all just orphans of one storm or another!*

At that moment a pair of mortals chose to roughhouse, snorting and chuckling as they pummeled each other in their seats in the wooden bleachers; one of them broke free and ran, scrambling apelike over the seats, until he lost his footing and fell with a horrendous crash that rolled and thundered in the air, echoing under the glassed dome, off the water and wet coping.

I saw Lewis go pale; I imagine my own countenance showed reflexive panic. After a frozen moment Lewis drew a deep breath.

"One storm or another," he murmured aloud. "Nothing to be afraid of here, after all. Is there? This structure will survive the quake. History says it will. Nothing but minor damage, really."

I nodded. Then, struck in one moment by the same thought, we lifted our horrified eyes to the ceiling, with its one hundred thousand panes of glass.

"I believe I've got a rail car to catch," I apologized, vaulting to the coping with what I hoped was not undignified haste.

"I've a luncheon engagement myself," Lewis said, gasping as he sprinted ahead of me to the grand staircase.

On the 16th of April I entertained friends, or at least my landlady received that impression; and what quiet and well-behaved fellows the gentlemen were, and how plain and respectable the ladies! No cigars, no raucous laughter, no drunkenness at all. Indeed, Mrs. McCarty assured me she would welcome them as lodgers at any time in the future, should they require desirable Bush Street rooms. I assured her they would be gratified at the news. Perhaps they might have been, if her boarding house were still standing in a week's time. History would decree otherwise, regrettably.

My sitting room resembled a council of war, with its central table on which was spread a copy of the Sanborn map of the Nob Hill area, up-to-date from the previous year. My subordinates stood or leaned over the table, listening intently as I bent with red chalk to delineate the placement of Hush Field generators.

"The generators will arrive in a baker's van at the corner of Clay and Taylor Street at midnight precisely," I informed them. "Delacort, your team will approach from your station at the end of Pleasant Street and take possession of them. There will be five generators. I want them placed at the following intersections: Bush and Jones, Clay and Jones, Clay and Powell, Bush and Powell and on California midway between Taylor and Mason." I put a firm letter X at each site. "The generators should be in place and switched on by no later than five minutes after midnight. Your people will remain in place to remove the generators at half-past three exactly, returning them to the baker's van, which will depart promptly. At that moment a private car will pull up to the same location to transport your team to the central collection point on Ocean Beach. Is that clear?"

"Perfectly, sir." Delacort saluted. Averill looked at her slightly askance and turned a worried face to me.

"What're they going to do if some cop comes along and wants to know what they're doing there at that time of night?"

"Any cop coming in range of the Hush Field will pass out, dummy," Philemon informed him. I frowned and cleared my throat. Cinema Standard (the language of the schoolroom) is not my preferred mode of expression.

"If you please, Philemon!"

"Yeah, sorry—"

"Your team will depart from their station at Joice Street at five minutes after midnight and proceed to the intersection of Mason and Sacramento, where a motorized drayer's wagon will be arriving. You will be responsible for the contents of the Flood mansion." I outlined it in red. "Your driver will provide you with a sterile containment receptacle for Item Number Thirty-Nine on your acquisitions list. Kindly see to it that this particular item is salvaged first and delivered to the driver separately."

"What's Item Thirty-Nine?" Averill inquired. There followed an awkward silence. Philemon raised his eyebrows at me. Company policy discourages field operatives from being told more than they strictly need to know regarding any given posting. Upon consideration, however, it seemed wisest to answer Averill's question; there was enough stress associated with this detail as it was without adding mysteries. I cleared my throat.

"The Flood mansion contains a 'Moorish' smoking room," I informed him. "Among its features is a lump of black stone carefully displayed in a glass case. Mr. Flood purchased it under the impression that it is an actual piece of the Qaaba from Mecca, chipped loose by an enterprising Yankee adventurer. He was, of course, defrauded; the stone is in fact a meteorite, and preliminary spectrographic analysis indicates it originated on Mars."

"Oh," said Averill, nodding sagely. I did not choose to add that plainly visible on the rock's surface is a fossilized crustacean of an unknown kind, or that the rock's rediscovery (in a museum owned by Dr. Zeus, incidentally) in the year 2210 will galvanize the Mars Colonization Effort into making real progress at last.

I bent over the map again and continued:

"All the items on your list are to be loaded into the wagon by twenty minutes after three. At that time, the wagon will depart for Ocean Beach and your team will follow in the private car provided. Understood?"

"Understood."

"Rodrigo, your team will depart from their Taylor Street station at five minutes after midnight as well. Your wagon will arrive at the corner of California and Taylor; you will proceed to salvage the Huntington mansion," I marked it on the map. "Due to the nature of your quarry you will be allotted ten additional minutes, but all listed items must be loaded and ready for removal by half-past three, at which time your private transport will arrive. Upon arrival at Ocean Beach you will be assisted by Philemon's team, who will already (I should hope) have loaded most of their salvage into the waiting boats."

"Yes, sir." Rodrigo made a slight bow.

"Freytag, your team will be stationed on Jones Street. You depart at five after midnight, like the rest, and your objective is the Crocker mansion, here." Freytag bent close to see as I shaded in her area. "Your wagon will pull up to Jones and California; you ought to be able to fill it in the allotted time of two hours and fifteen minutes precisely, and be ready to depart for Ocean Beach without incident. Loong? Averill?"

"Sir!" Both immortals stood to attention.

"Your teams will disperse from their stations along Clay and Pine Streets and salvage the lesser targets shown here, here, here, and here—" I chalked circles around them. "I leave to your best judgment individual personnel assignments. Two wagons will arrive on Clay Street at one o'clock precisely and two more will arrive on Pine five minutes later. You ought to find them more than adequate for your purposes. You will need to do a certain amount of running to and fro to coordinate the efforts of your ladies and gentlemen, but it can't be helped."

"I don't anticipate difficulties, sir," Loong assured me.

"No indeed; but remember the immensity of this event shadow." I set down the chalk and wiped my hands on a handkerchief. "Your private transports will be waiting at the corner of Bush and Jones by half-past three. *Please arrive promptly.*"

"Yes, sir." Averill looked earnest.

"In the entirely likely event that any particular team completes its task ahead of schedule, and has free space in its wagon after all the listed salvage has been accounted for, I will expect that team to lend its assistance to Mme. D'Araignee and her teams at the Mark Hopkins Institute." I swept them with a meaningful stare. "Gentlemen doing so can expect my personal thanks and commendation in their personnel files."

That impressed them, I could see. The favorable notice of one's superiors is invariably one's ticket to the better sort of assignment. Clearing my throat, I continued:

"I anticipate arriving at no later than half-past two to oversee the final stages of removal. Kindly remain at your transports until I transmit your signal to depart for the central collection point. Have you any further questions, ladies and gentlemen?"

"None, sir," Averill said, and the others nodded agreement.

"Then it's settled," I told them, and carefully folded shut the mapbook. "A word of warning to you all: you may become aware of precursors to the shock in the course of the evening. History will record a particularly nasty seismic disturbance at two A.M. in particular, and another at five. Control your natural panic, please. Upsetting as you may find these incidents, they will present no danger whatsoever, will in fact go unnoticed by such mortals as happen to be awake at that hour."

Averill put up his hand. "I read the horses will be able to feel it," he said, a little nervously. "I read they'll go mad."

I shrugged. "Undoubtedly why we have been obliged to confine ourselves to motor transport. Of course, *we* are no brute beasts. I have every confidence that we will all resist any irrational impulses toward flight before the job is finished.

"Now then! You may attend to the removal of your personal effects and prepare for the evening's festivities. I shouldn't lunch tomorrow; you'll want to save your appetites for the banquet at Cliff House. I understand it's going to be rather a Roman experience!"

The tension broken, they laughed; and if Averill laughed a bit too loudly, it must be remembered that he was still young. As immortals go, that is.

Astute mortals might have detected something slightly out of the ordinary on that Tuesday, the 17th of April; certainly the hired-van drivers must have noticed an increase in business, as they were dispatched to house after house in every district of the city to pick up nearly identical loads, these being two or three ordinary-looking trunks and one crate precisely fifty centimeters long, twenty centimeters wide and twenty centimeters high, in which a credenza might fit snugly. And it would be extraordinary if none of them remarked upon the fact that all these same consignments were directed to the same location on the waterfront, the berth of the steamer *Mayfair*.

Certainly in some cases mortal landladies noticed trunks being taken down flights of stairs, and put anxious questions to certain of their tenants regarding hasty removal; but their fears were laid to rest by smiling lies and ready cash.

And did anyone notice, as twilight fell, when persons in immaculate evening dress were suddenly to be seen in nearly every street? Doubtful; for it was, after all, the second night of the opera season, and with the Metropolitan company in town all of Society had turned out to do them honor. If a certain number of them converged on a certain warehouse in an obscure district, and departed therefrom shortly afterward in gleaming automobiles, that was unlikely to excite much interest in observers either.

I myself guided a brisk little four-cylinder Franklin through the streets, bracing myself as it bumped over the cable car tracks, and steered down Gough with the intention of turning at Fulton and following it out to the beach. At the corner of Geary I glimpsed for a moment a tall figure in a red coat, and wondered what it was doing so far from the theater district; but a glance over my shoulder made it plain that I was mistaken. The red-clad figure shambling along was no more than a bum, albeit one of considerable stature. I dismissed him easily from my thoughts as I contemplated the O'Neil family's outing to the theater.

Had I a warm, sentimental sensation thinking of them, remembering Ella's face aglow when she saw me present her father with the tickets? Certainly not. One magical evening out was scarcely going to make up for their ghastly deaths, in whatever cosmic scale might be supposed to balance such things. Best not to dwell on *that* aspect of it all. No, it was the convenience of their absence from home that occupied my musings, and the best way to take advantage of it with regard to my mission.

At the end of Fulton I turned right, in the purple glow of evening over the vast

Pacific. Far out to sea—well beyond the sight of mortal eyes—the Company transport ships lay at anchor, waiting only for the cover of full darkness to approach the shore. In a few hours I'd be on board one of them, steaming off in the direction of the Farallones to catch my air transport, with no thought for the smoking ruin of the place I'd lived in so many harrowing weeks.

Cliff House loomed above me, its turreted mass a blaze of light. I saw with some irritation that the long uphill approach was crowded with carriages and automobiles, drawn in on a diagonal; I was obliged to go up as far as the rail depot before I could find a place to leave my motor, and walk back downhill past the Baths.

I daresay the waiters at Cliff House could not recall an evening when so large a party, of such unusual persons, had dined with such hysterical gaiety as on this 17th of April, 1906.

If I recall correctly, the reservation had been made in the name of an international convention of seismologists. San Francisco was ever the most cosmopolitan of cities, so the restaurant staff expressed no surprise when elegantly attired persons of every known color began arriving in carriages and automobiles. If anyone remarked upon a certain indefinable similarity in appearance amongst the conventioneers that transcended race, why, that might be explained by their common avocation—whatever seismology might be; no one on the staff had any clear idea. Only the queer nervousness of the guests was impossible to account for, the tendency toward uneasy giggling, the sudden frozen silences and dilated pupils.

I think I can speak for my fellow operatives when I say that we were determined to enjoy ourselves, terror notwithstanding. We deserved the treat, every one of us; we faced a long night of hard work, the culmination of months of labor, under circumstances of mental strain that would test the resolution of the most hardened mercenaries. The least we were owed was an evening of silk hats and tiaras.

There was a positive chatter of communication on the ether as I approached. We were all here, or in the act of arriving; not since leaving school had I been in such a crowd of my own kind. I thought how we were to feast here, a company of immortals in an airy castle perched on the edge of the Uttermost West, and flit away well before sunrise. It is occasionally pleasant to embody a myth.

I saw Mme. D'Araignee stepping down from a carriage, evidently arriving with other members of the Hopkins operation team. No bulky Russian sea captain in sight, of course, yet; I hastened to her side and tipped my hat.

"Madame, will you do me the honor of allowing me to escort you within?"

"M'sieur Victor." She gave me a dazzling smile. She wore a gown of pale bluegreen silk, a shade much in fashion that season, which brought out beautifully certain copper hues in her intensely black skin. Diamonds winked from the breathing shadow of her bosom. She took my arm and we proceeded inside, where we had the remarkable experience of having to shout our transmissions to one another, so crowded was the ether:

I am very pleased to inform you I have arranged for an automobile for your use this evening, I told her, as we paused at the cloakroom for checks.

Oh, I am so glad! I do hope you weren't put to unnecessary trouble.

Through the door to the dining room we caught glimpses of napery like snow, folded in a wilderness of sharp little peaks, with here and there a gilt epergne rising above them.

Not what I'd call unnecessary trouble, no, though it proved impossible to requisition anything at this late date. However, I did have a vehicle allocated for my own personal use and that fine runabout is entirely at your disposal.

Merci, merci mille temps! But will this not impede your own mission?

Not at all, dear lady. I shall be obliged to you for transportation as far as the Palace, I think, after we've dined; but since my mission involves nothing more strenuous than carrying off a child, I anticipate strolling back across the city with ease.

You are too kind, my friend.

A gentleman could do no less. I pulled out a chair for her.

We chatted pleasantly of trifling matters as the rest of the guests arrived. We studied the porcelain menu in some astonishment—the Company had spent a fortune here tonight, certainly enough to have allotted me one extra automobile. I was rather nettled, but my irritation was mollified somewhat by the anticipation of our *carte du jour*:

Green Turtle Soup	Consommé Divinesse

Salmon in Sauce Veloute   Trout Almondine   Crab Cocktail

Braised Sweetbreads   Roast Quail Andaluz

Le Faux Mousse   Faison Lucullus

Early Green Peas   White Asparagus   Risotto Milanese

Roast Saddle of Venison with Port Wine Jelly

Curried Tomatoes   Watercress Salad

Chicken Marengo   Plovers' Eggs   Virginia Ham Croquettes

Lobster Salad   Oysters in Variety

Gateau d'Or et Argent   Assorted Fruits in Season

Rose Snow   Tulip Jellies   Water Ices

Surprise Yerba Buena

All accompanied, of course, by the appropriate vintages, and service *à la russe*. We *were* being rewarded.

A shift in the black rock, miles down, needle-thin fissures screaming through stone, perdurable clay bulging like the head of a monstrous child engaging for birth, straining, straining, STRAINING!

The smiling chatter stopped dead. The waiters looked around, confused, at that elegant assembly frozen like mannequins. Not a scrape of chair moving, not a chime of crystal against china. Only the sound that we alone listened to: the cello-string far below us, tuning for the dance of the wrath of God. I found myself staring across the room directly into Lewis's eyes, where he had halted at the doorway in mid-step. The immortal lady on his arm was as still as a painted image, a perfect profile by Da Vinci.

The orchestra conductor mistook our silence for a cue of some kind. He turned hurriedly to his musicians and they struck up a little waltz tune, light gracious accompaniment to our festivities. With a boom and a rush of vacuum the service doors parted, as the first of the waiters burst through with tureens and silver buckets of ice. Champagne corks popped like artillery. As the noises roared into our silence, an immortal in white lace and spangles shrieked; she turned it into a high trilling laugh, placing her slender hand upon her throat.

So conversation resumed, and a server appeared at my elbow with a napkined bottle. I held up my glass for the champagne. Mme. D'Araignee and I clinked an unspoken toast and drank fervently.

Twice more while we dined on those good things, the awful warning came. As the venison roast was served forth, its dish of port jelly began to shimmer and vibrate — too subtly for the mortal waiters to notice more than a pretty play of light, but *we* saw. On the second occasion the oysters had just come to the table, and what subaudible pandemonium of clattering there was: half-shell against half-shell with the sound of basalt cliffs grinding together, and the staccato rattle of all the little sauceboats with their scarlet and yellow and pink and green contents; though of course the mortal waiters couldn't hear it. Not even the patient horses waiting in their carriage-traces heard it yet. But the sparkling bubbles ascended more swiftly through the glasses of champagne.

The waiters began to move along the tables bearing trays: little cut-crystal goblets of pink ices, or red and amber jellies, or fresh strawberries drenched in liqueur, or cakes. We heard the ringing note of a dessert spoon against a wineglass, signaling us all to attention.

The Chief Project Facilitator rose to address us. Labienus stood poised and smiling in faultless white tie and tuxedo. As he waited for the babble of voices to fade he took out his gold Chronometer on its chain, studied its tiny screen, then snapped it shut and returned it to the pocket of his white silk waistcoat.

"My fellow Seismologists." His voice was quiet, yet without raising it he reached all corners of the room. Commanding legions confers a certain ease in public speaking. "Ladies." He bowed. "I trust you've enjoyed the bill of fare. I know that, as I dined, I was reminded of the fact that perhaps in no other city in the world could such a feast be so gathered, so prepared, so served to such a remarkable gathering. Where but here by the Golden Gate can one banquet in a splendor that beggars the Old World, on delicacies presented by masters of culinary sophistication hired from all civilized nations — all the while in sight of forested hills where savages roamed *within living memory*, across a bay that *within living memory* was innocent of any sail?

"So swiftly has she risen, this great city, as though magically conjured by djinni out of thin air. Justifiably her citizens might expect to wake tomorrow in a wilderness, and find that this gorgeous citadel had been as insubstantial as their dreams."

Archly exchanged glances between some of our operatives as his irony was appreciated.

"But if that *were* to come to pass — if they *were* to wake alone, unhoused and shivering upon a stony promontory, facing into a cold northern ocean and a hostile gale—why, you know as well as I do that within a few short years the citizens of San Francisco would create their city anew, with spires soaring ever closer to Heaven, and mansions yet more gracious."

Of course we knew it, but the poor mortal waiters didn't. I am afraid some of our younger operatives were base enough to smirk.

"Let us marvel, ladies and gentlemen, at this phoenix of a city, at once ephemeral and abiding. Let us drink to the imperishable spirit of her citizens. I give you the City of San Francisco."

"The City of San Francisco," we chorused, raising our glasses high.

"And I *give* you," smiling he extended his hand, "The City of San Francisco!"

Beaming the waiters wheeled it in, on a vast silver cart: an ornate confection of pastry, of spun-sugar and marzipan and candies, a perfect model of the City. It was possible to discern a tiny Ferry Building rising above chocolate wharves, and a tiny Palace, and Nob Hill reproduced in sugared peel and nonpareils. Across the familiar grid of streets Golden Gate Park was done in green fondant, and beyond it was the hill where Sutro Park rose in nougat and candied violets, and beyond that Cliff House itself, in astonishing detail.

We applauded.

Then she was destroyed, that beautiful city, with a silver cake knife and serving wedge, and parceled out to us in neat slices. One had to commend Labienus' sense of humor, to say nothing of his sense of ritual.

It was expected that we would wish to dance, after dining; the ballroom had been reserved for our use, and at some point during dessert the orchestra had discreetly risen and carried their instruments away to the dais.

I thought the idea of dancing in rather poor taste, under the circumstances, and apparently many of my fellow operatives agreed with me; but Averill and some of the other young ones got out on the floor eagerly enough, and soon the stately polonaise gave way to ragtime tunes and two-stepping.

Under the pretense of going for a smoke I stepped out on the terrace, to breathe the clean night air and metabolize my portion of magnificent excess in peace. By ones and twos several of the older immortals followed me; soon there was quite an assemblage of us out there between two worlds, between the dark water surging around Seal Rock and the brilliant magic lantern of the ballroom.

"Victor?" Mme. D'Araignee was making her way to me through the crowd. Her slippers, together with her diamonds, had gone into the leather case she was carrying, and she had donned sensible walking shoes; she had buttoned a long motorist's duster over her evening gown. The radiant Queen of the Night stood now before me as the Efficient Modern Woman.

"You didn't care to dance either, I see," she remarked.

"Not I, no," I replied. We stood for a moment looking in at the giddy whirl. I saw Averill prance by in the arms of an immortal sylph in pink satin; their faces were flushed and merry. Don't think them heartless, Reader. They did not understand yet. Horror, for Averill, was still a lonely prairie and a burning wagon; for the girl, still a soldier with a bayonet in a deserted orchard. *Those* nightmares weren't here in this bright room with its bouncing music, and so all must be right with the world.

But we were old ones, Mme. D'Araignee and I, and we stood outside in the dark and watched them dance.

Down, miles down, the slick water on the clay face and the widening fissure in darkness, dead shale trembling like an exhausted limb, granite crumbling, rock cracking with the strain and crying out in a voice that rose up, and up at last through the red brick, through the tile and parquet, into the warm air and the music!

The mortal musicians played on, but the dancers faltered. Some of them stopped, looking around in confusion; some of them only missed a step or two and then plunged back into the dance with greater abandon, determined to celebrate something.

Mme. D'Araignee shivered. I threw my unlit cigar over the parapet into the sea.

"Shall we go, Nan?" I offered her my arm. She took it readily and we left Cliff House.

Outside on the carriage drive, and all the way up the steep hill to where my motor was parked, the waiting horses were tossing their heads and whickering uneasily.

Mme. D'Araignee took the wheel, easily guiding us back down into the City through the spangled night.

Even now, at the Grand Opera House, Enrico Caruso was striking a pose before a vast Spanish mountain range rendered on canvas and raising his carbine to threaten poor Bessie Abott. Even now, at the Mechanic's Pavilion, the Grand Prize Masked Carnival was in full swing, with throngs of costumed roller-skaters whirling around the rink that would be a triage hospital in twelve hours and a pile of smoking ashes in twenty-four. Even now, the clock on the face of Old St. Mary's Church—bearing its warning legend SON OBSERVE THE TIME AND FLY FROM EVIL—was counting out the minutes left for heedless passers-by. Even now, the O'Neil children were sitting forward in their seats, scarcely able to breathe as the cruel Toymaker recited the incantation that would bring his creations to life.

And we rounded the corner at Divisadero and sped down Market, with Prospero's *après*-pageant speech ringing in our ears. At the corner of Third I pointed and Mme. D'Araignee worked the clutch, steered over to the curb and trod on the brake pedal.

"You're quite sure you won't need a ride back?" she inquired over the chatter of the cylinders. I put my legs out and leapt down to the pavement.

"Perfectly sure, Nan." I shot my cuffs and adjusted the drape of my coat. Reaching into the seat I took my stick and silk hat. "Give my seat to the Muse of Painting. I'm off to lurk in shadows like a gentleman."

"*Bonne chance,* then, Victor." She eased up on the brake, clutched, and cranked the wheel over so the Franklin swung around in a wide arc to retrace its course up Market Street. I tipped my hat and bowed; with a cheery wave and a double honk on the Franklin's horn, she steered away into the night.

So far, so good. The night was yet young and there were plenty of debonair socialites in evening dress on the street, arriving and departing from the restaurants, the hotels, the theaters. For a block I was one of their number; then I accomplished my disappearance down a black alleyway into another world, to thread my way through the boarding-house warren.

Rats were out and scuttling everywhere, sensing the coming disaster infallibly. In some buildings they were cascading down the stairs like trickling water. Cats ignored them and drunkards stood watching in stupefied amazement, but there was nobody else to remark upon it; these streets did not invite promenaders.

I found the O'Neils' building and made my way up through the unlit stairwell, here and there kicking vermin out of my way. I left the landing and proceeded down the corridor, past doors tight shut showing only feeble lines of light at floor level to mark where the occupants were at home. I heard snores; I heard weeping; I heard a drunken quarrel; I heard a voice raised in wistful melody.

No light at the O'Neils' door, naturally; none at the door immediately opposite theirs. I scanned the room beyond but could discern no occupant. Drawing out a skeleton key from my waistcoat pocket, I gained entrance and shut the door after me.

No tenant at all; good. It was death-cold in there and black as pitch, for a roller shade had been drawn down on the one window. A slight tug sent it wobbling upward but failed to let much more light into the room. Not that I needed light to see my Chronometer as I checked it; half-past eleven, and even now my teams were assembling at their stations on Nob Hill. I leaned against a wall, folded my arms and composed myself to wait.

Time passed slowly for me, but in Toyland it sped by. Songs and dances, glittering processions came to their inevitable close; fairies took wing. Innocence was rewarded and wickedness resoundingly punished. The last of the ingenious special effects guttered out, the curtain descended, the orchestra fell silent, the house lights came up. A little while the magic lingered, as the O'Neil family made their way out through the lobby, a little while it hung around them like a perfume in the atmosphere of red velvet and gilt and fashionably attired strangers, until they were borne out through the doors by the receding tide of the crowd. Then the magic left them, evaporating upward into the night and the fog, and they got their bearings and made their way home along the dark streets.

I heard them, coming heavily up the stairs, O'Neil and Mary each carrying a child. Down the corridor their footsteps came, and stopped outside.

"Slide down now, Ella, Daddy's got to open the door."

I heard the sound of a key fumbling in darkness for its lock, and a drowsy little voice singing about Toyland, the paradise of childhood to which you can never return.

"Hush, Ella, you'll wake the neighbors."

"Donal's asleep. He missed the ending." Ella's voice was sad. "And it was such a beautiful, beautiful ending. Don't you think it was a beautiful ending, Daddy?"

"Sure it was, darling." Their voices receded a bit as they crossed the threshold. I heard a clink and the sputtering hiss of a match; there was the faintest glimmer of illumination down by the floor.

"Sssh, sh, sh. Home again. Help Mummy get his boots off, Ella, there's a dear."

"I'll just step across to Mrs. Varian's and collect the baby."

"Mind you remember his blanket."

"I will that."

Footsteps in the corridor again, discreet rapping on a panel, a whispered conversation in darkness and a sleepy wail; then returning footsteps and a pair of doors closing. Then, more muffled but still distinct to me, the sound of the O'Neils going to bed.

Their lamps were blown out. Their whispers ceased. Still I waited, listening as the minutes ticked away for their mortal souls to rest.

Half-past one on the morning of Wednesday, the 18th of April in the year 1906, in the City of San Francisco. Francis O'Neil and his wife and their children asleep finally and forever, and the world had finished with them. In the gray morning, at precisely fourteen minutes after the hour of five, this boarding house would lurch forward into the street, bricks tumbling as mortar blew out like talcum powder, rotten timbers snapping, and that would be the end of Frank's strength and Mary's care and Ella's dreams, the end of the brief unhappy baby, and no-one would remember them but me.

And, perhaps, Donal. I stepped across the hall and let myself into their room, perfectly silent.

The children lay in their trundle on the floor, next to their parents' bed. Donal slept on the outer edge, curled on his side, both hands tucked under his chin. I stood for a moment observing, analyzing their alpha patterns. When I was satisfied that no casual noise would awaken them, I bent and lifted Donal from his bed. He sighed but slept on. After a moment's hesitation I drew the blanket up around Ella's shoulders.

I stood back. The boy wore a nightshirt and long black stockings, but the night was cold. Frank's coat hung over the back of a chair: I appropriated it to wrap his son. Shifting Donal to one arm, I backed out of the room and shut the door.

Finished.

No sleeper in that building woke to hear our rapid descent of the stairs. On the first landing a drunk sat upright, leaning his head on the railings, sound asleep with his lower jaw dropped open like a corpse's. We fled lightly past him, Donal and I, and he never moved.

Away through the maze, then, away forever from the dirt and stench and poverty of that place. In twelve hours it would have ceased to exist, and the wind would scatter white ashes so the dead could never be named nor numbered.

Even Market Street was dark now, its theaters shut down. Over at the Grand Opera House on Mission, Enrico Caruso's costumes hung neatly in his dark dressing room, ready for a performance of *La Boheme* that would never take place. Up at the Mechanic's Pavilion, the weary janitor surveyed the confetti and other festive debris littering the skating rink and decided to sweep it up in the morning. Toyland, at the Columbia, was shut away in its properties room; fairy tinsel, butterfly wings, bear heads peering down from dusty shelves into the darkness.

Even now my resolute gentlemen and ladies were despoiling Nob Hill, flitting through its darkened drawing rooms at hyperspeed like so many whirring ghosts, bearing with them winking gilt and crystal, calfskin and morocco, canvas and brass, all the very best that money could buy but couldn't hope to preserve against the hour to come. Without the Franklin I'd have a tedious walk uphill to join them, but at a brisk pace I might arrive with time to spare.

Donal stretched and muttered in his sleep. I shifted him to my other shoulder, changed hands on my walking-stick, and was about to hurry on when I caught a whiff of some familiar scent on the air. I halted.

It was not a pleasant scent. It was harsh, musky, like blood or sweat but neither; like an animal smell, but other; it summoned in me a sudden terror and confusion. When I tried to identify it, however, I had only a mental image of a bear costume hanging on a hook, the head looking down from a shelf. When had I seen *that*? I hadn't seen that! *Whose memories were these?*

I controlled myself with an effort. Some psychic disturbance was responsible for this, my own nerves were contributing to this, there was no real danger. Why, of course: it must be nearly two o'clock, when the first of the major subsonic disruptions would occur.

Yes, here it came now. I could hear nearby horses begin to scream and stamp frantically, I could feel the paving-bricks grind against one another under the soles of my boots, and the air groaned as though buried giants were praying to God for release.

Yes, I thought, this must be it. I balanced my stick against my knee and drew out my Chronometer, trying to verify the time. As I peered at it the door of a stable directly across the street burst open, and a white mare came charging out, hooves thundering. Donal jerked and cried.

Timing is everything. My assailant chose that perfect moment of distraction to strike. I was enveloped in a choking wave of *that smell* as a hand closed on my face and pulled my head back. Instantly I clawed at it, twisted my head to bite; but a vast arm was wrapping around me from the other side and cold steel entered my throat, opened the artery, wrenched as it was pulled out again.

So swiftly had this occurred that my stick was still falling through midair, had not yet struck the pavement. Donal was pulled upward and backward, torn from me, and I heard his terrified cry mingle with the clatter of the stick as it landed, the rumbling earth, the running horse, a howling laughter I knew but could not place. I was sinking to my knees, clutching at my cut throat as my blood fountained out over the starched front of my dress shirt and stained the diamond stud so it winked like Mars. Ares, God of War. *Thor.* I was conscious of a terrible anger as I descended to the shadows and curled into Fugue.

"Will you get on to this, now? Throat cut and he's not been robbed! Here's his watch, for Christ's sake!"

"Stroke of luck for us, anyhow."

I sat up and glared at them. The two mortal thieves backed away from me, horrified; then one mustered enough nerve to dart in again, aiming a kick at me while he made a grab for my Chronometer. I caught his wrist and broke it. He jumped back, stifling an agonized yell; his companion took to his heels and after only a second's hesitation he followed.

I remained where I was, huddled on the pavement, running a self-diagnostic. The edges of my windpipe and jugular artery had closed and were healing nicely at hyperspeed; if the thieves hadn't roused me from Fugue I'd be whole now. Blood production had sped up to replace that now dyeing the front of my previously immaculate shirt. The exterior skin of my throat was even now self-suturing, but I was still too weak to rise.

My hat and stick remained where they had fallen, but of Donal or my assailant there was no sign. I licked my dry lips. There was a vile taste in my mouth. My Chronometer told me it was a quarter past two. I dragged myself to the base of a wall and leaned there, half-swooning, drowning in unwelcome remembrance.

That smell. Sweat, blood, the Animal, and smoke. Yes, they'd called it the Summer of Smoke, that year the world ended. What world had that been? The world where I was a little prince, or nearly so; better if my mother hadn't been a Danish slave, but my father had no sons by his lady wife, and so I had fine clothes and a gold pin for my cloak.

When I went to climb on the beached longship and play with the gear, a warrior threatened me with his fist; then another man told him he'd better not, for I was Baldulf's brat. *That* made him back down in a hurry. And once, my father set me on the table and put his gold cup in my hand, but I nearly dropped it, it was so heavy. He held it for me and I tasted the mead and his companions laughed, beating on the table. The ash-white lady, though, looked down at the floor and wrung her hands.

She told me sometimes that if I wasn't good the Bear would come for me. She was the only one who would ever dare to talk to me that way. And then he *had* come, the Bear and his slaughtering knights. All in one day I saw our tent burned and my father's head staring from a pike. Screaming, smoke and fire, and a banner bearing a red dragon that snaked like a living flame, I remember.

My mother had caught me up and was running for the forest, but she was a plump girl and could not get up the speed. Two knights chased after us on horseback, whooping like madmen. Just under the shadow of the oaks, they caught us. My mother fell and rolled, loosing her hold on me, and screamed for me to run; then one of the knights was off his horse and on her. The other knight got down too and stood watching them, laughing merrily. One of her slippers had come off and her bare toes kicked at the air until she died.

I had been sobbing threats, I had been hurling stones and handfuls of oak-mast at the knights, and now I ran at the one on my mother and attacked him with my teeth and nails. He reared up on his elbows to shake me off; but the other knight reached down and plucked me up as easily as if I'd been a kitten. He held me at his eye level while I shrieked and spat at him. His shrill laughter dropped to a chuckle, but never stopped.

A *big* shaven face, no beard, no mustache, colorless fair hair cropped. Head of a strange helm-shape, tremendous projecting nose and brows, and his wide gleeful eyes so pale a blue as to be colorless, like one of my father's hounds. He had enormous broad cheekbones and strange teeth. That smell, that almost-animal smell, was coming from him. *That* had been where I'd first encountered it, hanging there in the grip of that knight.

The other knight had got up and came forward with his knife drawn and ready for me, but my captor held out his huge gauntleted hand.

"*Siste!*" he told him pleasantly. "*Siste, comes.*"

The other knight growled something and brandished his knife. My captor's eyes sparkled; he batted playfully at my assailant, who flew backward into a tree and lay there twitching, blood running from his ears. Left in peace, my knight held me up and sniffed at me. He sat down and ran his hands all over me, taking his gauntlets off to squeeze my skull until I feared it would break like an egg. I had stopped fighting, but I whimpered and tried to wriggle away.

"Do you want to live, little boy?" he asked me in perfectly accented Saxon. He had a high-pitched voice, nasally resonant.

"Yes," I replied, shocked motionless.

"Then be good and do not try to run away from me. I will preserve you from death. Do you understand?"

"Yes."

"Good." He forced my mouth open and examined my teeth. Apparently satisfied, he got up, thrusting me under his arm. Taking the two horses' bridles, he walked back to the war-camp of the Bear with long rolling strides.

It was growing dark, and new fires had been lit. We passed pickets who challenged my captor, and he answered them with smiles and bantering remarks. At last he stopped before a tent and gave a barking order, whereupon a groom hurried out to take the horses and led them away for him. Two other knights sat nearby, leaning back wearily as their squires took off their armor for them. One pointed at me and asked a question.

My captor grinned and said something in fluting reply, hugging me to his chest. One knight smiled a little, but the other scowled and spat into the fire. As my captor bore me into his tent I heard someone mutter "*Romani!*" in a disgusted tone.

It was dark in the tent, and there was no one there to see as he stripped off my clothes and continued his examinations. I attempted to fight again but he held me still and asked, very quietly, "Are you a stupid child? Have you forgot what I said?"

"No." I was so frightened and furious I was trembling, and I hated the smell of him, so close in there.

"Then listen to me again, Saxon child. I will not hurt you, neither will I outrage you. But if you want to die, keep struggling."

I held still then and stood silent, hating him. He seemed quite unconcerned about that; he gave me a cup of wine and a hard cake, and ignored me while I ate and drank. All his attention was on the two knights outside. When he heard them depart into their respective tents, he wrapped me in a cloak and bore me out into the night again.

At the other end of the camp there was a very fine tent, pitched a little distance from the others. Two men stood before it, deep in conversation. After a moment one went away. The other remained outside the tent a moment, breathing the night air, looking up at the stars. When he lifted the flap and made to go inside, my captor stepped forward.

"*Salve*, Emres."

"*Salve*, Budu," replied the other. He was a tall man and elderly—I thought: his hair and eyebrows were white. His face, however, was smooth and unlined, and there was an easy suppleness to his movements. He was very well-dressed, as Britons went. They had a brief conversation and then the one called Emres raised the flap of the tent again, gesturing us inside.

It was so brilliantly lit in there it dazzled my eyes. I was again unrobed, in that white glare, but I dared do no more than clench my fists as the old one examined me. His hands were remarkably soft and clean, and *he* did not smell bad. He stuck me with a pin and dabbed the blood onto the tongue of a little god he had, sitting on his chest; it clicked for a moment and then chattered to him in a tinny voice. My captor and he had a conversation in a swift tongue quite unlike the Latin they'd been using until that time. At its conclusion, Emres pointed at me and asked a question. My captor shrugged. He turned his big head to look at me.

"What is your name, little boy?" he asked in Saxon.

"Bricta, son of Baldulf," I told him. He looked back at Emres.

"*Ecce Victor*," he said.

The taste in my mouth was unbearable. I hadn't wanted this recollection, this squalid history! I much preferred Time to begin with that first memory of the silver ship that rose skyward from the circle of stones, taking me away to the gleaming hospital and the sweet-faced nurses.

I got unsteadily to my feet, groping after my hat and stick. As I did so I heard the unmistakable sound of an automobile approaching. In another second a light runabout rattled around the corner and pulled up before me. Labienus sat behind the wheel, no longer the jovial Master of Ceremonies. He was all hard-eyed centurion now.

"We received your distress signal. Report, please, Victor."

"I was attacked," I said dully.

"Tsk! Rather obviously."

"I . . . I know it sounds improbable, sir, but I believe my assailant was another operative," I explained. To my surprise he merely nodded.

"We know his identity. You'll notice he's sending quite a distinct signal."

"Yes." I looked down the street in wonderment. The signal lay on the air like a trail of green smoke. Why would he signal? "He's . . . somewhere in Chinatown."

"Exactly," agreed Labienus. "Well, Victor, what do you intend to do about this?"

"Sir?" I looked back at him, confused. Something was wrong here, some business I hadn't been briefed about, perhaps? But why—?

"Come, come, man, you've a mission to complete! He took the mortal boy! Surely you've formed a plan to rescue him?" he prompted.

The hideous taste welled in my mouth. I suppressed an urge to expectorate.

"My team on Nob Hill is more than competent to complete the salvage there without my supervision," I said, attempting to sound coolly rational. "That being the case, I believe, sir, that I shall seek out the scoundrel who did this to me and jolly well *kill* him. Figuratively speaking, of course."

"Very good. And?"

"And, of course, recapture my mortal recruit and deliver him to the Collection Point as planned and according to schedule," I said. "Sir."

"See that you do." Labienus worked both clutch and brake expertly and edged his motor forward, cylinders idling. "Report to my cabin on the *Thunderer* at seven hundred hours for a private debriefing. Is that clear?"

"Perfectly clear, sir." So there was some mystery to be explained. Very well.

"You are dismissed."

"Sir." I doffed my hat and watched as he drove smoothly away up Market Street.

I replaced my hat and turned in the direction of the signal, probing. My dizziness was fading, burned away by my growing sense of outrage. The filthy old devil, how dare he do this to me? What was he playing at? I began to walk briskly again, my speed increasing with my strength.

Of course, the vow to kill him hadn't been meant literally. We do not die. But I'd find some way of paying him out in full measure, I hadn't the slightest doubt about that. He had the edge on me in strength, but I was swifter and in full possession of my faculties, whereas *he* was probably drooling mad, the old troll.

Yes, mad, that was the only explanation. There had always been rumors that some of the oldest operatives were flawed somehow, those created earliest, before the Augmentation Process had been perfected. Budu had been one of the oldest I'd ever met. He had been created more than forty thousand years ago, before the human races had produced their present assortment of representatives.

Now that I thought of it, I hadn't seen an operative of his racial type *in the field* in years. They held desk jobs at Company bases, or were Air Transport pilots. I'd assumed this was simply because the modern mortal race was now too different for Budu's type to pass unnoticed. What if the true reason was that the Company had decided not to take chances with the earlier models? What if there was some risk that all of that particular class were inherently unstable?

Good God! No wonder I was expected to handle this matter without assistance. Undoubtedly our masters wanted the whole affair resolved as quietly as possible. They could count on my discretion; I only hoped my ability met their expectations.

Following the signal, I turned left at the corner of Market and Grant. The green trail led straight up Grant as far as Sacramento. What was his game? He was drawing me straight into the depths of the Celestial quarter, a place where I'd be conspicuous were it daylight, but at no particular disadvantage otherwise.

He must intend some kind of dialogue with me. The fact that he had taken a hostage indicated that he wanted our meeting on his terms, under his control. That he felt he needed a hostage could be taken as a sign of weakness on his part. Had his strength begun to fail somehow? Not if his attack on me had been any indication. Though it had been largely a matter of speed and leverage. . . .

I came to the corner of Grant and Sacramento. The signal turned to the left again. It traveled up a block, where it could be observed emanating from a darkened doorway. I stood considering it for a moment, tapping my stick impatiently against my boot. I spat into the gutter, but it did not take the taste from my mouth.

I walked slowly uphill past the shops that sold black and scarlet lacquerware and green jade. Here was the Baptist mission, smelling of starch and good intentions. From this lodging-house doorway a heavy perfume of joss sticks; from this doorway a reek of preserved fish. And from *this* doorway . . .

It stood ajar. A narrow corridor went straight back into darkness, with a narrower stair ascending to the left. The bottommost stair tread had been thrown open like the lid of a piano bench, revealing a black void below.

I scanned. He was down there, and making no attempt to hide himself. Donal was there with him, still alive. There were no other signs of mortal life, however.

I paced forward into the darkness and stood looking down. Chill air was coming up from below. It stank like a crypt. Rungs leading down into a passageway were just visible, by a wavering pool of green light. So was a staring dead face, contorted into a grimace of rage.

After a moment's consideration, I removed my hat and set it on the second step. My stick I resolved to take with me, although its sword would be useless against my opponent. No point in any further delay; it was time to descend into yet another hell.

At the bottom of the ladder the light was a little stronger. It revealed more bodies lying in a subterranean passage of brick plastered over and painted a dull green. The dead had been young men, and seemed to have died fighting, within the last few hours. They were smashed like so many insects. The light that made this plain was emanating from a wide doorway that opened off the passage, some ten feet further on. The smell of death was strongest in there.

"Come in, Victor," said a voice.

I went as far as the doorway and looked.

In that low-ceilinged chamber of bare plaster, in the fitful glow of one oil lamp, more dead men were scattered. These were all elderly Chinese, skeletally emaciated, and they had been dead some hours and they had not died quietly. One leaned in a chair beside the little table with the flickering lamp; one was hung up on a hook that protruded from a wall; one lay half-in, half-out of a cupboard passage, his arm flung out as though beckoning. Three were sprawled on the floor beside slatwood bunks, in postures suggesting they had been slain whilst in the lethargy of their drug and tossed from the couches like rags. The apparatus of the opium-den lay here and there; a gold-wrapped brick of the poisonous substance, broken pipes, burnt dishes, long matches, bits of wire.

And there, beyond them, sat the monster of my long nightmares.

"You don't like my horrible parlor," chuckled Budu. "Your little white nose has squeezed nearly shut, your nostrils look like a fish's gills."

"It's just the sort of nest you'd make for yourself, you murdering old fool," I told him. He frowned at me.

"I have never murdered," he told me seriously. "But these were murderers, and thieves. Who else would keep such a fine secret cellar, eh? A good place for a private meeting!" He leaned back against the wall, lounging at his ease across the top tier of a bunk, waving enormous mud-caked boots. His dress consisted of stained bluejean trousers, a vast shapeless red coat made from a blanket, and a battered black felt hat. He had let his hair and beard grow long; they trailed down like pale moss over his bare hairy chest. He looked rather like St. Nicholas turned monster.

Donal sat stiffly beside him. Budu had placed his great hand about the boy's neck, as easily as I might take hold of an axe handle.

"Uncle Jimmy," moaned Donal.

"Explain yourself, sir," I addressed Budu, keeping my voice level and cold. He responded with gales of delighted laughter.

"*I* was the Briton, and *you* were the little barbarian!" he said. "Look at us now!"

I stepped into the room, having scanned for traps. "I followed your signal," I told him. "You certainly made it plain enough. May I ask why you thought it was necessary to cut my throat?"

He shrugged, regarding me with hooded eyes. "How else to get your attention but to take your quarry from you? And how to do that but by disabling you temporarily? What harm did it do? Spoiled your nice white shirt, yes, and made you angry!" He chuckled again.

I tapped my stick in impatience. "What was your purpose in calling me here, old man?"

"To tell you a few truths, and see what you do when you've heard them. You were wondering about us, we oldest Old Ones, wondering what became of us all. You were thinking we're like badly made clockwork toys, and our Great Toymakers decided to pull us off the shelves of the toyshop." He stretched luxuriously. Donal tried to turn his head to stare at him, but was held fast as the old creature continued:

"No, no, no. We're not badly made. I was better made than *you*, little man. It's a question of purpose." He thrust his prognathous face forward at me through the gloom. "I was made a war-axe. They made you a shovel. Is the metaphor plain enough for you?"

"I take your meaning." I moved a step closer.

"You've been told all your life that our masters wish only to save things, books and pretty pictures and children, and for this purpose we were made, to creep into houses like mice and steal away loot before Time can eat it."

"That's an oversimplification, but essentially true."

"Is it?" He stroked his beard in amusement. I could see the red lines across the back of his hand where I'd clawed him. He hadn't bothered to heal them yet. "You pompous creature, in your nice clothes. You were made to save things, Victor. *I* wasn't. Now, hear the truth: I, and all my kind, were made because our perfect and benign masters wanted killers once. Can you guess why?"

"Well, let me see." I swallowed back bile. "You say you're not flawed. Yet it's fairly common knowledge that flawed immortals were produced, during the first experimentations with the Process. What did the Company do about them? Perhaps you were created as a means of eliminating them."

"Good guess." He nodded his head. "But wrong. They were never killed, those poor failed things. I've seen them, screaming in little steel boxes. No. Guess again."

"Then . . . perhaps at one time it was necessary to have agents whose specialty was Defense," I tried. "Prior to the dawn of civilization."

"Whee! An easy guess. You fool, of course it was! You think our masters waited, so gentle and pure, for sweet reason to persuade men to evolve? Oh, no. Too many wolves were preying on the sheep. They needed operatives who could kill, who could happily kill fierce primitives so the peaceful ones could weave baskets and paint bison on walls." He grinned at me with those enormous teeth, and went on:

"We made Civilization dawn, I and my kind! We pushed that bright ball over the horizon at last, and we did it by *killing!* If a man raised his hand against his neighbor, we cut it off. If a tribe painted themselves for war, we washed their faces with their own blood. Shall I tell you of the races of men you'll never see? They wouldn't learn peace, and so we were sent in to slay them, man, woman, and child!"

"You mean," I exhaled, "the Company decided to accelerate Mankind's progress by selectively weeding out its sociopathic members. And if it did? We've all heard rumors of something like that. It may be necessary from time to time even now. Not a pretty thought, but one can see the reasons. If you hadn't done it, mankind might have remained in a state of savagery forever." I took another step forward.

"We did good work," he said plaintively. "And we weren't hypocrites. It was fun." His pale gaze wandered past me to the doorway. There was a momentary flicker of something like uneasiness in his eyes, some ripple across the surface of his vast calm.

"What is the point of telling me this, may I ask?" I pressed.

"To show you that you serve lying and ungrateful masters, child," he replied, his attention returning to me. "Stupid masters. They've no understanding of this world they rule. Once we cleared the field so they could plant, how did they reward us? We had been heroes. We became looters. And you should see how they punished us, the ones who argued! No more pruning the vine, they told us, let it grow how it will. You're only to gather the fruit now, they told us. Was that fair? Was it, when we'd been created to gather heads?"

"No, I daresay it wasn't. But you adapted, didn't you?" To my dismay I was shaking with emotion. "You found ways to satisfy your urges in the Company's service. You'd taken your share of heads the day you caught me!"

"Rescued you," he corrected me. "You were only a little animal, and if I hadn't taken you away you'd have grown into a big animal like your father. There were lice crawling in his hair when I stuck his head on the pike. There was food in his beard!"

I spat in his face. I couldn't stop myself. The next second I was sick with mortification, to be provoked into such operatic behavior, and dabbed hurriedly at my chin with a handkerchief; Budu merely wiped his face with the back of his hand and smiled, content to have reduced my stature.

"Your anger changes nothing. Your father was a dirty beast. He was an oath-breaker and an invader too, as were all his people. You've been taught your history, you know all this! So don't judge me for enjoying what I did to exterminate his race. And, see, see what happened when I was ordered to stop killing Saxons! When Arthur died, Roman order died with him. All that we'd won at Badon Hill was lost and the Saxon hordes returned, never to leave. What sense did it make, to have given our aid for a while to one civilized tribe and then leave it to be destroyed?" His gaze traveled past me to the doorway again. Who was he expecting? They weren't coming to his aid, that much was clear.

"We do not involve ourselves in the petty territorial squabbles of mortals," I recited. "We do not embrace their causes. We move amongst them, saving what we can, but we are never such fools as to be drawn into their disputes."

"Yes, you're quoting Company Policy to me. But don't you see that your fine impartiality has no purpose? It accomplishes nothing! It's wasteful! You know the house will burn, so you creep in like thieves and steal the furniture beforehand, and then watch the flames. Wouldn't it be more efficient use of your time to prevent the fire in the first place?" He paused a moment and looked at the back of his hand with a slight frown. I saw the red lines there fade to pink as he set them to healing over.

"It would be more efficient, yes," I said, "but for one slight difficulty. You couldn't prevent the fire happening. It isn't possible to change history."

"*Recorded* history." He bared his big teeth in amusement once more. "It isn't possible to change *recorded* history. And do you think even that sacred rule's as unbreakable as you've been told? I have made the history that was written and read. It disappoints me. I will make something new now."

"Shall you really?" I folded my arms. Doubtless he was going to start bragging about being a god. It went with the profile of this sort of lunatic.

"Yes, and you'll help me if you're wise. Listen to me. In the time before history was written down, in those days, our masters were bold. All mortals have inherited the legend that there was once a golden age when men lived simply in meadows, and the Earth was uncrowded and clean, and there was no war, but only arts of peace.

"But when recorded history began—when we were forbidden to exterminate the undesirables—that paradise was lost. And our masters let it be lost, and that is the condemnation I fling in their teeth." He drew a deep breath.

"Your point, sir?"

"I'll make an end of recorded history. I can so decimate the races of men that their golden age will come again, and never again will there be enough of them to ravage one another or the garden they inhabit. And we immortals will be their keepers. Victor, little Victor, how long have you lived? Aren't you tired of watching them fight and starve? You creep among them like a scavenger, but you could walk among them like—"

"Like a god?" I sneered.

"I had been about to say, an angel." Budu sneered back. "I remember the service I was created for. Do you, little man? Or have you ever even known? Such luxuries you've had, among the poor mortals! Have you never felt the urge to *really* help them? But the time's soon approaching when you can."

"Ridiculous," I stated. "You know as well as I do that history won't stop. There'll be just as much warfare and mortal misery in this new century as in the centuries before, and nothing anyone can do will alter one event." I gauged the pressure of his fingers on Donal's neck. How quickly could I move to get them loose?

"Not one event? You think so? Maybe." He looked sly. "But our masters will turn what can't be changed to their own advantage, and why can't I? Think of the great slaughters to come, Victor. How do you know I won't be working there? How do you know I haven't been at work already? How do you know I haven't got disciples among our people, weary as I am of our masters' blundering, ready as I am to mutiny?"

"Because history states otherwise," I told him flatly. "There will be no mutiny, no War in Heaven if you like. Civilization will prevail. It is recorded that it will."

"Is it?" He grinned. "And can you tell me who recorded it? Maybe *I* did. Maybe I will, after I win. Victor, such a simple trick, but it's never occurred to you. History is only writing, and *one can write lies!*"

I stared at him. No, in fact, it never had occurred to me. He rocked to and fro in his merriment, dragging Donal with him. Silent tears streamed down the child's face.

Budu lurched forward, fixing me with his gaze. "Listen now. I have my followers, but we need more. You'll join me because you're clever, and you're weary of this horror too, and you owe me the duty of a son, for I saved you from death. You're a Facilitator and know the codes to order Company equipment. You'll work in secret, you'll obtain certain things for me, and we'll take mortal children and work the Augmentation Process on them, and raise them as our own operatives, for our purposes, loyal to *us. Then* we'll pull the weeds from the Garden. *Then* we'll geld the bull and make him pull the plow. *Then* we'll slaughter the wolf that preys on the herd. Just as we used to do! There will be Order.

"For this reason I came as a beggar to this city and followed you, watching you. Now I've made you listen to me." He looked at the doorway again. "Tell me I'm not a fool, little Victor, tell me I haven't walked into this trap with you to no purpose."

"What will you do if I refuse?" I demanded. "Break the child's neck?"

This was too much for the boy, who whimpered like a rabbit and started forward convulsively. Budu looked down, scowling as though he had forgotten about him. "Are you a stupid child?" he asked Donal. "Do you want to die?"

I cannot excuse my next act, though he drove me to it; he, and the horror of the place, and the time that was slipping away and bringing this doomed city down about our ears if we tarried. I charged him, howling like the animal he was.

He reared back; but instead of closing about Donal's throat, his fingers twitched harmlessly. As his weight shifted, his right arm dropped to his side, heavy as lead. My charge threw him backward so that his head struck the wall with a resounding thud.

All the laughter died in his eyes, and they focused inward as he ran his self-diagnostic. I caught up Donal in my arms and backed away with him, panting.

Budu looked out at me.

"A virus," he informed me. "It was in your saliva. It's producing inert matter even now, at remarkable speed, that's blocking my neuroreceptors. I don't think it will kill me, but I doubt if even your masters could tell. I'm sure they hope so. You're surprised. You had no knowledge of this weapon inside yourself?"

"None," I said.

Budu was nodding thoughtfully, or perhaps he was beginning to be unable to hold his head up. "They didn't tell you about this talent of yours, because if you'd known about it, I would have seen it in your thoughts, and then I'd never have let you spit on me. At the very least I wouldn't have wiped it away with my wounded hand."

"A civilized man would have used a handkerchief," I could not resist observing.

He giggled, but his voice was weaker when he spoke.

"Well. I guess we'll see now if our masters have at long last found a way to unmake their creations. Or *I* will see; you can't stay in this dangerous place to watch the outcome, I know. But you'll wish you had, in the years to come, you'll wish you knew whether or not I was still watching you, following you. For I know your defense against me now, think of that! And I know who betrayed me, with his clever virus." Budu's pale eyes widened. "I was wrong! The rest of them may be shovels, but you, little Victor—you were made a poisoned knife. *Victor Veneficus!*" he added, and laughed thickly at his joke. "Oh, tell him—never sleep. If I live—"

"We're going now, Donal Og, Uncle Jimmy'll get you safe out of here," I said to the child, turning from Budu to thread my way between the stinking corpses on the floor.

I heard Budu cough once as his vocal centers went, and then the ether was filled with a cascade of images: A naked child squatting on a clay floor, staring through darkness at a looming figure in a bearskin. Flames devouring brush huts, goatskin tents, cottages, halls, palaces, shops, restaurants, hotels. Soldiers in every conceivable kind of uniform, with every known weapon, in every posture of attack or defense the human form could assume.

If these were his memories, if this was the end of his life, there was no emotion of sorrow accompanying the images; no fear, no weariness, no relief either. Instead, a loud yammering laughter grew ever louder, and deafened the inner ear at the last image: a hulking brute in a bearskin, squatting beside a fire, turning and turning in his thick fingers a gleaming golden axe; and on the blade of the axe was written the word *VIRUS*.

Halfway up the ladder, the trap opening was occluded by a face that looked down at me and then drew back. I came up with all speed; I faced a small mob of Chinese, grim men with bronze hatchets. They had not expected to see a man in evening dress carrying a child.

I addressed them in Cantonese, for I could see they were natives of that province.

"The devil who killed your grandfathers is still down there. He is asleep and will not wake up. You can safely cut him to pieces now."

I took up my hat and left the mortals standing there, looking uncertainly from my departing form to the dark hole in the stair.

The air was beginning to freshen with the scent of dawn. I had little more than an hour to get across the city. In something close to panic I began to run up Sacramento, broadcasting a General Assistance Signal. Had my salvage teams waited for me? Donal clung to me and did not make a sound.

Before I had gone three blocks I heard the noise of an automobile echoing loud between the buildings. It was climbing up Sacramento toward me. I turned to meet it. Over the glare of its brass headlamps I saw Pan Wen-Shi. His tuxedo and shirtfront, unlike mine, were still as spotless as when he'd left the Company banquet. On the seat beside him was a tiny almond-eyed girl. He braked and shifted, putting out a hand to prevent her from tumbling off and rolling away downhill.

"Climb in," he shouted. I vaulted the running board and toppled into the back seat with Donal. Pan stepped on the gas and we cranked forward again.

"Much obliged to you for the ride," I said, settling myself securely and attempting to pry Donal's arms loose from my neck. "Had a bit of difficulty."

"So had I. We must tell one another our stories someday," Pan acknowledged, rounding the corner at Powell and taking us down toward Geary. The little girl had turned in her seat and was staring at us. Donal was quivering and hiding his eyes.

"Now then, Donal Og, now then," I crooned to him. "You've been a brave boy and you're all safe again. And isn't this grand fun? We're going for a ride in a real motor-car!" Under my words was a soothing frequency to blur his memory of the last two hours.

"Bad Toymaker gone?" asked the little muffled voice.

"Sure he is, Donal, and we've escaped entirely."

He consented to lower his hands, but shrank back at the sight of the others. "Who's that?"

"Why, that's a little China doll that's escaped the old Toymaker, same as you, and that's the kind Chinaman who helped her. They're taking us to the sea, where we'll escape on a big ship."

He stared at them doubtfully. "I want Mummy," he said, tears forming in his eyes.

The little girl, who till this moment had been solemn in fascination, suddenly dimpled into a lovely smile and laughed like a silver bell. She pointed a finger at him and made a long babbling pronouncement, neither in Cantonese nor Mandarin. For emphasis, she reached down beside her and flung something at him over the back of the seat, with a triumphant cry of *"Dah!"* It was a wrapped bar of Ghirardelli's, only a little gummy at one corner where she'd been teething on it. I caught it in midair.

"See now, Donal, the nice little girl is giving us chocolates!" I tore off the wrapper hastily and gave him a piece. She reached out a demanding hand and I gave her some as well. "Chocolates and an automobile ride and a big ship! Aren't you the lucky boy, then?"

He sat quiet, watching the gregarious baby and nibbling at his treat. His memories were fading. As we rattled up Geary he looked at me with wondering eyes.

"Where Ella?" he asked me.

When I had caught my breath, I replied:

"She couldn't come to Toyland, Donal Og. But you're a lucky, lucky boy, for you will. You'll have splendid adventures and never grow old. Won't that be fun, now?"

He looked into my face, not knowing what he saw there. "Yes," he answered in a tiny voice.

Lucky boy, yes, borne away in a mechanical chariot, away from the perishable mortal world, and all the pretty nurses will smile over you and perhaps sing you to sleep before they take you off to surgery. And when you wake, you'll have been Improved; you'll be ever so much cleverer, Donal, than poor mortal monkeys like your father. A biomechanical marvel fit to stride through this new century in company with the internal combustion engine and the flying machine.

And you'll be so happy, boy, and at peace, knowing about the wonderful work you'll have to do for the Company; much happier than poor Ella would ever have been, with her wild heart, her restlessness and anger. Surely no kindness to give her eternal life, when life's stupidities and injustice could never be escaped?

. . . But you'll enjoy your immortality, Donal Og. You will, if you don't become a thing like me.

The words came into my mind unbidden, and I shuddered in my seat. Mustn't think of this just now: too much to do. Perhaps the whole incident had been some sort of hallucination? There was no foul taste in my mouth, no viral poison sizzling under my glib tongue. The experience might have been some fantastic nightmare brought on by stress, but for the blood staining my elegant evening attire.

I was a gentleman, after all. No gentleman did such things.

Pan bore left at Mason, rode the brakes all the way down to Fulton, turned right and accelerated. We sped on, desperate to leave the past.

There were still whaleboats drawn up on the sand, still wagons waiting there, and shirtsleeved immortals hurriedly loading boxes from wagon to boat. We'd nearly left it too late: those were my people, that was my Nob Hill salvage arrayed in splendor amid the driftwood and broken shells. There were still a pair of steamers riding at anchor beyond Seal Rock, though most of the fleet had already put out to sea and could be glimpsed as tiny lights on the gray horizon, making for the Farallones. As we came within range of the Hush Field both of the children slumped into abrupt and welcome unconsciousness.

We jittered to a stop just short of the tavern, where an impatient operative from the Company's motor agency took charge of the automobile. Pan and I jumped out, caught up our respective children, and ran down the beach.

Past the wagons loaded with rich jetsam of the Gilded Age, we ran: lined up in the morning gloom and salt wind were the grand pianos, the crystal chandeliers, the paintings in gilt frames, the antique furniture. Statuary classical and modern; gold plate and tapestries. Cases of rare wines, crates of phonograph cylinders, of books and papers, waited like refugees to escape the coming morning.

I glimpsed Averill, struggling through the sand with his arms full of priceless things. He was sobbing loudly as he worked; tears coursed down his cheeks, his eyes were wide with terror, but his body served him like the clockwork toy, like the *fine machine* it was, and bore him ceaselessly back and forth between the wagon and the boat until his appointed task should be done.

"Sir! Where did you get to?" he said, gasping. "We waited and waited—and now it's gonna cut loose any second and we're still not done!"

"Couldn't be helped, old man!" I told him as we scuttled past. "Carry on! I have every faith in you!"

I shut my ears to his cry of dismay and ran on. A boat reserved for passengers still waited in the surf. Pan and I made for the boarding officer and gave our identification.

"You've cut it damned close, gentlemen," he grumbled.

"Unavoidable," I told him. His gaze fell on my gore-drenched shirt and he blinked, but waved us to our places. Seconds later we were seated securely, and the oarsmen pulled and sent us bounding out on the receding tide to the *Thunderer* where she lay at anchor.

We'd done it, we were away from that fated city where even now bronze hatchets were completing the final betrayal—

No. A gentleman does not betray others. Nor does he leave his subordinates to deal with the consequences of his misfortune.

Donal shivered in the stiff breeze, waking slowly. Frank's coat had been lost, somewhere in Chinatown; I shrugged out of my dinner jacket and put it around Donal's shoulders. He drew closer to me, but his attention was caught by the operatives working on the shore. As he watched, something disturbed the earth and the sand began to flurry and shift. Another warning was sounding up from below.

The rumbling carried to us over the roar of the sea, as did the shouts of the operatives trying to finish the loading. One wagon settled forward a few inches, causing the unfortunate precipitation of a massive antique clock into the arms of the immortals who had been gingerly easing it down. They arrested its flight, but the shock or perhaps merely the striking hour set in motion its parade of tiny golden automata. Out came its revolving platforms, its trumpeting angels, its pirouetting lovers, its minute Death with raised scythe and hourglass. Crazily it chimed FIVE.

Pan and I exchanged glances. He checked his Chronometer. Our boatmen increased the vigor of their strokes.

Moment by moment the East was growing brighter, disclosing operatives massed on the deck of the *Thunderer*. Their faces were turned to regard the sleeping city. Pan and I were helped on deck and our mortal charges handed up after us; a pair of white-coifed nurses stepped forward.

"Agent Pan? Agent Victor?" inquired one, as the other checked a list.

"Here, now, Donal, we're on our ship at last, and here's a lovely fairy to look after you." I thrust him into her waiting arms. The other received the baby from Pan, and the little girl went without complaint; but as his nurse turned to carry him below decks, Donal twisted in her arms and reached out a desperate hand for me.

"Uncle Jimmy!" he screamed. I turned away quickly as she bore him off. Really, it was for the best.

I made my way along the rail and emerged on the aft deck, where I nearly ran into Nan D'Araignee. She did not see me, however; she was fervently kissing a great bearded fellow in a brass-buttoned blue coat, which he had opened to wrap about them both, making a warm protected place for her in his arms. He looked up and saw me. His eyes, timid and kindly, widened, and he nodded in recognition.

"Kalugin," I acknowledged with brittle courtesy, tipping my hat. I edged on past them quickly, but not so quickly as to suggest I was fleeing. What had I to flee from? Not guilt, certainly. No gentleman dishonorably covets another gentleman's lady.

As I reached the aft saloon we felt it beginning, with the rising surge that lifted the *Thunderer* at its mooring and threatened to swamp the fleeing whaleboats; we heard the roar coming up from the earth, and in the City some mortals sat up in their beds and frowned at what they could sense but not quite hear yet.

I clung to the rail of the *Thunderer*. My fellow operatives were hurrying to the stern of the ship to be witness to History, and nearly every face bore an expression compounded of mingled horror and eagerness. There were one or two who turned away, averting their eyes. There were those like me, sick and exhausted, who merely stared.

And really, from where we lay offshore, there was not much to *see*; no DeMille spectacle; no more at first than a puff of dust rising into the air. But very clear across the water we heard the rumbling, and then the roar of bricks coming down, and steel snapping, and timbers groaning, and the high sweet shattering of glass, and the tolling in all discordance of bronze-throated bells. Loud as the Last Trumpet, but not loud enough to drown out the screams of the dying. No, the roar of the earthquake even paused for a space, as if to let us hear mortal agony more clearly; then the little we had been able to see of the City was concealed in a roiling fog the color of a bloodstain.

I turned away, and chanced to look up at the open doorway of a stateroom on the deck above. There stood Labienus, watching the death of three thousand mortals with an avid stare. That was when I knew, and knew beyond question, whose weapon I was.

I hadn't escaped. My splendid mansion, with all its gilded conceits, had collapsed in a rain of bricks and broken plaster.

A hand settled on my shoulder and I dropped my gaze to behold Lewis, of all people, looking into my face with compassion.

"I know," he murmured, "I know, old fellow. Too much horror to bear. At least it's finished now, for those poor mortals and for us. At least we've done our jobs. Brace up! Can I get you a drink?"

What did he recognize in my sick white face? Not the features of a man who had emptied a phial into an innocent-looking cup of wine, and given it to him under pretense of calming his nerves. Why, I'd always been a poisoner, hadn't I? But it had happened long ago, and he had no memory of it anyway. I'd seen to that. And Lewis would never suspect me of such behavior in any case. We were both gentlemen, after all.

"No, thank you," I replied, "I believe I'll just take the air for a little while out here. It's a fine restorative to the nerves, you know. Sea air."

"So it is," he agreed, stepping back. "That's the spirit! And it's not as though you could have done anything more. You know what they say: History cannot be changed." He gave me a final helpful thump on the arm and moved away, clinging to the rail as the deck pitched.

Alone, I fixed my eyes on the wide horizon of the cold and perfect sea. I drew in a deep breath of chill air.

One can write lies. And live them.

Two operatives in uniform were making their way toward me through the press of the crowd. I looked across at them.

"Executive Facilitator Victor?"

I nodded. They shouldered into place, one on either side of me.

"Sir, your presence is urgently requested. Mr. Labienus sends his apologies for unavoidably revising your schedule," one of them recited.

"Certainly." I exhaled. "By all means, gentlemen, let us go."

We made our way across deck to the forward compartments, avoiding the hatches where the crew were busily loading down the Art, the Music, the Literature, the fine flowering of the Humanity that we had, after all, been created to save.

Daniel Abraham, "Jaycee," *Asimov's*, December.
——, & Michaela Roessner, Sage Walker, Walter Jon Williams, "Tauromaquia," *Event Horizon*, August/September.
Brian Aldiss, "An Apollo Asteroid," *Moon Shots*.
Poul Anderson, "The Shrine for Lost Children," *F&SF*, October/November.
Michael Armstrong, "Recalled to Home," *Asimov's*, April.
——, "Of Bitches Born," *Not of Woman Born*.
Eleanor Arnason, "The Actors," *F&SF*, December.
——, "The Grammarian's Five Daughters," *Realms of Fantasy*, June.
——, "Stellar Harvest," *Asimov's*, April.
Constance Ash, "The Leopard's Garden," *Not of Woman Born*.
Paolo Bacigalupi, "A Pocketful of Dharma," *F&SF*, February.
Kage Baker, "The Fourth Branch," *Amazing*, Summer.
——, "The Queen in the Hill," *Realms of Fantasy*, December.
——, "Smart Alec," *Asimov's*, September.
Tony Ballantyne, "Soldier.exe," *Interzone*, June.
John Barnes, "Bang On!" *Apostrophes & Apocalypses*.
——, "Enrico Fermi and the Dead Cat," *Apostrophes & Apocalypses*.
William Barton, "Soldier's Home," *Asimov's*, May.
Stephen Baxter, "Huddle," *F&SF*, May.
——, "The Plain of Bones," *Interzone*, February.
——, "Saddle Point: The Face of Kintu," *Science Fiction Age*, May.
——, "Spindrift," *Asimov's*, March.
Greg Bear, "The Way of All Ghosts," *Far Horizons*.
Chris Beckett, "Valour," *Interzone*, March.
M. Shayne Bell, "The Game," *Realms of Fantasy*, April.
Gregory Benford, "A Hunger for the Infinite," *Far Horizons*.
Judith Berman, "The Window," *Asimov's*, August.
Terry Bisson, "macs," *F&SF*, October/November.
——, "Smoother," *F&SF*, January.
Paul Blake, "Watching the Angels," *Altair Four*.
Nelson Bond, "Proof of the Pudding," *Asimov's*, October/November.
Ben Bova, "Red Sky at Morning," *Analog*, May.
T. Coraghessan Boyle, "After the Plague," *Playboy*, September.
Scott Bradfield, "Dazzle Redux," *F&SF*, December.
Elizabeth Braswell, "The Bride," *Amazing*, Winter.
David Brin, "Temptation," *Far Horizons*.
Keith Brooke & Eric Brown, "The Flight of the Oh Carrollian," *Interzone*, July.
Eric Brown, "Dark Calvary," *Science Fiction Age*, January.

——, "Hunting the Slarque," *Interzone*, March.

——, "Steps Along the Way," *Moon Shots*.

——, "Venus Macabre," *Aboriginal SF*, Winter.

Stephen L. Burns, "Vultures," *Analog*, February.

Pat Cadigan, & Kathleen Ann Goonan, Paul Witcover, Sean Stewart, "Camera Obscura," *Event Horizon*, April/May.

Orson Scott Card, "Heal Thyself," *Amazing*, Summer.

——, "Investment Counselor," *Far Horizons*.

——, "Vessel," *F&SF*, December.

Amy Sterling Casil, "Letters from Arles," *Talebones*, Winter.

Adam-Troy Castro & Jerry Oltion, "The Astronaut from Wyoming," *Analog*, July/August.

Robert R. Chase, "Heat," *Analog*, December.

Rob Chilson, "The Hestwood," *F&SF*, April.

Rick Cook, "The Host of the Air," *Analog*, March.

Bruce Coville, "The Giant's Tooth," *Realms of Fantasy*, December.

Albert E. Cowdrey, "Revenge," *F&SF*, May.

Robert Cox, "The Grandmaster's Last Crusade," *Aurealis* 24.

Tony Daniel, "In from the Commons," *Asimov's*, October/November.

——, "Mystery Box," *Asimov's*, April.

Don D'Ammassa, "Wormdance," *Asimov's*, May.

Stephen Dedman, "A Single Shadow," *Weird Tales*, Summer.

——, "The Lady Macbeth Blues," *Interzone*, October.

——, "Unequal Laws," *Science Fiction Age*, March.

A. M. Dellamonica, "The Dark Hour," *Tesseracts*[8].

Nicholas A. DiChario, "Movin' On," *Weird Tales*, Spring.

——, "Sarajevo," *F&SF*, March.

Paul Di Filippo, "Angelmakers," *Interzone*, March.

——, "Fax," *Pirate Writings* 17.

Cory Doctorow, "Home Again, Home Again," *Tesseracts*[8].

——, "Visit the Sins," *Asimov's*, June.

Terry Dowling, "The View in Nancy's Window," *Interzone*, August.

Gardner Dozois, "A Knight of Ghosts and Shadows," *Asimov's*, October/November.

L. Timmel Duchamp, "Living Trust," *Asimov's*, February.

Andy Duncan, "The Executioners' Guild," *Asimov's*, August.

——, "Fortitude," *Realms of Fantasy*, June.

——, "From Alfano's Reliquary," *Weird Tales*, Fall.

——, "Grand Guignol," *Weird Tales*, Winter.

S. N. Dyer, "Original Sin," *Asimov's*, January.

Scott Edelman, "The Last Man on the Moon," *Moon Shots*.

Kandis Elliot, "TCoB," *Analog*, September.

Harlan Ellison, "Objects of Desire in the Mirror Are Closer Than They Appear," *F&SF*, October/November.

Timons Esaias, "Lilith, Searching," *The Age of Reason*.

John Ezzy, "The Old God Begins to Reassert Himself," *Aurealis* 24.

Gregory Feeley, "Ladies in Their Letters," *Asimov's*, June.

Gemma Files, "Blood Makes Noise," *TransVersions* 11.

Sheila Finch, "No Brighter Glory," *F&SF*, April.

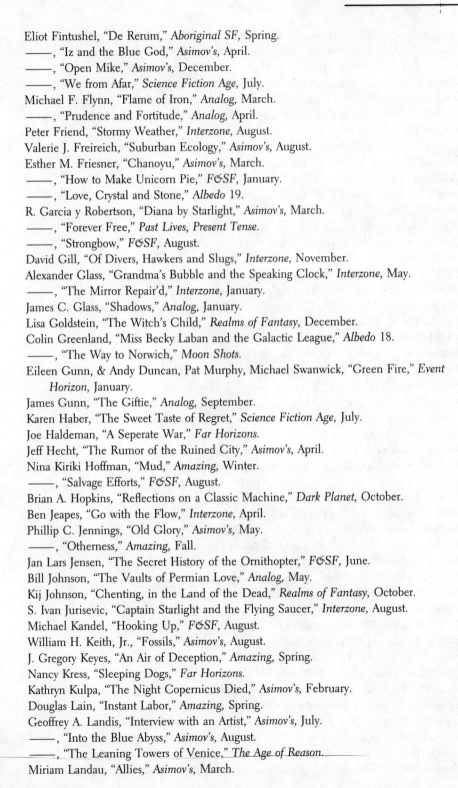

Eliot Fintushel, "De Rerum," *Aboriginal SF*, Spring.
——, "Iz and the Blue God," *Asimov's*, April.
——, "Open Mike," *Asimov's*, December.
——, "We from Afar," *Science Fiction Age*, July.
Michael F. Flynn, "Flame of Iron," *Analog*, March.
——, "Prudence and Fortitude," *Analog*, April.
Peter Friend, "Stormy Weather," *Interzone*, August.
Valerie J. Freireich, "Suburban Ecology," *Asimov's*, August.
Esther M. Friesner, "Chanoyu," *Asimov's*, March.
——, "How to Make Unicorn Pie," *F&SF*, January.
——, "Love, Crystal and Stone," *Albedo* 19.
R. Garcia y Robertson, "Diana by Starlight," *Asimov's*, March.
——, "Forever Free," *Past Lives, Present Tense*.
——, "Strongbow," *F&SF*, August.
David Gill, "Of Divers, Hawkers and Slugs," *Interzone*, November.
Alexander Glass, "Grandma's Bubble and the Speaking Clock," *Interzone*, May.
——, "The Mirror Repair'd," *Interzone*, January.
James C. Glass, "Shadows," *Analog*, January.
Lisa Goldstein, "The Witch's Child," *Realms of Fantasy*, December.
Colin Greenland, "Miss Becky Laban and the Galactic League," *Albedo* 18.
——, "The Way to Norwich," *Moon Shots*.
Eileen Gunn, & Andy Duncan, Pat Murphy, Michael Swanwick, "Green Fire," *Event Horizon*, January.
James Gunn, "The Giftie," *Analog*, September.
Karen Haber, "The Sweet Taste of Regret," *Science Fiction Age*, July.
Joe Haldeman, "A Seperate War," *Far Horizons*.
Jeff Hecht, "The Rumor of the Ruined City," *Asimov's*, April.
Nina Kiriki Hoffman, "Mud," *Amazing*, Winter.
——, "Salvage Efforts," *F&SF*, August.
Brian A. Hopkins, "Reflections on a Classic Machine," *Dark Planet*, October.
Ben Jeapes, "Go with the Flow," *Interzone*, April.
Phillip C. Jennings, "Old Glory," *Asimov's*, May.
——, "Otherness," *Amazing*, Fall.
Jan Lars Jensen, "The Secret History of the Ornithopter," *F&SF*, June.
Bill Johnson, "The Vaults of Permian Love," *Analog*, May.
Kij Johnson, "Chenting, in the Land of the Dead," *Realms of Fantasy*, October.
S. Ivan Jurisevic, "Captain Starlight and the Flying Saucer," *Interzone*, August.
Michael Kandel, "Hooking Up," *F&SF*, August.
William H. Keith, Jr., "Fossils," *Asimov's*, August.
J. Gregory Keyes, "An Air of Deception," *Amazing*, Spring.
Nancy Kress, "Sleeping Dogs," *Far Horizons*.
Kathryn Kulpa, "The Night Copernicus Died," *Asimov's*, February.
Douglas Lain, "Instant Labor," *Amazing*, Spring.
Geoffrey A. Landis, "Interview with an Artist," *Asimov's*, July.
——, "Into the Blue Abyss," *Asimov's*, August.
——, "The Leaning Towers of Venice," *The Age of Reason*.
Miriam Landau, "Allies," *Asimov's*, March.

Chris Lawson, "Chinese Rooms," *Eidolon* 28.

Tanith Lee, "Scarlet and Gold," *Weird Tales*, Summer.

——, "Where Does the Town Go at Night?" *Interzone*, September.

Ursula K. Le Guin, "Darkrose and Diamond," *F&SF*, October/November.

——, "Old Music and the Slave Woman," *Far Horizons*.

Jonathan Lethem, James Patrick Kelly, & John Kessel, "Ninety Percent of Everything," *F&SF*, September.

Kelly Link, "The Girl Detective," *Event Horizon*, March.

Richard A. Lupoff, "31.12.99," *Interzone*, September.

Ian R. MacLeod, "The Chop Girl," *Asimov's*, December.

Paul J. McAuley, "Alien TV," *Interzone*, April.

——, "Before the Flood," *Interzone*, May.

——, "Naming the Dead," *Interzone*, November.

——, & Michael Marshall Smith, Jeff VanderMeer, "Dead Stringer for Love," *Event Horizon*, June/August.

Sally McBride, "Speaking Sea," *Tesseracts*[8].

Anne McCaffery, "The Ship That Returned," *Far Horizons*.

Wil McCarthy, "Once Upon a Matter Crushed," *Science Fiction Age*, July.

Jack McDevitt, "Dead in the Water," *Not of Woman Born*.

Ian McDonald, "Breakfast on the Moon, with Georges," *Moon Shots*.

Christopher McKitterick, "Circles of Light and Shadow," *Analog*, February.

Elisabeth Malartre, "Evolution Never Sleeps," *Asimov's*, July.

Barry N. Malzberg, "Shiva," *Science Fiction Age*, May.

Joseph Manzione, "Emperor Penguins," *Analog*, July/August.

David Marusek, "Cabbages and Kales, or, How We Downsized North America," *Asimov's*, February.

——, "Yurek Rutz, Yurek Rutz, Yurek Rutz," *Asimov's*, January.

Kathleen M. Massie-Ferch, "Moon Hunters," *Moon Shots*.

Michael Meddor, "The Wizard Retires," *F&SF*, September.

Yves Meynard, "Within the Mechanism," *Tesseracts*[8].

Lyda Morehouse, "Twelve Traditions," *Science Fiction Age*, May.

Andrew Morris, "Emotional Bypass," *Eidolon* 28.

Derryl Murphy, "Northwest Passage," *Realms of Fantasy*, February.

Vera Nazarian, "Rossia Moya," *The Age of Reason*.

Kim Newman, "Angel Down, Sussex," *Interzone*, November.

Simon Ng, "The Heart Drummer," *Eidolon* 28.

David Nickle, "Ground-Bound," *On Spec*, Spring.

G. David Nordley, "Democritus' Violin," *Analog*, April.

——, "Mustardseed," *Asimov's*, September.

——, "The Touch," *The Age of Reason*.

Jerry Oltion, "Biosphere," *F&SF*, June.

Susan Palwick, "Judith's Flowers," *Not of Woman Born*.

Severna Park, "The Breadfruit Empire," *Event Horizon*, May.

——, "Harbingers," *Event Horizon*, January.

Richard Parks, "Take a Long Step," *Realms of Fantasy*, April.

Ursula Pflug, "Gone with the Sea," *Tesseracts*[8].

Frederik Pohl, "The Boy Who Would Live Forever," *Far Horizons*.

Tom Purdom, "Fossil Games," *Asimov's*, February.
——, "Woman's Work," *Asimov's*, August.
Wolf Read, "The Trees of Verità," *Analog*, June.
Robert Reed, "At the Corner of Darwin and Eternity," *Interzone*, October.
——, "Baby's Fire," *Asimov's*, July.
——, "The Challenger," *Science Fiction Age*, May.
——, "Game of the Century," *F&SF*, May.
——, "Human Bay," *Asimov's*, May.
——, "Mac and Me," *Asimov's*, February.
——, "Nodaway," *Asimov's*, September.
——, "What It Is," *Science Fiction Age*, September.
——, "Will Be," *F&SF*, January.
Jessica Wynne Reisman, "Raney's Hounds," *Realms of Fantasy*, October.
Mike Resnick, "Hunting the Snark," *Asimov's*, December.
Alastair Reynolds, "Angels of Ashes," *Asimov's*, July.
——, "Viper," *Asimov's*, December.
Uncle River, "The Dashing About Flying Box People," *Analog*, April.
Kim Stanley Robinson, "Arthur Sternbach Brings the Curveball to Mars," *Asimov's*,
    August.
——, "Maya and Desmond," *The Martians*.
——, "Sexual Dimorphism," *Asimov's*, June.
——, "What Matters," *The Martians*.
Bruce Holland Rogers, "How the Highland People Came to Be," *Realms of Fantasy*,
    August.
Chuck Rothman, "Sundials," *Aboriginal SF*, Fall.
Diana Rowland, "Extant," *The Age of Reason*.
Rudy Rucker & Paul Di Filippo, "The Square Root of Pythagoras," *Science Fiction Age*,
    November.
Kristine Kathryn Rusch, "Bonding," *Asimov's*, April.
——, "Flowers and the Last Hurrah," *Analog*, March.
——, "Relics," *Past Lives, Present Tense*.
——, "The Women of Whale Rock," *F&SF*, March.
Richard Paul Russo, "Watching Lear Dream," *F&SF*, July.
William Sanders, "Dirty Little Cowards," *Asimov's*, June.
——, "Jennifer, Just Before Midnight," *F&SF*, August.
James Sarafin, "A Clarity in the Ice," *F&SF*, June.
Pamela Sargent, "Hillary Orbits Venus," *Amazing*, Spring.
Nisi Shawl, "The Pragmatical Princess," *Asimov's*, January.
Robert Sheckley, "Visions of the Green Moon," *Moon Shots*.
Charles Sheffield, "With McAndrew, Out of Focus," *Science Fiction Age*, March.
Rick Shelley, "At the Zoo," *Analog*, June.
——, "The Alien," *Asimov's*, March.
Lucius Shepard, "Crocodile Rock," *F&SF*, October/November.
Lewis Shiner, "Lizard Men of Los Angeles," *F&SF*, July.
W. M. Shockley, "By Non-Hatred Only," *Asimov's*, July.
William Shunn, "Stalin's Candy," *Realms of Fantasy*, June.
Robert Silverberg, "Getting to Know the Dragon," *Far Horizons*.

——, "Travelers," *Amazing*, Summer.

Leah Silverman, "Deep Blue Sea," *On Spec*, Spring.

Dan Simmons, "Orphans of the Helix," *Far Horizons*.

Janni Lee Simner, "Raising Jenny," *Not of Woman Born*.

Dave Smeds, "A Raven on My Shoulder," *The Age of Reason*.

Brian Stableford, "Another Branch of the Family Tree," *Asimov's*, July.

——, "Ashes and Tombstones," *Moon Shots*.

——, "The Gateway of Eternity," *Interzone*, January/February.

——, "Hidden Agendas," *Asimov's*, September.

——, "Ice and Fire," *Albedo* 18.

——, "The Oracle," *Asimov's*, May.

——, "The Secret Exhibition," *Weird Tales*, Fall.

Allen Steele, "The Exile of Evening Star," *Asimov's*, January.

——, "Green Acres," *Science Fiction Age*, March.

——, "Her Own Private Sitcom," *Analog*, January.

Lucy Sussex, "The Queen of Erewhon," *F&SF*, September.

Michael Swanwick, "Ancient Engines," *Asimov's*, February.

——, "Riding the Giganotosaur," *Asimov's*, October/November.

Jennifer Swift, "Living History," *Interzone*, February.

Tais Teng, "Crowned by Lightning," *Albedo* 18.

Michael Thomas, "The Time Thief," *F&SF*, December.

Mark W. Tiedemann, "Chasing Sacrifice," *Science Fiction Age*, January.

——, "Gallo," *Asimov's*, March.

——, "Texture of Other Ways," *Science Fiction Age*, September.

Lois Tilton, "Dragons' Teeth," *Asimov's*, January.

——, "Midnight," *The Age of Reason*.

——, "The Scientific Community," *Asimov's*, September.

Shane Tourtellotte, "Live Bait," *Analog*, July/August.

Harry Turtledove, "Forty, Counting Down," *Asimov's*, December.

——, "Twenty-one, Counting Up," *Analog*, December.

Mary A. Turzillo, "Mars Is No Place for Children," *Science Fiction Age*, May.

James Van Pelt, "The Diorama," *TransVersions* 11.

Richard Wadholm, "The Ice Forest," *Asimov's*, January.

Howard Waldrop, "The Dynasters Vol. 1, On the Downs," *F&SF*, October/November.

——, "London, Paris, Banana . . .", *Amazing*, Winter.

Kyla Ward, "The Feast," *Aurealis* 24.

Ian Watson, "Caucus Winter," *F&SF*, January.

——, "Three-Legged Dog," *Interzone*, May.

Lawrence Watt-Evans, "He's Only Human," *Science Fiction Age*, September.

Andrew Weiner, "The Identity Factory," *Science Fiction Age*, January.

K. D. Wentworth, "The Embians," *F&SF*, May.

——, "The Girl Who Loved Fire," *Realms of Fantasy*, August.

Ramona Louise Wheeler, "That Sleeper in the Heart," *Analog*, October.

Rick Wilber, "Imagine Jimmy," *F&SF*, April.

Kate Wilhelm, "The Happiest Day of Her Life," *F&SF*, October/November.

Walter Jon Williams, "Argonautica," *Asimov's*, October/November.

Jack Williamson, "Engines of Creation," *Science Fiction Age*, September.

Connie Willis, "The Winds of Marble Arch," *Asimov's*, October/November.
F. Paul Wilson, "Aftershock," *Realms of Fantasy*, December.
Robin Wilson, "The Grift of the Magellanae," *F&SF*, March.
——, "Sole Mortal Thing of Worth Immortal," *Science Fiction Age*, July.
Laurel Winter, "Sky Eyes," *F&SF*, March.
Gene Wolfe, "Fish Story," *F&SF*, October/November.
——, "Has Anybody Seen Junie Moon?" *Moon Shots*.
Sarah Zettel, "Kinds of Strangers," *Analog*, October.
——, "Means of Survival," *Analog*, March.
Zoran Zivkovic, "The Astronomer," *Interzone*, June.